The Fluxion Trilogy
Three stories about life, duty, legacy, and most of all: science

Benjamin M. Weilert

The Fluxion Trilogy

First Name Basis
Paperback: https://www.createspace.com/3621328
Kindle e-Book: http://www.amazon.com/dp/B005XMENLC
Other e-books: http://www.smashwords.com/books/view/322038

Second to None
Paperback: https://www.createspace.com/3697801
Kindle e-Book: http://www.amazon.com/dp/B008A2FYA6
Other e-books: http://www.smashwords.com/books/view/322042

The Third Degree
Paperback: https://www.createspace.com/3847908
Kindle e-Book: http://www.amazon.com/dp/B00D5DC8CW
Other e-books: http://www.smashwords.com/books/view/322046

The Fluxion Trilogy Anthology
Hardcover: http://www.lulu.com/shop/benjamin-weilert/the-fluxion-trilogy/hardcover/product-21465264.html
Paperback: https://www.createspace.com/4558753
Kindle e-Book: http://www.amazon.com/dp/B00IPWUZ9G
Other e-books: http://www.smashwords.com/books/view/413708

The Constellation Trilogy
Coming Soon!

Connect with us online!
Follow on twitter: https://twitter.com/BMWtheAuthor
Like on facebook: https://www.facebook.com/BMWtheAuthor

Copyright © 2014 Benjamin M. Weilert

All rights reserved.

ISBN: 978-1-304-69182-8

DEDICATION

To the teachers who make learning fun

To Max,

I hope you enjoy this, as I know your love of science easily surpasses mine.

— Eg̃ M. Weily

CONTENTS

Contents   i

Acknowledgements   iii

FIRST NAME BASIS

Chapter 1:   IN   1

Chapter 2:   Lunacy   14

Chapter 3:   Rebirth   28

Chapter 4:   Monster   50

Chapter 5:   Escape   82

Chapter 6:   Heavy   90

Chapter 7:   Light   105

Chapter 8:   SIN   120

Epilogue: Oath   144

SECOND TO NONE

Prologue: The Beginning   149

Chapter 1:   Gathering Assembly   152

Chapter 2:   Family Blood   169

Chapter 3:   Forest Fluent   190

Chapter 4:   Imaginary Number   207

Chapter 5:   Extinguished Soul   235

Chapter 6:   Recruiting Switch   254

Chapter 7:	Training's Reward	272
Chapter 8:	War	289
Epilogue:	Millennial Erasure	310

THE THIRD DEGREE

Chapter 1:	The Missing Key	319
Chapter 2:	Collecting the Players	334
Chapter 3:	The Fixed Oasis	344
Chapter 4:	Fight the Fire	365
Chapter 5:	The Son's Birth	398
Chapter 6:	Destroying the Statues	423
Chapter 7:	The Third Degree	440
Epilogue:	Ending the Story	449

APPENDIX

Section 1:	Introduction	455
Section 2:	Characters	457
Section 3:	Settings	493
Section 4:	Items	504
Section 5:	Organizations	518
Section 6:	Maps	529
Section 7:	Timeline	533

ACKNOWLEDGMENTS

"God saw all that he had made, and it was good." — Genesis 1:31

The book that you now hold in your hands has been a labor of love for four years. If you had asked me before that whether or not I would write a novel, let alone three of them, I would have never thought it possible. And yet, here we are with all three novels written and collected into the anthology known as *The Fluxion Trilogy*.

If there was one reason for my expedient and briefly prolific writing career, it would be due to National Novel Writing Month (or NaNoWriMo for short). Each year I plan my work for November, then I sit down and crank out the first draft of a novel in 30 days. This community helps put words on paper for those who have always dreamed of writing their own novel. Of course, I would be amiss to exclude the mention of my cousin, Gretchen Sauvey, for introducing me to this incredible organized chaos.

And yet, once the draft is written, there's still a lot of work to do before I publish. Even though I do multiple edits on my manuscripts, there are still things I miss, so I am forever indebted to the following individuals for reading my first drafts and providing me with notes on how to make them better: Robert West, Scott Burger, Gary Liebowitz, and Elyce Westby. A special shout-out needs to go to Cindy Hipps, who has helped edit two of the three novels contained within this anthology.

As was the case in the Acknowledgement sections of each individual novel, I need to recognize my parents, who raised me and taught me to strive for excellence in everything I do. Their individual influences on my life have made it possible for me to be logical with plots (from my father) and creative with words (from my mother). I have always appreciated their support in my many endeavors.

Finally, I want to acknowledge all the friends, family, and readers who have given my writing a chance. I realize that there may be better books out there, but the fact that you've taken the time to read what I've written makes me happy. I love discussing my novels with people and I love the reactions I get from them when they read them.

First Name Basis
A story about life, love, honor, and most of all: science

Chapter 1

IN

The sky was unusually blue that day. Not a cloud in the sky. The only white disrupting the monochromatic expanse belonged to the seagulls circling around a caravel, aimlessly drifting towards the shore. The sails were torn and the riggings battered. A cursory glance would reveal that the ship was deserted. With one exception. On the deck laid a man in his late 20's, clad in a white jacket. Underneath the open jacket, he wore a black shirt with a pair of crossed bones adorning his chest. The clothing he wore was functional, and it showed the many years of its use. Clean shaven with rugged features, his face revealed his youth and yet, an unusual shock of white hair held out of his face by a simple headband made one question the man's true age. He was not awake. Not moving. Just lying there.

○

It was a pretty ordinary day for Irene. The young woman had an ordinary look and did ordinary things around the house to help her father. Irene was in the kitchen baking apple pies, her apron smudged with flour and sugar. Standing back up from putting a pie in the oven, she let out a sigh and brushed an errant strand of red hair out of her face and set it back behind her ear. She was about to clean up when she was interrupted by the ruckus of seagulls on her father's pier. She looked out the window to see what was upsetting the birds and could immediately tell that it was no longer going to be an ordinary day.

○

Isaac awoke with a start. As he lay on an unfamiliar bed, he began to examine his surroundings, aglow with the golden twilight. He lay in a simple room with very few features. Besides the bed he was on, there was a lone chair in the corner with his white jacket tenderly placed over its back. The last rays of the sun's light were streaming in through the open window where Irene was standing, looking out over the pier. She could tell that her patient was now awake.

"Good morning, sunshine. That is if you could call it morning anymore. You've caused quite the stir today." Irene turned around and sat on the windowsill as she motioned to the scene outside, "I hope you don't mind the precautions we've taken to insure your payment of our damages."

Isaac sat up and tried to lean forward so that he could see outside and figure out what she was talking about. However, the chain on his right wrist was attached to the metal frame of the headboard, thus preventing him from getting a good look. Realizing the futility in struggling, he lay back down on the bed.

Staring up at the ceiling, Isaac spoke to the woman, "How long was I out?"

"That's hard to tell. You were already out when we found you on your ship. Since then it's been about six or seven hours."

"Wait. 'We'?"

"My father and I."

"So I made it to shore?"

"Yes, sir. And what an entrance *that* was. I'm not sure anyone will be able to top it. At least, I *hope* no one tries to top it. You should've been awake to see it, it was pretty memorable. Then again, I can assume as much from a pirate."

"What? I'm not a pirate."

"Then what about those crossbones on your chest?"

"I'll have you know that this is my family's coat of arms, thank you very much."

"So your family was comprised of pirates?"

With a frustrated sigh, Isaac changed the topic, "So anyways, if I made it to shore, what town did I end up in?"

"You've arrived at New Town. Home of the 'Square G shrine' and 'Pierre's Pier'." Irene finished her marketing speech and came over to the bed to replace the cold compress on Isaac's forehead. With an agile movement, Isaac grabbed her wrist with his right hand while at the same moment using his left hand to check his forehead.

An intense look came into his green eyes as he shouted, "Where is it!?"

Frightened by the sudden change in her patient, Irene squeaked out, "Where is what?"

"The headband I was wearing! Where is it! How much have you seen?"

Irene dutifully answered him, "It's on the chair, along with your coat. I'm sorry, sir. I didn't mean anything by it. You were running a fever and were mumbling incoherently, so I had to do something." Suddenly regaining some of her courage, she said, "And don't you start taking this tone with me. Not only did I help you out, but you owe us for the pier. Furthermore-" Just as quickly as she regained her courage, the color dropped out of her face when she realized that Isaac had grasped her wrist with his right arm. The same arm that was moments ago chained to the bed frame.

Isaac realized this fact as well. Now that he was no longer restrained, Isaac got up, grabbed his coat, tied his headband back on, and opened the door to leave. Irene shouted at him, "What about your debt?!"

Without turning around or missing a beat, Isaac replied, "Sell my boat. I don't need it anymore." He slammed the door and was gone. As Isaac left the dock house he noticed his boat "parked" on the pier. He now understood why his entrance was memorable. In a mess of splinters and shattered planks, his boat had made itself a part of the pier. The bow of his ship was mere feet from the window where Irene was standing, glaring at him. As the waves came and rocked the boat, the pier groaned and cracked in protest. Smirking at the gawkers to the scene, he pulled the hood of his coat up over his head and melded into the crowd.

New Town was a bustling city at night. People were outside, enjoying the cool of the evening. As was his custom after arriving in a new location, Isaac needed to connect into the information network of the town. Briskly walking by the variety of vendors who used the port to their advantage, Isaac kept searching for his "go-to" place for information. Glancing from side to side as he strode down the street, he finally decided on a peculiarly shaped tavern by the name of Taurus. Entering underneath the large sign with a rather intimidating bull branded onto it, Isaac surveyed the scene in the boisterous tavern.

Taurus was a two-level bar that was of a circular construction. The outer circle was where the booths and tables were located and the inner circle held the bar. Food and drinks were delivered from upstairs via a dumbwaiter that was conveniently placed in the bar portion of the tavern. Taking one casual lap around the tavern, he examined the patrons. Gruff men, buxom women, mysterious figures in dark cloaks. One of the mysterious figures seemed to be a woman who made it a point to make it look like she was not watching him. Finally, Isaac found an empty seat at the bar and sat down. A giant of a bartender came over and gruffly said, "What'll you have, stranger?"

"Some hot food; cold alcohol; and peace and quiet." Isaac said as he placed three gold coins on the bar. The bartender saw that he was dealing with a wise guy, so he took the payment and went to inform the upstairs staff of the order.

Across the bar, set up against the central pillar of the building, sat a stately grandfather clock. The clock was originally owned by the founding proprietor of the tavern, as made clear on the brass plaque above it. Isaac took advantage of the rhythm of the device to pace his eavesdropping.

A talent that Isaac had developed over the years was the ability to be able to listen into specific conversations, even in the raucous atmosphere of a busy tavern. After all, with the flow of liquor came the flow of unrestrained information. He started at his 12 o clock, eyes focused straight ahead.

Tick.

"Did you hear about the new adviser that came in to help out the city of Topal?"

"Yeah. Supposedly he just showed up and was ready to help after King Sadim died."

"Too bad there aren't more volunteers like that in the world."

Tock.

3 o clock, eyes to the periphery on his right.

Tick.

"It's a tragedy all the crime that's happening these days. Not one day goes by when I don't hear about some murder somewhere or a battle in a faraway war."

"At least we can be glad that some of the worst criminals are locked away in 'The Box'. Remember the 'Crimson Front'? That guy could not be stopped. It's a good thing Testament was there to take care of him."

Tock.

6 o clock, eyes closed as he focused behind him.

Tick.

"I'm not sure I can leave my livestock out in the fields overnight anymore. Have you heard of the sheep being slaughtered over in the Posea Pasture?"

"Where is that again?"

"You know, right at the base of the Pythagorean Triangle. Of course, maybe that's the whole problem. I don't trust that area."

Tock.

9 o clock, eyes to the periphery on his left.

Tick.

"I really don't like how we're being treated by those folks from Testament. I mean, it seems kind of insulting that they'd just hole themselves up in their Eagle's Nest and not come down to help out the common folk."

"True, but you have to remember that things were much worse during the Reign of Robert."

"Yeah, but I can't say that I approve of that Mayor Felix they've put in charge. First of all-"

Tock.

12 o clock.

A steaming plate of something unrecognizable landed in front of Isaac, disrupting his focused eavesdropping. He started in on the meal and was satisfied. Apparently unaware of how hungry he really was, he ravenously finished the plate and lifted it toward the bartender, who had been standing there the whole time. Stunned at the appetite of the strange man, the bartender silently took the empty plate and went to retrieve some more food for the voracious customer.

As Isaac began to drink, the tavern became deathly quiet. Even the humid and musky atmosphere seemed to stiffen at the sudden change in the ambiance. The swinging doors were squeaking as they informed the crowd of a new patron. The only other sound in the tavern was Isaac gulping down his drink. From behind him came a slurred and booming voice, "Hey thur, man. Yous sure like yer drink, doncha?" The owner of the voice was a large, athletic man with a grizzled beard and hair lopsidedly parted to the left. His hazel eyes were unfocused and he wobbled as he stood in the doorway. Isaac kept drinking, trying to ignore the man behind him. "Why doncha buy a round for all these folks?"

Finishing his drink and slamming the mug down on the bar, Isaac let out a satisfied sigh. "No thanks, I was just leaving." As he tried to pass by, the drunk wobbled and caught Isaac's shoulder, bringing him to his knees.

Holding Isaac down, the man continued, "I don think ya understand what I'm askin', mistur. I want ya ta buy drinks fer all the people here, which includes me."

Isaac pulled up his right foot as he covertly removed something from its boot. With his head down, Isaac responded, "Yes, I heard you. But like I said, I was just leaving. I will give you something to remember me by, though."

The drunk above him smiled and began to say, "Well, that's more like-"

With a sudden movement, Isaac sprang to the air, bringing his right fist squarely into the drunk's lower jaw. Landing with a spinning flourish, Isaac waited to hear the heavy "thud" of his opponent. Isaac now stood above his harasser, right fist defiantly in the air. Opening his fist, he let a handful of coins fall onto the man's chest. Pushing through the swinging door, Isaac looked back over his shoulder and said, "Keep the change."

Everyone in the tavern was shocked beyond belief. Their eyes were wide and mouths agape. Almost as one organism, they looked at the man knocked out on the floor, then up at the swinging door. The bartender had enough sense about him to run after Isaac. He took two steps into the street and realized the futility of trying to find the stranger. He yelled into the crowd, "You don't know what you've done! That was a powerful man you've just crossed! They don't call him 'Flint Fist' Felix for nothing!" Hearing no response, the bartender just shook his head and headed back to tend to his tavern.

○

The moonlight of the evening gave Isaac an eerie glow as it lit his white hair and jacket. He was hiking up the trail to the Square G shrine. Standing at the top of the hill was an apple tree with a katana stuck in its base. The hilt of the katana protruding from the trunk was the only indication that there was even a sword there at all. On the trunk of the tree was carved a square "G", beneath which was written a quote, "No one escapes the Black Demon's grasp."

Before the tree, Isaac bowed his head and sat cross-legged in front of the inscription. He lifted his head and began to soliloquize, "I don't normally believe in fate. I believe that for every consequence, there is an action which drives it. Maybe now I am starting to realize that fate can be that action. The fact that I arrived at this town somewhat by chance shows that there are stronger forces than myself at work here."

"I've always admired you and the work you have done. In fact, I would have to consider you a mentor. A teacher. A guide and influence into my own work. Not only for your talent, but for your ability to stand up for what is right, even if it means opposing those who are more powerful than you are." A cloud covered the moon and, with the darkness of the night, brought some reality to Isaac. He sighed and shook his head, "Look at me. I'm talking to a tree as if he were actually here in front of me."

Isaac got up and turned around to leave. Emerging from its temporary blockage, the light of the moon revealed a very agitated man who now stood before him. Felix's voice was a low grumble as he spoke to the calm and controlled Isaac, "How dare you. How dare you insult me like that in front of my people. Don't you know that image is half of maintaining power? Don't you know that your little stunt will start to give them ideas? I didn't threaten my way into the position of Mayor with the intention of being humiliated by a punk like you." The time spent knocked out on the tavern floor had obviously sobered the man.

Making a motion to leave, Isaac was stopped by Felix's booming shout, "Hold it! I didn't say you could leave." Felix reached into his pockets and pulled out a pair of gloves. Putting the gloves on, he continued, "Now that you know image is half the battle of maintaining power, I will give you a first-hand demonstration of the second half." Winding up his right fist, Felix lunged with his full force at Isaac, who had decided to take the right hook instead of dodging.

A moment later, Isaac was on the ground, spitting blood and at least one molar out of his mouth. He couldn't tell what stars were in the sky and what stars were in his head. Giving one good cough, he leaned over to get up, "Very well, so you've got a mean right. I'll give you that." Slipping two small daggers from his jacket sleeves into his hands, Isaac stood and motioned for Felix to come again.

Felix ran toward Isaac, but as he got closer, his footwork became sloppy and unpredictable. Isaac took a few wide swings at the man, but managed to miss every time. The weaving of his opponent mimicked a boxer but had the attributes of one adept at fighting while drunk. Another solid punch from Felix into Isaac's stomach took the wind out of him.

Back on the ground, Isaac held his side. At least two broken ribs. His previous interaction with Felix did not prepare him for the true strength of the man. Or was it more than that? The blows somehow seemed harder than they should. Getting back up, Isaac smirked and goaded, "Is that all you've got?"

Provoked by Isaac's summons, Felix smiled and dashed at the white haired man. Isaac was prepared now. He knew to watch the joints, mainly shoulders and hips, to know where the blows would come from. Isaac brought his knives up to block a left hook. Upon impact, he was expecting Felix to recoil at the cuts the daggers would have inflicted. Instead, there were sparks. Isaac was able to get his knives away in time to prevent injuring himself, but Felix's blow continued on target.

Standing over Isaac, Felix started to gloat, "They don't call me 'Flint Fist' Felix for nothing, little man." He pulled on the left glove and flexed his fingers, which made grinding sounds, almost like stone. No, wait. They *were* stone. The moonlight glinted off of the dark stone surface now exposed through the cut in the glove caused by Isaac's knives. The moonlight also revealed a disk encircled by an embroidered snake embedded on the back of the glove.

Having now gotten a better look at Felix's glove, Isaac knew what he was up against. "Where did you get those gloves?" he asked.

"I don't think you've got the right to ask me any questions right now. Maybe if you defeat me, I'll let you in on a little secret."

"Very well." Isaac threw down his daggers and ran for the tree. This was a desperate, last-ditch effort, but Isaac hoped fate was still on his side. With Felix in hot pursuit, Isaac knew that he should never turn his back on a stronger foe. He knew to not run into a corner. He knew everything depended on this one chance.

Arriving at the shrine, Isaac began pulling at the hilt of the katana embedded in the tree. Felix was gaining ground and had nearly caught up. Suddenly, the resistance of the tree gave way and the sword quickly slashed upward, catching Felix by surprise and slicing a large gash across his abdomen and chest. The roles were now reversed. Felix lay on the ground, gripping his wound as Isaac stood over him, letting the moonlight glint off the black blade mere centimeters from Felix's throat.

"Talk."

"OK, OK, you win." Felix groaned in pain, "A strange man like yourself came to town one day and told me that there's a cave just outside of town that's filled with a lot of ancient items. These gloves were in there, along with a lot of treasure. However, you need a password to get in." Felix flinched as Isaac moved the blade away and took a swipe at a low-hanging limb on the apple tree.

Felix squeaked out, "It's, 'Where there's a Will, there's a way'!"

"Thanks." Isaac tossed an apple at Felix while he took a bite out of his own. He headed back to town, branch and sword in tow.

When Isaac was out of sight, Felix grinned and took a bite out of the apple. Speaking softly to himself, Felix mused, "Fool. I'll trap you in that cave and you'll never bother me again."

Sitting in an ordinary rocking chair and knitting an ordinary scarf, Irene was still thinking about what had happened earlier that night as evidenced by the scowl on her forehead. She was just about to head upstairs and go to bed when she heard a shy knock on the front door. Curiosity led her to open the door and see who would be knocking at this time of night.

Standing before her was Isaac, battered and bruised, with a tree branch in one hand and a sword in the other. He looked downcast as he had given up his pride by simply knocking on the door. Irene leaned against the doorframe and scoffed, "And what brings you back here after the way you've treated me and my father's pier?"

Staring at the ground, Isaac softly answered, "Apparently word gets around this town pretty quickly. Apparently making a fool of your Mayor is frowned upon. And apparently the inns won't have anything to do with an injured man." Looking up at Irene and her skeptical expression, Isaac continued, "I know I've been an enigmatic jerk, but could you forgive me and let me stay here tonight?"

Smiling at the gesture, Irene stepped inside to let Isaac in, "I suppose we can make an arrangement."

Limping through the open door, Isaac returned the smile and asked, "Thanks, but can we forego the chains this time?"

○

Pierre was a portly, balding, bearded man who looked down on Isaac with concern. A rough hand stroked a grey beard, peppered with some red hair still clinging to the vestiges of his youth, "Those injuries still look pretty bad, *monsieur*. Are you sure you should be leaving so soon?"

Partially wrapped in bandages and kneeling down to tie his boots, Isaac replied, "Yes, I'm sure. I've got my path pretty well laid out now. I'll heal on the way to my next destination."

"At least stay one more day and let Irene tend to your broken ribs."

"I can't. I've already overstayed my welcome. Besides, it's better if I leave now while she's out. I'm terrible at goodbyes." Isaac headed out the door and made his way to the edge of town.

Pierre stood in the doorway and just shook his head. He then turned to the workers who were dismantling Isaac's ship, using the resulting lumber to rebuild his pier. "*Sacrebleu!* Come on you lazy bums, keep working!"

Isaac strode along the path out of town with his new sword, Kuroni, secured in the elaborately designed scabbard on his left hip. The yellow edging of the cover encapsulated a deep blue base coat, on top of which was painted the boughs of an apple tree at the throat of the sheath. A lone, shiny red apple was painted at the tip. New Town was full of many skilled craftsmen, so it wasn't difficult to find a woodworker who could take the branch from the apple tree and fashion it to hold the katana from the same tree.

His plan was to check on the cave to see if there were any clues as to the whereabouts of the legendary Fluents. From there, he was going to head east toward the source of his journey's purpose. As he walked along, he noticed that he was being followed. With a quick motion, he unsheathed Kuroni and pointed it at the one tailing him.

At the sight of Irene, Isaac let down his guard. She had a stern look on her face as she came closer. "How could you leave without saying goodbye, Isaac?"

"I'm not good at goodbyes."

"At least tell me where you're going."

"I can't."

"Then let me come with you." Irene sighed as she continued, "I've lived such an ordinary life that I feel I need to get out and experience the world. I know that if I follow you, I'll get some of the adventure I've been craving. It must be fate that you came here. After all, who else would sail a boat all by themselves only to let it crash into a pier? If you'd just let me tag along-"

Isaac was shouting now, "I can't!"

Irene looked surprised and a little hurt. Isaac let out a deep sigh and put his hands on her shoulders. "I'm sorry; I shouldn't have reacted like that."

The two sat down on a downed log lining the path. Isaac explained, "First of all, I don't believe in fate, if something happens, it happens for a reason. Each action a consequence of another. Secondly, you've seen what's under this headband, haven't you?" He pointed at the headband he was wearing. The fabric was white with the design of a red lion's face in mid-roar set the middle of his forehead.

"Yeah, but I don't see what-"

"It's a reminder. A reminder that I must take this burden alone. This will be a dangerous endeavor, and I can't lose anyone else. I've discovered this power, and now it's my duty to make sure that the world is not controlled by it." Isaac stood and turned away from Irene.

"I don't know how I may appear to the world; but to myself, I seem to have been only like a boy playing on the sea-shore, and diverting myself by finding a smoother pebble or a prettier shell than ordinary. All the while, the great undiscovered ocean of truth lies in front of me, waiting to be examined." As he took a step to leave, Irene also got up.

"Wait!" She held out her hand, balled into a fist with the exception of her pinky. "Promise me. Swear that you'll come back. Even if it is your burden to bear, don't throw your life away on it."

Isaac smiled at the childish act and brought forth his hand, linking pinkies with Irene. "This is *my* reminder. My reminder that you've promised to come back and tell me about your extraordinary adventure." Isaac nodded, turned around and proceeded on his way. Irene stood there, watching him leave. With a short laugh, she turned back toward town and spoke softly to herself, "Maybe it's for the best. If those are the types of adventures I would be getting into, I'm not too sure I would look good with white hair."

It took a little while to find the entrance to the cave Felix described. Hidden behind a dense clump of aspen trees was a small vestibule carved out of the rock of the hill. It looked natural enough, but stood out when compared against the natural formations nearby. The door to the cave was hardly distinguishable from the rest of the rock, but there was a small gap that was visible upon closer inspection.

Isaac tapped on the door with his knuckles, half expecting someone to come and answer his knock. Standing away from the door for clearance purposes, Isaac spoke the password with confidence, "Where there's a Will, there's a way!" Nothing. As his brow furrowed, Isaac waited for a response from the rock. Just as he took a step forward, there came a low rumble emanating from the door. Cracking and grinding noises started to come from the rock with increasing frequency and volume. Slowly, the door slid away, revealing the mouth of the cave, ominously beckoning Isaac to enter. Looking around to make sure no one was following him, Isaac ventured into the cave.

Upon entering the cave, Isaac could see that much more effort was put into the construction of the interior than the exterior. The light of the day streamed in, revealing elaborate relief carvings in the walls and a majestic, mosaic floor. As Isaac took his first steps into the cave, he could tell that no one had visited it in a very long time. Dust and cobwebs covered everything. The only indication of his presence was his footprints. Brushing away some of the dust from the wall to his left, Isaac began to examine the carving.

However, his examination was short-lived as his light source suddenly cut off. With a much quicker movement than it had taken to open, the door to the cave had shut, trapping Isaac inside. Deciding to make the best of the situation, Isaac felt around for something he could use as a torch. Blindly feeling the walls, he eventually came upon an unlit torch. Removing the torch from its holder, Isaac twirled it around above him, collecting some cobwebs for kindling. Feeling around in his pockets, Isaac produced a match, which he used to light his new-found light source. As his eyes re-adjusted to the light, Isaac was startled by the anguished visage of a man, mere inches from his face. Brushing off the carving on the wall, he could see a pictorial story of what had happened to this statue of a man.

Long ago, when the Armies of Amedeo were battling against The Triumvirate, certain experiments were performed on some of the soldiers to give them the strength to withstand the supernatural attacks of The Triumvirate. Isaac was well aware of these powers, as he had re-discovered them after the Millennial Erasure had made their use the stuff of legends and myths. These powers were called fluxions. Men who did not have the fortitude to withstand the power of the fluxion were taken over by its power. This man was just such an example. In trying to create an army full of men as strong as stone, some of them did not make the cut, so to speak.

Continuing further into the cave, Isaac arrived at a room full of scrolls. Slumped in the corner sat a skeleton, still wearing the tattered remains of a lumberjack's uniform. Isaac placed the torch in a holder on the wall and began to peruse the scrolls. Historical records, battle reports, maps. None of these pieces of information were of any use to Isaac. Feeling somewhat defeated, Isaac sat down next to the skeleton and asked, "You don't happen to know where I can find information on fluxions, would you?" Feeling kind of silly for having talked to a skeleton, Isaac got back up and returned to the entrance of the cave.

Once again, he spoke the password. Nothing. And not the nothing that had happened before, truly nothing happened. Isaac became frustrated with the door as he shouted the password at it multiple times. Still nothing. Now he knew why Felix had given him the information about the cave so easily. There was no way out. Or, at least there was a different method for getting out. Upon further examination of the inside of the door, Isaac found two distinguishing marks. One was what looked like a peephole in the shape of a "Q". Isaac put his eye up against it to see if he could see anything. Only darkness. The other mark was obviously a keyhole.

Apparently this cave had some security to keep its treasures safe. In order to get into the cave there was a spoken password that was needed, but in order to get out, one needed a key. This way even people who heard the password and saw how it led to a cave would not be able to escape once inside. Isaac began to panic. The bandages around his chest felt like they were constricting him, preventing him from breathing properly. Frantically, he tore at the bandages until they were all strewn about on the floor. Finally able to take a few deep breaths, he eventually calmed down. Now that his anxiety attack was over, he started to think of a solution.

Kneeling down in front of the keyhole, Isaac tried using one of his daggers to pick the lock. Unfortunately, due to the ancient nature of the mechanism, this lock could not be picked by modern means. Standing back from his failure, Isaac thought of another plan. Surely if someone had forgotten their key, there must be a spare somewhere in the cave for such emergencies. The only logical place Isaac could think of to hide such a key was the room full of scrolls. Grabbing the torch, he headed back to the room from which he came.

Pulling down scrolls from their cubbyholes, Isaac was making a mess of the place. Strewn about the floor were reports in dead languages, diagrams of various knots, and maps of roads no longer traveled. Having emptied the walls of their scrolls, Isaac once again sat down next to the skeleton. He turned and looked at the pitiful collection of bones. A flash of a future state where two skeletons were sitting in a room full of disheveled scrolls gave Isaac a shudder. Noticing the name tag on the skeleton's ragged clothes, Isaac brushed off some of the dust to read it. Jason.

The disturbance of the skeleton caused it to shift and fall away from Isaac. Apparently he was too enthralled with the room before to have noticed that

Jason was holding a scroll. This wasn't a scroll like the others, it looked more like something he had torn out of an existing scroll and used for his own purposes. Isaac gently removed the paper from the gloved hand. Opening it, he could see that Jason had written his last thoughts upon the paper. This is what it said:

To the one who finds my body:

It is sad to think that my best friend has betrayed me, and there is nothing I can do about it. He kept bragging about a cave full of treasures and I eventually called him on it.

He said there was a glove in the cave that could let you through any locked door you wanted. We always loved mischief, and that glove seemed like just the ticket. When we got in the cave and found the glove, I was still skeptical. And yet, I suppose curiosity killed this cat.

As I put the glove on my right hand, I wondered how it worked, and how in the world it would let us through any door we wanted. Before I could ask my friend for more information, my hand started to get incredibly hot. The fingers in the glove were becoming stiff and it was painful to move them. My hand started to swell, and I screamed out in pain.

Seeing that I was in trouble, my friend immediately ran away. I tried to run after him, but I was trying too hard to get the glove off of my hand.

Eventually the pain died down, but now I was trapped. My friend must have known the other password to get out, because I tried the one we used to get in, and it didn't work. Now I'm starving, and I think that's exactly how I'll die.

I had no regrets in this life, with the exception of this damned glove.

- Jason

Isaac finished reading the testimony and looked down at the skeleton's right hand. Sure enough, the glove was still there. Time and decay had removed the fingers of the glove to reveal an interesting phenomenon. All of the fingers were fused straight, almost like white shafts. At the end of the fingers were what looked like bone spurs. What remained of the glove was perhaps the most telling of the circumstances of the man's pain.

On the back of the glove there was a small key embroidered into the fabric. Surrounding the key was the design of a snake that was biting its own tail. Isaac knew that this was a prime example of a fluxion. The key was the core of the glove, and the snake in an uroboros configuration was the seal that transferred the power of the key to the user's hand. It was true that the glove would let you unlock any door, but that was only through the sacrifice of the user's right hand. All of Jason's fingers were now keys. Apologizing to Jason, Isaac took the glove, hand and all, and broke it off from the skeleton's wrist. Grabbing the torch, he headed back to the cave's entrance for one last-ditch effort.

Arriving back at the door, Isaac was disappointed to learn that Jason's keys did not fit in the keyhole. Thumb. No luck. Index finger. Failure. Middle finger. Nope. Ring finger. Wrong. Pinky. Incorrect. Isaac was just about to lose his cool again when he noticed something peculiar about the design of the uroboros. Most of the uroboros seals were of the snake eating the entirety of its tail. However, this design had the snake not biting its tail, but biting closer to the end of its body. This produced what looked like a "Q" on the back of the glove.

Fresh out of ideas, Isaac figured that he would give it a shot. Inserting Jason's thumb into the Q-shaped peephole, Isaac found that it was a perfect fit. He turned the key and the door rumbled open. Letting out a sigh of relief, Isaac grabbed the torch and prepared to leave the cave.

Chapter 2

Lunacy

As the stone door opened, Isaac could feel the cool air outside stream into the cave. Stepping across the threshold, he sensed that something was amiss. The door behind him slammed shut, and the resulting breeze from that action blew out the torch. Darkness. Isaac was confused at this new development because he was almost certain that he did not spend enough time in the cave for it now to be evening. Furthermore, the vegetation that had been around the entrance of the cave was no longer present. Instead, there was a carpet of very short and thick grey grass.

Venturing out from the vestibule of the entrance, Isaac looked to the sky to try and get his bearings. Perhaps it was the unusually large number of stars that he could now see or perhaps it was the absence of the moon in the sky, but Isaac could not manage to recognize any celestial bodies. Walking further out and allowing his eyes to adjust to the dim lighting provided by the multitude of stars, he saw that the path he had taken to get to the cave was no longer there. Or, more accurately, it was a different path which looked like it had been the path less traveled.

Isaac became frustrated at these new developments. He was certain that it shouldn't be this dark outside for the amount of time he was in the cave. He was also certain that only a few days ago the moon had been about three-quarters full, which was not the case since there was no moon to be seen. Off in the distance, Isaac heard the lowing of cattle and decided that if there were cows, there was a strong possibility of people nearby to ask for directions.

The hike along the path helped to warm Isaac up from the colder weather. Once he arrived at the pasture where the cows were grazing, he found that he was out of breath. Another strange development. It almost felt as if the air were thinner here, which shouldn't be the case for how close to the sea the cave had been. As such, he felt light headed. Actually, he just felt lighter overall.

Isaac looked about the pasture to see that it was a very wide expanse, unmarred by the presence of trees. Far off in the distance, he could make out the ridges of a very uniform mountain range. From behind him came the whistling of a bird. Or at least it sounded like a bird.

"Hey, mister! What are you doing all the way out here?" The voice was young, and whistled on every "s".

Turning around, Isaac answered, "Excuse me?"

Behind him stood a boy, about 12 years old, arms akimbo in a questioning stance. The boy's arms were covered with a dark grey shirt, on top of which was worn a plain white T-shirt. His short brown hair was brushed back in an attempt to control its wispy nature. A pair of brown eyes squinted as they examined the stranger in front of him. "I asked what you were doing out here. People don't usually hang out at Jules Crater unless they have to."

Finding a rock to sit down on, Isaac rested and replied, "I just came out of a cave nearby and was trying to get my bearings. I figured that if I headed towards the cows, then someone might be here who could help me."

"Well, you came to the right place. I'm always a big help." The boy smiled, revealing a grin with a single front tooth missing. Extending his hand, the boy continued, "The name's Erwin."

Accepting Erwin's handshake, Isaac replied, "Isaac. Nice to meet you."

"So, what's with the sword? You some sort of samurai?"

Isaac slid part of the sword out from its hilt on his hip and explained, "No, I'm not a samurai, but I suppose you could say I am a warrior of sorts."

"What's that hole for?" Erwin was referring to a hole in the blade of the katana, slightly above the hand guard.

Sticking his finger through the hole and wiggling it around, Isaac explained, "This is the spot for a fluxion core. See this design on the edge of the hole?" Isaac pointed to a knotted uroboros seal with a vortex-like design surrounding the hole. "That's an uroboros seal. It's meant to keep the power of the fluxion core in check."

"That's great, but what do fla-flo-fl . . . what do the powers do?"

"Fluxions are changes to the basic construction of an object. Depending on what I put in this hole, I could have a sword with fire powers, or lightning powers, or water powers. Each power depends on the core that is used." Sheathing the sword, Isaac continued, "Of course, fluxions can be used in other things as well, not just swords. For instance, if you put a fluxion on a glove, your hand could gain the special powers, like being hard as stone."

"Why's there still a hole in your sword? Why haven't you filled it with something yet?"

"You certainly are an inquisitive boy, aren't you?" Erwin smiled at the compliment. Isaac went on to explain, "I'm actually looking for a very special type of fluxion for this sword. Some powers are so powerful that they are considered to be legendary. These powers are called Fluents."

Isaac stood up and gestured to the sky, "Two such Fluents are what have shaped the universe and what keep it running. That's why I was in that cave I mentioned earlier. I was looking for some information on the whereabouts of the Fluents. Unfortunately, most all the scrolls were in a language I was unable to read."

Erwin perked up at the mention of scrolls. "Scrolls? Scrolls on what?"

"Well, the two scrolls I'm looking for have to do with the Fluent of Darkness and the Fluent of Light."

"I know where that is."

"What?"

"I know where that is. The Light scroll."

Shocked and stunned at this development, Isaac eagerly asked, "Where is it?"

"It's kind of a far ways away, up on the Peak of Eternal Light."

"I don't care how far away it is. Can you take me there?"

"Yup, but it's thousands of miles north of here, I don't think you'd want to travel that far or for that long."

"Believe me; I feel it would be worth it."

Looking down to the ground, Erwin thought for a moment on how to proceed. Quietly, he asked, "Can you keep a secret?"

"Yes, but why?"

"Well, I've got a way we can get to the Peak really fast, but my mom says I shouldn't use the shortcut."

Kneeling to get to Erwin's eye-level, Isaac said, "I promise. I'll keep your secret."

Smiling at his honesty, Erwin grabbed Isaac's hand and said, "Let's go!"

Isaac thought he was out of breath before. After Erwin grabbed his hand, his vision went blurry and he heard a rushing sound in his ears. It felt like he had the wind literally taken out of his lungs. Seconds later, everything had stopped moving. Gasping for air and squinting at the blinding light, he spoke between deep breaths, "What . . . was . . . that?"

Timidly fidgeting with the dirt on the ground with the toe of his shoe, Erwin said, "That's my shortcut. I can go anywhere I want to, and quickly. In fact, there are some times I feel I'm everywhere and nowhere all at once. I call it 'jumping'."

Swallowing hard and regaining his composure, Isaac asked, "You remember our conversation about fluxions, right? You don't happen to have something with that snake design on it, do you?"

Lifting up his T-shirt to show the design on the long-sleeve shirt underneath, Erwin sheepishly said, "You mean this, right?"

There, embroidered around an orb of swirling air, was an uroboros design that mimicked the swirling of the core. Pulling his shirt back down again, Erwin said, "My mom says that I scare the townspeople with my wind. I get scolded when I use it, and afterward I feel I don't like jumping, and I'm sorry I ever had anything to do with it." Looking up at Isaac, Erwin pleaded with him, "That's why you can't tell my secret! If my mom knew I was still using it, she'd take it away."

Smiling an understanding smile, Isaac patted the boy on the head, "I promised, didn't I? Besides, were here, aren't we? That's what I wanted all along. Now let's go get that Light scroll." Erwin perked right up and the two of them headed for the summit.

The Peak of Eternal Light was an unusual place. It was obvious that the copious amounts of light were used for settlements elsewhere unseen. Large energy collecting stations were periodically set around the base of the mountain. Each of these stations seemed to send its power out and into the ground through some very thick cables.

No matter which part of the mountain you were on, you could look up and see the sun. In the light, one could clearly see the grey grass and the white dirt it was growing from. Oddly enough, it was easier to breathe on top of the Peak of Eternal Light than it was back at Jules Crater. Still, even though the sun was shining, the sky was very dark and black.

Arriving at the summit of the mountain, Erwin and Isaac found a shrine which looked promising. Upon further examination, nothing useful was there. Whatever had been there had been taken away a long time ago. Isaac was focused on examining the entirety of the shrine so that he could be sure that the Light scroll wasn't hidden somewhere on it. Erwin had occupied himself by throwing small pebbles off of the Peak. Finally, Isaac gave up and sat down, resting his back on the shrine. He had become so enthralled with the search for the scroll that he didn't notice a more important point of his surroundings.

Out in the expanse of the sky was a large moon. Isaac hadn't noticed it until now, but the moon was a very beautiful sight. It looked like a blue gem, swirling with white wisps of cotton. All at once, all the pieces came together. The extremely starry sky. The darkness. The grey grass and white dirt. Jules Crater. The azure and emerald orb in the sky.

The reason Isaac could not see the moon was because Isaac was on the moon.

At this stupendous realization, Isaac's head began to swim with the implications, which caused him to start hyperventilating. Soon afterward, he passed out.

○

Isaac awoke with a start. Another strange room. He reflected that he had better not be making a habit of passing out and waking up in strange beds. At

17

least this time he wasn't chained to it. The room was dark and he could hear the soft conversation of multiple voices in the other room. He creaked open the door and looked out. A group of four women were sitting around a coffee table having tea. The woman sitting on a plain black chair got up and approached Isaac. She was wearing all black, with the exception of a white bonnet. The features of her face were worn with worry. She did not smile.

"Won't you come and have some tea?"

Isaac emerged from the room and said, "Yes, please, miss. . ."

"Call me Carroll. These are my friends, Diana, Phoebe, and Claire." Each woman made a motion at the mention of their respective names.

Isaac went over to the sofa and sat between Phoebe and Claire as Carroll went to the kitchen to prepare some more tea. A striped cat bounded up to the sofa and came to rest on Isaac's lap. From the kitchen, Carroll spoke to Isaac, "Erwin brought you in here. He's always bringing strange things home, but I must say that an unconscious man is a first for him. I just hope he wasn't using that wind power of his. It drives the locals mad with all the whistling he does when he uses it."

Isaac nervously glanced toward his feet. Carroll re-entered the room carrying a tray and a fresh pot of tea. As she poured Isaac a cup, she asked, "What brings you to the town of Alden, mister-"

"Isaac. It's a long story really, and I'd rather not get into it right now."

"That's fine." Carroll finished pouring, dropped in two sugar cubes and handed the cup to Isaac. As he sipped, he made a face. "Is there anything wrong with the tea, Isaac?" Carroll inquired.

"No, the tea is fine. I just can't help thinking that with how dark it is outside that it's not the right time for tea."

Phoebe turned to Isaac and explained, "It's not that late, in fact it's almost four in the afternoon. We just came off of our light month, so things will be dark for a while."

"Light month?"

This time Diana answered, "You must really not be from around here. You see, our town gets sunlight for about one month and darkness for the month afterward. During the light month, it gets very warm and the air is fresh. We use that latent warmth and fresh air to get us through the dark month, which we usually spend underground. In fact, most of our work is done underground, just to keep everything unified."

Claire interjected, "It didn't always use to be that way though. When the tragedy of Edmond's comet about a decade ago put all of Herbert crater into chaos, we didn't think we'd ever have order again."

Carroll sat down and poured herself a cup of tea. "You can thank Priest Werner for getting us back on the right track. When he started Operation Alsos, he unified us all together under the religion of the comet. He told us that since we were spared by the comet, we should pray to it so that its relatives might not come and finish us off. I suppose it's appropriate that he set up the shrine on the very site of the impact and named it after Edmond, the man who discovered the comet in the first place."

Getting back on topic, Phoebe spoke, "Werner was the one who set up all the underground dairy facilities. Most of the men work there, and the boys tend to the cattle out in the pastures."

Isaac ate some cheese and crackers and remarked, "That's some stupendous cheese. I'm assuming it came from those dairies?" The women nodded. Isaac continued, "Speaking of boys tending to cattle in the pastures, that's where I met Erwin."

Carroll tried to smile, but looked worried, "Oh, that's nice."

"Where is Erwin, anyways?"

"Who knows? When he brought you home, he whistled and took off. If I had to guess, he's probably out playing with his friend, Eugene."

Finishing his tea, Isaac got up from the sofa, displacing the cat that was sleeping on his lap, "Thanks for the tea, Carroll. It was delightful. Now, if you'll excuse me, I think I'm going to go out and walk around for a bit." He went into the bedroom and emerged with his sword on his hip.

"You don't need that weapon to go outside. Alden is a very peaceful town."

"I'm sure it is, but one can never be too careful or prepared." As Isaac left the home, the cat slipped out, followed him for a few blocks, and disappeared.

Walking the streets of Alden, Isaac noticed all the houses looked the same. They were all constructed with the same adobe style. This seemed to make sense to him, since he had not seen a single tree since he arrived on the moon. The moon.

Isaac mused on his situation. He was unsure on how he had gotten on the moon, but he was certain that he needed to find a way back to earth so that he could continue on his quest. Reaching the edge of town, he saw that he was close to the edge of the crater. Continuing on, he decided to climb to the ridge and get a better view of the area.

Walking on the moon was a strange experience. The light feeling of his body made him somewhat clumsy, and he found that despite the handicap, his endurance was much more than it used to be. As he started to climb the ridge, Isaac noticed someone was already sitting on top. Arriving at the crest of the ridge, Isaac found that it was Erwin.

At the sight of Isaac, Erwin perked up, "You're OK! I was worried when you started sleeping up on the Peak and I couldn't wake you. I hope you didn't mind me taking you home."

"Not at all. You have a very nice mother."

Erwin smiled, but it soon vanished, "So, what are you doing up here, Isaac?"

"I thought I could get a better view of the surroundings from up here. Yourself?"

"I come here to think sometimes." Erwin turned from the crater, approached the opposite edge of the ridge and leaned on an invisible wall.

Isaac was confused, but soon was able to figure out this phenomenon when he went over to the edge to join Erwin. It wasn't an invisible wall. Not quite. Isaac put his hand on what appeared to be a glass barrier. Looking up, he could see that the barrier enclosed the entirety of the crater, almost like a bubble. Kneeling down, he examined the base of the glass bubble. There was evidence of some rapid heat generation. Isaac figured that the glass bubbles were made when the craters were formed. The heat released by the event turned the soil into glass.

Reaching down to the ground, Isaac picked up some of the dirt and ground it between his fingers. He then sniffed and tasted the dirt. Just as he thought. The soil was the entire reason there could be people living up here. When the sun heated the soil, the two parts of its composition removed the waste in the air and created more oxygen, respectively. That's why the air seemed fresh after the light month and why the air was so thick at the Peak of Eternal Light.

Erwin spoke, interrupting Isaac's examination of the soil, "My mom said that I was born shortly before this crater was formed. My father was the one who discovered the comet that created it, but there was nothing he could do to stop it. This glass wall is all I really have to remember him by, not that I even got a chance to know him in the first place. I sometimes feel like I was born into this environment: I don't know where I came from or where I'm going or who I am."

Isaac had stood back up and put his hand on Erwin's shoulder, "Well, you turned out just fine. In my opinion, even if you didn't know your dad, I'm sure he would be proud of you." Erwin's smile returned, wider than ever.

Turning back from the glass bubble, Isaac looked out over the vista of Herbert crater. He could see the nearby town of Alden, but the really impressive sight was the effects of Edmond's comet. It looked like someone had dropped a huge rock in a pond and the resulting wave became frozen in place. In the center of the crater was a lone hill, surrounded by water. The water was most likely the remains of the icy comet that created the basin. With no wind to disturb it, the water was still and reflected the multitude of stars above it, making the hill seem like a lone world unto itself.

Isaac looked over to Erwin, standing beside him, "I know we just met, but you wouldn't happen to know anyone who could help me get back to where I came from, would you?"

Erwin nodded, "Yup. See that island in the middle of the crater, that's Edmond shrine. Priest Werner should be able to help you. Say, where are you from anyways?"

"Do you remember when we were on the Peak of Eternal Light?" Erwin nodded. "That blue moon in the sky is where I'm from."

Erwin's eyes widened, "Wow! That's pretty cool! So how'd you end up here, if you came from all the way up there?"

"I don't know. That's what I'm trying to figure out. Maybe this Priest Werner can help me out with that. Come on, let's go." With that said, the two took the path down off the ridge and back into town.

○

"Knight to Queen Four." A man in a simple black robe, adorned with a circuitry of white light, sat at a small table on which was a game of chess, already in progress. Opposite the man sat a mirror image of himself, the grey, slicked back hair, pronounced nose, and grey eyes mimicking his opponent. The second man did not look happy.

"Checkmate." The first man knocked over the black king, triumphantly crossed his arms and leaned back in his chair. His voice was articulate, but unable to hide the thick accent of his origins.

From the door came a voice, "Excuse me, mister . . ."

Startled by the interruption, the first man got up from the table with a start. The second man and the white light on the robe were no longer there. "Don't you know you should knock before entering someone's office?"

"I'm sorry, father. I should have known better." Erwin examined his shoelaces in shame.

Isaac tousled Erwin's hair and said, "Lessons learned, my friend." Extending his hand to the Priest, he said, "You must be Priest Werner. My name is Isaac. I was told by my friend Erwin here that you might be able to help me."

Accepting the handshake, Werner said, "Of course. I've helped his town so much as it is, it's only natural to come to me with any problems that might arise. Come, sit."

Werner went behind his desk and sat down as Isaac and Erwin took the seats in front of the desk. "What can I help you with, my sons?"

Isaac began, "I know this may seem somewhat strange, but I'd like to get back home."

"That's not strange at all. Where are you from?"

"You know that blue orb that you can see from the Peak of Eternal Light? There."

"Oh my. That is a tough one. Well, let us start with how you came to be with us and work our way backward."

"Let's see. I entered a cave, became trapped, and used this key to get out." Isaac pulled Jason's hand from his pocket. However, only four of the fingers were left. He reached into the pocket again to only find the dusty remains of the key he had used. Letting the dust fall through his fingers, Isaac lamented, "Well, this *was* a key."

"That is unfortunate; however, I think that any of the keys should work."

"How's that?"

"Come, let me show you something." Priest Werner got up and beckoned the two follow him to the sanctuary.

The sanctuary was a marvelous sight to behold. There was no roof, which made the canopy of stars the sanctuary's ceiling. The floor was merely the polished rock which was formed after the comet had struck the moon. Tiny pieces of phosphorescent glass were embedded in the smooth surface and seemed to glow and twinkle just like the stars above did. Lastly, a collection of fireflies buzzed about in the open air of the sanctuary, completing the magnificent, all surrounding sparkling ambiance of the place.

Isaac was taken in by the spectacle of the room and felt a little dizzy with the overload of sparkling objects. Priest Werner stood behind the altar and knelt down to open a sliding door. He ran his finger along the edges of the scrolls contained inside, found the one he was looking for and pulled it out. Opening the scroll he selected, Werner laid it on the altar and spread it out for his two visitors to see.

"As you can see, those keys you have are similar to the ones shown here." Werner pointed to the picture of a peculiar looking key which was shown going into a hole shaped like a "Q". "According to the text, these keyholes are to open what are called 'Q-Portals'. These portals could lead anywhere. Apparently, the exit location of the portal is somewhat dependent on the key that is used, but all the keys should work in all of the keyholes. And yet, there is a probable chance that where you end up is entirely random. It will never be possible by pure reasoning to arrive at some absolutely certain location."

Focusing on the diagrams shown on the scroll, Isaac asked, "So, is it possible that if you know where an exit of a Q-Portal is, that you can use that exit as an entrance to another one?"

Priest Werner nodded, and pointing to a line with an arrow head on each end, he said, "Entrance and exit are both the same door, and the apparent duality arises in the limitations of our language." Pointing to a section of ancient text, he continued, "However, this paragraph warns the user of the limitations of the Q-Portals. 'Once a Q-Portal is used, it may be impossible to return to the location where he started'."

"Wait, you can read this?"

"Why of course. Can't you?"

"No, this is a dead language where I come from."

"Well, this is the only written language I've ever known."

Piecing together some of the information, Isaac pondered aloud, "Do you think that perhaps the ancient people from my world used the Q-Portals to come here? It would explain why the language hasn't transformed over the years. It would also explain why I was able to get here as well."

"That may be true, young lad. If we have all the pieces; we can know, as a matter of principle, the past in all its details."

"Do you have any more of these scrolls?"

"Why certainly. They're right here in this cabinet."

As the two men pulled out the scrolls and delved into their meaning, Erwin was meandering around the sanctuary, bored at the research of the two. He tried to catch some of the fireflies, which entertained him for a moment. When he looked back up at Isaac and Werner, they were both frowning. Apparently they had come upon a roadblock in their research.

"Are you sure these are the only scrolls you have? I'm looking for one in particular."

"*Ja*, I'm sure. Most of these are historical documents, and we've already gone over the few useful scrolls to your situation."

Erwin overheard their conversation and butted in, "What about that one?" As he pointed past the men, Isaac turned around and saw there was one more scroll held by a statue placed on an upper pedestal. The statue's other hand held a small, black orb.

Priest Werner frowned and shook his head, "*Nein*. I can't let you see that scroll. That scroll is part of the basis of our religion. Its contents are too sacred to be read. When combined with the remains of Edmond's comet, we simple people can have something to hope in."

Approaching the upper sanctum, Isaac said, "Well, if I'm just going to leave soon anyways, what harm would it be if I took a little peek." Priest Werner appeared in front of Isaac, blocking his path, almost as if he congealed from the air.

"I cannot let you do that. If I let every traveler who comes in here have a look at our sacred document, it would lose its impact as a sacred document." The white circle on the priest's robe began to glow, and a "–" became visible in the center of the circle.

This development greatly concerned Isaac. Of all the Number-fluxions, the "lost" Numbers were by far the most powerful. Of course, the reason they were called "lost" wasn't because they had been forgotten or hidden, but merely because they did not actually possess a number. In his research, he found it would be possible to create any of the Number-fluxions with the three lost Numbers. And yet, since the power and unpredictability of the lost numbers was so great, no one had ever been able to attempt the creative maneuver.

Still, of the three lost Numbers, "–" was the most dangerous. Not only could it imitate Lambda's power, but there were multitudes of other effects that it could create. Isaac hoped Werner did not know the extent of the power he possessed.

Snapping out of his deep thoughts, Isaac realized that Werner had materialized in front of him. He knew what this meant, but just to be sure he was seeing things correctly, he glanced over his shoulder at Erwin to ask if he saw the same thing and to warn him that they were now in a dangerous situation.

The truth was that Erwin saw the same thing, but in a different location. Apparently, when Werner went to block Isaac, he never moved from where he was originally standing. Now there were two of them.

Isaac didn't want to give away too much of what he knew, so he merely pointed at Priest Werner's chest and asked, "That's a Number-fluxion, isn't it?"

Werner's face became very serious as he said, "*Ja*, indeed it is. I seem to have underestimated you, Isaac." A sly smile crept over his face as he continued, "Are you a fan of games?"

Erwin, being naive of the situation, raised his hand and said, "I do! I love games."

Isaac glared at Erwin, but the damage was already done. Priest Werner continued, "Splendid! I have a game that we can all play. If I win, I get to keep those keys of yours, and you'll have to find your own way back home."

Sensing that there was soon to be no way out of this predicament, Isaac agreed, "And if I win, you'll let me see the scroll *and* the remains of the comet."

Werner, confident in his own abilities concurred, "So be it. Now the game is this: Are you familiar with the game of 'Tag'?" As he spoke, his simple robe began to glow with an intricate linear design emanating from the fluxion core. He walked down to the front pew and sat down, "All you have to do is catch me." Every empty seat on every empty pew was now filled with identical Priest Werners, "The real me, that is."

Jumping into action, Isaac sprinted toward the first pew where Werner originally sat down. Lunging toward Werner, the image suddenly disappeared as Isaac fell to the ground. An echo of many voices rang out around him, "I wouldn't be so foolish as to let it be that easy, now would I?"

Standing up and brushing himself off, Isaac took a deep breath and began to observe. All the Werners looked the same and they all made the same movements. This meant that if Isaac knew the location of the real one, he'd be able to catch him. Panning across the seats, Isaac saw something strange on the fringes of the sanctuary. The Werners who were sitting there were close enough to the fireflies that when the insects tried to land on them, they merely passed through the images. These were obviously not the real Werner.

Suddenly, all the Werners began swatting at their face and exclaimed, "*Ach! Stupid bug!*" One of the fireflies ran right into the face of the real Werner. As his focus was on other things, some of the images began to disappear. Near the back of the sanctuary, Isaac could see one of the remaining Werners swatting at a firefly. That was the real one.

"Erwin!" Isaac shouted, "That's the real one, grab him!"

As Erwin grabbed Priest Werner, the rest of the images vanished. Erwin was overly pleased with his success, "Cool! We win!"

"Not so fast, young man. My wager was with the white-haired gentleman over there. He has to tag me in order to win."

Rolling his eyes, Isaac strolled over to the Priest, still being held by Erwin. As he got closer, the image of the priest became hazy. "Hurry, Isaac! He's doing something weird." Isaac picked up the pace and was close enough to touch Werner when he was thrown back against the altar. Likewise, Erwin was forcefully thrown to the back of the sanctuary.

Still hazy, Priest Werner chided the two, "Oh, I'm sorry. I forgot to explain more of my power to you. You see, my power is the power of uncertainty. When you know how fast I'm moving, you'll have no idea where I am. However . . ." At this dramatic juncture, Werner punched the nearby pew, reducing it to rubble and debris, "Once you know where I am, there is no telling how fast I can move."

Coughing from the sudden blow, Isaac got up and set his feet apart for a fighting stance, "Erwin!"

Similarly, Erwin got up from the back of the room and replied, "Yeah, Isaac?"

"Remember what you explained to me when we arrived at the Peak of Eternal Light?" Erwin opened his mouth to speak. "Don't tell me, Erwin! *Remember.*" Erwin nodded. Isaac drew Kuroni from its sheath and readied himself. This would be the final move.

"You need to hurry now, there's not much time left." Priest Werner was pacing up and down the aisles, as were his clones.

Isaac charged down the main aisle of the sanctuary, "Now, Erwin!" Within moments, the entire area was filled with wind, and Erwin was nowhere to be seen. As the real Werner cowered from this sudden development, from behind him, Erwin appeared and the wind stopped. They had caught him in the middle of the sanctuary. "Good job! Now it's my turn." Leaping into the air, Isaac brought the sword down in a mighty slash.

Priest Werner cowered from the blow and yelled out an anguished cry. When he realized that he was under no physical harm, he opened his eyes. Isaac poked Werner right in the middle of the forehead, "Checkmate." Werner let out a sigh and slumped to the ground, defeated. He now noticed that the glow had gone from his fluxion core and that he was powerless.

Isaac used the tip of his sword to show the cut he made through the Priest's robe, severing one of the many circuits of the fluxion, "When you spread out the power like that, there's a greater chance you'll leave yourself open." Isaac sheathed Kuroni with a "ka-chink" and headed to the upper sanctum.

Grabbing the scroll and the orb, Isaac came back to the altar. As Werner woefully approached the altar, Isaac set down the scroll and opened it up. Emblazoned on the scroll was a large design of a triangular knot of an uroboros. On one side of the design was a beam of light entering the triangle, with multiple light beams emanating from the opposite side of the triangle. There was a number inside the shape: six.

Erwin joined the two and looked at the scroll, "Hey, that's the scroll we were looking for earlier!"

Isaac scowled at Priest Werner, "You didn't happen to steal this from the Peak of Eternal Light, did you?"

Werner shamefully hung his head and mumbled, "*Ja.*"

Pointing to the text surrounding the design, Isaac commanded, "Read."

"It says here that the design on this Light scroll is for the 'Fluent of Light'. The power is not to create light, or to destroy it, but rather to separate it."

"Good. That will do." Isaac rolled up the scroll and put it under his arm. He now held the remains of the comet between his index finger and thumb and said, "Now explain this."

Werner sighed again and secretly regretted gambling his religious position of power, "That is all that remains of Edmond's comet. All of the energy that went into creating this crater has been forcefully condensed into that orb you are holding. I suppose it is merely a reminder of the power of gravity in the universe."

Isaac made a double-take, "Wait, what did you say?"

"It's a reminder of the gravity of the universe. The only reason that the comet has any power at all is because there's a great source of gravity controlling its movements."

It couldn't be that simple. Isaac pulled out Kuroni just enough so that the hole for the core was exposed. Taking the comet, he put the orb into the hole. A perfect fit. As the power activated for a moment, Erwin and Werner took an involuntary step toward Isaac. Everyone looked at each other in astonishment.

○

"I'm sorry, but no." Isaac was packing his things and getting ready to use the Q-Portal and get back on track. Carroll was watching him and pleading with him.

"Please take him with you. Erwin has no future here. If he stays here, he'll only end up working in the dairies, and I know he's too restless to be happy doing that."

"I can't bring anyone else along on my journey. I'm already responsible for far too much, and I can't spend my spare time babysitting someone."

"But it wouldn't be like that! He may be mischievous at times, but he's always trying to help others and doesn't want to be a burden on anyone." Carroll solemnly looked down at her feet. She knew that she couldn't take care of Erwin for much longer.

"Listen. I've already turned down one other person who wanted to come with me, and I don't plan to come back here, so let's just let Erwin live his life, instead of planning his life for him."

Isaac opened the door started to leave, but stopped at Carroll's last attempt, "Wait! I know he's not going to ask to come, which is why I'm asking you to take him. At the very least just let him through the door and let him try to make his own life away from here."

"I'll think about it." Isaac closed the door and started walking down the main street.

Carroll re-opened the door and watched the white-haired man walk away. Talking to herself, she said, "But he needs a father figure so badly, and you remind me of Edmond so much I feel that you'd be good for him." As the tears started to well up in her eyes, the cat came waltzing through the open door and rubbed up against her leg. Picking up the striped feline, Carroll went inside and closed the door.

Arriving at the top of the ridge, Isaac once again found Erwin with a glazed look in his eyes, daydreaming over the vast expanse of the crater. "Hey, Erwin, you ready?"

Deep in thought, Erwin was a little startled, "What? Oh. Yup, let's go." Grabbing Isaac's hand, they both departed to Jules Crater.

Sputtering and gasping for air, Isaac said, "I don't think I'll ever be able to get a hang of that." Regaining his composure, Isaac extended his hand to Erwin for a parting handshake, "Well, Erwin, it's been a pleasure. I really appreciated your help back there." He pulled out the Light scroll and said, "I wouldn't have been able to get this without your help."

Looking down at his feet, Erwin mumbled, "You're welcome."

Tousling Erwin's hair, Isaac said, "Come on, perk up, bud. You've got a mother who is relying on you to be the man of the house." Erwin kept looking at his feet as Isaac walked away.

Isaac looked at the stone door that he had come through not too long ago. Examining it closely, he noticed the same Q-shaped hole on this side of the door. Pulling out Jason's hand, Isaac assessed what options he had left, now that the thumb key was gone. He figured that any key was good as any other so he picked the ring finger and put it into the keyhole. When he turned the key, the door opened as quickly as it had before. With no torch to light his path, Isaac felt his way blindly into the cave.

A few steps across the threshold, Isaac could see some light further in. As had happened before, the door quickly shut, resulting in a blast of wind. He was committed now, for better or for worse. He could immediately feel that his body was heavier than it was before and that there was more air to breathe. The air was fresh and had a hint of saltwater. He must be close to the sea. Hope rose in his chest as he continued along the cave.

Chapter 3

Rebirth

Even though many of the sensations told Isaac he was back on earth, there was a certainty that he had not returned to the Q-Portal near New Town. The structure of this cave was too well defined and too deep to be the same entrance he used before. The light streaming in from the entrance of the cave showed that there were passages branching off of the main tunnel he was occupying. Approaching the entrance of the cave, Isaac's eyes adjusted to the increasing light intensity.

It was a good thing Isaac cautiously approached the entrance of the cave, because this particular cave was set within a cliff. When Isaac examined the drop off, he whistled in astonishment. From behind him, Isaac sensed the presence of another person, who came running at him. No, not at him, past him. This individual was most interested in coming out of the cave. So interested, that the person did not notice the entrance was a precipice. Isaac noticed just in time, "Erwin!"

Reaching out and grabbing the back of Erwin's shirt, Isaac caught the boy before he could fall over the edge. Pulling him back, Isaac let go of the shirt and let Erwin fall to the floor of the cave. Nonchalantly, Erwin said, "Wow, is it just me, or does everything feel heavier?"

A mixture of anger and frustration boiled up in Isaac as he chided Erwin, "What are you doing here? You're supposed to stay behind!" He then realized the wind which blew shut the Q-Portal was stronger than the first time. It must have been Erwin.

Erwin got up and retorted, "You don't get to tell me what to do! You're not my dad! Besides, you and I both know that we make an excellent team." Isaac opened his mouth to speak and had his finger pointed, ready to lecture; but he stopped, unable to find the words.

From outside, the two could hear a voice, "Whoa there boy! Whoa, Supages!"

They looked at each other and had the same response, "Hide!" Finding a connecting tunnel, Isaac and Erwin hid out of sight and peeked around the corner to see what was going to happen. Appearing in the entrance of the cave was a man riding a white horse. Wait. Riding a bird. Wait. Riding a horse with the wings of a bird.

The horse landed and folded its wings. Its rider dismounted and grabbed the reigns, "Whoa, boy. What's got you spooked?" The man was young and well-tanned. A shock of disheveled blonde hair looked like a halo on the man due to the back-lighting of the cave entrance. As the man examined the cave, Isaac and Erwin pulled back from their peeking position. Unfortunately, the man noticed.

"Hey! Is someone here?" Slowly approaching the hiding place of the two, the man turned the corner to find Isaac and Erwin both standing in the shadows with their hands up.

Erwin spoke, "You caught us."

"What are you two doing in my house?"

Isaac stepped forward, hands still in the air and tried to offer an explanation, "It's actually kind of a long story, but we were just leaving anyways." The man approached with his horse-bird and walked right by the two. It seems the location they chose to hide from a man on a horse was the stable for said horse. Isaac and Erwin awkwardly looked at each other, obviously embarrassed.

As the man gave his horse some hay and brushed its neck to calm it down, he said, "Well, about the only way you're getting out of this cave is by this mighty steed, but I'm assuming that if you could get up here, you could easily get down."

"Well, like I said, it's a long story."

Pulling up a stool and sitting down, the man replied, "I've got time."

Back in the living quarters of the cave, the man said, "That's certainly an unbelievable story, but I feel you're both honest enough, so I'll just decide to believe you."

Breathing a sigh of relief, Isaac spoke, "So, now that you know about us, could you tell us where we are?"

Standing up and gesturing to the surroundings, the man said, "You are in the humble abode of Sucari, banished subject of the 5th Kingdom and the city of Topal."

Isaac was interested at this development, "Wait, did you say the 5th Kingdom?"

"Yeah, I did. Here, I'll show you." The group headed back to the entrance of the cave. As they stood at the edge of the cliff, Sucari pointed out the walled fortress off in the distance. "That's Topal, the capital city. Supages and I have taken up residence in the Holy Cliffs after our banishment. No one comes here because of the legends, but so far we haven't seen any reason to believe those myths."

Isaac looked despondent as he mumbled, "Great. I overshot it."

Erwin was curious of this statement, "What do you mean?"

Kneeling down, Isaac began to draw a map on the dirt floor. "See, this point here is where I started. I was heading east to get to this point, but now I'm way down here, south-east of where I was heading. Now I've got to travel much further than I had originally anticipated."

Erwin now knelt beside Isaac, "Well, that stinks."

Standing back up, Isaac said, "True, but we may be able to take advantage of the situation." Turning to Sucari, he asked, "You said that no one disturbs you here because of some legends. What legends are you referring to?"

"Well, the legends are only part of why people don't come by here. You've seen the ordeal one would need to endure just to reach this cave. At any rate, there is a story that the Holy Cliffs are home to the Gates of Hell."

Erwin was impressed, "Wow, really?"

Sucari continued, "The legend states that somewhere in these Holy Cliffs is a monster that sometimes is described as a giant man, sometimes as a bull and every combination in between. At any rate, the monster in the cliffs is in charge of something called 'Hellfire', because supposedly it's a fire that can't be put out."

Isaac nodded and said, "Just what I thought. I've heard of that legend, I just needed some confirmation." Pulling out a sheet of paper, he scribbled some instructions on it and folded it over. "Erwin, I want you to go and follow these instructions." He handed the note to Erwin and turned to Sucari, "I'd like to go into Topal to pick up some supplies and to get some information."

Sucari was skeptical, "I don't know how easy that's going to be. Topal is a very exclusive community, and they're often afraid of outsiders. I suppose I can take you to the edge of town, but you'll have to go it alone from there since I've been-"

"What the heck?" Erwin loudly interrupted, "You can't possibly expect me to do this, Isaac."

"Sure I do. I've seen what you can do, and I know you can do it."

"You're not trying to get rid of me?"

"No, I believe we're stuck with each other now."

"That's fine. I'll be going now." Erwin got up and ran toward the entrance of the cave, from which he took a great leap. Sucari was surprised by this and was about to call out after him when Isaac stopped Sucari with an outstretched hand.

They both approached the edge of the cave and saw that Erwin was nowhere to be seen. "Don't worry about him; he can take care of himself. Now, how are we going to get to the edge of town?"

Sucari was still stunned at the disappearing boy, but quickly snapped out of it. "Supages doesn't seem to be too spooked by you, so you'll ride him. That is, unless you also have some sort of odd way of getting down from here like your friend does."

"You're just giving me your horse? What about yourself?"

"Don't worry about me; I can take care of myself."

Smiling at his clever new friend, Isaac made his way to the stable. The two men readied the horse with its saddle and brought it out to the entrance of the cave. Isaac was now mounted on the horse, which had sprouted wings from its saddle, ready to fly. Sucari took a few steps back into the cave and gave a loud yell. As the horse galloped toward the edge of the cliff, Sucari was running alongside. In one motion, all three leapt into the air and were on their way.

○

When Erwin jumped off the precipice, he turned into wind and swept across the face of the Holy Cliffs. Isaac was right; he was the one for the job. The Holy Cliffs were an interesting sight. The composition of the stone was such that much of the cliffs had caves pockmarked across their surface. Erwin hadn't noticed in the dim light of Sucari's cave, but the white stone almost had a light blue tint to it.

Even though he was not used to the increased gravity of his new surroundings, Erwin felt at home flying through the air. When he felt the rush of an updraft beneath him, it was an exhilarating experience, almost as if he had found a lost family member.

After a momentary period of flying free, Erwin got to work. Down at ground level, Erwin took out the note Isaac had written. On it were the instructions, "Find the fire. If you get into trouble, use your wind." As he panned across the wide expanse of the cliffs, he located the different caves and made a mental note of their whereabouts. He took a readied stance and turned to wind.

He spent only a moment at the mouth of each cave, quickly breezing from one entry to another. Soon, the amount of places left to check dwindled down until there was only a handful left. It was in these last few caves that he found the doors.

Standing before the ominous doors gave Erwin second thoughts on whether or not he would successfully complete his mission. Engraved in relief on the face of the two doors was a scene of a half-man, half-bull who was terrorizing a village. All of the villagers had looks of horror on their faces as they ran from the monster. Most of the villagers were also on fire.

Taking a deep breath, Erwin leaned against the doors and, after some effort, was able to push them open a crack. "Here goes nothing," he said as he squeezed through the crack and into the darkness.

Yelling over the wind of the flight to the city, Isaac conversed with Sucari, "I didn't know you had a Blood-fluxion."

"Yeah, this vest was a gift from my father. He used it to escape from prison." The vest to which Isaac was referring was white and had a blood-red orb on its back. Surrounding the orb were two snakes, each biting the other's tail, resulting in a Level 2 uroboros seal. Sprouting from the back of the vest was a pair of wings. These wings were large and gave Sucari sufficient lift, but were also proportional to his frame.

"I suppose you adjusted the design for your horse, right?" Isaac pointed at the horn of the saddle, which had the same orb and uroboros design.

"I did, but Supages is definitely better at flying than I am. There's a certain level of control that I haven't been able to master yet."

The trio landed outside of town and Isaac dismounted. Sucari grabbed Supages' reigns and said, "This is as far as I can take you, and even this is a bit too close."

"What exactly did you do to get banished?"

"I was accused of killing the King." A look of concern came into Isaac's eyes, and Sucari noticed, "Look, I said that I was *accused* of killing the King, that doesn't mean I actually killed him. I was set up. Framed. And I'm not too happy about it either. Death is not the worst that can happen, apparently."

"Very well, I'll take your word for it."

"What other word do you have? At any rate, go and talk with Niccolo, he's the heir to the throne and will take over in a week when he turns 18."

Isaac pulled the white hood of his jacket over his head and headed for the gate. Sucari made one last warning, "One more thing: if you run into Allan, don't believe a word he says." Nodding in acknowledgement, Isaac entered the city of Topal.

Among the bustling streets of Topal, Isaac could tell that he was not wanted there. Everywhere he walked, he could see people watching him, seeing through him with their eyes. Not the least of which was a woman in a dark cloak. When he approached the woman, she stole around a corner and disappeared into the crowd.

The main streets radially emanated from the palace on the hill, which made finding his way an easy task. As he walked along the streets, he was hoping to pick up some of the gossip and hearsay just like he had been able to get while in the bar at New Town; but whenever he got close to anyone, they became quiet and waited for him to pass by.

When he arrived at the palace, he wasn't quite sure how to proceed. Due to the recent death of their King, security had been increased. Guards were patrolling the perimeter wall of the palace, both on the ground and on the top of the wall. They would notice him approaching and he wouldn't have a good story to get him out of any trouble. He couldn't just waltz into the throne room and say, "Hey everyone, I'm Isaac and my friend who you banished from your Kingdom told me to come in here and talk to Niccolo." Wait. Maybe that might just work.

Approaching the main gate of the palace, two guards stopped him. "Where do ya' think you're goin'?" the guard on the left gruffly asked Isaac.

"I'm going to go see Niccolo. I was told that I should talk to him."

The right guard leaned down and looked hard at Isaac's face and said, "Is that so? Well I don't suppose you'd have an appointment card, now would you?" As the right guard was talking, the left one motioned for another guard to come and assist them. After talking to the new guard, the left guard went into the palace, while the new guard took his place.

Isaac needed to stall for time or figure a way out of his predicament, so he turned to idle banter. "Lovely weather we're having."

"We're in a drought, thank you very much."

Clearing his throat, Isaac tried another tactic, "How about that local sports team?"

"Killed yesterday at an opponent's arena."

With each failed attempt, the guards got closer to Isaac and reached for their weapons. He only had one last ditch idea, "So, Allan was telling me yesterday how you guards need to be better compensated for all the great work you're doing."

The guards loosened up a bit, but still eyed him with curious eyes. The new guard spoke, "Really? And how do you know Allan?"

"Allan? Oh, Allan and I go way back. We, uh. We were partners. Yeah, partners in the security industry."

From the inside of the palace came a voice, "Isaac?"

Isaac perked up at the mention of his name, "Yes?" The guards turned around to see a rather smartly dressed man in black approaching them. He had wild, gracefully combed black hair and a neatly trimmed moustache. His face was thin, with a pair of dark eyes deeply set below a wide forehead.

"Allan, do you know this man?"

"Of course I do! We go way back." Both guards looked at each other and shrugged. Isaac passed by the two burly gentlemen and pulled back the hood of his jacket. Allan came down from the stairs and put his arm around Isaac, "I didn't know you were in town. How long have you been here?"

"A few hours now."

"Well, come inside, I'll show you around the palace."

○

Erwin was amazed at the labyrinth that he had stumbled upon. He kept walking but didn't seem to be getting anywhere. If he knew where he was going, he could just use his wind powers and jump there. But alas, that was a limitation of his fluxion: he needed to know where he was going in order to jump.

As he walked the twisting and intersecting halls, he started wondering what the whole monster story was about. Even though he was able to see pretty well in the dark, after being so accustomed to it for weeks at a time, he was worried that he might run into the half-man, half-bull.

His steps echoed off of the stone walls and he started to think about what Isaac meant by "If you get in trouble." Still, Isaac did seem to be confident in Erwin's abilities, and that made him smile. As he turned a corner, he saw some light emanating from further down the hall. It was something different, so he decided to continue on toward it.

As he approached the source of the light, the ceiling seemed to get higher and the walls seemed to grow further apart until Erwin was standing in a vast chamber. In the center of the room was a statue of the half-man, half-bull. The statue was holding the source of the light. In its hands was an orb that contained a flickering fire.

Erwin was staring up at the sight of the statue when he heard a voice. Due to the acoustics of the room, he couldn't tell where it was coming from, "This beast went by many names. Satan. Lotup Sedah. The Devil. Lucifer. Hades. Tecumseh. Pluto. Chi. But the name he was probably best known for was the name of Ruatonim." From behind the statue appeared a bearded man, who finished his monologue, "The core in his hands is known as Hellfire, and I suppose thou art here to take it?"

Erwin was a little astonished with regards to this man's calm demeanor, "Maybe I am. What's it to you?"

"We don't get many visitors in Ruatonim's Maze, so when someone actually makes it this far it's usually because they are after the orb."

"So, if people do occasionally come here, why is the orb still there?"

"That's simple. No one has yet been able to defeat me." With this bold statement, the man pulled out a glove and put it on his right hand. "Before we begin, thou must know that I am called Pruthesemo."

"Why must I know that?"

"Because it is best to know the name of the man who will kill thee."

○

The palace of the 5th Kingdom was extravagant and made anyone walking around in it feel very insignificant. Isaac followed Allan, who was giving a tour to his longtime friend, "Down this hallway is the aviary. We keep many varieties of exotic birds there." Isaac seemed disinterested with the tourist speech and was more interested in finding a spot where he could pull Allan aside.

Finally, in a grand hall lined by many large columns, Isaac grabbed Allan and pulled him behind one of the pillars, "What's your deal, Edgar?"

A little surprised by the sudden interrogation, Allan replied, "I'm not sure what you're asking, Isaac."

Pushing Allan further up the pillar, Isaac sternly asked, "What are you doing in the 5th Kingdom, and why did you change your name to 'Allan'?"

Chuckling softly, Allan replied, "Well, after we parted ways, I did a lot of thinking and have decided to make a positive change in my life. When I was Edgar, I was a drain on society, now as Allan I can help contribute to it."

"That's not how I remember it, Edgar."

"Please, stop calling me that. My name is Allan now, and everyone here has come to respect me and what I've done to help the Kingdom through the tragedy of losing its King."

Letting Allan go, Isaac skeptically grumbled, "Very well, I suppose someone like you can change his act. Just know that I've got my eye on you."

"All right. Now, you wanted to meet Niccolo, is that correct?" Nodding in agreement, Isaac followed Allan as they continued down the grand hall toward the royal chamber.

○

Erwin was out of breath from running. He didn't want to fight this man and he didn't want to use his fluxion until he could figure out more of his opponent's skills. So far, Erwin could deduce that Pruthesemo was fast. But the way that he ran was kind of odd. Instead of lifting his feet, he merely glided along the floor, skating on his boots. Erwin noticed there was a trail of residue from Pruthesemo's boots. Perhaps that's the reason he was so fast.

"Thou can't run away from me forever, you know."

"You don't have to keep chasing me."

"But I can't let thou leave now. Now that thou hast seen the Hellfire orb, thou might be liable to tell others where it is. Then where will we be?"

"I won't tell, I promise!"

"I cannot take that chance." Pruthesemo tugged on the glove on his right hand. The glove was odd in that it covered most of his hand, with the exception of his fingertips. On the back of the glove was a yellow disk with the number "16" engraved on it. Erwin noticed this and thought back to his fight with Priest Werner. What did Isaac call that? A "Number-fluxion"? It didn't really matter what it was called, all Erwin knew was that things were about to get interesting.

Pruthesemo took his right hand and started dragging its fingertips along the wall as he skated along. All of his fingers were now ablaze: five matches at the end of his palm. Erwin was surprised, but soon the surprise changed to disappointment, "Is that all?"

"Nay. Not in the slightest." Pruthesemo leaned down and touched the trail of residue from his boots. In moments, the entire room was ablaze with his fire. Erwin noticed a little too late that he was standing in one of the residue

35

paths that Pruthesemo had made. When his shoes caught fire, he kicked them off and ran to the statue of Ruatonim and started to climb. He didn't have much time.

Sitting in the palms that were holding the Hellfire orb, Erwin took a moment to assess his condition. Now that he didn't have his shoes, things would be very uncomfortable. He noticed that some of the residue was also on his clothing. Feeling it between his fingers, he now knew what it was. Oil. Erwin deduced that Pruthesemo's boots must be equipped with fluxions on their soles, which would produce the oil for him to skate on, while simultaneously providing fuel for his fire hand.

"Get down from there and defeat me! Thou cannot get away, even if thou possess the orb."

Erwin felt he was ready to take Isaac's advice. Meeting Pruthesemo's gaze, Erwin said, "You want to be defeated? You've got it!" Turning into wind, Erwin flew around the chamber, causing the flames to get bigger.

Pruthesemo was amazed at what he saw. In a moment the child had disappeared and in another moment he was engulfed by his own flames, which had grown out of control. He too had to kick off his boots in order to keep the flames from climbing up his body, but the damage was already done. His clothing was ablaze and the increased heat of the room burned his bare feet. Rolling around on the ground, Pruthesemo was screaming, "It burns! I cannot make it stop! Thou win! Thou win! Just get rid of the flames!"

Erwin rematerialized and now realized that he may have overdone it. The room was filling with smoke, and his bare feet were also being burned by the scorching stone floor. He was trying to concentrate in the blazing inferno, but found it difficult to breathe. "Isaac said to use my wind power if I got in trouble, and I thought that's what he meant," Erwin thought. "Now I'm in more trouble than if I hadn't used it at all." Erwin couldn't ignore the screams of his opponent and he couldn't possibly escape with the orb considering the condition of the room.

He kept thinking of Isaac, "Come on, Erwin, think! You were with Isaac for a few days in your home town, what would he do?"

○

Finally arriving at the throne room, Allan had reverted to his tourist guide mode, "This is the memorial statue of King Sadim." He gestured toward a life-size statue of a very regal looking man, made entirely out of gold, "He brought the Kingdom out of poverty with the help of his golden glove." Isaac could see that the statue's left hand wore a glove with a numbered disk on its back. This Number-fluxion was "79".

Isaac spoke up, "It must be nice belonging to a Kingdom that has two Number-fluxions. You remember that there are only so many of them around, right?"

Allan nodded, "Indeed. The noble '54' fluxion is kept in the Royal archive. If it were ever lost, this Kingdom would lose its holding as the 5th Kingdom."

"Allan, is that you?" The voice came from another room, and soon a young man entered the throne room. His brown hair was cut extremely short and he wore a red robe ornately adorned with gold embroidery. It was obvious that this young man was royalty.

"Ah, Niccolo, I've been looking for you. I'd like you to meet my friend, Isaac." Niccolo bowed, and Isaac did the same in respect. "He's just come to Topal and wanted to meet you as soon as he got in."

"I'm flattered, Isaac."

"Well, it's not every day that you get to meet the future King of the 5th Kingdom."

"Please, it is not the title of 'King' that makes me illustrious, but men, like my father, who make the title of 'King' illustrious. Also, we prefer the term 'Republic' over Kingdom. A ruler is useless unless he has the help of his subjects."

"I'm curious: who is running the Republic until you turn 18?"

"Well, technically Allan is, in his official capacity as Royal adviser. But don't think that I'll get rid of him after my birthday next week. I've always thought that the first method of estimating the intelligence of a ruler is to look at the men he has around him."

"So, I'm sure that you've got some big changes planned for your rule, right?"

"Quite the contrary, Isaac. You need to remember that there is nothing more difficult to take in hand, more perilous to conduct, or more uncertain in its success, than to take the lead in the introduction of a new order of things."

Isaac turned to Allan and said, "For seventeen, he's certainly a very wise man."

"Indeed. He already knows that the beginning is the most important part of the work and as such has been preparing for his coronation."

"I hope I'll be here long enough to attend."

Allan slapped a hand on Isaac's back and said, "Please, we insist. In fact, you should stay in the palace while you're here."

"I'm flattered, but I need to check with the rest of my party before committing to anything."

"Well, you and your friends are welcome to the palace while you are here. I'll inform the guards immediately."

After bows were once again exchanged, Allan escorted Isaac out of the throne room. At the entrance to the room, Isaac tripped over a tile which was slightly out of place. Allan was overly apologetic, "Oh my goodness, I'll have the maintenance crew look into fixing that immediately." Isaac watched Allan closely, and saw that he was sweating at this minor incident.

"What did he always say? Come on, Erwin, remember!" The situation in the fiery room was getting worse as Erwin was trying to figure out what to do. Suddenly, Isaac's voice entered into Erwin's memory, "For every action there is an equal and opposite reaction." That was it! If the wind had made the flames bigger, maybe removing the wind would make the flames go away.

Erwin ran to the entrance of the room and turned into his wind form. He was able to use the many tunnels of the maze to hold the air that was in the blazing chamber. Blowing the air out of the room deprived the fire of its fuel source, and it quickly died down and stopped.

Running over to Pruthesemo, Erwin turned him over and found that he was severely burned. Most of his beard was gone and the majority of his skin was red and black. Coughing out congratulations, Pruthesemo spoke, "Thou hast passed. Take the orb and go."

"Why would you do this? Why would you go through so much trouble just to protect an orb?"

With a raspy voice, Pruthesemo explained, "I wasn't protecting the orb; I was protecting those who would want to use it." With a cough and a wheeze, he continued, "My wife, Cinderella, was the previous bearer of the power, but her will was far too weak. I watched as she was engulfed by the power and burned to death." A weak smile came over his lips, "I guess now I know how it feels."

"You're not going to die! You can't die! I didn't want to kill anyone!" Erwin was crying over Pruthesemo, the teardrops that hit his skin immediately turned to steam due to the latent heat of the burns.

"When thou giveth the orb to the person who sent thou, please let them know everything." A racking cough caught Pruthesemo and he knew he didn't have long, "Please, before thou leave, tell me thy name."

"No! I can't!"

Pruthesemo was firm, "Please! Just tell me thy name!"

"Erwin." He spoke softly and tried to hold back all the emotions that were building up.

Pruthesemo smiled and said, "Erwin. What a kind name." With a long and drawn out breath, he was gone.

Erwin set his jaw, went over to the statue and picked up the orb. Hiccups of sobs escaped his throat as he walked out of the room and back into the maze. When he saw Isaac again, they'd need to have a serious talk.

○

Isaac left Topal by the main city gate. Sucari had been riding Supages around the perimeter of the city when he came upon Isaac, "Whoa, dude! What happened? You look really mad."

Trying to get rid of the scowl on his face, Isaac took a deep breath and let it out slowly. The technique didn't quite work. The scowl was gone, but he still had an intense look of seriousness across his face, "I'm sorry, but I got riled up in there. I'll explain everything when we get back together with Erwin."

Not wanting to press any further, Sucari got off of Supages and let Isaac ride. Sucari and Supages both sprouted their wings and took a running start to lift off toward the Holy Cliffs. Isaac was focused on the task of flying the horse, but Sucari could tell that the man in white was deep in thought. He was piecing together a puzzle which still had many pieces missing.

When Isaac and Sucari landed back in Sucari's cave, a gust of wind came in behind them and Erwin was standing there at the cave entrance. Once again, Sucari could tell something was wrong, but he wasn't going to point it out this time.

Turning around, Isaac saw Erwin standing there and said, "Oh good, you're back. Did you get it?"

Erwin put forward his clenched fist, turned it over and opened it to reveal the orb, flickering with fire. As Isaac reached for the orb, Erwin closed his hand again and brought it to his chest, "You have some explaining to do, Isaac." His stern look caught Isaac by surprise, but there was an understanding in Isaac's return gaze.

"Let's get settled and then we'll discuss our path forward." Erwin nodded in silent agreement, and Sucari just stared at the two serious individuals.

All three men sat in the living area of Sucari's cave. Isaac had pulled out some paper to take notes, "I'll start with the information I've gathered, then maybe we can fill in the missing pieces." Erwin and Sucari nodded in consensus. "Let's start with the most important point first: Prince Niccolo is in danger. I have reason to believe that he may be killed within the next few days."

Sucari shouted out in surprise, "What? How can you be sure?"

"Remember when you told me to not trust anything that a man named Allan had to say?"

"Yeah, but that's only because he was the reason I was banished."

"Interesting. Please, explain."

"Well, when King Sadim died, it was obvious that it wasn't an accident. All the evidence led to an intruder coming into his bedroom and poisoning him in his sleep. In order to restore order to the Kingdom, they needed to find the culprit, and fast. Since Niccolo and I were long-time friends and I hung around the palace a lot, I was immediately labeled the prime suspect. I found it odd how they would listen to the testimony of a man like Allan, who had only been here a few months, but ignored everything I had to say in my defense. Fortunately, my friendship with Niccolo was useful in that they merely banished me from the Kingdom, instead of executing me. Although some days I almost wish they had just gone ahead and done that instead."

"I see. That makes an interesting development."

"How so?"

"I met Niccolo and had a chance to talk with him."

"How did you manage to do that? Security around the palace must be incredibly tight by now."

"It was, and I really didn't have a way to get in, so I resorted to lying."

Sucari suspiciously looked at Isaac, "What kind of lie did you tell?"

Shamefully averting his gaze, Isaac admitted, "I said that I knew Allan."

"Why would you say that?"

"That's not even the worst part. I do actually know Allan, although I didn't know it at the time."

Sucari's opinion of Isaac was quickly dropping, "And how did you know this scumbag, Isaac?"

"Firstly, when I knew Allan, he didn't have that name. When I knew him, his name was Edgar. Edgar was my assistant during the Dark Year after my–" Isaac paused for a second to carefully choose his words, "My first assistant left. We were researching the fluxions and how they worked. Edgar was the first person I was able to successfully equip with a fluxion. But the power went straight to his head. He let the fluxion corrupt his mind and I had to get it away from him."

Isaac leaned forward and massaged his temples as he continued, "It's difficult to destroy something important like that, but I needed to for the greater good. The power I had given Edgar was an Elemental-fluxion. White sand. The battle was difficult, but I was able to use some fire to turn the sand to glass. This gave me an opening to strike at the core of his fluxion. Afterward, I exiled him from the island of the 4th Kingdom. Since then, it appears as though he has changed his name and his ways. I tend to disagree with that the last part, considering your story, Sucari."

Leaning back in his chair, Isaac spoke to Erwin, "Why don't you tell us what happened with the Hellfire orb?"

In a monotonous voice, Erwin gave his account, "I found the place easily enough, and the maze took a little time to navigate, but I eventually found where the orb was located." He looked up at Isaac, "But I wasn't expecting someone to be there protecting it. His name was Pruthesemo." Isaac could already tell where this story was heading. Erwin continued, "Your note said to use my wind powers if I got in trouble, but I didn't know that they would react with Pruthesemo's fire like they did." Erwin started to get choked up, "Why did you need the fire orb, Isaac? Why?"

"I had heard stories during my research of an Elemental-fluxion with the power of fire. The stories put its location in the Holy Cliffs of the 5th Kingdom, but no one who went looking for it came back. That's why I told you to use your wind powers if you got in trouble. I figured you could run away."

"You still haven't answered my question!" The tears were running freely now.

"I didn't want to risk the chance that it would get into the wrong hands."

"That's precisely what Pruthesemo was there for! He was protecting us. Protecting all of us. He knew the orb was too powerful for humans to wield. He watched his wife burn to death right in front of him. Can you even imagine what that would be like, Isaac? Can you?" Isaac averted his gaze from Erwin and his eyes glazed over in a distant memory. Erwin's speech became rapid. He was on the breaking point, "Well, I can! I killed him, Isaac! I killed Pruthesemo! I didn't want to, it just happened! You and your stupid advice caused me to kill someone and now I wish I had never come with you!"

Isaac dropped to his knees and pulled Erwin to his chest. He whispered into Erwin's ear, "I'm sorry." With a wail, Erwin let go. Sobs racked his body and he released his grip of the Hellfire orb, which dropped to the floor and rolled over to where Sucari was sitting. Sucari picked it up and examined it. He felt the past that the orb had endured; the centuries of pain that it had caused. For so long it had been used for injustice.

When Erwin had finished crying, Isaac laid out his plan, "Firstly, I think we should all be made aware of the historical significance of the Hellfire orb. I'm sure at least one of you has heard of The Triumvirate," Sucari nodded, but Erwin shook his head. "The Triumvirate was a group of three people who lived more than one thousand years ago. These people all possessed the powers we now call fluxions. Now, their sealing methods were more primitive than what I have discovered over the years, which is why the story of The Triumvirate has attained its legendary status." On the floor of the cave, Isaac drew three symbols: λ, ψ, and χ. Starting from the left, Isaac explained, "Lambda had the power of lightning, Psi had the power to control waves," pausing on the final symbol, he continued, "Chi controlled fire. The Hellfire orb is the core of Chi's power."

Standing up from his crouching position, Isaac moved on to his second point, "Now, in regards to Prince Niccolo: having known Edgar for some time, I have a pretty good idea what he has planned." Isaac turned and looked at Sucari, "Edgar is probably the person who killed King Sadim and used you as a scapegoat to hide his true intentions. Since he is currently the acting King for the 5th Kingdom, all he would need to do to cement his rule would be to kill the heir to the throne before the coronation ceremony. This is why Niccolo is in immediate danger. His birthday is mere days away, so Edgar will make his move soon."

Placing his hand on Sucari's shoulder, Isaac continued, "Sucari, you may be able to kill two birds with one stone. If you want to save your friend's life *and* clear your name, you will have to defeat Edgar."

Erwin spoke up, "So, what does saving Niccolo have to do with the Hellfire orb?"

Isaac took the orb and held it up to Sucari, "I have a good suspicion that since Edgar once had the Elemental-fluxion of sand, that he may have regained the power. All he would have needed to do would be to get a new core and recreate the seal. Since he helped me develop both, I see no reason why he wouldn't obtain that power again. As such, about the only way to defeat the power of sand is with fire." Locking eyes with Sucari, Isaac made an offer, "Sucari, I can give you that power, but you need to trust me. Erwin has made us all aware of the risks of this fluxion, but I know how to seal the core so that the user is not in danger."

Sucari held Isaac's gaze, "I'll do it. Not just for revenge. Not just to save my friend. But to bring meaning to the sacrifices that have already occurred."

Squeezing his shoulder, Isaac said, "Excellent. Now, all I need from you is your flight vest and some sewing materials. While I work on that, I'll go over the rest of my plan."

○

The next day, the group was flying back to Topal to confront Allan. Isaac and Erwin were on Supages, and Sucari was once again using his flight vest to glide through the air. As he rolled from side to side, Sucari was elated, "I can't believe how easy it is to fly now!"

Isaac yelled back, "It's simple really. The seal that you had on there was too primitive. With two snakes, there are two points where the fluxion has a chance to get out, and it's harder to control that way. My method utilizes one snake, but also uses the knotting method discovered by James and Garland. This way space is used much more efficiently."

"What knot did you use on my vest?"

"That is a 6-2 knot. The higher the first number is, the tighter the seal is. With a tighter seal, there is less chance for the fluxion's power to escape unexpectedly. The second number has to do with the number of cores that are tied together. I chose the 6-2 knot because I wanted you to have access to enough of your Blood-fluxion's power without letting the Elemental-fluxion get out of control."

Sucari tapped on the Hellfire orb that was set in the front of his vest, "Does that mean I can use my wings and the fire at the same time?"

"It most certainly does."

"Most excellent."

Isaac pointed to the ground, "There's the palace. We'll meet up with you when we're done, so do your best to keep Allan occupied until we get there."

"Gotcha." With that final word, Sucari banked away and dove toward the palace. As he got closer, he found an open courtyard to land in. He flipped over from his head-first dive and landed in the middle of the shallow courtyard pool with a dramatic splash. Standing up from his crouched landing position, Sucari stepped out of the pool and started to walk through the palace, a dripping path of water following behind him.

Strangely enough, there were no guards patrolling the hallways as Sucari made his way to the throne room. There, seated on the throne, was Allan. He got up when Sucari entered the room and started stuttering, "W-W-What are you doing here? You've been banished from the 5th Kingdom. Don't you know that everyone has a purpose in this town? Someone who commits regicide is not a welcome purpose."

"Funny you should talk to me about regicide and not belonging, since you just waltzed right into this Kingdom and killed the King yourself."

"Those are some pretty strong accusations, Sucari. Don't forget that I still have the upper hand here. If the guards catch you anywhere in this city, you are liable to be executed, no matter who your friends are."

"True, if there *were* any guards around. I haven't run into a single one on my way here."

"Let's just say they're protecting the final piece of my plan. I have great faith in fools: self-confidence my friends will call it."

"Friends like Isaac? Right, Edgar?"

○

Isaac was tying up Supages outside a side entrance to the palace as Erwin was petting the horse. With a tight tug on the reigns to check the knot, Isaac hoisted a bag onto his shoulder and said, "Done. Let's go." The two looked around to confirm that they were alone as they entered the side door. Inside, they had a choice. A staircase led upward, and another down. Isaac and Erwin hurried down the stairs to the basement of the palace.

Once in the basement, they hurried along until they came upon the main door of the dungeon. Drawing Kuroni, slashing at the lock and sheathing the katana in one movement, Isaac didn't miss a step and burst through the door with Erwin hot on his tail. Turning to Erwin, Isaac said, "Look in the right cells, and I'll look in the left ones. Remember, he's about 17 years old."

"Right." Erwin ran along the corridor, stopping at every cell to look at the prisoners being held there. All were very gruff men, some with scars, some bald, some covered with tattoos, some a combination of all three. When he turned the corner at the end of the hall, he immediately pulled back once he realized what they were up against. Whispering across the aisle, Erwin got Isaac's attention, "Psst! Isaac! Around the corner. It looks like you were right."

Joining Erwin on the right side of the cells, they peeked around the corner to see a very secure cell at the end of the hall, surrounded by a multitude of guards. "That's got to be it. No one would put that much security on the cell of a common criminal." With the disturbance of the two intruding men, the dungeon had begun to get loud with the yells and calls of the prisoners. They didn't have much time to act.

A guard who was protecting the cell came over to yell at the noisy prisoners. When the guard turned the corner, Isaac grabbed him by the chest and flipped the guard over his head and onto the ground. The guard landed with an, "Ooof," and was down. The other guards noticed something was up and came to check out the situation. Isaac set the bag he was carrying down and said, "OK, Erwin. You're on." Pulling out Kuroni, he slashed open the bag, spilling its contents of sand on the floor, "Don't stop until I give you the signal." Erwin turned to wind and picked up the sand, creating a very convenient sandstorm in the dungeon's tight quarters.

Isaac closed his eyes and turned his sword around to the blunt side. He didn't want to kill anyone, but he couldn't risk the hassle of surreptitiously getting in and out of a palace dungeon. The guards were all attempting to cover their faces in the midst of the sandstorm. With his eyes still closed, Isaac relied on the power of his sword to find the guards for him. He swung around wildly. Contact. One down. The Gravity core came in handy, as it pulled his opponents toward him. Contact. Two, no three down. With the extra force provided by the fluxion, Isaac easily took down the entire detail of guards in no time. Isaac made a bird call and the wind stopped. The sand hung in the air for a moment and fell to the ground all at once.

Erwin was impressed as they made their way to the cell at the end of the hall, "Wow. You're pretty good at this."

"Years of practice, my friend." Arriving at the cell, Isaac pulled open a tiny door and looked inside. Before him was a pair of eyes staring back at him.

"What's going on out there?" It was Niccolo.

Finding the keys on one of the guards, Erwin unlocked the door and helped Isaac open the heavy barrier. Niccolo timidly peeked out and immediately recognized Isaac. "Isaac! What are you doing here? What happened to all my guards?"

"They'll be all right. They may be a little sore in the morning, but they're fine."

"But they were protecting me! Allan said until I'm crowned King that I'm in extreme danger, so he put me in the most secure place in the palace."

"Well, he's certainly right, but you've misunderstood him."

"Excuse me?"

"You'll just have to trust me and come along." Grabbing Niccolo's hand, the trio escaped from the prison. As they ran through the halls of the basement, robes and coats trailing behind them in their escape, Isaac suddenly stopped, "Wait, what was that?"

"That's the Royal archive. It's where the token of our Kingdom is held."

"Can we go inside, for a quick moment?"

"You're pressing your luck, Isaac."

"Just trust me on this."

"Very well." Producing an ornate key which hung on a gold chain around his neck, Niccolo unlocked the door and let everyone in. Inside the archive were numerous treasures and rarities, but the one which piqued Isaac's interest was the hilt of a sword stuck in a stone.

"I thought this had been lost centuries ago, but it was probably here the whole time." Isaac gingerly felt the engraved "4" in the rock and moved his hand toward the grip of the hilt.

Erwin asked, "What is it?"

"The 4th Kingdom has a legend about a sword stuck in a stone. 'Whoever pulls the 10 Caliber Sword out of the Ragna Rock is to become the King.' When it disappeared, the entire Kingdom went through tremendous turmoil, which is precisely why I bet the 5th Kingdom stole it in the first place."

"Hey! I'll thank you very much to not slander my homeland like that," Niccolo said indignantly.

"My apologies." As he pulled on the hilt of the broadsword, Isaac strained at the effort.

Niccolo objected, "What are you doing? I thought you just came in here to look around!"

"Considering the predicament we are currently in, I think an extra weapon should come in handy." Grabbing the hilt with two hands, he pulled with all his might, at which point the sword came out of the stone, sending Isaac to the floor. "I did it! I didn't think it would be that simple." As he looked at his prize, he knew immediately why it had given away so easily. In his hand, he held the hilt and about three inches of sword. The rest had broken off in the stone after years of stagnation.

Dusting himself off, Isaac resigned himself to disappointment. Tucking the sword away, he said to Niccolo, "I hope you don't mind if I take this, do you?"

"We'll see. For right now you have a lot of explaining to do." A large shock came through the room, "What was that?"

"Where are we right now?"

"In the Royal archi-"

"No, I mean what are we underneath?"

"The throne room. The archive was put here to prevent people from tunneling up into it." Another large shock.

"Then we have to get up there. We haven't much time."

Sucari thought he knew what he was getting into. It sounded so simple: defeat a man who might have sand powers. Allan was taunting him now, "Did you really think a birdbrain kid like you would be able to fight me? I must say though, you've performed admirably, despite our difference in power."

Breathing heavily, Sucari couldn't think of a good comeback. He was too busy trying to think of a plan. Allan's black sand prevented him from flying, since the grit was irritating on his wings. He also couldn't land any solid blows, since Allan was able to turn parts of his body into sand, thereby reducing the impact force. There was only one option left. Sucari took a deep breath and calmed his body. Clenching his right fist, he focused his new power into a point at the end of his knuckles. The fist was soon ablaze.

Allan arched his eyebrows and remarked, "It would appear that you have been talking to Isaac. I remember him using that parlor trick on me many years ago. Unfortunately for you, it's not going to work anymore."

Sucari clenched his left fist, and now both were aflame. He ran toward Allan and started swinging his fists of fire. Allan deftly dodged every assault and was laughing, "What good will fire do if you can't even land a punch?" As Sucari fought with the fire fluxion, he became more aware of its capabilities. He pulled back his right arm for a jab to Allan's torso. With a sudden burst of orange flame from his elbow, he used the power to accelerate his fire punch with the hope of catching Allan off guard.

The punch ended just short of its intended target. Allan had blocked the fiery fist with his open palm, which was now a dense pack of black sand, "You see; that's not going to work either. I told you before that the fire isn't going to work anymore. This black sand was forged by the power of volcanoes, making it unaffected by fire." The sand started seeping from Allan's hand and onto Sucari's fist, but didn't manage to get far as Sucari pulled back and took a few steps back to give him some distance from his foe.

Shaking his hand, Allan said, "That actually stung a little bit." In a retaliatory attack, Allan put out both his hands, and within moments, Sucari was surrounded by black sand. Before the sand engulfed him, Sucari sprouted his wings, now ablaze with fire, and used them to shield his body from the attack. When Allan withdrew the sand, a dome of thin black glass covered Sucari.

Allan started pacing the room, "I don't see why you are so adamant on defeating me. You've already been banished from the Kingdom, and no matter what you do here, you're breaking the law. Defeating me will not get your citizenship back. And by the end of tomorrow I will rule this Kingdom and have final say in all matters."

Breaking through the glass bubble, Sucari said, "That's precisely why I have to defeat you. I love this Kingdom too much to let you fulfill your dream of ruining it."

"You are not wrong, when you say that my plan has been a dream. In fact, all that we see or feel is merely a dream within a dream. I'm just trying to get this Kingdom to wake up and realize that it's a different world now and different people run it."

"You're mad."

"No, I am merely a dreamer who dreams by day. As such, I am cognizant of many things which escape those who dream only by night. I see this world as it truly is, so why do you say that I am mad?"

Briskly walking into the throne room, Isaac spoke, "Because power and evil have gone to your head, Edgar."

For a moment, Allan scowled at Isaac, but let it transform into a smirk, "True, Isaac. But as, in ethics, evil is a consequence of good, are you not to blame for me being evil? If you are truly good, as you say, then by your idiom of actions producing consequences, then the mere state of *you* being good means that *I* must be evil."

From behind Isaac came another voice, "If you openly admit that, I am sorry that I ever trusted you in the first place." Taking a step to the side, Niccolo appeared beside Isaac, his hazel eyes showing his disappointment, sadness, and resolution.

A few stray strands of hair were brushed back with his hand as Allan was suddenly caught trying to explain himself, "Evil is only in the eye of the beholder, Niccolo. This man in front of me who killed your father has come back. He's the evil one here, probably intending to kill you as well."

"I don't think so." With one fluid motion, Isaac drew Kuroni and drove the point of the sword into the tile floor in front of him.

"What are you doing?" Allan screamed.

"Exposing you for the liar you are." Using the sword as a handle, Isaac pulled back the large tile to reveal a chamber underneath the floor. Hidden in the chamber was the former King Sadim, entirely turned to gold with a horrific expression on his face. The tile landed to the side with a large thud. "I noticed you became nervous when I tripped over this tile on my previous visit. I also noticed that the roof of the Royal archive had a different resonance in this one spot, thanks to the ruckus you two were making up here."

Hopping down into the hole, Isaac examined the golden corpse. The core was set in the former King's glove, but there was no uroboros seal around it, "Just as I had figured. Only someone like you would know that by removing the seal the fluxion would take over the host's body. With the King turned to gold, an autopsy would be impossible. Very clever, Edgar."

Allan finally snapped. Turning most of his body to sand, he rushed toward Isaac and Niccolo screaming, "Even if I was caught by your meddling, it won't matter if you're all dead! I'll just have to move my plan forward and kill Niccolo right now!" The only obstacle to Allan's plan was Sucari, standing between the madman and the Prince.

"I'm not going to let you hurt my friends!" With a renewed vigor, Sucari became engulfed in flames, but no longer were the flames a passive orange. Now the fire around the winged warrior was an intense shade of blue. Allan managed to pull back, but not after allowing his leg to turn to black glass in the process.

In defiance of his predicament, Allan smashed the leg on the ground, scattering tiny shards of black glass across the tile floor. A whirlwind of sand was now holding him up. Isaac noticed this phenomenon and shouted to Sucari, "Be careful! That's his most powerful attack: the Dove of Sand!"

Allan laughed maniacally, "You're wrong once again, Isaac. Now I call it 'The Raven of Death.' Nevermore will any of you stand in my way." From his back, the swirling sand seemed to form two ominous wings. "Now this is interesting! A raven versus an eagle. Let's see who the stronger bird is!"

Sucari shouted in retaliation, "I am no longer considered an eagle! From the shame of banishment I have come back. From the ashes of defeat I will rise victorious. I am Sucari, the blue phoenix!"

In one tremendous moment, the two men came at each other and battled. Sand and fire intermixed overhead in one dizzying spectacle: granular black in conflict with a flowing and brilliant blue. Erwin, who had also been behind Isaac, took a step forward, ready to help. Isaac put out his hand to hold Erwin back, "This is their fight. Let Sucari finish this for his own honor."

The black sand was raining down now as tiny beads of glass. As the increased heat of the blue fire rendered Allan's fluxion useless, a single opening revealed itself and Sucari took it. With the accelerated punch he used earlier, Sucari landed a successful blow on Allan's sternum. Allan was thrown to the ground and coughed up a mouthful of blood. The core of black sand had protected him from any further damage, but was now shattered and being carried away by the wind. He attempted to get up; eyes focused on Sucari through disheveled hair, but ran out of energy and collapsed on the marble floor.

○

Days later, at the coronation ceremony, Isaac and Erwin were in the back of the palace cathedral, feeling a little nostalgic from their own adventures in another cathedral only a week ago. The priest at the front of the sanctuary placed a five-pointed crown on Niccolo's head and announced to the crowd, "Today I confer the title of King of the 5th Kingdom on Niccolo. Long live the King!" The audience shouted in unison, "Long live King Niccolo!" followed by intense cheering.

At the reception, Sucari approached Niccolo, with Supages in tow, "I didn't know what to get a new King on the day of his coronation, so I suppose Supages will have to do."

"But Supages is your horse! I can't accept a gift like that."

"Please, I insist. Besides, I've gotten better at flying recently and I'm sure you'll love riding him through the sky as much as I have."

Niccolo stepped down from the throne and embraced Sucari, "You've already given me so much, my friend." Pulling back and holding Sucari at arm's length, Niccolo proclaimed in a loud voice, "My first act as King of the Republic is to reinstate Sucari as one of its citizens!"

The crowd that was mingling around gave a loud, "Huzzah!" in agreement.

Isaac and Erwin came over to join Niccolo and Sucari. Extending his hand in a congratulatory handshake, Isaac said, "I look forward to your long and wise reign, King Niccolo."

"We are looking for a new Royal adviser, you know. Why don't you stay here and fill that role, Isaac?"

"I'd love to, but I have more important tasks that I need to accomplish."

"Well, I wish you luck on your journey and welcome you all to visit Topal any time you're in the area. Consider yourselves honorary citizens."

Erwin chimed in, "You can count on it!"

○

Back at his cave, Sucari was saying goodbye to Isaac and Erwin, "I can't express how grateful I am for your help."

"Don't mention it. Once I knew Edgar was involved, I had to lend my assistance."

"So, where will you both go now?"

"We're too far south to walk to our destination," Isaac pulled out the remaining Q-Portal keys from his pocket. The ring finger key had turned to dust, just as the thumb key had done before it. Turning to Erwin, Isaac smiled, "Do you feel lucky?"

Erwin smiled back, "Life's a game of chance, isn't it?"

Choosing the middle finger key, Isaac opened the door in Sucari's cave. In the darkness of the cave, the pitch black beyond the door seemed to pull Isaac and Erwin toward it. Sucari was stunned that there was a passage like this in his cave. He was unsure where his guests were going as they ventured forth into the darkness.

"Wait!" The two travelers stopped and turned around. Sucari blurted out, "Take me with you!"

Isaac was once again hesitant, but Erwin was insistent, "Come on Isaac, we can always use another person on our journey. Besides, isn't the best way to make sure the Hellfire orb doesn't get into the wrong hands is if he's with us?"

Sighing reluctantly, Isaac said, "Very well, you can come along."

Sucari rushed back into his room and emerged with a bag, already packed and ready to go. Isaac let a smile curve on his lips as he motioned with a nod for Sucari to lead the way. Sticking his fist out in front of him with the thumb in the air, Sucari turned the thumb to fire, creating enough light to see by, and led the group into the unknown destination of the Q-Portal.

Chapter 4

Monster

When the trio emerged from the cave, they found themselves on a sweeping mountain pasture. The lush green grass swished in waves as the wind swept through it. A small cottage was the only nearby structure, but a small alpine village sat a little further down the valley. Isaac did not recognize this area, so he led the way toward the cottage to see if the owner could tell them where they ended up.

The cottage was made of stone and had a thatched roof. A waist-high stone wall encircled the house and soon the group could tell why. As they approached, the bleating sounds of sheep could be heard from behind the building. Following the wall around, the trio found the owner of the cottage in the back, shearing his sheep, "Well hullo there strangers. You wouldn't mind giving an old man a hand, would ya?" The man's short, curly white hair was offset by his dark skin, no doubt obtained by years spent outside tending his flock. Even though his face looked a little deformed and he had a hunched back, the shepherd had a kind and wise look about him. Isaac led the way by vaulting over the stone wall and heading over to where the man was sitting.

"We'll help, but only if you tell us a few things."

"Why sure, sonny. What do you want to know?"

"We're kind of lost at the moment. Could you tell us where we are?"

"I'd imagine that a pirate like yourself would be lost in this area since there's no ports around." Isaac decided it would take too long to correct the man and merely shook his head. "Well anyways, this here is Posea Pasture. I'm Posea, nice to meet you. I'd shake your hand, but I kind of have them full at the moment." The sheep he was holding struggled a little bit as he sheared off its wool.

Erwin was intrigued by this group of animals so he asked, "What animals are these? They eat grass like cows, but are too small and fluffy."

The old man was almost offended, "Sheesh, son! These are sheep. Where were you born, the moon?" Erwin opened his mouth to answer, but Isaac clapped his hand over the open mouth before anything could come out.

With his other hand, Isaac pointed to the nearby mountain, rising up above the pasture and into the clouds, "What's that mountain called?"

"Why that there is Asp Peak. It's just one of the three peaks that make up the Pythagorean Triangle."

Pulling out a map from his back pocket, Isaac spread it on the ground and found the location, "Well it looks like I'm a lot closer to where I need to go, but it's still a ways to the north."

"Why don't you gents come and take a sheep and start shearing? Here, I'll show you how to do one." As the trio eventually caught a sheep a piece, Posea gave a demonstration on how to shear a sheep. As he worked, he opined about the current state of shepherding in the valley, "I tell ya boys, this year's been rough for the wool industry. There's been an errant wolf killing a lot of our sheep, but we haven't been able to catch it. Of course, it only strikes about once a month, so we tend to get nervous when the time approaches. I still think that it's that monster what lives up in the mountains. He's got to eat at some point, and I guess sheep are just easy prey."

Isaac was intently listening to the man, but the other two were focused on trying to shear their respective sheep. Sucari finished his sheep, but noticed something strange, "Hey, Isaac! Come over here and look at this!"

Posea got up and joined Isaac over Sucari's sheep, "That's odd. I don't remember branding the sheep like that." Right behind the shoulder blades of the sheep was a blood red core surrounded by an uroboros seal branded into the sheep's flesh. Lower down on the sheep's back was another brand with the number "359".

Turning to look at the old man, Isaac asked, "You didn't put either of those brands on this sheep?"

"No sir, I did not. And I don't like the look of that blood boil either." Isaac reached down and twisted the orb out of the uroboros seal. The sheep bleated in fright, but soon calmed down. Moving the orb around in his hand, Isaac could see that there was something else inside it besides the blood.

"I hope you don't mind if I keep this, do you?"

"No please, go right ahead." Isaac pocketed the orb and got back to shearing sheep. The rest of them did likewise.

As they finished the last of the sheep, a hearty woman appeared at the back door and told them that dinner was on. Posea got up, wiped his brow and said, "You boys should stay here tonight before you continue on your journey. I insist."

After dinner, Isaac, Erwin, and Sucari fell asleep in a large feather bed set up in the attic. The handmade quilt covering the bed was warm and cozy. Around midnight, Isaac felt a breeze over his exposed face and noticed that the window was open. Going over to close it, he glanced outside and saw Erwin sitting on the stone wall. Putting on his white jacket, Isaac quietly went downstairs and made his way outside.

Erwin was staring up at the full moon, deep in thought when Isaac approached him, "It's kind of chilly out tonight, aren't you cold?"

"Huh? Nope, I'm fine." Turning back to the moon, Erwin thought out loud, "I can't believe how far away the moon seems from here." He reached out his hand, almost as if trying to grab it, "This side of the moon looks so strange to me, almost like another world." Turning to Isaac, Erwin asked, "Is this what it was like when you saw the earth?"

"A little bit."

"I wonder how my mom's doing up there."

"I'm sure she's doing just fine. She's a strong woman." Isaac unconsciously put his hands in his pockets as he leaned against the stone wall. Finding the orb he put in there earlier, he pulled it out and started examining it. The reflection of the moon caught the glint of the stone in the orb and immediately, all the pieces clicked into place.

Isaac gasped in shock, which prompted Erwin to ask, "What is it?"

"I know where the wolves were coming from." Holding up the orb, he explained, "This must be a Blood-fluxion for a wolf. But there's more to it than that. The stone shard inside the core is actually a piece of the moon."

"Wait a minute, how did a piece of the moon get down here?"

"Remember how Edmond's comet struck the moon?"

"Yup."

"Well, here on earth, that event triggered what we all know as 'The Dark Year'. The debris that was created when Edmond's comet hit the moon blocked out the light of the sun for an entire year. When the Dark Year ended, that debris either burned up in our atmosphere or it fell to the ground. This is one of those pieces that fell to the ground."

"But what does that have to do with the wolves?"

"Don't you see? The wolves were appearing about once a month, right around the full moon. It seems that the moon fragment acts as a trigger for the Blood-fluxion. Really quite ingenious when you think about it."

"But it's almost a full moon tonight!"

"Then we'll have to make sure to protect the sheep from any more of these wolves. But that's not the part that worries me. It's the number."

"What number?"

"The sheep we found this Blood-fluxion on had a number branded on its back. If the number isn't arbitrary, if it's actually used for counting purposes, then there may be more than three hundred other sheep just like it. Three hundred other sheep that someone wants to turn into wolves tonight."

"Who would do something like that? I mean, that's a lot of sheep to modify without anyone noticing."

"Whoever it is, they've got to be close-by. I recall that Posea mentioned something about a monster up in the mountains. It's not much to go by, but we could try looking there first thing in the morning."

"If we're going to go searching in the mountains tomorrow, shouldn't we get some sleep? And how are we going to keep the wolves away if we're sleeping?"

"Good point. You go wake up Sucari and I'll get some things prepared."

When Erwin got back into the attic, he found it difficult to wake Sucari. Eventually, he awoke and was escorted downstairs. When they met Isaac at the wall, Sucari groggily asked, "What's going on?"

"We need your fire." Isaac pointed to a thin row of grass which was laid out on the top of the wall. "We need to get some sleep, but before we can do that, we need to make sure the sheep are protected from any wolves."

Sucari just blankly stared at Isaac and lit the line of grass, "Next time, don't bother waking me and just rub two sticks together, would you?"

After explaining to a hysterical Posea the reasoning behind creating a ring of fire around his house, everyone got back to bed and had a good night's sleep. At least what was left of the night. During a late breakfast, Isaac explained the wolf phenomenon to Posea, "You see; this orb would turn that sheep into a wolf during a full moon. I have a hunch there are other sheep in this pasture that have the same problem. I suggest you tell the other shepherds this information. You all shear your sheep around the same time, am I correct?"

"That's right. But what should they do if they find one of those orbs on their sheep?"

"It just needs to be removed. That should make the transformation stop."

"What are y'all going to do now?"

"We're going up to the top of Asp Peak to see if we can find out who is behind this."

"Oh, I do hope you'll reconsider. That Pythagorean Triangle is very mysterious. I've heard of people who go there and never come back. There are legends that the snakes swallow travelers whole. I'm not even going to mention the dragon sightings that occasionally occur around there."

Isaac smirked and looked at his two comrades, "I think we'll be all right." The trio got up from the table, thanked Posea and his wife for their hospitality, gathered their things and headed toward the trailhead for the Asp Peak summit.

As they hiked away, packs full of supplies and food for a few days of adventure, Posea and his wife stood at their doorway and watched. Without looking away, Posea mused, "Those are either the three bravest or three craziest people I have ever met," turning to go back in the house, he added, "I think it may be the latter."

The trail up to the summit of Asp Peak was a grueling one. It started out gradually climbing up the mountain, but as the incline increased, so did the amount of rocks the group had to hike on. After about an hour of hiking, the trio was ready for a break. As they sat on some rocks, they were able to get a good view of the valley they had just been in. Everything was green and lush: the grass, the trees, the moss. It soon became obvious that the trees of the valley were used to build the small towns and cottages scattered around. As the trees became scarce, rocks were used to build some of the newer buildings. In the absence of trees, the lush grass had filled in nicely and now created a rolling green carpet between the grey, rocky peaks.

Looking up, they could see that they had a long day ahead of them. The trail, which up until now had been a rather direct route up the mountain, began to switchback, slowly snaking across the face of the mountain and all the way up into the clouds. The clouds were still hanging on the peaks, obscuring the true height of the mountains. Erwin was already tired of the hike, "Isaac, why can't Sucari and I just go ahead and wait for you to catch up?"

"That's simple. We need to stay together in case something happens. Plus, it wouldn't be good for the local population of the valley to see a magically appearing and disappearing boy or a human with wings."

"But if we were up past the clouds where they couldn't see us, then could we use our fluxions?"

"We'll see."

Another hour of hiking later, the group took another break. The hike was difficult, so they did not talk with each other while hiking, as the majority of their conversations would need to fit between gasping breaths. This time, Sucari spoke up, "So Isaac, since you seem to be so well versed in history and mythology, you wouldn't happen to know any back story to the Pythagorean Triangle, would you?"

"As a matter of fact, I do know a little, but it's mainly lore about how the Triangle got its name. A long time ago, perhaps even before The Triumvirate got started, there was a beautiful woman named Gorgon. A wizard was infatuated with her and when she shunned his advances, he placed a curse on her. The curse had two levels. The first level was that her hair was turned into a teeming pack of pythons, so that her beauty would be severely hindered. This is the reason we now refer to her as Pythagoras. If, for some reason, an individual were to find her beautiful, even despite the hair of pythons, the second curse would take effect. Anyone who would look at her and be attracted to her would be turned to stone."

Erwin scoffed, "Pfft. That's ridiculous."

Isaac nodded and continued, "I know, but that's not the end of the legend. After a while, Pythagoras learned that she could also turn those who found her repulsive into stone. Her pride and her curse made her an outcast. It was around this time that she began taming snakes. The pythons on her head allowed her to command other snakes as well, and after a while she was able to control them all and was deemed Queen of the Snakes."

Sucari, who had been paying attention asked, "Is that why the mountain we're climbing is named after a snake?"

"That's right. The final part of the story says that the three most powerful snakes, Asp, Boa and Cobra, were fighting. Each one disliked one of the others. When Pythagoras heard about their squabble, she warned them that if they kept fighting, she would have to discipline them. When they bit each other's tails, Pythagoras turned them all to stone. When she realized that she could not return them from their petrified states, she decided to take her curse away from the world by looking into a mirror and turning herself into stone. These final events are what gave us the Pythagorean Triangle and the Pythagoras tree." Isaac finished his story and everyone was silent in contemplation. Standing up and doing a short bit of stretching, Isaac said, "Well, we should probably keep moving."

Now three hours since they had left Posea's house, the travelers were taking yet another break. They were getting close to the clouds which hung overhead and would probably be in them or past them by their next break. Erwin, who had become the whiner of the group, sat down with a grunt, "Humph. Why are we doing this again?"

Sucari reminded Erwin, "It's because we want to find out who's behind those sheep turning into wolves."

"Nope, not that. Why are we following Isaac? He hasn't really told us where he's going or why he's going there."

With a sigh, Isaac sat down and said, "I suppose you both want an explanation." They both nodded. "Very well. This whole adventure started back during the end of the Reign of Robert. You know the story, right?" Once again, Sucari nodded his head in agreement and Erwin shook his head in confusion, "About forty years ago, a man named Robert started taking over the continent we are now on. With each piece of land he gained, he felt that he needed to steal the land adjacent to it, and so on and so forth. For many years, he ruled with a tyrannical iron hook."

Erwin was confused, "Hook?"

"Yes, hook. Robert had lost his right hand after stealing something as a child, but apparently having his hand cut off was not enough to deter him from stealing later in life. Anyways, soon after a few years of Robert's reign, a resistance group began to form. This group is named Testament and is the very same group I am trying to stop."

Sucari interrupted, "Wait a minute. I've heard of Testament. They're the good guys. I mean, you yourself just told us that they resisted Robert."

"Yes, I did say that, and yes, they were at one time fighting for justice. However, this was before they started using fluxions. You see, back in my homeland of the 4th Kingdom, I was researching the fluxions, trying to figure out how they worked and why they had apparently vanished into obscurity. When the Dark Year hit, I took to my research full force to see if I could find a solution. By the end of the Dark Year, when the problem had worked itself out, I had put the finishing touches on my research. My conclusions were that the fluxions were too dangerous to use unless the proper seal was placed upon them. I kept this revelation to myself, in the hope that the fluxions would still remain hidden from the world."

Sucari seemed worried and asked, "Wait a minute. The fluxion I was using to fly with was dangerous?"

"As it was, yes. The sealing technique was primitive, and was apparently a similar technique which was used millennia ago when the fluxions were in common use."

Erwin jumped in, "But aren't the fluxions in common use today as well?"

"Yes, they are. Fluxions are the main reason the Reign of Robert ended. Someone in Testament must have been researching the fluxions, much like I was, but ended up using them for more militarized purposes. As is the case after wars, what was once used to fight is adjusted to advance society, and that is why fluxions are so common now."

Sucari spoke up, "So what if fluxions are a part of our society? Isn't that a good thing?"

"I am not defining fluxions as 'good' or 'bad' things, since that depends on the user. What I have noticed is that in the absence of the unified control of Robert, the continent has split up into anarchistic colonies which are being silently controlled by Testament and its knowledge of the fluxions. I need to stop Testament so that history does not repeat itself."

Erwin had caught on and gave a conclusion, "Then if we're trying to figure out who is behind the fluxion that turns sheep into wolves, then maybe we can find a link to Testament?"

"That's right."

Sucari seemed skeptical, "Well, I'll have to take your word for it. I'll still come along, but only because I've got two of these fluxions and if anything goes wrong, I'll have someone knowledgeable who can help me."

Erwin's hand shot into the air, "Me too!"

Isaac seemed a little despondent at this revelation, "Well, I'm glad you guys are sticking around so I can be your mechanic."

The hike through the layer of clouds was almost maddening. Not only did the moisture hang in the air and cling to their bodies, but it deadened the sounds they made. There was a silence in the clouds. A silence so loud it was deafening. Even though the visibility was extremely poor, the group managed to keep on the trail, finding occasional cairns to confirm that they were on the right path.

Suddenly, they were up and out of the clouds. Having been in a state of sensory deprivation, everything seemed sharper. The scenery, the sounds, the rocks. Fortunately, the summit could be seen just above where the trio was standing. It wasn't more than an hour's hike away, but Erwin and Sucari both had severe cases of "peak fever" and used their alternative forms of transportation to get them to the top.

As Isaac came trudging up the trail, rocks clattering away as he took each step, the advance party was already enjoying their packed lunch. When Isaac approached the summit, Sucari tossed a piece of fruit at him, "Try the dried figs, they're pretty good."

Taking a bite out of the fig, Isaac nodded in agreement. He swallowed and said, "You guys find anything interesting up here?"

Erwin spoke up, "Nope, there's nothing but this pile of rocks."

"I see. I suppose since you two were so eager to get to the top, you didn't notice the cave."

"Cave? What cave?" Erwin came down from the top to see where Isaac was pointing. There, just below the summit, was an opening. A narrow gash in the side of the peak, just wide enough to let someone slide through.

When Sucari came down and saw the opening of the cave as well, he suggested, "Shall we go inside and see what we can find?" As the group approached the mouth of the cave, they could see that, in conjunction with the pile of rocks on the summit, the cave made the mountaintop look like the head of a snake. There was a ridge which came off of the right side of the mouth and gave the impression that the snake was biting the tail of the ridge. Sucari observed this and said, "This must be where that legend came from. It certainly does look like a snake biting another snake's tail."

When the trio made it inside the cave, they found that it was very difficult to see with the minimal light that was let in through the mouth of the cave. Sucari held his hand aloft and set it on fire to act as a torch. With the aid of Sucari's light, they could see two shining pieces of metal stuck in a pedestal in the middle of the surprisingly open room. Erwin walked up to the pedestal and was about to touch them when Isaac calmly mentioned, "You should be careful touching those: they're sharp." Erwin immediately pulled his hand away and waited for Isaac and Sucari to join him at the pedestal.

"Judging from what I know about these mountains, I suppose that those would be the 'Asp's Fangs'." Isaac wrapped his cloak around the right fang and managed to work it free. Repeating the process with the left fang, he continued his explanation, "During the era of The Triumvirate and the Armies of Amedeo, the six most powerful swords were broken into pieces and scattered across the continent. At the time, The Triumvirate had been using the three peaks of the Pythagorean Triangle as a headquarters, so the most logical place to put most of the pieces was upon the peaks." Isaac looked around to make sure that no one else was there, "I guess the protector of the fangs has long since gone on his way, which is good news for us."

Erwin curiously asked, "What were the names of those two swords?"

Isaac opened up his cloak to reveal the two broken shards, "Judging from the designs, the right fang was known as 'Red Flood', and the left fang was known as 'Green Legion'."

Sucari was hesitant, "So, why are we taking these?"

With his hand on Kuroni, Isaac explained, "There are two sides to every coin. An action and a reaction. Black and white. Kuroni is my black." Producing the hilt of the 10 Caliber Sword he received in Topal, Isaac continued, "With the Light scroll that Erwin helped me obtain, I'd like to repair this sword and imbed in it the Fluent described on that scroll. It will be my white. With the strengths of these legendary swords, the sum will become greater than its individual parts."

When the trio saw there was nothing else to the cave, they exited and held a meeting at the top of the Asp Peak. Erwin asked, "So, what do we do now?" The sun was beginning its march down toward the horizon, bathing the area in a golden glow.

"I suggest that we split up and go to the other peaks to find the other fangs. These two fragments won't be enough to create the sword I want." Facing toward the cloudy space trapped by the triangle and pointing to the closer peak on the right, Isaac continued, "Sucari, you and Erwin should take the ridge to Boa Peak," he now pointed to the mountain on the left, "While I head over to Cobra Peak. When you get done at Boa Peak, meet me on Cobra Peak."

Erwin protested, "But if we're meeting you on Cobra Peak, we've got to travel much further than you do."

Isaac looked at Erwin with eyes that didn't want to take any more complaining, "You both have powers that let you travel quickly to the other peaks, while I have to walk there. Since we're above the clouds, you should be able to use them without anyone else seeing you do so. I think I'm being pretty reasonable here."

Crossing his arms in defiance, Erwin pouted, despite being told that he could use his powers again. Isaac put his hand out and motioned for the other two to join him, "Very well, team. Let's meet back by nightfall." All three hands went up in the air as the two teams departed.

Erwin hovered above the ground, everything below his waist had turned to wind, and it was starting to creep Sucari out, "Hey, could you not do that?"

"Do what?"

"That . . . half-body thing you've got going on there. It's kind of creepy."

Sighing in annoyance, Erwin's legs rematerialized, but he still hovered along the path, "I'm not going to stop hovering, if that's all right with you."

"That's fine."

The Asp Ridge between Asp Peak and Boa Peak dipped down into the clouds. When they came down into the foggy haze again, they found that it was more difficult to see than before. Even though Sucari's beating wings and Erwin's wind displaced some of the cloud around them, it merely filled in again as quickly as it had left. Just like in every other situation where it was difficult to see, Sucari used his fire fluxion to light the way. Since the clouds were kind of difficult to fly in, he was using his hands to assist his wings. As such, he turned his hair to fire to light their path.

Turning around to see the glow coming from Sucari's head, Erwin exclaimed, "Wow! That's pretty cool! I didn't know you could do that!"

Sucari seemed just as surprised, "Neither did I." The halo produced by the fire illuminated some of the clouds and made it easier to see their path. Soon, the traveling partners were out of the clouds and more than half way toward their destination.

Erwin wondered aloud, "Do you think that another reason why these mountains are named after snakes is because of these wavy ridges between them?"

"I suppose. All the more reason why the legend sounds plausible."

The two traveled on in silence, both deep in thought. The only sounds heard were the flapping of Sucari's wings and the gentle breeze of Erwin's wind. Erwin looked over the left side of the ridge to the vast expanse between the three peaks, "I wonder what's down there."

Sucari shrugged and said, "Beats me. Probably another village, another pasture. The same stuff that's on this side of the ridges."

Finally, Sucari and Erwin arrived at the summit of Boa Peak. They found a cave of somewhat similar exterior to the one that was on Asp Peak. Squeezing inside, they found that the interior was similar as well. Mimicking what he saw Isaac do with the sword shards on Asp Peak, Erwin took off his short-sleeved shirt and used it to pull the fangs from the pedestal. They both stood there silently, waiting for something to happen. Nothing did, so they left.

When they emerged from the cave, carrying the sword fragments in Erwin's shirt, the sun was not far away from the horizon. As the sky darkened, the clouds on the outside of the triangle began to descend into their respective valleys, exposing the Boa Ridge and the path ahead of them. Sucari stood on the summit, arms crossed, and took in a deep breath and let it out with a satisfied sigh, "Well, we did what we needed to here. Let's keep going."

After a short while, Erwin broke the silence, "Why do you think Isaac split us up like he did?"

"What do you mean?"

"Well, before on the trail up to the top of Asp Peak, he told us to all stay together. Why was it that once we were above the clouds, he suddenly decided we should split up?"

"I think he just wanted to cover more ground by having us take different paths. It would take much longer for all of us to travel together with the paths split up like they are."

Erwin didn't seem convinced, "I suppose so."

"You're thinking it might be something else?"

"Well, I kind of forced Isaac to take me along with him, and he didn't necessarily ask you to come with us. I just wonder if he's trying to ditch us by having us go on different paths."

Sucari laughed, but secretly that seed of doubt had now been planted in the back of his head, "Don't be ridiculous. After all we've been through together, he wouldn't leave us."

Erwin smiled, deciding to give Isaac the benefit of the doubt, "Yup, I guess you're right."

"At any rate, we'll know when we get to Cobra Peak, won't we?"

○

Over on Cobra Ridge, Isaac was steadily trudging along toward the summit in front of him. He wasn't sure if it was the exertion of the many hours of hiking, or the vertical distance he had covered in that time, but his breath was becoming short and his heart was pounding in his head. The hike to the bottom of the saddle between the two peaks was easy enough, although having to pick his way through large boulders was tedious and tiring. Now, as he stood on the saddle, looking up at the climb ahead of him, he wondered what in the world he was doing there.

Taking a brief walking break by putting his hands on his head and allowing himself to get some good, deep breaths in his lungs, Isaac noticed that he was behind schedule. When he was descending the ridge to the low part of the saddle, he was chasing the clouds down as well. Now he could see that the clouds inside the perimeter of the Pythagorean Triangle kept their altitude at just a little below the ridges of the three mountains. However, the clouds outside the perimeter had lowered into the valley. As twilight encroached, Isaac could see the golden glow of the village below, as it lit its lampposts and prepared for a foggy evening. Of course, since the clouds obscured his view of the village, all he could see was the hazy glow beneath him.

Taking one last deep breath, he looked up at the path ahead of him, shook his head and trudged onward. The exposure on the path was somewhat extreme, as there was just enough of a ledge for him to walk on, and any missed step would send him into the abyss of the triangle. Side stepping along the ledge, with his back to the cold stone ridge, Isaac slowly made his way up to the summit of Cobra Peak. Coincidentally, being forced to carefully maneuver along the path meant that he was not overexerting himself like he had been for the previous part of the day. He wondered if his young companions were the reason behind his exhaustion, since he no longer had the energy they possessed and had to push himself to just keep up with it. The moon was already starting to rise when he arrived at the summit.

As was the case on Asp Peak, there was a similar cave on the summit of Cobra Peak. However, this cave had a hole in its roof, probably due to the many years of weathering it had endured. Isaac squeezed inside through the mouth of the cave and saw there were fangs here as well. Even though the setup was the same as the other cave, there were a few disconcerting differences. In a corner of the cave was a pile of bones which Isaac readily assumed were the remains of the Guardian of the Fangs. The walls, now well lit, revealed a multitude of tally marks, their white lines covering the entirety of the cave. Approaching the pedestal, Isaac examined the sword shards by the light of the moon streaming in through the hole in the cave's roof. Judging from the markings on the metal, these two fangs were pieces of "Yellow Flash" and "Violet Violence". If that was the case, then what Erwin and Sucari found were probably pieces of "Blue Division" and "Orange Crush."

Isaac took off his coat and was about to remove the sword fragments from the pedestal, when a piece of metal glinted in the moonlight behind him. This warning gave him enough time to pull his sword out. Unfortunately, the katana stuck in the scabbard, so the whole item was drawn, which proved to be a very clumsy block. Nevertheless, it was a successful block. The metal that had tipped Isaac off was now in full view and shown to be the visor of a helmet. Sans the helmet, just the visor remained. The visor was blocking his assailant's eyes, but that didn't matter because otherwise it would have blocked his mouth, which was now gripped around the scabbard of Isaac's sword.

The light grey hood of the assailant covered the rest of his features, but Isaac wasn't focused on that at the moment. He could see that not only were his opponent's canine teeth longer than usual, but they seemed to be producing a toxic substance, as shown by the discoloration of the lacquer on the scabbard. It was taking all of Isaac's strength to repel the attack. He needed some distance, so he placed a hearty kick into the torso of his enemy, which sent the man flying back into the wall of the cave. When the man hit the wall, the visor fell from his eyes and covered the unusually sharp teeth. However, the blood-red stare that now peered out from under the hood was less encouraging.

Finally producing Kuroni from its sheath, Isaac readied himself to fight, "You must be one of the Guardians of the Fangs. Probably the last of them, considering there was no one on Asp Peak." The thought of Erwin and Sucari facing a similar foe entered Isaac's head, and worried him for a moment.

Talking through the iron visor made the hooded man's voice sound very metallic, "Guardian of the Fangs? Is that who that guy was? I think you'd be better off if he was your opponent instead of facing me." As he got up and brushed himself off, he readied himself for battle as well. With another mighty leap, the man lunged at Isaac.

From behind the pedestal, Isaac swung Kuroni, striking the sword fragments and flinging them at his enemy. The shards spun through the air, catching the man's garments and arresting his attack in mid-air. Now pinned against the wall of the cave, the man struggled to get himself free, but Isaac was already there in front of him, the tip of Kuroni deftly placed near the man's throat, "It would be wise if you stopped struggling and answered a few questions for me."

The red eyes squinted in hate, but then softened when he realized that he was defeated. Inching closer, Isaac interrogated the man, "First off, what is your name, and what are you doing here?"

"My name is Vlad, and I believe that the second part is none of your business."

"I'm making it my business." The cold, steel blade of Isaac's sword now rested on Vlad's neck.

With a sigh, Vlad submitted sarcastically, "If you must know, I'm living up here so that I can terrorize the nearby villages."

Isaac was not amused. "I'm serious. What are you doing here?"

"Have you ever been an outcast, ah . . ." Vlad motioned that he did not know to whom he was speaking.

"Isaac."

"Well, I am an outcast partly of my own choosing. After having to deal with so many plebeians, I decided to just accept what they thought about me. I became tired of having to deal with people. From Abraham the butcher and his finely cut stakes, but more than rough persona, to George the vicar and his movement to have me labeled as a monster. I decided that if someone of my intelligence and skill was not appreciated, then I would make people appreciate it."

"Why would your local priest try and have you labeled as a monster?"

"I would assume it would be for a number of reasons. Although I think his main reason was because I am a part of the Order of the Dragon, and he didn't want his town to have any association with it at all."

"I'm surprised there are still any members of the Order of the Dragon left. I thought that Triumvirate ally died out centuries ago."

"No, we're not dead yet. Although I may be the last of the Order, so I suppose you can't really call it an 'order' anymore."

Suddenly, a tremor shook the cave which caused Isaac to back away momentarily from Vlad. Seeing this as an opportunity, Vlad took hold of the metal shards which were holding him to the wall and pulled them out. Isaac realized he still had some unanswered questions and his source of answers might now get away. As cracks began to appear all around the cave, Isaac dashed toward Vlad and tackled him back into the wall. With the integrity of the cave quickly diminishing, the wall gave way, allowing the two men out into the open of the summit. Soon afterward, the cave collapsed.

With the confusion of the resulting dust cloud to his advantage, Isaac once again quickly grabbed the sword fragments, pinned down Vlad's arms against the ground, and put a forceful foot down on his chest. In the distance came the shouts of two familiar individuals, "Isaac! Are you over there?" Sucari flew in above the dust and landed before Isaac and Vlad, "Hey, Erwin! I found them."

Appearing suddenly alongside Sucari in a gust of wind, Erwin asked, "Are you all right, Isaac? Wait. Who's this guy?"

Once again in a dominant position, Isaac answered, "I'm fine, but Vlad here still has some explaining to do."

As the dust and rumbling settled, Vlad realized he was now outnumbered, "I've told you what you wanted to know already, so will you please lay off?"

The unfiltered light of the moon gave Isaac a better chance to examine Vlad. Underneath the light grey hooded cloak, Vlad was fully clothed in black so that none of his skin was exposed. The one exception was his neck, which was craned back at the presence of Kuroni. Strangely enough, the neck seemed to be protected by a layer of white scales. The visor was covering his eyes, but the fangs of his mouth were clearly exposed. In the center of his chest was set a red Blood-fluxion core surrounded by an uroboros seal. It was a standard seal, except the snake on the seal had feet and wings.

"You never answered my second question, Vlad. Why are you here?"

"Are you familiar with the battle of Paul versus Harter?"

"A little, but I don't see what that has to do with it."

"Harter was my father. He was killed by Paul, and so I am here for revenge. I know that Paul is supposed to be around this area, but I haven't been able to find him."

Erwin was curious, "How long have you been looking for him?"

Looking over at the child, Vlad frankly replied, "1,095 days."

The trio of travelers was shocked by this answer. Sucari asked, "How do you know that so accurately?"

"I used to be an accountant, so I keep my records very thoroughly."

Glaring at Erwin for creating a tangent, Isaac tried to get back on topic, "What do you know about Paul?"

"I know that he was last seen at the Pythagorean Triangle, that he specializes in Blood-fluxions and that he stole my father's position in Testament."

Isaac was concerned with this development, "Choose your next words wisely, Vlad. Do you intend to avenge your father and reclaim his position in Testament?"

"Yes and no. I will avenge my father, but I do not want to join Testament. In fact, if Testament were to be destroyed, I'd feel like my vengeance would be complete. They're the ones who sent him to fight Paul alone, so I can't really forgive them either."

At last, Isaac realized that Vlad's goals coincided with his own. Pulling out the sword fragments, Isaac offered Vlad a hand to help him to his feet, "Good answer, although it doesn't explain why you attacked me."

Standing up and brushing off some of the debris from the collapsed cave, Vlad answered, "That's easy. I love to fight. It keeps my skills sharp. You just looked like the kind of man who would be a good sparring partner."

"I see. Well, at any rate, it looks like some of our goals are aligned, so you can come with us if you'd like." Isaac introduced everyone and got back to business, "I assume that you guys found the sword fragments, right?" Sucari produced the sword fragments they had found on Boa Peak. Isaac examined them and nodded, "Just as I had suspected. These are pieces from 'Blue Division' and 'Orange Crush'," looking up at Erwin and Sucari, he asked, "You didn't run into any trouble back there, did you?"

Erwin replied, "Nope. It was quiet, just like the first mountain. Nothing like what's happened over here."

All three travelers turned and looked at Vlad, who was adjusting his visor. Isaac took a step forward toward the man, "I'm curious about that Blood-fluxion that you have on your chest. Where did you get it?"

Looking down at the embedded object, Vlad explained, "This is the mark of those in the Order of the Dragon. It's what gives its members the characteristics of a dragon. Although I must admit that I haven't been able to fly yet."

"What kind of characteristics?" Erwin inquired. Vlad pulled up his visor to show the set of fangs, at which point Erwin's imagination got the better of him as he exclaimed, "You haven't sucked someone's blood out, have you?" Vlad was amused by this and just shook his head as he let the visor back down.

Isaac was still a little confused. He straightened up and explained, "Well, what you have is a Blood-fluxion, and judging from what I've seen, it seems to be of the Snake variety, which probably would explain why you can't fly. But what I can't figure out is how your fangs were able to damage the sheath of my sword like they did."

"What do you mean?" Isaac pulled out the scabbard and showed the two markings where the paint had been discolored. "Awesome! I was unaware they could do that!"

"It's almost as if your fangs were secreting a type of poison." Inspiration suddenly struck Isaac, "Vlad, where did you find that cloak?"

"This? I found it in the cave. That skeleton wasn't getting much use out of it, so I just took it."

Isaac circled around to the back of Vlad and held up the hood of the cloak. Just as he suspected. On the back of the hood was a V-shaped uroboros seal. The point of the "V" was where the core was sewn into the hood, but the ends of the V looked like they transferred the energy of the core to the inside of the hood. Isaac smiled and said, "The Guardians of the Fangs certainly went all out with this snake theme." A thought then came to Isaac, "Although, I suppose that if you changed the core then it could be used to breathe fire instead."

Sucari had been thoughtful for a while and spoke up, "But what do you think caused that earthquake? We certainly can't be safe up here if there's going to be more of them."

Isaac was thoughtful for a moment, "You're right, but considering the time of night and the current conditions, our best option is most likely to stay put. We've had a long day that led to some good finds, but no real leads toward solving the 'wolf in sheep's clothing' problem. We'll just have to sleep up here tonight and go back down into the valley tomorrow morning." Looking at the pile of debris that now constituted the summit of Cobra Peak, he continued, "I hope you all like sleeping under the stars."

The next morning found the four huddled together, leaning against a small stone wall they had built the night before. Vlad awoke first and let out an anguished groan at the sight of the sun. The sound woke the three travelers and they all started to get up while Vlad was trying to wrap his cloak in such a way that his face was covered. With the aid of the visor, which was now across his eyes, he managed to cover all his exposed skin and ended up looking like a mummy. He then went over to the pile of rubble and started digging as if he was searching for something. Upon finding what he was looking for, he checked to make sure that it still functioned correctly and hid it away in a long pocket on his leg. After a little more digging, he found a white coat and tossed it to Isaac, who brushed it off and put it on.

Erwin went to the edge of the peak and stretched his arms. After he rubbed the sleep out of his eyes, he let them adjust to the morning light. He had to blink a few times to make sure he was seeing things correctly. The clouds which were held in the Pythagorean Triangle were now gone. Oddly enough, the clouds outside the Triangle still hung lazily over the villages, slowly sloshing in the valley. "Hey guys! Come look at this!" Erwin yelled over his shoulder.

"Not so loud, Erwin," Sucari said as he made his way over to the edge of the summit. "OK, that *is* interesting." Isaac and Vlad eventually made their way over and stared in silent amazement at the spectacle before them.

Vlad was dumbfounded, "Well now I just feel stupid. I never even knew anything was down there after all those years of searching."

Deep within the confines of the Pythagorean Triangle, no longer obscured by clouds, was a vast lake. In the center of the lake was a doughnut-shaped island made from very tall cliffs. Off in the distance, one could see a winding trail coming down from the low point of Asp Ridge and down to a small plot of land at the base of Boa Peak. The land looked like it had been heavily modified by man to make it into a dock for the vast lake of the Triangle. It was difficult to know where the original land ended, but the docks were orderly and gave the plot a square shape.

Thinking out loud, Sucari postulated, "Hmmm. We must have passed that fork in the trail when we were in the clouds. It's certainly far away from here."

Isaac bent down and picked up his pack, "Well we'd better get moving then, shouldn't we?" As he set off on Boa Ridge, the others scrambled to gather their things and join him.

As the group hiked, Vlad made his way up to Isaac, who was leading the pack. His voice was muffled by the cloak he had used to cover his sensitive skin, "You certainly know a lot about these strange seals. I didn't even know that this cloak could make my fangs poisonous."

"Yes, they're kind of my specialty."

Not being quite sure how to breach the subject, Vlad nervously asked, "Do you mind telling me about your white hair? Are you an albino?"

Softly chuckling, Isaac replied, "No, not quite. But the real reason is a bit more-"

"So Vlad, if you've been around here for so long, you probably know a lot about the area, right?" Erwin had caught up to Vlad and Isaac and interrupted their conversation. Sucari was close behind.

"I suppose so."

Pointing to the dock far below, Erwin asked, "What's that dock called?"

"I haven't the foggiest idea."

Under his breath, Sucari mumbled, "A lot of help he is."

"Now hold on, Sucari. Let's give him the benefit of the doubt. He is somewhat of a local, so there is a chance he'll know something about the wolves turning into sheep." Isaac looked at Vlad, who seemed to divert his gaze, "You *do* know something, don't you?"

"I only know that I am not responsible for killing those sheep. I don't care how many people think you are a monster; I know that I'm innocent." The other three looked at Vlad, waiting for a further explanation. With a sigh, he continued, "When the sheep were being slaughtered, it was a simple explanation to blame the monster who lived on the mountain."

Focusing on the task at hand, Isaac said, "Well, it doesn't really matter right now. Let's just keep moving and see if we can learn anything at that dock down there."

Most of the day was spent on the trail, much like the day before had been. Isaac, Erwin, and Sucari were tired of walking. They were also tired of the food they had packed. They craved the comfort food they had eaten the day before at Posea's house. From their higher perspective, they could observe the depths of the lake and see all the fish that were swimming within it. As they finished hiking down the trail from Asp Ridge, they hoped that someone on the dock had some of those fresh fish to eat. Unfortunately, it looked like they would be lucky to even find someone living there. The group split up and began to search the area.

Rectangular, two story buildings were built right up to the boardwalk of the dock which, strangely enough, had no boats docked at it. Erwin leaned over the wooden railing and looked down into the calm waters. There in the depths were many small boats, broken to pieces. Erwin wondered how they got to be that way. Were they sunk because of some bad weather? Misuse? Inactivity? Were they even sunk on purpose? Turning away from the railing, Erwin kept walking along the boardwalk.

Vlad took to the shadows, checking all the alleys and dark areas which abutted Boa Peak. He found it strange that most of the buildings were similar in construction to the ones he knew back home. These perhaps had more rocks in their construction, but there was obviously a fair amount of wood used as well. He looked up to the ridge they had come from and wondered if the wood was brought all the way down here from the valley or if this small plot of land had originally been wooded. At any rate, there didn't seem to be any other land that could produce trees. Maybe the island in the middle of the lake had some resources on it?

Isaac was a little worried at how quiet the area seemed. Usually, even abandoned areas had some forms of life. Cats, raccoons, dogs, rats. Some sort of animal life usually hung around, clinging to the remains of civilization. Here there was nothing. He looked inside the minimal number of restaurants and shops and found them oddly preserved. Almost as if everyone got up and decided to leave on a whim.

Sucari slowly walked along the streets, casually glancing at the buildings around him. He suddenly noticed that he was in some sort of square. The clearing seemed to be in the center of the area and its only population was a lone, odd looking tree. It almost looked like a woman whose hair was spread out above her in branches loaded with fruit. Sucari reached up and grabbed one of the pieces of fruit and took a bite out of it. His face puckered up at the sour flavor and citrus aftertaste. Still, it was the first time in a few days that he had eaten fresh fruit, so he finished eating it. When he was left with the inedible remains, he looked around for a place to throw them away and noticed the square was unusually clean for having a fruit bearing tree in it. Judging by the lack of people in the area, he would have thought the ground would have been covered in rotten fruit.

Erwin heard Sucari's voice echoing from the buildings, "Hey guys! I found some food!" As he turned to go, he thought he saw something move out in the lake. Disregarding it, he followed the sound of Sucari's voice. Isaac turned to meet up with Sucari but did a double-take at a door in his peripheral vision. He could have sworn he saw someone peeking out from it. Continuing on toward the square, he chalked the eerie feeling up to his mind playing tricks on him. Vlad emerged from the shadows of a nearby alley and saw that Sucari was sitting underneath a tree which was very familiar to him, "Oh, I see you found the Pythagoras tree."

Sucari looked up at the tree and said, "Is that what this is?"

Nodding in acknowledgment, Vlad continued, "Indeed," he knocked on the trunk of the tree, "The bark is very hard, almost like stone, which I suppose is where the name came from."

Everyone finally made it to the tree and each one of them grabbed a piece of fruit from its boughs. As they were eating, Erwin noticed that there was a small stone plaque behind the tree. On it he read:

>This tree was planted to commemorate the epic battle of
>Paul versus Harter:
>'It's my way or the Heighway'

"Hey guys, come look at this." As the others gathered around, Erwin pointed to the plaque, "Do you think this is where the battle was fought?"

Sucari responded, "It's possible. But memorials can sometimes be set up far from the events that they are memorializing, so unless we meet someone from this area, we'll never be sure." When Sucari stood up from examining the plaque he saw an old man with slicked back grey hair standing in the square with a wild look in his eyes, "Uh, guys. We have company."

○

"I'm sorry for startling you all like that, but I don't get many visitors here at Tanilats Dock." The man was cooking some fish as the four visitors sat around a kitchen table. Even though a lone lantern dimly lit the dark room, one could see that the walls of the man's house were covered with memorabilia of greater times of a fishing industry long since gone from the docks.

Erwin piped in, "I'll say. I bet you don't get any residents either."

Isaac gave Erwin a cautionary look and apologized, "I'm sorry for my young friend's lack of tact, um . . ."

"It's Jacques. Here's your food." Placing the sizzling skillet on the table, Jacques let the four guys dig in. Jacques was fit for his age, but his tanned, leathery, wrinkled skin did not lie about how old he was. The blue scarf he wore around his neck brought out the deep azure color of his eyes. His accent was distinct, but still understandable, "When the fishing industry at Tanilats came to an abrupt end, I found that I was the only one crazy enough to stay down here. But sometimes we are lucky enough to know that our lives have been changed, to discard the old, embrace the new, and turn headlong down an immutable course. I still keep my skills up as a fisherman, but now that everyone is gone, I can focus on my writing."

Perking up at the mention of something literary, Isaac asked, "Writing? What of?"

"Fishing stories, mainly. But I do occasionally branch out to other topics. I recall that one of my better works took place at a bull fight."

Erwin was glad to have something to contribute to the conversation, "Oh, I love bull fights. Two beasts charging headlong at each other is fun to watch."

Jacques chuckled, "That's not quite what a bull fight is, but OK."

As Erwin tilted his head to the side in confusion, Sucari asked, "So, what happened with the fishing industry? I didn't see any boats at the docks when we were hiking down here."

"Oh, it's just that stupid Sea Dragon that started infesting these waters shortly after the Dark Year."

Quickly doing the math in his head, Isaac asked, "So you've been here by yourself for almost ten years now, haven't you?"

"*Oui*, I suppose I have, haven't I? At any rate, since I don't have any competition, I can usually catch what I need right around the dock."

Vlad asked, "You don't happen to know if a Dr. Paul has been around this area, do you?"

"You've all seen that plaque by the Pythagoras tree, right?" They nodded, "That Paul sometimes calls himself Dr. Paul. More recently he's taken to the moniker of 'Number 5'."

Isaac looked up and was about to speak when Vlad asked a follow up question, "So, you know Dr. Paul?"

"*Non*, not personally, but he occasionally showed up here in Tanilats. I want to say he lived in town, but there was never any record of him having a residence here. I don't think he lived on Sievuvus, considering the terrain."

Sucari asked, "Sievuvus?"

"*Oui*, it's the island in the middle of the lake. Not only is the slope too steep to land a boat there, but I've been around it enough times to know that there are no buildings anywhere on the island."

Isaac opened his mouth to ask a question, but was interrupted by a sudden jolt that shook the house. Erwin blurted out, "What was that? Is it another earthquake?"

Everyone ran out of the house and on to the boardwalk. By the light of the sky they could see a large serpent rearing its head out of the water. Jacques swore, "*Merde*, it's that *fils de pute* Sea Dragon again." The group gave him a look, "I'm sorry, pardon my French. Let me get my harpoon."

"Wait!" Isaac held out his hand to stop Jacques, "We'll take care of this." Isaac had noticed that there was a fluxion on the top of the serpent's head. When he glanced at Erwin and Sucari, they nodded in silent understanding.

Sucari sprouted his wings, which surprised Jacques, "*Mon Dieu!*" Isaac drew Kuroni and spread his arms out so Sucari could grab his shoulders and hold on. Erwin vaporized in an instant and began creating a swirling vortex where Sucari was standing with Isaac. Using the force of Erwin's wind, Sucari quickly climbed into the sky.

When the effects of the wind started to wean, Sucari's feet caught fire and were used to boost the pair even higher into the air. Isaac shouted over his shoulder, "OK . . . now!"

Letting go of Isaac, Sucari pushed his friend away and let him start his freefall toward the Sea Dragon. As he picked up speed, ripping through the air, Isaac let out a battle cry. Erwin, rematerialized on the boardwalk, watched the scene unfold, "Go Isaac!" Isaac's mighty yell reached a crescendo when he used Kuroni to strike the core of the fluxion, breaking it into a multitude of pieces and knocking the Sea Dragon's head back into the lake. Jacques stood on the dock, dumbstruck by the spectacle which just took place before his eyes. He stood open-mouthed as he was sprinkled by the rain resulting from the serpent's defeat.

Sucari caught Isaac and brought him back to the dock. The trio of warriors exchanged celebratory cheers and pats on the back when they were interrupted by Vlad's yelling, "Guys! You're not done yet!"

Emerging once again from the lake, the Sea Dragon shook its head and let out a deafening roar. Everyone craned their necks upward as it pulled back its head to strike. In an explosion of rocks, debris, and dust, the Sea Dragon collided with one of the buildings. Leaping out of the way, Sucari yelled across the monster to Isaac, "Is it just me, or is this thing bigger now?"

Isaac yelled back, "It certainly seems that way."

Erwin did not want to be left out of the conversation, "Then what did breaking the core do?"

Dodging the whipping tail of the Sea Dragon, Isaac tried to give an explanation, "If I knew what the fluxion was, I'd know what power the serpent was given. Judging from the increase in size, it must have been keeping the Sea Dragon in a shrunken state."

Erwin still wasn't satisfied, "Then why did we break the core?!"

"I'm sorry, but I *thought* that breaking the fluxion would prevent any further problems in our battle."

"Well, it didn't."

Sucari was annoyed at this bickering, "Guys! I think we have more pressing matters right now, and it doesn't matt- ooof!" The serpent's tail caught him off guard and flung him to the lake.

"Sucari!" both Isaac and Erwin exclaimed. Looking at the monstrous beast lifting its head once again, hissing at its enemies, they turned back to each other and nodded that they needed to get their act together.

"Isaac!" Running over to where the group was standing, Vlad spread out his arms and focused on the jacket he was wearing. A pair of white, leathery webbed wings grew from his arms and connected to his torso, "You guys have given me an idea."

Isaac was confused. "Are those wings? Snakes don't have wings, so what could be causing that?"

Vlad shrugged, "That's your specialty, not mine."

"But you said you couldn't fly."

"Well, that's half correct. I can't fly upward, but I can glide downward."

"Great! How long can you stay in the air?"

"It depends on how high I start from, but I can usually stay aloft for at least five minutes."

Turning to Erwin, Isaac commanded, "Erwin, do what you did before. Get Vlad as high as you can." With a salute, Erwin turned to wind and sent Vlad up into the sky. Yelling up to Vlad, Isaac gave some instructions, "Vlad! Fly out from the dock and get the Sea Dragon to follow you!"

"Sure thing!" With a bit of ecstatic pleasure, he added, "I've been waiting for a good fight like this for quite some time." Reaching into his pocket, he pulled out a short sharpened rod that he expanded out to a full length of about six feet. He threw the spear at the monster where it stuck in the slippery flesh, causing the beast to roar out in pain and anger. Taunting the serpent, he got it to follow him further out into the lake.

Sucari landed back on the boardwalk, dripping wet, "Are we ready to fight again? The monster, I mean."

The two others looked apologetic enough. Isaac huddled them together behind some cover and began going over the next plan. A few moments later, he broke the huddle and called to Jacques, "Jacques! Do you have a boat I can use?"

"*Non*. All the boats have been destroyed. But I think I may be able to do you one better." As he joined the huddle, Isaac finished with his plan.

Vlad was now far away from Tanilats and was having trouble staying aloft. When he saw the men on the dock disperse in different directions, he knew he wouldn't have to wait much longer. At least that's what the first round with the Sea Dragon led him to believe.

Erwin leapt off of the dock and turned to wind. As he moved across the water, a wave followed behind him almost like the wake from a boat. When the wave was about to get to the serpent, it died down, but now the water around the monster was starting to swirl. The Sea Dragon was still distracted with Vlad flitting about its head, but soon it began to notice the changing currents of the water. A short burst of wind lifted Vlad higher and gave him a chance to stabilize his flight and return to the dock.

Simultaneously, Sucari now leapt off of the dock and flew toward the increasing maelstrom while Jacques, equipped with nothing but his scarf and Isaac's sword, dove into the lake. As Sucari approached the serpent, he let the tip of his left wing dip into the water as orange fire spread from his vest to his wings. Underneath the surface of the water, Jacques swam quickly and swiftly through the depths, never once breaching the surface for a breath of air.

The Sea Dragon was now no longer interested in Vlad, who had glided back to the dock where Isaac was standing with his arms clasped behind him in approval. Instead, it was focused on Sucari, who was flying counterclockwise around the serpent, with the flow of the ever increasing whirlpool. This was much more interesting to the monster's reptilian brain. Isaac kept his eyes focused on the scene in front of him and addressed Vlad, "Do you still have that cloak you found on the mountaintop?"

"Of course."

"Excellent. Here's what I want you to do."

Back at the whirlpool, the water was starting to boil. The fire from Sucari's wing was heating the swirling water around the discombobulated serpent. Erwin shouted in his wind form, which sounded like it was coming from everywhere, "I hope Jacques and Vlad are ready. We only have a small window of opportunity here, and it's already getting a little too hot for my tastes."

At the bottom of the lake, Jacques approached the Sea Dragon, which had neatly coiled itself from having to constantly turn around to track Sucari's movements. Stealthily approaching the beast, Jacques could feel the warm water above him as he struggled against the ever increasing current. Lifting the black blade of Kuroni above his head, Jacques brought the katana down through the serpent's tail and into the lake bed. He then quickly left the scene for the rest of the plan to unfold.

When the Sea Dragon's tail was pierced by Kuroni, it let out an agonizingly loud roar. Erwin pulled back from creating the whirlpool and yelled, "That's the signal! Go!" The gravity fluxion imbedded in Kuroni took over Erwin's job and quickly created an even greater whirlpool than was already there. Sucari kept flying, but started to focus his energy into the vest. Almost instantaneously, the fire on his wings turned blue and the swirling mass of water shot up in a cyclone of steam.

Vlad was poised and ready to rejoin the battle. Erwin's wind suddenly came from behind and shot Vlad out toward the fray, where he quickly approached the pillar of steam and flew right into the eye of it. Inside the swirling mass of superheated vapor, the Sea Dragon looked confused and in a great deal of pain. The heat of the air inside the steam tornado told Vlad that he would only have one shot at this. Approaching the serpent from behind, he grabbed on to his spear, still stuck in its smooth and slimy back. Using this grip, he opened his mouth wide and bit the monster directly behind its head. Now in even more pain, the Sea Dragon flailed about, trying to dislodge Vlad, but he hung tight, at last being able to fully submit to the power of his Blood-fluxion.

Sucari pulled up from his holding pattern and let the fire on his wings dissipate. As he and Erwin hovered above the water, Jacques came up from underneath to see what was happening. The steam quickly stopped and cleared, revealing the Sea Serpent still standing, its head straight up into the air. Still clinging to the back of the monster was Vlad. The whirlpool below churned away.

Erwin was the first to say something, "Did we win?"

Sucari was doubtful as well, "It's hard to tell."

Stiffened like a tree, the Sea Dragon began to lean and proceeded to fall over into the lake. The rigor mortis of the beast pulled Kuroni from the lake bed, ceasing the swirling action it was creating. Due to the increased length and size of the monster, it fell just short of the dock of Tanilats where Isaac was standing.

Vlad was breathing heavily through his nose, as his mouth was still clamped onto the Sea Dragon. Isaac congratulated him on a job well done, "Good job, Vlad." No response. "You can let go now." Nothing. "Vlad!" Shocked from his primitive state, Vlad recoiled and took in a deep breath of air. Looking at Isaac, Vlad flashed a nervous smile with his fangs, still fresh with the monster's blood. Then his visor dropped, once again revealing a pair of twinkling red eyes.

With everyone back on the boardwalk, exchanging congratulations, most of the group was curious about Jacques' accoutrement. The navy blue scarf was tightly wrapped around his neck, but at one end there was a Blood-fluxion. This was what really piqued everyone's curiosity. Erwin was begging, "Please, Jacques, just show us how it works."

Jacques was hesitant because, after years of being a fisherman, he knew what the effects of using his scarf out of water might be. Finally, he caved and gave a short demonstration. Suddenly, the scarf around his neck produced three vent-like openings on each side of his neck, six in total. They were gills. The rest of the group was impressed, but Isaac seemed skeptical.

When they approached the railing of the boardwalk and looked at the dead serpent, Erwin noticed something interesting, "Isaac, look!" As he pointed, everyone's eyes fell on the broken core of the Sea Dragon and followed the line of the serpent's body to a marking many of them had seen before. It was a number. The number five.

Sucari postulated an explanation, "Do you think that number means there aren't over 350 wolves masquerading as sheep, but rather 350 monsters out there, wreaking havoc on the world?" Everyone shuddered at the idea. Not because they had to put up with the beast in front of them, but rather because there was no way of truly knowing the answer.

Turning to Jacques, Isaac said, "And yet, knowing that this monster was lurking in the lake, you decided to stay in Tanilats, even though there were no boats and no working fishing equipment. One does wonder how you managed to survive so long on only the fruit of the Pythagoras tree and the few fish you could catch from the dock." Jacques began to look nervous. "Furthermore, I'd like to know where you got that impressive scarf of yours." The others now turned and looked at Jacques with questioning eyes.

Finally cracking underneath the pressure, Jacques blurted out, "I got it from Paul, OK? Are you happy now?"

Isaac pressed on, "No, it's more than that. You know more about this Sea Dragon than you're letting on, and I have a sneaking suspicion that it's connected to Dr. Paul. As are you."

Jacques could see there was no way out now so he let out a deep sigh, sat down on the boardwalk and leaned his back up against the stone wall of a nearby building, "*Oui*, you're right. Paul used to live here on Tanilats long ago, but he left the area to go pursue his education in veterinary medicine. We didn't hear from him for a long time, but suddenly one day he returned. He only stayed long enough to get a boat and row out to the island of Sievuvus. After that, he occasionally came to the docks to sell clothing to fund his research and his experiments."

Pointing at Vlad and Sucari, Jacques continued, "You both have some of those clothes," he fingered his scarf nostalgically, "As do I. Soon the fishermen at Tanilats started coming back, not with fish, but with stories of the Sea Dragon that now lurked in the lake. Shortly afterward, the fishermen left Tanilats. However, they also left with their stories and soon a Monsieur Harter came to town."

Vlad became overly interested and asked, "What happened to Harter?"

"It was a few years after the Dark Year ended that Harter flew in on a winged dragon named Heighway and wanted to meet with Dr. Paul. When he flew over to Sievuvus, neither he nor his dragon ever returned. A few days later, Dr. Paul came back to Tanilats and set up the monument you already know. He then left the area and returned a few months later with the nickname of 'Number 5'. It's been five years and I haven't seen him since." Vlad seemed despondent at this news, but at the same time hopeful that he might still be able to get his revenge.

Isaac was deep in thought while listening to Jacques' story. He then asked, "Do you think Dr. Paul is still on Sievuvus?"

Jacques shrugged, "I suppose so, but there's no real way to land on the island." After a moment, he continued, "Well . . ."

Isaac prodded, "'Well', what?"

"Well, there's no way to the island by any conventional means."

"Explain."

"As I'm sure you can see, the island is comprised of very tall and very steep cliffs. However, the center of the island is hollowed out."

Sucari spoke up, "We saw that when we were on the ridge."

"Anyways, because of the cliffs, it is very difficult to climb over and into the heart of the island. Even flying over the walls takes a certain amount of skill, due to turbulent air currents caused by the cliffs and surrounding mountains. It seems that the only way in or out of the island is through an underwater tunnel. I've been through it once, and it's far too long for anyone to swim through just by holding their breath."

"So, do you think he was using this Sea Dragon to get from the island to Tanilats?" Isaac asked.

"*C'est possible.* I never actually saw him with the Sea Dragon, but it would explain why the, what did you call it? 'Fluxion'? Made the Sea Dragon smaller."

"How's that?"

"It's a very narrow tunnel."

Everyone was quiet, deep in thoughtful contemplation. Isaac spoke up, "Erwin? How long can you stay in your wind form?"

"A couple of minutes, why?"

"Jacques, how long does it take to swim through the tunnel?"

"A couple of minutes."

"I think we may have a solution on our hands." Walking out on the dead serpent, Isaac pulled his sword from its tail and said, "I think it's time we paid Dr. Paul a visit."

Everyone had gotten to the edge of Sievuvus by their preferred means. Sucari flew, Jacques and Isaac swam, and Erwin breezed along the surface of the lake, assisting Vlad in gliding to the island. Everyone was now treading water at the edge of the cliffs. Isaac gave Erwin instructions, "All right, now Erwin, what I need you to do is to create a bubble of air and slowly bring it down into the water. Remember, you're going to need to be very focused on maintaining the size and shape of the bubble, lest the pressure of the surrounding water becomes too great."

Erwin nodded and disappeared into the wind. At first nothing was visible, but soon the group could hear the torrential wind above their heads. As the bubble of air descended into the water, creating an indent on the surface of the lake, Isaac gave them their orders, "All right, now let's follow Jacques' lead through the tunnel. Remember to keep your head in Erwin's air bubble and just breathe normally."

As they descended into the lake, the bubble followed and was swallowed up by the water. Moments later, the surface of the lake was serene once again, almost as if no one had been there at all. In the depths, it was difficult to see where they were headed, not only due to the lack of light, but because the black mass of rock in front of them gave no hints as to the whereabouts of its secret passage. Following behind Jacques, the rest of the group watched as he swam toward the wall and disappeared into it.

When the group approached the wall where Jacques disappeared, they could see the mouth of the tunnel. He was right, it was narrow. In fact, it was narrow enough that the bubble Erwin created filled a portion of the tunnel with air and the group could proceed on foot. For the most part, the tunnel was straight, but it did take some turns and sharp climbs. Some of the members of the group felt a little weird walking in a tunnel bounded by two walls of water, but soon light from the end of the tunnel gave them a motivation to press on toward the end.

Emerging in a small, shallow pool, the group sat on the banks of the pool and wrung their clothes dry. Sucari turned to fire in an instant, causing all the water clinging to him to evaporate. Vlad noticed this and muttered, "Lucky."

Jacques stood knee deep in the water and said, "I've shown you this far, but I'm not coming with you. Dr. Paul said he'd kill me if he caught me on this island again." Jacques turned around, dove into the tunnel, and was gone. Isaac tried to stop Jacques from leaving, but moments later an earthquake shook the island. This dislodged some rocks from the cliff walls which fell and blocked the tunnel. After everything settled again, Isaac looked at their predicament and said, "I wish he hadn't left. His stories didn't seem to quite match up." Turning to the heart of the island, he continued, "I've got a bad feeling about this."

"Isn't it odd that we've felt two earthquakes in as many days?" Sucari wondered.

"I suppose so, but let's not focus on that for the moment."

From the trees behind them, the group heard a loud bark, "Halt! Who are you?" Emerging from the trees was a blue eyed man with a white beard who was dressed in a uniform and wearing a red collar. He sniffed the air and said, "Most of you are not from around here, are you?

Isaac stepped forward, "No, we are travelers here to see Dr. Paul."

"Dr. Paul," the man twitched in a moment of pain, "I mean Number 5 doesn't take kindly to visitors. Especially foreign visitors."

"We're here to discuss his work on these pieces of clothing." Isaac pointed at Vlad and Sucari, who both motioned toward their jacket and vest, respectively.

"I'll see what I can do. Follow me." As the group traveled through the forest, the man introduced himself, "I'm Ivan, Dr. Paul," twitch, "I mean, Number 5's assistant."

Erwin noticed the twitch again and asked, "Why do you twitch when you talk about Dr. Paul?"

"Well, Dr. Paul," twitch, "I mean, Number 5 doesn't like being called by that name anymore, so when I do, he usually slaps me with the back of his hand and tells me to call him 'Number 5'. I guess I've just gotten so used to him slapping me that it feels like he's slapping me every time I don't call him Number 5."

Soon, the group came upon clearing in the forest where there was a small hut and a large log cabin. Entering the log cabin, Ivan called out, "Number 5! You've got visitors." The cabin was dark, but a lot larger on the inside than it looked from the outside. Various open flames scattered about the room showed it to be some sort of laboratory. Emerging from a pile of books in the back of the room, a heavy-set, balding gentleman in a smart white suit yelled at his assistant, "How many times have I told you not to bring people back to my lab?"

"I'm sorry, sir, but-"

"But nothing. I thought moving to this island would stop visitors from intruding, but it seems I was wrong." Taking off his glasses and pinching his nose he said, "Very well, go and prepare some tea or something."

Cowering and quickly moving to the side of the room, Ivan responded, "*Da*, sir."

Approaching Dr. Paul, Isaac gave an introduction, "Dr. Paul, we've come to talk to you about these flight suits you've made."

"Please, it's Number 5." Putting his glasses back on, he came over to Vlad and Sucari and examined their clothes, "I see." Pointing at Vlad's jacket, he said, "This was my Bat Wing Jacket, but it seems to have been modified with a slightly different seal." Looking up at Vlad, he didn't recognize the covered man; despite silently recognizing the mark of the Order of the Dragon. Vlad was having difficulty hiding his anger; fortunately, the hood of his cloak hid his features in darkness. With his jaw set and his eyes filled with a fierce look of hatred, he stood there as Paul turned around, "One of my great flying suits. However-" he now pointed at Sucari, "I don't recall having this uroboros seal on the Eagle Wing Vest." He came closer to Sucari and examined the stitching on the vest. Looking up at him, he asked, "Did you do this?"

Isaac spoke up, "No, I did."

"This is a very good job. I didn't think to use knotting techniques to fuse two fluxions into one piece of clothing, but this is very clever. Very clever indeed. Takes me back to my days researching the Blood-fluxions."

"So, what made you decide to switch from studying veterinary science to fluxions?"

"How did you know that I used to study veterinary science?"

Isaac was hesitant for a moment, "Jacques told us."

Sighing, Dr. Paul said, "Him again, eh? He's probably why you all are on my island." No one could look him in the eyes. "Very well, since you're here, I suppose you'd like to have a look around. Now, where is Ivan with our tea? Ivan!" When he picked up a bell and rang it, Ivan came hurriedly over to the group with a tray full of tea cups and other tea necessities. As Ivan poured, everyone took a cup and Dr. Paul continued, "Let's take this outside, shall we?"

Opening the back door, Dr. Paul let everyone filter outside to the animal cages held out back, "When I learned what the Blood-fluxions could do, I decided to put my knowledge of animals to practical use. I mean, who hasn't wanted to fly like a bird, or swim like a fish? With the Blood-fluxions, I could evolve men! I could create gods! But as you can see, I had to start small and work my way up."

Walking through the aisles of cages, there were some very interesting looking animals. There was a kangaroo with the ears and tail of a rabbit, a pig with the skin of an armadillo, a moose with the face of a piranha, a dog with three heads, a horse with the horn of a narwhal, a beaver with the bill of a duck. Each animal had an obvious Blood-fluxion implant with a different number branded beneath the uroboros seal. To those who had seen the number on the sheep, it was a comfort to know that none of the numbers surpassed its 359. Still, many of these animals were sorry sights.

"At first, I started out small, mixing two animals together. Some of the animals rejected the fluxions and didn't change, but some of the animals were too weak and the fluxion completely took them over, turning them into the other animal. These here are the successes. And yet, I needed a new challenge. I needed to be able to control the bloodlust of carnivorous animals. This was much more difficult, but I managed to make some progress. More progress recently, though."

Erwin spoke up, "Like that sheep-wolf we found in Posea's pasture?" Isaac moaned at Erwin's naiveté. "What?"

Dr. Paul was a bit surprised, "You mean you've already seen one of them? What was it like?"

Sucari answered, "It was apparently killing some of the other sheep in the valley during every full moon."

"Oh, excellent. Just excellent." Everyone looked at Dr. Paul with concern, "You see; I was trying to figure out a way to control when the transformations took place, and that's when I came upon the idea of using moon fragments in the cores." Suddenly realizing he was on a tangent, Dr. Paul came back on topic, "Anyways, after a while I managed to figure out how to control what part of the Blood-fluxion would be produced and that's when I started creating the clothing infused with Blood-fluxion powers."

Erwin had wandered off a bit, but stopped at one of the large cages at the end of the aisle. The cage had many broken chains and restraints. The bars had been bent back like something had escaped. In the cage next to it was a terrifying monster. A dragon with two heads was lying on the floor of its cage, sleeping. The number below its seal was a two, "Hey guys, what do you make of this?" Everyone came over to the cage and looked inside. Most of them gasped at the sight of it.

Dr. Paul seemed very proud of his accomplishment, "Yes, my Twindragon is one of my best creations. I've named the left head Horace and the right head Donald." The left head of the dragon looked like it was spliced onto the body of the other dragon, "I took Harter's dragon, what was it called again? Heighway? Anyways, I took its head, renamed it Horace and fused it to Donald's body. He wanted me to give my research to Testament and I told him no."

Isaac perked up at the mention of Testament. Was Paul really open about discussing this with strangers? He decided to press on and see how much Paul would divulge, "Wait, did you say Testament?"

"I did. When Harter came here, he was their Number 5. Apparently he wasn't going to take 'no' for an answer, so I had to use Donald and my Sea Dragon to defeat him. When I went to Testament's main base and gave them the remains of their member, they immediately gave me his position. Even though I didn't meet all of the requirements to join, they let me in at the Number 5 spot I had vacated for them. Of course, I took them up on their offer, because I didn't really like how Robert was running things." Vlad's anger was now building to almost unbearable levels as he listened to Dr. Paul being so glib about his father's death.

Erwin was confused, "But how did Harter get to your island if the only way in is through that sea tunnel?"

Dr. Paul ignored the fact that Jacques had given away the secret of the entrance to Sievuvus and answered Erwin's question, "Simple, he flew in from the-" As he looked up, his face went pale, "Ivan!"

Ivan came running at his master's call, "*Da*, sir?"

"How long have the clouds not been there?"

"About a day or so, sir."

"Why didn't you tell me about this?!"

"I didn't know it was important."

"You've been living on this island for *how* many years? Has the sky ever been clear?"

"*Nyet.*"

"So you think that the one day it's clear outside, you might want to tell me about it?"

"Sorry, sir."

Another tremor of an earthquake shook the island. Dr. Paul's face got even whiter. He grabbed Isaac and asked, "Has your group been on the Pythagorean Peaks?"

"We were there just a while ago before we came down here."

"When you were on the peaks, did you take anything?"

"The Fangs of the Snakes. Why?"

Red color flushed Dr. Paul's face as he worked into a frenzy, "You fool! Those swords were sealing in the volcano!"

Sucari picked up on the last word, "Volcano? What volcano?"

Screaming in hysteria now, Dr. Paul explained, "This volcano! Sievuvus is a dead volcano! It was sealed by the uroboros connections of the Pythagorean Triangle back in the days of The Triumvirate. If the seal is broken, then the volcano can become active again! Which is exactly what is happening now!"

Suddenly, a wave of calm came over Dr. Paul as he realized the easiest way to get rid of these people, who now knew too much, was to let them die in the eruption of the volcano. That way he could get rid of the evidence of his crimes against nature and the one mistake that got away. "If you'll excuse me, I think I'm going to gather some things and escape now."

The group noticed this sudden change and surrounded him. Vlad could no longer hold his anger in anymore. Charging toward Dr. Paul from behind with his spear drawn and at the ready, Vlad yelled, "You're not going anywhere until I can get my revenge!" In a forceful motion, Paul swung his right arm backward and hit Vlad squarely in the chest. The strike was powerful enough to toss Vlad into some of the nearby cages, thereby denting the thick bars in the process. The reason for the sudden increase in strength was immediately obvious, as the arm was thick with muscle and now covered with dark brown fur.

Sighing in annoyance and rolling his eyes, Dr. Paul could tell that he'd just have to kill everyone and then escape. "I really didn't want to use this today, but it looks like I'll have to kill you all before I can leave." As he stood in the center of the circle, his body began to change. His right arm transformed into that of a bear. His left into that of a lion. His clothing was being ripped to shreds as his legs transformed into those of a leopard. From his back sprouted the wings of a condor. The tail of a crocodile also appeared. His torso now looked like it was from a gorilla. His face was a hodgepodge of other animal traits. The eyes of a hawk, the teeth of a tiger, the nose of a wolf. Now standing before the group was a monster the likes of which they had never seen and never wanted to see again.

Turning to look at Vlad, Dr. Paul scoffed, "So you must be the son of that pathetic Harter. The emblem of the Order of the Dragon was a dead giveaway, by the way. I'd like to study the effects of the modification to the Bat Wing jacket, but I'd much rather finish exterminating the remnants of the Order of the Dragon. Maybe you can die as pathetically as your father did."

The goading of Dr. Paul gave Vlad the strength to stand back up and attack again. With a whip of his tail, Paul sent Vlad flying over to the others, who caught their comrade.

Vlad was now livid, but Isaac put a hand on his shoulder to keep him from getting back up. He whispered, "I know it hurts your pride, but let me carry your revenge for you. Just stay and watch." Isaac kept a steady gaze at Dr. Paul and said, "Everyone! Go and try to find a Q-Portal! It may be our only option at this point. Just pray that there's one here, otherwise we may have no way to escape."

As Erwin and Sucari ran off, Dr. Paul gave a very slow and guttural laugh, "Q-Portals? You've got to be kidding me. Those are the stuff of fairy tales and bedtime stories."

Isaac pulled tight his white headband and answered, "I'm not about to be lectured by a collage from a zoo."

Dr. Paul's voice was a low growl now, "And why not? Animals have many powers humans don't. They're better than us in many aspects and I've merely taken them and infused their power into myself. You should bow before me, because I am now a god."

"You may have gained the powers of the beasts, but you may have lost the one thing that makes us all human."

"Oh, what's that?"

"Rational thought."

Another guttural laugh, "Ha ha ha. You slay me."

"My plans exactly." With a sudden movement, Isaac drew Kuroni and was slashing at the monster Dr. Paul had become. For as large as Paul was, he certainly moved quickly enough and easily dodged all of Isaac's attacks. A right from the bear arm caught Isaac by the chest, ripping open his shirt. A kick from the leopard legs sent Isaac flying into the empty cage with bent bars.

With the wind knocked out of him and the wound on his chest starting to bleed more profusely, Isaac was starting to lose consciousness. In the back of his head, Isaac could hear the calm and soothing voice of a woman, "Isaac . . . Isaac . . ." Shaking it off, Isaac got up and out of the cage. Paul was looking very impatient. Running at Paul, Isaac lifted Kuroni over his head and thrust it into the ground, using the hilt as a handle to deliver a dual foot kick into Paul's abdomen. The attack didn't seem to faze Paul as he grabbed Isaac and threw him into the air. With a mighty leap, and the aid of his condor wings, Paul met Isaac in the air and pounded Isaac back to the ground with a punch of his entwined hands.

The voice was back in Isaac's head, "Isaac, let me help you."

"No, Marie. I need to fight this alone."

"But Isaac, you're never alone. You have friends who need you, just like I did."

The ground began to rumble again and steam started venting from cracks appearing in the ground. There wasn't much time left to waste. With renewed vigor, Isaac got up and held Kuroni tightly. Everything started to move toward the sword, even Paul who was still flying in the air, "An impressive sword you have there, but unless you can hit me with it, it really isn't very useful, now is it?" When Paul was pulled within range, Isaac let fly with a mighty slash, many times faster than any he had done before. The sword caught one of Paul's legs and caused him to land.

"It is an impressive sword, *Paul*. Not only does it have the power to pull like gravity does, but it has gravity's power to accelerate as well."

"I see I'm going to have to get a little more serious now." Paul lunged at Isaac and was going for the jugular when the flash of Kuroni's blade blocked the attack. Isaac was barely holding the strength of Paul's mighty body back when the crocodile tail came from behind and tripped Isaac, bringing him to the ground with a thud. Paul was now on top of Isaac. Pulling his head back, Paul head-butted Isaac and everything went dark.

Isaac awoke with a start at the feeling of someone shaking him. It was Vlad, "Isaac! You need to get up! We've found the Q-Portal you asked for." Struggling to his feet, Isaac reached in his pocket and found Jason's keys. Only two left. Erwin and Sucari were standing nearby, examining the body of Paul, who lay defeated on the ground. The temperature was increasing rapidly and there was a greater rumbling in the ground, continuing to build in intensity.

When the other two noticed that Isaac was up, they came running over. Sucari said, "We found the Q-Portal over in the small hut by the log cabin, but we still need to hurry." Assisting Isaac, the group headed over to the hut as a stream of lava erupted not far away. Inside the hut was a small bedroom setup which had been ransacked by Sucari as he looked for the Q-Portal. Underneath the bed was the shape of a door and the distinctive Q-Portal keyhole.

Isaac found it ironic that Dr. Paul had been sleeping over one of the Q-Portals he scoffed at not existing. Choosing the index finger, Isaac struggled to get it into the keyhole. Erwin was a little frantic now, "Come on, Isaac! Hurry!" The key was in and the door swung open, creating a hole in the floor. Everyone jumped in and landed in a dimly lit room.

Sucari was providing direction now, "We need to close the door, quickly!" As Vlad and Erwin helped Sucari close the door in the ceiling, Isaac lay on the cool floor of the room, wondering what had just happened.

Chapter 5

Escape

With the door shut, the temperature of the room dropped to its normal level and most everyone stood there, breathing heavily, their adrenaline still rushing. Vlad let out a short laugh as he said, "Those finger keys you guys have are certainly pretty handy in a pinch, but where are we exactly?"

Isaac, still spread eagle on the floor explained, "Don't know. In all the times I've used the keys, I've never immediately known where I ended up. But I must say that the floor and ceiling combination is a new one for me." As he held the key, Isaac watched as it started to crumble and eventually turn to dust.

Erwin and Sucari were still catching their breath, but took the time spent resting to look at their surroundings. The room they were in was very sterile and very plain. The walls were made with large bricks, painted white. On one wall was a shelving unit which held white sheets. Another wall was lined with buckets, brooms and mops. Everything was covered in a layer of dust and held to the walls with cobwebs. They were in a janitorial closet of some sort, one that had not been used in a long time. The only light they had was a thin strip that peeked in underneath the door.

Helping Isaac up, Sucari smiled and said, "I guess Posea was right after all. We went into the Pythagorean Triangle, but we didn't really come out of it."

"I suppose you're right. Just more fodder for the myth. Although, I bet our disappearance will be a mere footnote compared to the volcano eruption." Trying to stand by his own power, Isaac found that he had taken more damage in the last battle than he had thought. His knees buckled and Sucari had to catch him before he fell to the ground.

"Whoa! Are you all right, Isaac?"

"Yes, I'll be fine. I just need to stretch my legs a little bit."

"I'm amazed you're even able to move. Dr. Paul was certainly a monster and I'm not quite sure how you managed to beat him." Erwin went and opened the door as Sucari helped Isaac walk out with the rest of the group.

Everyone had to blink their eyes a few times to get used to the whitewashed walls of the large hallway in which they were now standing. The tall, barred windows let in plenty of light and bathed the opposite walls in the light of the setting sun.

"I'm not sure I like the looks of this," Erwin said nervously. The walls opposite the windows were an array of prison cells, three stories high; their bars brown and rusted. The occasional drip of water or scurrying of rats could be heard echoing through the space, but otherwise it was silent.

Still holding on to Sucari's shoulder, Isaac was reassuring, "I wouldn't worry about it. This prison doesn't look like it's been used in many years. I would wager that there's nobody here but us." Looking longingly at the empty beds in the cells, Isaac continued, "And I would bet nobody wants to come to an abandoned prison, so we're probably pretty safe here. Let's get some sleep and see about getting out of here tomorrow." Everyone nodded in agreement as each of them went to find a cell to sleep in for the night.

○

Isaac stood in a vast field filled with white wildflowers. He wasn't sure how he got there, but it felt very familiar to him. Sitting underneath a tree at the edge of the meadow was a beautiful woman, wearing a white sun dress, blending in with the beauty of the flowers. She looked up from the book she was reading and realized that Isaac was nearby. At this realization, she stood up and started to run toward him, her long black hair flowing behind her. When Isaac realized who it was, he began running as well, tears in his eyes.

However, moments before they met, she turned into a light blue vapor and started to float into the sky. No, that wasn't quite right. The vaporous form of the woman stayed in the same spot, Isaac was falling. The ground had given out beneath him, and a flurry of white petals swirled around him as he fell. His heart started to beat faster; he tried to scream but didn't have the breath. He dared not look down lest he see the ground rush up to meet him. He could hear the echo of her voice calling his name, "Isaac . . . Isaac . . . Isaac . . ."

"Isaac!" Vlad was shaking Isaac in his cell when he finally awoke and grabbed Vlad's arms. His grip was tight and as his surroundings became clear to him, he loosened his grip. "Are you all right?" Vlad inquired.

Wiping the cold sweat from his forehead, Isaac mumbled, "Yes. I'm fine." Regaining his composure, he asked, "What's up?" The prison was still dark, but the light of the moon gave enough light to see by.

Vlad whispered, "I hear music. Someone else is here."

Isaac held his breath for a moment to try and listen without being interrupted by his breathing. Vlad was right. It was faint, but there was the sound of a pipe organ being played. The song was deep and powerful, but certainly bore a morose tone. Looking up into Vlad's red eyes, Isaac asked, "Do you want to check it out?" When Vlad nodded, Isaac sat up and grunted in pain. He knew he would be sore, but he couldn't have anticipated being *this* sore, "I'm going to need some help if you want me to come along." Vlad extended his arm for assistance, Isaac grabbed it and pulled himself upright.

Vlad asked, "Should we get Erwin and Sucari as well?"

Isaac shook his head, "No, let them sleep. Yesterday was a long day."

As the two men shuffled toward the music in silence, Isaac could tell that Vlad was hesitant to tell him something. Finally, Vlad got up the nerve to break the silence, "Um . . ."

"Yes?"

Even though it went against all the pride in his body, Vlad mumbled, "Thanks for stepping in back there." He coughed to clear his throat, "I mean, I didn't have a chance against Paul, so I'm glad that at least one of us took him out."

Isaac chuckled, "Yeah, people *that* crazy shouldn't be allowed to continue with their plans."

"No, I'm serious. I was so focused on revenge that I thought my anger could give me the power to defeat him. You made it obvious that I was foolish to pursue that vengeance."

Isaac smiled and nodded at the heartfelt thanks. The walking was helping Isaac loosen up and now he wasn't leaning on Vlad as much as he had been when they started their search.

Feeling a little more comfortable around Isaac, Vlad asked another question, "So, why do you wear that headband?"

"Excuse me?"

"That headband. It's got a red lion on it. I assume it stands for something."

Sighing in relief, Isaac said, "Oh, this? It's the mark of the Brotherhood of the Scarlet Lion. Back in the 4th Kingdom, where I'm originally from, it was a society of individuals who had been singled out by the King to represent the 4th Kingdom. Not only on the battlefield, but in diplomacy and other areas as well. For my work in fluxions, I was inducted into the Brotherhood and am now a proud member."

"That's awesome. So, how do you get it to glow red?"

"What?" Isaac was becoming more nervous.

"Well, when you were fighting Dr. Paul, the mouth of the lion was glowing red."

Pushing Vlad up against one of the walls, Isaac became very serious, "OK, Vlad. You need to tell me exactly what you saw when I was fighting Dr. Paul."

Vlad's confidence was now gone, "Wh-wh-what do you mean?"

"No more questions. Talk!" Isaac was very gruff now and it was scaring Vlad.

"I didn't see anything, I swear!"

"You and I both know that's a lie."

"All right, fine. When you were fighting Dr. Paul, you had your eyes closed, almost like you were asleep, but you were fighting extremely well. Your movements were very fluid, almost as if you were dancing. A dodge, an attack, a block. All were done in a single and continuous movement. Even if I wanted to help you fight, I would have obviously gotten in the way. Also, for some reason your hair had turned black."

"What about the headband?"

"Like I said before, it was glowing red in the lion's mouth, but when you defeated Dr. Paul, the light faded and you fell to the ground. I had to shake you to get you to wake up, which was odd because you had just been moving only moments before."

"None of you took off my headband, did you?"

"No! We were too much in a hurry to get out of there to care about something trivial like that."

Breathing a sigh of relief and pulling back from Vlad, Isaac said, "This headband is very important to me for many reasons. Let's leave it at that."

"But what about that fighting style?"

Thinking for a second on how to best answer that question, since he knew Erwin and Sucari probably saw some of it as well, Isaac replied, "It's a very special technique in which you remove one of your senses to heighten the other four. That's why my eyes were closed: I could hear and feel Dr. Paul's movement much better when I wasn't relying on my sight." Accepting the answer, Vlad started walking toward the sound of music, leaving Isaac behind. Isaac knew he wouldn't be able to hide some things for very much longer and wondered how long he could get away with it.

When he caught up to Vlad again, the silence between the two had returned. Trying to cover over what had just happened, Vlad broke the silence again, "I've been meaning to ask you about Sucari's flight vest."

"What about it?"

"Well, Dr. Paul said you had adjusted the seal somehow, and I've seen that Sucari can fly a lot better than I can."

"He probably has more experience at it, Vlad."

"Maybe, but if you could adjust my seal as well, maybe I might actually be able to lift off, instead of just gliding."

"That's certainly a possibility, but you must know that working on the seal of a fluxion is very risky work. If it's not done correctly, the fluxion might not work. Or worse, it might take you over."

Vlad was deep in thought about this choice. After a moment he spoke up, "I don't care. I want you to adjust my seal."

"Very well. Although, I must say that I'm a little confused about your powers. At first I thought that you had some sort of snake Blood-fluxion, but the wings don't fit that hypothesis." Musing on the given information, he came upon a solution, "Unless . . ."

"Unless what?"

"Unless there's the blood of more than one species in the core. That would be possible, but also seriously tricky to successfully pull off. Maybe your adjusted uroboros seal helps to keep the two blood types separate. If I had to guess, there's at least snake and bat blood in there, but there may be others that we're not aware of yet." Isaac's voice had been building in excitement, "All right. I'll definitely do it. I'm eager to try something out and this is a perfect opportunity to do so. But right now we need to focus on finding out where that music is coming from."

The music of the organ was hard to track because the solid brick walls of the prison, coupled with the maze-like structure of the facility, made finding its source more difficult than either Isaac or Vlad had anticipated. It had been a few hours since they started searching, but they finally arrived at the wing where it seemed most likely to be coming from.

Vlad read aloud the quote above the large doorway, "'Abandon hope, all ye who enter here.' Wow, that's pretty ominous."

"'Hope.' 'Hope.' Why does that sound familiar?" As Vlad reached for the handle on the door, Isaac remembered, "Oh, right! The 'Hope' Wing of 'The Box' was where the worst prisoners were kept. I think I know where we are now."

Vlad stopped and pulled away from the door, "What do you mean, 'worst prisoners'?"

"Well, Pandora Prison, more lovingly known as 'The Box', housed some of the most evil criminals ever. The quote on the door wasn't necessarily for the prisoners going in, although that was a large part of it. It was more as a warning to visitors and guards. This wing is called the 'Hope Wing' because if you have to abandon your hope, this is the last place you can leave it."

Pulling further away from the door, Vlad was no longer sure he wanted to know where the music was coming from. Isaac continued, "Of course, it's been empty since the Prison closed down after the Dark Year, so I'm sure there's nothing to worry about." As Isaac finished his sentence, the music came to a sudden stop, and an anguished yell came reverberating from beyond the door.

"On second thought, let's just get the others and leave. Now that we know where we are." Vlad was quickly walking backward toward the hall they just came from.

"I think I'll join you on that plan," Isaac said as he also backed away from the door.

The music picked back up again, a few bars before the place where it stopped. From behind them came a voice, "So this is where that music was coming from!"

Both Isaac and Vlad jumped and turned around to find Erwin standing in the hallway, "What? Why are you both so jumpy? Let's go see what's behind the door." Before they could stop him, Erwin had opened the large door and headed into the Hope Wing. They merely stood there, mouths agape at what had just happened. Isaac finally got enough sense about him to run after Erwin. Vlad just stood there, hesitant at the beckoning darkness beyond the open door.

Even though he was starting to get over the soreness of his muscles, Isaac could not keep up with Erwin and was eventually able to catch him at the end of the hall. This hall, like all the others, was empty, but there was obviously music coming from the solid door at the end of the hallway. Grabbing Erwin, Isaac yelled in a whisper, "Erwin! It's not safe here! Let's go get Sucari and get out of here."

Erwin seemed disappointed, "You mean you don't want to find out who's making this music?"

"Not considering where we are."

"Well, *I* do." Erwin reached out and opened the solid metal door. It creaked loudly on its heavy hinges, which hadn't been used in many years. The music stopped as the door came fully ajar. Taking a few steps inside, Erwin could see that the music was indeed coming from this particular cell. There was a rather impressive pipe organ taking up the back wall of the cell. A small window near the ceiling let in the light of the approaching dawn.

At the bench of the organ sat a man who was restrained with chains and fetters, but still could move about freely enough to play the keys of the organ. Ignoring the interruption, the man continued where he left off, the chains rattling as his hands moved across the keys. When he came to the part where he stopped previously, the chains were pulled taut as he struggled to reach the last key of the bar. The anguished cry came again, but this time it was followed by a metallic voice, "This is maddening torture! If only I could reach that middle C!"

Erwin approached one of the chains and loosened it. The man's hand, no longer held back, hit the key with a satisfying result. With a sigh, the man said, "I have been waiting five years to hear that note. Thank you."

Isaac came in the cell and noticed the scene in front of him. More importantly, he noticed that there were a few sets of broken chains already attached to the man's legs and arms, "Erwin," he said slowly, "You might not want to do that."

"Why not, Isaac? I'm just helping him out."

"Yes, but I'm sure he's being restrained for a reason. I swear, one of these days your curiosity is going to get you kil-."

The metallic voice interrupted, "Isaac? Did you say Isaac?"

Erwin was smug now, "See! If he knows you he can't be too bad, can he?"

"Erwin, I've never met this person before."

"Come on Master Isaac, how can you not remember me? You were like a father to me. Although, I must say that your voice does sound a little different from how I remember it. Erwin, is it? Could you loosen these chains so I can get a good look at my Master?"

"Sure thing!"

"Erwin!" But it was too late, Erwin had pulled the pin in the back of the cell that was holding all of the chains in place, and as they clattered to the floor, Isaac was now the one who stood still in terror.

Standing from the bench, the light of the morning caught the form of the man and reflected off his skin. When he turned around, a pair of luminescent green eyes examined the white haired Isaac in front of him. Black patches of old, dried blood covered most of the front of the man's shiny exterior. On his chest was the serial number: R-3N3.

"No, you are correct. You are not Master Isaac. Sorry for the misunderstanding." Bowing slightly, the man introduced himself, "I am R-3N3."

Isaac cautiously approached the man and put his hand on the shiny bicep. It was cold to the touch. Isaac recoiled in shock, "You're not human . . . are you?"

"What do you mean?"

"You're cold. Almost like you're made of metal."

"That does not mean I am not human. I move. I have thoughts. I think, therefore I am human."

"But how is that possible?"

R-3N3 pulled the pins out of his shackles to give his hands freer movement, he then opened his chest where he revealed a Blood-fluxion with a seal that connected into a network of other seals which seemed to run throughout his hollow body. The main seal had two snake heads trying to eat the core, instead of the standard tail-biting setup. Beneath the core of the fluxion was a number. The number one.

Isaac was concerned at the sight of the seal and the number, "You don't happen to know Dr. Paul, do you?"

"Negative, who is that?"

Letting out a sigh of relief, Isaac said, "Well, if you don't know him it really doesn't matter." Turning to go, Isaac said, "Come on, Erwin. Let's get the others and get out of here."

"You mean we're just going to leave him here?"

"Considering the circumstances, I think we should err on the side of caution. Would you please close the door behind you?"

Approaching the metal man, Erwin asked, "Why are you in here? Did you do something wrong?"

"Oh, I have not done anything wrong."

Isaac was getting frustrated now, "Really? Then why were you in the most secure part of the most secure prison on the continent?"

"Testament put me here."

"And why did they do that?"

"They said I broke the first rule. But I did not; I was obeying the first rule."

"And what is this 'first rule'?"

"Master Isaac told me that the first rule to live by is to not kill anyone else. If someone is killing someone else, I must step in and stop them."

"Are there any other rules?"

"Only two others. The second rule is that I should be obedient, unless I am told to kill someone. The third rule is that I should protect myself, but only if I am still obedient and I am not killing anyone."

Isaac was thoughtful, "I see." He was thinking that if Testament put R-3N3 away, there was probably a good reason for it. However, he figured the enemy of his enemy could be his friend. When it came right down to it, Isaac had a sneaking suspicion he knew who the man was, or more accurately what the man was called long ago. "Very well, R-3N3. You can come with us."

"Splendid! You will not regret it."

When the trio left the Hope Wing of the prison, Vlad and Sucari were just running in from the hall. Vlad was out of breath, "Oh thank goodness! When the music stopped and you guys didn't come back out, I thought something dreadful had happened, so I went and got Sucari for backup."

Sucari seemed a little irritated for being left out, "And who, might I ask, is this?"

"I am R-3N3, it is a pleasure to meet you."

"He's coming with us on our journey," Erwin said.

"Oh? And I suppose we know where we are now?"

Isaac gave an assuring pat on Sucari's shoulder and said, "Just . . . don't worry about it." Shrugging it off, Sucari went over to shake R-3N3's hand. He was shocked at how cold the hand was. He was about to say something, but Isaac beat him to it as he pulled out a map, "Yes, he's a little different."

Spreading the map on the guard's desk, Isaac pointed to the center of the map, "We're here, in Pandora Prison. If I remember correctly, the prison is located just north of the town of Mathiston." Pointing to a dot a little bit to the north and east of where they were, he said, "This is where we need to go. It's not too far away. Maybe a day's journey on foot."

Erwin was excited to get going, "Well, what are we waiting for? Let's go!" As he ran off, the others begrudgingly followed. R-3N3 however, was just as excited and followed Erwin down the corridors and to the main gate. When everyone caught up, Erwin was trying to push the doors open. He stopped for a moment and told the rest of the group, "It's locked."

R-3N3 looked up and down at the double doors and said, "Let me try." Putting a hand on each door, he began to push. The groaning sound of metal bending built to a crescendo until, with a loud burst, the doors swung open. As the group filed through the open doors, Isaac looked at the bent lock on the door, then at R-3N3. Things may have just gotten more interesting.

Erwin was patting R-3N3 on the back as they made their way to the outer wall, "Way to go, Artie!" Isaac looked down at the map. Next stop, Armor Village.

Chapter 6

Heavy

As Isaac walked along the road to Armor Village, he realized that for someone who was trying to defeat Testament all alone, he was doing a lousy job of it. Since he started on his journey, he had picked up a curious wind child, a blue phoenix, a lone dragon and a sentient suit of armor. He hoped he would reach his destination soon, before any more misfits decided to tag along.

Suddenly remembering an earlier conversation, Isaac turned to Vlad and offered, "Let me start working on that flight jacket seal for you."

"All right." As Vlad took off the jacket, he accidentally knocked back his hood, revealing a head of white hair.

R-3N3 was intrigued by this, "Isaac, you and Vlad are so young, but you both have white hair. Is it for the same reason?"

Isaac was pulling out the stitching on the current uroboros seal on the jacket as he replied, "Probably not. Vlad's an albino. Right, Vlad?"

Quickly pulling the hood back up over his head, Vlad said, "Indeed. That's why I have red eyes as well. With part of the Blood-fluxion being that of a bat, I really don't do well in sunlight."

Focused on his work, Isaac commented, "Besides, my hair's got a little bit of a light blue aura to it. In the right light, that is." Getting up, Isaac started walking on the road again, "With the road as defined as it is, I can work on this as we hike. Let's get going."

"Shouldn't we wait for Erwin?" Sucari asked.

"What do you mean?"

"He's not here."

"Well, then where is he?"

"Heck if I know."

With a sigh, Isaac realized Erwin's curious nature may have caused the child to wander off. In fact, it seemed strange that Erwin didn't chime in during the albino conversation earlier. All the more proof of his absence. "I guess we should turn around and try to find him. And we were making excellent time too."

Having just started on their way back to search for Erwin, a timid gust of wind promptly blew past them. There stood Erwin, right in the middle of the road. He looked a little embarrassed as he realized that everyone had begun to backtrack to try and find him.

"And where might you have run off to?" Isaac inquired.

As Erwin walked past the group, he replied curtly, "What does it matter? I'm here now, let's go."

Concerned that this might be the first signs of a pre-pubescent rebellion, Isaac responded, "It's easy to get lost in these thick woods."

"But the road is so straight that I'd have a hard time getting lost. Besides, I can catch up quickly with my wind powers."

"You know you shouldn't rely on your powers like that. If you need us to stop, just say so."

"You're not my dad! Don't tell me what to do!" Turning on his heels, Erwin faced the group. His face was red with frustration and embarrassment. Everyone was silent.

Turning back around, Erwin continued on toward Armor Village. Mumbling beneath his breath, he said, "We don't need to stop for me to go to the bathroom." In awkward silence, everyone continued hiking.

As the group continued on the road, the forest became more and more dense. Where once one could look into the trees and see sunlight, soon the only view of the sky was directly above them, almost as if the road had been cut out of the forest. There were a variety of trees in this forest, ranging from deciduous to coniferous, each hearty trees in their own right. Isaac noticed the change in the forest and made an offhand comment, "We must have crossed the border into Timberland, which means we're nearing our destination."

Biting off the thread, Isaac finished sewing the new seal on Vlad's flight jacket and tossed it over to the albino, "Here you go, Vlad. I've put a 7-3 seal on your fluxion, partly because of the mixed blood, but also so that you can use the poison hood without any side effects. I'm also not sure if there are any other powers in that core, so the seal is designed with that unknown in mind. At the very least, you should be able to use both the snake and bat fluxions at the same time."

Putting on the jacket again, Vlad immediately tried it out. Extending his arms out from his sides, his wings quickly formed in the space between his arms and torso, "Indeed. The wings respond much quicker than they used to," he paused for a moment, feeling the inside of his mouth with his tongue, "And it looks like I can control the fangs too."

Erwin's amazement made him blurt out, "Are you sure you've never sucked anyone's blood?" Everyone chuckled, the previous argument quickly fading away from their memory.

The group continued walking, but the trees surrounding their path started to look sickly and dried. The dirt of the road had gradually turned to a yellow color from the tan that it had originally been. The temperature had increased significantly since earlier, and now most of the group was sweating. The smell of rotten eggs wafted through the air. Erwin was disgusted by this new smell, "Phew! What is that stench?"

"We must be near an active volcano, which would also explain the state of the trees in this area," Isaac explained. R-3N3 stopped for a moment; then quickly ran ahead of the group. Everyone else noticed this and ran after him. When he stopped, he held his hand against the trunk of a tree which seemed to be made out of metal.

"I saw this tree further up the path, and I wondered why it looked the same as my skin." R-3N3 rapped on the bark with his knuckles, which made a clinking sound. The group encircled the strange tree. For the most part, the tree looked exactly like a cottonwood, just with very few leaves and made entirely of a shiny metal.

Erwin reached out to touch the tree when Isaac shouted out, "Don't do that!" Recoiling in surprise, Erwin turned around and glared at Isaac, who picked up a stick off the ground and approached the tree. Strangely enough, Kuroni rattled slightly in its sheath, almost anticipating what was going to happen. Pressing the end of the stick onto the trunk of the tree, the stick caught fire moments later. "That tree is extremely hot. If it's made of metal, which seems to be the case, then the geothermal heat of the volcano is going to transfer to the tree a lot easier than any of the other trees around here." Cradling his hand, Erwin silently moved away from the tree.

Vlad, a little further along the road, called out, "Hey! There are more of those trees over here!" Sure enough, the forest gradually turned from an organic one to a metallic one. The travelers were careful to avoid touching any of the trees, after the apt demonstration Isaac gave earlier. Once the entirety of the forest seemed to be made of metal, the group came across a gate blocking the road. Isaac pulled out the map and examined it closely, "Well, this is definitely the right road, so I guess we'll just have to hop the fence and continue on." Taking the lead, Isaac vaulted the gate and kept walking on the road toward Armor Village.

Continuing on the path, the metal trees started to dwindle. A multitude of metallic stumps evidenced the previous population of the forest. Of the trees which remained, most of them were stripped of their branches. The forest looked more like a pit of spikes than a collection of trees. As the group was walking, something zipped by Isaac's head and made a metallic clink against one of the trees. Isaac seemed unfazed by the near-miss as he kept walking. R-3N3 found the object stuck to the tree and pulled it off of the trunk. Examining the object, it appeared to be some sort of throwing star or shuriken. "Isaac, you may want to take a look at this."

When Isaac turned around, a sudden barrage of throwing stars assaulted the group. The projectiles seemed to be coming from every direction, weaving through the trees on predetermined paths. Drawing his sword, Isaac managed to block a few of the incoming projectiles as he yelled, "We've got to keep going! Hurry!" The group of travelers picked up the pace as the barrage continued. As quickly as it had begun, the attack stopped.

Catching his breath, Isaac asked, "Is anyone hurt?" Everyone checked themselves and found that there were no injuries. However, one of the throwing stars had managed to stick against R-3N3's metal exterior. Isaac peeled the shuriken off of R-3N3's back and examined it. There didn't seem to be anything abnormal about its construction, although it felt lighter than it looked.

A little further along the path, Sucari noticed a copper-colored coil in the middle of the road, "Hey guys, I think I may have just found a snake."

Tossing the shuriken to the side, it inexplicably flew toward R-3N3 and stuck once again to his back. Determining that this phenomenon would have to be examined later, Isaac approached the copper coil with both hands on his sword. As he came closer, the coil seemed to retreat away but then flew into the air and snapped at Isaac. Blocking with Kuroni, the copper object coiled around the sword and started making a buzzing sound. Isaac grunted and fell to his knees. When the others came over to try and help him, he stuttered, "D-D-Don't touch me! I'm b-b-being shocked." He let go of his katana, letting it drop to the ground. Removing his jacket, he wrapped his hands in it and picked up the sword again.

Following the tail of the animated copper object around the tree, it soon became clear that it was a whip being controlled by a clean-shaven man clad in dark green flannel and a bright yellow vest. His calm, brown eyes matched the color and disposition of his hair. Seeing that his foe thwarted the stun technique, the man scoffed, "Humph. Pretty clever. Most people wouldn't have made it past Rigel's attack." As Isaac drew closer to the man, the man drew closer to the tree. When Isaac threateningly pointed Kuroni at the man, a sudden force pulled the sword to the nearby tree. His attempts to free the sword from the invisible grasp of the tree were fruitless. The man smiled, "However, very few make it past me."

Sucari could hear the man talking around the corner and came over to join Isaac. Assessing the situation, Sucari reached out for the copper whip. The man in the yellow vest warned, "I wouldn't do that if I were you. You don't want to end up like your friend, do you?" Ignoring the advice, Sucari grabbed the whip and turned the palm of his hand to fire. Moments later, the man let out an exclamation and let go of the whip. However, the whip remained taut. Looking further around the tree, Sucari saw that the whip was in fact one long cord, with one end wrapped around one of the trees and the other end wrapped around Isaac's sword.

Clenching his fist and turning the ball of knuckles into a fiery fist, Sucari calmly said, "You might want to let him go. Lest any more of us decide to step in." Vlad stepped out from behind Sucari and snapped his retractable spear to its full length.

Defiant to the end, the man said, "And why should I? You're all trespassing in the Dendritic Forest."

R-3N3 turned the corner and joined Sucari, "Sir, we do apologize for trespassing, but we are merely travelers on our way to Armor Village."

Seeing R-3N3's metal skin, the man apologized, "Oh, I'm sorry. I thought you were here to steal some of this forest's Dendrites." As he uncoiled one end of the whip from the tree, Isaac's sword became unstuck from the nearby trunk.

Sheathing the katana, Isaac called out to Erwin, "You can come out now. The fighting's over."

The man in yellow turned his head and yelled into the woods, "Rigel! You can come out as well; they're not here to steal the Dendrites." Out from the forest came Erwin, followed by a tall, muscular man who was wearing armor on his chest and a pumpkin-shaped helmet on his head. On his waist he wore two sacks which were full of throwing stars. The man in yellow came up to Rigel and put a hearty slap on his back, "I'm Michael, and this here is Rigel. He doesn't talk much." Isaac went through his group and introduced everyone to Michael and Rigel.

Michael coiled the two ends of his whip and fastened a coil on the left and right sides of his belt. Turning to his partner, he said, "Well, Rigel, should we head into town?" Rigel nodded and soon a strange thing started to happen. His legs started to look like they were getting bigger, and eventually they split to a front and back pair of legs. The back pair kept extending backward as everything below his waist started to resemble the body of a horse. Rigel was now quite the sight. Combined with the armored upper half, the horse-like bottom half made him an even more intimidating figure. Michael hopped on Rigel's horseback and said, "OK, guys. Follow us."

As the group continued on their way toward Armor Village, Isaac struck up a conversation with Michael, "What did you call these trees again?"

"Dendrites. They're a special type of tree only found in this area. That's why we try and protect the Dendritic Forest as much as we can, since they're a limited resource."

"Resource? Resource for what?"

"Armor. They don't call it 'Armor Village' for nothing. We use the metal from the Dendrites to create the masterpieces that make the village famous." Turning to R-3N3, Michael continued, "In fact, I bet everyone in the village would like to check out your armor. It looks very slick and form-fitting."

R-3N3 seemed confused, "Armor? I am not wearing armor."

"But your body is covered in metal."

Isaac stepped in, "Artie is a special case. Let's just leave it at that." Pulling off the throwing star which was still stuck to R-3N3, he held it up and continued, "But what I can't figure out is why Rigel's shuriken stuck to the trees like that."

"Oh, that's easy. This area, just like the three other Molten Forests, is highly magnetized. It just happens that since Dendrites are metal, they pick up that magnetism better than in the other Molten Forests."

"Wait, back up. What are the Molten Forests?"

"Well, this area of Timberland has a lot of access to geothermal power. This means that the earth's crust is thinner here compared to other areas of the country. As such, the magma of the earth's core is closer to the surface, creating some interesting molten materials. These materials are then absorbed by the robust plant life, which then takes the properties of the molten material when it cools. This area just happened to be over a seam of metal. Other Molten Forests are made of rock or glass. Since the plants are destroyed in the process, it's difficult to get new plants to grow to replenish the forest. This is why we need to protect the Dendritic Forest."

The group came upon another gate, similar to the one they jumped earlier. On this gate was an obvious "No Trespassing" sign. Emerging from the Dendritic Forest, the landscape opened up to reveal a quaint little village, at the base of which was an enormous chain that led to an island floating in the sky above a vast lake. Three additional chains were attached between the island and three other spots spaced around the shore of the lake. All the travelers looked up at the floating island, amazed at the spectacle it beheld. Isaac knew he was close. This floating island was known as the Eagle's Nest, and it was the main base for Testament.

Arriving in Armor Village, the group was led through the streets, past the blacksmiths and the foundries, right to the largest house in town. Michael dismounted Rigel and opened the front door. Inside, a woman with short, wavy blonde hair greeted Michael with a kiss on the cheek. She wore green armor on her upper torso, replete with breastplate and arms. Her long skirt swished back and forth as she invited the rest of the group into the house, "Come in, everyone! Make yourselves at home. I'll get some more chairs and we can begin eating dinner. Honestly, Mike. You need to warn me when you bring so many guests over."

With a peck on her cheek, Michael replied, "Sorry, Milo. Even I wasn't expecting to bring this many people home." The group followed Milo to the dining room where two men were sitting, having a heated discussion. Both men had short, frazzled, sandy blonde hair with mutton chop sideburns outlining their cheeks. The men looked almost identical, except that each of them had armor covering one side of their body.

Milo stood behind them and put her hands on her hips, "Why don't you boys stop fighting and go find some more chairs for us."

In unison, the two men said, "OK, sis," got up and left the room.

When they had gone, Michael turned to the group and explained, "Those guys are Milo's younger brothers. Carl is the one wearing the blue armor on his right side. Fred is the one with the red armor on the left side."

After Carl and Fred returned with some more chairs, Milo re-entered the dining room with a roast and said, "OK, let's eat!"

The travelers enjoyed the home-cooked meal, since many of them hadn't had a good meal in many days. When everyone finished eating, the conversations began. Milo went around the table, pouring coffee. When she stopped at R-3N3, who had not eaten anything during dinner, she asked, "You feeling all right, hon? You hardly touched your dinner."

R-3N3 replied, "Oh, I do not really eat much. But thank you anyways."

"No, I understand. You're just like the rest of us. Rigel has difficulty eating as well. All of us Armorites know what it's like to go through life like you do."

Sipping his coffee, Isaac entered the conversation, "I don't think you all understand Artie's condition."

Milo took off her right arm with her left arm, revealing that nothing was there, "No, we understand completely." Carl and Fred removed their armored arms, and Rigel removed his helmet. In each case, the body part covered by armor was missing. Isaac spat out his coffee in surprise. Reattaching her arm, Milo gently touched R-3N3 on the shoulder, "Why don't you show us what you're missing?"

Reluctantly, R-3N3 pulled back the door on his chest to reveal his hollow interior. The Armor Village natives gasped at the sight. Fred stuttered out a question, "H-h-how is that possible?"

Isaac, who had regained his composure, replied, "Probably the same way you all do it: through a Blood-fluxion. What I can't figure out is how you all can do it without the extensive seal work that Artie has." Carl came over to where Isaac was sitting, and allowed him to examine the area where his shoulder should have been. Implanted in the skin, which was scarred from a previous surgical procedure, was a Blood-fluxion. However, instead of the red core which was the distinguishing mark of the Blood-fluxion, the core in Carl's shoulder looked like green goop.

Carl sat down and explained, "A large majority of the people born in this village are born with birth defects. Milo was born without arms, Rigel without a head, and Fred and I were Siamese Twins. We think it may have to do with the magnetic properties of the area. But at any rate, in order to function as a society, we needed to find ways to solve these defects."

Fred spoke up, interrupting Carl, "So what we found is that, if we implant the powers of insects on the missing area, we can control the armor that covers it."

Isaac was thoughtful, "I see. The Blood-fluxions of the insects take advantage of their exoskeleton characteristics to let you all lead normal lives."

Nodding in agreement, Fred continued, "It gets even better than that. Not only can we control the missing limb, but we gain the strengths of the insects.

I've got the power of the Hercules beetle, Carl's got the Atlas beetle and Milo has the Praying Mantis," he looked over at Rigel, "We're not really sure what he's got."

R-3N3 spoke up, "But if you all have armor, why does Michael not have any?"

"Oh, I'm not from around here," was Michael's reply. "I'm from the 3rd Kingdom, over on the west coast of the continent. I joined the family business of being a lumberjack, but when my grandfather, Jason, mysteriously disappeared many years ago, I decided to pick up shop and move to Timberland. I heard that Timberland had trees which could not be cut down, and I just had to see if I could break that myth." Putting his arm around Milo and giving her a squeeze, Michael continued, "That's when I found Milo and fell in love. I've lived here ever since."

Isaac thought part of Michael's story seemed familiar, but tucked away the connection when Fred changed the flow of the conversation, "So, Sucari, I noticed that you have the Hellfire orb. I'm assuming you've met Pruthesemo?"

"Nah, I didn't meet anyone by that name. Besides, Erwin found the Hellfire orb for me."

"I've known Pruthesemo from a long time ago. After Cindy died, he was traveling down south when he stopped at Armor Village. I found him on the outskirts of town, being attacked by an eagle that was pecking at his stomach. When I chased off the eagle, we became good friends." Turning to Erwin, Fred said, "I'm assuming you and Pruthesemo are really good friends if he let you take the Hellfire orb. How is Pruthesemo these days?"

Erwin looked away, his eyes filling with emotion as he mumbled, "He's in a better place now."

"Oh, that's good, because I heard from my mother that he was dead. I guess she was just mistaken."

Carl spoke up, "Come on, Fred. You know mom's been dead for a long time now."

"I know, but I've seen her angel a few times. She comes to me during the night and tells me things."

"Fred, why don't we choose another topic of conversation?"

"Hey, just because you carry the weight of running the armor industry in this village, don't go telling me what we should talk about." Fred was becoming agitated.

As was Carl, "I only took the job because you tricked me into it! You know I'd much rather be a cartographer!"

"It's not my fault that you're such a pushover!"

Raising her voice for a brief moment, Milo yelled, "Enough! Besides, it's late, so let's end the conversation and let our guests get to bed." Turning to the group of travelers, she apologized, "I'm sorry for my little brothers' behavior. I hope you all don't mind sleeping out in the stables, but we don't have nearly enough space for you all to sleep in the house."

Isaac replied, "That's fine. We're used to sleeping wherever we can find a place to lay our heads." Isaac, Erwin, Sucari, Vlad, and R-3N3 all stood at once and followed Milo outside. The main stable had a large sign over its entrance with the name "Luvnac" burned into it. The Luvnac stables were large and replete with the tools necessary to the art of blacksmithing. In the center of the room was a fire pit which had burned down to warm, red coals. Milo went into the back room and emerged with some blankets. As each traveler received a blanket, they thanked Milo and proceeded to find a place to lie down and sleep.

○

The night was peaceful and the sky was clear. As everyone slept, a lone figure appeared on the edge of the lake underneath the Eagle's Nest. He didn't stop, he just kept walking, but he didn't sink. Each step was taken on the surface of the lake. When he was directly beneath the floating island, he ascended on a clear, shining pillar up to the Eagle's Nest.

A few hours later, a large bird flew from the floating island and down to Armor Village. Fred awoke with the feeling that someone was in his room, which was an accurate feeling because someone was. A woman, softly lit by the light of the breaking dawn streaming in through the open window, stood at the end of Fred's bed. She was beautiful and had long, flowing blonde hair and wore a serene white robe. On her back was a pair of white wings. She spoke in a soft voice, "Fred, are you awake?"

"Mother? Yes, I'm awake."

"Good. I've got something to tell you."

"Now wait a minute, mother. You told me Pruthesemo was dead, but Erwin told me that he wasn't."

"That's what I've got to tell you. Erwin killed Pruthesemo."

"What?! How do you know that?"

"Listen, you idiot! You saved Pruthesemo's life before, and that life has been snuffed out. Just take care of it, all right?"

Fred quietly replied, "Yes, mother."

"Good." The woman turned, leapt out of the window and was gone.

○

The following morning, everyone woke up to a thin layer of snow on the ground. During breakfast, Michael commented on the oddity, "It looks like Helge was right. That coot of a weatherman is always predicting snow, and it looks like for once he was correct."

Milo sipped some tea and mused, "Well, a broken watch is right twice a day, isn't it honey?"

Finishing his breakfast, Fred asked Erwin, "Hey, you want to go see something pretty cool?"

"Sure!" Erwin and Fred got up and left the house.

Turning to Isaac, Milo asked, "So, where are you off to next?"

Isaac pulled out the sword fragments he had collected at the Pythagorean Triangle and asked, "Well, I was wondering if there was a blacksmith in town that could help me with these sword fragments?"

"Oh, our expertise here isn't weapons, it's armor. You're going to need to go to the Granite Grove just a little bit northwest from here. That's where some of the world's greatest swordsmiths are located."

"Then I suppose Granite Grove is our next destination." Isaac wrapped the sword fragments back up and headed out to the stables. Before he left the room, he thanked Milo for repairing the damage his shirt had sustained when he fought Paul, to which Milo merely nodded and smiled in acceptance of his thanks.

Inside the Luvnac stables, Sucari was watching one of the blacksmiths at work. He was fascinated at what a simple application of fire could do to a sheet of metal. Sucari could sense Isaac behind him, but didn't turn around, mesmerized by the glowing steel.

"We're heading to Granite Grove. Gather your things and let's get going." When Sucari turned around, Isaac was already gone, off to find another member of his crew. Soon, a variety of footprints were seen in the snow, heading toward the edge of town. As the group walked along the lakeside path, the trees flocked with snow started to change again. From the occasional metal tree, the forest once again gained its hearty, organic theme. Eventually, a rogue petrified tree, dark from the melted snow signaled to the group that they were nearing the next village.

A light breeze rustled through the trees, dislodging some of the snow held on their boughs. As it plopped on the ground, R-3N3 asked, "Are we forgetting someone?" The group stopped and thought for a moment.

Isaac slapped his forehead and said, "Erwin." Letting out a sigh, he continued, "If he was mad then, he's *really* going to be mad now. I don't even think he knows where we're going."

Just then, the large chain which connected the Eagle's Nest to Armor Village broke. The explosive sound sent rumbling thunder and echoes throughout the valley as the floating island shook from the shock. Part of the chain fell into the lake and broke the ice covering the surface. The other section of chain hung limply from the Eagle's Nest, swaying back and forth as the island tried to settle. Isaac wished he was prepared for this destructive event on Testament's base. As it was, he was short one sword and one member of his crew. Even if this occurrence was an opportunity, Isaac could not take advantage of it. He could sense that something was seriously wrong. Starting to run back toward Armor Village, Isaac screamed over his shoulder, "We have to go back! I don't have a good feeling about this!"

Erwin followed Fred down the narrow path to the base of the large chain that was holding up the island hovering above the lake. Running past Fred to the large metal link embedded in the ground, Erwin was amazed, "Wow! Is this really holding up that island?"

"It is. Along with those three other chains. They just appeared one day about three years ago. About a week later, a large explosion separated Ralph Island from the middle of the lake, the chains went taut and lifted it into the air. It was after that event when people started calling it 'the Eagle's Nest'."

Still looking at the chain and its path up to the island, Erwin asked, "Is the island held up by magnetism?"

"Yes it is. How do you know that?"

"Michael was telling us about the magnetic properties of the Dendritic Forest when he found us there."

"Really? Can you tell me something else? How did Pruthesemo die?"

"What?" Before Erwin could turn around, he heard a hissing sound, followed by a cold hand on his back. The hissing sound increased as he felt a burning sensation on his back. Suddenly, there was a small explosion and Erwin was on the ground. Taking a second to regain his breath, Erwin pushed himself off of the ground and turned over to a sitting position. Fred still stood there, his armored left hand smoking from the explosion. The smoke was blown away to reveal a silvery-white disk with a "3" engraved on it, set within the palm of his red gauntlet.

Coughing out an exclamation, Erwin asked, "What was that for?"

In an almost monotonous growl, Fred said, "Don't play coy with me. Mother explained everything. I know he's dead. I know that *you* know he's dead. I know because *you* killed him. So now tell me: how did Pruthesemo die?"

Standing up, Erwin looked Fred straight in the eyes with a look of pain and regret, "OK, I killed him. I didn't mean to, but I made his fire go out of control and it burned him to death." Erwin's face became hot as he held back his tears. Taking a deep breath, he choked out, "I held him in my arms when he died."

Fred looked at the ground and said, "I see." As Erwin ran by Fred toward the village, Fred grabbed the left wrist of his armor and twisted the hand off. The arm and hand were connected by a chain. Swirling the left fist over his head, Fred threw it at Erwin. As he was running, Erwin heard the hissing sound again and turned around to see the left hand coming at him. When he jumped to the side to evade the attack, the hand followed. It grabbed him by the foot. Another explosion.

As Erwin once again lay on the ground, the hand of armor seemed to float through the air, back to Fred's arm. Fred's right hand was covered in a glove and was gripping the metal forearm of his left side. When the hand was retrieved, Fred twisted it back in place. He slowly walked toward Erwin, providing an explanation, "I bet you wonder why I'm doing this. Well, this little disk in my hand is what I like to call the 'Li-berator'. I use it to free the truth from people. I also use it to free people from their sins."

Erwin was starting to panic. With tears running down his face, he screamed, "I'm sorry, OK! What more do you want?! I already have Pruthesemo's death to carry, isn't that enough?" He got up and turned his injured leg into wind to try and escape to Armor Village. Screaming out in his panic to the only person he knew could help, Erwin yelled toward the village, "Isaac! Help me!" This time, Fred put his right hand on the forearm of his left arm and opened the left palm. Erwin was uncontrollably pulled backward toward the menacing hand. His clothes seemed to be working against him. Once again, the hissing, cold hand, hot spot, and explosion put Erwin on the ground.

Fred still stood there, a stoic expression on his face, "But I'm trying to help you Erwin. I'm trying to help relieve you of your burden. I want to liberate your pain." Erwin spat out blood. The first explosion broke a few ribs, the second his ankle, the third was probably his collarbone. Erwin knew he was in bad shape and needed to escape as soon as possible.

When Erwin turned to wind, Fred said, "I know all about your powers." He once again put out his left palm, but this time his right hand he placed up on the horned shoulder of his armor. "You may seem to be like the wind, everywhere and nowhere, but that's merely a misnomer." As he spoke, the large chain of the island started to groan. "Do you know why blood is red? It has iron in it which rusts when it comes in contact with air. Iron that I can control with my magnetic glove."

The chain continued to resist the magnetic pull as Erwin started to materialize again, being held in the air by the force of the magnetism amplified by Fred's armor. Just like the chain, Fred's armor began to groan underneath the extreme forces induced upon it. As Erwin became more and more visible, the left arm of the armor started to collapse in on itself. Finally, Erwin was completely there, hovering in the air, blood dripping from his pores. His mouth was open in a scream that would not come due to the immensity of the pain.

Fred finally saw that his prey was back and gave one last final push to finish his task. Unfortunately, the magnetic fluxion couldn't handle it. Just as the large chain was pulled apart, the core of the fluxion cracked. Erwin was released from his mid-air hold and fell to the ground. Fred came over to where Erwin was lying, gasping for air. He leaned down and whispered, "I saved Pruthesemo's life so he could live it, not so that it would be snuffed out by the likes of you." Standing up, Fred turned and walked toward the village, leaving Erwin to die.

Isaac was running on pure adrenaline now. With the rest of his group close behind, he ran through Armor Village and headed toward the base of the chain. Seeing Erwin on the ground, Isaac ran to him and knelt beside him. The others stopped a little bit away and stood there, horrified by Erwin's condition. An enraged whisper came through Isaac's clenched teeth, "Who did this to you?"

With a rasp, Erwin replied, "Fred." Isaac got up, the fury building in his chest, but stopped when Erwin continued, "Wait. Don't take your anger out on him. He was just doing what he thought was right. I probably deserved this."

Isaac was having trouble talking now, "No one deserves this. No one deserves what he's done to you."

He turned to go again, but once more, Erwin stopped him, "No, don't go. I've been alone most of my life, so just let me spend these last moments with my only friends." The others slowly approached and put their hands on Isaac's shoulders, at which point he let go and started to cry.

It was becoming more of a struggle for Erwin to talk, "Don't cry, Isaac. Now I can die with no regrets." He smiled and whistled through his trademark gap on that final "s" and was gone. Isaac's knees buckled and he wept openly over the lifeless body. When he had finished, hiccupping the last sobs, Isaac picked up Erwin's limp body and headed to Armor Village.

Very calmly, he spoke to the others who followed behind, "Search the village. Find Fred. We need an explanation. Sucari, come with me." Isaac headed into the Luvnac stables and set Erwin on one of the empty forges, "Light it, Sucari."

"But, wait a minute-"

"Don't question me. Just do it." The emotion had drained from Isaac's voice. Looking down at his feet, Sucari thrust his hand into the bed of charcoal and seconds later the pile was ablaze. He pulled out his hand and headed toward the house as Isaac stood there, watching the flames engulf Erwin's body. Vlad and R-3N3 met Sucari at the door to the stables and just shook their heads.

Fred's gait was a little limped as he arrived back in Armor Village. Apparently, the effects of the magnetic fluxion had not only crushed his arm, but had shortened his left leg as well. When he got into his bedroom, there was already somebody there, waiting for him. "So, did you take care of Erwin?" The woman in the white robe was sitting in a chair in the corner of the room.

"I did. He'll be dead soon."

"You mean you didn't kill him?"

"I would have finished it, but the magnetic core broke. I'll just have to get Carl's magnet glove to replace it, even if his is the opposite pole."

"I don't care about your stupid glove, or your armor, or anything about you. You've screwed up, Fred."

"Come now, mother. Stop saying those things."

"No, you've royally messed up. Isaac has probably found Erwin by now and was told that you were responsible. He's probably on his way to kill *you* now."

"Do you think so?"

"I'm certain of it."

"Fine, I'll go and finish up." As Fred headed to the door, the woman put on a white glove with four rings on the fingers. Two on the index finger, one on the middle finger, one on the thumb. It was a Gottfried Gun.

When he was at the door, she said, "No, there's too great of a chance that Isaac will trace this back to Testament, if he hasn't already. I'll just have to clean up your mess." The woman pointed at the back of Fred's head and snapped her fingers. A sudden blast from her hand shot through Fred's head and lodged itself in the door. Fred limply fell to the floor.

Downstairs, the woman could hear Milo talking to some people who had just burst into the house, "Fred just got in. He looked in pretty bad shape. What's going on?" Hurried steps up the stairs heralded the arrival of three people. By now the woman had already left the room by the window, flying once again toward the Eagle's Nest.

The door opened a crack, but was blocked by Fred's body. When R-3N3 and Vlad finally managed to get into the room and found Fred dead on the floor, they quickly closed the door and whispered to Milo. She screamed in shock and immediately fainted.

○

Standing on the steps outside the small chapel of Armor Village, Isaac held a can containing Erwin's remains. The doors to the chapel were held open, and inside R-3N3 was on the organ playing a solemn dirge. Isaac spoke calmly and with purpose, "This was not an accident. One of our close friends was killed today, and it is most likely the result of our proximity to Testament's base on the Eagle's Nest. When I met Erwin, I never intended for him to come with me. And yet, he was a valuable asset to our team. As with every one of us, he was a misfit. But was he truly a misfit, or did he just not fit in with normalcy? I think the misfit is merely someone who fits in with greatness, instead of normalcy."

Pausing and looking toward the sky, Isaac continued, "I'm not sure if his mother will ever know that his life was taken so soon after leaving his home, but it is probably for the best. What I do know is we should press on and confront Testament, lest Erwin's sacrifice be for naught." A wind came through the town and Isaac turned over the can with Erwin's ashes, letting them ride on the breeze, "I commit Erwin to the wind. His home and his natural element. Now he will be everywhere and nowhere and always within our hearts."

Everyone stood there on the steps to the chapel as R-3N3 continued to play, the wind running through their hair and fluttering their clothes. Michael approached Isaac and said, "That's a fine eulogy, and I'm sure Erwin would have agreed. I'm proud of you Isaac, because the most important thing about right now is to know how to take things quietly. You've got a daunting task in front of you, but you should still give it a try, for who knows what is possible? And yet, I have far more confidence in you, who works mentally and bodily at a matter, than in six people who merely talk about it."

Isaac nodded and R-3N3 finished playing. When R-3N3 met with the others at the entrance to the chapel, they all exchanged glances and silently started to head once again toward the Granite Grove. Nothing more needed to be said. Michael, Milo, Rigel, and Carl stood in the street, watching the emotionally wounded warriors leave the village.

Suddenly, a high pitched whistle came from above the travelers which led to a steel rod about three feet long and an inch in diameter forcefully planting itself in front of them. When the dust settled, the group had stopped in front of the metal rod which had a lone piece of fabric tied to its end. On the fabric was the monogrammed initial of "H". Taking the fabric between his fingers, Isaac looked at the monogram, trying to recall where he had seen it before. When he finally remembered, a smile came across his lips, "Hey guys, do you want to take a little detour?"

Chapter 7

Light

Hiking along the Ferdinand Freeway from Armor Village to the Crystal Woods, Sucari spoke up, "OK, so who *exactly* are we going out of our way to meet?"

Isaac pulled out the piece of fabric and said, "This," waving the fabric in the air, "is the calling card of my good friend, Hermann. He's an excellent sniper who I've known for some time, and I think he may be able to assist us on this final leg of our journey."

Vlad jumped in, "Wait. You mean the metal rod that almost impaled us was shot by a *sniper?*"

"Only the best." Turning the corner, the group came upon a large mansion on a hill. Pointing up at the gigantic house, Isaac said, "There it is. Maurits Manor, our best bet of finding Hermann." Walking up to the enormous front doors, Isaac lifted the heavy obsidian door knocker and let it drop against the door with a loud "thud."

Moments later, footsteps were heard inside and the door was opened a crack. A butler asked, "Yes? What business do you have at Maurits Manor?"

Pulling out the fabric, Isaac handed it to the butler and said, "We're here to see Hermann. Is he in?"

Seeing the monogrammed "H", the butler said, "Ah, I see. Well, you'd best come in then." Opening the door further, the butler obsequiously motioned for the group to enter. As everyone passed by the smartly dressed butler in his pressed clothes, his brown eyes, set beneath a bushy unibrow, watched each individual enter the mansion. His bearded face was set as he examined the guests. Wavy chestnut hair topped off the image of the butler as the last guest entered and the large door was once again closed.

Inside the Manor, the front hall was vast and ornately decorated. On the floor was an expensive Wactaw Carpet. Pedestals lining the sides of the hallway displayed a variety of priceless items. An intricate Gaston Tea Set. A bold

Benoit Chess Set. An oddly shaped Karl Sponge. As the group walked through the artifacts and antiques, the butler explained, "You may call me Cornelis. I am the butler of Lord John, current owner of the Maurits Manor."

Isaac quickened his pace to walk side-by-side with Cornelis, "That's quite interesting, but what about Hermann? He's still living here, right?"

The butler stopped and turned to Isaac, "No, I'm afraid that Hermann passed away some time ago."

Taken aback by the tragic news, Isaac asked, "Then who could have used his calling card on us?"

"I'm not entirely certain, but I believe your answer may lie on the roof of the Manor." Turning to the others, he added, "You are free to roam the halls of the Manor, just keep out of the Chapelle Wing where Lord John is currently resting." Cornelis turned, went up the grandiose Roger Staircase and was gone.

Isaac turned around and looked at the group, "Well, I'm going to the roof to see if I can figure out who's using Hermann's techniques. You're all welcome to join me if you'd like."

"I'll come along," Sucari answered.

"I think I'm going to look around a bit," Vlad said. He quickly glanced around the room and asked, "Hey, where's Artie?"

○

When R-3N3 heard the name "John", he had a pretty good guess about the other moniker John had used when he first met him. Very quietly, R-3N3 reduced his walking speed so the rest of the group had passed him. Checking to see if anyone was watching, he stole away to another room of the Manor.

Quickly running down the hallways, R-3N3's green eyes scanned the rooms he could see through their open doors. Library. Observatory. Aviary. Kitchen. A vast array of bedrooms interspersed between. All of the rooms were empty. Finally, he came upon a simple closed door on the west side of the house. He tried the knob. Locked. Twisting with a little more force, the door moaned as the knob and lock broke with a loud crack. The door lazily swung open. From inside the room came the call, "Who's there?"

R-3N3 deftly maneuvered through the door and into the room, making no sounds as his feet progressed along the lush, burgundy carpet. The room was of fair size, but the defining feature was its walls. Three of the walls were comprised entirely of stained glass. The glass told the stories of epic adventures of long ago. Battles between armies and gods. Fights of good against evil. The encroaching sunset gave the room a brilliant glow as the intruder very slowly made his way to the lone chair situated in the middle of the room.

Making his way to the front side of the chair, R-3N3 confirmed what he had thought all along. There in the chair sat an old man, his white hair edging a mostly bald head and adorning his upper lip. On each eye he wore a black eye patch, their straps creating an "X" on his forehead that was aligned with a similarly shaped scar. After his first inquiry, the man was silent, almost as if he was listening for something. This was John. When R-3N3 and John had first met, John was better known as "Number 3."

Standing in front of the old man, a slew of emotions came rising up in R-3N3's body. His eyes turned from green to red as he pulled back his right fist for a mighty punch. With a quick motion, R-3N3 let fly with his assault. Just as quickly, both of John's arms flew into the air to block the attack. However, only one hand caught R-3N3's fist, the other was grasping at an invisible object. John spoke with a taunting tone, "Now, now boys. It's not fair to gang up on an old man like me."

John lifted his legs and thrust them out at his assailants, sending both of them flying. R-3N3 landed in a corner of the room. The sound of another person landing across the room was also heard; however, when R-3N3 turned to look, no one was there. Putting his feet back on the floor, John got up from his chair and strode to the empty side of the room, "I'd suggest you go back to Harry, Snellius. I'm not going to be leaving this spot so easily." The sound of footsteps could be heard running out of the room as the door was shut with a slam. Yet again, R-3N3 saw nothing.

Still talking to the empty side of the room, John slowly turned around to face R-3N3, "Now. You, on the other hand, are familiar. But I can't seem to figure out how you might have managed to escape. It's not every day that you fight with a metallic hollow man like yourself, Crimson Front."

Eyes still glowing red, R-3N3's voice was stern, "Let us just say you and I have unfinished business which I could not attend to while I was locked away in The Box."

R-3N3 got up, but John was immediately there in front of him. When did it happen? Did R-3N3 blink? No one could be that fast. John raised his right hand over his head and R-3N3 winced when it was brought down on his shoulder. However, it wasn't a hard hit, but a comforting pat. John said, "I know. What we did to you back then was unacceptable. We shouldn't have attacked Mathiston. We shouldn't have killed those innocent people. I can understand why you would want to fight. Why you wouldn't back down. We may have killed a lot of people that day, but your front was stained with our blood as well. I was amazed that you killed Number 10, although Conrad's ability to see through things was more of a tactical asset rather than a fighting one."

John led R-3N3 to the window opposite the chair he was sitting in moments ago, "But Testament isn't who I am anymore. It started changing right around that incident, and I needed to get out. Fortunately, I was able to escape, but it's odd how destiny works. Here I am, sitting in my Manor, while they plot away on that island. I'm so tired, I can't muster the strength to resist them anymore."

R-3N3's eyes faded from red back to their green glow as John continued, "Perhaps I spend too much time here, feeling the light. I love how the energy of the yellow, the cool of the blue, the passion of the red all can be felt. In all honesty, I'm glad that I lost my sight, because it's given me a chance to see the world in a whole new way. That's how I knew both of you were in the room. My senses have been acutely trained and now I don't even need my sight to keep a few whippersnappers in check. Come, let's find Cornelis and get you a room to stay in tonight."

○

Up three flights of stairs, Isaac and Sucari finally found the access door to the roof. Once outside, they found a lone girl, bent over a rabbit's hutch. She had long black hair that fell to her shoulders. She also wore a conservative, knee-length pleated skirt with the only odd traits about her appearance being the twin quivers she had strapped to the calves of each of her legs. Approaching her from behind, Isaac asked, "Excuse me, miss. Do you know where I can find the owner of this handkerchief?"

When she turned around, holding a white rabbit, Sucari was struck dumbfounded by her beauty. She wore a pair of glasses on her head as a headband to hold her hair back and smiled warmly as she asked, "What's that?" Isaac held out the fabric with the monogrammed "H" on it. She took it and examined it, "Oh, this is mine."

Isaac questioned her, "But this is Hermann's trademark, what are you doing with it? Furthermore, what are you doing with his glasses?"

The girl giggled as she replied, "Oh, well you see, I'm Hermann's daughter, Hellen." Her face turned sour for a moment, "But I don't really like that name. My father was the one who was obsessed with rhyming. Please, just call me Robin." She put the rabbit back in the hutch which had a nameplate with the name "Adrien" emblazoned on it.

"Well, you certainly have your father's eyes. I'm so sorry to hear he's passed away. Is your mother still around?"

She bowed her head in remembrance but then perked back up, "Oh, she's here in the house with me. Let's go find her."

Before they made it off the roof, a man wearing winged sandals and a top hat landed on the roof and slid to a stop. The name on his coat said "Lewis". He dug around in his messenger's bag and found the letter he was looking for. Pulling it out, he said, "Transcontinental Express Airmail delivery for John."

Robin took the letter and said, "I'll give it to him." Lewis tipped his hat to Robin and took a few running strides, using the last one to leap off the roof. Wings once again sprouted from his shoes, and the shiny silver soles of the sandals shone in the sunset. Opening the access door to the roof, Robin said, "Let's go find John and give him his mail." Isaac followed behind, but Sucari was still stunned speechless.

Finally, he realized they had gone and he ran after them with a, "Hey, wait up!"

○

Snellius stood at the wood-paneled back wall of a large office. Both the left and right walls were full mirrors, giving the smoky room an infinite feel. At the large mahogany desk on the side of the room opposite where Snellius was standing sat a man, reclining in his office chair, feet up on the desk. He had slicked back black hair, was smoking a cigar, and was shuffling a deck of cards with one hand. In the ashtray on the desk was another cigar, already lit and slowly burning. The nameplate on the desk said "Governor Harry."

With a flick of his wrist, Harry threw a card at Snellius, which just missed his shoulder and stuck in the wall behind him. Ace of spades. "First of all, Snellius!" Harry yelled, "I don't know why you bothered to come back here unless you could confirm to me that John is dead."

Stuttering out an explanation, Snellius said, "I t-t-tried to kill him, Harry, but he noticed me."

Another card whizzed by, nicking some of Snellius' hair. Two of diamonds. "What the deuce? How can a man who can't see notice someone who is wearing an invisibility suit?"

"I d-d-don't know how he did it! The suit helped me easily infiltrate the Manor and I was trying to take advantage of the other guy who was there, but-"

Another card nicked Snellius' ear. Joker. "You mean there was some other joker there too? And John beat *both* of you? Just how weak are you?"

"Owww," was the wimpy reply as Snellius held his hand to the nicked ear and continued, "I'm s-s-sorry Erik, but-"

"You are not to call me by that name!" With Harry in a fury, Snellius finally ducked at the fourth and fifth cards that embedded themselves in the wall behind him. Jack of hearts and King of clubs. As his temper cooled, Harry continued, "Now, do you want to become part of Testament or not, jack? You and I both know that the only ways to do that are to be recruited or to kill one of their members. I just so happen to need John to gracefully step aside so I can claim Maurits Manor as my own, so it works out to both our advantages if you actually kill him. Don't forget who the kingpin of this operation is."

Nervously nodding, Snellius just stood there. Harry became irritated at his presence, "Get out of here, will ya?" Snellius hurriedly opened the door and left the room. Harry just rolled his eyes, sighed, and said, "Sheesh. You can't find good help these days, can you?"

○

Isaac and Sucari were following Robin through the vast halls of Maurits Manor. She stopped at every room to see if her mother was in any of them. Sucari couldn't keep his eyes off of the young woman, her charm had him mesmerized. Finally, they found her in the greenhouse. She was watering some white flowers when the group entered. Robin went over and gave her mother a hug, "Hi, mom. We've got visitors."

The mother turned around and a look of shock came across Isaac's face. The mother's expression turned to one of recognition, "Isaac! Why, I haven't seen you in years." Her face became solemn for a moment, "I'm so sorry for what happened to Marie. Did you know she wrote to me just before she passed? I think it would be good for you to read what she wrote."

Isaac finally shook himself out of his stupor, "Maria, you and Marie always amazed me with your similarities. I'm convinced that you two were the closest to being identical twins, despite actually being born a decade apart." Turning to Robin, he said, "And it looks like your daughter has inherited your beauty as well." Both women blushed at the compliment, "Of course, Hermann always had eyes for you, Maria. It just took him a while to gather up the courage to express it."

The solemn look came across Maria's face once again, "Yes, it's so tragic how he was taken from us, but there's little we can do now. Hindsight is 20/20 after all." Maria noticed Robin was holding the letter that the delivery man had given her, "Is that a letter for John?"

Fidgeting with the letter, Robin examined it and said, "It is. But I wonder who could have sent it. This envelope is pretty fancy."

John and R-3N3 entered the room and came to join the group. From what he had overheard, John said, "I hope that's not another letter from Harry. That hypocrite is just trying to use his political power to push me out of this house."

Maria took the letter from Robin and opened it. She gasped when she began to read it. Everyone gave her a look, but John finally said, "Well, what does it say?" Clearing her throat, Maria read:

Dear Son,

    We tire of continually asking you to come back to the 2nd Kingdom. We understand you've betrayed us by stealing our noble Number-fluxion and joining the ranks of Testament. That will still be a part of your past. However, we've heard you have since left Testament and we would like you to come back and take over the rule of the 2nd Kingdom. We love you and want you come back to the city of The Meadows.

Love,
King Edward and Queen Lalande of the 2nd Kingdom

"Amazing. What was that about? Are you the heir to the 2nd Kingdom's throne?" R-3N3 asked.

John looked down in shame, "Yes, but that's not who I am anymore. If my parents saw who I've really become, then I doubt they'd really want me back. Here, follow me." John exited the greenhouse and made his way through the corridors of the Manor. Finally, he came upon the library where he removed a box from a shelf set about waist high. Opening it, he revealed the "10" Number-fluxion disk and its setting in the palm of a glove.

"I stole the Royal power of the 2nd Kingdom when I heard that Testament was recruiting members to fight Robert. I was so much of an idealist then; I never knew this same power would eventually make me blind."

From behind one of the aisles, Vlad emerged and apologized, "I'm sorry for intruding, but I didn't want to keep listening in without your knowledge."

Isaac shook his head, "Not at all. It's a good thing you're here. Now that we're all together, why don't we get a better explanation of what's going on here. What's this about someone wanting this mansion?"

John put the box back on the shelf and began to explain, "Well, you see, there are actually two things in play right now. One is Harry. He's recently become Governor of this area. When he was campaigning, he showed the public what they wanted to see, but now that he's in office he's shown that he's only in it for himself. As such, he has decided that Maurits Manor should be the new Governor's Mansion."

"This leads us to the second problem: Snellius. Snellius wants to join the ranks of the New Testament, but in order to do so, he'd either have to be recruited, which is unlikely, or kill one of the current or former members of Testament. If he were to kill me, he would immediately surpass my rank as Number 3 and become Number 2 of Testament. The only person who would be higher would be Number 1 himself. Harry knows this, and has helped Snellius in his attempts to kill me."

R-3N3 interrupted, "It is true. He has some sort of invisibility suit or something. He was in the room when I-" he hesitated for a moment, ". . . met John."

Isaac gathered the situation and offered a solution, "So, what you're saying is that if we take care of Harry and Snellius, you'll get to live here in peace and quiet, right?"

"Pretty much, yes."

"Well, we'll help you out, but only for more information on Testament."

"Why do you want that?" John's face scrunched into a scowl, "You're not thinking of joining them as well, are you?"

"Not at all. Quite the opposite really."

"Excellent. Then it's a deal." Isaac and John shook hands and the agreement was set.

The capital city of Morgana was quiet at dusk. The team of travelers slid through the streets and alleys and eventually ended up at the capitol building. A lone light high in the building remained on. Harry was still there. Using R-3N3's strength, the group made its way through the heavy doors of the capitol and into the rotunda.

Their footsteps on the marble floor echoed through the building, but when they all stopped in the center of the room, the footsteps persisted. R-3N3 whispered, "That must be Snellius. Be careful everyone."

Suddenly, R-3N3 was on the floor, tripped by the invisible leg of Snellius. A faint chuckling was heard as Isaac gave out commands, "Sucari, follow me. Vlad and Artie, take care of business here."

The other three nodded and said in unison, "Right!" Isaac made his way to the spiral staircase which led to the second floor of the building. Sucari was close behind him. R-3N3 got up and made his way to the edge of the room as Vlad proceeded to the opposite side. When they were both in position, R-3N3's eyes began to glow brighter, producing a beam of light that emanated to Vlad on the other side. The two fighters then sidled along the edge of the room, always staying opposite the other. Finally, results.

"Stop!" Vlad yelled when he noticed an abnormality in the room. The light that R-3N3's eyes were giving off was bent and sent to another part of the room. The point where the light was bent was where Snellius was standing. Vlad and R-3N3 quickly approached that point, which vanished just as quickly as it was noticed.

Snellius' voice echoed throughout the room, "There's no point in trying. You're just going to lose eventually anyways."

Vlad whispered to R-3N3, "I think I've got another plan. Just try to keep up." Vlad held his hands out and the wings appeared on his jacket. Slowly, a mist began to form on the floor of the rotunda and swirled around the marble surface. It flowed around in a very fluid fashion, revealing everyone who was standing there, including the invisible Snellius. He noticed this and began running, eddies of mist following behind his steps.

Observing the obvious trail of mist, the two fighters cornered Snellius against one of the walls of the rotunda. Both were pushed back by unexpected heavy punches. Even though they knew where Snellius was, they still couldn't tell what he was capable of. Snellius was taunting now, "This suit is by far the best thing that has happened to me. With it I can change the density of anything around me, even my own punches, as I'm sure you both are now aware."

R-3N3 recovered quickly, a dent in his chest being the only damage. Vlad however, disappeared into the mist, which rose to even higher levels. Now Snellius was starting to become nervous, as he became the one who couldn't see his assailants. Using the powers of the vampire bat fluxion, Vlad had gained excellent hearing and now had the upper hand. Swirling the mist around Snellius, Vlad made short, quick punches at vital areas. Ribs, stomach, throat, knees. Finally Snellius was down on the ground, pleading with the two to be merciful, "I was only following orders!"

Picking up Snellius and lifting him into the air, R-3N3 managed to snag some of the invisibility suit, which broke the fluxion core with a crunch, revealing a very scared Snellius. R-3N3 pulled Snellius in close and from behind, Vlad appeared. His red eyes glistened behind the armored visor and his sharpened smile whispered, "So are we." In one fluid motion, R-3N3 slammed Snellius onto the ground, cracking the marble floor as well as Snellius' sternum. The mist gradually disappeared as Vlad returned to normal. He chuckled at their victory.

"I did not know you could turn to mist."

"I didn't know either. But you have to admit it was pretty awesome."

"Affirmative, I suppose." Some yelling was heard upstairs, so the two left Snellius, unconscious on the floor, as they ran up the spiral staircase to the second level.

○

Since Harry's office was the only one with the light on, it was easy for Isaac and Sucari to find it on the second floor. Once inside the office, though, they found that their battle would be a little different from the ones they had fought before. Harry was sitting behind his desk, but this time he seemed a little hazy and out of focus. Isaac approached the desk and slammed his palms down on it, "Listen Harry, you don't know what you're getting into when you start dealing with Testament."

"Oh, I'm pretty sure I know exactly what I'm doing. I figure it this way: if I can get a man on the inside, when Testament takes over and unites us under its rule, I'm pretty much set for life."

Isaac lunged across the desk and grabbed at Harry, only to get a handful of smoke. As Harry was laughing at Isaac's futile attempt, the smoky image reappeared with Isaac's hand right through the middle of it. Not wanting to take any more of Harry's games, Isaac gave his command, "Sucari, you know what to do." Sucari nodded and his wings emerged from his back. With a mighty flap, the smoke was gone. Isaac made his way to the other side of the desk and crouched down behind the chair. There, tucked in the space underneath the desk, was Harry.

When Isaac pulled Harry out from underneath the desk, Harry let out a frightened howl, "Don't hurt me! I don't know what you want!"

"I want you to stop trying to take John's house." Harry nodded hurriedly. "I want you to stop trying to get involved with Testament." More nodding. "And I want you to promise me that you'll start working for your constituents and not for your own gain." The nodding stopped, as Harry had to contemplate what that really meant.

With a swift punch into Harry's gut, Isaac made his final point. Harry lay on the ground, moaning in pain as Isaac stood over him, "After all, they don't call you a civil servant for nothing."

When Isaac met up with Sucari at the back of the room, Vlad and R-3N3 arrived at the doorway. They looked around and saw nothing, but heard the moaning behind the desk. R-3N3 spoke up, "Did you guys win?"

Sucari responded, "Yeah. Did you?"

Vlad chimed in, "Of course!"

Isaac said, "Good. Let's go back."

○

Back at Maurits Manor, the night was in full swing as the weary travelers each found empty rooms and collapsed from a long day of traveling and fighting. At breakfast, Maria was bringing out some food to the dining room when she asked Isaac, "So, now that you've taken care of Harry, where are you headed to next?"

"Well, this was somewhat of a detour for us, as we were heading to Granite Grove to have a sword made."

John spoke up, "Why would you go there?"

Isaac seemed confused, "Because the people in Armor Village said that's where the best swordsmiths were located."

Chuckling softly, John said, "Well, their information is a little dated, I suppose. Granite Grove hasn't been the best since David moved to the Crystal Woods outside of Morgana."

"So you mean this David is the best swordsmith in the area?"

"Why of course!"

The group perked up as this meant they wouldn't have to backtrack all the way to the other side of the lake. Maria put a folded letter by Isaac's side and whispered in his ear, "This is Marie's letter. Please take it and read it." Isaac nodded in recognition.

When everyone had finished with breakfast, John stood up from the head of the banquet table. "Well, now that we've had our breakfast, why don't we go down and visit David and see if he can make this sword of yours." As the travelers got up to leave, John said, "Maria, Robin, you should come too. It's nice to get out of this stuffy house once in a while." The two women got up and joined the tail end of the group as they left the Manor.

Just a little bit outside of town, near the base of the giant chain connected to the Eagle's Nest, stood a small house and stable that David the swordsmith used for his modest operation. David was chopping wood outside when the large group approached. He looked up and wiped the sweat from his brow. When he recognized John, he ran to greet the old man, "John! What a pleasant surprise. Although, I do wish you would warn me when you want to bring so many people over." Entering his house, he called to his wife, "Rachel! We have company!"

Drying her hands on her apron, Rachel entered the room, "Oh my! This certainly is a lot of people. Let's go outside and I'll bring out some refreshments." Everyone sat down on the lush lawn as Rachel came back out with a tray of ice waters.

"So," Isaac sipped his drink as he talked to David, "John tells me you're the best swordsmith around."

"Well, I don't know about the *best* swordsmith."

Rachel laughed, "Oh, come now, David. Don't be so modest. They didn't call you the King of Spades for nothing."

"Yeah, but that's back when I was fixing farming equipment. It wasn't until the war against Robert that I found out my skills could transfer to swordsmithing so easily. Besides, you're hardly one to talk, Queen of Diamonds."

Isaac almost choked on his drink, "Wait, you mean *you're* the Queen of Diamonds?"

Doing a small curtsy, Rachel said, "Guilty as charged."

"If that's the case, then things may have finally turned to my favor." Isaac pulled out the sword fragments and the Light scroll and laid them on the lawn. David and Rachel came over to examine the items.

David noticed immediately what the sword fragments were, "How did you get these? I thought the legendary blades had been lost centuries ago." Kneeling down and picking up the hilt of the 4th Kingdom's legendary sword, he marveled, "And this is the famous 10 Caliber Sword embedded in the Ragna Rock . . . although it doesn't seem so impressive as it is right now."

"That's where I need your help. I want to take these seven sword fragments and fuse them together to make one mighty sword."

David frowned as he stood back up. With his hands in his pockets, he said, "That's a tall order for a swordsmith, even a swordsmith like myself."

Rachel came from behind and put her arm through David's, "*I* know you can do it, honey." Looking at Isaac, she asked, "But why am *I* important?"

Unrolling the Light scroll, Isaac pointed at the triangular shape surrounded by the intertwining uroboros seal, "I need you to make this. It's the core for the Fluent of Light."

Rachel and David looked at the pieces on their lawn, then at each other, and nodded. Together they said, "We'll do it." Gathering up the fragments and the scroll, they headed into the stable to begin their work.

Finding his wallet, Isaac fumbled with the coins inside, "I'm sorry that I can't pay you more for this."

David turned and replied over his shoulder, "Oh please, any friend of John's needn't bother with paying us, and besides-" turning back to the stable, he continued, "it's not every day you get an opportunity to work with such exquisite materials."

Isaac almost felt naked without the sword fragments and Light scroll on his person, but he felt Marie's letter in his pocket and knew that now was as good a time as any to let everyone know what had happened, "Since we're so close by, why don't we go check out the Crystal Woods?" Everyone nodded in agreement as they left the house and the couple working in the stable.

The Crystal Woods were certainly heralded as the most beautiful of the Petrified Forests. Molten sand had turned to glass and was sucked up into the trees, creating a dazzling display of light amidst the translucent trunks. As everyone marveled in the splendor of the forest, Isaac pulled out the letter from his late wife.

Clearing his throat, Isaac spoke, "We've all traveled together for some time now, and I believe you all deserve an explanation." Everyone stopped examining the trees and gave Isaac their attention. "We're getting ready for the fight of our lives, and I need you to know why this fight is so important."

"Well, it's about time if you ask me," Sucari said as he came over and sat down against the trunk of a nearby tree.

"I was just fine with the opportunity to fight, but if there's a reason then I guess I'll listen," Vlad interjected as he leaned against another tree.

"I am sure we all have our own reasons for fighting Testament, so I am curious what Isaac's is," R-3N3 replied as he took a few steps toward the group.

Opening the envelope containing Marie's letter, Isaac began his story, "This all started about ten years ago during the Dark Year..."

○

"Come on, Isaac, we're almost there!" the beautiful woman with the long black hair and sparkling blue eyes said as she hiked along the path. The sky was dark with the particulate of the moon blocking out the light of the sun, but up ahead a strange glow was emanating from just beyond the hill.

Isaac was standing at the base of a giant statue of two men, grasping each other's wrists, "I'm coming, Marie. Just give me a minute." His hair was a chestnut brown that emphasized his youth.

When he caught up, Marie chided him, "You need to be less curious about people and more curious about ideas."

"I *am* curious about ideas. I just feel we need to recognize the great men who discovered them."

"Well, stop drooling over the James Garland Arch and let's go check out the Thurston Ring." As the couple crested the hill, they came upon a ring of upright stones, the center of which was illuminated. It was almost as if daylight was still bathing the area in its brilliance. Marie ran to the center of the ring and spun around, her dress spinning with her like a bell. "All my life, the new sights of Nature like this make me rejoice like a child. It seems like so long ago that we had any sunlight, this is definitely refreshing."

Feeling one of the stone pillars, Isaac seemed confused, "But what do you think is causing it? I mean, just the circular shape isn't enough to capture light like this. There's got to be more to it than that."

Marie ran to an opening on one side of the ring and pointed at the ground, "Look at this! Maybe this is the key." There on the ground was the image of a snake's head eating its tail carved into the ground. "Perhaps the uroboros design is the seal for the light, holding it in the confines of the circle."

Isaac joined her and said, "Of course! Each time the core is used, the seal would naturally get smaller, thus restricting the power of the core." Taking a few moments to soak in the discovery, Isaac turned to Marie, "I think we may be ready."

Back at their house, Isaac was putting the finishing touches on the seal for the "88" Number-fluxion. The fluxion was set in the center of a vest, its singular uroboros seal surrounding the Number Disk being the only defining feature of the clothing item. Isaac was still a little skeptical, "Are you sure you want to do this, Marie? It could be dangerous. Once you activate the core, there's no going back. If you can't control it, then I'm afraid that-"

"Nothing in life is to be feared, Isaac. It is only to be understood. Now is the time to understand more, so that we may fear less." Marie lifted the vest over her head and slipped it on over her clothes. She adjusted it so the core was situated in the middle of her chest. Nodding at Isaac, she said, "I'm ready." The core of the fluxion began to glow a brilliant white. A light blue aura enveloped Marie as she shouted, "It's working! Isaac, it's working!"

Isaac was ecstatic, until he noticed her skin starting to turn white. Marie also noticed this and exclaimed, "What's happening?"

"It must be the seal! It's still incomplete!" The shining white of her skin spread to her hair, turning it white. Combined with the light blue aura surrounding her, Marie looked like an angel. Clawing at the vest, Isaac attempted to remove the core, the seal and finally the vest itself. Each attempt was a failure and as small, brittle fractures started appearing on Marie's arms, Isaac knew it was hopeless. Dropping to his knees, Isaac hugged his wife's mid-section, "I can't lose you! I don't know how to go on without you!"

Marie put her hand on Isaac's head and tried to comfort him, "Now Isaac, you must. You need to continue our work so that others won't have to suffer. Humanity will draw more good than evil from this new discovery. You have to make sure of that." Isaac held on to her tighter as his hair started to turn white from Marie's touch. Quickly, like a cloud passing in front of the sun, the white of Marie's body turned to black. Starting at her fingertips and spreading to the rest of her body, the effect was fatal. Her last words were whispered, almost inaudible, "Goodbye, Isaac." Just as quickly as the blackness had spread, her body turned to dust and was blown away through the open window. Isaac huddled himself into a ball and lay there on the floor, weeping at his loss.

The group at the Crystal Woods didn't know how to respond. Each of them sincerely felt empathetic toward Isaac, but none of them could truly understand his pain. Reaching up to his headband, he untied it and let it fall to the crystalline grass. Beneath the covering of the headband was the core of a Blood-fluxion. However, the familiar uroboros-based seal was a little bit different than all the others which had been seen up until that point. The seal was of a single snake, tattooed around the crown of his head. However, this snake had two heads, both of which were trying to devour the Blood-fluxion core.

"This is a Soul-fusion fluxion. It is considered to be the taboo of all fluxions. The blood core contains Marie's blood. When I use it, I use a little bit of her presence within me." Turning to Sucari and Vlad, Isaac explained, "When you saw me fighting with Dr. Paul, it was really Marie doing the fighting, since I had blacked out. She took over my body and completed what I could not finish. However, as is the case with any fluxion, each time I use it there are risks. I may never be able to regain control. Worst of all, each time I use it, I lose a little piece of Marie that can never be regained. I worry that soon I'll lose her forever."

Unfolding the letter Marie had written to her sister, Isaac summarized, "I was unaware of this letter until Maria gave it to me, but it seems Marie knew all along that what she was doing would most likely end with her death. In this letter, she tells Maria that I would probably stop the research completely. And yet she says, 'Isaac never notices what has been done; he only sees what remains to be done.' She was right. I knew that if I wanted to prevent others from being taken over by the power of the fluxion, I would have to figure out how to control it."

"Days later, in a stupor, I made it back to the Thurston Ring, but I did not go inside it. No, this time I climbed to the shoulders of the James Garland Arch. It was on this arch where I saw something I had not noticed before. Underneath the circular pattern of the Thurston Ring was a weaving pattern. The uroboros was a long, knotted snake, but still retained its unity. It was in this realization that I knew what the missing piece was. If I had seen further into the solution of the mystery, it was only by standing on the shoulders of the giants."

Looking at R-3N3, Isaac continued, "The fluxion you have inside you is the same Soul-fusion fluxion that I have. The reason these fluxions are so taboo is that they desecrate the human soul in order to work. I have the feeling you were the product of Testament's research and even if they did not succeed with you, they would not stop trying to use the Soul-fusion fluxion to create an army of invincible men like yourself. My journey originally began as a quest to stop Testament's military use of fluxions, but after having met you, I can see that the problem with Testament is far more serious than I originally anticipated."

Isaac folded the letter and put it back in his pocket. "So, now you know. Now you know why I can't allow Testament to use the fluxions the way they have been. Now you know why I've been fighting alone all this time. Now you know what must be done to finish this."

Everyone was silent when David and Rachel came rushing into the Crystal Woods carrying the newly forged sword. David carried two sledgehammers crossed on his back and Rachel still wore her twin Number-fluxions with the "6" disks on the palms of the thick leather gloves. The sword was an enormous and beautiful piece of work that shimmered in the light of the forest. The tip had a triangular diamond core inside the uroboros seal from the Light scroll. David handed the sword to Isaac, "I call it 'Hikari Shichidai', or 'The Seventh Light'." Holding the sword in admiration, Isaac said, "All right. Let's get ready, everyone . . ." he lifted the sword above his head, "For battle!"

Chapter 8

SIN

The sun was setting as the group headed back to David's house. the Eagle's Nest shimmered in the reflected waves of the lake beneath it as everyone once again sat on the front lawn. Isaac was still admiring his new weapon and had a lot of questions about its manufacturing, "How did you make this so fast? I know you're good, but there has to be a limit."

David laughed a hearty laugh as he pulled out his twin sledgehammers and twirled them around in his hands as if they were nothing more than batons, "When you need to repair weapons on the battlefield, time is of the essence. And yet, I can't take all the credit. Rachel usually helps me carbonize the swords I make with her gloves, but this time you gave her quite the challenge."

Gripping her wrist and moving her hand around, Rachel chimed in, "It certainly took more focus to get that diamond core in the tip of the sword, not to mention the design surrounding it. I'm not used to doing that kind of precision or using my gloves with that much pressure. Why do you need a diamond in your sword anyway?"

Holding the sword up to the setting sun, Isaac let the diamond produce small rainbows on the ground, "That's simple. Because of the diamond and the uroboros design, this sword is now so sharp that it can cut light itself."

John was the last to join the group. He clapped his hands to get everyone's attention, "All right, everyone. Gather 'round. It's time I tell you what you're up against." As everyone got up and circled around him, John squatted down and began to draw some designs in the dirt. "It's been a while since I've been out of the organization, but I'll try and remember as much as I can. I could only run away, but if I can help you all take down those scoundrels, then perhaps I can retire in peace."

Pointing to the center of the circle he had drawn, John began, "Your final destination will probably be the center of Ralph Island. This is where Number 1 resides. Let me rephrase that. It's where that mutinous Thomson, who has decided to run this 'New Testament', is most likely hiding. After all the work Thurston put into the Old Testament and all the good we did to free the world from the Reign of Robert, now we're right back where we started."

Isaac interrupted, "Wait. Thurston? As in *the* Thurston? Was he the man whom the Thurston Ring was named after?"

John seemed impressed, "You know your stuff, son. He's the very same. At any rate, Thomson is probably going to be your most difficult challenge; but unfortunately, he's not the only one on the island. Some of you may remember the raid on Pandora Prison many years ago. Thomson was looking for some additions to the group, and he figured The Box would be the best place to find them. However, when Thomson let them out, the town of Mathiston ended up being the site of their first rampage. Our metal friend, R-3N3 can tell us all about that, I'm sure."

Taking the cue, R-3N3 spoke up, "When they escaped, I tried to keep them from killing the villagers, but in order to do that, I had to kill some of them. I just kept fighting until they were able to stop me. When I woke up, I was chained in the empty prison."

"I'm unsure how many are still with Thomson, but there are three who I feel would be on the island. The first one I can think of is the reason why Ralph Island is floating before us. He's not an official Testament member, but he's dangerous nonetheless. He goes by the name of 'Alfred the Peacemaker', probably because he'll fight you until you surrender peacefully."

Pointing to another one of the markings on the illustrated island, John continued, "Another one of the escapees is 'Grigori the Reaper'. Many know him by the misnomer, 'The Grim Reaper'. Once again, he's not an official member, as many of them have left or have been killed. Even so, my advice would be to avoid fighting him at all costs. I'm not sure why, but apparently he cannot die."

Sucari seemed a little impatient, "OK, that's great, but you're forgetting one important thing: how are we supposed to even get to the island? Not all of us can fly."

John tapped the drawing of the chains, "You only have one option. The chains are the only link to the ground, and therefore are the only way to get to the island from here. Of course, Thomson knows of this weakness, which is why he has Valerie working for him. Valerie is a beautiful and cunning woman. She controls the most skilled army of female warriors, The Kyries. If The Kyries attack while you're on the chains, you might not make it to the island."

Isaac was furiously writing down notes. When he caught up, he looked up from his pad of paper and asked, "Is there anyone else?"

"Like I said before, most of the Old Testament has left or died. I don't know if Ralph is still around, since his island was completely taken over once it was lifted into the sky. I think he may be the highest number still around. Number 8, I think. There were a few lower numbers, like Gottfried, who might still be around, but they were mainly support members of the group."

Flipping the pad of paper closed, Isaac said, "Excellent. We'll attack at dawn." Turning to David, he asked, "I know you may not have much room, but can we stay here for the night?"

John interjected, "Dave, it'll only be the four of them. The rest of us should probably get back to Maurits Manor."

"Now wait a minute!" Robin seemed offended, "Why can't I stay? Why can't I fight? Von says my technique is excellent, and I know I'll be able to help out."

Maria placed a hand on Robin's shoulder and tried to calm her, "Now Hellen, the battlefield is no place for a lady."

Brushing her hand off, Robin pleaded with her mother, "But mom, this is my chance to fight for dad's sake. Surely you don't want Testament to take away more men like him? Don't you miss him? Don't you wish he was still alive?"

Maria started to tear up and was about to respond, but John cut her off, "Robin, I think it's best if you sit this one out. I know what these men are up against, and I'm sure your mother doesn't want to lose you as well."

Robin was furious now, "At least let me try! If I can't fight along Isaac and Vlad and R-3N3 and-" her eyes locked with Sucari's for a brief moment and she blushed, "a-a-and Sucari, then I'll feel worthless."

John was stern in his reply, "Listen. As long as you are a resident in my mansion, you will do as I say, and that's final." Turning and walking on the path back to the Manor, John commanded, "So let's go."

As John, Maria, and a reluctant Robin left, the rest of the group stood there in silence. Finally, Rachel broke the awkwardness and said, "Let's see if we can't find somewhere for you to sleep."

○

In the early darkness of the morning, Isaac was getting ready. Kuroni was attached to his left hip. The white coat slid over his arms and onto his back. With no time to make a scabbard for the unusually long Hikari Shichidai, he simply strapped it to his back with the handle extending above his right shoulder. Picking up the Scarlet Lion headband, he paused for a moment before putting it on his forehead and tying it off in the back.

Quietly opening the door, Isaac found the others already prepared and waiting for him. In silent agreement, they followed him out of the house and to the base of the giant chain. The chain was large enough that there was room to walk along its lengths comfortably. Even the grade at which the links rose into the air was gentle enough as to not be a struggle to climb. The chain gave a little as the group began their ascension.

As was the case in the Dendritic Forest, the magnetism of the chain was a phenomenon they had to deal with. Isaac occasionally had to pull his swords off of the chains when they became stuck. R-3N3 had the most difficult battle with the magnetic force, since his entire body was comprised of metal. Still, he took it a step at a time, making progress along with the others.

The sun was rising now and the warriors were about one third of the way along the chain to the Eagle's Nest. R-3N3 tripped after a struggle against one of the links and was pulled to the link with a loud clang. The noise seemed to trigger a flock of black birds flying out from the island. No, not quite birds. The flock flew like birds, but they were too big to be any normal bird. Isaac looked up and realized they may now be in trouble, "It's The Kyries! Get ready, everyone!"

Only a few dozen strong, The Kyries had the definite advantage over the group on the chain. The flock all wore flight vests like the one Sucari wore, except their wings were black like a raven's. A blonde woman in a white dress stood on the edge of the island, commanding the battalion of flying women. The first assault came straight down the chain. Isaac yelled, "Duck!" As Sucari and Vlad followed suit by crouching close to the chain, R-3N3 suddenly stood up from the release of one of his feet from the magnetism.

When The Kyries hit, they only managed to hit R-3N3, who steadfastly remained on the chain, albeit he was on the bottom of it now. The change in position shook the chain, giving the others all the more reason to hold on. On the second attack, The Kyries banked near the edge of the lake and made their approach from the opposite direction of their first assault. Sucari tapped Vlad on the shoulder as he sprouted his wings. If the fight was in the air, they had to fight on The Kyries' turf.

Sucari and Vlad leapt off of opposite sides of the chain and prepared to engage the onslaught. Right before The Kyries clashed with Sucari and Vlad, an object zipped by and struck one of the Kyries in the chest, breaking the fluxion core and turning the woman into a raven. In the confusion, Vlad and Sucari took advantage of the situation. In a flurry of fire and mist, the two warriors were fighting against the odds. Again, another object zipped by, breaking another core. Another raven now flew away. Isaac noticed this and yelled to R-3N3 over the din of the battle above them, "Can you see where those shots are coming from?"

R-3N3 focused his eyes as another shot zipped by and removed another Kyrie from the fight, "There! They are coming from Maurits Manor!"

This caught Sucari's attention, "What?" In his moment of distraction, one of the Kyries got a shot off with her Gottfried Gun, grazing Sucari's right wing. When Sucari landed on the chain he grimaced and shouted to R-3N3, "Can you see who it is?" Another shot, another raven.

Out of his peripheral vision, Sucari saw the blonde woman leap off the edge of the island and sprout a set of brilliantly white wings. With a few flaps, she began to dive toward the mansion. R-3N3 yelled, "Robin! She is on the roof with . . . what is that? It looks like she has an enormous crossbow."

The pieces came together in Sucari's head, and he knew that Robin was in trouble, "Vlad! Give us more mist!"

"All right, Sucari!" Suddenly the group was enveloped with mist. Puncturing the hazy orb, Sucari flew out and toward the Manor.

The remaining Kyries landed on the chain and Isaac pulled out Kuroni from his left hip, "Now it's my turn."

The wind was blowing past Sucari as he rushed toward Maurits Manor. With a flap of his wings, a shooting pain racked his body, almost interrupting his flight. He gritted his teeth and bore it as he used his fire to accelerate his body below the waist. His wings were merely guides for the incredible speed. He saw the blonde woman getting closer to Robin and could hear shots of the Gottfried Guns which the blonde wore on both her hands. Robin was trying to shoot down the woman, but kept missing.

Finally, a shot got through. Robin was hit! Sucari saw this and realized he wouldn't be able to get there before the woman did. With renewed vigor, the fire turned a brilliant blue and moments later Sucari's head was embedded in the ribs of the blonde. He could hear cracking, not only of bone, but of glass as well. In a flurry of feathers, the woman turned into a dove and flew away, limping in defeat.

Landing on the roof, Sucari was breathing heavily as Robin sat there, clutching her right shoulder. "Are you OK, Robin?" As he helped her up, he noticed there were only a few arrows left in the quivers she had strapped to her calves. Looking over to the giant crossbow which lay on the roof, he looked back at Robin and said, "You really helped us out there. I don't know how to thank y-"

Sucari was surprised by a kiss on the lips. Robin pulled back and shyly said, "You saved my life, there's no need for thanks." Sucari stood there in stunned silence yet again. Robin adjusted her glasses, which now rested on her nose. The frames around each lens were in the form of uroboros snakes. On the bridge of the frames was a number: 20/1. She sighed in relief as she said, "Looks like they managed to fight off the rest of The Kyries. You'd better get back and join them."

Snapping out of the sudden daze, Sucari walked to the edge of the roof. "Oh, and Sucari," Robin said, "Come back to me alive, won't you?" Without looking back, he nodded and jumped off the edge. In a blaze of blue fire, he was on his way back to the Eagle's Nest.

The rest of the group was waiting for Sucari at the top of the chain they had just climbed. R-3N3 asked Sucari, "So, how is Robin?"

"She's fine," he blushed, "I mean, she's been shot, but it was only a graze, so she'll be OK." Isaac just rolled his eyes at the fumbling young man, turned, and started heading toward the daunting edifice set up on the middle of the island. The forest on the island thinned as the group advanced toward the encircling stone wall of Testament Tower. Even without the wind block of the trees, the air was unusually calm. Every brick used in the construction of the facility was a dark black color. When the warriors came to the metal gate of the outer wall, it was obvious the black color was due to the soot of a great fire that seemed to have taken place many years ago.

Rapping on the metal gate with the back of his hand, Isaac sized it up and turned to R-3N3, "All right, Artie. You're up." R-3N3 took a few steps toward the gate and examined it for hand holds. Bending down, he grasped the bottom of the gate and, with a mighty effort, slowly lifted the barrier above his head. When everyone had passed through the gate, R-3N3 let it down with a loud clang. Inside the outer wall of the compound was a rather odd sight. The area between the wall and the Testament Tower was covered in neatly groomed grass. A moat was next to the tower, fed by a waterfall that seemed to seep out of the structure of the building at a uniform height of about eight feet. The waterfall appeared to continue around the perimeter of the tower.

A small koi pond was ahead of them, fed by some bamboo piping from the nearby waterfall. A piece of bamboo was hinged so that when it filled with water it would dump the water into the pond. When the water had drained from the bamboo, it would fall back to its starting position with a loud "clack". A red, lacquered wooden bridge crossed the moat and ended at an opening in the tower.

In front of the koi pond was a man sitting cross-legged and dressed in a red kasaya. His tattooed hands rested on his knees with the palms facing up, the thumb and index finger on each hand forming a circle. Instead of fingernails, his thumbs had gem-like implants. Across his lap lay a staff of the same red color as the bridge a little further beyond the man. Each end of the staff had a fluxion embedded in it. The man wore a mask with a mischievous smile.

Clack.

When the group silently headed toward the bridge, they noticed that the man did not stir or seem to notice them. As they approached him, there was a slight breeze which gave Sucari chills down his spine. Muffled behind the mask, the man spoke, "Are you cold, young man?"

Clack.

The sitting man reached up and removed his mask, revealing a very calm and blank face. "Why don't you gentlemen join me in some silent meditation? The grass is soft and the running water is relaxing."

Isaac kept walking to the entrance of the tower as he replied, "I'm sorry, but we can't right now, we've got plans."

Clack.

Some blades of grass zipped by Isaac's face, almost like needles fired from a dart gun. He looked over to where the man was sitting. He hadn't moved, but still sat, staring at the group, "I'm afraid I can't allow you to enter the tower. Now, won't you come and sit down?"

Clack.

Excited to start fighting, Vlad spoke up, "You guys go on ahead, I'll provide some cover." Everyone nodded in agreement. When they broke away, Isaac, Sucari, and R-3N3 started slowly shuffling toward the entrance of the tower. A mist appeared over the moat and began to billow out onto the grass. When it became thick enough that they could no longer see the sitting man, Vlad disappeared into the mist, "Now!" he yelled, "Go now!"

Clack.

After a few minutes, Vlad was certain the others had gotten through and were now inside. The mist subsided and now the man before him was standing, his staff in his right hand, "Why did you have to let them escape? Now I've got to deal with you, don't I? Why can't we just all get along?"

Vlad pulled up the visor to cover his eyes as he said, "Then you must be Alfred the Peacekeeper."

In the same monotonous voice, Alfred replied, "I am."

Clack.

When Isaac and the rest ran for the entrance of the tower, even the cover of Vlad's mist didn't seem to prevent the onslaught of accelerated blades of grass. Fortunately, none of the projectiles hit anyone, and instead were heard bouncing off of the stone wall of the tower with high pitched pings. Out of the mist and into the darkness the trio ran. The entry hallway was dark, but there was a faint light at the end that spurred them on. As the group crossed over into the room, the darkness soon seemed like a friendlier environment.

The vast room where the three now found themselves was lined with a multitude of skulls. Each skull had a various number of candles in it. Some in the eyes, some in the mouth, a few in the nose. A majority of the candles were lit, giving the room its dim lighting. In the center of the room sat a man in a chair, his head resting on his right palm. In his left hand, he held a jet black staff upright and at an angle to the chair. He wore a black robe which seemed to be ragged from years of use. On his face he wore a mask of a sad skull.

As the warriors were examining the eerie room, the man in the chair noticed and sat up, "That's strange. Usually Alfred doesn't let anyone get this far." Removing the mask from his face, the man revealed the scars of years of battle. A long scar ran across the left side of his face, right through his now milky white eye. A long, grizzled and scraggly beard clung to his chin. "I suppose I should probably clean up after his mistakes. Like I always do."

Sucari and R-3N3 were terrified of the man before them. Leaning over to Sucari, R-3N3 whispered, "I think this may be Grigori the Reaper."

Sucari replied, "If it is, we need to run away. But where would we run?"

Isaac could hear the hushed conversation and pointed, "There, behind him. Can you see that staircase? I bet Thomson is on the top floor. Why don't you two go on ahead and I'll catch up."

R-3N3 was shocked, "Are you crazy? How are you going to get away if he can't be killed?"

A sinister look came across Isaac's face, "Oh, I've got some new tricks I want to try out. You know, as a warm-up."

Sucari placed his hand on R-3N3's shoulder and just shook his head, "There's no reasoning with Isaac, so let's just trust in his abilities." When they started jogging toward the entrance to the stairs, Grigori tapped his staff on the floor and a large, straight blade emerged from the staff and was now perpendicular to it. It looked like a very angular scythe. He got up and started on his way to cut off Sucari and R-3N3 from their escape.

Isaac intercepted Grigori as the others made it to the stairs and started their climb up the tower. In a raspy and thick voice, Grigori objected, "This isn't a game, sonny." A grin crept over the undamaged right side of his face, "But if you want to play, I suppose I have some time."

Grasping the hilts of his two swords, Kuroni with his right hand and Hikari Shichidai with his left, Isaac replied, "I wouldn't have it any other way."

○

Sucari and R-3N3 were running up the staircase, two steps at a time. The stairs curved along the outside of the tower and by the time they were at the top of them, Sucari was out of breath. They both knew that in the brief opening Isaac gave them, they needed to get as far away from that room as they could. But now they stood before a large double door with a more dangerous man lurking behind it.

With a deep breath, Sucari and R-3N3 both took a door and pushed it open. Inside, the room was large and circular, just like the one below it. However, this room was lined by a colonnade which held up a domed roof. Everything was constructed with a smooth, white marble. From behind one of the columns appeared a man, smartly dressed in a white suit, "So, it seems that my opponents today are Sucari and the Crimson Front. Oh wait; you like to be called 'Artie' now, don't you?" His breath formed little clouds as he spoke.

R-3N3 growled at Thomson, "You don't have the right to call me that."

Sucari was still flustered by the fact that the man in front of them already knew who they were. Thomson could sense this from Sucari's body language and gave an explanation, "You see, Sucari, information is paramount to maintaining power. I've had Val's Kyries observing Isaac from the shadows all the way back when he started interfering with my plans. I still can't figure out how he jumped around from place to place, but what I'm more interested in is how you all managed to get past her and her warriors."

Regaining his composure, Sucari replied, "Was Val that blonde woman? If so, then that bird has flown away. I made sure of it."

A flash of intense anger came to Thomson's eyes, but quickly cooled, "I see. Now, can you two please close that door? You're letting the heat in."

"We would rather have it stay open," R-3N3 said.

"Very well." Thomson sighed while looking at his pocket watch, "Now, I've got some important things I need to take care of; so if you don't mind, I'm going to speed this process along a little." The air began to crackle as the temperature of the room began to rapidly drop. Steam started appearing on Sucari's skin and the moisture in the atmosphere began to solidify and fall as snow.

As Thomson walked toward the duo, he explained, "See, I've got this ability that I like to call the 'Zero Hour.' I'll give you both sixty minutes to try and stay alive, and if you succeed at that, I'll let you go on your merry little way. However, I've rarely had anyone get past five minutes. The Crimson Front here only lasted for half of that."

"Sucari! We need to act fast while his attack is still taking shape!" R-3N3 was yelling over his shoulder as he charged at Thomson. He wound up for a running punch, but began to significantly slow down as he approached his target. Soon he had stopped completely.

Thomson arrived at the spot where R-3N3 had frozen and tapped on the metallic body, "Tsk, tsk. Some things never learn. That human Blood-fluxion that Dr. Paul developed only works if the blood is flowing, not when it's frozen." With a short laugh, Thomson continued on toward Sucari, fog gathering at his feet and spilling out of the open door, "It's too bad none of your group excels at ranged combat. Otherwise, you might have stood a chance against any of us."

Frozen with fear and racked with shivers, Sucari stood there while his brain was telling him to run, to fight, to do something. A blast from outside shook the tower and shook Sucari out of his daze. With a burst of blue flame, Sucari was now engulfed and ready for battle. Thomson seemed un-phased by both the explosion and Sucari's change. Cupping his hands together, Thomson started forming what looked like a snowball out of nothing but the air. When the ball, which had a purple tint, had grown to a reasonable size, Thomson threw it at Sucari.

Thinking nothing of it, Sucari let the flames on his body return the snowball to its natural state. Except that the snowball didn't melt into water, it vaporized into something else. The flames where the ball had hit on Sucari's chest disappeared and Sucari found that he was suffocating. Thomson was already forming another ball in his hands. This time the ball looked bluer and smaller than its predecessor. All the while, Thomson was lecturing, "These aren't normal snowballs. That one was solidified air. Nitrogen to be exact. Your fire needs Oxygen to function, as do your lungs. But don't worry; air is also composed of Oxygen."

With a more forceful effort, Thomson threw the new snowball at Sucari, who tried to dodge, but to no avail. The ball caught fire and exploded, throwing Sucari across the room and into a column. Once again, Thomson was forming another snowball, "And yet, with how necessary it is for life, it's certainly highly flammable."

Sucari got up from the floor and spat out some blood from his mouth. With a sharp crack, the blood froze in mid-air and ricocheted off of the floor with a "ping." Looking to the open door, Sucari wondered when Isaac was coming to help them.

○

Uncrossing his arms, Isaac's first attack was quick. The acceleration from Kuroni's Gravity-fluxion and the latent speed of Hikari Shichidai gave him the advantage he needed to land the first blow. And yet, it didn't seem to have any effect on Grigori. Seeing that Isaac was confused, Grigori laughed, "Bwa ha ha. What a rookie mistake." With a wide swipe of his scythe, Grigori caught Isaac's coat just as he evaded with a backwards jump.

Folding the blade back into the staff, Grigori spoke to Isaac, "You know, lad, I'm feeling pretty generous today, so why don't you give me your best shot. I'll just stand here and take it." Isaac was leery on this proposal, but eventually decided he was going to take every opportunity he could. He sheathed Kuroni and held Hikari Shichidai with both hands. Strangely enough, even though Hikari Shichidai was the larger of the two swords, it felt lighter than Kuroni did.

With a running start, Isaac lifted the broadsword over his head and brought it down on Grigori's neck, making a diagonal slice down the man's body. It was a clean cut, and soon Grigori's head and right arm lay on the floor. However, Grigori's body was still standing. The disembodied head began to laugh as it started to fade away. At the same time, the head and arm that were once missing from his body began to re-appear much in the same manner that they were disappearing from the floor.

An explosion from outside shook the tower, and Isaac instinctively looked toward the arch where he had entered the room. Grigori once again tapped his staff on the ground, revealing the scythe blade, "You should really pay attention to your own battle, bean-sprout." Isaac evaded like before, but did so a little too late, as Grigori's attack caught part of Isaac's right shoulder.

Isaac began to feel chills, not from the wound he had sustained, but from the entrance to the stairs. There was a fog which clung to the floor, pouring from the upper staircase. It swirled around in little eddies on the floor as it continued to the downward stairs. It seemed like everyone was in the midst of their battle, and Isaac got the feeling none of his friends were managing very well. This gave him all the more reason to fight harder against his current foe.

Once again charging at Grigori, Isaac ducked underneath the switchblade scythe's slash and brought down his own across Grigori's body. This time Isaac's attack took off the head and left arm. He figured that, at the very least, he'd be able to prevent Grigori from attacking in that brief period when the separated body parts reappeared. But Grigori's main body didn't stand still this time. While it was still missing its head and left arm, it started swiping at Isaac with its right arm.

When the body was fully functioning again, Isaac noticed his attacks were doing something, but not to the body. The ragged cloak that Grigori wore had four distinctive cuts in it which were not there when the battle began. Through one of the cuts, Isaac could see through the cloak to Grigori's chest. There, embedded over his heart, was a broken pocket watch surrounded by an uroboros seal.

Now Isaac knew why Grigori could not be killed. The broken watch maintained the same state, and as the core of the fluxion over his heart, it transferred its eternal powers to Grigori. Any alterations to his physical form would just fade away to the equilibrium state that his body was in when the fluxion was activated. Taking a few steps backwards to maintain a safe distance to think at, Isaac began to formulate a plan of attack. That's when he noticed something peculiar about the broken watch.

Vlad was starting to have his doubts about staying behind. Granted, he was able to assist the others by allowing them to get by Alfred, but now he was stuck having to deal with The Peacemaker when there must have been more exciting enemies to battle inside the tower. Eager to get into battle, Vlad produced his spear and charged at the man in red. With a thrust of his weapon, Vlad had hoped to make contact, but Alfred easily side-stepped the attack and grabbed on to the shaft. Vlad tried to free his spear from Alfred's grip, but was having difficulty in doing so. In fact, he was having difficulty holding on to the spear at all as it felt like it was being pulled away from him. Suddenly, his grip gave way and the spear shot into the air and arced over the wall where it most likely landed in the nearby woods. With his opponent disarmed, The Peacemaker started his offensive. At first, Vlad did his best to dodge the attacks from Alfred's staff, but it soon became obvious to him that he couldn't keep dodging attacks forever.

Or could he? Vlad didn't need to defeat Alfred; he just needed to keep him occupied until the others came back. Seeing an opening, Vlad turned and ran away. He just needed to keep his distance and everything would be all right.

When Vlad began to run away, Alfred yelled after him, "Don't you know you should never show an enemy your back?" Taking a wide stance, Alfred held his staff horizontally. His left hand was palm up, holding the end of the staff with his index finger and thumb. His right hand grasped the opposite end of the staff and seemed to be resisting an invisible pull on the weapon. Taking aim at his fleeing prey, Alfred released his right hand's grip on the staff.

In a flash of red, the staff disappeared from his hands and shot at a frightening speed toward Vlad's unsuspecting back. Fortunately for Vlad, the air resistance against the staff gave him enough warning to enable him to leap away from the attack. As the red flash whistled by, Vlad watched as the staff hit the outer wall and immediately exploded. Rubble and debris flew out from the wall and the ground shook from the explosion. Some of the stone shrapnel hit Vlad, knocking him on his back and knocking the wind out of his lungs.

Alfred calmly walked past Vlad and over to the huge gap that now marred the uniformity of the outer wall. His staff was stuck in the rubble, pointing up to the sky. Grabbing the weapon, he turned around and made his way toward Vlad.

Taking deep breaths, Vlad stared up through his visor, slats of light showing him the clear sky above. He tasted something acidic in his mouth and could only assume it was his blood. When Alfred arrived at Vlad, he put his foot on Vlad's chest and leaned down to talk, "You see, I don't even have to hit you in order to win. My dynamite staff and acceleration tattoos are more than enough to take care of the likes of you." Vlad gathered up the sour tasting liquid in his mouth and spat in Alfred's face. Alfred recoiled in pain and screamed out similarly. With the pressure released from his chest, Vlad rolled over and bit into Alfred's leg.

More screaming, more pain. Alfred had lost his calm demeanor and was livid now, "What *was* that? Did you just spit poison in my eyes?" Kicking Vlad off of his leg, Alfred ripped part of his kasaya and bent down to tie up his wound. Seeing the large holes where the elongated canines had pierced his flesh, Alfred asked, "What the heck are you?"

Vlad stood up and brushed himself off, "I'm a dragon. Why do you ask?" Something snapped in Alfred as he grabbed the end of his staff with both hands and swung it at Vlad like a bat. Vlad didn't have enough time to get away. He closed his eyes and winced in anticipation of the impact, but the impact never came. Instead, the ricocheted sound of metal against the dynamite staff was heard. A breeze swept by Vlad's head as the staff passed, missing him by inches.

Opening his eyes, he could see his savior, standing on the pile of detritus that once was part of the encircling wall. Alfred turned around to see who had interfered and was met with a bespectacled gaze from a black haired girl with an enormous crossbow in her hands and twin quivers strapped to her calves. She shouted to Alfred, "Don't you know you should never show an enemy your back?"

Vlad yelled out in elation, "Robin!"

Robin hopped down from the pile and started walking toward the fighters, "Are you OK, Vlad? I got here as quickly as I could, but the front gate was locked."

Alfred took a few steps back and casually placed his staff over his shoulders, his arms draped over the ends. Taking a deep breath, he calmed himself and said, "Fighting a girl and a dragon won't be much of a challenge, but if I have a thousand ideas on how to defeat them and only one manages to kill them both, I will be satisfied." With a loud click, Alfred broke his staff over his shoulders, each piece showing a clean separation from the other. He now held an end in each hand and, with a quick motion outward, allowed the two hidden swords to be unsheathed, their coverings clattering to the ground behind him. Striking a fighting pose with the two swords, Alfred said, "Now, let's see if I can get you both to rest in peace."

Isaac wasn't entirely sure that the thin, silvery thread which was coming out of the broken watch in Grigori's chest was what he thought it was, but at this point he had few options. In one fluid motion, Isaac pulled Kuroni from its scabbard, lifted it into the air and thrust the tip into the floor. After returning his broadsword to his back, Isaac began doing leg stretches. Grigori was confused by these actions, "So, you're giving up, are you? If that's the case, maybe I should get serious so I can get back to sleep."

Flipping the scythe over, he tapped it against the floor and another blade emerged from the staff. It was perpendicular like the other blade, but just happened to be on the opposite side of the staff. Isaac knew he had his work cut out for him now. With a dash, he ran toward Grigori and evaded the first swipe of the switchblade scythe. Getting up close to Grigori, Isaac grabbed at the silver thread. As a reflex, Grigori pulled back and asked, "What are you doing? Have you gone mad?"

Looking down at his clenched fist, Isaac saw he had succeeded. The silver thread was now in his grasp. Looking up at Grigori, Isaac said, "Quite the contrary. I've just gained the advantage." Taking a few steps backward, he bent down and tied the thread to Kuroni's black blade.

Grigori was still confused, "You say you've gained an advantage and now you've resorted to pantomime? What are you doing, tying an invisible bow to your sword? Are you going to give it to me as a present for when I win? *Nyet*, I'm pretty sure you've lost," holding his scythe in a ready position Grigori added, "And soon it won't just be your marbles that you've lost."

Isaac stood up and took a step forward, just within the range of Grigori's attacks. Now he was ready to see if the thread was truly the Time Thread. Grigori took the bait and began swiping at Isaac with his switchblade scythe, fully utilizing its two straight blades. With each attack, Isaac took a step or two backwards and began leading Grigori in a circle around Kuroni.

The changes were small, but it confirmed what Isaac had thought: one of the slashes from Hikari Shichidai separated the frozen Time Thread from the fluxion in Grigori's chest. Grigori's hair was slowly getting greyer, which showed that as the Time Thread was pulled from his chest, time once again began to atrophy his body. Now it was only a matter of patience and careful evasion until Isaac would win.

As Isaac guided Grigori around Kuroni, the ravages of time became more apparent. Grigori was unaware of the changes to his body. At least he was unaware until he took a step forward and his femur shattered: a victim of osteoporosis. By now his hair was almost pure white, and the wrinkles on his face were deep and furrowed. Isaac approached the fallen legend and Grigori tried to attack, which only resulted in his arms breaking as well. With his bones essentially turned to dust, Grigori moaned on the floor, "What have you done?"

Gripping the thread in his hand, Isaac replied, "I didn't do anything. You've merely paid the price for ignoring the rules of time. For every action, there is a consequence." With a firm tug on the Time Thread, Isaac pulled the end out of Grigori's chest and threw the thread on the floor. Grigori's vacant eyes stared up at the ceiling as Isaac went over and pulled Kuroni out of the ground. Removing the Time Thread from the blade and sheathing the katana on his left hip, Isaac made his way to the stairs. At the arch, he leaned over to one of the skulls and blew out the candle in the right eye.

Standing at a crossroads of upstairs and downstairs, Isaac looked up toward where R-3N3 and Sucari had headed. He no longer felt the chill emanating from upstairs like he did before. Looking down into the darkness of the basement stairs, Isaac followed them to his next battle. He figured that if his comrades had won or lost, Thomson wasn't anything more than a puppet and didn't deserve any of his attention. He really needed to find the man responsible for the surge of fluxion use in the world. He needed to find Gottfried.

○

Even with the threat of the snowballs, Sucari had to keep his flames going to prevent eventually freezing to death. And yet, with the blue flames covering his body, Sucari could feel the cold seeping through the fire. He wasn't sure how long Isaac would take to come and help them, but he knew that two against one was better than his current situation. Running over to R-3N3, Sucari sprouted his wings and used them to cover the cold, metal body with fire.

Regaining consciousness, R-3N3 asked, "What happened? Did I get him?"

Sucari shook his head, "Nah, you froze long before you got to him, so you need to stay close to me in order to keep from getting frozen again."

"I see. Thank you."

From across the room, Thomson was taunting them, "Two whole minutes! I'm impressed. You've only got fifty-eight more to go."

"You've fought him before, Artie. Any ideas?"

"Yes, I have fought him before, but that does not mean I know how to beat him."

"I wonder what Isaac would do in this situation?"

Thomson was preparing another snowball, "I don't know what you two are whispering about, but I wish you'd give up and die already. I thought if I had

133

Erwin killed it would deter everyone from putting up a fight. I guess you all don't realize how dangerous it is to oppose Testament."

Sucari gasped in mortified anger, "What did you say about Erwin?"

"I had him killed."

"You mean that you were just using Fred?"

"Oh, come on. Once we have the world under our control, people will be lining up to be used by Testament."

Sucari's throat tightened as his anger grew. In a controlled whisper, he spoke to R-3N3, "Artie, I've made up my mind. We're not only going to survive his 'Zero Hour', we're going to take him out. Now listen carefully."

Thomson had finished forming his snowball and was tossing it in the air, waiting for his opponents to make a move, "It looks like you've surpassed your previous record, Artie. Although, I don't know if I can count it since you had to be revived."

With a loud and angry shout, Sucari's flames transformed from the almost sedate blue to a fantastic white. He almost looked like an angel, clad in a brilliant light. And yet, he wasn't the only one shining. R-3N3's metal body glowed red with the residual heat absorbed from Sucari's wings. In a swirl of fire, R-3N3 once again ran toward Thomson, a mighty punch wound up and ready to be delivered.

Surprised by the sudden change in the two warriors, Thomson threw his snowball at R-3N3. Unfortunately, his effort had no effect as it was a Nitrogen ball. R-3N3's body continued to glow and his charge remained unhindered from the lack of Oxygen. In the last moment before the impact, Thomson crossed his arms in front of his chest as R-3N3's fist made contact.

R-3N3 remained steady as his body began to cool, steam rising from his outstretched fist. Thomson had been pushed back a few feet and steam was rising from his arms due to the transferred heat of the punch. Retreating to Sucari, R-3N3 asked, "OK, what is next?"

Putting his hand on one of the pillars, Sucari said, "Now we play his game by *our* rules."

Grabbing the column with his hand engulfed in white fire, Sucari produced balls of molten marble and handed them to R-3N3 who said, "Now we are talking!" With a simple wind-up, he launched one of the marble balls at Thomson. As the projectile passed through the frigid air, it rapidly cooled, crackling along its path. By the time it had reached Thomson, the ball had taken a drop-like shape and was once again hard as stone.

Thomson dodged the first shot as it impacted the column behind him, bursting into shrapnel and leaving a fair sized dent in the pillar. Running along the colonnade, the barrage of molten marble shots kept coming at Thomson. Suddenly, the assault stopped as Sucari noticed that the roof wasn't going to hold up much longer under this kind of abuse to the columns.

"OK, Artie. I'll finish this."

"But I need to avenge what happened in Mathiston, and what happened to Erwin."

"I know that. Let me assume those burdens. Just trust me." Closing his eyes and controlling his breathing, Sucari vanished in a flash. He immediately appeared before Thomson, the white-hot intensity of the flames engulfing his body paling in comparison to the fire in his eyes.

Everything happened so quickly that it was difficult to know what had occurred. Each action was accelerated by a flash of white fire. With incredible force and speed, Sucari punched Thomson into the air and intercepted him in the middle of the room, slamming his body to the ground, cracking the marble underneath. Flying up to the apex of the dome, Sucari crouched down against the ceiling and shot down to deliver a final blow. As Sucari's shoulder impacted Thomson's abdomen, the integrity of the room began to fail. Cracks raced along the floor and up to the compromised columns.

R-3N3 saw what was happening and ran over to Sucari and the unconscious Thomson as the floor gave way beneath them. When they landed in Grigori's chamber, the resulting shockwave blew out all the candles in the skulls. As the dust settled and Thomson's room crumbled to ruin above them, everything faded to darkness.

○

Even though the battle had turned to two against one, the odds were still against Robin and Vlad. It was almost as if Alfred really wasn't trying before. Now he was serious. Vlad didn't want to get too close to Alfred, but he needed to be the bait to draw any attention away from Robin while she attacked. The back and forth between close range and long range attacks finally forced Alfred to make a decision.

Turning from Vlad, Alfred ran toward Robin. In a panic, she fired a shot into the air as Alfred lunged at her. Blocking his swords with her crossbow, she called out to Vlad, "A little help?" When Vlad came running to save Robin, Alfred turned his head and pointed one of his swords at Vlad. Releasing his grip on the handle, he let the sword fly through his hand, accelerated like his staff had been before. Vlad was too close to completely dodge and it tore away the cloak on his left side, leaving a deep gash and revealing the pale white skin of his shoulder. Clutching at his injury, not only for the wound, but for the instant burn that the sunlight brought, Vlad stopped his advance.

Turning back to Robin, Alfred gripped the hilt of his other sword and held it above his head, the fluxion on the end of the hilt poised for an attack, "Now normally I don't attack little girls, and normally I don't use this in such close range, but today really hasn't been a normal day, now has it?" Lifting the hilt for his strike, Alfred heard a whistling noise above him and was almost able to look up when the metal rod that Robin shot into the air earlier came zipping down to his head, instantly knocking him unconscious.

Robin got up, dusted herself off and said, "The spot directly above a person is their worst blind spot." She then laughed, as if she had planned that bit of luck all along. Vlad just stared in disbelief. Ripping off part of his hood, Vlad began to cover his bleeding shoulder. Robin jogged over to Vlad and asked, "Are you OK?"

"I'll manage."

"Where are the others?"

"Probably still inside the tower."

She was already running to the entrance, "Let's go help them out!"

Vlad was taken by surprise and tried hard to catch up, "Hey! Wait a minute!"

When they arrived at the tower, a large blast from inside blew a cloud of dust from the entrance, knocking both of them on their backs. Terrified that something had gone wrong, Robin was quickly back up and running into the tower. It was dark inside the tunnel, but she just kept running forward. Eventually, she arrived at Grigori's room and slowed down as she breathed in some of the dust from the roof collapse.

With a cough, she choked out, "Sucari? Artie? Isaac? Is anyone there?"

The two blinking green lights of R-3N3's eyes opened, providing a small amount of light, "Robin? What are you doing here?"

"That doesn't matter right now. Where is everybody?" R-3N3 looked down at the lifeless pile of bodies that was Sucari and Thomson.

Robin became panicked. She ran over to where Sucari lay and held his body close to hers. Screaming through sobs and tears, she cried, "No! Sucari! Didn't I tell you to come back alive?"

Sucari stirred and moaned, "Ugh. Not so loud. And what's with all this ringing in my ears?"

"Sucari!" Robin hugged him tightly and he grimaced at the pain of a broken collarbone and a gunshot wound.

Suddenly, the hug was over and an open handed slap was brought across Sucari's face. Snapped out of his daze, he yelled, "What was that for?!"

Sternly, Robin replied, "That's for making me worry, stupid." She then laughed and resumed hugging Sucari.

R-3N3 had gotten up and examined the damage. Thomson lay defeated on the chunk of marble that had fallen from the ceiling of their current room. A body that looked like a decrepit version of Grigori lay a little further away from them, debris lightly covering his body.

Sucari noticed it was incredibly dark in the room, so he lit his hair on fire to provide some extra light. Robin was taken aback by this sudden development, "I didn't know you could do that."

"Yeah, it's one of my many talents."

When Robin got a good look at the room they were in, she clutched Sucari's arm in fear, "Where are we?"

R-3N3 answered, "We are in the room of Grigori the Reaper, the immortal man who apparently has been defeated by Isaac. Now the real question is: where is Isaac?"

A rumble deep beneath them violently shook the tower and caused more of the ceiling to fall to the floor. Sucari struggled to his feet and said, "Isaac can take care of himself, but we'd better leave this tower if we want to live to see him again."

R-3N3 nodded as he picked up the two lifeless bodies of Thomson and Grigori and held them over his shoulders, "Agreed. Let us depart." The group of warriors hurriedly made their way out of the darkness. Once outside, they climbed through the hole in the wall that Alfred had created and piled the bodies of Thomson and Grigori next to Alfred.

Another shockwave shook the ground, which dislodged one of the support chains from the edge of the island. The chain rose into the air and stood vertically, no longer hindered by the weight of the island. Sucari commanded his friends, "We need to get off of this island. *Now.*"

Robin was worried, "But what about Isaac?"

"Again, he can take care of himself."

"But-"

Vlad chimed in, "I agree, we need to escape before something else happens."

Robin pouted for a moment, but eventually followed everyone to the chain that connected the Eagle's Nest to the ground outside of David's house. Going down the chain was much easier than the journey up it, especially with the increased tension of the load it now had to bear. With everyone safely on the ground again, David came out of his house and met the group, "I'm assuming everything went well, but-" looking at those in front of him, he noticed someone was missing, "Where's Isaac?"

Suddenly, the chain began to rattle and the last two links to the island broke. The scene that everyone watched seemed to unfold in slow motion. As the chains which once held the island aloft began their journey to an upright position, the island itself fell into the lake. They all watched as an enormous wave rapidly approached them. David yelled out, "Everyone! Grab on to the house!"

The wave came and receded, but the lake definitely had a different coastline now. As the fish of the lake flopped around on the ground, everyone yelled in unison, "Isaac!" Sucari, Vlad, and R-3N3 dove into the lake and began to swim across to the island.

David yelled after them, "Wait a minute! Some of you are injured, and I'm pretty sure R-3N3 can't swim!"

R-3N3 just sank to the bottom of the lake and bashfully walked back to shore as the other two struggled their way to the island. David just shook his head and turned to Robin, "Now, didn't John tell you not to get involved?"

Robin shyly bowed her head and mumbled, "Yeah."

"Well, if you're going to break the rules, you might as well go all the way. Let's get a boat so those idiots don't drown." Perking up, Robin ran over to the nearby dock and started untying the rowboat held there.

○

Isaac arrived at the bottom of the stairs and stood before a large and ominous metal door. Finding it was unlocked, he pushed on the door and passed unhindered into the room beyond. The room was large and circular, just like the others in Testament Tower. A rim of lights lit the ceiling, the reflected ambiance illuminating the room.

Scattered throughout the room were various tables and benches, each with their own variety of materials spread out upon them. Scrolls, glass orbs, various metal implements. Isaac was looking around, soaking in the surroundings when he heard a voice ahead of him, "Not bad, right? Although I bet it pales in comparison to the laboratory you performed your work in, Isaac."

Crouched over a table, the man stood upright and held his back in an attempt to work out a knot in the muscles of his lower back. His hair was short, tightly curled and dark black. He wore a black coat which looked a lot like the one Isaac was wearing.

Isaac kept advancing into the room, but was at the ready, should anything happen, "And you must be Gottfried. The Onyx Eagle. Inventor of the Gottfried Gun. Number 4 of Testament."

Gottfried chuckled, "Oh please. My reputation can't precede me that much, especially to The Scarlet Lion." The ceiling above them shook as Thomson's battle came to a close. "It looks like your friends have lost."

"Don't sell my friends short. They may be misfits, but they're *my* misfits. But enough about them, why do *you* work for Testament?"

"Isn't it obvious? I'm not working for them; they're merely my guinea pigs. What good is research without test subjects? What good is an army without weapons? I hold all the power, I control the weapons. Besides, wouldn't the world be a better place if we are united together under a single organization?"

"You know that doesn't work. That's why Testament overthrew Robert."

Gottfried scoffed, "Bah! That fool? *Nein*, Robert destroyed himself, we just sped the process along."

"Then why did you start spreading the fluxions?"

"You're right. Nothing exists and nothing happens without a reason. Our reason was to become gods."

"But you're wrong. They haven't produced gods, they've merely spread evil!"

"I do not believe that a world without evil, preferable in order to ours, is possible; otherwise it would have been preferred."

"Fluxions are not what Nature intended for man. Why do you think the world fell into the Millennial Erasure after the fall of The Triumvirate?"

"Nature? Nature does not make leaps of progress. Nature takes too long to get to the point. Every substance in Nature is a world apart, independent of everything. I have merely combined those substances to progress man to the status of gods, independent of all rules."

"Without rules, there is no order. There is no consequence for actions, be they good or bad. Besides, your method of sealing the fluxions is all wrong."

"Oh? And I suppose you've found a better way."

"I have studied the seals. You have not."

"Fine. Let us fight, without further ado, to see who is right."

Isaac smiled as he gripped the hilts of his two swords. With a leap, he was upon Gottfried. He pulled his swords out and slashed them both across Gottfried's body. Isaac saw a familiar sight as the swords came upon resistance. Sparks.

Unfazed by Isaac's first attack, Gottfried looked around his laboratory and said, "It's far too cluttered in here to fight. Let me take care of that." Widening his stance, he held his fist aloft and followed the pose with a punch to the floor. A shockwave shook the floor, and pushed everything to the edges of the room. Isaac had to jump over the wave as it carried tables and equipment with it.

Isaac landed at the edge of the now cleared room and said, "That doesn't make any sense! Psi's power has been lost on the bottom of the ocean for centuries, how did you find it?"

"You can't be serious. If you found Chi's Hellfire orb, why wouldn't it be possible for me to find Psi's Seawave orb? Besides, you're only partly right."

"What do you mean?"

"Psi's power to control waves wasn't as unique as everyone thinks it is. The same with Chi's power of fire and Lambda's power of lightning. There is one power that combines all powers together."

"You mean The Omnipotence? Even within legends, its existence was a myth."

"True, it did sound too good to be true. And yet, if one were to find such an awesome power, how would one control it? Gottfried pulled back his torn shirt to reveal a large dark disk embedded in his chest. The disk swirled with dark vortices and colors. Surrounding the disk was an uroboros seal consisting of over one hundred snakes tattooed on his skin and radiating out to the rest of his body.

Isaac was shocked by this revelation, "You idiot! With that many snakes, how will the power be contained?"

"Why would I want to contain this power? Besides, the multitude of snakes composing this seal contains the power well enough."

"No, you're wrong! Fluxions need to be controlled. At their base concept, they're changing the composition of your body. That many snakes provide far too many outlets for the core's power to escape."

"*Ja*, if you're a weakling."

Isaac could see he wasn't getting through to Gottfried. He could also see he couldn't win this fight by himself. Closing his eyes, he focused on the fluxion embedded in his forehead. His heart rate steadied as he began the process of activating the Soul-fusion fluxion.

Badump.

"Marie? Are you there Marie?"

Badump.

"Of course, Isaac. You know I'm always with you."

Badump.

"I need your help. I can't do this alone."

Badump.

"Oh? Why the sudden change of heart?"

Badump.

"I've come to realize I have something to protect now. I have my friends, and I didn't realize how much some of them meant to me until it was too late."

Badump.

"I'm proud of you Isaac; you've grown so much on your journey. I've enjoyed watching you open up again. Watching you live again."

Badump.

"Well, I might not be alive if Gottfried kills me here. That's why I need us to fight him. Together. I know the risks, and I'm willing to sacrifice myself if it will save my friends and stop this menace standing before me."

Badump.

Gottfried was becoming annoyed by the white-haired man in front of him who seemed to be ignoring his presence. Another punch to the floor sent a shockwave of stone and tile rushing toward Isaac. The mouth of the lion on Isaac's headband began to glow red. Right before Gottfried's attack hit, he opened his eyes and leapt into the air, bringing his swords once again down across Gottfried's body. Sparks once again ensued as his skin had turned to flint.

"Don't you ever learn? That's not going to work on-" Gottfried was cut short when he realized that a small crack had appeared on his left shoulder. Blood began to trickle down his chest. Looking up from his injury toward Isaac, Gottfried saw his opponent's appearance had changed. Now his eyes gazed with determination beneath the glowing red headband. One eye was green, like it had always been, but the other was now blue. A streak of black interrupted his uniformly white hair.

Gottfried was intrigued, "Oho? I thought you were better than that, Isaac. Although, I must say that using the forbidden Soul-fusion fluxion on a living person is a new one for me."

"Don't speak to *me* about forbidden techniques; I've seen your foray into the realm of the Soul-fusion fluxion. You were trying to recreate the Army of Amedeo, weren't you?"

"And if I was? Not only would I get it right this time, but it would truly be invincible. It's unfortunate I delegated that responsibility to Number 5. I thought his experience in Blood-fluxions would prove useful, but his pride screwed up the whole operation." With a sigh, Gottfried got back on topic, "Of course, this is no time to talk. I need to silence you before I go and confirm that your friends are dead."

The core of The Omnipotence began to glow as two numbers appeared on its surface. The number 6 drifted toward his left and the number 1 drifted toward his right. As the numbers reached their respective edges, the circuitry of snakes began to glow. Putting four fingers from his right hand into his left palm, Gottfried focused his energy into his hands. Many of the Number-fluxions were rare and most were unstable, so Isaac was worried that if Gottfried was combining the power of two Number-fluxions that the result could be disastrous. At any rate, he saw this as a sign his opponent was preparing an attack and took to resuming his assault.

Charging toward Gottfried, Isaac's swords were out and extended behind him. With a swirling motion, Isaac swung Kuroni at Gottfried, who dodged backward, but was unable to dodge the slash of the longer Hikari Shichidai as the momentum of Kuroni brought the other sword quickly through the remainder of the spinning attack. A few of the snake heads on the uroboros seal disappeared, but Gottfried, hands still in position, did not seem to be dissuaded by this development, "Are you sure you actually hit me? I mean the *real* me." Around the room, a veritable army of Gottfrieds stood at the ready, all in the same pose, the Omnipotence core swirling on each of them.

Isaac had no time to deal with multiple opponents, so he simply picked the nearest Gottfried clone and attacked it. He swung his swords and made contact. Unfortunately, the resistance felt different. From the gaping wound on Gottfried's body, sand started seeping out. Was that how he created the multiples? As Isaac pondered the situation, he felt a sting on his back. Turning around, he saw another one of the Gottfried clones with large, clawed hands. Shreds of Isaac's coat were caught on the claws. Isaac figured Gottfried could quickly change from one fluxion to another and any combination in between.

He slashed with Kuroni at another clone, who simply grabbed the sword. Attempting to free the katana seemed to be too much of a struggle, so Isaac let go of the weapon, stepped back and drew his broadsword. He jumped toward Gottfried, ready to slash at his foe. At that moment, the clone let go of Kuroni and sent it flying toward Isaac with an invisible, magnetic force. Catching the hilt of the katana in mid-air, Isaac landed and brought both blades down into the multitude of clones. Standing back up, Isaac shook his hair out of his eyes. It now had more black than white in it.

The chorus of voices said, "Enough! I am finally ready for my attack." The multitude of bodies disappeared. Isaac was left alone in the room. Looking around the laboratory, Isaac was having trouble concentrating. He was becoming dizzy and couldn't focus his eyesight. Finally, Gottfried appeared in front of him and he charged forward, the twin swords once again slashing across Gottfried's body. Gottfried smiled as Isaac had fallen into his trap.

Sparks once again filled the air at the interaction of flint and steel. In a flash, the room was white and hot. Gottfried had been filling the room with an invisible gas and had now allowed Isaac to ignite it. Lying on the floor, smoldering and coughing, Isaac's hair was now almost completely black, but not from the explosion. Standing over his opponent, Gottfried seemed unfazed by the explosion, his singed clothing smoking on his unharmed body, "Just give up, Isaac. You can't win; you just don't have enough fluxions to battle the legion of powers I possess." Using his swords to help him stand back up, Isaac struggled to his feet.

The island continued to shake after Gottfried's attack and soon the feeling of weightlessness came upon them. Isaac knew he had his opportunity. Using the pull of Kuroni, he floated over to Gottfried and used Hikari Shichidai to slash at Gottfried's uroboros seal. More snake heads were now gone, and Isaac could tell he was making progress. About one third of the snake heads were now incapacitated. With no way to tell how long the floating would continue, Isaac prepared for another attack. That's when the island landed.

With a jolt, everything fell back to the floor at once. Cracks started appearing in the ceiling and dirt started seeping through. Isaac knew that time was of the essence. Gottfried regained his composure and also realized that his laboratory would soon be his tomb. Holding his right hand above his head, it began to crackle with the sound of electricity being gathered to the fist. Opening his hand, he released the lightning, sending it toward Isaac.

Isaac threw Kuroni to the side and let it stick in the wall, attracting the electric attack originally intended for his body. Gracefully, a head full of black hair bouncing at every step, he charged in toward Gottfried and gave Hikari Shichidai one final thrust. The sword hit its target: the central core of The Omnipotence. With eyes wide open in shock, Gottfried looked down at the glimmering sword that had been shoved into his body. He then began to laugh manically, "The Omnipotence is one of the legendary Fluents! It can't be broken so easily."

Smirking in his knowledge, Isaac provided a rebuttal, "Yes, but when faced against another Fluent, how does it stack up?"

"What?"

"The Light Fluent has the ability to split anything it comes in contact with. The Omnipotence is merely a collection of tiny powers, and the sum of their slivers gives it strength. But what if those tiny powers are split up?"

Gottfried put his hand up to his face and watched as it fluctuated between many different powers. Blood-fluxions. Number-fluxions. Elemental-fluxions. Each came and went rapidly, and outside of his control. This same change was happening all over his body as he yelled, "A Light Fluent? Why have I never heard of anything like that?"

"Like I said, I've studied the seals. You have not." With a twist, Isaac pushed the broadsword through Gottfried's body.

With an anguished scream, Gottfried burst into a multitude of tiny bits of stuff, each bit representing a fluxion contained in The Omnipotence. Now that Gottfried was defeated, Isaac let out a sigh of relief. A piercing headache grabbed Isaac and brought him to his knees.

"Goodbye, Isaac."

"Marie! I can't lose you again."

"I'm sorry, but once more I have to leave you. We've had good times, but you need to move on. Your friends are depending on you to lead the future you have created." Collapsing on the floor, Isaac lost consciousness as his hair faded back to its original white color.

Epilogue

Oath

Isaac awoke in a comfortable bed in an elaborate room. As he lay in the bed, he thought to himself that if he was going to make a habit of waking up in strange beds, it might just be for the best.

"He's awake!"

Looking around the room, Isaac saw that everyone was gathered around his bed. Sucari. Vlad. R-3N3. Robin. Maria. John. David. Rachel. Even Cornelis was there. They all looked exhausted. Some of them looked like they had been crying. This was on top of the fact that many of them were bandaged up from their fights with Testament.

Sitting up in the bed, Isaac asked, "Where am I?"

John replied, "You're back at Maurits Manor. And I must say you've given us all quite a scare."

"What do you mean?"

"You've been asleep for two days now."

"And everyone has been by my side this whole time?"

"Well, not all of us, but your companions certainly have been." Looking around at the friends he had gathered, Isaac smiled and fell back into bed.

Robin chimed in, "When we found you, the room you were in was in pretty bad shape. It collapsed right after we left."

"What about my headband?"

Looking down mournfully, Maria answered, "You still have it, but I'm afraid Marie's spirit is now black, instead of red."

"I know. We said our goodbyes for the last time." Sensing that the room was getting depressed, Isaac continued with his questions, "So, what happened to the island? There was some weird stuff going on during my fight, but I'm not sure if it was Gottfried's power or something else."

Vlad explained, "It fell from the sky. The chains all broke and it landed back in the lake it originally came from."

"Did everyone get off the island before then?"

Sucari answered, "We did, but when we saw the island fall, we immediately headed back to get you. In fact, we figured you could take care of yourself, which is why we didn't come to help you in your fight."

Closing his eyes with a pleased sigh, Isaac said, "As long as everyone's safe, I'm happy." As he fell back asleep, everyone quietly left the room.

Days later, Isaac was on the roof of Maurits Manor, enjoying a clear day of sunshine. Everyone else also gathered on the roof; even Vlad, who was there for the social atmosphere. John was leaning against the walled edge of the roof when he asked the question that had been on everyone's mind, "So, now that Testament is essentially gone, what does everyone plan on doing? You're all welcome to stay here if you like, but I just wonder if people are waiting for you back home."

Sucari answered first, "Well, I for one am going to take you up on your offer to stay here. I have nothing to go back to in the 5th Kingdom, whereas here-" Sucari trailed off, as he turned to smile at Robin, their hands intertwined.

"I would like to go and check out the Granite Grove," was Vlad's reply, "Afterwards, I might try and get back into some accounting somewhere in the area."

R-3N3 very matter-of-factly said, "I should probably move down to Armor Village, considering that my body is essentially *all* armor." Everyone laughed at his honesty. Then all eyes were on Isaac.

"What do you plan to do, Isaac? Are you going to help spread the fluxions for good instead of evil, like Testament was doing?"

"No. I've done a lot of thinking, and I think it would be best for the human race stop using fluxions. They've caused too much trouble and more often than not have fallen into the wrong hands. It's probably why fluxions were forgotten about during the Millennial Erasure."

Putting his hands in his pockets, Isaac found something he had completely forgotten about. He pulled out the last finger of Jason the lumberjack. The pinky finger. Maria was curious about the odd shaped key that Isaac produced, "Oooh, what's that?"

Tenderly rolling the key in his fingers, Isaac let nostalgia take over, "It's a promise I made long ago. A promise I need to keep."

Irene was in the kitchen, baking apple pies. She couldn't remember the last time she made apple pies, but it was a good change of pace to the hectic life on the Pier. It seemed that every other day someone came in to New Town with some news or other. She had heard about Niccolo rising to power in the 5th Kingdom, the suspicious circumstances around the volcano eruption in the Pythagorean Triangle, Harry of Morgana finally living up to his campaign promises.

She had also heard about the fall of the Eagle's Nest. Staring blankly out the kitchen window, she could see the hill where the Square G shrine still sat, its sword long since missing. The breeze was blowing through the boughs of the apple tree and it brought her attention to the color of the sky. It was unusually blue that day. She remembered the last time the sky was this blue. That was the day she met Isaac.

Secretly, she hoped he would come back someday, but that was probably pretty unlikely. After all, who kept silly little pinky swear promises anymore? A knock at the front door shook Irene out of her daydream. Her father answered the door and after exclaiming, "*Sacrebleu!*" he called for her, "Irene, you have a visitor."

Drying her hands on her apron, she made her way to the front door, where a man with unusually white hair stood, his pinky in the air, "It looks like I may have to start believing in fate. What do you think, Irene?" The shock was too much for her, and she fainted.

Second to None

A story about friendship, duty, betrayal, and most of all: science

Prologue

The Beginning

"Where to begin? Where to begin?" Isaac sipped his tea as he sat contemplating where to start his story. For a man with white hair, Isaac certainly didn't look old. His rugged features and well-worn clothes told only part of the story he was mulling over in his head. Sitting across from Isaac was Irene, an ordinary looking young woman who had tied her red hair neatly in a bun on the back of her head. She wore a plain, light-blue sun dress, which was protected by a plain, white apron, smudged with flour and sugar. Next to her was her balding, bearded, and portly father, Pierre, who wore the sturdy and drab clothes of an experienced dock worker. Setting down the teacup and saucer on the coffee table, Isaac continued, "I suppose the best place to start would be the beginning."

"You might as well, considering how little we know about you." Irene spoke with a tinge of frustration in her voice. After all, Isaac was the one who decided to sail across the channel alone, thereby single-handedly crashing his boat into her father's pier. Furthermore, after he left the scene of the accident, he picked a fight with the local mayor and disappeared for almost six months. When he arrived back on their doorstep, both Irene and Pierre were astonished to find the white-haired man back in their house.

Sighing and giving a slight chuckle, Isaac understood Irene's annoyance, "That's true, the old me was kind of a loner. I've changed since then and I would like to give you a proper explanation. However, the beginning of my story goes back much further than when I arrived at New Town. It all began-" a knock on the door interrupted Isaac's introduction.

Pierre got up to answer the door, and Irene took this chance to interject before Isaac got too far into his story, "From what I already know about you, I have to ask: how much of an adventure did you *really* have? Day after day, I kept reading the papers and some strange stuff was happening out in the world. I just want to know how much of it you had a part in."

"Do you have anything in mind?"

"What about that alleged plot to kill the heir of the 5th Kingdom?" She leaned forward in her seat.

"Yes, I was there, but-"

"And the eruption of Sievuvus?" Her speech was becoming more rapid.

"I was nearby, but my story-"

"The destruction of the Eagle's Nest?!" She was practically shouting in Isaac's face.

"Yes! But this story goes back further-"

Pierre re-entered the room with a man who was carrying a long, wrapped package. He gave his daughter a confused look as she demurely sat back down and brushed an errant strand of red hair back behind her ear. The guest, oblivious to the situation, took a few steps into the room and unwrapped the package, revealing two swords.

One sword was a katana with a black hilt and a beautifully lacquered sheath which depicted an apple tree. A notch in the sheath revealed a dark black orb which seemed to absorb even the light that landed on it. The other sword was a broadsword in a half-sheath which ran the length of the blade and held the tip, but was open on the right side. Of course, the unique sheath was due to the sword's excessive length making it difficult to wield from a full scabbard. As was the case with the katana, the sheath accommodated the unique properties of the broadsword and was a stark white piece beautifully decorated and accented with seven colorful straps to hold the sword in place, each one a different color of the spectrum.

Isaac stood and walked across the room to receive the swords. He was excited to get his weapons back, since he felt naked without the pieces of steel that saw him through some tough battles. The guest who brought the swords handed them to Isaac, "I just touched up the paint on the katana sheath for you, since it only had a little bit of damage on the lacquer. I'm not sure what could have caused that discoloration, but I haven't seen any damage like it ever before."

Removing the katana known as Kuroni from its scabbard, Isaac examined the jet black blade as the man continued, "We re-sharpened the blade and gave the hilt a new binding as well. You really used that sword a lot in just a few months, so just try to be more careful in the future. As for your other sword-"

Isaac pulled out Hikari Shichidai, the sword crafted by David, the master swordsmith, as the guest continued, "The unusual size of this sword was a bit of an issue we had to figure out how to deal with, but I think what we came up with will work pretty well. The seven leather straps help keep it in the scabbard, but easily detach when the sword is needed." Holding the tip of the sword up to the light, the room was suddenly filled with small rainbows. The rainbows came from the triangular, diamond core embedded in the tip of the sword, surrounded by a twisted and knotted design of a single snake biting its tail. "Strangely enough, we didn't need to sharpen that one, as it was plenty sharp already. Sharper than anything I'd ever seen."

Putting both swords back in their respective scabbards, Isaac set them in the corner of the room behind a chair that held his trademark white coat and headband, the latter of which bore the seal of the Brotherhood of the Scarlet Lion, a red lion with its mouth open in mid-roar. Thanking the man and paying the fee for his swords, Isaac sat back down and picked up the teacup and saucer he had set down on the coffee table. Pierre came back in the room after showing their guest out and sat back down next to his daughter.

Taking another sip of tea, Isaac got back on track, "As I was saying, it would be best if I started my story at the beginning, by which I mean the *very* beginning." Sip. "I'm sure you're both aware of the legend of The Triumvirate, right? Well, it was around that time when the fluxions first appeared."

"Fluxions? What are those?" Irene once again leaned forward with anticipation.

Pointing at his forehead, Isaac brought their attention to the black disk embedded there, surrounded by a tattoo of two snake heads trying to eat the disk, "I know you're already familiar with this design on my forehead. *This* is a fluxion. There are many fluxions, each with different powers. And yet, their use has never been quite as prevalent since the time of The Triumvirate. Around the same time, the Armies of Amedeo were being gathered, and research was being done to create what are known as Fluents."

Standing up and going over to the corner of the room, Isaac picked up his broadsword and once again pulled it out of its sheath. Laying it on the table in front of them, he continued, "One of the Fluents that was created was the Fluent of Light. This uroboros design, coupled with the diamond core, created a power that could cut anything apart, even light itself. The history this design has seen spans back before the Millennial Erasure, when fluxions and Fluents vanished into obscurity and the stories of their power became known to us as mere myths and legends."

Staring into the brilliant diamond core of Hikari Shichidai, Isaac became a little nostalgic, "But truth, in this case, is almost stranger than fiction."

Chapter 1

Gathering Assembly

"Now are you *sure* you want me to do this? I mean, even overlooking the fact that I am highly skilled with a sword, you are crazy to allow me to attack you while being completely unarmed." A tall, lean man, clad in black leather gear and holding a rapier in his left hand stood in a clearing made in the midst of a crowded laboratory. His black hair was parted down the middle of his head, and a neatly trimmed moustache adorned his upper lip.

"Yes, Nikola. And I don't want you to hold back. I won't be able to test the true capabilities of this power unless you have enough resolution to try and kill me." Standing opposite the first man was another, who was slightly more athletic and sported a pair of rectangular glasses. He wore no protective gear other than a simple suit vest. The only thing out of the ordinary about him was a chain around his neck from which dangled an orb. The orb swam with electric tendrils, each of which looked like it was trying to escape its glass container. Pulling his long, dark brown hair back and tying it in a ponytail, the man took a ready stance for Nikola's attacks.

The third man in the room was a bit older than the other two, who were both in their early 30's. His brown hair was wild, but his dark, thick eyebrows were furrowed with concern. He sat in a worn chair at the edge of the cleared circle, "Ben, I'd have to agree with Nikola here. While we know you can use the Skybolt orb, we're still unsure of its limitations, let alone your own."

"Thomas, that's *precisely* why we need to test it, and there's no better way to accomplish a realistic test than a realistic battle." Turning to his opponent, the man known as Benjamin goaded Nikola on, "Unless you're scared your reputation might be ruined if I *do* manage to survive your 'highly skilled sword.' Or is that title merely empty words, Nik?"

Straightening up and getting into a fighting stance, Nikola shook his head as he glared across the clearing, "Don't go making excuses when I end up killing you." Benjamin stood at the ready and motioned with his hand for Nikola to start.

Within three steps, Nikola was upon Benjamin. His thrusts were quick, but lacked the intent to kill. At first, Benjamin kept his feet in the same place, merely moving his torso to dodge the attacks, but soon the frenzy of battle had reached full swing and he had to take a few steps back. As his thrusts kept missing their mark, Nikola became frustrated and began to aim toward more vital points on Benjamin's body. Almost as if they were in a deadly ballet, Benjamin reacted to each swing of Nikola's rapier. With subsequent swings, the sword came closer and closer to actually making contact.

When the orb around his neck began to glow, and the electricity seemed to get more excited, Benjamin's dodges became more fluid and a greater gap was being created between the two. With a scoff, Benjamin taunted his opponent, "I've just now started using the orb, and you couldn't cut me down before then?"

With more fuel on the fire of his ego, Nikola smirked, "Then maybe I should *really* get serious, now that you've decided to actually try." The speed of both combatants quickly increased, and soon their movements were mere blurs. For a fraction of a moment, the electric orb flickered. Nikola, fully immersed in the battle, saw his opportunity as he brought his rapier upward in a slash aimed to hit Benjamin fully across his torso.

As the Skybolt orb regained its power, Benjamin took a half step backward. However, a full step was what he truly needed to fully dodge the attack. The rapier missed his body, but continued upward and made contact with Benjamin's face. While the entire action took less than a second, the result was soon obvious: Benjamin had lost.

A spurt of blood erupted from Benjamin's face as he fell backward onto the ground. Nikola now stood over Benjamin, the tip of his sword pointed at his defeated opponent, "What did I tell you? You can't win against me unarmed."

"Nikola, seriously!" Thomas got out of his chair and rushed over to Benjamin's side. From his pocket, Thomas pulled out a cloth, ready to help stop the bleeding on the face of his friend. "You've won, now please help me tend to his injury. You probably put his eye out." On the floor lay Benjamin's glasses, a clean cut through the right lens showed that even glass couldn't withstand the quick, finishing blow.

With the cloth firmly held against the right side of his head, Benjamin began to laugh. "I didn't think it would work, but I guess I proved myself wrong."

Nikola and Thomas looked at each other with confusion. Speaking up, Thomas asked, "What do you mean? You *meant* to get injured?"

"No, not quite." Pulling aside the cloth on his face revealed that his wound was a mere surface scratch. Granted, it was deep enough that it would eventually leave a scar, but the bleeding had already stopped. Starting at the right side of his chin, his cheek was sliced open in a line that headed toward his eye; and yet, just before the wound would have hit his eye, the direction changed. The line of the injury now headed toward his right ear just long enough to avoid hitting the eye, after which it continued up to the temple and into his hairline. Taken as a whole, the wound Benjamin wore on the right side of his face resembled the zigzagging pattern of a bolt of lightning.

Nikola was surprised at this development, "I don't understand. I was *sure* that I had a clean hit. How did the line of your wound change direction?"

"It's simple, really. In fact, it's the same reason I was able to dodge your attacks for so long. I was using the power in the Skybolt orb to enhance my own nervous system. My body was able to move and adapt to its surroundings much quicker with the electrical stimulus it received from the lightning core. When your sword came in contact with my face, the defensive nature of my nervous system caused me to turn my head so that you would avoid hitting my eye. Even though your slash was incredibly quick, my reaction speed was increased, so I managed to save my eye from getting injured."

Still kneeling beside Benjamin, Thomas was intrigued, "Astounding, just astounding. I'm amazed at how quickly you've been able to adapt the powers of that orb. You've truly been a great help in furthering the advancement of society."

Turning around on his heels, Nikola scoffed, "*Tsk!* Your idea of advancing society is so boring. It's all about making our lives more comfortable. This power can do much more than that!"

Standing up and heading over to Nikola, Thomas tried to talk some sense into the younger man, "Now, Nikola, I may only be ten years older than you are, but I created this castle on the outskirts of Menlo as a bastion of new and practical ideas that can help us get more out of life. I'm sorry if your ideas are a little too extravagant, but I still depend on your insights and inputs."

"You know, for someone who the commoners are calling a wizard, you certainly have no sense of magic. I would much rather take this power and use it to become a magician, astounding those lesser than myself with illusions of grandeur."

"This is no power to be trifled with, Nikola!" Thomas was starting to get riled up by his subordinate's insolence. "While it may have great potential to do good, the destructive power of the Skybolt orb is far too great to treat its opportunity so glibly. I am thankful that Benjamin has volunteered to help us understand its power and limitations, considering the many years and valuable people that it has destroyed. I don't know how he controls it, but I'd rather not take any risks on the off chance that-"

"Hey guys, we have a visitor." Benjamin motioned over to the maze of equipment and the butler who was finding his way to the clearing in the middle of the room. Taking a deep breath, Thomas made his way to the perimeter of the clearing and started to push tables and benches aside to help clear the way. Nikola, still sulking at the lecture he had just been given, made his way to the nearest window.

Finally making his way through the equipment, the butler delivered a newspaper and a note to Thomas. Excusing the butler, Thomas opened the note and read, while Benjamin slipped the newspaper out from under Thomas' arm and began to read as well. The note was written in a confident and feminine script and read as follows:

Thomas,

I have heard rumors of the amazing work you are doing with electricity and would like to discuss some potential projects with you at your convenience. I will be in Menlo in a few days, and I hope you can accommodate my request to meet.

Sincerely,
Mary

Closing the note and slipping it into his back pocket, Thomas looked up to see Benjamin immersed in the paper, "We really should get that wound looked at, you know." Nodding, Benjamin silently kept reading. Thomas looked around the room for Nikola, but found he had already left. Gently grabbing Benjamin by the elbow, he said, "Let's go."

On their way to the infirmary, Thomas and Benjamin headed through the library, where most of the staff of Menlo Castle did their research. As the two men passed by, a few of the staffers looked up from the books they were reading, but most kept to their work. Benjamin still had his nose in the paper. Thomas cleared his throat and began an apology, "I'm sorry you had to see me like that back there. I just get frustrated with Nikola from time to time. The young sometimes have no perspective. Even though I only have ten years on you, I've seen enough tragedy for a lifetime."

Pulling down the paper from Benjamin's face, Thomas stopped walking and looked him straight in the eye, "I saw what happened back there, Ben. The Skybolt orb gave out on you for a moment, and that's why you got injured. You need to be more careful with this power, I've seen you take far too many risks with it."

Smiling at Thomas' sincerity, Benjamin gave him a reassuring slap on the back, "Don't worry about me, Tom. I've got things under control."

Loosening up, Thomas chuckled, "OK, I guess I can give you the benefit of the doubt." Pointing a warning finger at Benjamin, he added, "But just this one time, do you hear me?"

Winking back, Benjamin replied, "Sure thing."

At the infirmary, the nurse was cleaning out the wound on Benjamin's face as Thomas talked about future plans, "Even though you don't need any stitches, I still want to wait a few days before we start on the next few experiments."

A hesitant look came across Benjamin's face as he interjected, "Well . . ."

"Well, what?"

"I don't know if I'm going to stick around here anymore."

"Is this about Nikola? He's just stubborn; I know he'll come around."

"No, this is something else." Producing the paper, Benjamin folded it over to show the article he was reading. The headline read: "Mysterious mountain Mystic makes mirrors." Continuing into the article, it was revealed that as people began to explore the mountains to the east, rumors had begun to emerge of a woman who sat on the surface of lakes, causing them to have no waves whatsoever. The result was often a lake which looked like a perfect mirror, reflecting the sky above and the image of a woman sitting cross-legged in the middle of the lake.

Thomas scoffed at the article, "That's just journalistic hype. They'll publish anything just to get a few extra readers."

"No, it's true. I'm sure of it."

"How are you sure?"

"Do you remember the article with the headline, 'Lightning lance leaves lucky librarian living'?"

"I do, but what-"

"That was me."

"What do you mean?" The nurse finished her procedure and began to busy herself in another part of the infirmary.

"Well before I arrived at Menlo Castle, I used to be a librarian. In fact, my former wife is still a librarian. We both worked at the Library of Delaxanair, when it went through a terrible thunderstorm. We were both on the roof trying to repair the serious leaks that had developed as a result of the storm. For a brief moment, I slipped on the roof and grabbed one of the spires to steady myself. Suddenly, the hair on the back of my neck started to tingle. In a bright flash, lightning struck and the next moment I found myself high in the sky. Once I gained my wits about where I was, I started to panic as I hurtled toward the ground. I could feel another bolt of lightning building in the clouds, and once again a bright flash transported me somewhere else. Luckily, it was on the ground, but it was so far away from the Library that it took me a while to get back."

"So, the librarian in the article wasn't you, but your former wife? Why 'former'?"

"When I arrived back at the Library a day later, I found my wife inside, sobbing uncontrollably. As I approached her, she looked up and her face turned white, like she had seen a ghost. Her sobs turned to screams, which eventually became unintelligible as it became apparent that she thought I had been vaporized by the lightning strike and had only returned to her as an apparition. Since I couldn't explain what happened either, I thought it best that I leave."

Staring at the ground, Benjamin continued, "After a while, I started to realize that part of the reason I was alive after the incident was that my body could take the form of and control a wide variety of materials. A lot of times it happened accidentally, but it happened so often that I knew I had made the right decision in leaving her." Looking a little despondent, Benjamin continued with a short laugh, "In the end, I'd rather she be safe than risk my newfound powers unintentionally hurting her. But at any rate, that's why I came to your castle: I wanted to know why I'm different. Now that I see there may be someone else out there like me, I have to find them."

Thomas smiled as he handed Benjamin back his rectangular glasses, the right lens held together with glue, "I understand. You need to know where you fit in this world. I'm just glad you were able to help further society while you were here."

After gathering his few belongings, Benjamin met Thomas at the gate of Menlo Castle. He reached up to his necklace and was about to give back the Skybolt orb when Thomas stopped him, "Please, take it with you. It's the least I can give you for your contribution."

"I'm sorry I have to leave so suddenly, but I don't know if the woman in the article will stay there for very long."

"Will you stop apologizing and leave already!" With a friendly push, Thomas shoved Benjamin out onto the bridge over the moat. When Benjamin gave a final wave and began walking off into the distance, Thomas yelled after him, "You're always welcome here, so don't forget to visit sometime!"

A few minutes later, Benjamin had entered the forest and could no longer be seen from the castle. Thomas turned around and headed back inside, closing the gate behind him.

Light streamed in from the large wooden doors as a muscular man clad in a military uniform entered the library. He wandered toward the front desk, glancing around at the impressive foyer of the Library of Delaxanair. When he arrived at the front desk, the head librarian looked up and asked with an unenthusiastic tone, "Can I help you?"

Startled out of his sightseeing, the man stuttered, "U-u-um, yeah. I'm looking for something."

This phrase seemed to trigger a switch in the librarian as she smiled and began a rehearsed, condescending, and sarcastic diatribe, "Well, have you tried looking for this *thing* before you ask me where it is? Even though I work here I do not know where *everything* is located. It's actually rather simple: these shelves hold books. The books are arranged by the author's *last* name. Subjects of said books can be found on the aisles." Under her breath she muttered, "That is assuming you can even *read*." Speaking back up, she continued, "Furthermore-"

"I'm sorry," the interruption caused the librarian's eyes to bulge and her lips to become taught across her teeth in a forced smile, "But I meant that I'm looking for where a meeting is being held." At once, a realization came to the librarian's face that quickly shifted into a look of embarrassment as her cheeks became flushed.

Standing up, she turned around, came out from behind the front desk and quietly said, "So sorry. This way please." As she led the man through the vast halls of the library, the soldier had another chance to look at his surroundings. There were shelves upon shelves of books for as far as he could see. Most shelves were so tall that the floors seemed like they divided up six solid stories of literature. On each row of shelves was a ladder on a rail which could be used to reach the books that were not easily accessible. The roof was arched above him and separated the library into two sides. Up ahead was a staircase that led up to the second level, and continued to zigzag all the way up to the top, where it seemed to disappear into the ceiling.

The entire time he followed the librarian, she did not say a single word until they climbed the stairs past the ceiling. Once above the main area of the library, a set of doors led to a long hallway. As she opened the doors, the librarian quietly said, "The meeting you are looking for is at the end of the hall." He turned to thank her, but she was already gone.

The hallway was lined with doors and none of them had any markings to designate what they were for or where they led to. Walking down the corridor, his steps echoed on the dark, tiled floor at a steady rhythm consistent with his military training. Arriving at the end of the hall, he knocked on the door and peeked inside. Within, he found a round room with a circular table, around which sat a variety of about twenty people who all looked over at him.

The only person standing up was a man clad in the simple clothes of an academic: a tweed jacket with leather patches on the elbows and a simple pair of grey slacks. When the man turned around to see what everyone was looking at, he immediately recognized the soldier, which caused him to remove a plain smoking pipe from his mouth and walk over to the door. With an open hand, he led the soldier in and said, "*Wunderbar!* You have arrived. Please, come in."

In the center of the table sat a bowl of fire, which lit the room fairly well, as the perimeter of small windows near the ceiling of the room did not do much to illuminate the space. The man who came over to the door had very wild, white hair, a thick moustache, and spoke with an accent. With his hand on the soldier's back, the man led him to the table and the last empty seat. As the soldier sat down, the man began his speech, "Now that we are all here, we can begin. In case you do not know who I am, my name is Albert. I have been tasked by Amedeo to bring together some of the greatest minds so we can solve two of his problems."

One of the men raised his hand and immediately began to ask a question, "With the exception of the soldier who just joined us, none of us are in Amedeo's army, so why is he asking us to help him?"

"*Ja*, that is a good question, Julius. While meaning no offence to Amedeo, his problems are not ones that can be solved by physical might, but rather by an intellectual pursuit. There is some irony in this because the first issue he wants us to solve has to do with increasing his military's size."

Another person at the table spoke up, "You can't be serious. Since when was having an army several myriad strong not enough to conquer any part of the world he would want?"

"You are right, Herbert, but that brings us to his second request, which I will defer explaining in lieu of a demonstration. James and Garland, could you both please pick up those weapons that are lying against the wall?" As the two men went over and picked up a sword a piece from a rack of various weapons, Albert put his hand on the trooper's shoulder. When the soldier looked up at Albert, he knew it was time to show his special ability.

As the warrior stood up and removed his uniform jacket, Albert explained, "This soldier's name is Arma Ress. He is a recent recruit to the Army of Amedeo." When Arma Ress took off his jacket, he revealed a very muscular physique, covered by a red undershirt. On his wrists, he wore iron bracelets and around his neck was an iron chain which held his military issue identification tags. "While Arma Ress is unarmed, I have been told that he cannot be injured by any of the weapons we have here. In fact, James and Garland, I would like you to attack him with those swords you have both just picked up."

The two men hesitantly looked at each other and shrugged. Rushing toward the soldier, both men swung their swords at the unarmed man. The room gasped as Arma Ress stopped their attacks with his bare hands. A loud clang brought many of the observers to their feet in astonishment. Both of Arma Ress' hands had turned into the very same iron that he wore around his wrists. Gripping the blades, he pulled the swords from the hands of his assailants and broke them like they were mere twigs.

"What on earth just happened, Albert?" A new voice rang out above the mumbling din of the others.

"This is precisely why Amedeo wants an army one septillion soldiers strong." The room became deathly silent at the shocking number.

The same voice as before spoke up again with a laugh, "*C'est ridicule!* Are you serious, Albert? One septillion soldiers? Not only are there not nearly that many people living on this planet, there isn't even enough surface area to store a septillion watermelons, let alone soldiers."

"A valid point, Jules. And, *ja*. He *does* want one septillion soldiers. Our task is to first figure out how to create the amount of soldiers he wants, followed by the task of figuring out where to keep them all."

This time a woman's voice broke through the grumbling, "So, what's your demonstration have to do with the second request?"

"I'll answer that with a question. Arma Ress, how did you stop the swords from cutting you?"

With his jacket half on again, Arma Ress answered, "I just focus some of my energy into my bracelets, and they turn my body into iron. If I put more energy into the bracelets, then more of my body turns to iron." Making his point, he clenched the fist on the arm not yet in his jacket, and within a few seconds his entire arm was comprised of iron.

Albert walked over to a door on the edge of the room as he explained, "Arma Ress exhibits the rare quality to be able to control any material he comes in contact with. Some he can control better than others, but he can control them all the same." Opening the door, Albert revealed the astonished visage of a man, frozen in a panicked pose, comprised entirely of stone. The room gasped and grew silent yet again, "This is not the work of a master sculptor, ladies and gentlemen. This was our first test subject. As you can see, once you put some of your energy into a material, it can quickly take over your body if you cannot control it. Our task is to figure out how we can harness this power without endangering the user."

Closing the door, Albert continued, "The world is a large and diverse place, so here is what I propose: first we find as many core powers as we can. It does not matter how trivial or how stupid the core might seem, we need a plentiful supply of energy sources to determine the range that these powers can occupy. Secondly, we work on sealing these cores to allow just enough energy through to the user to be useful. This core and seal combination shall be known as a 'fluxion'."

"Now, these fluxions may prove useful in accomplishing our first task, so I would like us to split up and work in three groups. The first group will go out and find areas we can use to hold vast armies. They will also work on recruiting and finding other ways of meeting the septillion soldier goal." Most of the group had sat back down at the table as they realized the sobering truth of how many people it might take to defeat someone like Arma Ress. Others were still up in arms at this ludicrous task. A few even decided they no longer wanted a part of this project, headed to the door, and were never seen again.

"The second group will be on a mission to find as many cores as possible. Remember, *anything* is possible, so do not turn anything down. Lastly, the third group will focus on the sealing procedure. They will also work on a top secret project that will require serious sealing methods." Albert rose again and started walking toward a grand piano which was set up in the corner of the room. "Since these tasks have been handed down from an Aquila-Class General, we have all been given the authority of Polaris-Class Generals in order to carry out this mission. Military resources are now at everyone's disposal to make these things happen." This revelation silenced the remaining naysayers.

Arriving at the piano, Albert paused, "In conclusion, some of you may be wondering why I was chosen as the leader of this research project. Well, you see, with a time limit placed on this project, I hold the keys to our transportation. Quite literally, in fact." Albert lifted a black and white key from the keyboard to reveal a hidden chamber in both keys. Removing the objects found in both keys, he held them up and said, "These are the keys to Q-Portals."

○

Benjamin hiked along the road with a bounce in his step. He knew he was special and he knew he was gifted with great power. He also knew he no longer had to be ashamed of this power. His past was behind him, and an intriguing future laid itself out in front of him. Always one to keep testing his abilities, he began to toy with the Skybolt orb he received from Thomas. He now knew he could enhance his nervous system to decrease his reaction time, but he wondered what other attributes he could affect with the electric power.

Crouching down in the middle of the road, he closed his eyes as he focused on the power dangling from his chest. When the orb began to glow, a moment later, he had vanished. High above the trees, Benjamin flew through the air, propelled by the sudden twitch the electricity brought to his legs. At the peak of his flight, he admired the fantastic view of his path ahead. He then realized that if he had gotten up that high, he would have to fall back to the ground.

In a panic, Benjamin flailed through the air, but to no avail. His body began to pick up speed and his panic increased proportionally. Closing his eyes, he focused again on the Skybolt orb. If this power had gotten him into this mess, it might just be able to get him out of it. A flash of light was followed by a deafening explosion. A rain of splinters and pine needles fell on Benjamin's face. With slight hesitation, he opened his eyes to see if he was still alive.

Lying flat on his back, the first thing he noticed was that the tall tree at the base of his feet was now sporting a large black gash down the side of its trunk. Also, it was on fire. This last development was something he could handle. Eventually. It took a bit of work, but Benjamin was able to finally put out the fire by using his enhanced muscular power to push the tree down, and then dousing the fire with dirt. He was startled when he heard a voice behind him, weak and feeble, "Ruatonim!"

The voice came from an old woman, hunched over and wrapped in a dark green cloak. She had collapsed against one of the fence posts along the path after seeing the whole scene with the fire and the tree unfold in front of her. Benjamin walked over to the woman and asked, "Ruatonim? What's that?"

Slightly confused, the woman explained in her raspy voice, "You can create fire, just like Ruatonim. Are you one of his disciples?"

"What? No. I've never heard of him."

The woman grabbed Benjamin by the front of his shirt, just above his vest, and brought him close. He noticed that she smelled of smoke and singed hair, "Then beware! I warn you of a monster who is half-man and half-bull. He erupts from the ground in an explosion of fire and rains down his fiery judgment on any village that does not live up to his standards! I am a refugee from such a village and have been wandering for weeks."

"That's awful. Is there anything I can do to help?" Benjamin backed away a little bit to help the old woman to her feet.

"Just stay away from his path of destruction. It is too late for me, but if you turn back now you might be able to avoid certain peril."

Examining the path ahead, Benjamin was conflicted with the warning of the old woman and his desire to find the Mystic of the eastern lakes. Turning back to the woman, he found she had already begun to wander off, mumbling something about the horrors she had seen. Deciding that her warnings were probably the delusions of a crazy wanderer, he chose to press on toward the mountains.

Glancing around to make sure that any other wandering villagers weren't around, Benjamin leaned against the fence post that the old woman had collapsed against. Looking over at the downed tree, its fire still smoldering under the dirt, Benjamin began to put some pieces together. He wasn't entirely certain, but he began to suspect that he had turned into lightning during his frantic free-fall. Luckily, there was more than one way to test this theory.

Turning his attention from the downed tree to his hand, and then to the barbed wire held up by the fence post, Benjamin recalled one of the experiments he performed while at Menlo Castle. Thomas was trying to find a more efficient and longer-lasting way to provide light after the sun had set. The experiment setup required Benjamin to hold small pieces of wire and run his electricity through them to see how long they would last under the electrical resistance. He deduced that if he could turn into lightning and strike a tree, he could turn into lightning and travel along the barbed wire.

With a bit of hesitance, Benjamin reached out and grabbed the wire between the barbs. He wasn't sure if he was going to travel in the correct direction along the wire when he attempted to turn into electricity, but it might as well be worth a try. Focusing on his hand, the wire began to spark at the barbs. Increasing the intensity of his focus, Benjamin concentrated on the flow of power from the orb around his neck to the hand gripping the wire. He abruptly disappeared and shot along the length of wire. Huge electrical discharges erupted along the wire at the regular intervals of the barbs, showing his rapid progress.

As suddenly as it had begun, Benjamin reached the end of the line and appeared with a bang. Sitting, stunned from the sudden stop, he checked his surroundings to see if he had made any progress. The post which held the end of the barbed wire fence also held a sign which informed him that he was now considerably closer to his destination. And yet, he found he was once again not alone, as someone else stood on the path, gawking at the scene that had unfolded in front of him.

The man had bright red hair which covered his head and most of his tanned face, the latter of which had a distinctive brow that gave his demeanor a serious look. The man's clothes were the worn and sturdy clothes of a man who worked outdoors, edged with traces of old mud and black marks of soot or ash. Despite his apparent lowly status, the man stood tall and proud. He held a pitchfork in his hand and was leaning on it as if he was using it as a walking stick.

Coming over to Benjamin and lending him a hand, the man helped him up as he asked, "Are you trying to get somewhere in a hurry?"

Brushing himself off, Benjamin replied, "Somewhat. I'm trying to get up to the mountains soon to check on a rumor based in those parts." Remembering the previous encounter with the old woman, Benjamin became skeptical, "You don't find it strange that I just appeared here out of nowhere?"

"Nah. I've seen a lot of crazy stuff in my time, so what you've done doesn't really surprise me. Anyways, it looks like you're headed in the same direction I'm heading, mister..."

"Benjamin. I assume you're going to check on the rumors up there as well?"

"Not quite. I'm actually traveling a little further north on a quest. My name is Tecumseh, by the way."

A little embarrassed that he didn't ask, Benjamin brought up a suggestion, "Why don't we travel together for a while, then? After all, the journey goes so much quicker with someone else to talk to."

"I'd be delighted, Benjamin." With that acceptance, the duo continued along the road.

○

In a dark room, Albert stood beneath a single spotlight and spoke, "It took a little bit of convincing, but they are all on board."

From the shadows came the reply, "*Splendido*. Keep me updated on your status and let me know when you can expect results."

With a short bow, Albert acknowledged the request, "*Jawohl*." Having finished his report, Albert turned and left the severely under-lit room. Another figure entered the spotlight as two other spotlights began to appear on either side of the existing one, illuminating where others were already standing. The three men were in uniform, but had adjusted their appearance to best suit their abilities and personalities.

On the right was a man who wore his uniform tightly. On his legs he wore three scabbards a piece, strapped to his thighs, the handles of the swords adjusted so that they would fit neatly between his fingers. His neatly trimmed goatee lined a smile which showed that he enjoyed what he did. On the left was a man who wore a large longbow on his back. The rest of his body sported as many quivers filled with arrows as would fit comfortably. Finally, the last man who had stepped forward to fill the initial spotlight wore the uniform perfectly, with the only addition being a black cape worn off of his shoulders. His long black hair was tied behind him and a scraggly beard tried to hide the many scars he had obtained in battle. To his side, he held a long, black staff.

The man still in shadow spoke to those before him, "You have all been identified as my best warriors, and I would like to reward your efforts." The three soldiers saluted and awaited their gifts. "Your first benefit is that you are now all Cross-Class Generals. However-" the shadow continued, "there are a few conditions associated with the rest of your rewards. The first condition is that you will have to go out and find your respective awards. As word comes back from Albert, I will let you know where to go to receive your prize."

The archer in the left spotlight spoke up, "Sir, does this mean we will be receiving fluxions?"

"*Si*, Braun. You will all be given the best of the best that are discovered from this research."

From the right spotlight, the swordsman asked a question, "So, after we go out and find these new powers, what are the other conditions, sir?"

"From Albert's briefing, you know that there exist individuals with the ability to use the fluxion cores without the fluxion seals. These individuals are known as the Naturals, as they can naturally use these powers without being consumed by them. In order to maintain military supremacy, I ask that you use your new powers to eradicate anyone who might be a Natural."

The last individual saluted and said, "Understood, General Amedeo, sir." He finished his salute, turned around and marched out of the room. The other two soldiers saluted and did the same.

On the trail to the mountain lakes, Benjamin had struck up a conversation with his traveling partner, "So, Tecumseh, I'm assuming you're from around here, correct?"

"Nah, I'm from the city of Topal further south. Actually, I lived more on the outskirts of town, since I was a farmer."

"That would explain the pitchfork."

"Yeah, things like this eventually become an extension of your body after a while."

"So, why did you decide to leave? Isn't this the prime growing season?"

"To be honest, I had become sick of living near Topal. Much like the other citizens, I suffered from poverty induced by constant taxation. What finally goaded me into leaving was the city's newest construction project: a giant wall that would have essentially cut off the poorer citizens from the center of the city. This upset many of us, but I decided to do something about it."

"So, there was a problem and you just left?"

"I didn't just leave," Tecumseh seemed indignant. "Have you heard of the Order of the Dragon?" Benjamin shook his head to indicate that he hadn't, "Well, the rumor is that they have a massive treasure horde that they keep locked away in a castle to the northwest. My goal is to try and find that treasure and use it to rise to power in Topal. After all, the wealthy already rule over the poor, so someone who was once poor could empathize with their plight."

"But what if the power and wealth corrupt you, and you end up being worse than the current leaders?"

"Nah, that won't happen. In obtaining riches from poverty, I would appreciate it more. If I can obtain and handle that much wealth wisely, I should certainly have enough responsibility to be a leader of men." An awkward silence followed, which caused Tecumseh to change topics, "Anyways, why are you heading to the mountains? You said something about a rumor, but I doubt it's the rumor I just shared with you."

Benjamin pushed his glasses up to the arch of his nose as he began, "That's right, my rumor has to do with the mountain Mystic. I read that there have been sightings of a strange phenomenon where lakes had their waves removed by a woman who sat on the surface of the water. At any rate, you've seen that I have a strange ability as well. After I found out I had this ability, I felt very alone, even in situations where I used to feel a sense of community. Now I just feel like I'm being judged. Like I'm feared as a monster. I'm really just looking for others who understand my unique situation. Without these powers, I'm just the same as everyone else, but *with* them I'm different enough that others fear me."

"I don't fear you. I actually think what you can do is pretty cool. But then again, I'm not entirely sure what you *can* do, exactly."

"That's just the point. I'm not entirely sure myself. I have decided to embrace this new power, to more completely understand it, to know what I'm truly capable of. I love nothing more than unlocking another ability I can use. This is why I went to Menlo Castle. I couldn't resist the opportunity to have my ability researched, examined, and expanded."

Since the sun was just about to set, Tecumseh made a suggestion, "Hey, it's going to get dark soon, so why don't we set up camp for the night?" Benjamin agreed and led them off the trail to a small clearing in the trees. After setting down their gear, both Benjamin and Tecumseh searched for some firewood to make a fire.

When Benjamin came back to their camp, he started constructing a fire pit, after which he arranged the firewood in the pit for optimum lighting ease. When Tecumseh came back, Benjamin went over to his bag to try and find something to light the fire. He found what he was looking for, but when he turned around, the pile he had created was already ablaze as Tecumseh stood back up.

Benjamin was confused, "Did you do that?" Tecumseh smiled and nodded, "How did you do that so fast?"

Putting his index and middle finger in the air, Tecumseh blew across the two fingers as they caught fire. Benjamin's eyebrows raised as he asked, "You're just like me . . . aren't you? Why didn't you tell me earlier?"

Tecumseh shrugged as he replied, "I thought that showing you would be more effective."

"It certainly was, but where do you get your power from?" Pulling on a chain from around his neck, Tecumseh revealed an orb that flickered with fire. Mesmerized with the fiery orb, Benjamin asked, "Can I try it?"

"Sure."

Reaching out to the orb, Benjamin grabbed it with his right hand and focused on his left hand. A small flame erupted from each one of his fingertips. It wasn't nearly as large a flame as Tecumseh created, but it was definitely a flame. With a thoughtful hum, Benjamin let go of the orb and the flames on his hand disappeared.

Tecumseh noticed the hum and asked, "What are you thinking?"

"Well, my attempt at flames wasn't nearly as big as what you can produce, so I'm curious whether or not that has to do with practice or if you and I have different affinities to different elements."

"That's a good question. I think once we find the Mystic who you read about in that article, we may be able to know the answer."

"Good call."

Benjamin and Tecumseh talked a little longer, eventually falling asleep next to the fire. Over the night, the fire died down and the warm coals kept the two Naturals from feeling the cold of the outdoors.

Since the summer season was in full swing, the glow of the sun soon began to illuminate the sky as the stars went back into hiding. Benjamin awoke with a start. He stopped for a moment and listened. A strange sound could be heard in the distance, and was possibly the reason for Benjamin's sudden awakening. Crawling over to Tecumseh, he asked, "Do you hear that?" After taking a moment to wake up and to switch his focus from sleeping to listening, Tecumseh sat up and cupped his hands around his ears.

The sound was faint, but there was an eerie feeling about it, almost like it came from every direction. "I hear it, but where is it coming from?" Tecumseh asked.

"It could be that the sound is echoing off of the mountains, but I'm trying to figure out what it is. It almost sounds like," Benjamin paused for a second to listen again, ". . . singing."

Taking another listen, Tecumseh agreed. Using some nearby dirt to douse their campfire, Tecumseh said, "You want to go check it out? Maybe it has something to do with the Mystic."

Benjamin nodded and gathered his things, "Since there's two of us, let's head in opposite directions, and we'll decide to go in the direction where the sound is louder."

"That's fine." Tecumseh headed west as Benjamin turned and went east. After a few paces, they turned and looked at each other. Benjamin made a motion that the sound was louder where he ended up. When Tecumseh caught up with Benjamin, they repeated the process in the north and south direction, with Tecumseh's southern direction being the louder one.

Using the information they had gathered, the duo decided to travel southeast toward the singing. The sun hadn't risen above the ridge of the mountains around them, but the sky was now a bright blue above the two travelers. As they got closer to the singing, they began to pick up a few words here and there, but the lyrics didn't make any sense yet. What did make sense was that the song was definitely sung by a woman.

The two men stood at the edge of a very thick grove of trees and could hear the song the loudest through the filter of the forest. As they made their way through the dense foliage, the lyrics of the song soon became clear. A beautiful soprano sang out in the wilderness, and this is what was sung:

> O those who come from nature's breast
> Let your power flow from rest
> That wars and fights cannot provide
> But comes from harmony at your side

As the woman kept singing, the trees began to clear from Benjamin and Tecumseh's path. Soon, they had emerged from the forest and came upon the sight of a lake, as still as glass and reflecting the scenery above it in its watery mirror. The source of the singing was now very obvious. There, sitting cross legged on the surface of the lake, was a woman in her mid-twenties who held on to a golden pole as she sang. Her hair was flaxen, bleached light by the constant exposure to sunlight. It rested gently on her shoulders and covered part of her face. She wore a blue dress that matched the color of the sky, which made her head and bare arms seem like they were almost hovering in mid-air.

When her song had finished and she took a breath to start again, she briefly opened her eyes, and saw the two men at the edge of the lake. This startled her and she fell into the water, creating a radiating set of waves. A moment later and hundreds of feet closer, she emerged from the lake, holding a golden trident in a position ready to attack. Through strands of wet hair, an intense pair of blue eyes looked back and forth at the two suspicious men. As waves lapped the shore and water dripped from her body, she asked, "Where did you guys come from?"

Benjamin cleared his throat, and the tip of the trident shifted over to him, "We heard you singing and followed your voice through the woods."

The girl's freckled face began to blush as she averted her gaze, "You mean you could hear me?"

"Of course, but it was really quite beautiful."

Tecumseh leaned over to Benjamin and whispered, "Should we tell her about the article in the paper?"

Even though the whisper was quiet, the girl heard what Tecumseh had said, "Are you guys here looking for the mountain Mystic?"

Benjamin could tell the young woman in front of him was flustered by talk of the article, "Well, yes-" the trident was once again up and this time closer to Benjamin's neck than it was before, "-but it's not what you think! We're not here to spread the word; we just want to know if you're like us."

The woman's eyes squinted, "What do you mean, 'like us'?"

Taking a step backward so as to give himself some room, Benjamin extended his right hand in front of him, fingers spread apart. Focusing on the orb hanging around his chest, the sphere of electricity began to glow as sparks ran up his hand from the webs of his fingers, each spark snapping as it reached the fingertips.

The girl was impressed, which ignited a bit of jealousy in Tecumseh, who went into a display with his fire that was incredibly showy. Almost too showy, as it seemed to frighten the girl he was trying to impress.

Determining that the two men were no threat, the girl thrust her trident into the ground and extended her hand, first to Benjamin and then to Tecumseh, "OK, I trust you both . . . for now. My name is Penneut Psinodeo, although if you'd like something more normal, you can call me Penny."

Benjamin accepted the handshake and introduced himself and his traveling partner, "It's a pleasure to meet you, Penny. I'm Benjamin and my fiery friend here is Tecumseh. Might I ask why you have such a long name?"

Penny smirked as she gave a short laugh, "Oh, that? Well, to tell you the truth, you two should probably have names like that as well, since you both have abilities. I'm not really good at creating those names, so we'll have to go see my mom." As she picked up her trident and headed into the woods, Penny shouted behind her, "Come on, slowpokes!"

Startled by the sudden change in attitude, the two men jogged for a short distance until they had caught up with Penny, their small band of travelers heading back into the dense woods.

Chapter 2

Family Blood

Emerging from a cave into a green mountain meadow, two of Albert's research team looked at each other and then back at the opening from which they had just emerged. The door had just shut with a gust of wind, and the change in lighting caused the two to shield their eyes from the sun. When it became comfortable to see again, the duo glanced around to try and figure out where they were.

The meadow was expansive but showed no signs of civilization. Further down the valley they could see a grove of pine trees, but the only things interrupting the sea of green grass that they were now standing in was a handful of glacial erratics, rocks that had been left behind in the formation of the area.

Looking up to the nearby mountains, the first man tapped his partner on the shoulder and pointed up at the closest peak, "That's the legendary Asp Peak, Jules. We must be at the Pythagorean Triangle." He was obviously the younger of the two men, probably no older than twenty years. His perfectly combed hair and bushy moustache seemed to accent a face full of energy and optimism atop a short and somewhat stocky frame.

Jules, the other man, had about 40 years on his young partner, as well as about 10 inches in height, but certainly less in terms of weight. A receding hairline was compensated for with a full beard, both of a light grey color. His eyes were set in a face that had gained knowledge and wisdom over the years. Jules saw that his partner was correct in deducing their location. He nodded as he examined the mountain top shaped like the head of a snake, and followed its wavy ridge over to its neighboring peak, similarly shaped like a snake's head, "You're right, Herbert. That must be Cobra Peak to the left." Glancing once more around the valley, Jules added, "Should we make our way to the top?"

"I don't see why not. Actually, I'm kind of interested about why this landmark is so legendary. It should be fun, don't you think?" Jules nodded as he made his way toward a barely distinguishable path up the side of Asp Peak.

As they hiked, they began to discuss their assignment, "Why do you think we were paired together to go look for fluxion cores, Herbert?"

"There could be any number of reasons. I mean, we have a few similarities. At the very least, I see by the ring on your left hand that you too are married."

Smiling at the thought of his lovely wife, Jules replied, "Indeed I am, however I don't know how long this assignment will be for, and I know that concerns Honorine."

"Yeah, I know Amy will just end up worrying the entire time I'm gone."

The two men chuckled as they reminisced about their home lives. After hiking in silence for a while, Herbert spoke up, "Those Q-Portals we're using for this assignment are pretty wild, aren't they?"

"They sure are. I'm actually pretty interested in them, as I've always wanted to travel around the world and see its sights. And yet, I didn't really want to spend all the time travelling from one place to another. I'd almost like to use these Q-Portals to travel around the world in eighty days. You know, really get to experience all that it has to offer without having to be constrained to a travel schedule."

"That would be pretty nice, but I still can't believe what I saw when Albert demonstrated their power. I'm amazed something like this even exists. It's truly a strange and mysterious world we live in." Nodding in agreement, Jules hiked along with Herbert toward Asp Peak.

○

Albert held up two keys. One black. One white. As everyone in the room observed the finger-length keys, he explained, "These are the keys to Q-Portals."

From across the room, Jules raised his hand as he asked a question, "If you don't mind my asking, what *are* Q-Portals?"

"An excellent question, Jules. Q-Portals are doors that are so named due to the shape of their keyhole. As you can see, the bit at the end of the shaft is curved outward. If you look at the key straight on, the shape it makes looks like a 'Q'. But, as the rest of the name suggests, these doors are portals. Portals linked by the very keys that open them."

Walking over to a nearby doorway that sported the distinguishing "Q" keyhole, Albert continued, "And yet, just talking about it is not quite enough. I really need to show you." Taking the white key he held in his hand, Albert inserted it into the keyhole and turned it sideways. Immediately, a door across the room opened up and a brilliant white light poured out from the doorway.

Standing before the enveloping darkness that was the antithesis of the white door, Albert continued his explanation, "You see; the white keys will open up white holes that are a specific distance away from the starting door. In order to use the Q-Portal, one need only-" stepping across the threshold of the black door, Albert immediately appeared at the entrance of the white one, "-step through the black hole created at the Q-Portal's origin."

The room had gotten used to being surprised, but still gawked with eyes wide and mouths agape. Now that Albert had crossed through the Q-Portal, both doors automatically shut with a burst of wind. Walking over to the table, Albert struck the white key he had just used against the edge of the table, producing a high-pitched note, "These keys have been made out of a very special and rare material which translates their wavelength to the amount of distance that can be traveled. The higher frequencies, such as this key I have just used, can be used to move between very short distances. As the pitch gets deeper, the frequencies get lower and one can move much further."

"Along with my partner Nathan, I have worked on perfecting these keys so that everyone here can quickly spread throughout the world and search for fluxion cores and sealing techniques. Nathan is known as the Bridgekeeper and I am known as the Keymaster. Since Nathan is not here, I will merely mention that the reason these portals are instantaneous transfers between spatial locations is because a bridge is made between the two doors when a single door is opened. This bridge utilizes the event horizon of both the black and white holes. These two holes have opposing polarities, so as to keep the universe in a neutral state, which is why when a single door is opened, another door with the opposite affinity must be created."

"Now, in terms of the keys, I cannot emphasize enough the importance to use the same key with the same door. If you want to return to the spot you started from, you must obey this simple rule." Holding up the white key, Albert resumed his discourse, "This also only applies to the white keys. These keys will teleport you to another location. However-" he now held up the shorter, black key, "the black keys will teleport someone to your location. As it is difficult to know where the other portal may open, I would advise against using these keys except in extreme emergencies."

Returning to the piano in the corner, Albert lifted the entire set of ivories to reveal an entire set of Q-Portal keys underneath, "If there are no questions, I would like you to pair up in the groups I have assigned to you and grab your set of Q-Portal keys." The room gradually got noisier as everyone tried to find their partner and as the sets of researchers received their keys to go out and explore the world.

Penny led Benjamin and Tecumseh east through the woods, although the two travelers weren't quite sure they knew where she was taking them. As the trio walked along, the forest started to awaken from its slumber. The chirrups of birds foraging for their first worm of the day and singing of their triumphs increased as the sun finally broke over the ridges of the mountains and began to stream down into the valley.

Feeling right at home, Penny returned a few of the bird calls, to which some of the birds sang back their own replies. Benjamin was impressed, "That's pretty good."

"Thanks, I've been practicing for some time now."

"Well, you make it look pretty simple."

"To be honest, it kind of is. After all, sound is just a compressive waveform. All you would need to do to imitate a sound is to match the waveform."

"I don't mean any offense, but that's a pretty smart thing to say, coming from a pretty girl like you."

Penny laughed, "I don't mean any offense." She imitated Benjamin's voice and inflection perfectly as she giggled, "You sound just like my dad." Benjamin chuckled at her impression of him.

Tecumseh was walking behind the two and felt left out of their conversation, so he inserted himself into a new topic for them to discuss. Making his way between the two, he asked, "So, Penny, what were you doing out there on the lake this morning?"

"Practicing. But to be honest, I've been told not to."

"Oh? Practicing what? Singing?"

Penny shrugged, "Yeah, partly. I was practicing more on my control of the waves."

Benjamin jumped in, and Tecumseh scowled as the conversation was taken away from him again, "Do you mean to say you were controlling the lake to the point that you could make it not produce any waves at all?"

"Not quite, but that's the result either way. No, what I'm doing is sensing the waves already present in the lake, then injecting my own waves to cancel those original waves out."

Tecumseh was determined to keep in the conversation, "How can you do that?"

Loosening the strap which held the trident on her back, Penny pulled out the golden weapon and flicked one of its prongs. Immediately, the forest was filled with the pure tone that was produced by the pointy implement. "This trident magnifies my power, and with it I can do things like remove the waves from water. However, I'm still not good at controlling it yet, which is why I've been practicing on these mountain lakes early in the morning. The waves of those lakes at that time of day are very calm, and I can easily control them."

As they continued walking and the forest became thinner, Penny seemed to grow despondent, "Of course, since I've been caught using my powers in the presence of those who don't understand, I've been forbidden from using them at all."

Knowing the freedom that his power gave him, Benjamin had to ask, "Who could possibly deny you the right to use your power?"

"Penneut Psinodeo!" The call came from further down the valley and, as the group breached the edge of the forest, they could see a small farmhouse carved out of the face of a steep cliff. As the valley stretched out before them, it became obvious that they were on the outskirts of a farm.

"Penneut Psinodeo!" Once again, the call came from the farmhouse, the tone slightly more concerned. More specifically, the call came from the woman who was standing on its porch. She was older, as evidenced by her grey hair which hung loosely from her head and down her back. And yet, she had aged gracefully as evidenced by her tall, slender body and that still had the lungs to call out for Penny.

"Here, mother!" Penny replied as she jogged to the house. The woman came down from the porch and met her daughter underneath the sign that hung above the opening in the fence surrounding the front yard. The sign read, "Rancho de la Sol."

"Where have you been, young lady? I hope you haven't been out on those lakes again." Taking a strand of Penny's hair and feeling it between her fingers, the mother could sense that her daughter would only have one chance of telling the truth.

Averting her gaze, Penny reluctantly answered, "Yes, mother."

"And I assume that these two gentlemen are from *another* newspaper, here to get the scoop on our whole little secret world out here? Am I right?"

Penny regained some confidence as she explained, "No! These guys are just like us. In fact, Benjamin has been on a journey to find more people like our family."

The mother was still skeptical as she approached the bespectacled man and squinted at him with a questioning stare, "Benjamin, eh? And what exactly is your specialty?"

As he had done before, Benjamin extended his hand and allowed the sparks of electricity to crawl up his fingers. Seeming adequately impressed, the mother turned to Tecumseh and asked, "And I'm assuming you're not from the papers either, are you, mister . . . "

"Tecumseh. And you're absolutely right." Having learned his lesson from before, Tecumseh dialed back his demonstration and merely lit the tips of his fingers on fire.

Having been convinced of their abilities, not only to manipulate the elements but to also keep mum about their home, the mother opened her arms for a group hug. As she squeezed all three of them, she gave an introduction, "Well, if you're one of us, then you are welcome to Rancho de la Sol." Releasing the trio from the hug, she continued, "I'm Penneut Psinodeo's mother, Trea Raiga." Making her way around the group, she ushered the two guests into the house, "It's time for breakfast, so why don't you join us?"

As they entered the home, the smell of baking bread and sizzling grease overwhelmed their senses. A young girl of about 18 emerged from the kitchen holding a pan of freshly baked muffins. Her pink apron swished as she walked over to the table and set the pan down in front of the centerpiece of a single wilting rose. Leaning down and whispering into Penny's ear, she said, "You need to bring back cuties like this more often, sis." Standing back up, she flashed Tecumseh a smile and a wink. He couldn't help noticing and smiled back.

In a loud whisper, Penny retorted, "Sue! That's not appropriate with mom around."

Unfortunately, Trea Raiga only overheard the last part of the conversation, "Penneut Psinodeo! I will remind you to refer to your sister by her full name of Suev Tideorphan. You should know that by reducing her name, you are treating her like all those who do not possess the powers we do."

Tired of being lectured by her mother, Penny mumbled, "Yes, mother," as she went into the kitchen to help prepare breakfast and to punch her sister in the arm.

Turning to her guests, Trea Raiga apologized, "I'm sorry if my daughter has been any trouble, but I can remember a time when I was just as belligerent."

Benjamin waved his hand to show that Penny had really been quite helpful, "No, not at all. In fact, Tecumseh and I wouldn't have known there was a full family of people like us until we met her."

"Ah, yes. That reminds me. Give me your hands, please." Slightly confused at this request, Benjamin hesitantly complied. "Your names are not befitting those who possess the powers that you do, so I need to find out what your true names are, the names that should come naturally to you." Closing her eyes, Trea Raiga began to concentrate on the hands she held. Benjamin could feel the flow of power from her hands, which was definitely a new experience for him. Suddenly, Trea Raiga opened her eyes and said, "Reptiju Suez."

Slightly confused, Benjamin said, "I beg your pardon?"

"Your name. It's really Reptiju Suez. At least that's what your body told me." Turning to Tecumseh, Trea Raiga repeated the process. When her eyes were closed, Trea Raiga scowled for a moment, but it disappeared by the time she opened her eyes, "Lotup Sedah."

Steps were heard on the staircase as a man came down from upstairs. He was as thin and tall as Trea Raiga, but wore a pair of round glasses high on his nose. Judging by his age, evidenced by the greying and receding hairline, neatly parted to the side, he had to be the father of the household, "I wasn't aware we had guests this morning, Trea Raiga."

Getting up from the table, Trea Raiga approached the man and gave him a quick peck on the cheek, "Penneut Psinodeo found these two gentlemen out in the woods and brought them home to meet us. They have the same powers that our children do. Their names are Reptiju Suez and Lotup Sedah."

"I see." As Benjamin and Tecumseh got up to shake the man's hand, he asked, "I don't mean any offense, but what were your names *before* you came to Rancho de la Sol?"

Trea Raiga seemed offended, "Gustav! Those are their true names and-"

Interrupting his wife, the man calmly said, "Trea Raiga, let the men speak."

Instead of answering, Tecumseh asked, "Wait. 'Gustav'? You mean that you don't have powers like the rest of us?"

"Nope. I'm just a regular old man. Although, what a normal guy like me could have done to deserve a family like this is beyond me."

"Well, perhaps luck is your power," Benjamin suggested.

Gustav laughed a hearty laugh at the mere thought of such a thing, "That's a good one. I'll have to remember that."

"A pleasure to help. I'm Benjamin by the way."

"Tecumseh." A hearty handshake followed each introduction.

"Say, fellas. Why don't you come with me and let's see if we can't find the rest of my family as we let these lovely ladies finish making breakfast." Both men nodded as they followed Gustav out the front door and into the field.

○

Jules and Herbert stood atop Asp Peak and were struck speechless by what they saw. Although, one would suppose that the sight of an enormous boat, balanced on the top of the mouth of a volcano, might tend to leave the viewer with no words to express their amazement. Nevertheless, the two researchers saw that if they were to try and get to the boat, they had an incredibly tough journey ahead of them.

The volcano in front of the two travelers was located in the middle of the three peaks of the Pythagorean Triangle, so named because the ridges between the mountains, combined with their respective summits, gave the appearance of three snakes biting each other's tails. Legends of the area told of a woman named Gorgon who was extremely prideful and was cursed for that character flaw. The curse was twofold. First, her hair turned into a teeming pack of pythons, thus causing most to call her by her new name, Pythagoras. Secondly, she could turn most things to stone. Therefore, a set of mountains that just happened to look like three stone snakes caused most people to refer to the area as the Pythagorean Triangle. However, a certain amount of mystery revolved around the mountains, as many who went into the triangle never came out, and others seemed to appear from the triangle out of nowhere.

Herbert was aware that the myths and legends might be against them, but he was determined to accomplish his directive. Looking down the ridges to the neighboring mountains, he tried to see how they could get down into the bowl where the volcano resided, belching up a lot of smoke and embers. When he caught sight of a switch-backed path which led down from the ridge between Asp Peak and Boa Peak to a small, wooded patch of land, he turned around to show Jules. However, Jules had disappeared. Concerned that something may have happened, Herbert shouted, "Jules! Jules, where are you?"

An echoed response came from a little further down the peak, "In here, Herbert!" Making his way down the mound of rocks, Herbert found that the voice was coming from a slit in the mountain which provided the visual effect of a snake's mouth. Crouching down and sliding through the opening, Herbert found himself inside the hollowed out summit of Asp Peak. Jules had produced a lantern from his pack and had lit it with a match so that he could see.

While Jules was examining the walls, Herbert took in the sight of the whole enclosure. The walls were smooth and rounded, and almost looked to be man-made. At the very least, the solitary pedestal in the middle of the room was most definitely not a natural occurrence. Jules turned around and could only see a silhouette, as Herbert was still standing at the entrance of the cave, illuminated by the outside light. "Come over here, and take a look at this." When Herbert approached, Jules held up the lantern to the wall and pointed out a unique feature.

"See this seam in the wall here? I think there may be a door to a tunnel leading down the ridge of the mountain. I would hope that a tunnel could get us up to the volcano, or at least closer to it. However-" Jules pointed to the keyhole set in the middle of the rock. He pulled out the white Q-Portal key and put the end of it near the hole, "Our key won't fit this hole. The key we have is Q-shaped, where this hole is obviously that of an i."

Herbert slapped the key away, "Even if it isn't the same fit, you shouldn't try to open it with that key. Just think about it for a minute: if we traveled half-way across the continent because of that key, I don't think using it in a different shaped keyhole will get us closer to the volcano. Now come on, I've found a way we can get over there." Jules was a little put off by the chiding, but blew out his lantern and followed Herbert back outside anyways.

As Herbert led the way down the mountain, Jules glanced over at the impressive boat teetering on the top of the volcano. It was an oddly shaped boat which looked like a quarter slice of watermelon that had the best part cut right off the top. As such, the curvature of the hull set in the mouth of the volcano looked like it was pretty stable. Of course, as is the case with many mountainous things, the scale of the boat was hard to judge. And yet, based on the nearby peaks, the boat looked to be about 150 yards long. Far longer than any normal boat would be.

Arriving at the small, square patch of land, the partners found that they had just finished the easiest part of their journey. Ahead of them was a vast expanse of boulders, most of which had fallen from the Pythagorean peaks and had come to rest in the bowl between them. Beyond that, was the volcano itself. The sheer face of the cone showed no openings or discernible ways to climb it. Deciding it was time for a break before starting on the rest of their journey, Herbert sat down at the edge of the grove of Pythagorean trees. The trees were named as such because their bark was extremely hard, like that of stone, and their form seemed to imitate that of a woman with long hair flowing into the air.

Jules plucked a few pieces of fruit from a nearby Pythagoras tree and tossed one to Herbert before sitting down himself. They both puckered up at the sour taste of the fruit, but the juicy and fresh attributes of the produce caused them both to finish eating. Looking forward at the boulder field, Jules sighed, "What are we doing here again?"

Herbert chuckled, "What do you mean? I thought you wanted to see the world. I would bet that most people have never seen anything like this."

"*Oui*, I did say that. But I never said anything about *walking* around the entire world. I'd much rather be in a balloon or a boat or a submarine or some sort of conveyance that would allow me to get somewhere without actually exerting myself like this."

Extending a hand to help Jules up, Herbert replied, "Well, we've all got to walk at some point. It builds character, you know." Looking to the sky to see the sun directly above them, then at the distance they had to cover, Herbert grabbed his pack, "I'd like to reach the volcano by sunset. Hopefully we can use its heat to keep us warm tonight, even if we can't manage to climb it today." Walking to the edge of the square patch of land, Herbert once again led the way toward the volcano.

Even though they had to pick their way across the boulders, the route was generally pretty flat. So, in the process of jumping from rock to rock, their progress was quicker than anticipated. Of course, the brief rest and small snack helped ready their bodies for the second leg of their trek. In no time at all, they were at the edge of the volcano as the sun disappeared behind Cobra Ridge, leaving the light of the sky to see by.

Since there was still some time before having to make camp, Jules gave a suggestion, "Let's walk around the edge of the volcano to see if there are any ways we can climb this beast. Then we'll have somewhere to start tomorrow if we find anything." Nodding in agreement, Herbert began to walk around the perimeter of the black mountain as Jules walked in the opposite direction.

Finally having some time to himself, Herbert began to think of his involvement in the fluxion project. He had a few ideas that he wondered if the fluxions would be able to make a reality. An invisibility suit? Perhaps. A way to travel to the future? Maybe. And yet, his most secret desire was to someday set foot on the moon. To be the first man to walk on its white, glowing surface. He felt that maybe his access to military resources might be able to fulfill his wish.

Of course, he easily related to the fear that a people more powerful than anyone else could imagine would be able to start a war to engulf the whole world. They needed to be crushed immediately, and he had a hunch the rumored treasures of the boat above him would be a big part of the Naturals' downfall.

When Jules appeared around the other side of the volcano, Herbert could tell there was no discernible way up the nearly vertical face of rock in front of them. He was just about to suggest that they set up camp when a rope ladder unfurled itself directly between them. Looking up toward the part of the boat which stuck out over the edge of the volcano, the partners could see that the rope ladder led all the way up the face of the mountain and into the dark hull of the enormous vessel.

Since both men had seen no options on how to climb the daunting edifice, they accepted the hempen help and began to ascend up the hand-made ladder. Once again, the scale of the mountain was deceptive as they slowly made their way up its face. As the ladder swayed with the blowing wind of the higher altitudes, both Jules and Herbert held on tightly and gradually made progress upward. By the time they arrived at the opening in the boat's hull, they were exhausted. How high had they climbed? Two thousand vertical feet? Three thousand vertical feet? It seemed like the climb would never end.

As they lay gasping for air on the wooden floor, the ladder suddenly began to be pulled in from outside. The speed at which the ladder was retrieved kept increasing until the last of it whipped through the hole and the trap door was slammed shut, leaving the two travelers in a state of confused darkness.

When the three men headed outside, the morning had come into full swing. Livestock could be heard lowing in the distance as the trio headed south to the fields. The various crops were growing well and were a few months away from harvest. Each crop was in its own circular patch and the patches were dotted up and down the valley. The entirety of the ranch was fairly well hidden from the rest of the world, as it sat up against at least two sheer cliffs, one to the north and the other to the east.

Despite the seclusion of the area, the crops seemed to grow, regardless of the reduced amount of sunlight they received due to their position in the valley. Of course, each crop was watered well from a pipework irrigation system that functioned off of the concept of center-pivot irrigation. Water from a nearby waterfall was fed to the main water line that zigzagged down the valley and hit the center of each crop's circle. A radial arm was attached to the point where the main pipe connected to the center of the crop. This arm was set up so that animals could pull it around the circle, thereby watering the whole crop.

Navigating through the maze of corn, wheat, barley, and oats, Gustav led his two guests as he called out to one of his children, "Tranus Sunroc! Where are you, son?"

From behind another patch of corn, the voice came out, "Over here, dad." When they walked around the perimeter of the crop, they found a man who was considerably older than his siblings. While the two children of Trea Raiga and Gustav they had already met were fairly young, Tranus Sunroc had to be at least 40. Small bits of grey in his untamed hair had started to appear and his tanned and leathery skin revealed that he was a hard worker who had labored in the fields for many years. A simple golden band on his left hand showed that he was married, although his wife was nowhere to be seen.

"It's time for breakfast, son." Gustav motioned to his two guests, "These gentlemen are Benjamin and Tecumseh. They will be joining us this morning."

Nodding in acknowledgement and shaking both their hands, Tranus Sunroc went back to the central-pivot irrigation system and untied the cow that was pulling the radial arm around the circle. Whispering in the animal's ear, Tranus Sunroc gave a few clicks with his tongue, and led the way back to the house.

While they walked, Gustav asked, "Do you know where Sunaru Suleac is this morning? I haven't seen him at the house."

"I'm not sure. I haven't seen him out here either. Let's just hope he's not causing any trouble."

Benjamin cleared his throat as he asked, "So, Tranus Sunroc, I'm assuming if you have a name like that, you also have a power to go with it, right?"

Tecumseh broke in, "I bet it's talking to animals."

Tranus Sunroc smiled as he answered, "Yes, I do have a power, but it's not talking to animals. That talent comes with time, as I'm sure you know. At least I'm assuming you're a farmer with that pitchfork you carry." Reaching out and letting his hand brush through some of the crops, he continued, "I suppose my power could be translated as a 'green thumb'." Looking over to his father, he said, "Being the firstborn, I suppose I took after mom in that respect."

With raised eyebrows, Gustav agreed, "Yes, but don't sell your mother short. I don't mean any offense, but while you do have a talent for growing things, I doubt you could bring stuff back from the dead like she can."

As the four men entered the yard, and while Tranus Sunroc tied the cow to the fence, they heard a scream from inside the house. Seconds later, a large round object flew out the window and landed in the yard. As the object hit the ground and rolled to a stop at their feet, everyone could see that it was a disembodied head.

Not wanting to scream out in fright, Benjamin and Tecumseh merely gasped at the disturbing sight. Tranus Sunroc and Gustav merely rolled their eyes. A small dust storm kicked up in the yard. As it moved toward the head, a headless body appeared from the swirling dirt. The head blinked a few times, then gave a mischievous grin as the body picked it up and set it on the stump of its neck. Tilting the newly attached head back and forth and around a few times for good measure, the sharply dressed man spoke, "Mom just can't take a joke, can she?"

Tranus Sunroc did not seem to be amused as he walked past, "You've got some bacon on your ear, Sunaru Suleac."

Feeling behind his ear, Sunaru Suleac pulled the bacon off his head and immediately ate it. Looking at Gustav, he asked, "Who are these guys?"

"Benjamin and Tecumseh. They'll be joining us for breakfast." Gustav now took his leave and made his way to the house, leaving his son with the guests.

Sunaru Suleac extended his hand and Tecumseh took it for a handshake. However, soon Sunaru Suleac's hand was all that he was shaking, as it had separated from his wrist. Slightly shocked, Tecumseh threw the hand on the ground and backed away as it disappeared with a swirl of dust and reappeared on the end of Sunaru Suleac's arm. Another big smile from the sharply dressed son, "I'm a bit of a magician, I should have you know."

When Benjamin shook Sunaru Suleac's hand, he let some of his electricity pass through his palm, giving the magician a bit of a shock. Pulling out of the handshake and giving Benjamin a look, he merely said, "Not a fan of tricks, are you?" as he headed into the house.

With Benjamin and Tecumseh close behind, they could hear Trea Raiga informing Gustav what had happened moments earlier, "That boy of ours nearly scared me half to death! I opened one of the platters and found his head just sitting there without his body. So I did what any normal person would do and threw it out the window. Seriously, Sunaru Suleac just doesn't have much tact, does he?"

Going over and giving his mother a kiss on the cheek, Sunaru Suleac teased, "You're no fun, mom." As he sat down, Trea Raiga just had to sigh and smile at her mischievous son. Looking over the spread of food on the table, she saw that everything was in order. Just as she was about to sit down, Trea Raiga noticed the wilted centerpiece and brushed her index finger along its stem. Filled with new life, the rose regained its color, its posture, and its beauty.

The rest of the family made it over to the table and sat down. They all joined hands and bowed their heads as Trea Raiga said a prayer, "Lord, bless this food that we are about to eat and bless the hands that made it. Please be with our sons, Arma Ress as he serves in the military; and Cremy Serehurm as he goes about his daily deliveries. Also, please be with Tranus Sunroc's wife, Morgana, while she works as Luvnac's apprentice. Amen." The amen was echoed by the other members of the family, followed by a squeeze of the hands.

The spread in front of them was impressive and was as delicious as it looked. During the meal, Suev Tideorphan asked, "So, Tecumseh, what are you searching for on your journey?"

Looking into the smiling girl's green eyes, Tecumseh had to divert his gaze for a moment of embarrassment, "W-w-w-well, I'm actually traveling up north in search of the treasure horde of the Order of the Dragon."

Tranus Sunroc spoke up, "That's going to be quite a dangerous journey. I hear their leader, Bram, is very manipulative and can control *actual* dragons. Of course, whether or not dragons really exist is another thing all together."

"Actually, now that you mention it," Trea Raiga interjected, "I've heard that Bram may have found a way to control powers, much like we can do naturally."

This piqued Benjamin's curiosity, "You mean that normal people could possibly use these powers? I've only heard of such events ending in tragedy.

What do you think could allow everyone else to be able to control our powers?"

"I'm not sure, Reptiju Suez. But what I do know is that our abilities lie in our genetic code. This is why, even though Gustav cannot use our powers, all of our children can." Getting up and taking some of the empty dishes to the kitchen, Trea Raiga continued, "A few years ago, when I was a part of-" she paused, choosing her next words carefully, "a group of fellow Naturals, a researcher by the name of Friedrich approached us and asked to study our blood. When he had finished his research, he had made an amazing discovery."

A knock on the front door startled Trea Raiga from her story. As the door opened, a young man of about 20 years peeked his head inside. A shout of joy came from the woman as she jumped up and ran over to the door and hugged the visitor, "Cremy Serehurm! You're home!"

Returning the hug, the man in a tan delivery uniform, complete with top hat accoutrement and sandals laced up to his knees, entered the house as he pulled out a letter from his back pocket, "If you're happy to see me, just wait until you read the letter Arma Ress sent us."

○

It took some time for Herbert and Jules to adjust to their new surroundings. Catching their breath, they both stood up and looked around. They stood inside the hull of the boat and found that whoever lived there had a lot of free time on their hands. Every surface had words carved in it, producing a somewhat dizzying effect as the flickering light of a single candle danced over the grooves of the letters.

What was stranger still was the lack of people in their immediate area. Considering the speed at which the ladder came to them and was retracted back into the hull, it almost felt like the boat itself was sentient and had summoned them into its depths. From behind them, a door closed and a lock was heard being latched. Running over to the now locked door, Herbert and Jules started pounding on the thick wooden barrier.

A small door opened at about eye level and the voice of a young boy was heard, "What do you guys want?"

Jules spoke up in a demanding voice, "What do you mean what do we want? You're the one who let us up here!"

"You didn't have to climb that ladder, you know."

Jules was becoming more frustrated with the boy, so Herbert intervened, "Let me try." Stepping up to the door, he smiled and asked politely, "Could you let us out, please? I'm sure if we could talk face-to-face that everything can be explained."

"*Non.* Try again."

Something snapped in Herbert and he kept smiling as he approached the door. With a sudden movement, he thrust his hand through the small opening in the door and reached around toward the handle on the other side. The boy let out a startled yell, and began to thrash at Herbert's arm. But it was too late, as Herbert had found the latch and unlocked the door. Soon, the two travelers were on the other side of the door and could get a better look at the boy who had trapped them.

The boy was about eleven years old and skinny as a rail. His height seemed a little disproportionate, but it looked like he would eventually grow into it. As Jules shut the door behind them, the boy cowered against a wall, "Don't hurt me! I was only joking around."

They now stood in a long hallway of a room, both sides of which seemed to hold mostly empty cages. A few animals rustled around but didn't make much noise, even with the scene unfolding in front of them. Again, every surface was carved with a plethora of words, no two words together making any coherent sense. Just a random assortment of expressions carved into the woodwork. The lighting was a little better, as there were more candles set at closer intervals. From the end of the long hall came another voice, much older this time, "Camille? Are you down there? What's going on?"

"It's my papa! Hide!" As Camille pushed Herbert and Jules into an empty cage, they could hear steps coming down the staircase at the end of the hall. Camille made his way down the corridor to meet his father at the bottom of the steps, "Nothing suspicious going on down here, papa. Just me and the animals." The man had flowing grey hair and a beard to match. He wore a simple grey robe and sandals on his feet.

"I hope you're not teaching the bears to dance again."

"*Non*, I'm not doing anything of the sort."

"Because, I've told you once before that these animals are part of a dwindling collection, and not to be paraded around in a 'Carnival of the Animals'." Something in their cage caused Jules to sneeze. This caught the attention of the old man, "Who else is down here, Camille?"

As the father walked further down the corridor, Camille was trying to get him to stop, "No one is down here, papa! I'm just practicing my ventriloquism. That's right!" By the time the old man had reached their cage, Camille was practically trying to push his dad back down the hall.

The man was surprised and intrigued to find two men hiding in one of his animal cells, "And who might you gentlemen be?"

Coming out of their cage, Jules introduced them, "My name is Jules and this is my partner, Herbert." Herbert waved when his name was mentioned. "We've come here on an expedition to find some potential power sources for a project that could change the entire world."

The man seemed to lighten up as he realized the men posed no threat, "I see. Then you must know my name is Noah and you must be here to see my collection of animals." Having done their homework, both men nodded. "Excellent. Come with me."

As they followed Noah up the stairs, they couldn't help noticing that the words continued. Noah noted their wandering eyes as he started his explanation, "You see, gentlemen, I am a collector. Just like how I enjoy collecting animals, I enjoy collecting words. Words are just as diverse as animals, you see. And even though animals like hippopotami, platypuses, and ostriches may seem strange and look funny, words like ambidextrous, pizzazz, and ubiquitous can seem just as strange and look just as funny."

When Herbert had put together a few pieces about their environment, he asked, "Why doesn't it smell like smoke in here?"

"That's easy, my boy. This ship is airtight so that it can float on water. As such, the airtight seal keeps unwanted smoke from seeping in, while allowing the heat of the volcano Sievuvus beneath us to keep everything warm." At the top of the stairs, the group came upon another corridor, this time filled with plants and lit by skylights in the ceiling. About half-way through the hallway was a woman in armor, watering some of the plants. The light of the rising full moon and setting sun reflecting off of her armor made her almost look like an angel. Noah approached her and gave her a kiss, "Joan, my love. These gentlemen are here to look at my collections for a research project that could change the world."

Politely bowing, Joan greeted the two travelers, "I hope you don't mind the heat in here, it's a bit hot for my tastes, but I'll stick with Noah even if I have to be a bit uncomfortable."

"Well, dear, maybe if you took off the armor, you wouldn't be so hot."

"Are you kidding? I've seen what animals you keep down there. I'd rather be safe than be comfortable."

Jules spoke up when he came to a realization, "By the way, where *are* all your animals? I noticed most of the cages down there were empty."

"Ah, a valid question, Jules. You see, when I started collecting animals, I found very quickly that, even in a boat this big, I would soon run out of space. There are a *lot* of animals out there. I made a decision a while ago to merely collect samples of their blood. Not only could I conserve on space, but the blood of an animal is its true essence. Its soul, if you will."

Jules and Herbert looked at each other and asked simultaneously, "Can we see that collection?"

"Of course! Camille, come with me as we show these gentlemen my collection." Going up one last flight of stairs, the group arrived on the roof of the boat where there sat an impressive shrine that looked like an arch. Beneath the arch was an elaborate and ornately decorated box. The lid of the box had four angel statues on each of the corners, their wings touching at the tips. Two bars were attached on the lid so that two people could lift it and set it to the side, revealing the impressive collection within.

Inside the golden box was a vast array of small glass orbs, each filled with a little bit of animal blood. Noah proudly stood over the box and boasted, "I call this collection 'The Spectrum', as it exhibits the full spectrum of all life on earth." Looking up at the two men, he mentioned, "If you would like, I can loan you this collection for your research, as I have a backup collection of these animals."

Herbert and Jules were elated that they had found such a goldmine of cores to use in the fluxion research, but soon their smiles vanished as they realized that getting the box back to headquarters might be somewhat difficult. However, before they could speak up, Joan appeared on the deck of the boat, looking worried, "Noah, *mon amour*, I was finishing up watering the plants when I heard the animals downstairs starting to make a lot of noise. I think they may be restless again and-" a sudden jolt on the deck caused everyone to lose their balance.

As if in slow motion, Joan began to fall off the side of the boat as Noah and Camille lunged out to try and catch her. They just missed grabbing her hand as she tumbled down toward the bubbling pit of lava below. Fortunately, as she fell, Joan caught the red-hot metal anchor which was hanging from the boat into the open mouth of the glowing volcano. Despite the sudden deceleration breaking many of her bones, she stopped short of the fiery depths beneath her.

Noah and Camille were speechless as they looked down at Joan's predicament. She yelled up to them, "I'm hurt! And I don't know how long I can hold on to this anchor! It's getting *really* hot down here!"

Herbert and Jules were acting quickly. They had found the water supply for the boat and had begun to throw it over the side of the ship in buckets. After the first few buckets evaporated before they did any good, the researchers set forth trying to destroy the tank of water. Noah was screaming, "What are you doing!? This is my boat and my home!"

Herbert sternly yelled back, "If you want your wife to live, then I suggest you help us!" Realizing his priorities, Noah ran over to a compartment in the deck where he pulled out a bunch of axes and handed them out to everyone. They hacked away at the tank, and eventually the water burst forth and fell to the boiling lava below. After the steam of the interaction cleared, a small island of black rock now floated in the middle of the sea of lava.

Yelling down to Joan, Herbert asked, "Can you drop down to that island?"

With no response, Jules observed, "*Non!* It looks like she's too injured, and now she's been burned by the steam used to create that island."

Noah was quickly losing his mind, "You're not helping! You're merely making things worse!"

Herbert was quickly losing his patience, "Well, I don't see you doing anything to help!"

Jules stepped in and provided a solution, "We're not getting anywhere by arguing, so let's try my plan. Noah, do you have any ropes that are long enough to get down there?" The old man nodded and, from another compartment in the deck, produced long ropes coiled around giant pillars. Pointing to the golden box, Jules continued, "Now, tie those ropes to the corners of the box."

Satisfied with the knots, Jules explained his plan, "*Tres bien*. Now look, Noah and Camille will lower Herbert and myself down with this box, which we will then use to lift Joan out of the volcano. Are we clear?" Everyone nodded as they got to work.

The descent was slow, but at least it was safe. Through the smoke and the embers, the two researchers descended as Noah and Camille lowered them down with a system of pulleys jury rigged on the deck of their boat. When they arrived at Joan, hanging on the chain of the anchor, she was in sorry shape. Most of her armor was dented and her exposed skin was bright red and starting to blister.

Herbert reached out to grab Joan and pull her into the box, but her armor had absorbed too much heat and was hot to the touch. In fact, it was practically glowing. Jules calmly spoke across the box, "Joan! You have to fall into the box so we can lift you up! Herbert! You and I have to hang on to the chain until the box can be lowered again." Looking up to Noah and Camille, Jules made a motion to let them know to lower the box just a little more.

In the delicate choreography of trying to get everyone in position, Joan slipped and fell into the lava of the volcano. Her death was quick, but excruciating. Noah and Camille saw Joan fall into the lava and, in their shock, let go of the ropes holding the box. As Herbert and Jules had not made it to the chain yet, they fell down to the small island of black rock they had created earlier.

Surprisingly, the box and its contents were not very damaged, but everyone's morale was. The failed rescuers could hear yelling and screaming from above them, but no distinct words made it down to their ears. Their situation looked bleak, as the small island they stood on had begun to sink into the molten rock. Herbert quickly thought of a solution, "Jules! Grab the Q-Portal key, and let's use it on this rock to get out of here!"

Feverishly searching his pockets, Jules' face became white when he could not find the right Q-Portal key. With wide eyes, he instead held the black Q-Portal key in front of them as Herbert yelled, "Where's the white one? We can't go back with a black key; we can only bring something else here with that one!" The color dropped out of his face as he too realized that the white key sat atop Asp Peak.

Grabbing the black key from Jules, Herbert rashly decided that doing something was better than doing nothing, "Let's use it anyway! Maybe we can force our way through to the other side!" Thrusting the key down into the black rock, it entered smoothly and was immediately turned. Cracks of white light appeared in a circle around where they were standing, followed by the deafening roar of a torrent of water emerging from the hole of light created by the black Q-Portal.

The rushing water was extremely cold in comparison to their surroundings, but soon began to absorb the heat of the lava as it started to solidify the molten rock. Struggling against the current, Jules yelled in sputters, "We need to make our way through the portal somehow! But with this water pouring out, how can we possibly make our way through?"

With the situation quickly deteriorating, Herbert coughed out, "I don't know!" When he looked down at the glowing light emanating from the Q-Portal he created, something glinted on the bottom of the quickly forming lake. "Wait a second! I've got an idea!" Diving down into the scalding water, Herbert swam toward the box containing Noah's prized collection, some of its orbs now being carried away by the torrent. Jules picked up on Herbert's plan and dove in after him.

Herbert arrived at the box and grabbed on. Not daring to leave his eyes open any more in the rushing, boiling stream, he pulled at the box and hoped that Jules had caught on. When the box lifted off the rock floor, Herbert knew it was now or never. Opening his eyes for a moment to get his bearings, he saw the white light of the Q-Portal and began to swim toward it, carrying "The Spectrum" with him. Once they arrived over the white hole, Herbert stopped swimming and began praying that the golden box would be heavy enough to drop them through the rapid water.

As they began to sink, Herbert instinctively closed his eyes, but immediately opened them when he felt the cold water on the other side of the portal. They had made it! But they weren't out of trouble just yet. The black hole they had miraculously emerged from was still pulling water into its darkness, and was creating quite the whirlpool. Keeping his directive in mind, Herbert quickly pulled off his shirt and began stuffing as many animal blood orbs into it as he could. Jules was doing the same. Just as the remnants of air burned in their lungs, they headed toward the surface of the water, carrying with them their tragic reward.

On the shore, they breathed heavily, occasionally coughing out the water they had accidentally swallowed. Herbert sat up and looked out over the surface of the water to see that their whirlpool was still there, a churning hole in the dark waters. He then glanced around at their surroundings. In the distance to the south, there stood the silhouette of the Library of Delaxanair, lit by the full moon above them. They had arrived back almost in the same spot they had started. Even though they would have loved to lay on the shore and stare at the full moon, they knew the situation they had created took priority.

Trea Raiga opened the letter from Arma Ress and read aloud,

Dear family:

While my time in the Army of Amedeo has been short, I have quickly shown that I am capable of great things. A few days after I joined, I was promoted to the rank of Orion-Class General. And to think it was all thanks to the inherent power within me.

I will be away from home for quite a while, as I have been tasked from my commanding officers to find others like myself to make the Army of Amedeo even more powerful than it already is. Be confident in the knowledge that I am safe and am helping to protect the world.

- Arma Ress

The soldier's mother smiled as she folded up the letter. Cremy Serehurm hung up his top hat and messenger's bag and sat down at the table, ready for some food. As had been the case with everyone else so far, Cremy Serehurm was introduced to Benjamin and Tecumseh and the table was soon revitalized with the sounds of conversation.

Benjamin tried to get back on the topic they had been on before they were interrupted, "So, Trea Raiga. You were saying something about Friedrich's discovery?"

"Ah, yes. Well, you see, Friedrich had discovered that our genetic code is comprised of strings of data. The interesting thing he found about our genetic strings was that, while normal people exhibited strings which were straight and disconnected, ours looped back on themselves. He postulated that the reason why we could use our powers and not be taken over by the overwhelming energy was that our genetic strings captured most of the energy. Sealing it, if you will. As such, we were able to call upon any power source we pleased and were also able to pass these special traits on to our children."

Benjamin was silent in meditation over this new information. He was intrigued that his own body was designed so it could harness the raw powers found in nature. Penny saw Benjamin deep in thought and asked him, "A penny for your thoughts?"

Smiling at the clever wordplay, Benjamin sat up in his seat and replied, "I was merely trying to think of where I should head next. After all, I'm here because I was searching for you." Penny blushed at this statement, "And now I've found many more who have the same powers I do. I don't feel quite as alone in this world anymore, and I wonder if I should keep searching for more people like us."

Tecumseh cleared his throat, "To be honest, I kind of liked traveling with you and if you don't mind, might I suggest you come with me to search up north for the Order of the Dragon?"

"That's an excellent idea, Tecumseh. Plus, if we can find Bram, we can find out how, or even if, he's able to control our powers without having the genetic strings necessary to do it naturally."

"Might I make a suggestion on how to get there?" Sunaru Suleac spoke up and everyone looked at him, which made him smirk at the attention, "I have heard of a way that you could get up north quickly, but since it is shrouded in mystery, no one is sure if it really exists."

Tranus Sunroc interjected, "You're not talking about that imaginary tunnel that takes people wherever their desires want, are you? I know you're really into being a magician, but the i-World is pure superstition."

"Well, not quite." Cremy Serehurm joined the conversation, "I've traveled around quite a bit, and I have heard rumors of it. The strange thing is that the rumors are highly concentrated around the Angular Mangroves, which leads one to believe that something having to do with the i-World must be in the area."

Benjamin looked at Tecumseh and said, "I've got nowhere to be, so why don't we try and find this i-World? Who knows, maybe it'll put us right at the treasure horde of the Order of the Dragon?"

"I'm game if you are."

As the two travelers got up from the table, Penny stood up too, "Let me come with you guys!"

"Penneut Psinodeo! What is with this sudden outburst?"

With a pleading look in her eyes, Penny tried to reason with her mother, "Mom, I'm twenty-five now, and it's time I left the safety and comfort of our ranch in favor of finding out what my purpose in life is. I think these two men will give me the opportunity I need to figure that out."

"Absolutely not. I will not have my oldest daughter traveling around to God knows where and-" a hand on Trea Raiga's shoulder quieted her.

Looking up behind her, Gustav was standing, "I think she's right, Trea Raiga. We shouldn't keep her sheltered like this. She needs to go out and make her own decisions. Make her own mistakes. Make her own life." Trea Raiga smiled at the wisdom of her husband and, in acceptance of her daughter's wishes, merely nodded.

Squealing with excitement, Penny hugged her parents then ran off to her room to gather her belongings for the journey ahead. Benjamin asked Cremy Serehurm, "So, where exactly are the Angular Mangroves? Since it looks like we're heading out soon, I'd like to know where to go."

"The Angular Mangroves are directly south of here, so if you just follow the Olympus River you should eventually end up in that general area."

Racing back down the stairs, Penny grabbed Benjamin and Tecumseh and pulled them out the front door. They just barely had enough time to grab their bags before they were outside and in the front yard. Once they were out into the fields, their pace slowed as Penny turned around to see her parents, brothers, and sister out on the front porch, watching her leave. With a wave of her hand, she waved goodbye and turned toward the path heading to the river. The family returned her wave and her siblings made their way back into the house. Gustav hugged Trea Raiga when he noticed tears in her eyes, "It's OK, dear. She's with some good men who will protect her."

"I'm sure you're right. It's just so hard to watch her grow up so fast like that." With a kiss on her forehead, Gustav pulled his wife into the house and shut the door.

Chapter 3

Forest Fluent

Albert closed and locked the door behind him as he made his way to the front of the room, "Thank you for waiting while I gave my report to the higher ups." Facing the small group of people, he continued, "You have all been chosen to work on this project based on your previous research. I cannot stress how extremely classified this part of the project will be. The sealing techniques we come up with in here will be the key to harnessing the power of the fluxions. If any of you breathe a word of this to anyone without the proper clearance, you will be convicted of treason and locked up in Pandora Prison until the day you die. Do I make myself clear?"

The room nodded in solemn unison as the small group looked hesitantly at each other. "*Wunderbar.* Now, to get everyone up to speed, let us go around the room and give an explanation of our research. Let us start with James and Garland. Correct me if I am wrong, but you two have managed to successfully seal sunlight, am I right?"

A plain man with no real distinguishing features was leaning against the wall and spoke in response, "That's right, Albert. Garland and I worked together over many years to perfect our sealing technique, which all started with a piqued interest in an aboriginal tribe from the southern continent."

From the opposite wall, a second, equally ordinary man began, "James and I heard some rumors a few years back about a tribe in the deepest depths of this southern continent which had a peculiar rite of passage for its men. Being the adventurous chaps that we are, we packed our bags and boarded a boat heading south."

At this point, James took over speaking, allowing Garland to pick up where he left off, "It took a bit of work to finally find their village, but eventually we came across the home of the Serpentes tribe. This tribe is primarily known for their snake handling religion, but this is where the interesting rite of passage came into play. We were fortunate to have arrived when the ceremony was taking place, and even more fortunate that they were also holding their ceremony for picking a new shaman chief."

"The rite of passage ceremony is certainly one of the more severe human activities out there, but the Serpentes found that it proved their boys were ready to become men. If they weren't, they were killed. The ceremony would proceed as follows: each boy who had turned eighteen that year was allowed an hour to prepare himself for the snake pit. This preparation entailed using war paint to draw snakes on their body."

"Once their time was up, they were thrown into their own individual pit of snakes. This is where the war paint preparation was supposed to pay off. When each boy fell into the pit of snakes, they were completely unarmed. And while there were small rocks in each pit, they were not nearly big enough to kill any snake. Of course, the point of the ceremony was not to *kill* snakes, but rather to not *be killed* by snakes."

"Those who were successful in their war paint preparation would grab some of the stones in their hands, and stand on some of the stones with their feet. Now, this is where things got interesting. The boys who had correctly applied their paint would turn into stone. As the snakes attacked, they could not bite the stone limbs. As a result, these boys would pass the test, be hoisted out of the pit, and have a great feast with the other men of the tribe."

"However, the boys who did not correctly paint their bodies would not be able to turn to stone or would only partially turn to stone, thereby leaving openings for the snakes to attack. Fortunately for these boys, the snake venom acted quickly and they did not have to suffer long. And yet, there was a third type of boy who would enter the pit and, due to lack of physical willpower, would turn to stone and could not turn back, as we have already seen an example of today."

"After their ceremony, we got a chance to look at the war paint of all the boys who had participated, both winners and losers. It seemed that those who successfully passed the test used the snake design as a type of circuitry along their body that connected to circles painted on their palms and the bottoms of their feet. These circles were also snakes, but exhibited an uroboros form where the snake head was biting its own tail."

"We came to realize the uroboros design was what harnessed and controlled the powers, as the boys who had died did not have this attribute in their war paint designs. This was also confirmed during the ceremony for their new shaman chief. While this rite of passage was similar to the one for the boys, only a single candidate would be tested at a time for the chief's position. The one other difference was that the potential shaman chief would not only have to keep the snakes from biting him, but he also had to turn into a snake. This latter requirement was usually done by killing one of the snakes and pouring its blood on a rock, which was then placed in the mouth, where an uroboros design was tattooed either on the man's tongue or the roof of his mouth, usually both."

Albert spoke up to confirm the lessons of their story, "So, what you are both saying is that in order to control the fluxions, three things are needed: a fluxion core, an uroboros seal, and human energy or will?"

Both James and Garland nodded, but then James continued the story, "Yes, but there's a bit more to our story that may be of interest. You see, when we arrived back home in the 4th Kingdom, we set to work on trying to test our theory. Since we did not want to experiment on people, due to what we had seen on the southern continent, we set about trying to seal sunlight. And while I had noticed the uroboros link before, Garland had come up with another novel idea."

"Our early trials of capturing sunlight produced results, but they were rather weak. There needed to be a way to allow the maximum amount of energy to be stored in a minimum amount of space. When I looked at the uroboros design, I noticed that the single exit point for the powers seemed to be at the link between the snake's head and tail. As such, the longer the snake you used; the more power you could store. However, the real trick in storing more power in less space was due to knotting. You see, if you took that really long snake and had it twist back upon itself, braiding and looping it over its entire length, then the snake that once took up an enormous amount of space now only took up a quarter or even a tenth of its previous area."

"We had done some preliminary tests of this knotted uroboros design and they seemed to work pretty well, so we set forth on producing our penultimate experiment. Out in the countryside, we carved the knotted uroboros design on the ground; then got some of the nearby villagers to stand up stone structures on top of the seal to make a sort of basket to catch the sunlight. On the summer solstice, when the sun was at its highest point, Garland and I knelt at the head of the seal and put our hands on the head and tail of the snake. When we put some of our energy into the seal, the lines on the ground began to glow, as did the stones set upon them."

"Holding the seal for a few minutes, we let the experiment soak in the sun; then we released our hold on the uroboros. That night, we stood in wonder underneath the darkness of the new moon. The circle of stones had held in the sunlight. Within the confines of the seal, the area looked like it was the middle of the day, bathed in sunlight."

Making a note on some paper, Albert asked again, "So, the important part of the seal is both the uroboros design *and* the knotting technique?"

Once again, James and Garland nodded, and once again James confirmed it, "That's right. In order to capture the full power of any fluxion core, the snake needs to be long enough to hold it all in, and that's where the knotting really works its magic."

A sigh was heard from the corner of the room. Everyone looked to the man sitting there as he leaned forward and cleared his throat, "That's a mighty fine story you boys have told us, but what's that got to do with me?" The man looked somewhat out of place, with his unkempt hair and beard flowing over the edges of his dark leather jacket. A look of boredom was worn on a face that normally would express serious toughness.

Albert acted as the master of ceremonies like he had always done, "Well, Dmitri, why not tell us what *your* research is about?"

Leaning back into his chair and putting his hand in his jacket, Dmitri pulled out a disk with the number "101" engraved on it, "Now, my story isn't quite as fancy as these two comrades, but it has to do with these disks. You see, I'm a collector by trade, and I've taken to collecting the Number Disks. This one in my hand here is just one of one hundred and twelve different Numbers." He put the disk back in his jacket and continued, "I don't have any fancy sealing techniques to bring to the table, but what I do have is on that table over there."

The group all got up and headed over to the table where a blanket covered a pile of something. Dmitri grabbed the corner of the cloth and pulled it off the table in a flourish. What was once covered was now revealed to be a series of stacked disks, all with numbers engraved on them. Also on the table were six swords, all of differing design and all with Number Disks embedded in their blades. There was also a strange device that looked like it could combine Number Disks to create other Number Disks.

"This here is my collection of Number Disks." Dmitri pulled out the "101" he had put in his pocket and set it on one of the piles, "I suppose my contribution to this whole project would have to be these disks and their inherent powers. These could be used as fluxion cores. However, I do have to make a confession."

"What is that?" Albert inquired.

"My collection is one disk short." He pointed to the very last pile, "I have yet to find the '112' disk anywhere, and since it is so incredibly rare, I was hoping I could use some military resources to try and find it."

James spoke up, "Couldn't we just make the '112' disk? Are there no methods to produce these disks?"

"Comrade, I'm impressed. That is a possibility, although-" going over to the strange device, Dmitri continued, "this device is the only thing that would be able to create something like that, and even though this device is incomplete, the amount of effort that would have to go into creating the '112' disk could be more than anyone has ever encountered before. Besides, I have heard rumors of where the '112' disk might be located."

Prodding on, Albert asked, "Where do you think it might be?"

"I've heard of an island in the clouds, where balance is the norm, and peace is considered best practice. It's called the Island of Stability. The '112' disk is supposedly on the exact center of the island."

From the back of the group, a timid figure quietly spoke, "I believe I may have a map to that island."

Most of the group missed it, but Dmitri caught what was said, almost as a double take, "Wait! Who said that?" He turned around to the group and the rest of the people parted to reveal a small man in a bowler hat with his hand half raised.

"I did. I have come into possession of a map to a Treasure Island which matches that description."

Albert stepped forward, "Excellent. Then Dmitri and Dr. Robert will head to the Island of Stability to complete Dmitri's Number Disk collection."

Dr. Robert was hesitant, "Um, do you think perhaps someone else could go in my place?"

Slapping the frail man on the back, Dmitri was insistent, "Nonsense, Doc! We're going on a grand adventure." He let out a loud shout, which scared Dr. Robert, "I'm so excited to finally complete my collection!"

Frenzied banging was heard at the door as Albert went over to see what the racket was all about. When he opened the door, he was just about to tell whoever was on the other side that they were interrupting a secret meeting when he noticed it was Herbert and Jules.

They looked absolutely ragged, and slightly burned as they stood there, hair wet, shirtless, and out of breath. Behind both of them, they carried their shirts, knotted and bulging with glass orbs filled with blood. When he recognized the two researchers, Albert opened the door a little wider and slid out into the hallway, "Herbert! Jules! You have returned with Noah's collection of Bloodfluxion cores." Noticing that they weren't quite happy about returning to the Library of Delaxanair, he asked, "What is wrong?"

In unison, the two men answered, "We may have a problem."

As the three Naturals traveled along the bank of the Olympus River, Penny was asking a barrage of questions to try and get to know her traveling partners, "So, where did you guys find your power cores?"

Tecumseh, once again trying to show off, answered first, "There's a labyrinth set within the Holy Cliffs outside of where I used to live. I went in there and powered through the maze, and this Hellfire orb was my prize. Well, at least one of my prizes. Take a look at this!" While still walking, his body began to transform. The changes started happening from his feet and worked upward until he stood as an impressive, nine foot tall half-man, half-bull creature, "When I take on this form, I gain the strength of a bull, which means I'm probably as powerful as twenty men put together!"

Politely nodding and smiling, Penny said, "That's nice, Tecumseh. What about you, Benjamin?"

"Well, I'm not so impressive as to have two power cores, but I did receive this Skybolt orb from a friend of mine who helped me figure out some of my powers. How about yourself, Penny?"

Slightly blushing that he had even asked, she answered, "I received this Seawave orb when I turned six. It was a birthday present from my parents. Six years later I received an animal core, like Tecumseh has."

"Oh? What animal?"

"It's a little embarrassing."

"We won't tell anyone, will we Tecumseh?"

"Nope. Not a word." Tecumseh made a motion of zipping his mouth closed as Benjamin motioned with an invisible lock and key.

Glancing down at the river, Penny mumbled, "A trout."

Benjamin was impressed, "Really? That's actually pretty cool. Can you swim upstream?"

Once again, Penny blushed, but it stayed a little longer than it did previously, "Well, I never tried it before, but I guess I might be able to."

"Why don't you go downstream and give us a demonstration?"

"Sure!" Penny handed her trident to Tecumseh and her bag to Benjamin as she jumped into the river. Through the clear water, the guys could see her legs start to grow scales and fuse together. Soon, the bottom half of her body was like that of a fish. Swimming downstream quickly, the guys lost sight of her and were curious as to when she would be coming back.

Some time passed and they wondered if anything was wrong. Looking at the rushing stream, then at each other, they both decided to start heading downstream along the bank of the river. Just as they started walking, Penny came leaping up the creek, jumping out of the water and quickly gaining headway against the opposing current. When she arrived where Benjamin and Tecumseh were standing, Benjamin was impressed, "What do you know! You *can* swim up-"

"You guys need to come with me, quickly!"

"What is it?"

"No time to explain!" When she jumped back into the river and swam away, Tecumseh turned into a bull and charged along the banks. Benjamin crouched down and closed his eyes as he focused his energy into his legs, which sprung him into the air. More confident in what he was capable of, he picked a spot to land that wouldn't damage anything. However, while he was in the air, he suddenly saw what Penny was talking about.

A little further down the river, there laid a village that had been destroyed. Most of the houses and huts were burnt, and there was an enormous hole in the middle of the settlement. Landing with a resounding boom outside of the village, Benjamin ran over to where Tecumseh and Penny had stopped. She was shaking her head and kept saying, "No no no-" as she knelt over the limp and lifeless body of one of the villagers who had collapsed at the edge of the river.

Tecumseh looked a little nervous as he stood behind Penny, "I'll go see if I can find anyone else around to help . . . or at least find some supplies." He quickly disappeared into the village as Benjamin came over to Penny.

"When I swam downstream, I came across this guy and he told me that someone had attacked his village. He looked in pretty bad shape, so I told him to just lie still until I could come back with some help." She sniffed back a sob, "I didn't want him to die while I was gone." Becoming frustrated, she placed her open right palm on his chest and shouted, "Just let me know who did this to you!" The man's chest began to undulate, back and forth underneath her hand.

Benjamin knew what she was doing, but he knew she was only pumping the man's blood for him. He knew that in order for him to live again, his heart had to be restarted. Pushing Penny to the side, Benjamin stepped in. In protest, she yelled, "What are you doing?"

Sternly answering, Benjamin calmly said, "Just let me take care of this." Rubbing his index and middle fingers together between both of his hands, sparks began to form. As he pulled his hands apart, an arc of electricity appeared between the two sets of fingers. With a sharp jab, Benjamin struck the man's chest, letting the arc of energy cross his heart. The man's body immediately tensed up and, as it landed back on the ground, the man gasped loudly for air as his eyelids popped open.

Penny was relieved and dumbfounded at the same time, "What did you do, Ben?"

"I restarted his heart. He should be all right now, assuming he wasn't out for too long." The man grabbed Benjamin's arm and a look of thanks and relief swept across his face, "Are you all right?"

"I am now, thanks to you." Looking over to Penny, he recognized her and said, "And especially thanks to you."

"Who did this to your village?" Benjamin inquired.

"It was some sort of monster, covered in fire. He erupted from the ground and asked to see our leader. When he went in to our leader's hut, it wasn't but two minutes until the hut was on fire and the monster had started setting other huts ablaze. Then he charged off into the forest, leaving a path of destruction in his wake."

Penny was curious, "But why did he set fire to everything? What did your leader say to him?"

"I don't know, but when the villagers saw their houses on fire, they grabbed everything they could and evacuated. I'm actually a little surprised that no one died."

Benjamin couldn't help but scoff, "Speak for yourself."

Chuckling at his near-death experience, the man agreed, "OK, so maybe I pushed myself a little too hard in trying to get all the fires out. But to my credit, they *are* all out now."

"You should probably get some rest, then try and find the rest of your village. I'm sure a lot of people are worried about you."

"You're probably right." When the man couldn't manage to get up, Benjamin and Penny helped him to his feet, then into one of the less damaged huts. When he had laid down, the man said, "I can't thank you enough for saving my life. Is there anything I can do for you?"

"In fact, there is something you can do. Can you tell us about the Angular Mangroves? How far away are they from here?"

"You're in luck, mister. This village is just north of the Angular Mangroves. To that point, this is an agricultural village that has been harvesting the square fruit of the mangroves for many generations."

"Excellent! Do you happen to know anything about the i-World? It is supposedly connected to the mangroves."

"Only rumors. It is said that if you find a tunnel underneath the trees, you should not go through it, as those who have done so in the past have never returned." The man saw Benjamin was deep in thought, "But I'm sure there's nothing like that out there. Why don't you go ahead and make your way to the mangroves? I think I should be able to take care of myself after some rest."

Nodding and making his way out of the hut, Benjamin went looking for Tecumseh. As Penny turned to follow him, the man spoke, "Thank you, miss. I owe my life to your quick thinking." She smiled and nodded as she left the hut, jogging to catch up to Benjamin. When they had left, the man laid down and immediately fell asleep.

Looking through the abandoned huts, Benjamin was having trouble finding Tecumseh. When Penny caught up to him, she noticed his concern. He shouted, "Tecumseh! Where did you go? We need to get moving."

From behind one of the huts, Tecumseh seemed to magically appear, "I'm here. Did you learn anything about the mangroves?"

"Yes. They're just south of here, so let's get going." As the three travelers made their way to the edge of the village, they could see the burnt path of the beast that attacked the village heading northwest. Stopping for a second of reflection, Benjamin wondered aloud, "I'm curious how many other villages ended up like this one?"

"It's just a natural part of life," Tecumseh remarked offhandedly. Both Benjamin and Penny turned and looked at him with concerned faces. A little flustered by their reaction, he caught himself, "Fire, I mean." Motioning out to the forest, he tried to explain, "Look at this forest, for instance. If fire didn't come through and burn out some of the death and decay, then the whole area would eventually suffer. Fire brings a new life to forests, and is a natural part of it."

Penny did not find Tecumseh's speech amusing, "Forests may be one thing, but villages and people's lives are something else completely."

Benjamin stepped in to avert the conflict, "Hey, let's just focus on our goal and get going. We don't have much daylight left." Wanting to end up on Benjamin's good side, Penny silently dropped the argument, grabbed her trident from Tecumseh, and began walking along the river once again. With a quick look at Tecumseh, Benjamin turned and followed after Penny, at which point he returned her bag. Tecumseh breathed a sigh of relief as he gripped his pitchfork and brought up the tail of the group.

○

The group of researchers stood on the roof of the library in the cool of the evening and watched as the sea to the north drained through the Q-Portal. Herbert explained, "We really didn't have many options at our disposal."

With a shout, Albert gained control of the situation, "All right! That is enough observing, let us get inside and try to figure out how to solve this problem." As the researchers were herded off of the roof, Albert grabbed Herbert and calmly told him what to do, "You need to go downstairs and get a message out to our leaders. Tell them that we have a situation which requires a company of their soldiers." Nodding in understanding and rushing down the stairs, Herbert was glad someone else was taking control of the problem he had created.

Back in the room where the classified discussion was taking place, Albert laid out what they knew, "All right, everyone. We have an open Q-Portal which links between here and the volcano of Sievuvus. While most Q-Portals close after someone has gone through them, this one remains open because the flow of water is keeping the door from shutting. Considering that Sievuvus is in the Pythagorean Triangle, how do we solve this problem?"

James and Garland realized they had a solution, "I've got it!" they shouted simultaneously.

"*Wunderbar*, what do we do?"

James took the lead, "Since the Pythagorean Triangle already looks like snakes, and they are already in an uroboros configuration, we'd just need to modify something at the site to seal the door closed."

Making sure all his bases were covered, Albert asked, "Even though there are two more snakes in the uroboros configuration, would this be a problem?"

"It shouldn't be. After all, we're just trying to seal it, and the ring of snakes should be all we need. But I'm not quite sure how we can complete the seal."

Garland offered his part of the solution, "Perhaps if we give the snakes some fangs, then it would represent the biting action to complete the circuit of the uroboros." He looked over at the table holding the Number Disks, "And I think I know what we can use as fangs."

"Now, wait a minute!" Dmitri yelled, gaining everybody's attention, "Everyone was given a white key *and* a black key. Why didn't you use the white key?"

Jules looked ashamed at this piece of information. He stared at his feet as he mumbled, "I lost it."

"You *lost* it? Well, isn't that just convenient."

Albert put his hand up to stop Dmitri's diatribe, "That is enough. We will just have to look for it when we are done sealing the Triangle."

Herbert burst through the door and spoke between breaths, "We've. Got. A company."

Pushing his way past Herbert, a high ranking officer of the Army of Amedeo made his way into the room, the four stars pinned on his uniform made it quickly known that he was the highest ranked person there, "My name is Gulogulo of Amedeo's Army. I was training some recruits nearby when I was informed of your predicament. How are we going to solve this, gentlemen?" Something on the table caught his eye, and he rushed over to confirm that what he was seeing was real, "This is incredible! Are these the six Noble Swords?"

Dmitri smugly sauntered over to the table, "That's right. They're part of my collection of Number Disks."

"I've tried to find these swords for years! When they disappeared from the 6 Kingdoms, I thought they were gone forever. And they're all here! The 1st Kingdom's Orange Crush, the 2nd Kingdom's Red Flood, the 3rd Kingdom's Violet Violence, the 4th Kingdom's Blue Division, the 5th Kingdom's Yellow Flash, and the 6th Kingdom's Green Legion." Turning to Dmitri, Gulogulo congratulated him, "You're a much greater collector than I am."

Approaching the table, Garland tried to delicately breach the subject of their solution, "Sir, we are going to use those swords to seal the Pythagorean Triangle."

"What? How? And more importantly, *why*?"

"Well, sir, we're suggesting that these six swords will be the fangs of the three snakes which will complete a circuit to seal an open Q-Portal."

"But these are the legendary swords! Each a masterpiece of the swordsmith Luvnac; you're surely not suggesting that we use them in this way?"

"Unfortunately, yes. Since the metals Luvnac used were sensitive to fluxion cores, it stands to reason they would make great conductors to complete a fluxion seal."

The color suddenly dropped out of Gulogulo's face, as he realized the swords he had been looking for would soon be out of his reach forever. Taking a deep breath and letting it out slowly, he calmed his nerves, "All right, I'll do it, but I want to make sure that anyone else who might find these swords won't be able to use them. We'll break each sword into pieces and use the tips of the blades for this operation. This way we can keep the Number Disks and also solve this problem."

Looking over to the doorway, Gulogulo motioned for some of his men to come in and grab the swords as he made his way over to Albert, "I don't necessarily like this plan, but if it's for the greater good of keeping this Army's reputation intact, then I'll do it."

"*Wunderbar.* Let us get you some keys and you will be on your way." Heading over to the piano, Albert lifted a few of the keys, "Herbert, Jules, what keys did I give you before?"

Pulling out the black key, Jules handed it over to Albert who examined it and gave it a flick to listen to its tone, "Ah, A4 and A4 flat. Which means-" he picked out one of the keys hidden within the piano keys, "B4 will get you close." He handed the white key to Gulogulo, who turned and motioned for his men to follow him. They saluted, then followed him into the hallway.

Albert was close behind, "Just put the key in the keyhole and step through the door once it opens. It is as simple as that. To return, merely do the same thing at the place where you come out." Without hesitation, Gulogulo put the key in the keyhole and waited for the door to open. The door swung swiftly open, revealing a black void. Before he went through the door, Albert had one last request, "And if you can find another one of those white keys out there, please bring it back with you."

With a nod, Gulogulo began to rush his soldiers through the open door. When the company arrived on the other side of the Q-Portal, they glanced up at the black silhouette of the mountain they had to climb. Some of them winced at the sight of it. Sensing the urgency conveyed by the researchers, Gulogulo ordered his men, "Come on, soldiers! Let's get up there ASAP!"

With a salute, the company shouted, "Yes, sir!" and began marching up the switchbacks to the top of the nearest mountain. Gulogulo saw this as a perfect opportunity to train his troops, so he ran them up the mountain with no breaks, except for those at the front of the line, and he only allowed them for the amount of time it took for the rest of the line to pass the frontrunners. While the trail was certainly long, and it took a while to get to the top, before they knew it, the company had arrived at the summit of Boa Peak.

"At ease, men," Gulogulo gave the order as he stood on the summit, inspecting the situation he had to fix. The volcano between the mountains was erupting, but not with lava. Instead, a steady flow of water was spilling over the top of the conical peak. The area between the mountains was starting to fill up with water, and there appeared to be a half-sunken enormous boat that had crashed upside down in the rapidly forming lake.

Pointing at two of his men, both of whom held a sword, he ordered, "Come with me." Making his way down into the cave of Boa Peak, Gulogulo led them into the darkness. Lighting a match, he got a look of the cave and saw it was strangely well made. Definitely too well made for nature to have done so. In the middle of the cave sat a pedestal. He decided it was as good a place as any. Taking one of the swords from his men, he drove it into the pedestal and bent it toward him. With a swift punch on the broad side of the sword, the weapon snapped in half.

Observing the process, the two soldiers repeated it with the other sword and handed the broken handle to their superior. Quickly perusing the cave, Gulogulo arrived at the conclusion that there was nothing else of importance there. When they exited the cave, he sighed as he held the hilts of the two broken swords, each one still having their Number Disk embedded within the metal of the blade that remained, "Blue Division and Orange Crush. Your lives were far too short."

When he arrived back at the top of the mountain, he gave his orders, "All of you split up. I want one of the soldiers who was just with me down there to follow one of the groups. They will give you instructions on what to do. Also-" he held up the white key, "be on the lookout for another one of these keys."

As the soldiers split up, he yelled after them, "Time is of the essence, men!" He watched as his company split up and made their way to the other peaks. As he sat atop Boa Peak, he took a look around at his location. With Sievuvus no longer spewing smoke into the sky, one could see far into the distance as well as the starry sky above, lit with the light of the full moon.

Not being too familiar with geography, he couldn't recognize any of the natural landmarks in the darkness. He did, however, notice the one man-made wonder which stood tall and proud, blocking out many of the stars to the north: The Tower of Lebab. He knew a little bit about the tower, like how it was built as a means to unify the nations under one language. Unfortunately, old habits die hard and the new language, along with the construction of the tower, were abandoned. He knew the Tower was now an asset of Amedeo's Army, but he never cared enough to get an explanation as to why.

As Gulogulo glanced down at his hands and the shattered blades he held in them, he began to wonder how he could get the swords remade. He knew if he went to Luvnac directly with the broken weapons, the master swordsmith would refuse his request outright. Perhaps if he had someone else try and fix the swords, he could add them to his collection. Maybe not as swords he would actually use, but swords he would hold as trophies. He just shook his head as he realized that only Luvnac could work with swords of this caliber.

Gulogulo snapped out of his sword daydream when he heard the faint and distant sounds of cheering coming from the other peaks. He looked down into the area confined by the Triangle and saw that the water had stopped erupting out of the volcano. It had actually begun to descend into the mouth of Sievuvus and the surface was now no longer visible from where he was standing. He had accomplished his mission and, even though it was somewhat banal for his rank, he now realized the reality of the power of the fluxion research that was going on for his eventual benefit.

When the company had regrouped on the top of Boa Peak, he congratulated his men, "Good work, soldiers. Now, let's go back." The men were definitely tired from the long night, but also pumped with adrenaline due to the exciting task they had accomplished. When they made it back through the Q-Portal and stood in the Library of Delaxanair, most of the night had passed. Standing before the researchers, General Gulogulo gave his report, "Crisis averted, as per the suggestions of this group."

The researchers were ecstatic; especially Herbert and Jules, who no longer had to worry about their mistake. Albert approached the General and asked, "Did you find the missing key?"

"I didn't find anything in the cave I searched. How about the rest of you?"

The two soldiers who had joined him in the cave of Boa Peak stepped forward, "Sir, we did not find any such object in either of the other caves, sir." Albert looked a little concerned about losing one of these special keys, but he decided that if there was anywhere to lose it, the Pythagorean Triangle was definitely one of the lower traffic areas to do so.

"If you no longer need our assistance, I shall be taking this company back to camp."

"*Nein*, we are good. Thank you for your hard work, General Gulogulo." As the company left the library, they could be heard cheering as Gulogulo promised to give them all some extra leave for their efforts.

Heading deeper into the Angular Mangroves proved to be a difficult task and Benjamin began to wonder how the villagers ever managed to harvest anything from this unyielding forest. The strangest thing about the forest was that its name fit it to a tee. While most trees have very natural curves and spread out above and below in very fluid forms, these trees were very sharp, abrupt and angular. And while there were a variety of angles that the roots and branches chose to take, most of the trees tended to prefer the right angle to anything else. To top off the apt descriptive adjective, the fruit found on said trees was perfectly cubic.

Since the Olympus River had terminated in the marshy area which the Angular Mangroves thrived in, the three travelers had to slog through quite a bit of muck. With the added detriment of no distinguishable path, no posted signs, and a rapidly increasing fog, Benjamin was quickly becoming leery about heading into the swamp. When he felt something on his back, he nearly jumped, until he realized it was Penny's hand, "I'm not sure these are the best conditions to find what we're looking for," she whispered.

"I'm going to have to agree with you there."

When Tecumseh caught up to the two, he passed them and felt that now was his time to shine, "Are you two chickening out on me? What's the problem? Is it the fog? I can deal with that." Lifting his pitchfork into the air, the tines caught fire and helped clear up some of the fog and to provide light where the setting sun had once illuminated their way.

Penny peeked around Benjamin and saw that, even though the area was lit better, the shadows produced by Tecumseh's flame danced and moved in ways that made her uncomfortable. Before she could voice her opinion, Benjamin pointed ahead of them, "Hey, look at that!" As he ran off, Penny was close behind, which left Tecumseh in the back yet again.

When Benjamin stopped, he stood before a large mangrove tree. While most of the other trees had roots starting about shin height, this enormous specimen had roots that started well above their heads. After Penny and

Tecumseh had caught up to Benjamin, he kept standing in front of the mangrove, mesmerized by its size, "It almost looks like an archway." Looking down from the tall roots of the tree, he noticed the supposed arch seemed to continue on into the darkness under the tree.

For some reason, Benjamin was inexplicably drawn to the darkness. As he started walking forward, Penny was concerned, "What are you doing, Benjamin!?" He stopped walking, but still looked dazed. "Benjamin!" she shouted again. With a jolt, Benjamin broke out of his trance, "What's going on, Ben?"

"I'm not sure. But I feel this is the way we need to go."

"Don't you remember what that villager said? He said a tunnel under the trees usually led to people disappearing. I'd really like it if you wouldn't disappear on us."

"But that's just it, don't you see?" Gesturing with an open hand to the square tunnel made up of mangrove roots, Benjamin continued, "Rumors are meant to hide something bigger. Something important. If you let fear take ahold of you, then just think of all the things you'd never get to understand. Besides-" he now extended his other hand to Tecumseh and Penny, "I won't disappear from you if you're with me."

Resigning herself to push down her fear, Penny stepped forward and made her way into the tunnel. With a nod of his head, Benjamin motioned for Tecumseh to follow along. Sighing with a sense of futility, Tecumseh followed Benjamin into the mangrove tunnel.

As the three strolled single file into the darkness ahead of them, the roots of the trees above them began to grow closer and closer together until they formed a solid wall of vegetation on each side, as well as above them. At this point, Tecumseh's pitchfork torch came in very handy, not necessarily for lighting their way, since the tunnel was straight and had no forks, but instead to keep the group's courage up.

It seemed like the trio had been walking for some time, so Tecumseh turned his head around to survey behind them and see how far they had come. He could no longer see any light, and now they were surrounded on both sides by darkness. He kept walking forward until he bumped into Benjamin, "Hey, why did we stop?" When Tecumseh turned around to look, he knew why. In front of them was a curved archway made of stone. In the keystone of the arch was embedded a circular disk with the symbol of "–" engraved on it.

"I think we may have arrived."

"Arrived? Arrived where?"

"At the entrance of the i-World." Once again, Benjamin was pulled by an invisible force into the darkness beyond the archway, and Penny wasn't far behind. They both stopped when they came upon a man standing on dry ground. The man had a very high forehead and a very neatly trimmed goatee. An " i " was emblazoned on his chest. When Tecumseh caught up, Benjamin turned around and asked, "Weren't you just behind us?"

"Yeah, but I'm not nearly as eager to tread into unknown territory as you are."

"Silence!" the mysterious man's voice was booming, and it immediately gained the trio's attention. "I am Sigmund, gatekeeper of the Imaginary World." As he spoke, the fog filled in behind them, leaving everyone in a small, disorienting circle, "Before me, I have three travelers who should wish to pass through this i-World, is this correct?"

Benjamin was the first to answer with confidence, "Yes."

Penny was a little more hesitant, "Yes."

Tecumseh was ready to just get on with it, "Yes."

"Each of you has a trial ahead of you, which must be handled alone, as each test is a personal battle between you and your inner self. Your fears, your desires, your weaknesses. Please choose your path wisely." Once again, the fog seemed to move as it revealed three stone archways behind where Sigmund was standing.

Tecumseh was tired of being the last of the group, so he charged on past Sigmund and directly into the left archway, which immediately disintegrated after he had passed through it. With the light of his pitchfork gone, Benjamin opened his hand and let a spark jump across his fingers, creating an arc between his thumb and index finger. There was less light than before, but it was sufficient, "Go ahead, Penny," Benjamin urged.

Penny was about to protest, "Don't worry. I'll be right behind you, and we'll meet up on the other side." Penny nodded as she chose the middle path, the arch falling apart much in the same way it had done when Tecumseh passed through. With only one path remaining, Benjamin chose the right path and passed through the last arch. When the structure crumbled behind him, leaving him in a smothering darkness, Benjamin knew this would be no ordinary trial.

○

With a sigh of relief, Albert closed the door to the windowless room and turned to the researchers, "Now, where were we?"

"I was about to head out with Dr. Robert to try and complete my collection," Dmitri frankly replied as he set down six Number Disks on the table. The same six Number Disks that had been in the six Noble Swords. Dmitri didn't care that he no longer had the weapons, as long as he had his Number Disks.

Nervously trying to delay the inevitable, Dr. Robert quietly interjected, "*Nae*, I believe the rest of the group has to introduce themselves, then Albert will tell us why we were gathered together." Dmitri grunted and rolled his eyes in exasperation.

A feminine voice seconded the motion, "That's right! Some of us haven't even been introduced yet." Everyone turned to behold the only woman in the room, her thin face set in an expression of haughty superiority. "In fact, I'm surprised I wasn't introduced *first*, since General Amedeo personally asked me to join this group of researchers."

Murmuring began to fill the room as Albert tried to be the mediator, "All right, Mary. Will you-"

"My name is Mary, and my specialty has to do with the human body." Shoving Albert aside, Mary took center stage in the small room, "I have spent many years researching ways to repair the body, even unto being able to reattach severed limbs. Through my research, I have found ways to make men stronger and faster. Amedeo approached me to help make his soldiers into the best the world has to offer, and I see now that he means to do so through these fluxions."

"*Wunderbar*, Mary. Now let us move on to the last-"

"Oh, you don't have to introduce him. He's my assistant."

"*Ja*, but I do believe that-"

Sighing in frustration, Mary yielded, "Fine! Mathison, *go*."

Stepping forward, the hunched man bowed and looked up, but did not look anyone in the eyes, "I am Mathison. I have helped Miss Mary with her research, and Amedeo has tasked me with a project to make a large amount of statues into soldiers."

Mary scoffed, "I'm not sure why he asked him to do that. It's probably something to keep him busy and out of our way."

Staring at his feet, Mathison mumbled, "Yes, ma'am."

As everyone stood there in awkward silence, Albert took this as a sign that all the introductions were over, "*Wunderbar*, now that everyone knows everyone else, it is finally time I tell you about the top secret part of this project."

Since they had kind of burst in on this meeting, Herbert asked, "Um, do we need to leave now?"

"*Nein*, you both have proven yourselves already and should be included in this important tasking. In fact, bring those orbs of blood over to the table with Dmitri's Number Disks on it." As Herbert and Jules lugged their makeshift bags over to the table, Albert began, "Now, we all know it is important to work in steps. It would be too easy to jump straight to the end result, but it is also important to know what you're working toward."

When Herbert and Jules sat down, Albert made his way to the table, "Our first step is to provide these fluxion cores with working seals so Amedeo's soldiers can enhance their power. As we have seen today, the uroboros seals discovered by James and Garland do work and we shall use them as the basis of this first step."

Picking up a blood orb and the "99" Number Disk, Albert continued, "However, the endgame that Amedeo would like to see is a fluxion core which combines the powers of all fluxions. This core shall be known as The Omnipotence." At this juncture, Albert put both of his hands together. Now holding the two fluxion cores between his hands, he added, "And yet, in order for there to be a balance, a way to make sure that if The Omnipotence falls into the wrong hands, it can be defeated, we must also create another core that can split The Omnipotence into its individual pieces."

Pulling his hands and the fluxion cores held therein apart, Albert set the cores back on the table as he wrapped up, "Since these two cores and their resulting seals will be more powerful than anything else out there, everyone's expertise will come into play. James and Garland's sealing techniques to keep the power in check. Dmitri's knowledge of the Number Disks. Mary's understanding of the human body. These are just a few examples, but each one of you has an important role in this project. And since these products will be the most powerful fluxions, we shall call them by a different name than the rest of the ordinary powers. They shall be known as 'Fluents'."

Chapter 4
Imaginary Number

Tecumseh heard the arch crumble behind him, but kept walking forward, despite the fact that he could not see where he was going. The fog had become thick and almost suffocating. Tecumseh couldn't even tell if he was in a large clearing with Benjamin and Penny or if he was all alone in a cramped room.

Suddenly, the fog cleared up and Tecumseh found himself with a child, around the age of six, standing in front of him. The child looked strangely familiar, with his shock of unkempt red hair resting on top of a mischievous face. Looking down at the child, Tecumseh gruffly asked, "Who are you?"

"Me? I am it."

"This isn't a game of tag, kid. Who are you really?"

When the arch crumbled behind Penny, she quickly turned around and tried to run back to where she thought the broken threshold once was. However, as she ran, she began to realize that she should have come across the door quite some time ago.

Already being somewhat nervous about heading into this mysterious area, Penny called out to her partners, "Benjamin! Tecumseh! Where are you guys?"

With her arms out in front of her, trying to feel her way through the dense fog, Penny stumbled into a small clearing in the clouds. Standing in the middle of the clearing was a young girl, about the age of six, with blonde hair and freckles, and wearing a blue dress.

Penny thought she recognized the girl, but was unsure as she asked, "Who are you?"

"Me? I am it."

"That can't be right. You look like me when I was a little girl."

The crumbling of the arch was the last sound that Benjamin heard. With a fog so incredibly thick, all the sounds which normally would accompany being in a marsh were now strangely absent.

Benjamin couldn't see but a foot in front of him, and this aspect of the fog was perhaps the most disorienting. In such situations, Benjamin knew to cautiously move forward, as standing still hardly solved anything.

Without warning, the fog cleared and before him stood a boy of about six, barefoot, wearing shorts and holding the string of a kite, which could be seen far above them in the void within the dense fog.

Benjamin recognized himself in the boy, but to make sure, still asked, "Who are you?"

"Me? I am it."

Benjamin thought this might be part of the trial, "*It*, is it?"

"It." The child was adamant.

"Fine. I don't really care anyways. Now, could you please tell me where to go from here, or do I have to find my own way?"

"You can't leave me until you've answered my question."

Tecumseh rolled his eyes and sighed, "Whatever. Ask away."

"You love Penny, don't you?"

This immediately flustered Tecumseh, "What do you mean?"

"It's pretty obvious."

"Oh? And how so?"

"The way you act around her. Trying to be tough, trying to impress her."

"Look, I'm just trying to get her to notice me. She's so into Benjamin, I can't seem to get a word in edgewise."

"Have you tried being bad?"

"What?"

"Girls love a bad boy. You've got to overshadow Benjamin by doing something outrageous. Something a good guy like Ben wouldn't do."

"It." The child was adamant.

"OK, it. Can you tell me where to find my friends? I think I may be lost in here and I'd like to leave soon."

"You can't leave me until you've answered my question."

Penny knelt down to the child, "What is your question?"

"You love Ben, don't you?"

Penny blushed as she looked away, "H-H-How do you know that?"

"It's pretty obvious."

Still looking away, she thought about the last day and how she was impressed by Benjamin's knowledge and kindness. Looking back at the child, she said, "I suppose it is."

"I don't see why you don't give Tecumseh a chance, I mean, why go for a guy out of your league, when you've got one who obviously wants you to notice him. He's totally into you."

A grimace went across Penny's face, "I know. But he's not really my type."

"It." The child was adamant.

"Is there anything you need from me so I can move on from here? I'm guessing that you're a trial I have to pass."

"You can't leave me until you've answered my question."

Nudging the glasses up his nose, Benjamin said, "Shoot."

"You love info, don't you?"

Benjamin was a little confused, "Yes . . . and your point is?"

"It's pretty obvious."

"Enlighten me."

"You never have any fun. All work and now play makes Ben a dull boy, after all."

"But if we do not learn, we cannot grow up, young man."

"Growing up is boring. You need more excitement in your life. You need to be more impulsive, less calculating."

Now Benjamin felt like he was lecturing, "Being impulsive is the hobby of someone with too much time on their hands. You need to plan your life so that no time goes to waste. Time is money after all, and people don't like to waste it."

"It's unfortunate that you've learned so much, but still so little about women."

Benjamin was taken a little aback by the sudden change in topic, "What do you mean?"

"Are you that dense? Why do you think Penny dropped everything she was doing, ran away from her family and joined you on a random journey?"

This question left Benjamin silent for a while. As the child stood there, staring at him, his kite fluttering high in the sky, Benjamin asked, "Is there anything else?"

"No. you may pass. But you must think about what we have discussed. After all, deep down inside you lies your most unchained desire, and I am it."

Benjamin squinted into the fog. He thought

"And what do you suggest?"

"Steal. Kill. Destroy. Or at least do those things in front of her for a change."

Now Tecumseh was starting to get mad. He pointed his pitchfork at the kid, "Listen, you little punk, I don't know how you know about that stuff, but I'd appreciate it if you wouldn't bring it up."

"Fine, Tecumseh. I really don't care either way. Besides, if things don't work out with Penny, you could always try her little sister. She was definitely checking you out."

"Look, I've got my priorities pretty well in check, kid. Now, are there any other questions?"

"No. You may pass. But you must think about what we have discussed. After all, deep down inside you lies your most unchained desire, and I am it."

Tecumseh watched as the child's image became hazy and eventually

What do you think would get Benjamin's attention?"

"You need to be more overt."

"That's a big word for a little kid."

"You know I'm right. Just like you noticed Tecumseh, why don't you use your . . . *ahem* . . . talents to attract Benjamin's attention?"

Penny didn't really like how often she was being embarrassed by this miniature version of herself, "Well, um"

"Trust me. Subtlety does not get through to men; you need to be more forward."

"I think I've had enough advice for one day. Do you have any more questions?"

"No. You may pass. But you must think about what we have discussed. After all, deep down inside you lies your most unchained desire, and I am it."

The child faded away into the fog, which soon enveloped Penny once melded into the wall of fog surrounding him. Just as quickly as it had opened up, the clearing in the fog was absorbed back into the cloud.

A glowing archway appeared in front of him, and Tecumseh took it as a sign that this was the way he needed to go. Once again, he passed through the arch as it crumbled behind him.

This time there were no clouds, only a vast black expanse that seemed to stretch out from him in every direction. As he walked forward, the only sound he could hear were his footsteps.

When he stopped for a moment to try and utilize his Hellfire orb to light his path, he noticed that the footsteps continued. Quickly spinning around in every direction, Tecumseh tried to see who else was there with him.

Soon, a shadowy figure approached. Tecumseh was relieved that by first impressions it was not that obnoxious kid. Still, since the shadow's identity wasn't immediately apparent to him, he

again. Still kneeling, Penny hugged her legs as her mind swam with the remnants of the frank discussion she had just had with what she believed to be her younger self.

The light from a glowing archway broke her concentration. As she hesitantly got up and approached the threshold, she hoped it would lead her out of this Imaginary World and reunite her with the rest of the group.

When the arch crumbled behind her, like it had done before, Penny found herself alone once more. This time she was not alone in the stifling moisture of the fog, but instead in the dizzying darkness of an endless expanse.

As she walked forward, she noticed that her steps echoed, but soon the echo began to have a life of its own, as it continued even when she had stopped.

A dark figure was walking toward her, and since it was not as disarming as a child, Penny pulled her trident out and took a defensive position as she

that maybe his glasses were the cause of the disappearance, so he took them off to clean them. When he put them on and looked again, there was no doubt: it had vanished.

However, in place of the child, a glowing archway stood, silently beckoning Benjamin to enter. When he passed through the arch, he wondered if there were going to be any more trials like the last one, or if he had passed safely through the Imaginary World.

As the arch crumbled behind him, Benjamin had a feeling that the trials were just beginning. Looking around at his new surroundings, Benjamin thought his eyes were playing tricks on him again, as the darkness gave no bearings.

Taking the first step forward, Benjamin immediately stopped when he noticed that the sound of his steps hit his ears before his feet hit the ground. And they kept coming. A black silhouette appeared from the darkness ahead of him as Benjamin curiously asked, "Who are you?"

The sound was faint at first, but soon it became loud enough to be distinguished as a rather maniacal laugh. Benjamin's eyes darted around the darkness to try and see if he could find the source of the disembodied laughter.

Little cracks seemed to appear on the dark exterior of the figure, which spread bright color to the blackness adjacent, pulling in the laughter from the atmosphere.

Benjamin's eyes were inquisitive as he began to recognize the being's true form.

---

cautiously asked, "Who are you?"

From the darkness a quiet, cackling laugh arose and spun around Penny and the mysterious figure. With each step forward, Penny became more and more nervous as the shape began to come more into focus.

The shadow began to be filled up with color, like it was being poured into a container. At the same time, the laughter spiraled into the figure, giving it an ominous voice.

Penny's eyes became wide as she began to recognize the being's true form.

---

asked, "Who are you?"

A slow, deep laugh echoed throughout the darkness, changing direction and pitch seemingly at random. As the laugh traveled around Tecumseh, the figure gradually took shape.

First, the edges of the shadow became sharp, followed by a slow infusion of color that spread up from the figure's feet. The laughter seemed to get closer until it landed on the figure before him.

Tecumseh's eyes narrowed as he began to recognize the being's true form.

"Would you hurry up already?" Dmitri was yelling back over his shoulder at Dr. Robert, who looked immensely out of place in the rocky, mountain valley. While Dmitri wore his standard "tough-guy" clothes, which did well outdoors, Dr. Robert still wore the clothes of an academic, complete with bow tie and sport jacket. The bowler hat he usually fiddled with in his hands was placed squarely on his head, covering the neat part straight down the middle of his dark hair.

What added to Dr. Robert's out of place persona was the pack he was wearing. He was such a small man that the same pack which Dmitri was wearing caused Dr. Robert to hunch over. The pack was proportionate to Dmitri's frame, but seemed to be consuming the weaker doctor.

"I apologize, but this sort of thing is not really my area of expertise."

"Well, maybe I should have just copied down your map and went by myself."

"I don't think that would have been wise. There are intricacies to this map that even I'm unsure of."

"Whatever. At any rate, let's get to that cottage up ahead and ask where we are. I'd like to know how much further I've got to put up with you."

Dr. Robert stopped at the insult, "If that's truly how you feel, then maybe I'll let you figure it out by yourself."

Frustrated that he had been paired with someone so opposite his personality, Dmitri purposely backtracked to where Dr. Robert was standing. He sighed and said, "I'm sorry. Now, can we please get going?"

"Certainly."

The two travelers made their way along a path cleared through the rocks of a mountain top. And while the mountain was tall, the mountains surrounding it were taller, and were all topped with snow. The cottage they were heading toward was made entirely of stones, and was quite the impressive structure. Of course, with as many rocks as the original builder had to work with up above the tree line, it was no wonder the house was as big as it was. And yet, with the plethora of rocks still on the ground, the house could have undoubtedly been much bigger than it was.

As the two men came nearer to the house, they heard the sound of music flowing from its open windows. When Dr. Robert approached the front door and knocked, the music kept playing. Dmitri pushed him aside as he pounded on the door, which obviously did the trick as the music came to an abrupt stop.

The door opened a crack and the voice of an old man could be heard from further in the house, "Who is it, Junior?"

"It appears to be some travelers."

"Well, let them in!" Opening the door further, the young man motioned for the duo of researchers to enter. The old man they had heard earlier walked into the main foyer of the house with his arms wide open, "*Willkommen*, gentlemen! Have you been traveling long? Please, come in and make yourselves at home." His grey hair was combed back over his head, and his clean-shaven face was sharp and cheery. He wore lederhosen with some simple musical embroidery on the sides.

Making their way into the house, Dmitri and Dr. Robert found two other men, about the same age as the one who answered the door. They were both holding instruments, and it became obvious that the two empty seats, which held two more instruments, were for the old man and his son.

The old man was rushing around as fast as he could, but finally remembered that he had forgotten to introduce everybody, "You must forgive me, but I just realized you do not know whose house you are in. I am Strauss, and this is my house," he chuckled at his rhyme, "These are my sons, Pachelbel, Sebastian, and Junior."

Each son motioned at the mention of his name, and the order seemed to go from oldest to youngest. And while the youngest son looked the most like his father, with the exception of a handlebar moustache, Sebastian's face was considerably rounder and Pachelbel's hairline was unfortunately receding. "What can I do for you fine gentlemen?"

Dmitri quickly answered, "We'd like to know where we are, Strauss. We've just found ourselves in this area and we're a little disoriented."

"Ah, I understand completely. In fact, we were lost up here once, until we made the best out of our situation and merely built our house up here. Even though my family and I were just trying to survive, somehow the beautiful scenery made it all worthwhile." Realizing he was rambling, Strauss caught himself, "I'm sorry, I seem to have gotten off topic. You are currently in the Slap Mountains. In fact-" hobbling over to the window, he pointed out the tallest peak, its summit obscured by thick clouds, "that is the famous Meadow Peak, which is ironic because there are no meadows anywhere near it." Again, Strauss burst out in laughter, and didn't seem to mind that no one else was laughing with him.

Looking up at the imposing edifice, Dr. Robert began to smile, "That's our mountain."

"Excuse me?" Strauss wiped away a tear as his expression turned from one of laughter to one of confusion.

Rolling back his left sleeve, Dr. Robert revealed a map which was seared around his forearm. As everyone gathered around, he pointed out some text that wrapped around his wrist, "See here, where it says the island is 'of all countries and therefore, no countries'? Well, Meadow Peak is known precisely for that attribute." Looking up from his arm, Dr. Robert now pointed toward the mountain, "See how its formation is that of a pyramid shape? Each of those four ridges are the boundaries between four different countries. Since it lies on the exact center of those boundaries, it cannot be claimed by any of them, and yet it shares land with all of them."

Dmitri was starting to get excited, "So, we made it close after all. Those portals are something else, I've gotta say."

As Dr. Robert rolled his sleeve back down and Dmitri headed for the door, Strauss did not want to seem like the ungracious host, "Wait! You can't leave so soon. Would you care for some cheese? How about some hot chocolate?"

"Thanks, but we're actually on a bit of a schedule that we need to keep." Dr. Robert joined Dmitri at the door as the two exited the cottage. They hiked along the cleared path until they came upon a crossroads and a sign which pointed them in the direction of Meadow Peak. As they walked, Dr. Robert spoke, "This is very promising. When I originally got this map, I was confused by the phrase that talked about an island in the clouds, but now it makes sense."

"You mean, you originally thought that since it was an island, it had to be in the water, right?"

"Pretty much. But if you think about it, clouds are made of water, so I wasn't too far off; I just got the phase of the water wrong. After all, I would assume that on the top of a mountain which rises above the clouds, it would seem like you were on an island in a sea of those clouds. And yet-"

"And yet, what?"

"If I've read the map correctly, the island is supposed to be much larger than the peak of a mountain, considering most mountains don't have very expansive summits. In fact, some are only large enough for one or two people to stand on top at a time." The two travelers walked in silence for a while, "But I'm sure we'll figure it out when we get up there."

When they came to another fork in the trail, the sign informed them that the trail up to the summit of Meadow Peak was in fact the border between the 5th and 6th Kingdoms. Standing at the saddle of the ridge, Dr. Robert looked up at the climb he had ahead of him and began to lose his nerve, "Maybe I'll just let you climb to the top. I'm sure you can figure it out once you're up there."

Grabbing Dr. Robert's arm, Dmitri pulled him along the path, "Don't chicken out on me now, Doc. After all, you've got the map. Can't do much without that." Dr. Robert merely groaned.

○

"Who am I? I am I." As the words came out of the hazy figure, the veil was lifted, and before Tecumseh stood none other than himself.

"No, you are obviously me."

"I know who I am."

As Tecumseh tried to step past his doppelganger, the doppelganger moved with him, mirroring his every action.

"Please let me pass."

"And where will you go, exactly?" Looking around at the emptiness

"Who am I? I am I." Upon hearing these words, Penny saw her face directly in front of her, staring back with no expression.

"This is crazy, you look just like me. What's going on?"

"I know who I am."

Looking up and down at her mirror image, Penny became self-conscious. While she was an attractive woman, she only managed to see her imperfections over the features that made her beautiful.

"Who am I? I am I." The silhouette in front of Benjamin took its final form and soon he was standing face to face with himself in the darkness.

"I didn't think I had a twin."

"I know who I am."

Benjamin moved his hand, which caused the person in front of him to mimic his motions. He was amazed at the synchronicity that this person had with him, and how this person had the same scar he had earned just a few surrounding him, Tecumseh gave in, "Fine. What do you want?"

"You can't leave me until you answer my question."

"This is starting to get really old. How many more quizzes do I have to take?"

"I'll ask the questions here."

"Then ask already."

"Why are you looking for the horde of the Order of the Dragon?"

Tecumseh's face scrunched up, "That's obvious. Because I'm poor. Because my family is poor. Anyone could tell you that you can't run a country without money, and I'm merely going to get some."

"Then what does that have to do with the villages you burned to the ground?"

"I'm keeping my answer. Even on the small scale of a village, if there's no one rich enough to support the village,

When she averted her eyes from the stare of her doppelganger, she asked, "Can I go now?"

"You can't leave me until you answer my question."

Penny sighed as she resigned herself, "Very well, how many questions do you have?"

"I'll ask the questions here."

Penny readied herself and met the gaze of her mirror image, "Ask away."

"Why did you leave your parents?"

"I'm twenty-five. I need to become an independent person at some point."

"But why now? Surely your parents provided for you. Surely they protected you. What would cause you to so impulsively decide to leave home?"

"Because there's more to this world than the farm life. I've been given this ability and I'd like to get out there and see what it can do."

"But why take the risk? Why head out on a journey that might have no end? Why join up with two guys who

days ago.

"I'm assuming I must pass some sort of test to move on, am I right?"

"You can't leave me until you answer my question."

"Another exam, huh? Will this one be oral as well, or will I have to write anything?"

"I'll ask the questions here."

"Fine by me. Let's begin."

"Why do you want to know more about your power?"

"Why indeed? I've got to live with this power, I might as well figure out what it can do."

"If this power is a mystery to you, you won't ever know if you've figured out everything about it."

"That's a risk I'll take."

"Exactly. You're always taking risks and those risks could get you killed. Life isn't something so glib that you should accidentally throw it away on something as trivial as power."

"But power isn't something trivial.

They might as well start over."

"And you think you're the one to administer judgment?"

"Why not?"

"I will warn you, Tecumseh: the path you are heading down will eventually lead to your destruction. If you stop right now, then there might be a chance that you'll be able to live a safe life."

"And who would ever want to live a safe life? That would be boring."

"Have it your way. All I am saying is that you have plenty of talent, and you are focusing it in the wrong directions."

"What do you know about anything?"

"I know more than you think. I am the constant observer. I am the restraint of it. *I* am I."

After a moment of silence, Tecumseh rudely asked, "Are you done?"

"Yes. You may pass." The figure began to fade to black into its darkened

you really know nothing about?"

"You can't gain anything if you don't take any risks once in a while."

"You are right, but the world is a large place; yet as such, it holds many unknown dangers."

"I guess they are merely ways that I can prove to myself I can lead an independent life."

"I am simply saying that I know your life might not end up the way you want it to. With love comes heartbreak. With power comes responsibility."

"And how do you know this?"

"I know more than you think. I am the constant observer. I am the restraint of it. *I* am I."

Penny was uncomfortable with how deep these conversations got, "Is that all?"

"Yes. You may pass." Just like her doppelganger began to appear from the

People spend their whole lives trying to gain it, whether through political means, physical means, or supernatural means."

"True, but with power comes responsibility. Not only responsibility to keep it under control and not exploit it, but responsibility to make sure that no one is hurt by it. And 'no one' tends to include its user."

A sudden twinge of pain ran through the scar on Benjamin's face. He touched it as he adjusted his glasses, "That's a good point, but sometimes we must use power so that evil can be conquered. After all, evil will prosper if good men do nothing. I'm sure that even someone like you knows this."

"I know more than you think. I am the constant observer. I am the restraint of it. *I* am I."

Noticing a pattern between the quizmasters, Benjamin asked, "That's it, right?"

"Yes. You may pass." Melding into the darkness that enveloped them, the doppelganger seemed to fuse with the surroundings until it was completely gone.

Once again, a glowing arch appeared out of the darkness and Benjamin walked through it, ready for the next trial. Although, he began to wonder if he would ever be able to leave this Imaginary World.

In stark contrast to the previous room of darkness, the next room past the crumbling arch was one of endless light. Closing his eyes to allow them time to adjust to the new surroundings, Benjamin stood still and listened.

Silence. No wind, no footsteps, no muffled sounds. Silence. Slowly opening his eyes, Benjamin checked to see if anyone else was there. No one. The area was as void as the last two initially were. Suddenly, a sound was heard. It was faint at first, but seemed to approach rapidly from all directions, rumbling high above his head. With a flash brighter than the brightness already in

feet upward, the darkness started swallowing up the figure in front of Penny until only an outline was left. Then that outline disappeared.

A new outline appeared a little further away from Penny. It was the outline of an arch, which was soon glowing with the same white light as the first one.

Knowing the drill by now, she passed through the arch and immediately had to shield her eyes. The new room was so bright that she didn't notice the same routine of the arch crumbling behind her.

Squinting at the abnormally bright expanse that surrounded her, Penny found herself once again alone in a strange place. Things had been so odd lately, she wasn't sure what to expect.

From above her came a flash of something sharp. When she jumped back and allowed the object to imbed itself in the floor, she saw that it looked like her trident.

form, eventually fading into the darkness that surrounded Tecumseh.

Appearing from the black was yet another glowing arch, which Tecumseh begrudgingly headed through. He was getting tired of the constant barrage of questions and wondered how many more tests he would have to take.

When he passed through the glowing arch, he was blinded by the bright light that now surrounded him. He now stood in a room that was in exact opposition to the room he had just been in.

Blinking a few times to readjust to the light, which still was too bright to directly look at, Tecumseh called out into the white void, "Whoever is out there to ask me questions about my personal life, let's get this over with quickly, OK?"

An explosion of fire erupted from the ground, which caused Tecumseh to back away and grab his pitchfork so that he could defend himself from the

the room, lightning struck behind Benjamin.

With each subsequent strike, the thunderclap caused Benjamin to recoil. Each assault seemed to come at a regular rhythm, so when the attacks stopped, he jumped away for no reason.

The break in the rhythm took a second to register in his mind before he realized that the battlefield was now completely devoid of sound. Tapping his right ear, Benjamin made sure that the extremely loud thunder had not made him go deaf. He now wondered if the trial was over and started looking for an exit.

Suddenly, a bolt of lightning struck directly in front of him, revealing another doppelganger who looked similar to the last one, but of a more ideal form.

"I'm confused. I thought you were from the last trial. Am I not done?"

"I am not the I you encountered

The ground began to shake underneath her feet, and as she regained her footing, Penny pulled out her own trident, ready to defend herself from the invisible assailant.

All at once, the rumbling faded, then stopped completely. Even though it was now absolutely quiet, the bright surroundings seemed to scream at Penny from every discernible direction.

With the only audible sounds being her heavy breathing and her heart beating in her ears, Penny started to panic. The silence was broken by a large shock in the ground, which caused her to stumble for a moment.

A wave of white approached, and standing on the crest was another doppelganger, similar to the previous one, except she was more beautiful and more skilled at controlling her powers.

"Aren't you I? Didn't I just pass your test?"

"I am not the I you encountered

---

unseen attacker.

Twice more the explosions of fire missed Tecumseh as he became adjusted to the light and adjusted to a fighting mode.

Then there was silence. This caught Tecumseh off guard more than the previous attacks had. He stood in the blinding white nothingness, waiting for the next assault. His muscles were starting to scream at him with the constant tension they seemed to be enduring.

The silence made Tecumseh nervous, and soon a single bead of sweat appeared on his forehead and rolled down his face.

A large explosion of fire erupted in front of him, and once more he beheld a figure who looked like himself, only slightly more attractive and powerful. The man almost looked like I.

"I've already answered your questions, what do you still want?"

"I am not the I you encountered

"Well, that took longer than I had expected." Dmitri sat down on a rock as he observed how far they had traveled on the trail up Meadow Peak. The stone cottage where they started was now a small, almost indistinguishable landmark, the light pouring out its windows being the only difference between it and the rest of the rocky terrain. Looking up, Dmitri saw nothing but clouds, almost as if he was sitting right below the roof of the sky. All around the area, the snowcapped peaks of other mountains stood silently beneath them, bathed in the moonlight.

Slowly but surely, Dr. Robert kept hiking up the ridge, one step after another, "I'm sorry if I'm not used to the arduous task of mountain climbing." He gasped for breath as he passed Dmitri, "After all, if people were meant to function this high above sea level, they would have been given bigger lungs." Not even hesitating for a moment, Dr. Robert continued to climb into the clouds.

"Hey! Don't you want to take a break?"

From the layer of clouds came the answer, "*Nae*, I've got too much momentum now to stop. I'm afraid that if I do stop, I won't be able to start again." The reply coming from the thick clouds almost made it sound like God himself was talking to Dmitri.

Sighing and taking one last look at the ground below, Dmitri got up and followed the path into the clouds. It was difficult to see due to the heavy cloud layer, on top of the fact that the only light out at that moment was the rising moon. Still, taking it slowly, Dmitri walked along, letting his eyes adjust to the low visibility. Fortunately, as had been the case all day, the path up Meadow Peak was as straight as the ridge it laid upon.

"How long do you think we'll be in the clouds, Rob?"

"First, that's *Doctor* Rob to you. I didn't spend five years of my life to not have that title included in my name. Secondly, I think the summit should be about one to two hundred feet above the point where we entered the clouds. At least, if I were to extrapolate the formation of the mountain I have seen up to this point."

Dmitri was a little taken aback by Dr. Robert's response. He didn't think the timid scientist was more than a weak body and introverted personality, but he was finding that at times the small man was so much more than that. Dmitri thought that maybe his rough personality was rubbing off on his partner, but it felt more like there was another, stronger person inside Dr.

Robert trying to get out.

Not one to enjoy any long stretches of awkward silence, Dmitri asked another question, even if he couldn't actually see who he was talking to, "So, how'd you get that map on your arm? It looks like it hurt."

"It did. When I was a child, I was playing with some kids near some seaside ruins when our ball fell down a hole. When I went to go get it, I reached down the hole and something latched onto my arm. I could feel it burning my skin, but I couldn't pull out my arm because the thing made it too big to pull out of the hole. When it finally let go, I had these strange markings on my arm. It wasn't until many years later that I realized that it was a map."

"So, why didn't you try and follow the map before now?"

"I suppose the traumatic experience of receiving the map did not make me eager to search for what it led to."

Dmitri was silent for a while as he couldn't really think of anything else to ask, so he just kept hiking up the trail, despite the silence. Actually, he was a little surprised that he hadn't caught up to Dr. Robert yet. Suddenly, he heard an exclamation ahead of him. "What is it?" he asked.

"We're at the top. Well . . . almost."

"What do you mean?" A few steps later, Dmitri almost ran into Dr. Robert as he stood on a small, flat area which was obviously the peak of the mountain as all four ridges seemed to converge on the square top. As they were still in the clouds, Dmitri thought they had just gone on a wild goose chase. That was, until he saw the pillar Dr. Robert was examining, "What is *that?*"

"I think this may be our way to the top."

"Aren't we already *at* the top?"

"Not if we're still in clouds. The island is described as an island in a sea of clouds, which would have to be above where we currently are. Here, just wait a second." Dr. Robert knelt down and lifted up the left leg of his pants where he fiddled with his left calf, eventually putting his hand into it and emerging with some matches.

Dmitri was certainly surprised, "Whoa! How did you do that?"

"Oh, this?" Dr. Robert rapped his knuckles against the leg, which produced a hollow, wooden sound, "I've got a fake leg, also attributed to my childhood." He laughed for a moment, "I guess I was a pretty accident prone kid." Dmitri couldn't help but smile at the loosening up of the Doctor, but now he knew what was causing the slight limp that Dr. Robert walked with.

With the matches in his right hand, Dr. Robert pulled back the sleeve which was covering the map on his left arm. Lighting a match, he held it up to his arm to examine the markings. Rolling his arm around to get the full text, he let out a pleased grunt when he found what he was looking for, "It says here 'Symmetry is balance. As below, so above.'"

"So, does this mean that from here, a whole other mountain is being held above us? A whole other mountain that we have to climb?"

"It would appear so." Putting out the match, Dr. Robert lit another as he examined the pillar on the peak. Eventually, he found what he was looking for, as he grabbed part of the column and pulled back a stone slab to reveal an opening in the pillar. The opening revealed a staircase spiraling up the shaft, which continued into the clouds. "Let's go."

Dr. Robert entered the staircase as Dmitri followed after him. After about ten steps up inside the pitch black column, the entire structure seemed to groan, creak, crack, and make any variety of noises to indicate that something bad was going to happen. Immediately turning around, Dr. Robert exclaimed, "Go back! Go back!" The two travelers hurriedly came back out on the top of the summit and waited for the noises from the pillar to stop.

"OK, so that's apparently *not* the way to do it." Dr. Robert pulled one more match from his pocket and lit it so he could further examine the entire pillar. Eventually, he found another door leading to another staircase, exactly opposite of the first one he had found, "Aha! I get it now."

"Get what?"

"The remark about symmetry not only applies to the mountain, which I can only assume looks like a large hourglass in its entirety, but also applies to everything else above this point. In order to remain balanced on this incredibly small area, we need to keep symmetry when we climb the staircase."

"That's great, but aren't I a bit heavier than you are?"

"Hmmm, you're right. How much do you weigh?"

"About 210."

"I'm 160, so it looks like I need to carry about 50 pounds worth of stuff while I climb. Here, give me your pack." As Dmitri handed his pack to Dr. Robert, who put it on his front, he made sure that he was carrying as little as possible so as to make the weight difference minimal, "OK, so if my pack was about twenty pounds, and yours was about twenty pounds, then I still need about ten more pounds."

Dr. Robert pointed to some rocks just off the top of the summit, "Pick up those four rocks and give them to me." When Dmitri handed the rocks to Dr. Robert, he weighed them in his hands and put them in his pockets, "OK, I think we're all set." The two travelers went their separate ways and each stepped into their respective spiral staircases.

The moment Dmitri stepped into the staircase, he heard a rapping sound that seemed to come from the other side. He then heard Dr. Robert's muffled voice through the rock, "Can you hear me, Dmitri?"

"*Da*," he yelled back.

"Good, now listen. In order to maintain balance, we need to be at the same level, which means that we have to climb these stairs at the same rate. It may be slow going, but in order to make sure we don't get off synch and don't get tired out too quickly, we need to set a beat that we can match each step with." Dmitri heard the rapping on the wall again as he matched the steady rhythm on his side by knocking on the wall.

"Excellent. Now, I don't know how long we'll be this close in our separate staircases, so just keep up the beat and don't stop for any reason. We'll know if we're off if we get that groaning and cracking that we got before. Now, are you ready?"

"*Da.*"

"Good. Now, on three. One. Two. Three. Step!" As both men took their first few steps, they nervously listened for the reaction of the mountain above them. Nothing. So far so good. After a while, the spiraling steps seemed to curve less and less as the radius of the staircase increased. Dr. Robert was glad he set up the plan to move up the stairs in a synchronized fashion, because he now knew that Dmitri was probably too far away to hear any more instructions.

Even though it was a bit slow, Dmitri did appreciate the fact that the pace was fast enough to make progress, but not so fast as to wear anyone down. And yet, climbing in the darkness was very disorienting. He couldn't tell how long he had been climbing in the small, confined space. He had lost count of how many steps he had taken long ago. The process seemed to be taking forever, but he kept reminding himself that when they reached the top of Meadow Peak, that was probably only the half-way point of their journey. At least he *hoped* they were more than half-way there.

With the monotony of climbing for what felt like days, both researchers almost didn't notice that they had arrived at another door, the light from outside seeping in through the cracks around its sides. Having been in a rhythm for so long, both men slid open the doors at the same time and stepped out into the sunlight of a rising sun. The spectacle was something else entirely. They stood on the edge of a perfectly circular island, surrounded by a sea of clouds. Looking across the island, they could see each other and waved in recognition of their achievement.

he ran toward his foe. Super-I dodged the first punch, a straight shot for his chest. He returned the initial assault with an uppercut deep into Tecumseh's stomach.

"Predictable. You've got to do better than that."

Coughing and gasping on the ground, Tecumseh gradually made his way back to standing as he grabbed his pitchfork. Using his fire as an accelerant on his arm, Tecumseh threw the pitchfork as hard as he could.

There wasn't much time to react, but Super-I managed to dodge again by using his fire to boost out of the path of the weapon. However, the fire was not the same orange color that was covering Tecumseh. Instead, the fire on Super-I was a brilliant blue.

"Wait! How did you do that?"

"You are not fully aware of the power you possess. Perhaps it is your at her assailant. Grabbing the trident in mid-air, Super-I twirled the weapon around and thrust it into the ground, creating a massive wave that knocked Penny down.

"Predictable. You've got to do better than that."

When Penny got back up, she pulled out her own trident and copied the attack that she had just seen her opponent perform. Penny wasn't sure what it was about battling this doppelganger, but it felt like she needed to prove herself by defeating this woman who looked like a perfect version of herself and who could fully control her powers.

As the wave of white quickly approached Super-I, she struck the ground, causing another wave to combine with the first one, instantly neutralizing it.

"Wait! How did you do that?"

"You are not fully aware of the power you possess. Perhaps it is your the improved mirror image in front of him. In a flash, Super-I had disappeared and reappeared to the side of Benjamin, where he struck at the small of Benjamin's back.

"Predictable. You've got to do better than that."

Being struck in such a vital spot left Benjamin on the ground for some time. When he eventually mustered enough strength to stand back up, Benjamin was surprised that his opponent did not attack him. He then realized that Super-I was merely defending himself.

Crouching down again, Benjamin sprung forth and turned into lightning. When he appeared again, Super-I was waiting. With a single finger, he shocked Benjamin on the forehead. His body went numb.

"Wait! How did you do that?"

"You are not fully aware of the power you possess. Perhaps it is your guilt holding you back."

"Guilt? What guilt?"

"The guilt of ruining so many lives."

"And what lives have I ruined?"

"Well, the lives of those villagers for one, Then there's always those closest to you. Lastly, you could be ruining your own life without knowing it."

"I think I'll be the judge of that."

Tecumseh was focused on trying to recreate the blue fire that his opponent had made earlier. With a bit more focus, Tecumseh's flames began to get bigger and hotter until they finally switched from orange to blue.

With a smirk, Tecumseh also used the Blood-fluxion in his possession to turn into a bull, covered in blue flames. Charging forward, propelled by the thrust of the blue fire, Tecumseh once again missed his target because Super-I once again increased the power of his flames.

When Tecumseh stopped charging, he saw what looked like an angel of light guilt holding you back."

"Guilt? What guilt?"

"The guilt that you are not perfect."

"What do you mean? I know I'm not perfect. No one is."

"True, but you are envious of those who are better than you are. Those who are prettier. Those who are smarter. Those who are more powerful."

"That may be true, but if we were all perfect, then where would our personality be? Our weaknesses bring forth our strengths and make us who we are."

Suddenly, a flash of inspiration hit Penny as she realized that her opponent had used the same technique she had used to calm the waves of the lakes back at home. If this was true, then it could be worked backwards as well.

Kneeling down, Penny struck the ground, causing a shockwave to shoot out toward her foe. A moment later, she struck the ground again, creating a faster shockwave. Super-I jumped into the air

guilt holding you back."

"Guilt? What guilt?"

"The guilt of squandering power."

"Squandering? How so?"

"You ran away from Thomas, who could have put your power to many more uses that will now never be realized because you have the Skybolt orb."

"That research could only go so far. In order to truly be able to help people, I needed to understand how it worked, and not necessarily rely on the results of it working."

As the feeling came back into Benjamin's body, he began to think of how he could defeat someone who, for all intents and purposes, was a perfected version of himself. After all, if Super-I was Benjamin, then he would already know all the moves Benjamin would make.

Benjamin's eyes widened as he realized that if they were the same, they must share the same weakness. He was

Going about fighting all wrong. He needed to get in closer.

Running forward, Benjamin was obviously not using the power that he held in the Skybolt orb, and Super-I noticed this, "Are you giving up already?"

"No. I'm just getting started." He made a swift right hook, followed by a left uppercut and began steadily throwing punches at his opponent.

Super-I easily dodged the assaults as Benjamin gradually increased their speed. Soon, he had to use his Skybolt orb to speed up his attacks to the point where his plan would work.

Eventually, Super-I also had to use his Skybolt orb to be able to dodge Benjamin's relentless assault. He knew it was a bit of a gamble, but Benjamin just had to hold out long enough for the weakness to present itself.

There it was! Benjamin was in luck as he noticed the Skybolt orb on his opponent flicker for just a brief

---

to avoid the waves.

When both shockwaves converged, a large wall of white flew at Super-I. But somehow in mid-air, she managed to jump again, thereby deftly dodging the attack.

Penny knew what had happened, because she used the same technique to walk on water. She smiled as she realized that this could be adapted to walk through the air. Still, it wouldn't be easy.

Once again, Penny gave the ground a one-two punch, but as the waves traveled, she leaped into the air. Once she had become airborne, she focused the energy of the Seawave orb into her feet and pushed off of the latent resistance in the air.

The resulting second jump pushed Penny toward her opponent, who had just dodged the large wave of ground. She was now close enough to land the finishing attack. Spreading out her hands, Penny quickly brought them

---

standing before him. This only excited him more, to see just how the Hellfire orb's power could be harnessed.

Focusing more on the orb at his chest, Tecumseh's fire went through the same cycle it did before, this time changing from blue to white.

Charging at his opponent again, his speed dramatically increased, Tecumseh barely missed, so he knew that he was close.

When Tecumseh charged again, his opponent scoffed, "You've already tried that. Don't you know it won't work?" As Tecumseh came up to full speed, he reverted back to his lighter human form, thereby increasing his speed even more from the latent momentum he had gained. As a result, he flew headlong into Super-I's torso, knocking him on the ground.

Walking up to the downed foe, Tecumseh was ready to finish him off. Standing above Super-I, he turned his arm into white fire and used it to

moment. That moment was all he needed to land an uppercut underneath Super-I's chin.

Benjamin clenched his jaw and closed his eyes as he knelt down and wound up for the finishing blow. It happened quickly, but it was a solid hit.

With his fist still in the air, and his eyes still closed, Benjamin waited to hear the "thud" of his opponent hitting the ground. When the sound never came, he slowly opened his eyes to see that with the exception of himself, the room was completely empty.

Super-I's voice echoed throughout the bright room, "You have done well. As your reward, you will be given a new weapon."

From the sky, a long-handled sledgehammer slowly descended until it hovered just a few feet away from him, its bright yellow lacquered handle holding up the silvery hammer head, the number "90" etched on its side. Benjamin didn't normally carry a

---

accelerate his punch into the face of the idealized version of himself.

When he connected, it did not feel like he made contact with Super-I. Instead it felt like he punched the ground. He knew he couldn't have missed at such a short distance, so he was surprised to see that not only had Super-I disappeared, but the ground was undamaged as well.

Super-I's voice echoed throughout the bright room, "You have done well. As your reward, you will be given a new weapon."

Looking around to find his pitchfork, Tecumseh noticed it was missing, but in its place, a beautifully designed pitchfork with a red lacquered handle hovered just a little bit away from where he was standing. The prongs seemed to be very shiny, as if

together, causing a concussive wave in the air that knocked Super-I to the ground.

When Penny landed, she couldn't see where her foe ended up. Furthermore, she couldn't find either of the tridents that were used in battle. She suddenly felt alone and wondered if she had actually won, or if Super-I was going to launch a surprise attack. Unable to take the deafening silence, Penny called out, "Did I win?"

Super-I's voice echoed throughout the bright room, "You have done well. As your reward, you will be given a new weapon."

Emerging from the ground was a trident that put her old weapon to shame. The blue lacquered handle held a golden head with three barbed tips. It hovered a few feet away from her. Penny was hesitant to grab a hovering trident, but hers had disappeared.

weapon, but approached regardless.

When Benjamin grabbed the floating weapon, Super-I's voice was heard once more, "Pursue your ideal. Fight for perfection. Become Super-I."

Holding the hammer in his hands, Benjamin wondered if there were any special properties that would accentuate his powers. When the ground shook and his surroundings changed, Benjamin knew something different was happening as he stood in a pillar of light, surrounded by darkness and shin deep in fog.

From the darkness in front of him, a strange creature appeared. The creature had the head of a woman, the body of a lioness, the wings of an eagle, and a tail that was a venomous serpent.

In a soothing voice, the creature spoke, "I am the Psychological Heightened eNigma, or PHN for short." The characters "PHN-3" appeared above her in white light.

"Having bested it, I, and Super-I,

When Penny grabbed the floating weapon, Super-I's voice was heard once more, "Pursue your ideal. Fight for perfection. Become Super-I."

Marveling at the workmanship on the trident, Penny didn't notice that no archway appeared. Instead, as the ground trembled, she became nervous as darkness seemed to pour out of the sky, and fog from the ground. Eventually, she stood in a pillar of light, surrounded by darkness and shin deep in fog.

From the darkness in front of her, a strange creature appeared. The creature had the head of a woman, the body of a lioness, the wings of an eagle, and a tail that was a venomous serpent.

In a soothing voice, the creature spoke, "I am the Psychological Heightened eNigma, or PHN for short." The characters "PHN-3" appeared above her in white light.

"Having bested it, I, and Super-I,

---

they had never been used.

When Tecumseh grabbed the floating weapon, Super-I's voice was heard once more, "Pursue your ideal. Fight for perfection. Become Super-I."

As he waited for the archway to appear, something strange happened instead. The ground began to rumble as a wall of darkness approached on all sides. Fog began seeping up from the ground and soon Tecumseh was standing in a pillar of light, surrounded by darkness and shin deep in fog.

From the darkness in front of him, a strange creature appeared. The creature had the head of a woman, the body of a lioness, the wings of an eagle, and a tail that was a venomous serpent.

In a soothing voice, the creature spoke, "I am the Psychological Heightened eNigma, or PHN for short." The characters "PHN-3" appeared above her in white light.

"Having bested it, I, and Super-I,

you have arrived at the final test." Tecumseh hoped that it was more fighting, as he wanted to test out his new weapon. At the very least, it looked like he would soon be done with the Imaginary World.

"That's fine, what is it?"

"There is only one question."

"Good, let's get it over with."

"Just know that if you answer incorrectly, you will be swallowed alive." The snake tail began to hiss and dance in the air.

"I don't care; just get on with it already."

"What walks on four legs in the morning, two legs by noon and three legs by the evening?"

Tecumseh was a little disappointed that he had to answer another quiz. Still, he began to think of what the answer might be.

The only animal he could think of that could remove and add legs would be some sort of reptile, but that wasn't

you have arrived at the final test." Penny was excited by this revelation, because it meant that soon she would be reunited with her friends. She had been in this world full of voids and questions for far too long.

"May I ask what the test is?"

"There is only one question."

"That's all? OK, I'm ready."

"Just know that if you answer incorrectly, you will be swallowed alive." The snake tail began to hiss and dance in the air.

Gulping back some fear, Penny nodded, "I'm ready."

"What is the sound of one hand clapping?"

Penny had to think hard about this question. All the rest of the quizzes had been somewhat personal, so she wasn't quite ready for this riddle.

She then realized that she had the power to answer the question. In order for a hand to clap, it needs to come in contact with something, "I have your

you have arrived at the final test." Thinking back on the past three trials, Benjamin realized that he faced some deep parts of his personality and he wondered if the others had fared as well as he had.

"Very well, what is the test?"

"There is only one question."

"Great. I'm tired of fighting."

"Just know that if you answer incorrectly, you will be swallowed alive." The snake tail began to hiss and dance in the air.

"Duly noted. Please ask away."

"If a tree falls in the forest and no one is around to hear it, does it make a sound?"

Benjamin thought he knew the answer, but the threat of being eaten alive caused him to think it over. One would tend to answer that it would make a sound, because that's what people observe, but if there are no observers, would there be no sound?

"The answer is 'yes'. While no one

quite right. Maybe the legs of a table? But tables don't walk. As he leaned on his new pitchfork, he came upon the answer.

"The answer is 'man'."

"That is correct." The number above PHN changed from "3" to "6". Suddenly, Tecumseh felt a burning sensation on the back of his left hand. The symbol χ appeared on his flesh in a flash of light.

The creature spoke again, "From today forth you shall be known as 'Chi the Powerful'. The symbol is to remind you that those with power can choose where they want to go in life. They are always at a crossroads. Make sure you choose wisely."

The ground shook again and Tecumseh noticed out of the corner of his eye that two more pillars of light were positioned to his right. Looking over, he saw Penny and Benjamin and was a little shocked that they were there. Were they really there the whole time?

answer." Taking her right hand, she struck the air, producing a shockwave of sound. Penny waited for the reverberating echoes of the blast to die down.

"That is correct." The number above PHN changed from "3" to "6". Suddenly, Penny felt a burning sensation on her chest. The symbol ψ appeared below her neck, just where she could barely see it.

The creature spoke again, "From today forth you shall be known as 'Psi the Sensitive'. The symbol is to remind you that just as your trident penetrates the water, so can water penetrate the earth. Finding the base of the issue can breed sensitivity."

The ground shook again and Penny noticed out of the corner of her eye that two more pillars of light were positioned on either side of her. Looking to the right and the left, she saw Tecumseh and Benjamin standing before the creature just as she was.

would hear it, the vibrations that a falling tree induces would create waves in the air, thereby creating 'sound'."

"That is correct." The number above PHN changed from "3" to "6". Suddenly, Benjamin felt a burning sensation on his face. The symbol λ appeared on the middle of his forehead.

The creature spoke again, "From today forth you shall be known as 'Lambda the Just'. The symbol is to remind you that Justice is always a fork in the path on life. You have the ability to choose: right or left. Right or wrong."

The ground shook again and Benjamin noticed out of the corner of his eye that two more pillars of light were positioned to his left. Looking over, he saw Tecumseh and Penny, both a little roughed up from their battles, just as he was. At least they were

PHN spoke, attracting everyone's attention once more, "As you three are the first group to successfully pass through the Imaginary World, you shall be known throughout the real world as 'The Triumvirate'."

In the darkness behind the creature, stained glass images of the three travelers appeared. Tecumseh's pitchfork also glowed as the symbol he was given appeared on the shiny silver metal head.

Below their stained glass images, three more portraits appeared, "You now join the ranks of three others: Breve the Lion, Umlaut the Dragon, and Tilde the Cardinal."

As he gazed upon the images, Tecumseh recognized one of the three portraits that appeared, which made him smile with new determination.

The ground rumbled one last time and the darkness began to envelop everything. The light vanished and the

Finally reunited, Penny smiled.

PHN spoke, attracting everyone's attention once more, "As you three are the first group to successfully pass through the Imaginary World, you shall be known throughout the real world as 'The Triumvirate'."

In the darkness behind the creature, stained glass images of the three travelers appeared. Penny's trident also glowed as the symbol she was given appeared on the golden head. A pure tone rang from the symbol.

Below their stained glass images, three more portraits appeared, "You now join the ranks of three others: Breve the Lion, Umlaut the Dragon, and Tilde the Cardinal."

As she gazed upon the images, Penny recognized one of the three portraits that appeared, which made a look of surprise come across her face.

The ground rumbled one last time and the darkness began to envelop everything. The light vanished and the

together again.

PHN spoke, attracting everyone's attention once more, "As you three are the first group to successfully pass through the Imaginary World, you shall be known throughout the real world as 'The Triumvirate'."

In the darkness behind the creature, stained glass images of the three travelers appeared. Benjamin's hammer also glowed as the symbol he was given appeared on the silvery head opposite the side with the "90".

Below their stained glass images, three more portraits appeared, "You now join the ranks of three others: Breve the Lion, Umlaut the Dragon, and Tilde the Cardinal."

As he gazed upon the images, Benjamin didn't recognize any of the three men, but he decided that he wanted to eventually meet them all.

The ground rumbled one last time and the darkness began to envelop everything. The light vanished and the fog disappeared. Soon, Tecumseh felt like he was falling, at which point he blacked out and fell asleep.

In his head he heard the voices of it, I, and Super-I as they said in unison, "Well done."

---

fog disappeared. Soon, Penny felt like she was falling, at which point she blacked out and fell asleep.

In her head she heard the voices of it, I, and Super-I as they said in unison, "Well done."

---

fog disappeared. Soon, Benjamin felt like he was falling, at which point he blacked out and fell asleep.

In his head he heard the voices of it, I, and Super-I as they said in unison, "Well done."

Dmitri and Dr. Robert stood on opposite sides of the island and soaked in the view. While they were in the darkness of the stairwells, the sun had managed to rise and now shone down on the architecturally impressive spectacle. They had both emerged from pillars set on the very edge of the island, each pillar holding a bowl full of fire. The rest of the island had many more pillars, just like the ones they came out of, arranged in concentric circles around a domed temple set up on the exact middle of the island. Each circle of columns sat on a terraced level leading down to the temple, which was quite a distance beneath where the two travelers were standing.

The number of pillars per terrace seemed to increase from the outside until about the fourth ring, when they became sparse again. Dr. Robert did a quick count of the rings, starting with the one he and Dmitri were standing on. Two. Eighteen. Thirty-two. Thirty-two. Eight. Two. Doing some quick addition in his head, he came up with the number 112. Dmitri's Number Disk had to be on this island, the pillars confirmed it. Among other things, the columns also confirmed they were indeed on the Island of Stability.

Since they were too far away to hear each other, Dr. Robert made some hand motions to indicate that they would climb down to the temple much in the same way they climbed up the spiral staircases. Dmitri motioned that he understood and the two began to descend down the terraces. Their progress was much quicker this time, since they could see each other and could thereby coordinate their movements better than before.

When they arrived at the temple, they found that it was merely another set of pillars that held up a domed roof. Stepping inside, they could see they were not alone. A man, balancing on one foot with both his hands pressed together in front of him, stood on what appeared to be the exact center of the island. Entering underneath the dome of the temple, Dmitri saw that the man was standing on the final Number Disk needed to complete his collection. In his excitement, he rushed forward, but Dr. Robert could not keep up, he could merely shout, "Wait!"

The entire island shifted, which threw everyone off balance. In adrenaline fueled panic, Dmitri retreated to where he started and waited for the island to settle. Dr. Robert yelled across the room, "How long have we been working to maintain this island's balance? You need to control yourself. Just take a look at your surroundings." Pointing upward, Dr. Robert made Dmitri aware of a sword dangling above the lone monk, the string holding it in place being so thin that it made the sword look like it was floating in space.

However, this sword was now swaying back and forth like a deadly pendulum above the monk's head. The monk seemed somewhat unfazed by all of this; the only change he exhibited was that he now stood on two feet, straddling the disk set in the floor with the number "112" clearly engraved on its surface. Dmitri pointed to the disk and said, "That's what we came for, so let's get it and get out."

"Well, now things are a little different, so we'll need to move closer with the rhythm of the sword." Dr. Robert took the first step as a demonstration, and Dmitri followed suit until they were both standing about an arm's distance away from the monk. Noticing that the monk had said nothing, even though the two travelers had been yelling for the past few minutes, Dr. Robert asked, "Excuse me, what is your name?"

"Niccolaus."

Dmitri was somewhat taken aback by the man's limited speech and abrupt responses, "You don't talk much, do you, Niccolaus?" The monk merely motioned to the engraving on the floor. It encircled the entire temple.

The engraving read, "Silence induces Neutrality. Neutrality induces Equilibrium. Equilibrium induces Balance. Balance induces Stability. Stability induces Peace. Peace induces Silence." The entire mantra ran back upon itself, creating an endless loop of equalities. Something caught Dmitri's eye as he read the text carved into the floor. Kneeling down, he noticed that the light glinted off the dot of the " i " in "neutrality" differently than the rest of the words.

When Dmitri pointed out the inconsistency to Dr. Robert, his partner merely said that they should take care of their original objective first before exploring anything else. Nodding in agreement, Dmitri crawled toward the disk positioned underneath Niccolaus. The monk certainly didn't seem to care, as he had closed his eyes and tried to ignore the intruders.

As Dmitri reached for the disk, Dr. Robert blurted out, "Stop!"

"What is it now?"

"We were evenly weighted when we came up here."

"So?"

"So, if you take that disk, you'll be heavier than me, and we won't be able to get back down."

"You're right. What do you suggest?"

"Let me take it."

"What? Why?"

"Don't worry. You'll get it eventually, when we get down from the Island of Stability. But for right now, trust me." Pulling out a rock from his pocket, Dr. Robert weighed it in his hand and determined that it must be about the weight of the disk. Reaching out and picking up the disk from the floor, Dr. Robert checked the weight in his hand and confirmed that the rock matched its weight, since he subsequently put the rock down in the spot where the disk once sat.

Without warning, the string holding up the swinging sword snapped, and the sword fell to the tile floor, embedding itself a few inches behind where Dr. Robert was crouched. He slowly stood up and turned around to examine the implement which almost ended his life. Shrugging, he said, "Since we're already taking things, I don't see why we can't take this as well." Reaching into his pockets once again, he pulled out a bigger rock and set it down on top of the one he had already placed beneath Niccolaus.

Pulling the sword out of the floor, he examined its markings and excitedly remarked, "This must be the legendary Sword of Selcomad!" Pointing to an "X" which was engraved on the blade, he continued, "See this mark? It shows that the size of this sword is ten. This is the 10 Caliber Sword of Selcomad." Reaching behind him, he tied the sword down to his pack and looked up to Dmitri, who was still frozen from the close call that his partner had recently encountered.

In fact, as Dmitri watched the sword fall toward Dr. Robert, he immediately began to wonder how he would be able to get off the Island of Stability. A myriad of scenarios ran through his mind until the weapon landed safely behind his partner. Dmitri had experienced quite enough of this island and wanted nothing more than to leave as soon as possible. But first there was the matter of the dot in the " i ".

Dr. Robert was once again giving orders after pulling out another rock from his pocket of the same size and heft as the first one he set beneath Niccolaus. Explaining their situation, Dr. Robert told Dmitri how to move, "OK, we need to move out and around until I can get to the dot in the " i ", at which point I'll put down another rock and pick it up. Understand?" Dmitri nodded as they began to shuffle about the temple.

When Dr. Robert arrived at the area of interest, he knelt down and picked up another Number Disk, replacing the displaced item with the rock he held in his other hand. A scowl furrowed Dr. Robert's brow as he stood up and held the disk for Dmitri to see, "It looks like a Number Disk, but I didn't think that they went any lower than one." Engraved on the disk's surface was the number "0".

Dmitri could hardly contain his excitement, but having already learned the folly of rushing in, he merely exclaimed, "That's one of the lost Number Disks!

I've been looking for them for almost as long as I've had my collection!" He was now eager to leave, considering that the sooner they left, the sooner he could have two new Number Disks in his collection, "I'll explain it later, but if we don't have anything else to do here, let's leave."

"Agreed." The two men slowly backed away from each other and soon were outside and on their way back down from the precariously positioned island.

Sighing in relief that the two men had finally left, Niccolaus shook his head and said only a single word, "Tourists."

Chapter 5

Extinguished Soul

Benjamin awoke with a start. Sitting on a cold, stone floor gave him shivers, so he stood up and began examining his surroundings. Darkness was the most prevalent attribute of where he found himself, so he wondered if he had actually left the Imaginary World at all. The one difference Benjamin did deduce was that, unlike the areas in the i-World, this spot was most definitely bounded.

A horizontal slit of dim light on the far side of the cave gave Benjamin enough light to see by. The room he found himself in was very smooth and appeared to be carved right out of the rock. A single stone pedestal stood in the middle of the room. Turning around to the back of the cave, Benjamin found the hammer which was given to him in the Imaginary World. He now knew that perhaps it had all been real, despite the very distinct possibility that it had all been a dream.

In his further examination of the room, something glinted on the floor, the light from outside reflecting off its surface. Bending down, Benjamin picked up what appeared to be a key, except the tooth of the key was a bit bent out of shape. The item looked so odd that Benjamin spent some time examining it. Without warning, a loud crash came from outside, almost like a tree falling over, but multiplied many times over.

Placing the key in the chest pocket of his vest and picking up his hammer, Benjamin rushed outside through the slit opening in the cave to see what had made the noise. As his eyes adjusted to the light of the full moon, he saw what had made the noise, and immediately backed away from the ledge on which he now found himself. Far beneath him, in a valley between three mountains, a large wooden ship had landed upside down next to what appeared to be a volcano spewing out . . . water? The water was flowing out of the mountain top and was beginning to fill the valley with darkness. Thinking quickly, Benjamin turned to lightning and, with a thunderous boom, landed on the upturned hull of the boat.

Quickly looking up and down the keel, Benjamin found a small hatch in the stern that he threw open and yelled in, "Is there anyone in here?" Only hearing the frenzied noises of animals, Benjamin decided it would be a good idea if he checked inside. Dropping down into the boat, the moonlight streaming in from the hatch above illuminated Benjamin in eerie spotlight, "Hello? Is there anybody there?"

The sound of voices could be barely heard over the din of animals, but it sounded like there was someone at the end of the corridor. Walking along what used to be the ceiling of the pitch-black hallway, Benjamin made his way to the other end as the voices became more distinct, "Do you think it's someone else from the Army come to finish us off?"

"Hello? Is anyone hurt?"

"Shoot! He heard us."

Benjamin heard scurrying as the people ran away, "Wait! I'm here to help." Running after them and down the up staircase, Benjamin eventually found an old man and a young boy who were cowering behind a pillar engraved with a plethora of words. The pillar used to hold up a glass roof, which had now become a glass floor, showing a steadily rising water level beneath them, shimmering in the moonlight. Benjamin didn't venture further out onto the glass, seeing as a lot of it had already broken in the fall.

Letting an arc of electricity jump across his fingers, Benjamin used the resulting light to show his face to the two behind the pillar, "My name is Benjamin and I want to help you. I heard your boat crash and I came to see if anyone was here."

The old man angrily growled, "You're not part of that murderous Army of Amedeo, are you?"

"What? No. What do you mean by *murderous?*"

"Two men came to me earlier today and I foolishly helped them out, and now my wife is dead and my home has been destroyed. They wore the mark of the Army of Amedeo."

The boy was more amazed by Benjamin's control over electricity, "Wow! How are you doing that?"

"Quiet, Camille. This is neither the time nor the place." Carefully walking back over the glass, the old man brought Camille with him to the safety of the stairwell where Benjamin was standing. As all three stood together, the man continued, "I must apologize for my curt attitude, but a lot has happened today. My name is Noah and this is my son, Camille. You said your name was Benjamin, am I right?"

"That's right, and I'm here to help you out of this boat."

"And how do you plan on doing this?"

"Probably in the same way I can control electricity."

A thought struck Noah, "Wait a minute. Are you one of those people who can naturally use the power inherently held in an object?" Before Benjamin had time to answer, Noah asked another question, "What's your favorite bird?"

"Um, a turkey?"

"No, that won't do at all. I mean what's your favorite bird that can fly long distances. Something like a dove or a raven or an eagle."

"Well, if I had to choose from those, I suppose it'd have to be a bald eagle."

"Excellent. Come with me." As Noah grabbed Benjamin's hand and pulled him upstairs to the bottom of the boat he explained, "Those scoundrels from the Army of Amedeo took off with my collection of animals after killing Joan; but fortunately for me, I keep a backup collection." When the group made it to the corridor lined with animal cages, Noah lit one of the upside-down candles and used it to examine the ceiling. When he stopped looking, he pointed to a plank that seemed to be just like all the others, "Help me get up there, will you?"

Camille and Benjamin lifted Noah up to the plank where he managed to pry it loose, letting a large amount of glass orbs fall from the ceiling. Being let back down, Noah searched through the random orbs on the floor until he came across the one he was looking for. Examining it closely in the candlelight, the name of the animal's blood contained in the orb was delicately etched on the outside. The one Noah picked up said "Bald Eagle."

Benjamin hadn't quite caught up to speed yet, "So, tell me again why you had two collections of every animal?"

"Because collecting is what I *do*. It is what gives me purpose in life." Handing the blood orb to Benjamin, Noah looked him straight in the eye, "And I am breaking my collection by giving this to you. I am only doing so on one condition: you find the two men who did this to us and you bring them to justice."

Silently accepting the core, Benjamin nodded as Noah spoke the one key word that seemed to resonate with Benjamin's soul as of late. Suddenly, the lighting in the dark room seemed to become brighter as Noah stared at Benjamin's forehead. From the hatch, two familiar voices could be heard, "Benjamin, are you there?" It was Penny.

"We saw you come down to this shipwreck, but we're not as fast as lightning, so it took some time to join you." Tecumseh was there as well.

"I'm here. I'm just helping out some people who were trapped inside." The other two members of The Triumvirate hopped down into the hull of the boat. All they could see was the glowing mark on Benjamin's forehead, which caused Penny and Tecumseh to realize that their marks were glowing as well. Not having time to delve into this mystery, the two newcomers were introduced to the boat's inhabitants, "This is Noah and his son Camille. These are my friends, Penny and Tecumseh." With the water level quickly rising, Benjamin cut to the chase, "So, Noah, are you guys ready to go?"

"I don't think that would be wise right now," Tecumseh warned.

"Oh? Is there something more pressing than getting out of a sinking boat?"

"There are some soldiers out there right now, and we're not sure what they're doing."

"What?" Noah was livid, "They've come back to finish the job. I knew it!"

Penny spoke up, "I don't think so. They looked like they were only on a mission up on the mountains. Tecumseh was lucky that it's dark out, since he just barely made it out of the peak they started on. They didn't look like they were interested in a wrecked boat."

Taking charge, Benjamin laid out a plan, "Very well. I don't think the water is rising fast enough for us to be worried if we stay up here in the hull. We'll just check outside occasionally to see if the soldiers have left yet, then when they're gone we'll get everyone to safety." Turning to Noah, he apologized, "I'm sorry, but you may have to leave your collection here for now and pick it up from the wreckage later."

"I have no problems with that, as long as you hold up your end of our deal."

Benjamin nodded as he pulled his friends into the other room where the open hatch was streaming in the light of the full moon. Lifting himself up through the opening, he took a quick peek to see where the soldiers were. As far as he could determine from the shadows, there were two sets of soldiers heading toward two different peaks. Coming back inside, he said, "It looks like we might be here for a bit."

Lowering his voice, Benjamin asked, "Did you experience what I did in the Imaginary World?"

Tecumseh answered first, "I think so. If what you experienced was encountering three versions of yourself followed by some crazy hybrid creature giving a quiz."

"That's what I encountered too," Penny replied.

Rubbing his forehead, Benjamin said, "It all felt so unreal, but at the same time almost eerily personal. And these marks add a whole other level of strangeness on top of everything else. You two didn't notice if your marks were glowing before, did you?"

"Nope, when I came out of the mountain cave, I couldn't see my mark, but it appeared when I met up with Tecumseh and it started glowing when we met up with you."

"Hmmm. There must be some sort of trigger to our marks whenever we get near someone else who has passed through the i-World."

The Triumvirate was quiet in thought until Tecumseh broke the silence when he noticed that Benjamin carried a hammer on his back, "Wow! Did you get that after the third trial?"

"I did, although I haven't really used many weapons before." Noticing the weapons that Penny and Tecumseh held, Benjamin saw that they were better looking than the ones they had before, "I see you both got upgrades to what you had when you entered the Imaginary World."

All three were silent for a while in deep contemplation, the only sounds heard being the animals and the rushing water. This time Penny broke the silence, "So, where do you think we are?"

"That's a good question. Let me ask Noah. Hey, Noah!"

Entering the room, Noah replied, "What is it, Benjamin?"

"Where exactly are we?"

"What do you mean?"

"Well, we all kind of just appeared here, and we don't really know where this is."

"Right now you're just outside of Sievuvus Volcano, which is where this boat was perched until just a short while ago. The volcano is set in the valley between the three peaks of the Pythagorean Triangle."

"Hmmm. Interesting. This means we headed more westward than northward when-" Benjamin was interrupted by the sound of cheering coming from outside. "I think whatever the soldiers came to do, they may have just finished." Lifting himself through the hatch just enough to see outside, Benjamin saw the shadowy groups of soldiers were retreating from the peaks which he had originally seen them heading towards. He also noticed something strange: the volcano that was overflowing with water had stopped flowing.

Coming back inside, Benjamin briefed the rest of the group, "The soldiers are retreating, and the volcano is no longer erupting with water." Looking at Noah, he asked, "Since this boat doesn't appear to be in any immediate danger any more, would you like to stay?"

"Are you kidding? This boat is a loss. I'll just gather some more things and we can go. In fact, if you could help me, Benjamin, I'd greatly appreciate it."

"No problem."

Benjamin left Penny and Tecumseh in order to follow Noah to another part of his boat. Opening up a closet, some linens spilled out, some of which Noah picked up and handed to Benjamin, "Now, Benjamin, if you are going to fulfill your promise, I would suggest that you head north from here to the Tower of Lebab. I have heard it is one of the many strongholds of the Army of Amedeo. There is a chance you might find the two who ruined my life there. Their names are Jules and Herbert. Jules is about my age, but Herbert is much younger. I don't necessarily mean for you to kill them, I just want them to be punished for killing my wife."

Nodding in agreement, Benjamin replied, "Understood."

When they returned to the hull of the boat, Noah bent down and gathered up the blood orbs that had spilled on the floor and put them in the sheets, which he then tied up and hoisted on his back, "All right, let's go."

Tecumseh made sure the coast was clear as he helped everyone out of the boat. When they stood on the outside, Benjamin asked, "How did you two get down here?"

"I used my fire to slow my descent after I jumped off the mountain," Tecumseh replied.

"I kind of did the same thing as Tecumseh, only with waves of air resistance."

Examining what needed to be evacuated from the overturned boat, Benjamin laid forth how they would proceed, "Very well, I want Penny to carry Camille, I'll carry Noah with the power of the eagle he recently gave me, and Tecumseh can carry the bag of blood orbs. Any objections?" No one answered, "Excellent. Let's get to it."

The operation went smoothly enough and soon everyone was standing on the top of Cobra Peak. Noah and Camille said their goodbyes and started to hike down into the green valley on the opposite side of the Pythagorean Triangle. Now that The Triumvirate was alone, Benjamin pointed to the tower blocking out some of the stars above the horizon to the north, "If we're to eventually get up north to try and find Bram, we need to head in that direction. Let's use that tower as a break point." Once again, nodding and silent acceptance were received as the group leapt off of the mountain and flew toward the mysterious black monolith ahead of them, their silhouettes briefly crossing the bright disk of the full moon before merging back into the starry, black sky.

Back at the Library of Delaxanair, Herbert and Jules were being debriefed and had arrived at the part of the questioning where they were asked if they had anything to say. Both were in separate rooms, but Herbert spoke up first with his youthful optimism, "I was thinking about how we could use some of the fluxions that Jules and I brought in. One of the ideas I had was that we could use the Blood-fluxion of a chameleon to create a camouflage suit that could be worn by soldiers doing covert operations. Something like an invisible man! I also thought if we were looking for somewhere to store a lot of soldiers in an interim period, why not the moon? I mean, there's gotta be tons of space up there, and with the Q-Portals, I think we might actually be able to make it there without too much-" Herbert was cut off when someone came in the room and let them know that Dmitri and Dr. Robert had come back.

Jules, on the other hand, had a few of the same ideas that Herbert expressed in the other room, "Have we considered the possibility of storing soldiers under the earth? I mean, if we don't just use the surface of the earth, but everything underneath it, possibly even down to the center, we could store many more soldiers than if we just left them in barracks above ground. And for that matter, why don't we use the moon to store people? I'm sure we could get there with the technology we have at our disposal. This way no one would ever find the stores of soldiers up there until we needed them for-" another man entered the room and informed Jules and his interviewer that Dmitri and Dr. Robert had returned.

Meeting back up, Herbert and Jules made their way to the room where everyone was working on developing the Fluents. Before even entering the room, they could hear Dmitri's booming voice down the hallway, "I can't believe that we managed not only to complete my collection of Number Disks, but to find one of the lost Number Disks as well! That was truly unexpected!"

Herbert had entered the room and couldn't help but ask, "What are the lost Number Disks? Obviously they can't be lost if you've found one of them."

With a guffaw, Dmitri explained, "*Nyet*, they aren't lost in that sense, my comrade! They're lost as in they don't fit in the normal set of Number Disks. For instance, this one that we found up there on the Island of Stability is the number '0', which most of us don't start counting at anyways. We start at one. And yet, the lost Number Disks are special in that they hold more power than the individual Number Disks do. In fact, this '0' has the ability to neutralize the effects of any Number-fluxion, so it might be very useful in creating the Fluent that can separate other fluxions."

Jules now entered the conversation, "You said there are lost Number Disks. That's plural. Do you know where the others are?"

"Well, I know where one more is," at this point, Dmitri pulled out a disk he had hanging around his neck on a chain. The symbol on the disk was "+", "This is one of the other lost Number Disks, which goes by the name of 'push'. Its main purpose is to counteract the power of the 'pull' lost Number Disk, which is perhaps the most powerful of the three because of its multiple powers. Lightning. Uncertainty. Magnetism. The pull disk has it all."

"So, correct me if I am wrong, but do these lost Number Disks have anything to do with this triangular stone?" Albert was at the table and was examining the carved piece of rock that had ornate designs engraved into it, along with three symbols: "–", "0", and "+".

Walking over to the table, Dmitri answered, "*Da*, that's right. This is known as the Philosopher's Stone. It is so named because philosophers have long speculated on the ability to create any Number Disk out of nothing but the power inherent in the three lost Number Disks. I found this artifact a long time ago, and now it looks like we might even be able to test it out to see if the philosophers were right." He paused for a moment of thought, "If only we knew where the '–' Number Disk was . . ." Looking over to the corner where Dr. Robert quietly sat, Dmitri yelled over to his partner, "Doc! You don't happen to know where I could find the disk I'm looking for, do ya?"

Not being a fan of crowds, Dr. Robert silently shook his head as Dmitri made his way over to the introverted scientist, "Let me tell you guys, this guy was incredible out there. He knew exactly what was what and what to do. We would have never been able to bring back the haul we did if Doc here didn't take control." Dr. Robert blushed at the compliment, but also at the fact that everyone was looking at him. Dmitri continued, "I mean, it was almost like he was a completely different person up there. It was amazing."

"Actually, Dmitri, you bring up a good point which is an excellent segue to something Mary has asked us to work on while she is out completing her mission." Albert let everyone gather around before he continued, "A lot of Mary's work was on how to make people stronger. It originally started with implanting healthy tissues; then led to transplanting whole organs. She has a theory that, just like the blood of animals can be used to make us more powerful, the blood of men could be used to enhance our strength as well."

"After all, there are many soldiers who can no longer fight because they are injured or cannot fight because they are merely weak. If we can get these soldiers into fighting condition, they can be added to the one-septillion goal. I am still not sure why General Amedeo thinks he need so many men, but I am pretty sure that if we can actually come up with that many soldiers, we will be greatly rewarded."

Clearing his throat, Albert continued, "At any rate, Mary left some sample cores that we can use and now that James and Garland have worked out a few seals, we think we're ready for testing."

"I think Doc Robert would be a great test subject," Dmitri shouted out, slapping the small man on the back.

"Now, Dmitri, it is not all right to volunteer other people like that. This is still not fully understood, so we are unsure of the effects that-"

"I'll do it," the Doctor's voice was soft, but it caused Albert to stop dead in his sentence.

"Are you sure? I mean, you do not have to do this just because Dmitri wanted you to."

"*Aye*, I'm sure. Who better to test strength than the weak?"

"*Wunderbar.*" Picking up a vest from a table set up on another wall of the room, Albert brought over the piece of clothing and gave it to Dr. Robert. The fabric was rough, but in the middle of the vest was a blood-red core which was surrounded by a single snake with two heads. Both heads were trying to eat each other and the blood core was the only thing holding them apart.

Dr. Robert took off his sport jacket and put on the bulky vest over his shirt. Albert gave some instructions, "Supposedly, all you have to do is focus some of your energy into the core on your chest and you should feel a change shortly afterward." Everyone backed away as Dr. Robert closed his eyes and began to focus his energy. The core began to glow red.

The change was gradual, but it was distinct. Dr. Robert began to grow taller. His clothes soon became tattered from increased muscle mass. His hair even managed to change color from brown to blonde. When he had finished changing, he sighed deeply, which sounded more like a growl to everyone, who all instinctively took another step backwards.

When Dr. Robert opened his eyes, Albert asked him, "How do you feel, Dr. Robert?"

"I don' know who dis Doc Robert is yur referrin' to. My name's Mister Louis."

Almost talking to himself, Albert mumbled, "Interesting. The soul trapped in the blood of the core takes over the host when the fluxion is used." Regaining the awareness of his surroundings, Albert spoke to Mr. Louis, "I see. Well, Mr. Louis, could you do us all a favor and focus a bit of your energy into that round object on your chest?"

Tilting his head in confusion, Mr. Louis looked down at his chest and found the glowing blood core embroidered in the vest he wore. He pointed at it and looked at Albert for approval. Albert nodded, confirming that the blood core was what Mr. Louis needed to focus on. When Mr. Louis closed his eyes, the light on the core began to fade and Mr. Louis slowly turned back into Dr. Robert. When the doctor had returned, he opened his eyes and looked around at everyone who seemed to be staring in shock, "Well? Did it work?"

Dmitri was the first to congratulate Dr. Robert, "You were amazing yet again, Doc! Truly amazing!"

"I agree." Albert turned to James and Garland and started giving further orders, "Let us see how many of these fluxions we can get a single person to use. I think we need to start around seven. Get that soldier who volunteered to work as a test subject in here. What was his name again? Dante? Well, whatever. We may have just managed to solve a few of our problems. Let us keep working on these fluxions. In fact, these are just amazing enough to warrant their own name. From now on, they shall be known as Soul-fusion fluxions." Clapping his hands together, Albert beamed with excitement, "We have got a lot of work to do."

○

All three members of The Triumvirate stood in front of the Tower of Lebab, their necks craned back in an attempt to see the top of the daunting structure. The repeating pattern of pillars supporting arches curved around the circular tower. These pillared layers seemed to propagate into the sky until they were too small to be distinctly seen.

Before the group was an opening, its black mouth seemed to beckon for them to enter the deserted building. While still staring upward, Benjamin spoke to the others, "I'm sorry if it took so long to get here. I could have sworn that a tower like this seemed closer than it was, merely based on how far above the horizon it stood. But at any rate, we're finally here, so let's take a break and look inside." Neither Penny nor Tecumseh broke their gaze with the tower until they realized that Benjamin had already made his way inside.

The interior of the tower was just as impressive as its outside façade. Up above, the open roof was a pinpoint of light which dimly lit the pillared archways that supported the inside ring of the tower. Benjamin put his hand on one of the pillars and felt the coolness of its stone construction. Looking below, he saw that the tower continued down into the earth, its repeating layers mirroring those that were held above.

As he peered down into the depths of the tower, he noticed there was a light which seemed to stare back at him. He was a little confused as he continued to watch, but soon two small dots blocked out part of the light as he heard a familiar voice, "Pretty impressive, isn't it?" Looking up, Benjamin adjusted his glasses, which had slid down his nose, and noticed that Tecumseh and Penny had joined him. Suddenly, the light made sense. It must have been a reflection of the light above.

Tecumseh continued, "Should we take a look around?"

Benjamin replied, "Sure. Let's split up so we can see more of the tower." With no arguments from the others, they all split up and began to explore the architectural behemoth.

With a flash, Benjamin had left the others behind as he decided to take the high road, heading toward the top of the tower. As he zigzagged back and forth across the opening in the center of the skyscraper, each lightning leap obviously gained him some elevation, but the top still hung far away above him. Eventually, the hole seemed to get bigger and suddenly Benjamin found himself standing outside once again.

When Benjamin left Penny and Tecumseh behind, Tecumseh smiled awkwardly at Penny, which caused her to merely turn and begin walking around the inner perimeter of the tower. When she turned back, Tecumseh had also disappeared. Breathing a sigh of relief, Penny came across a strange contraption in one of the pillars. The column seemed to be hollowed out so that it could hold what looked like an auger. In fact, it looked like there was a spiral staircase in this pillar, except the staircase had no stairs.

After Penny had shunned him, Tecumseh leapt off the railing around the inner perimeter and descended into the depths of the tower. Something Tecumseh found strange was how a large structure like the Tower of Lebab could be so completely useless. So far, he couldn't tell why this tower was made or what it could even be used for. Walking along one of the many layers, Tecumseh found a simple door that seemed to blend right in to the wall opposite the opening in the middle of the stronghold. The door matched the curve of the structure, so it was almost indistinguishable, except for the handle on its right side. Feeling particularly exploratory, Tecumseh reached out, opened the door, and went inside.

The wind whistled by as Benjamin stood shivering on the top of the tower. He took gasping breaths as he tried to fill his lungs with the sparse amount of oxygen that remained so high above the earth. Taking a look around, Benjamin saw that, even though he was an extremely long distance from the ground, those who had built the tower had planned to go even higher. Organized piles of abandoned stones and hardened mortar were scattered around the edges of the roof, its wide expanse allowing for many to work at once. Among the construction materials was a beautifully crafted bell, its surface tarnished after years of sitting out in the elements. Heading over to the edge of the tower, Benjamin wanted to know how far he could see.

Penny was intrigued by this spiraled pillar and had managed to find another one directly adjacent to the first one she had found, except that its helix went in the opposite direction. Next to each hollowed out pillar, alongside the railing around the center of the tower, was a lever. Penny's intuition told her these levers surely had to do with these strange pillars, her only curiosity being what action the levers actually produced. Since the entire tower was abandoned, she decided that it wouldn't hurt to give one of the levers a pull. As she grabbed the first lever, Penny could feel a pulsating wave that felt like it was connected to the lever, albeit very far away.

When Tecumseh let the door close behind him with a dull thud, he found himself surrounded by darkness. He really hoped that no one would come out and ask him any questions. Holding up his pitchfork, he set the head ablaze, illuminating the entire area. He was a little surprised that this technique worked much better with his new pitchfork, but more surprised by what he saw. Before him stood a veritable army of statues, their grim visages set in stone, their armor sturdy but dusty. As he walked by the numerous rows of soldier statues, he began to speculate that every layer of this tower was filled with these silent warriors.

Gazing out over the vast expanse, Benjamin was impressed with the height of the tower on which he stood. From his lofty vantage point, he could even see the curvature of the earth, although it was very slight. Perhaps what was even more impressive was that, even though the tower stood so tall, Benjamin could feel no movement, despite the constant blowing of the wind. Letting his mind wander, Benjamin began to think about the people who built this tower. Why did they make it so tall? Why did they never finish? Why is it abandoned now? Benjamin was pulled out of his thoughts when a grinding sound was heard behind him. Turning around, he saw that the inside of one of the pillars was rotating. He hoped this was due to some action on the part of one of his partners, but wondered if they weren't completely alone.

Pulling the lever took a little bit of effort, as it had not been moved in a long time. When the resistance gave way, Penny found herself on the floor with a bruised tailbone. And yet, the result was certainly worth the slight injury. The inside of the pillar now rotated, which caused the spiral to spin upward. Penny began to wonder if the forces she felt through the lever were held back by a latch controlled by it. Perhaps there was some sort of underground stream which was causing the movement of the spiral. If that was the case, then what was the other lever for?

Lifting his lit pitchfork into the air, Tecumseh tried to get a sense of how big the area was, but the darkness seemed to propagate onwards past the light he created. After a while, Tecumseh felt he had probably walked past the outer perimeter of the tower, which just impressed on him how expansive the room really was. Observing the construction of the chamber, he noticed that some of the pillars weren't quite as well made as the first ones he encountered. When he approached one of these new pillars, he noticed that it seemed to be carved out of the rock itself. Small marks on the column revealed that it was dug out by hand, almost like a man-sized mole had removed the rock adjacent to it. Taking another look around, Tecumseh realized that whoever had the resources to carve out more underground storage space for an endless army of soldier statues could have the resources to fulfill his dreams. As he thought on these things, he faintly heard his name being called and headed back toward the door he entered earlier.

With a fluttering of his eagle wings, Benjamin descended down the tower until he came across Penny, who had just pulled the second lever. When Benjamin landed next to her, he could see that the spiral in the pillar next to the lever she just pulled had just started moving. Now both spirals were moving, each in a different direction, "I see you've found this tower's set of Archimedes Elevators," Benjamin remarked.

"It appears that I have."

"Do you know where Tecumseh went?"

"Nope, do you?"

"No."

"Should we call him?"

"I'm ready to go, so that's probably not a bad idea."

Pushing the levers back into their original positions, Penny managed to stop the noisy Archimedes Elevators before calling out to Tecumseh. After a few attempts by the both of them, they heard a door open on a level beneath where they were standing. Tecumseh approached the railing and looked upward toward them, "What is it?"

"Penny and I are ready to go, are you done?"

Using his fire to boost up to the ground level, Tecumseh landed in front of them and replied, "Not quite. I think there's something you both need to see."

Leading the two others around the tower, Tecumseh eventually found another door, similar to the one he found below. Opening the door, he led them into the darkness and illuminated the room with his pitchfork. Penny gasped when she saw the multitude of stone soldiers and Benjamin was silent with concern. Tecumseh could see that the room downstairs was definitely bigger than this one, which only confirmed in his mind what he already knew.

"I have a feeling that every level of this tower is filled with these soldiers. Now, whether or not they can be used for war yet, I don't know. But what I do know is that they are the property of the Army of Amedeo, as shown by the symbol 'N_A' on their shoulders."

"What should we do?" Penny asked.

"I think we need to destroy this tower."

Benjamin snapped out of his daze, "What? This tower is part of history. We can't just destroy it."

"Face it, Ben. No one has used this tower for years, and now that it *is* being used, I don't think the world would like to be taken over by a legion of stone soldiers."

"Granted, but how do you expect us to destroy this tower? It's obviously very well built."

"That's true, but I'm thinking that we use the tower's height to its disadvantage. After all, the supports at the bottom of the tower must have tremendous weight placed on them all the time. However-"

"What?"

"Well, I know that both of your powers can't really do much in this situation. If the tower is truly as sturdy as you say it is, Ben, then Penny's waves will just pass right through it. And let's not even start on the uselessness of lightning on stone."

Penny was starting to piece it together, "Are you suggesting that you destroy the tower by yourself? That's suicide!"

"I am, and it may be. But I can't just stand around here and let this opportunity pass us by. I need to sacrifice my power for the greater good of the world." Opening the door again, Tecumseh led them out into the inner circle of the tower and leaned against the railing, "There's no arguing with me. You'd both better get to safety so you aren't trapped in the resulting destruction. I'll try and bring it down as an implosion, but I can't make any promises."

Benjamin, having accepted that he was useless in this situation, even though he wanted to help destroy Amedeo's Army, gave Tecumseh his nod of approval. Tecumseh nodded back and took a step forward. In a quick motion, he grabbed Penny and gave her a kiss on the lips. Letting go and jumping up on the railing, Tecumseh simply said, "Goodbye," as he leaned backward and dove into the pit below.

Penny was shocked and could hardly contain her surprise as she ran to the railing to look down at Tecumseh's descent. As she saw his body turn into flames and start changing colors from orange to blue, Penny felt a tug on her arm as Benjamin tried to get her to follow him out of the tower. Instantly, the entire center of the tower was engulfed in flames which grew in intensity as the two remaining members of The Triumvirate ran out of the entrance of the Tower of Lebab.

In a spectacular display, white fire shot out of every level of the tower and climbed all the way to the top. A great moaning sound was heard as cracks began to appear on the ground. With a sudden jolt, the tower dropped a level, then began to accelerate into its own grave, pillars and stones crumbling and falling quickly down from the sky.

Benjamin had managed to get Penny away from the destruction and they both crouched behind some cover as the scene in front of them unfolded. With a loud thud, a cloud of dust kicked up and covered everything in a blinding haze. Covering his mouth with his sleeve, Benjamin was coughing as he got up and walked blindly toward the destructive scene. As he slowly picked his way through the debris; at once, all the dust disappeared with a loud boom.

Turning around, Benjamin saw Penny with her hands together and deduced that she was the one who cleared the dust.

They both headed to the crumbled pile of the tower, their Triumvirate symbols still glowing. The clattering of settling rubble was heard far below them as they tried to lift rocks off of the small pile which was now all that remained of the mighty tower. Penny fell back and sat down on a rock, exhausted by the effort as Benjamin worked away at the unrelenting pile. When she noticed that the light from their symbols had faded, and all that remained was the black mark obtained when only two of them were together, she softly spoke, "Stop, Benjamin."

"I can't. Even when there's no hope."

"Just *stop!*" Penny's voice cracked as tears started streaming down her cheeks. She was surprised by the sudden tears and wiped them away with her arm. Regaining her composure, she continued, "Even though we traveled together, I don't think either of us really understood what Tecumseh was all about. I think it's best that we accept his sacrifice and move on."

Benjamin could tell that Penny's words did not match with what she was feeling, so he merely dropped the matter and sat down next to her, "I guess we should go ahead and continue on with our journey. Maybe we can get some more people to join us in fighting against Amedeo's Army. And even if they don't manage to contribute quite like Tecumseh did, I'm sure that we can build a resistance to this absurd military power."

Sniffing away the last of her unexpected tears, Penny looked Benjamin in the eyes, "Ben, I think that may be our best option right now. To be completely honest with you, when we passed through the Imaginary World, I recognized one of the people who passed through before us. The one who was known as Tilde the Cardinal is a friend of my family. He goes by the name of Antonio. I'm sure that we could gain a lot of help if we go find him."

"We can go and find Antonio after we find Bram."

"What? I thought Tecumseh was the only one who wanted to find the Order of the Dragon."

"True, he did want to find the Order, but I want to find Bram. I wanted to confirm if the rumors of a non-Natural using these powers is true or not. Heck, we might even be able to get him to join our cause." Lifting up Penny's chin, Benjamin gave her some encouragement, "After we find Bram, then we'll go find Antonio, OK?"

A faint smile appeared on Penny's lips as she nodded, "OK."

Standing up and turning to look over the ruins of the Tower of Lebab, Benjamin nodded, "It sounds like we have our plan." Helping Penny to her feet, he continued, "Well, we'd better get to it then." Sprouting his eagle wings, Benjamin began to fly north once more with Penny right by his side.

Arriving at the gate of Menlo Castle, Mary pulled a long rope to ring the bell to let the residents of said castle know of her arrival. Mary was a tall woman, mainly due to her posture. With a very stiff face, her black dress matched the darkness in her eyes. She impatiently stood at the gate, tapping her toe rapidly until at last someone came and answered the door. The man who answered was also smartly dressed in black, which matched his neatly combed hair with the part right down the center of his head, "Can I help you?"

"I should certainly hope so, after having me wait for so long."

"Excuse me?"

"Surely you received the note I sent weeks ago informing you of my arrival?"

"I'm sorry, I don't own this castle; I merely work here."

"Then please be so kind as to move aside and take me to Thomas." The man was so shocked at the forward manner of the woman that he instinctively stepped aside and motioned for her to enter. As she walked toward the entrance, without looking back, she shouted behind her, "Mathison, my bags, please."

When the woman mentioned someone else's name, the man in black did a double take as it seemed that a hunched man holding two large bags almost appeared out of nowhere. Despite his hunch, his face was kind, even if the pronounced brow did make him seem somewhat dim-witted. Mathison waddled toward the door and mumbled, "Yes, Master Mary."

With everyone inside the castle, the man snapped out of his daze and introduced himself, "I'm Nikola, by the way, and-"

"Well, Nikola, if you could take me to Thomas as soon as possible, I would greatly appreciate it. We have many things to discuss."

Put off by Mary's attitude, Nikola decided that she would get the long tour of Menlo Castle, "Right this way, ma'am." As he led Mary through the winding corridors, he asked, "So, what is it you are so insistent on seeing Thomas about?"

With a frustrated sigh, Mary answered, "If you *must* know, I am interested in the electric power he is researching. I think I may have some groundbreaking, albeit somewhat unorthodox, research that could be done with that power."

"I see. Well unfortunately, I don't think we can help you with that anymore."

"And why not?"

Taking a turn and opening a door, Nikola led the group into a large room with an imposing device occupying one of the walls and running up into the ceiling, "You see, that device there is what we used to originally make the Skybolt orb. However, Alessandro, the creator of the orb, died in its creative process, taking his secret manufacturing technique to the grave. On top of that, a man by the name of Benjamin came in here, gained Thomas' trust, and stole the orb right out from under us. So, you see, I don't think Thomas can help you here."

"Is that a fact?"

"It is, but I do believe that *I* can do you one better."

"Oh? And what can you do?"

"Well, for one thing, I am Thomas' best assistant. And in my work with the Skybolt orb, I have come up with some unorthodox research opportunities of my own." Nikola led the group back out of the room and on an alternate route to the front of the castle where they started.

"You couldn't possibly have ideas more outrageous than mine, young man."

"Try me."

Mary was starting to warm up to the unrelenting repartee that Nikola was providing her, "How would you like to be a god?"

This stopped Nikola in his tracks, "A god? I merely wanted to be a magician, but I must confess that being a god would be a lot more fun. What do you have in mind?"

"The answer is simple . . ." for the first time since they started their conversation, Mary turned and looked at Nikola, ". . . life." Nikola raised his eyebrow as Mary continued, "In order to control man, one must control life. The ability to take life away pales in comparison with the power to give it."

"And how would the Skybolt orb manage to give life, might I ask?"

"Surely you must know what a mishandling of that power would do to a body. It is that same power which runs our nervous system and it is that same power which can stimulate a brain and start a heart. With that power, one can raise a body from the dead."

A sly grin crept across Nikola's face as he continued leading the group once again toward the entrance, "I see. If that's the case, then I myself may be able to help you."

"Are you sure that Thomas couldn't help us more?"

"Believe me; he would never go for something as incredible as what you are describing. Now, if you'll just trust me, I can help you attain your dream."

"You're on, Nikola." Mary suddenly realized that they were back at the entrance to the castle and that Nikola had led them literally and metaphorically right where he wanted them to go. This caused Mary to smile as she let out a short laugh, "Lead the way."

"With pleasure." The two of them left the castle as Mathison slowly brought up the rear, not complaining, but certainly not enjoying his lot in life.

A short hike away, Nikola led Mary to a small shack further up in the mountains. Dark clouds were advancing as the warmth of the morning had induced a thunderstorm, an occurrence that happened almost daily at this elevation. The shack had once been a church but, due to its inconvenient location, was abandoned long ago. Outside, it began to rain, creating little pools of mud in the cemetery adjacent to the church, its graves far surpassing the age of the wooden structure.

Inside the building, Nikola was rearranging some of the furniture and equipment to get ready for the proof of concept experiment to take place. Mary stood by the window and watched him work, occasionally throwing a glance outside to see how Mathison was doing on digging up her side of the experiment. Turning back to Nikola, who was adjusting a large metal orb above a makeshift table, Mary spoke offhandedly, "It's quite fortunate that your laboratory is in this location, otherwise it might have been a while before we could get to work."

Absorbed in his preparation, Nikola continued his adjustments as he replied, "Well, I must admit that this idea may have had a faint glimmer in the back of my subconscious somewhere, so it's really no surprise that I ended up here."

The door swung open and Mathison dragged in a giant of a body. The man must have been eight feet tall when he was alive, but now his limp form was easily pulled into the church, "This was the most recent grave I could find, Master Mary. I hope this will do." Plopping the corpse down on the makeshift table, Mary and Nikola gathered around their experiment.

A loud crash was heard outside, signaling the start of the thunderstorm. Nikola began to hurry around the church, adjusting equipment and getting things in position, "You'd better get that body ready quickly, as these thunderstorms don't last long up here." His advice was heeded before he even gave it, as Mary had opened up one of the large bags that she had Mathison carry. She had begun to remove the sections of decay, sew up any remaining holes, and attach metal rods in strategic points on the body.

As she worked, Mary made another offhand comment, "This corpse is really well preserved. It's almost as if it hasn't been dead but a few hours."

Mathison started to think this remark was aimed at him until Nikola replied to her comment, "That's partly due to the environment up here. A lot of organic material doesn't get a chance to grow; and the tundra these bodies are buried in acts more like a tomb than a grave."

The storm was a cacophonous monster roaring outside the small building when Nikola glanced up from his equipment and saw blue sky not far off on the horizon. Yelling over the noise of the thunder, he asked, "Are you done yet?"

Pulling a needle through one last stitch and biting off the surgical string, Mary replied, "Just finished!"

"Great!" Nikola pulled a lever, which opened up the cross on the top of the steeple, revealing a six-foot tall metal coil. The end of the coil fed into a network of wires in the ceiling of the church and down to the large metal orb hovering above the cadaver. Nikola knew that with the storm already having progressed this far, they'd only have one shot at this today.

Within seconds, Nikola knew they had succeeded. In a single moment, the hair on the back of his neck stood straight up, a bright flash blinded his vision, and a deafening boom managed to push him to the floor. Lightning had struck the coil on the roof and had traveled through the web of wires, down to the metal orb, where it made the final jump to the six rods embedded in the corpse's body. The body involuntarily convulsed upward, creating an arch on the table. When all the electricity had drained from the sky into the corpse, the body returned to its inverse prostrate position. A single second had elapsed.

Standing back up, Nikola found that the others had also been knocked down by the sheer power of the strike. As the storm marched away, its roars echoing off of the nearby mountains, Nikola took a deep breath and remarked, "It's quite the rush, isn't it?"

Mary wasn't interested in the rush involved with the dangerous situation they had just subjected themselves to; instead, she was interested in whether or not she had succeeded. Kneeling down next to the body, she looked across the corpse to see if there were any signs of life. A moving chest, a beating heart, anything. As light began to stream into the small mountain chapel, Mary noticed that the body's right hand twitched. She held her breath as she watched the hand, hoping that it wasn't just her imagination.

Once again, the hand moved, but this time it slowly made its way to the forehead of the formerly inanimate body. A low groan was heard from the ex-cadaver as it sat up and mumbled something unintelligible. Jumping up in elation, Mary hugged Nikola as she exclaimed, "It worked! It worked! It's alive!"

"I honestly didn't think it would work. Alessandro made it look so difficult, but I suppose having an organic container for the lightning works a lot better than an inorganic one like a glass orb."

The monster of a man stood up and was still mumbling incoherently. Mary remained standing there, an amazed look plastered on her face, as she watched her creation, "We shall call him Victor, for we have obtained victory over death. And to the victor go the spoils of life." Turning suddenly to Nikola, she had a look of inspiration in her eyes, "What about the rest of the graves? You said that most bodies were fairly well preserved. Do you think we'd be able to bring them all back to life at once?"

Nikola frowned as he tried to think through the issues that would come with increasing the scale of the experiment. However, the frown gradually disappeared as he began to work out how to do it, "It could be done-" he paused and started his sentence again, "It could be done, merely by using the capacitance that is inherent in the earth's crust. We'd just need to set up the bodies beforehand and rig the coil to multiply the voltage, but it could be done."

"Then what are we waiting for? Let's get to work!" Turning to Mathison, Mary barked orders, "Mathison! Get Victor out there and teach him how to dig up graves. Unless you want to dig them all up yourself, that is."

"Yes, master." Mathison obsequiously grabbed Victor's hand and led him outside where he began to show the incoherent man what to do.

After a few days of continual work, of which the only times not spent working were spent eating or sleeping, the group of four was ready to perform the coup de grace. With the telltale black clouds approaching, everyone retreated to the safety of the church. This time, the entire setup was outside, with the exception of a single switch that Nikola held in his hand. Each and every grave had been dug up, the corpses repaired and readied with the metal rods, then re-buried to take advantage of the soil's natural capacitance.

The large coil which once sat atop the chapel now stood in the middle of the graveyard. The web of wires now wove its way from the coil to all of the respective headstones. As rain started to sprinkle the freshly turned mounds of dirt, the first lightning strike hit the coil. The sheer intensity of the event hadn't decreased since the first time it had happened, but this time one strike would not be enough. They would need lightning to strike the same place multiple times.

As the storm progressed, more and more electricity was stored into the coil and the network of wires. So much electricity was stored, in fact, that many of the wires began to glow with anticipation. When the storm had passed, Nikola handed the switch to Mary and asked, "Would you do the honors?"

"With pleasure." Flipping the switch, Mary and the others watched as the stored energy made its final leap into the ground. The light from the web of wires faded and everyone waited with bated breath for the first sign of success or failure. After a few minutes, Mary became despondent, "I guess it didn't work this time. Maybe we should just go back to doing this one body at a time-"

Victor, who was slowly starting to re-grasp his verbal faculties, dumbly said, "Look!" as he pointed out the window. There in the graveyard, the piles of dirt began to stir. Stiffened hands reached out to fresh air and soil fell away from bodies sitting up for the first time in ages. A harmonious din of groaning accompanied the rising of the formerly dead.

Mary was even more excited than last time as she jumped up and down, "We are gods! Honest to goodness *gods!*"

Nikola was still stunned at this scientific achievement as he monotonously replied, "I'm not even sure where to go from here."

"That's simple." A smile crept across Mary's face as she grabbed Nikola's shoulder, "We join the army."

Chapter 6

Recruiting Switch

Benjamin and Penny hesitantly knocked on the door of the enormous castle which seemed to almost erupt out of the mountainside. Each villager they had talked to shuddered and most ran away screaming at the mention of the name "Bram." After finally getting enough information, they learned that he lived in the most out-of-place building in perhaps the whole countryside. With most villages residing nearby being comprised of small wooden huts, one did have to wonder how someone could afford the resources to make such an extravagant castle.

After standing in front of the tall, wooden doors for a few minutes, Benjamin leaned forward to lift the heavy doorknocker again, but found that the door now opened of its own accord. As such, Benjamin tripped his way into the vast hall just beyond the entrance. When Penny joined Benjamin inside the castle, the door seemed to automatically close in response. The foyer was dimly lit, with most of the light coming from a multitude of white wax candles set in chandeliers far above the exquisite tile floor.

Something didn't seem quite right to Benjamin as he took a few steps further in and called out into the emptiness, "Hello! Is anyone there?" More silence, "We're looking for Bram, and we were told that he lived in this castle." Even more silence.

Penny turned to Benjamin and pleaded with him, "Maybe we should just go. We're probably trespassing right now, and this may have just been a ruse by the villagers to get us to stop asking about Bram. Perhaps Antonio-" the sound of a door closing far away in a distant passage interrupted Penny's thoughts. Without saying a word, Benjamin grabbed Penny's wrist and led the way up the impressive staircase at the end of the hall.

When the path diverged to the left and the right, Benjamin turned to Penny and asked, "How sensitively can you feel waves?"

"What do you mean?"

"I'm asking if you can feel footsteps from far away."

Thinking for a moment, Penny replied, "I don't think I've ever tried, but it's worth a shot." Kneeling down and placing her hand on the floor, Penny focused on the Seawave orb that she wore on a necklace. A few moments later, she perked up, "Aha! I think I've got something, but I can't tell from which direction it's coming from. Here, give me a second." Placing her other hand on the floor, she repeated the process; after which, she looked up toward the top of the left staircase, "Whoever is here is up these stairs, and they're moving quicker than before."

Benjamin took the lead as he headed up the stairs, but was almost immediately stopped by a strange sound which seemed to be coming from above them, "Is that squeaking? No, not quite. What is that?" All at once, a black teeming cloud of bats seemed to pour out from the ceiling above them, causing both Benjamin and Penny to crouch on the ground.

When the barrage of bats had stopped, they both hesitantly stood up and found that they were no longer alone. Standing at the top of the stairs was an extravagantly dressed man, his black hair was slicked back and he wore a similarly shaded cape, hung from his shoulders. A pair of sharp, green eyes peered down a pointed nose at the two trespassers, "May I ask what you are doing here?" The man began to slowly walk down the stairs toward the pair.

The imposing aura of the man caused Benjamin to stutter, "W-w-we're just looking for Bram of the Order of the Dragon, a-a-and we were told-" Benjamin stopped mid-sentence when he noticed that a ¨ mark appeared on the man's neck. As he approached closer to them, it began to glow and Benjamin realized where he had seen the mark before, "You're Umlaut the Dragon, aren't you?"

This remark stopped the man in his tracks, "How do you know that name?"

Pointing at his forehead, Benjamin showed the λ that resided there, "I got this mark going through the Imaginary World, which is exactly where I learned about you."

"Oh? And what did it call you?"

"Lambda the Just."

Penny didn't want to be excluded from this, so she stepped out from behind Benjamin and timidly replied, "Psi the Sensitive."

"Ah, so *two* of you made it through and decided to find me, is that it?"

Not wanting to hang around much longer, Penny answered, "Not really. We were trying to find Bram, so unless you're him, we're out of luck."

As she turned to go, anticipating the answer she wanted to hear, Penny was stopped short by the man's response, "Yes, I am Bram. I am *also* Umlaut the Dragon. I am *also* the founder of the Order of the Dragon. Now I must apologize for my rude questioning, but you must realize that I don't get many guests around here. Now that my butler Alfred has left, I have lost the subtle eloquence of conversation." Bram turned and began to go back up the stairs, "Please join me upstairs as I try to get my bats to return to their belfry."

Benjamin readily followed, but Penny still had her doubts and only kept up with them so she could be with Benjamin.

As they climbed the stairs, Benjamin began to talk with Bram, "So, is it true that the Order of the Dragon has a massive horde of treasure somewhere?"

Bram laughed a short laugh, "*Ha!* No, that was merely some misinterpretation. When I started the organization, our motto was 'The greatest treasure is held in a chest'."

"So, there's no large pile of money and treasure somewhere? Considering the state of your house, I find that a little hard to believe."

"I obtained my wealth *far* before I ever ventured out and received my i-World status as 'Dragon'. Besides, money isn't the greatest treasure."

"Then what?"

Tapping on his sternum, Bram explained, "It's heart. We're all given this gift at birth and if we use it to its full potential, then we can get more treasure out of life than any amount of money could buy."

Penny groaned at the cheesy line as she tried to change the topic, "I've heard you can control dragons. Is this true, or merely something someone misunderstood because of your i-World name?"

"I think it's best if I just show you." Arriving at the top of the stairs and opening the solitary door that blocked their path, Bram led them into a room filled with tree branches and a wide variety of snakes. Penny had just about had it with this castle full of bats and snakes and merely grabbed on to Benjamin's arm to keep herself from screaming out in disgust.

Grabbing a harness from the wall, Bram showed Benjamin and Penny the cylindrical device, "This design here is the mark of the Order of the Dragon. It shows a dragon eating its own tail to symbolize a unity between beginning and ending. However, the real trick comes with the addition of the core that the uroboros dragon encircles." Walking up to one of the branches which held a lazily slithering python, Bram put the harness on the snake, which immediately sprouted wings like a bat.

Penny cowered, but Benjamin was truly interested in this development, "What's in the core? Is it blood from the bats that you keep?"

"That's right! How did you guess?"

"Well, I've seen similar effects elsewhere. In fact, if you'd let me hold that harness, I can show you." When Bram removed the harness from the python, the wings disappeared. Holding the blood core in his hand, Benjamin focused his energy into the disk as his hand began to change. With a flourish, Benjamin revealed that his hand had changed into the wing of a bat.

This impressed Bram as he exclaimed, "That's amazing! How do you do that?"

"Just like your snake harnesses the blood of the bats, I can do pretty much the same thing, but without the need of your symbol." Bram was speechless as he examined Benjamin's hand, "What I find more impressive is how you can get the snakes to control the bat blood. It was my understanding that very few people like myself could actually use these cores."

Looking up from Benjamin's hand, Bram postulated, "Maybe the control has to do with the symbol surrounding it. I'm not completely sure, but I know what's worked in the past."

Penny cleared her throat to remind Benjamin why they were there, "Oh, that's right. Bram, we've come to ask for your help. You see, we've discovered that the Army of Amedeo has been building up their military power, and we assume there may be a movement to take over the world soon. Now that I know you have passed through the Imaginary World like we have, I would really appreciate it if you could lend us your help."

Bram appeared downcast as he turned away, "I'm sorry, but I don't fight."

"But surely the Order-"

"We're not founded on principles of war, Lambda. We are founded on the principles of peace."

"But-"

"I think it'd be best if you left now."

Penny was more than ready to get out of the castle as she dragged Benjamin back down the stairs and out the front door. When she saw how despondent he had become, she smiled and touched his shoulder, "Cheer up, Ben. We don't need someone like Bram, with all his creepy animals. I'm certain that Antonio can help us." A small smile appeared on Benjamin's face as he nodded. In moments, they were off to find Antonio.

When Amedeo heard the news that the Tower of Lebab had fallen, he immediately called for his best soldier and set out to the scene of the disaster. When Amedeo and Grigori arrived at the site of the once mighty structure, all they found was a humble pile of rubble. The entire tower had collapsed in on itself and filled the caverns beneath it.

Amedeo was somewhat short, but he held himself with a presence that would intimidate almost anyone. And while he was not very handsome, with his thinning hair carefully combed over his head, a large and sharp nose poking out from his face, and eyes that seemed to bug out from the large bags underneath them, the sharp look in those dark eyes revealed a man who was always thinking. Always planning. Always plotting.

The commander-in-chief sighed as he climbed up on the ruins and examined the damage done, "This tower was too strong to fall at the hands of anything natural. Someone must have been able to find a weakness, but I can't imagine any of the other armies out there would have the manpower to exploit something like that." With another sigh, Amedeo jumped down from the pile and headed back to where Grigori was still standing at attention, "I suppose we'll have to figure out a way to salvage what we can from this, but it's not going to be easy."

"Sir, I think you'd better look behind you." Turning around, Amedeo watched as the ground nearby began to smoke. Soon, not only was the ground smoking, but it was glowing red. Amedeo almost took a step toward the glowing dirt until Grigori stepped in front of him to block his path. The strange phenomenon continued until the ground suddenly burst open and the molten rock fell into the cavern below.

Slowly emerging from the underground darkness was a man covered entirely in fire. With a deep sigh, the fire went out and he looked up at the two military men standing in front of him. A sly smile crept across his face as he spoke to the Aquila-Class General, "You must be Amedeo. I had a feeling you'd eventually show up."

Grigori was appalled at the man's glib attitude, "How dare a mere man such as yourself speak to General Amedeo like that! And furthermore, what are you doing here? This area is strictly property of the Army of Amedeo."

Looking past Grigori, the man spoke once more to Amedeo, "Do you want to call off your lap dog? I'm actually here to join your side." Motioning to the pile of rubble behind him, the man continued, "I just needed to do something drastic to get your attention. After all, I admire someone who came from such humble beginnings like myself. Someone who lusts for power and influence like you do."

The man began to pace toward Amedeo, making Grigori tense up with every step, "When you worked your way up to the head of the tiny militia that protected a worthless figurehead of a King, I'm sure you realized you could do whatever you wanted. Through propaganda, threats, and downright blatant lies, you started to grow that militia into an army. And yet, other nations weren't going to stand by and let that happen. With each assault against your army, you grew your forces to outnumber your opponent and eventually absorb them completely. Now, I know that others may see your tactics as martial bullying, but when I see the kind of numbers you've gathered here, I can't help but get excited at what your endgame might be."

Amedeo was intrigued by this man and the almost intimate knowledge he had of his rise to power. A smile came across his face and a twinkle entered his eyes as he immediately thought of a test that would result in a win-win situation for himself, "What is your name?"

"How about you just call me Chi the Powerful of The Triumvirate."

"OK, Chi, you've gotten my attention. Under normal conditions, I would have you killed for being a Natural, let alone for knowing so much about my tactics, but if you can be of some use to me, I'll let you join." He held up his index finger as he continued, "However, in order to serve in my army, you need only pass one requirement."

"You're on."

Pointing at his subordinate, Amedeo challenged, "Defeat my best soldier, Grigori. I'm sure he'd love to fight you after that 'lap dog' comment you made earlier."

Both Grigori and Chi smiled as they prepared to fight. When Chi pulled out his pitchfork, Grigori grasped his black staff in a fighting position, "I see you were also once a farmer, Chi. Just know that while you may hold the title of 'powerful', I hold the title of 'reaper'."

With a scoff, Chi replied, "And I suppose you think that staff will be enough to take me on-" without allowing Chi to finish, Grigori had begun his attack. Chi was fortunate enough to get his weapon in place just in time to block the quick thrust.

As the two warriors struggled against each other, Grigori responded, "Oh, this staff is more than enough to take out the likes of you." Kicking the bottom of his weapon, Grigori produced a long, straight blade which sprung from the shaft of the otherwise innocuous looking rod. Since both fighters were so close, Chi had barely enough time to dodge, but he managed to evade the attack with a short burst of fire from his mouth.

When the two men separated, Chi noticed that some of Grigori's hair was singed as an after effect of his evasion, "Just let me know if this fight is getting too hot for you, Mr. Reaper." With Grigori's switchblade scythe revealed, Chi was a little more guarded and stood at a distance that would require one of them to make the next move.

After a few moments, it seemed to Chi that Grigori was biding his time, waiting for his opponent to reveal something. Engulfing his body in flames, Chi pushed some of the fire to strategic points on his body to accelerate his movements and launch his attack. Even though Chi was moving faster, Grigori was easily keeping up and even managed to get in a few attacks of his own.

Swinging his scythe from the outside, Grigori's weapon was stopped once again by the shaft of Chi's Pitchfork. With the blade and shaft nested against the pitchfork's handle, Grigori used this pivot point to throw the shaft away from Chi, who took this as a sign of surrender, "Giving up so soon?" When the scythe's shaft whipped around, Grigori grabbed the bladed end of the weapon and pulled it toward himself. Chi heard a familiar click and managed to leap out of the way with the assistance of some blue fire erupting from his feet.

High above the soldier, Chi hovered for a moment before descending back to the earth. He saw that the weapon Grigori now held was a dual-bladed scythe, each blade a straight edge perpendicularly attached to the black staff. Each blade was on the opposite end and side of the staff as compared to its brother. Grigori now held Chi's Pitchfork in his other hand as he examined the implement, "The workmanship on this is quite exquisite, but it is useless in a fight." As Chi landed, Grigori threw the pitchfork to the side and began to approach his opponent, twirling the scythe in an exhibition of handling skill.

Now covered in blue flames, Chi's pride had been bruised enough times that he knew it was time to end this battle. Closing his eyes, he focused all his energy into the Hellfire orb he held near his chest. Grigori picked up his pace as he headed toward Chi, "Giving up so soon?" he mockingly asked. With a mighty wind-up, Grigori swung his scythe at Chi, but didn't connect with anything as he became blinded by a flash of white light.

When he regained his sight, another flash occurred as Chi reappeared in front of him. Grigori tried to attack, but it was far too late. A searing pain ran up the left side of his head and blackness soon followed from his left eye. In that single moment, Grigori knew he had suffered defeat and had failed his commanding officer. Before him stood Chi, clad in a brilliantly white fire, holding his pitchfork close to Grigori's body, its metal prongs also exhibiting the same white light and emanating an uncomfortable amount of heat.

Holding his hand against the left side of his face and cautiously watching Chi with his right eye, Grigori could hear the slow applause of General Amedeo gradually growing louder behind him, "*Magnifico!* You've done well, Chi. You shall have your wish as long as you let my man live." Chi backed away and soon all the flames had disappeared. Grigori could feel Amedeo's hand on his shoulder as he whispered something inaudible in his soldier's ear.

When Amedeo arrived at Chi, his hand extended for a congratulatory handshake, Chi had pulled out something from one of his pockets and gave it to Amedeo during the exchange, "This is one of my gifts to you for allowing me to fight on your side, and as a token to apologize for destroying your tower." Opening his hand, Amedeo found a small disk with a "–" mark on it. The item looked familiar to him, but he knew that his research team would be able to put it to good use.

"The gift of your fighting ability is more than enough, but I will accept this as a tribute to our cause. Now the Naturals don't stand a chance against us."

"That leads me to my second gift. However, this one comes with a condition."

"Oh? And what might that be?"

"I have come in contact with many others like myself who can use the power I have displayed for you here. Others who you have called 'Naturals'."

"And the condition?"

"Let me personally eliminate these Naturals to make sure your superiority remains intact."

This development pleased Amedeo and he let a smile creep across his face as he gave the order, "Make it so. And since you will do this act for me, and since you have proven your power to me, I will make you my second in command. Whatever you need from my army will be given to you. The only one who can tell you otherwise is me."

This development pleased Chi immensely, as a smile once again crept across his face. He had gone all in and had emerged victorious beyond what he had hoped. Erasing the smile and standing at attention, Chi gave his first salute as the newest member of the Army of Amedeo.

Now it was Benjamin's turn to be skeptical, "Are you sure that Antonio can help us fight?" The two members of The Triumvirate had just knocked on the large wooden doors of a modest monastery and were waiting for someone to let them in.

"I'm sure of it. While mom rarely spoke of Antonio, the few anecdotes she did tell me were certainly impressive. And at the very least-"

A small opening slid open in the door and a voice came from the darkness, "What do you seek?"

Penny stepped over to the opening and leaned down to talk into it, "We're here to meet with Antonio."

"What business do you have with The Red Priest?"

"He's a friend of my mother's and we need to ask him something." The opening snapped shut as Penny and Benjamin were left standing there in awkward silence.

After a few moments of this, Benjamin spoke up, "Maybe we're at the wrong monastery. After all-" a deep groaning sound drowned out the rest of Benjamin's sentence as the massive wooden doors began to open. They creaked to a stop as the opening between them became big enough for a person to enter. An arm clad in a simple brown robe emerged from the darkness beyond the doors and beckoned the two to enter.

When the doors had been closed and their eyes had become used to the decreased light, Benjamin and Penny found themselves in a simply constructed hallway. Lined with lit candles, the flickering lights caused their shadows to dance on the walls. The hooded monk's face was obscured, but his voice emerged simply from the darkness, "Follow me." He then turned and began to walk down the corridor, leading the two visitors through the eerily quiet building.

As they followed, Benjamin and Penny investigated their surroundings. Benjamin noticed that the monastery was incredibly old, not only by its architecture, but by the layer of black soot which coated the ceiling above the candles. Penny, on the other hand, noticed that all the walls were bare, and bore no religious accoutrement aside from the unending line of candles. Soon, a bit of natural light began to appear from a doorway further down the hall.

When their guide arrived at the open door, he stood at its threshold, blocking their path, "Father Antonio, you have visitors." He backed away and allowed the guests to pass through the door.

"Thank you, Thelonious," was the man's reply. The door led to an open-sky garden where a man clad in a bright red cassock stood with his back to the visitors. Upon his head, he wore a zucchetto of similar color, which seemed to blend into the red, curly hair it sat upon. He was holding his palm in the air toward the single tree which stood in the middle of the area. From a nest in the tree, a cardinal hopped down from its home and fluttered off the branch to land on the man's hand, pecking seed out of the open palm.

As Benjamin and Penny approached, their i-World symbols began to glow, which confirmed to them what they had already suspected. When they came even closer, they could see through the red robes, the faint light of a symbol glowing on the man's back. The ~ that appeared confirmed Antonio was Tilde the Cardinal.

"Uncle Antonio!" Penny exclaimed, which caused the bird to fly away to the safety of its nest.

"Is that Penneut Psinodeo? What brings you here, my child?" Antonio turned around with a smile on his face, which quickly disappeared when he saw the glowing symbols on his visitors, "Where did you get those marks?"

Benjamin stepped forward, "That's actually what we've come here to talk about." Antonio gave him a stern look as Benjamin continued to explain, "You see, we've been through the Imaginary World as well, and we know from experience that it is not an easy journey to accomplish. We also know that there is a force being gathered that is liable to overthrow the entire world. We need powerful men like yourself to join our fight, or we will surely fail."

Antonio sighed as he sat down on a stone bench beneath the tree, "I think you may be mistaken. While I did make it through the Imaginary World, that was a very long time ago."

Penny spoke up, "But I heard from my mother that you were a great influence on her. Is that not true?"

"Well, that might be true, but my involvement with Trea Raiga was more of a managerial position than one of a fighting comrade. You see, in my younger days I was in charge of a group that fought for justice, much like you're trying to do today. We were known as 'Seasoned Compass'."

Benjamin became excited, "I've heard of them! They're the four most powerful people on the planet. Are you saying you weren't one of them?"

"That's right. I merely ran the group. I had no special powers like Haru Higashi and the rest of them." Antonio looked over at Penny, who had a confused look on her face, "Oh, that's right. I bet your mother never told you her code name. While she was in Seasoned Compass, Trea Raiga was known as Haru Higashi."

"You've obviously disbanded since then, so do you know where the rest of the members are?"

"I've only been able to keep track of two of them. Obviously, Haru Higashi is one, and the other is Fuyu Kita. I believe his real name is William, but I could never confirm it from him. As far as the other two, Natsu Minami and Aki Nishi, I'm not sure where they've gone."

"So, where does Fuyu Kita live?"

"Actually, not far from here, although I wouldn't recommend attempting to visit him."

"Why not?"

"He's kind of a hermit. Since we disbanded, he's holed himself up in a cave on the top of Mount Jack."

"You mean the mountain that's perpetually covered in ice?"

"That's the one."

After a moment of thought, Benjamin spoke, "Could you come with us to convince him to join our cause?"

"Unfortunately, *non*. While I do admire your sense of justice like I once had, I have sworn to the ideals of non-violence. Going to war goes against those ideals. Plus, I cannot leave the monastery because of my commitment here. However-" Antonio stood up and removed a gold ring from his finger, "I can let you have this. I had it made shortly after I became Tilde the Cardinal. It was my seal for Seasoned Compass. Show him this and hopefully he'll listen to you."

Dejectedly accepting the ring, Benjamin quietly replied, "Thank you." He turned to go and called for Penny to follow, "Let's get going. We've got another long day ahead of us."

Hugging Antonio, Penny said, "It was good to see you again, Uncle Antonio."

"It was good to see you too, Penneut Psinodeo. Give your mother my regards when you see her again."

"I will." Penny turned to follow Benjamin, who had already made his way into the dark corridors of the monastery. Sensing that the strangers had left, the red bird hopped out of its nest and fluttered down to a lower branch where it gave a short chirrup. Antonio looked at his feathered friend and smiled as he reached into his pocket for some more bird seed.

○

The Library of Delaxanair was buzzing with excitement. Not only were great strides in fluxion research being accomplished, but General Amedeo had sent an announcement that he would personally be stopping by to check on the progress. The researchers were talking amongst each other about the different breakthroughs they had discovered.

"I am certain that General Amedeo will be most pleased with my contribution, since the soldiers I have created can feel no pain and are quite the unstoppable force." Mary proudly touted her achievements as Victor sat awkwardly in a chair behind her.

"While I do admit that your entrance with an army of the reanimated dead was certainly a flashy way to go about returning here, I think part of the credit should go to Nikola as well," Albert replied as he nodded at the newest member of the group.

Not wanting to be outdone, Mary spoke up again, "True, but if I hadn't brought Mathison along with me, we'd never have figured out how to use the Soul-fusion fluxion on inanimate objects to make them come to life. If my soldiers are unstoppable, then surely his are invincible." Mathison blushed at the compliment, the first he had ever received, let alone from Mary. And yet, the stone soldier who had been one of the first failed experiments was now Mathison's servant because of the application of the Soul-fusion fluxion.

Dmitri wanted to move the conversation off of the narcissistic woman, "*Da*, but let's not forget that as a *group* we figured out how to create and harness the very first Fluent, the Fluent of Light."

Mary replied with a smirk, "Oh? And how's the other Fluent coming? The Fluent of Darkness isn't even close to being complete; even after *all* of you worked on it." With a short laugh, she continued, "By the way, how's that Number Disk-creating rock coming along?" With no clever retort, Dmitri silently scowled at Mary.

The door opened and everyone became silent. When the group of researchers realized that it was just General Gulogulo, they went back to their conversations. Albert approached the high ranking officer, "We are glad to see you again, General."

"Am I the first one here?"

"What do you mean?"

Pulling out a letter with General Amedeo's "N_A" seal on it, Gulogulo explained, "I was told that it was time to receive my fluxion for the coming war."

"*Coming* war? I thought this research was merely to be used as a deterrent."

"Apparently something happened which requires our immediate attention. I've been told that two other Cross-Class Generals will be coming to receive fluxions as well. We may not be far from battle, although against what or whom I have yet to surmise."

The door opened again, revealing another highly decorated General who carried a large longbow on his back. He silently held open the door as two more Generals entered. This time everyone became silent and stayed that way as they watched the injured General enter the room, his bandaged face giving many of them something to think about.

General Amedeo approached Albert and commanded, "Give me a status update, then I'll address the rest of the group." The researchers overheard this order and quietly left the room, the last of them shutting the door on the lead researcher and the four Generals. Sitting down at the front of the room, Amedeo asked, "So, what do you have for me?"

"We have made a lot of progress, but we are far from the goals you have set for us."

"I see. Maybe this will help your team," reaching inside his jacket, Amedeo pulled out the "−" lost Number Disk and set it on the table.

Albert's eyes became wide as he realized that this was one of the missing pieces to their research, "Where did that come from?"

"I'll tell you later. First, let me know just how close you've come to getting me my septillion-man army."

"Well, while they are not all quite battle capable yet, we believe we have found a few techniques to help meet your goal."

"OK, then how much do you have right now?"

"We are at a little more than 60%."

Doing some calculations in his head, Amedeo took a moment to respond, "That may have to do for now. What ways are you using the fluxions to get that number?"

"We have three methods, two of which are somewhat similar. The first method was discovered by Nikola and Mary and involved resurrecting the dead. These re-animated corpses are completely loyal, extremely strong, and feel no pain. Part of my estimate relies on them going to more cemeteries to create more soldiers."

"I see. Good work. Go on."

"Secondly, many of your soldiers who have been discharged due to injury could be fixed so they could fight again. Now, keep in mind, these injuries involve loss of limbs so the sheer joy of being repaired may give these men the fortitude to fight for you again."

"Good use of existing resources, I like that. What's the final method?"

"Well, as you tasked us to do, we have managed to make soldiers by infusing a soul with an inanimate object. Statues work well, but so do suits of armor. Pretty much anything that's human shaped. Mathison was behind this part of our research, but our only problem now is finding enough blood cores to meet the quota."

Standing up, Amedeo began to give orders, "This last method is easy to utilize. Send out a command to all my troops that they need to give some blood to the cause. Hopefully they won't need to give too much, am I right?" Albert nodded in agreement. "Also, go into the prisons and get as much blood as you can from there. I especially want you to use the prisoners in Pandora Prison. In fact, if they're going to be executed anyways, just drain all of their blood and use it to make more blood cores. I've got a lot of statuesque soldiers that need these blood cores in order to work, so make it happen."

Motioning to the Generals who had been silently standing at attention, Amedeo asked Albert, "I assume you've prepared what I've asked for?" Nodding in confirmation, Albert went over to a safe in the corner of the room and knelt down to open it. When it was open, he took out three folders and, using his best deductions, gave the folders to their respective Generals. Each folder was red in color and had "Top Secret" emblazoned in black ink on the cover. "If you wouldn't mind giving an explanation," Amedeo suggested.

Clearing his throat, Albert began, "Gentlemen, the dossiers you now hold contain all the information needed to obtain your fluxion. Some require more work than others, but that work is important to the whole mission we are trying to accomplish here."

Tossing down the folder on the table, the General with the longbow turned to leave, "I'm powerful enough as it is. Just tell me when and where and I'll fight."

As the door closed, Albert looked over to Amedeo, who did not look pleased, "Do not worry, sir. We will make sure that General Braun's ammunition uses the fluxions we have developed." When Amedeo's expression changed for the better, Albert turned to the injured General and continued, "Now, I am assuming that you are General Grigori, since I have already met General Gulogulo." A small nod confirmed the fact. "Your fluxion is something I personally oversaw. However, the installation process could be tricky or even life threatening."

Grigori gruffly responded, "What do you mean 'installation process'?"

"Well, you see, before I started my research here, I had discovered the part of the body known as the 'Time Thread'. It is a very fine string that slowly emanates from a person's body. Since it moves away from a everybody at the speed of light, the faster you move, the slower it leaves your body, thereby making you remain younger longer. The fluxion core that you need ties into the Time Thread and keeps it from leaving your body, essentially making you immortal. However, the only way to do this is through a process which essentially boils down to open heart surgery. Plus, the person who supposedly has this fluxion core is not quite right in the head."

Amedeo spoke up, "I'd like to accompany Grigori on his quest to obtain the core, and I'd like you to come along as well so we can give Grigori his fluxion as soon as possible. Do you have anyone else who could come along with us for assistance?"

"I think Herbert may just be the right person for this, so I will let him know."

Grigori spoke up, "Is this what you meant when you whispered, 'I'll make it so you won't ever lose again' in my ear?"

Amedeo was frank, "It is."

Turning to Gulogulo, Albert continued, "As for you, your reward comes with a bit more work behind it. You are going to be accompanied by Mathison and a soldier who has one of our fluxion prosthetics. They are both needed to convince Luvnac to cooperate with us."

"Did you say *Luvnac*? As in *the* legendary swordsmith, Luvnac?"

"That is correct. However, he has long since stopped making swords and has instead turned to producing armors. We need these armors built to Mathison's specifications so we can use them for part of your army. I believe the amputee soldier will help convince him to make as many armors as possible."

"I still don't understand what my reward is."

"Before Luvnac began making armors, he made one last sword. This sword was forged with the purest of a specific type of metal. The nickname we have given this metal is 'fluxionite'. It was this same metal that he used to make the six Noble Swords. As such, the properties that his final sword possesses allow for the power of fluxions to be fully harnessed by the wielder. And yet-"

"You mean there's more?"

"*Ja*, but this is the final task. Our intelligence suggests that Luvnac knows where a certain individual known only by the codename 'Aki Nishi' is located. This individual has an extremely powerful Elemental-fluxion core. In fact, he may have the *most* powerful fluxion core. Once you obtain Luvnac's final sword, you will need to find Aki Nishi and get his fluxion core. I doubt that either will give you these items without a fight, so I hope you are up to it. You are free to decline this mission like Braun did."

A large grin was plastered on Gulogulo's face as he replied, "*Non*, I look forward to this."

Amedeo seemed a little impatient, "Is that all? Then let's bring everyone else in so I can talk to them." Albert understood that his superior's time was valuable, so he hurried over to the door to let everyone back in. Once they were settled, Amedeo began to speak, "You have all done very well so far. But just know that you're not finished yet. The time on which I need to call upon all your valiant efforts quickly approaches." Walking over to Grigori, Amedeo continued, "I know you have all seen what a Natural can do, but let me emphasize why we need to match their power."

Nodding at Grigori, the soldier understood the gesture and began to remove the bandage on his head, revealing a white scar that ran up the right side of his face, the now milky-white eye staring straight ahead. The room gasped and some hesitantly approached to look at the damage.

Dmitri was the first to say anything, "That's something else. It looks like the wound was immediately cauterized. What could do something like that?"

"Not 'what', 'who'," was Amedeo's reply.

Nikola, having experienced something similar, spoke out, "You mean a *person* did this? I've given my fair share of facial scars, but none looked quite like this."

Jules was the next one to interject, "But surely, against the most powerful soldier in Amedeo's Army, this person must have much worse wounds, shouldn't he?"

Grigori looked down, a glazed look of dejection entering his good eye. Amedeo merely shook his head, "General Grigori's defeat was sound and quick. He didn't even manage to hit his opponent even once." The room grew silent again.

"Well, I certainly don't want to be fighting against these Naturals, if that's the case," Mary remarked.

"Don't you see? This is the reason why your research is so important!" Amedeo was fired up, "If we can control the fluxion cores like they do, then we can actually stand a chance against them!" Calming down a bit, he continued, "I'm sending the Naturals an ultimatum. They have one week to answer us; and as such, we have one week to perfect our research." Finishing his speech, Amedeo motioned for his soldiers to follow as he left the room.

Stunned with the quick deadline, Albert snapped out of a small stupor and started giving orders, "Mathison, I want you to go with General Gulogulo and follow him wherever he needs to go. Herbert, you and I will accompany General Amedeo and General Grigori. Dmitri, I have something that you will find most useful. The rest of you already know what you should be doing, so get to it!"

○

The morning was still dim as the rising sun struggled to break through the light layer of clouds. Benjamin and Penny strolled along a familiar path through the woods toward Rancho de la Sol. Accidentally brushing against a tree, Benjamin cringed and held his bandaged left shoulder. Penny was concerned, "Are you still hurt? I thought once we treated it, the pain would stop."

With a short laugh, Benjamin replied, "I thought so too." He took a deep breath and attempted to control the pain. Rubbing the injured shoulder, he tried to lighten the mood, "Although I must say I've never been given the cold shoulder *quite* like that before."

"That still doesn't excuse William's behavior. I would have thought that someone who worked with my mom and Uncle Antonio would have better manners than that."

For a moment, Benjamin was thoughtful, then he spoke, "I've been wondering about something. Something about Antonio and Bram."

"What, like if they know who Breve the Lion is?"

"Well, that's part of it, but since we didn't ask if Antonio knew Bram, then we can't be sure if there's a connection at all. At least we know there's not a connection like we had as The Triumvirate." Both were silent for a while as they thought of the loss of their comrade. Benjamin snapped out of the temporary daze and continued, "Anyways, I was wondering if everyone who passed through the Imaginary World was given a weapon like we were. I mean, I know we were special, like I said before, but I still wonder how many similarities we share with the others."

"I'm sure we can ask my mom once we get back. I know that she's got a lot of explaining to do." With a sigh, Penny changed her tone, "I find it hard to believe she was ever a part of a group like that, and I wonder if she's kept in contact with any of the other members, since William and Antonio certainly didn't know anything."

Continuing on the mountain path, both travelers found that the ground was moist from the recent rain, and the atmosphere seemed to emanate a refreshing feeling, but also an eerie feeling of solemnity. As they hiked, Benjamin glanced over at Penny and recalled the first time they had met. It seemed so long ago, but it couldn't have been more than a few weeks. They had been through so much together. In fact, Benjamin couldn't recall the last person he had spent this much time with.

Something in Penny's demeanor suddenly changed, almost as if she had realized something she had forgotten. She quickly came to a stop and put out her arm in front of Benjamin to signal that he needed to stop with her. Looking around at their surroundings, Benjamin didn't notice anything amiss, "Is there something wrong?" he whispered with no understanding of why he was talking so softly.

"It's strange . . ."

"What is?"

"The Kármán Line is gone."

"Kármán *what?*"

"Kármán Line. It's a little difficult to explain, but it is part of the reason why our home can be hidden so well. If it's not there, then-" Penny trailed off as pieces of information began to fall into place in her mind. She slowly began to walk along the path again, her pace rapidly increasing until she was running at full sprint toward the edge of the forest.

"Hey! Wait up!" Benjamin was running after Penny, which was no easy task in the forest of her youth, let alone a forest illuminated with the dim light of sunrise. Soon, he burst out of the trees and almost ran into Penny, who was standing a short distance from the clearing, breathing heavily, "Could you please tell me what's going on?" Benjamin was yelling now, but Penny didn't seem to hear, she abruptly started sprinting down the hill into the valley.

Taking a moment to survey the landscape, Benjamin's eyes grew wide with shock. Where there had once been a thriving ranch, replete with crops and livestock, there was now a desolate and burnt swath of land. The few remnants of anything significant were charred black, and most seemed like crooked fingers bunched together, reaching for the light orange sky. Pools of still water dotted the area, reflecting the clearing sky amidst such devastating destruction.

When he had finally realized where Penny was going, Benjamin knew he needed to act fast. In a flash, he turned to lightning and struck the ground of the front yard of her house, his hands outstretched to block her path. She just kept running, and collided with him, at which point he wrapped his arms around her to get her to stop. Behind him lay a black pile of rubble, the soot of a recent fire washed off in a few spots from the morning rain. No longer the quaint home of a family, Benjamin suspected that the ruins were now her family's tomb. He held her tighter to prevent her from seeing what she already knew was there.

Suddenly, the resistance was gone. Sobs racked Penny's body as her knees gave out and she collapsed to the ground. For a moment, her shoulders heaved. Her eyes were clenched shut and her mouth stood agape, but no sound came out. With a gasp of air, she let out a scream. Pebbles on the ground seemed to rattle in response to the yell. The cry was broken only by the last of her breath exiting her lungs, at which point she gasped again and continued to weep.

Benjamin couldn't help but feel a tight knot develop in his throat as he stood over the grieving woman. When he knelt down to talk to Penny, she grabbed him and dug her face into his chest, where he could feel the tears seeping through his vest and shirt. Placing a gentle hand on her back, Benjamin let Penny release all her grief. When her inhalations became less staccato, she took a deep breath and let out a long sigh. Pulling away from Benjamin, she gazed up into the man's face. With red eyes and puffy cheeks, a look of helplessness stood predominant on her face.

Quietly, almost hesitant to say anything lest she break into sobs again, she whispered, "Why did this happen? Who do I have left?" A strength slowly returned to her voice as her grief turned into anger, "What can I do about any of it!?" Tears began to gather in her eyes as she stared at Benjamin's stoic expression.

In a comforting tone, Benjamin spoke, "Odds are, you still have a brother. I know you have a sister-in-law," he paused, "And you have me."

This last comment brought a smile to her face as she let out a short laugh, "I'm sorry. I'm not laughing at you, I'm laughing at myself." The smile slowly vanished when she began to think about the situation, "Still, it doesn't make any sense."

"What doesn't?"

"The Kármán Line should have stopped any intruders."

"All right, I have to ask again: what *is* the Kármán Line?"

Penny scratched her head as she tried to think of the best way to explain, "Well, one of my mother's powers is an invisible barrier that protects the entire area. Most people encounter the barrier and decide to go in a different direction. Others try to brave the resistance the barrier induces, but those people don't make it very far."

"So, if this line was around your home, how come Tecumseh and I didn't notice it?"

"That's because I was with you. The barrier can be accessed by those who are already known by my mother, so I was kind of like your pass into the area."

"It would stand to reason then, that whoever did this to your family was already known by your mother."

"I suppose so, but I can't think of anyone who would want to hurt this family."

"Well, maybe someone made it all the way through the barrier. Maybe there was a large force that was able to overwhelm the Kármán Line and do this atrocious act."

"That may be a possibility, but who on earth would storm our humble home?"

"The only group that I can think of would be the Army of Amedeo. They've been up to no good recently, and I'm sure they probably had a reason to do this to your family, although I'm not sure what reason that could possibly be."

"That's just the thing, though. I know for a fact my family was by no means weak. We all could use powers that any normal person couldn't reasonably defeat. I think they may have been surprised. Maybe your first theory about a known intruder is right."

Both were silent for a moment while they contemplated the situation. Benjamin perked up when he thought of an idea, "While we don't necessarily know why this happened to your family, we can do something about it."

"What could we possibly do?"

"We can train. We can become masters of our powers. We can make sure that whoever was after your family cannot possibly defeat us."

"How do you think we could possibly become that powerful?"

"I have a friend who has helped me hone my powers, and I think he may be able to help us again."

"I'm game if you are. Anything to help me avenge my family will be a welcome adjustment." With these words, Penny stood up and started walking away from the charred remains of her former life.

Chapter 7

Training's Reward

Gulogulo once again opened the map from the dossier he had received and examined it. This couldn't possibly be right. According to the map, Luvnac was holed up in Daniel Volcano. Everyone knew the origins of this volcano. They all knew how a meteor struck the earth in an area where the crust was at its thinnest, thereby allowing a lot of pent up volcanic energy to erupt from the ground, creating the unmistakable geographic formation. The top of the volcano happened to rise above the crater that created it, providing the illusion that the ground was almost fluid, stopped in time at the moment after the meteor had struck.

Mathison peered over Gulogulo's shoulder at the map and asked, "Is anything wrong?"

This snapped Gulogulo out of his thoughts as he looked at his traveling partners, "*Non*, I was just checking to make sure we were in the right area." The soldier commanded to accompany these two on their journey stoically remained silent and so far had just followed orders.

The trees were thick in the realm of Timberland, but the daunting edifice of the volcano could be seen in the distance. When the group reached the edge of the crater, they couldn't help but gasp at the sight before them. The edge of the forest came to a sudden stop and dropped at the perimeter of the crater. Everything was yellow and everything smelled of sulfur past the crater's threshold. Examining the volcano placed in the center of the crater, Mathison pointed at one of the openings in the side of the imposing mountain, "Look at that one opening, it's not venting steam like the others. Perhaps that's where we need to go."

Gulogulo merely nodded as he began to guide the group down into the crater. Even though he had travelled with Mathison for a short time, he found the hunchbacked man to be intelligent and knowledgeable. In fact, it was almost as if his entire personality changed when he was away from Mary.

Where once there was obsequiousness and cowering, now there was confidence and a commanding spirit. Gulogulo silently thought on these things as the others came along behind him.

After a few hours of hiking, it became extremely obvious that they were approaching an active volcano. The sulfurous smell and the heat had increased to almost unbearable levels. With the cave's entrance looming in front of the group, they hurried up the slope of the mountain with the hope that the small bit of protection would provide a respite from the sufferable conditions.

Scrambling the last few yards to the cave's opening, the three men sighed in relief as the cooler temperatures began to take effect. Staring deeper into the darkness of the cave, Gulogulo's eyes began to adjust to the new lighting conditions and eventually he saw the faint outline of a door, lined with the yellow glow of light beyond it. Silently leading the rest of the group, Gulogulo slowly approached the door and cautiously opened it.

When they entered the room beyond, everyone's eyes became wide as they examined the humble blacksmith stable. Oddly enough, they could sense no one's presence until two cool blades presented themselves on the necks of Gulogulo and the soldier. The figures behind the army men were completely hidden by their intended targets, the only part of their bodies that showed were their arms, both strong, but both very different. From behind Gulogulo came a gruff voice, "I've got nothing to do with you military folk anymore, so I'd advise you to leave the same way you've come in."

Mathison turned around to see the predicament they were in and tried to reason with the man, "Look, sir, we're not here to cause trouble. We've come with a request."

This time, the other individual spoke from behind the soldier with a voice markedly higher and softer than the first, "We know what you want. It never differs. Militaries are always demanding swords, spears, and arrows. Weapons! Always weapons!"

With his hands out in a defenseless position, Mathison tried to explain, "No! In fact, we want you to make the exact opposite."

At this revelation, the blades dropped from the necks of the two men, who quickly grabbed the weapons and turned around to join Mathison. They now had a chance to get a good look at the two people who had a brief command of their lives. The person behind Gulogulo was an old man, his white hair stained black through years of blacksmithing. In fact, the profession not only kept him in shape, which denied his true age to most people, but its artificial coloring of his hair made him seem even younger.

Now, the other individual was a bit more of a shock to the group of travelers. While the blacksmith's apron hid a lot, one could see that this individual was in fact a woman, her demure face smudged with black stains of coal. And while her arms were well defined from the labor involved with her profession, there was a softness that still accompanied them, even down to her hands, the left of which bore the telltale ring of a married woman. After the army men got over their preconceived notions about blacksmiths, Gulogulo stepped forward and bowed in an act of humility, "I apologize for trespassing, but we come with a request directly from General Amedeo. I am General Gulogulo, and I would assume that you are Luvnac, is that right?"

The man skeptically examined the high ranking officer and shortly replied, "That's right." With a glance at the other two invaders of his space, he looked back at Gulogulo, "I guess the army's intelligence is as sharp as ever. Most people aren't supposed to know who I am, let alone where I work." With a motion, Luvnac introduced the woman to his right, "This is my apprentice, Morgana." At the mention of her name, Morgana gave a slight curtsey. With the introductions out of the way, Luvnac got back to business, "So, if you gentlemen don't want us to make weapons, what *do* you want us to make?"

Mathison stepped forward and explained, "We know that you don't want to make weapons anymore, after you've personally seen them kill a number of people. We also know that, as a result of your aversion for weaponry, you have delved into the realm of armor. As such, we have come to the conclusion that you wish to prevent others from being hurt by weapons, be they yours or someone else's."

"Right on all counts, but I'm still not convinced. Once someone has been injured, there's no way to get that capability back."

"Yes, that *used* to be true." Looking over to the soldier, Mathison nodded, which was the signal for the infantry man to remove the armor covering his right arm.

When the soldier touched the armor, he immediately recoiled. In their journey into the volcano, the metal had become incredibly hot. Luvnac saw what he was trying to do and came over to assist, "Here, let me help." With his bare hands, he managed to twist off the soldier's armor, which immediately clattered to the floor when Luvnac found that beneath the metal coating was absolutely nothing. Morgana gasped and put her hands over her mouth to hide the look of shock on her face.

Luvnac stuttered at the realization that something strange was going on, "B-b-b-but your arm! It was just moving a moment ago! I saw it myself! What's going on here?"

Mathison calmly approached the soldier and pulled back the protective cloth which the man wore between his body and his armor. There, embedded in the skin at the shoulder, was a glass orb filled with a green goop. A series of snakes encircled the orb and emanated out to where the armor once connected to the man's body. Pointing down at the piece of armor on the ground, Mathison explained, "You see, we have figured out a way to give back what has been taken away. We just need you to make more armor so that more soldiers like this man can live normal lives."

Picking up the metal arm, Luvnac looked inside and saw more of the circuitry of snakes etched on the inside of the armor. Humbly re-attaching the arm on the soldier, Luvnac watched as the man regained control of the prosthetic limb, flexing its various parts and joints. Luvnac was completely dumbfounded, "Remarkable. Just remarkable." Looking up at Mathison, he asked, "But how does it work?"

"It's kind of complicated, and I'll try to explain it better later, but suffice it to say that we've harnessed the powers of insect exoskeletons."

"And you want me to make armors so you can give them to soldiers like this?"

"That's right. Although, we really need as many full sets as possible."

"How soon?"

"Six days."

Luvnac let out a long sigh as he thought about what would be needed to fill this order, "I can't promise you any specific number, but we'll try to make as many as we can." Turning to Morgana, Luvnac began barking orders, "Get the hearth warmed up and scrounge for as much metal as we can find. We'll need to get more as we progress, but let's work with what we have right now."

Everyone moved into the other room and began diligently working. Upon further inspection of this new room where the work was to be performed, it became obvious why Luvnac worked in a volcano. Areas of the room were carefully shut off, but a series of mechanisms would lead one to believe that the very hot magma of Daniel Volcano was used to help speed any metalworking processes along.

When Luvnac began to grab pieces of metal with his bare hands in preparation for starting work, Mathison chimed in, "I don't mean to question your process, but don't you need protective gear in order to work on the metal?"

Luvnac continued getting ready and merely chuckled, "There's no need. You see, I'm very adept at controlling heat." The pieces of metal in his hands began to glow, as if they were being heated by his touch alone. In fact, his hands produced a faint reddish glow which was obviously the source of the increased temperatures.

As he started in on his work, molding the malleable metal with his hands, Luvnac began to monologue, "I've always been a strong proponent for the usefulness of fire. It can do so many things to make our lives better. When I made the six Noble Swords, I meant for them to be gifts of peace. Pretty soon, all the Kingdoms were asking me to make more swords. I happily obliged, since I was foolish and young. I just wanted to feel needed. It wasn't until I saw the results of my work that I realized just how naive I had been."

For a moment, he paused as he continued to reminisce, "I didn't know Jerry or Joe very well, or at all for that matter, but they opened my eyes to the harm that my creations were liable to produce." Dousing one of the pieces he was working on into a bucket of water, Luvnac waited for the steam to clear before continuing on his work and his story, "After I delivered a shipment of weapons to the 4th Kingdom, I was allowed to see the Sechilla Ceremony which was held on the Island Kingdom every thirty-six years. Two men would fight for the right to have an 'S' emblazoned on their chest that symbolized their strength and apparent invulnerability."

Picking up a hammer, Luvnac placed the piece of metal down on an anvil and began to pound it into shape, "The year I witnessed the event was the first that the Number Disks had been allowed. While Jerry wielded the sword I had made, Blue Division, Joe sported a full set of armor which gave him the nickname, 'The man of steel.' Both were excellent fighters, and both were allowed to use the '36' Number Disk, which was the noble Number Disk associated with the 4th Kingdom."

Stopping to wipe the sweat off his brow, Luvnac took a breath and continued, "What I witnessed was perhaps the most intense battle I had ever seen. The two men fought each other with such vigor, and yet the irony of their use of the Number Disks was that the '36' Number Disk is actually its own weakness. While the blue light that is produced on any item using that particular Number Disk is essentially a high-powered laser, extended use of the disk revealed its narcotic properties, which is extremely dangerous when in the heat of battle."

"In the end, both men were destroyed by their drive to be the best, partly fueled by the tremendous power that I had helped create. It was then that I vowed never to make another weapon, but only to create those objects that would protect. After all, the best offense is a good defense. Once the world sees the futility in fighting, my goal will be realized."

Setting aside the first piece of armor, Luvnac started on the next piece. Mathison was amazed at how quickly Luvnac worked, and he knew that in six days he would produce more than enough armor to fulfill General Amedeo's desires. Luvnac pointed at Mathison and gave an order, "I need you guys to go out and get me a lot more metal if I'm to make these armors for you. Morgana will draw up a map that will lead you to the Dendritic Forest. Once you're there, you'll need to cut down a bunch of the trees and bring them back here. You'll need to keep doing this until I've run out of time. It would be best if all three of you did this while Morgana and I worked here." Looking around, Luvnac remarked, "Hey, where's the General?"

Thomas gave Benjamin a big hug when he arrived back at Menlo Castle, "I'm so glad to see you again, Ben! And you've brought a friend." Penny was hesitant, but unable to avoid Thomas' greeting hug.

"Thomas, I'd like you to meet Penneut Psinodeo, although she likes to be called Penny." Benjamin smiled at the confused look on Penny's face, "Penny, the man hugging you right now is Thomas."

Finally able to get out of the hug, Penny snidely remarked, "Thanks. I've figured that out by now."

As Thomas led the way inside, he asked, "What's it been, a few weeks now? Why are you back here? I'm assuming that you've found-" Thomas stopped walking as he put the pieces together. He turned around, looked Benjamin in the eye, and whispered "Is Penny who you were looking for?"

Benjamin nodded and Thomas became very excited. The excitement quickly waned when Thomas noticed that Benjamin looked a bit down, "It's not that simple, Tom. She's pretty much the last person in her family who's still alive."

"Was this before or after you met her?"

"After." Benjamin paused and let out a brief sigh, "It was really bad, Thomas. I don't think this was an accident, it was a message. But to who and from whom I don't quite know yet. That's why we're here. We need to train. We need to get stronger. Whoever was after her family is probably after us as well." Thomas was silent as he absorbed all this new information.

Benjamin perked up as he asked, "Has Nikola had a chance to cool down yet? I'm really looking forward to a rematch."

"Actually, it's funny that you mention that."

"How so?"

"Well, a few days after you had left, he just up and disappeared. No note. No warning. Nothing."

"Really? I wouldn't peg him for the type who would do that."

Thomas sighed, "I don't know. Maybe it had to do with you taking the Skybolt orb. I'm just not sure where he could have gone."

Further up the hallway, Penny had already reached the main courtyard and was amazed at its spectacle. When the two men caught up, her neck was craned back, admiring the architecture above. Thomas approached her, and she immediately recoiled, hoping that he wasn't going to give another hug. He laughed as he assured her of his intentions, "Don't worry, I've gotten my hugs out already."

When she let down her guard, she smiled and gave a short laugh, "Sorry."

"Don't worry about it. At any rate, from what I have already deduced, you are someone like Benjamin who can use these strange powers without injuring yourself."

Penny was a little surprised, "That's right."

"And if I may go so far as to guess your inherent ability, I would say that it is the ability to control waves, am I right?"

Now Penny was stunned, "R-r-right." Looking at Benjamin, she asked, "How did he know that?"

With his hands up in an unknowing gesture, Benjamin said, "Beats me."

"Simple deductive logic, my friends. Anyways, since Benjamin has told me you both have come here to train, I have something that would be right down your alley." Walking over to a suit of armor set outside a nearby arch, Thomas began to explain, "My former apprentice, Nikola, was working on a device that could destroy almost anything. He said that it worked on the concept of resonance, or using the natural frequency of an item against itself."

Flicking the suit of armor produced a deep sound, at which Thomas continued, "He reasoned that if you could match this frequency, the waves trapped inside the material would build upon themselves until they finally tore the item apart. He was never able to find something that could create the desired frequencies, but I have a feeling you may be able to."

Taking a step forward, Penny placed her hand on the armor and closed her eyes. Soon, the armor began making a noise, deeper than the one they heard earlier. Eventually, the tone matched and began to grow louder. Benjamin and Thomas watched as the armor began to vibrate and undulate, until it exploded without warning into a mass of shrapnel. Everyone tried to get to cover, but the event happened so quickly that they were just lucky enough to not get hit by anything.

Thomas stared at the remains of the armor and whispered under his breath, "Amazing." Looking up, he smiled and said, "I think you're off to a good start, Penny. Especially for your first try." She smiled in response, but looked to the sky as she heard a familiar voice off in the distance. Everyone else looked skyward to see a man skating through the air, his sandals sporting sprouted wings which helped keep him aloft. When he got nearer to the ground, the wings disappeared and he landed forcefully.

The tan delivery uniform and top hat seemed familiar to Benjamin, but what he now noticed was that the uniform was from the Army of Amedeo. Before he could approach the man, Penny had leapt forward and gave the visitor a tight hug. Through her tears, she sobbed, "Cremy Serehurm! You're alive!"

Returning the hug, the man seemed confused, "Of course I'm alive, sis. Why wouldn't I be?"

"You mean you don't know?"

"Know what?"

Penny became choked up and tried to speak, but was unable to get anything out. Benjamin stepped forward and solemnly explained, "Your family has been killed. The entirety of Rancho de la Sol has been razed to the ground."

Pushing Penny away, Cremy Serehurm just shook his head in disbelief, "No. That can't be true. Who would do such a thing?"

"It's true. We saw it with our own eyes. Also, we're not sure who did it, but we plan on finding out." Taking a step closer, Benjamin questioned the delivery boy, "By the way, have you always been with the Army of Amedeo?"

"Of course I have. Just got a promotion too." Lifting up his right foot, Cremy Serehurm revealed a silvery metal disk embedded in the sole of his sandal. The disk had the number "80" engraved on it and the metal inside seemed to flow, "These things make landing so much easier. Gives me some cushion and some weight to drop me from the sky."

"So, if you're a part of the Army of Amedeo, then I'm assuming that your brother . . . who was it again?"

"Arma Ress."

"Yes. Him. I'm assuming that he also doesn't know your family's been killed, am I right?"

Remembering why he was there, Cremy Serehurm reached into his messenger's bag and pulled out a note, "Well, if he did, I need to talk to him about that." Handing the note to Penny, he continued, "Speaking of Arma Ress, I was told by my superiors that this note is from him and it was supposed to get to you as soon as possible."

When Penny grabbed the note and began tearing into the envelope, the delivery boy started to express his frustration, "I wish you'd told us where you were going. It took me two days to track you down, and I was only able to find you here based off of an old address where Benjamin was known to have resided." Pausing for a moment, he glanced around and asked, "Hey, where's that other guy? Tecumseh, was it?"

"This is not good." Penny was fiercely gripping the note as she read, "I have a feeling that someone knows what Tecumseh did. This note isn't *from* Arma Ress, it's a ransom from the Army *for* Arma Ress."

"What? Give me that." Cremy Serehurm grabbed the note and eventually got it out of Penny's hands. His face began to tighten as a severe frown grew on his brow. Through clenched teeth, he spoke, "They set me up! Well this tears it. I'm going AWOL."

Benjamin felt left out of the loop, "Well, what does it say?" Cremy Serehurm handed the note to Benjamin, who immediately began to read:

To Penneut Psinodeo:

    Your brother, Arma Ress, Orion-Class General of the Army of Amedeo has been charged with treason after he single-handedly destroyed military property. He will be executed in the valley of the Tower of Lebab, the site of his treasonous act. This execution will occur in seven days unless the necessary funds to expunge his record are received. We apologize for any inconvenience.

Aquila-Class General
Amedeo

When Benjamin noticed the date on the note, he saw that they had a mere five days left. He knew that this was retaliation for what Tecumseh had done, and now Penny's family was paying for it. He knew that he needed to gather as many people together as soon as possible, "Cremy Serehurm, how fast can you travel?"

"I'm the fastest person on the planet. Does that answer your question?"

"It does. I'm going to get a bunch of letters together which I need you to deliver. I hope you don't mind swapping sides now, do you?"

"Not in the slightest."

"Excellent. Just deliver my letters and let me help your brother. At this rate, if we do not hang together, we will hang separately." Turning to Thomas, he continued, "Tom, what do you have for me in terms of training?"

An excited smile came across Thomas' face as he said, "I've got a few interesting and unique applications I'd like you to try out. Let's start with the difficult ones first. Are you familiar with the legend of the Fire of Saint Erasmus?"

Confused at this development, Benjamin answered, "I am, but I don't see what fire has to do-"

With an open palm, Thomas signaled for Benjamin to stop talking, "It's not really fire. It's electricity. If you can master forming it into a ball, we can really start getting somewhere." Benjamin looked down at his open palm and soon a smile appeared on his face that matched the smile of his mentor.

"How much longer until we get there?" Herbert was sweating profusely as he followed the group through the sandstone canyon, the heat of the sun beating down from directly above them. Everyone else didn't want to waste any energy answering him, so they trudged on in silence. The striations on the curved walls showed evidence that the wind had made it through the canyon much quicker than they were.

Of course, no wind was currently present, and Herbert wished that it was. Even if it kicked up sand, the movement of air over his exhausted body would feel good. He even figured that if the sand was bad enough, it would force the others to stop for a moment, giving him enough time to rest. A sudden sound startled Herbert and he instinctively shouted out, "What was that!?"

The loud tolling of a bell could be heard, and its repeated tones penetrated every echo of the canyon. The effect was quite disorienting, not only due to its volume, but due to the ambiguity of its direction. As Herbert spun around, trying to find the source of the sound, despite having his hands clapped over his ears, he suddenly realized that he had lost the rest of the group.

After the twelfth toll of the bell, the area became deathly silent. Herbert was panicking as he ran along the path of the canyon. Fortunately, due to the geography, one had very few options in terms of direction. Turning a corner, Herbert almost ran into the rest of the group, each of them standing still, staring up at a solitary obelisk in the middle of a wide opening, a crossroads for a few different canyons.

Being the last to arrive, Herbert was the last to get a look at the structure in front of them. When the others started heading toward its base, Herbert was still trying to figure out what it was. The pillar almost looked like it was a part of the canyon, but past a certain height it was obviously man-made. When his gaze reached the top of the tower, he now knew where the loud sound had come from earlier. Atop the pillar, far above the upper surface of the canyon, sat a clock, its four faces showing the time: five minutes past twelve.

Albert led the way to the strange clock tower and seemed to disappear into the sandstone pillar. One by one, the others disappeared into the obelisk. As Herbert caught up, he managed to slip in right before the stone door snapped shut. Letting his eyesight get used to the dimmer lighting, Herbert blinked a few times and saw that the interior of the structure was hollow. The only way up was by a spiral staircase carved into the rock wall. Everyone had already begun to climb toward the source of light at the top of the column.

By the time the group reached the top, Herbert had completely caught up. Now all four of the travelers stood in the interior of the clock, its many moving parts clicking and rotating to keep the time. A large bell hung from the top of the room directly over a smaller building. The group now stood in front of the solitary door for this small structure inside the clock tower.

Albert led the way once again and opened the door. Everyone neatly filed into the building and Albert shut the door behind them. At first appearances, the one-room shack was a shop which specialized in clocks and watches. And yet, most of the clocks seemed to drip from the walls, melting away from the nails that held them up. The clocks on the counters were no different, their forms seeming to flow in a very fluid manner toward the floor. Observing all these melting clocks, Herbert wondered if the heat of the canyon contributed to their current state, and then he wondered why one would put a clock shop out in the middle of a desert to begin with.

In the back corner of the room, his back to the group, hunched over his work, sat a man who yelled in preference to turning around, "*¡Váyase!* We're closed today. Please come again some other time."

"I think you can make an exception," Albert yelled back, knowing of the man's hearing problem.

Albert's voice caused the man in the corner to straighten up and to slowly turn around to see if his ears had deceived him. The man had black hair, slicked back from his forehead, which now crinkled up as his dark eyes grew wide. He had a peculiar, pencil-thin moustache that curled up from the edges of his mouth which had begun to smile in recognition of Albert, "*Mi viejo amigo! ¿Cómo estás?*"

Shaking hands with the man, Albert introduced the rest of the group, "Salvador, this is Aquila-Class General Amedeo and two of his officers, Cross-Class General Grigori and Polaris-Class General Herbert."

Salvador realized that his guests were far more distinguished than he had thought and that his initial greeting had been incredibly uncouth. Bowing in a sign of respect, Salvador spoke, but still louder than he should have, "*Lo siento*, General Amedeo. Please let me know how I can be of assistance to you."

"Please, get up. I'm here merely to observe. Albert will let you know what you will do for us."

"I see. You've moved up in the world, Albert. What do you need my help with?"

"We need a watch."

"As you can see, I have many of those. Of course, for *you* the watch will be pro bono. Is this for a retirement? A promotion?"

"It is for a Time Thread stasis experiment."

The color dropped out of Salvador's face as he got close to Albert and harshly whispered, "That is not something one should joke about."

"I am not joking."

Salvador could see by the look in Albert's eyes that he was excited at this opportunity, so he merely sighed and moved over to the counter where he began to look through the collection of watches for the one that would do what Albert wanted. Finally, he found the piece he was looking for and held it up. The design of the watch was simple, but the spider-web cracks across the face of the piece revealed its broken status.

General Amedeo was confused, "Albert, are you sure you know what you're doing?"

Taking the watch from Salvador and examining it, Albert replied, "*Ja*, This will do nicely. I believe that this is my specialty, General. Please let me do my work. Now, Grigori, if you do not mind." Albert motioned to one of the counters, which Salvador and Herbert quickly cleared of all its watches, most of them spilling onto the floor. Grigori took off his shirt and laid down on the countertop. On another counter, Albert opened up a bag of implements and began setting some aside.

While still making preparations, Albert began giving orders, "Herbert, I want you to ready the uroboros brand. We are going to need everything to go quickly and smoothly if this is to work." Herbert grabbed a metal implement and headed outside to heat the device in the scorching sun.

"Salvador, I am going to need you to apply the anesthetic." Grabbing a small glass vial and a wooden dowel, Salvador headed over to where Grigori was laying. Taking a cloth, he doused it with the liquid in the vial and began rubbing the moistened cloth on Grigori's chest. He then held out the wooden dowel, splintered and worn from many uses. Grigori understood and opened his mouth so he could bite down on the peg.

Completed with his preparations, Albert came over to Grigori's side and set down a few instruments, as well as the broken pocket watch. Flipping the watch over, he popped the back cover off and found the main spring. Taking a deep breath and looking once again at everything, he turned to yell out the door, "Herbert! We are about to begin!" Grabbing his scalpel, Albert brought it over Grigori's chest and paused one last time before starting the procedure.

Plunging the knife into Grigori's flesh, Albert cut along the skin that had been discolored by the local anesthetic. Grigori already had an extraordinary tolerance for pain, so he had yet to bite down on the wood in his mouth, but remained still, staring at the ceiling. Blood started pooling at the incision, which Salvador wiped off with a cloth. Putting down the scalpel, Albert picked up his forceps and opened the incision, hoping that this dangerous operation wouldn't take any nasty turns.

With a furrowed brow, Albert peered into Grigori's chest cavity and found the beating heart within. Picking up the scalpel again, he made a small incision near the top of the heart's protective sac. Salvador once again wiped away as much blood as he could. The stress of the operation was starting to get to Albert, who was sweating more than normal, especially considering the ambient temperature in the room. Moving his head back and forth to try and get a better view, Albert started to hold his breath for each second that he couldn't find the vital Time Thread.

Suddenly, a glint of something thin and silvery caught Albert's eye and he let out his breath. Grabbing another pair of forceps, he carefully pinched the fine thread and began to pull. This caused Grigori to convulse in pain, and he bit down hard on the wooden dowel between his teeth. A bit of blood spurted out of the wound, and a small tinge of grey appeared in Grigori's scraggly hair. Placing the open pocket watch next to the incision, Albert calmly took the silvery thread and wound it around the shaft of the main spring. Closing the back of the watch, Albert called for Herbert, "We are almost done! Get in here!"

The next part of the operation was the tricky part. After sewing up the innermost incisions, Albert spread the top incision open to allow room for the installation of the watch. Footsteps were heard from outside as Herbert came into the room holding the metal device, now no longer black but a glowing soft red color. Forcing the watch into the incision once again caused Grigori to tense up in pain. Without looking up, Albert grabbed the brand from Herbert and pushed the hot end into Grigori's flesh around the newly inserted pocket watch.

For one last time, Grigori gritted his teeth on the wood and waited for the pain to be over. Soon, he let out a deep breath as Albert began bandaging the seared flesh on his patient's chest. Everyone else let out their breath as well, as they had all been holding it in while the operation took place. The tension in the room began to lighten as Grigori spat out the wooden dowel and asked, "How long until we know it works?"

Finishing up the bandage, Albert frankly replied, "We cannot really be sure in a situation like this. Only time will tell if the surgery was a success, but considering how well you are doing right after it, I should think that you could know in a few days when the ultimatum to the Naturals runs out."

Despite the throbbing in his chest as the anesthetic began to wear off, Grigori didn't feel any different. He wondered if this was the oldest he would ever be. If anything, Grigori felt numb. Was this what immortality felt like?

When Luvnac went into his monologue, Gulogulo quietly slipped away to another part of the cave. He approached several doors and silently opened them to see what was inside. By the third door, he found what he was looking for. Slipping into the room and closing the door behind him, he found a candle and proceeded to light it. The room he now stood in was Luvnac's office. The walls were lined with framed pictures and letters, bookshelves were filled to capacity with a number of metalworking books, and a desk was covered with an unorganized mess of papers.

Gulogulo had been holding in his excitement for so long, he was glad he could finally let some of it out. He was actually standing in the office of Luvnac, the creator of the six Noble Swords. Getting to meet his hero made Gulogulo unbearably giddy, but he had a mission he needed to accomplish. Taking a deep breath, he gathered his emotions and began to look through the room.

One of the pictures caught his eye and he leaned in to get a closer look. The picture was of five individuals, four men and a woman. The caption under the picture read, "'Seasoned Compass.' From left to right: Haru Higashi, Natsu Minami, Aki Nishi, Fuyu Kita. Back row: Antonio." Even though it was obviously taken some time ago, Gulogulo saw that the one designated as Natsu Minami was in fact Luvnac. This confirmed that Luvnac at least knew who Aki Nishi was.

Looking down on the disorganized desk, Gulogulo began to read the bits and pieces of text that were visible. Finally, something caught his eye. Even though the rest of the letter was covered, the name "Aki Nishi" was clearly visible. Grabbing the letter and sliding it out from underneath the stack of other papers, Gulogulo began to read. Apparently, it was some sort of correspondence between Luvnac and his former Seasoned Compass counterpart. Flipping the letter over, he found the return address: Granite Grove. Pulling out the map of the area, Gulogulo scanned it to make sure that he recognized the name from the map.

Putting his finger down on an area to the northwest of Daniel Volcano, Gulogulo confirmed what he had thought. Granite Grove was nearby. Folding up the map and the letter, he put both in his pocket. Now that he knew where Aki Nishi was, Gulogulo began looking for Luvnac's final sword.

Scanning the room, he tried to think where he would put something that valuable. Bending down, he looked underneath the furniture, but to no avail. Just as he was about to get frustrated, Gulogulo noticed something different about the top of the bookcase. The light from the candle didn't create the right shadows. Reaching up over the top of the shelves, his hand hit something.

Grabbing the item from the top of the cabinet, Gulogulo brought it down and a smile immediately formed on his lips. In a solid black, wooden scabbard sat the curved blade designated as Luvnac's last. Feeling the smooth finish on the sheath, his hand instinctively went to the handle. Directly below the hilt of the sword was an engraved symbol on the scabbard. Gulogulo remembered a little bit of this foreign language, and he whispered, "Kuroni." If his translation was correct, it meant "Black Demon."

Pulling the sword from its sheath, Gulogulo marveled at its craftsmanship. The blade was as black as its scabbard, maybe even darker. A swirling design of snakes encircled a hole in the blade near the hilt. Suddenly, a realization came to Gulogulo. If he was to take this sword, how could he make it look like he didn't? Or at least, how could he delay anyone from finding out? Looking down at the sheath, he arrived at his solution.

Reaching on top of the bookcase again, he set the scabbard back where he first felt it. Blowing out the candle, Gulogulo opened the door a crack to let some light in and set the candle back where he initially found it. Slipping out into the hallway, he made his way to the entrance of the cave. Hopefully, Luvnac would be so engrossed in his work that Gulogulo could get back before anyone noticed. Hopping off the ledge of the cave's threshold, he slid down the slope of the volcano and made his way to the path he had used to get there.

After a short hike, Gulogulo came across a sign that indicated Granite Grove was down the right fork of the trail. The Dendritic Forest and Crystal Woods were also designated as being to the right, but Gulogulo didn't really care about those areas. As he kept hiking, the landscape began to change again. What was once a full forest now started to look sickly. The soil started to turn more of a yellow color, just like it was near the volcano.

Soon, the trees began to shine in the sunlight, their metal trunks and branches providing some oddly beautiful scenery. Gulogulo's swords began to rattle in their sheathes and it seemed that Kuroni was being inexplicably drawn toward the trees. And yet, he kept pace and eventually made it out of the metal forest. Before long, he now stood on the shore of a lake. A small island silently sat in the middle of the body of water. Examining the shoreline, he could see that there were similarly strange forests to the left and right sides of the lake. Since the trees to the right seemed to be made of glass, he decided to head toward the forest which looked more like stone.

As Gulogulo strode toward the stone trees, he began to think. While he was loyal to the Army of Amedeo and had been treated well during his service, he couldn't help shaking the feeling that some of the orders he had been given were wrong. He didn't want to oppose the ones that had given him the opportunities to see so many great things and to receive so many incredible weapons. And yet, he could relate with the fear of the unknown. Whoever had managed to injure Grigori like that had to be incredibly powerful. What if he encountered someone just as powerful? What if Aki Nishi *was* that powerful?

By the time he had worked through his thoughts, Gulogulo had arrived at the Granite Grove. Now that he stood in the rocky forest, he wasn't quite sure where to go from here. The strange silence of the petrified trees made every step he took sound insurmountably louder than it should have. Gradually, Gulogulo began to notice that his swords were being pulled again, but not like the last time. This time they weren't pulled toward the trunks of the trees, they seemed to be pulled to a single point ahead of him.

Soon, his entire body was being pulled toward that unseen point. Turning and trying to escape proved to be fruitless as the resistance grew stronger. When his foot slipped, Gulogulo found himself being pulled toward the unknown with a new ferocity. Digging his fingers into the soil proved to be a futile effort in trying to stop his acceleration. Then he stopped. Unexpectedly, he heard laughing from behind him. He flipped over to his back and sat up to see who was there.

A man in bright, warm colors with a shock of red hair covering his head and face sat on the fractured trunk of a fallen, petrified tree. He was a bit portly and the guffaws he made were making his belly jiggle a little bit. Taking a breath and sighing, the man spoke, "I've not had that much fun in a while. Thanks for indulging me, stranger."

Getting up and brushing himself off, Gulogulo mumbled, "Don't mention it."

"Oh, but you see, things are so quiet here in the Granite Grove. We don't get many visitors in these parts, so I usually make it a habit of having a bit of fun with them."

"I see." Deciding to take a stab in the dark, Gulogulo asked, "You wouldn't happen to be Aki Nishi, would you?"

All at once, a look of nostalgia and hesitation came over the man's face, "I haven't heard that name in a long time." Beholding the military man in front of him, he asked, "Who wants to know?"

"Cross-Class General Gulogulo of the Army of Amedeo."

"Well, General Gulogulo, you are correct. I am Aki Nishi."

"Then I would assume what you just used was a fluxion core, am I right?"

"I'm not sure I know what a fluxion core is, but I do use something to do what I did."

"Can I have it?" Gulogulo put his hands down at his sides, right above the handles of the six swords he had strapped to his legs, "Just make sure that you choose your answer wisely."

Aki Nishi laughed again and pulled out a black orb that he held around his neck, "You want this trinket? Even though I found it from Daniel Volcano, the only significance it holds is one of nostalgia."

"Are you sure? Won't you be unable to perform your trickery without it?"

He shrugged, "Maybe. To be honest, I've kind of been tired of carrying its burden. If you want it, you can have it."

"Really?" This caused Gulogulo to drop his guard.

"Yeah, really." Aki Nishi grabbed the orb and suddenly Gulogulo was pulled toward the clenched fist. His right hand was pulled forward against his will, at which point Aki Nishi opened his fist and let the black orb fall into the open palm. Stunned at the sheer density of the object, Gulogulo just held the sphere in his hand and stared at the blackness which almost seemed to suck in the light around it.

Slowly pulling out Kuroni from the strap on his back, Gulogulo's world seemed to slow down as he encountered an internal crisis, "This man just gave me the source of his power. He's completely defenseless."

The tip of the sword cleared the strap, "How do you know he doesn't have a back-up somewhere? Maybe that's a fake and he still has the real one."

He brought the sword in front of him, "He's just a normal person. He laughs like us, has fun like us, has memories like us."

Gulogulo let go of the orb he now gripped in his fingers, "But that doesn't mean he's completely innocent. What do you really know of his past?"

The orb seemed to hang in the air as it dropped toward Kuroni, "And what about his past? Maybe he's got a family, maybe he's just trying to survive."

Mating together with precision, the orb was now set in Kuroni's blade, "*Non!* He's a Natural! They're bound to kill us all! Didn't you see what they did to Grigori?"

Aki Nishi noticed the sword that Gulogulo pulled from his back, "Hey, that's Natsu Minami's final sword. Are you some sort of Seasoned Compass fan?"

Gulogulo looked up at the man in front of him, all emotion had left his face. His eyes were blank and stared straight forward as he brought Kuroni into a fighting stance.

Aki Nishi could see that something was wrong, "Whoa! What are you doing, man? I gave you what you wanted, right?"

Blinking a few times and shaking his head, Gulogulo smiled and said, "Of course you did. *Grazie.*" He lowered the tip of the sword and proceeded to tie it on his back. Turning to go, Gulogulo waved as he left the man in the woods. Suddenly, he heard a high pitched whistle above him. Where had he heard that sound before? When he realized and turned back around, it was already too late. The hefty body of Aki Nishi fell to its knees then followed its momentum forward, landing prostrate on the ground.

The feathered fletching of the solitary arrow that had lodged itself in Aki Nishi's head gave away its origin. Footsteps came from behind Gulogulo and passed him as he stared at the dead body in front of him. Placing a foot at the base of the arrow, a man in uniform pulled out the projectile and proceeded to wipe it on a small cloth. Gulogulo was furious now that he had arrived at the decision of his moral dilemma, "Braun! What on earth are you doing?"

"I'm cleaning up your mess. Orders are orders."

"Did you follow me this entire time?"

"Not the entire time, but enough."

"Why did you kill him? He wasn't a threat to anyone."

"Look, I don't care. Once I let the arrow off my bow, it's out of my hands."

"Don't be so glib! He was a human being."

Braun pushed Gulogulo against one of the granite trees, "He was a *Natural!* We were *commanded* to get rid of them." Stepping away, Braun returned the arrow to the quiver on his back, "We've got a week before we fight against the rest of the Naturals. I suggest you take a long hard look at yourself and find out which side you're on, G.G."

Gulogulo just scowled at his military peer as he disappeared back into the woods, his shadow cast by the setting sun blending into the shadows of the trees. Under his breath he spoke, "You don't have the right to call me that. Perhaps you've made my decision for me." After burying Aki Nishi's body, Gulogulo headed back to the lake and started to return to Daniel Volcano.

He walked in a daze, deep in thought until he heard his name called out, "General Gulogulo?" Snapping out of his thoughts, he found that he had arrived back in the Dendritic Forest where Mathison and the soldier were cutting down some metal trees. Mathison spoke again, "What are you doing out here? Did you already know that we needed to get more metal for Luvnac? That's pretty good, sir."

Deciding to run with it, Gulogulo laughed, "Yeah, I guess I was just a bit ahead of the game."

"That's great. Well, let's get this raw material back to Luvnac so he can make more armors. I gotta tell you sir, they're already looking great. General Amedeo will be very pleased."

Gulogulo had the feeling that Amedeo would be pleased, but not about everything.

Chapter 8

War

"What do you mean it's probably a trap?" Thomas was livid with Benjamin, who had just revealed this small piece of information.

"Well, Penny and I know for a fact that Arma Ress didn't destroy the Tower of Lebab, and since we're the only people who *do* know who the real culprit was, I'm assuming this is the army's ploy to gain that information. The only thing I can't figure out is how they know that *we* know."

"For your information, this revelation could have come in handy much earlier."

"True, but you'd probably have come anyways."

Thomas took a second to think about it and realized that he would be there just out of sheer curiosity, "But why do you think the army has targeted-" Penny hushed Thomas as she pointed over the ridge. All three of them peeked over to see the scene down in the valley. A large fissure in the ground was spewing up a constant curtain of black smoke where the tower once stood. The area was deserted with the exception of a solitary object sitting in the empty field.

Pulling back behind the ridge, Thomas sighed in relief, "I was half-expecting to see the entire army standing there in the valley. Maybe they're just bluffing. Considering our minimal numbers and your stance on armor, I certainly hope so."

Almost a rehearsed line by now, Benjamin answered, "The armor would only slow me down. My power relies on me being as light as possible."

Penny was still looking over the ridge at the scene below, "This doesn't make sense. Obviously someone was here after we were, since there's now a big crack in the ground spewing up smoke . . . which would explain the odor we were smelling for the last few miles."

289

Thomas was trying to be optimistic, "Maybe something in the earth was affected when the tower fell, and it didn't reach the surface until after you'd left."

"Nope, that's not what I'm worried about. It's that thing down there. I think it's a person."

Standing up, Benjamin stretched his arms and said, "Well, why don't we go down and have a look?" Hopping over the ridge, he began to slide the scree down into the valley. Penny jumped over right behind him. Thomas shook his head and, after a deep sigh, vaulted over the ridge to join the other two.

When they got closer to the object, it became more obvious that it was a person, kneeling on the ground, slumped over and wearing a military uniform. Penny was the first to realize who it was as she ran past Benjamin. When she arrived at the body, she screamed out in agony. Benjamin recognized the scream. As he ran past the trembling pebbles, he didn't need to guess that the soldier was likely Arma Ress.

Penny clutched the form of her brother, who didn't even look human anymore. His skin was a flaky, reddish brown, but still somewhat metallic. Small pools of dried blood left their black stain on the ground beneath his chest, which was obviously the cause of his death. A gaping hole now stood in the spot where his heart was once protected. Whispering to the silent form, Penny chided her brother, "You know that you rust if you get wet. You know your weakness, so why didn't you show the wisdom of an older brother? Why didn't you run away?"

As Benjamin approached Penny, she suddenly stood up, a fierce look of anger in her teary eyes. Benjamin was slightly taken aback by her change in attitude. When Thomas caught up, he leaned over to Benjamin and asked, "What's wrong?"

Penny let out a mighty yell. The ground shook in response. To the sky, she addressed her query, "What do you want? Why are you killing my family? Show yourself!" After a few moments of waiting, the echoes of her cry had died down and all that could be heard was Penny's heavy breathing and the slow billowing of smoke from the nearby fissure. She gave one last call, "I'm still here! You're not done yet!"

Benjamin cautiously approached Penny and said, "I think we're the only ones here."

"Oh, how wrong you are, Benjamin." From behind the curtain of smoke came a voice. Soon after, a silhouette followed and before long, a military officer in full battle armor appeared and stood before them, his beady eyes accentuating the smirk he wore on his face, "I believe I am the one you are looking for, Penneut Psinodeo." He stopped advancing and announced, "I am Amedeo."

From a nearby hill, General Gulogulo scanned the surroundings with his telescope. The black curtain of smoke made it somewhat difficult to see, but fortunately he was at a position to observe both sides of the upcoming battle. Something caught his attention. Three people off in the distance jumped over a ridge and began sliding down the scree of the mountain to the field below. Collapsing the telescope and putting it in his back pouch, Gulogulo turned to the group of men behind him.

"OK, look. This thing's going to get started soon, but you all need to stay up here. I don't care what happens down there, you're only supposed to be observers. In fact, you're not even supposed to be here at all."

Albert was the spokesman for the group, which included Dmitri, Herbert, Jules, Dr. Robert, Julius, and Mathison, "We understand, but *you* must understand that we want to see what all our research has gone toward. We want to see the fruits of our labor."

"Very well." Turning to give the signal to the mass of soldiers below, Gulogulo gave one last word over his shoulder, "Just be aware that you might not like what you see." With a leap, he began to run down the side of the hill. Just as he was reaching the edge of the group of soldiers stationed behind the smoke, he heard the scream of a woman followed by some angry words.

Meeting up with the army commanders at the front line, Gulogulo gave his report to General Amedeo, "They've arrived. I'm assuming that you've made the woman pretty mad."

"Most likely. How many are there?"

"Only three."

Amedeo arched his eyebrow as he responded with a chuckle, "This may be easier than I thought." With a motion of his hand, he commanded two soldiers to lower a plank across the fissure in the ground.

From the other side of the smoke, a voice could be heard, "I think we're the only ones here."

Amedeo made an assumption based on all available data as he began to cross the chasm, "Oh, how wrong you are, Benjamin." With each step over the temporary bridge, Amedeo began to get more excited. He had put a lot of effort into exterminating the Naturals and now his dream to remove all obstacles in his path had almost come to fruition. Arriving at the other side of the smoke wall, Amedeo saw the three individuals, staring at him with confusion and apprehension. Looking at the woman, Amedeo responded, "I believe I am the one you are looking for, Penneut Psinodeo." He stopped and put his hands out in a gesture of welcoming, "I am Amedeo."

With a slight bow, Amedeo finished his introduction and was immediately in the clutches of Penny, who growled at him through clenched teeth, "Why did you kill my family?"

"I believe that I am not the one who has killed your family."

"What do you mean? I thought you just said-"

"I know what I said, but may I just say that this should go as a lesson to you."

"A lesson?"

"*Si.* Choose your friends wisely."

"What does that mean?"

"You'll find out soon enough." Pushing Penny to the side, Amedeo snapped his fingers and an array of planks suddenly bridged the smoky gap. More silhouettes appeared as the army began to cross the gap that hid them from view.

Thomas began to understand their plight and took a few steps back, "I knew we should have tried harder to find more people to join us. If Nikola was here, then we'd be at least a little better off."

"Oh, but I *am* here, Thomas." From behind a line of soldiers, Nikola and Mary appeared.

"Nik! Where the heck have you been?" Thomas took a second look at Nikola's clothes and realized what he had come to fear, "Why have you joined this army?"

"Why? You ask *why?* Isn't it obvious?" Sweeping his hand to show the soldiers now behind him, Nikola yelled out, "Here I can research the way *I* want to. I could do things that you would never have let me do. Here I have freedom. Here I am God." Benjamin let out a scoff which gained Nikola's attention, "Oh, and you think you're a god with your lightning powers? Who was it that gave you the scar on your face again?"

Penny had never seen Benjamin lose at anything, so when Nikola revealed this piece of information, she was shocked, "Is that true, Ben?"

Nikola seemed to have hit a nerve, "Yes, but that was a long time ago. I've mastered my powers since then." The soldiers continued to cross the chasm and started to surround the small group.

As Benjamin headed toward where he last saw Amedeo, Nikola called out, "Running away again, are we?"

Without turning around, Benjamin replied, "You no longer interest me, Nik." Leaping into the air, Benjamin sprouted his wings and flew higher to get a better look at the field. He could hear Nikola yelling from far below, but he didn't care anymore. He needed answers. Amedeo was easy to spot with his highly decorated armor. When Benjamin found him, he let the lightning crackle over his body as he turned into a bolt of electricity, crashing down before the army commander. He let his wings disappear in a flurry of sparks as he pulled out his sledgehammer and began to walk toward the Aquila-Class General.

All the soldiers backed away from Benjamin, clearly stunned at the spectacle they just beheld. Whispers of "thunderbird" ran through the ranks. Amedeo could see that Benjamin meant business, which was why he was backing away at the same rate that Benjamin was approaching, "You may not give Penny a straight answer, Amedeo; but I will get answers out of you, even if we've got to do it the hard way."

"No need for violence, Benjamin. What do you want to know?"

"Why did you kill her family?"

"You, of all people, should know the raw power that the Naturals can harness. How many men would it take to equal your power? One thousand? One billion? One *septillion?* Do you know how terrifying it is knowing that there are beings out there that could wipe out entire nations? I'm doing humanity a favor."

"Humanity? Are we not *all* humans?"

Amedeo stopped backing up, "*Non!* You are *not* human! You're a monster, a freak of nature, an anomaly. I'm merely trying to fix the anomaly."

Benjamin had heard enough. Readying his hammer, he burst forth toward the General, ready to attack. In the split second it took him to close the distance between them, Benjamin noticed that Amedeo didn't flinch, didn't back away, and didn't show any signs of retreating. Suddenly, his vision went white and he felt a sharp pain at the bottom of his chin. When he regained his vision, he found a soldier, nearly as decorated as Amedeo, standing between them.

The soldier was twirling a black lacquered staff in a display of skill. Amedeo stood behind the soldier and chided Benjamin, "If you want to get to me, there's a whole army of soldiers you need to get through first. But to save you some time, I'll let you play with General Grigori for a while." As Amedeo backed away, Grigori extended an open palm and motioned for Benjamin to make the next move.

○

When Benjamin jumped into the sky, Nikola was furious, "How dare you ignore me! You're just a coward! You couldn't beat me if you tried!"

Thomas spoke with force, "Enough, Nikola! He's more capable than you'll ever be."

"Oh? And I suppose you've got the fortitude to back up those words, old man?"

"Certainly."

"Well, I'm not alone out here, so I hope you can deal with Mary as well."

Mary laughed at this comment, "Hah! Please, I don't need to fight when I've got Victor and my army of the undead to fight for me."

Nikola smiled, "Well, there you have it then."

Thomas turned to Penny and whispered, "We need to work together here. I'll take on Nikola, so I'll need you to deal with Mary and her soldiers. I have no doubt that you've got what it takes. Just remember that once their armor is gone, they're pretty much done for."

Penny nodded, but became a little hesitant when a giant of a man slowly lumbered out of the crowd behind Mary. When Penny turned to ask Thomas one last question, she found that he was already gone, battling against Nikola in a frenzy of fencing between two foils.

Mary looked down her nose at Penny and chided her, "Why don't you go home, little girl? The battlefield is no place to play."

"I wholeheartedly agree." Penny knew that if she were to survive, she first needed to defeat the big one called Victor. Judging by how he moved, he was slow, but that may only be due to his enormous armor. She knew that if he landed a hit on her, it would be over.

Rushing in, Penny used her speed to her advantage. With a swift, open palm strike, she hit Victor in the breastplate, causing the giant to lose balance and fall backward. When he hit the ground, his armor was still vibrating from the sudden strike. He slowly got back to his feet, but Penny found that she already had the upper hand.

When Victor swung his huge arm at Penny, she deftly ducked underneath the assault and delivered another blow, this time to his knees. Mary was starting to become irritated with her creation, "Victor! You need to get serious about this fight, and *fast!*" Dumbly nodding, Victor stood once again and waited for Penny's next attack. When she came at him, he managed to catch her hand and lift her body high into the air.

With no footing, Penny flailed frantically, trying to get loose from her opponent's grasp. Mary was cheering from the sidelines, "Crush her, Victor! *Crush her!*" The giant wrapped his arms around Penny and began to squeeze. As she felt the air being forcefully pushed out of her lungs, Penny didn't have much time to react. With her free arm, she pulled out her trident and stabbed it into Victor's side, between two pieces of armor.

What normally would have elicited a reaction in a normal person produced nothing on the giant. As Penny started to black out, she put her palm on the breastplate of Victor's armor and concentrated on the metal. A pure tone rang out from the armor and suddenly it broke into pieces, allowing Penny to slip out from Victor's grasp. She grabbed her trident on the way down to the ground, pulling it out of Victor's side.

Mary's mouth stood agape as she watched the shrapnel of Victor's armor fall to the ground. Penny took this slight opening to advance on Victor. With a quick flurry of strikes to the body, she managed to push him back toward the chasm of smoke from which he appeared. Even though the hits she landed didn't seem to hurt Victor, it did move him in the direction she needed him to go.

As he approached the edge of the wall of smoke, Victor glanced down and saw the tongues of fire down below. This caused him to freak out. It was a slow grunt, but he spoke loudly enough to distract Penny, "No! Fire!" She wasn't quite sure how to deal with this, but was knocked to the side in the brief moment when Victor became cognizant of his surroundings. The tide had turned on Penny and now she was being pushed back as Victor put more distance between himself and the fire below.

When Penny took a moment to think about what just happened, she got an idea. It would need to be quick, but if it worked, the difficult fight would be over. Sticking her trident in the ground to free up both hands, Penny rushed in and used both palms to strike at Victor's exposed abdomen. This action pushed Victor back toward the fault, but before he could fully freak out again, Penny squatted down and struck the ground with both hands, pushing it toward her foe.

The wave of ground rushed forward and caught Victor off balance, which caused him to fall backward into the fiery pit. As he fell, the last word he uttered was a long, "Nooooo!" as the flames rose to consume their meal. Penny let out a sigh as she went over to pick up her trident from the ground.

Mary's face was white with terror. When she came to the full realization that her trump card was gone, she ordered the rest of her minions to attack. Even though they moved slowly like Victor, the vast number of soldiers closing in on Penny ended up being too much for her. Soon, she was surrounded and had no room to move. No room to escape.

Even though the General standing in front of him seemed to have seen better days, Benjamin noticed that there was no hesitation on his opponent's end. Still, Benjamin took a short moment to plan out how he was going to attack. There was an obvious blind spot on the General's left side, as shown by the milky-white orb that was once a working eye; set in the middle of a long scar on his face. He also noticed that there were bandages underneath his armor. Was someone this injured so confident in his skills, or was there something else at play here?

First thing was first: he needed to figure out how to break that staff. A weaponless soldier was usually a useless soldier. Lifting his hammer above him, Benjamin charged in and swung down toward Grigori's head. Just as he had hoped, Grigori blocked with the staff. However, the weapon didn't break like he thought it would. A few more attacks to the staff proved to be fruitless, so Benjamin decided to start attacking the soldier directly.

Taking advantage of the natural blind spot, Benjamin shifted to Grigori's left side and thrust the head of his hammer toward Grigori's torso. Almost as if he had seen it coming, Grigori shifted to dodge the blow and grabbed the shaft of the hammer as he pulled Benjamin in close. Pounding the staff to the ground, a click made a blade appear from the shaft, just missing Benjamin's arm. Letting go of the hammer and backing away, Benjamin now knew there was more to this fighter than what initial appearances led him to believe.

"I'm feeling generous today, so why don't you take your weapon back?" Grigori tossed the hammer back toward Benjamin, who picked it up and held the head of the hammer in his left hand.

"I'm not going to complain, but you might start to once I'm done." Benjamin let electricity flow into his left hand and into the metal of the hammer. With a quick movement of his hand down the shaft of the weapon, the metal followed. Benjamin no longer had a hammer, but a rudimentary sword, still with the mark of "90" engraved upon its surface.

"Oho? Now things are getting interesting." Flipping over his switchblade scythe, Grigori tapped the other end on the ground and revealed the second blade of his weapon. Benjamin hoped that there weren't any more tricks involved with the black staff as he charged back into battle. This time Benjamin used the Skybolt orb to speed up his motions, but Grigori seemed to answer every attack with a block. Every movement of both fighters was fluid, a constant ebb and flow from attacks to dodges.

Suddenly, Benjamin stopped and backed away. His gaze rose into the air as he sprouted his wings and flew to the sky. Grigori was angered by this, "Why are you running? Come back here and fight me like a man!" A large shadow appeared over Grigori and quickly swept past him, causing him to turn around and immediately change his attitude. A wall of ground and soldiers was sweeping toward him, and he didn't have enough time to react.

Lying flat on his back, in a mass of bodies and rubble, Grigori wondered what other strange powers were being used on the battlefield as he got to his feet. Benjamin seized this brief moment of confusion to attack. In a burst of energy, Benjamin landed in front of Grigori in a kneeling stance. Leaping to the air, Benjamin brought his sword upward, slicing through Grigori's wrists. Taking a few steps back, Benjamin was sure of his victory, "Give it up, General. Let me fight Amedeo. Let me stop his insane drive to eradicate me and my friends."

Clutching his severed limbs close to his body, Grigori moaned in pain, which slowly transformed into a maniacal laugh, "Ha ha ha! I was hoping that I would get to test out my new power today, and you've helped prove that I have nothing to worry about any more." The hands which were once lying on the ground had disappeared and Grigori now held his arms out to show that the damage Benjamin had inflicted was no longer there.

Picking up his switchblade scythe, Grigori commanded the stunned soldiers who encircled the fighting area, "Seize the Natural!" Quickly gaining their wits just a moment before Benjamin regained his, the soldiers grabbed the Natural and held him back. He struggled to get out of their grasp, but there were too many to resist. In his struggle, he banged against many of the soldiers' armor, which not only felt different but sounded different as well. Almost hollow. Using a last ditch effort, Benjamin focused on the Skybolt orb and let its electricity flow over his body, hoping to shock his captors.

The electricity spread through most of the armored soldiers, but one in particular seemed to glow with a light that Benjamin had seen once before in Menlo Castle. It was at that moment when Benjamin noticed these armored soldiers all had different numbered disks embedded in their chests. The number of the glowing soldier was "74", which gave Benjamin reason to wonder what the other numbers would do.

Still, the effect of the electricity was not what Benjamin had hoped for: nothing happened. The soldiers didn't move an inch and Grigori slowly approached the defenseless man with a sly grin. Pointing at the scar on his face, he began to monologue, "If you had fought me just weeks earlier like your friend had, you might have left a mark. But that's no longer going to be the case."

"What? What friend?"

"Chi the Powerful."

Benjamin had to think for a moment, "That's impossible, he's dead. He sacrificed his life to bring down your Tower of Lebab."

With a short laugh, Grigori ceased his approach, "How much did you really know about your traveling partner? Oh well, it's not going to matter for much longer anyways." Lifting his scythe over his head, Grigori brought down the weapon with intent to kill.

Benjamin closed his eyes and prepared for the worst, but when the pain didn't come, he slowly opened his eyes to see another warrior between himself and Grigori. The soldier was equally decorated, but held six swords in his two hands, repelling Grigori's attack. The two Generals struggled as the new arrival grunted at Grigori, "You'd go so far as to execute this man without giving him a fair chance to fight?"

"Are you serious, Gulogulo? Not only does he have no chance of winning against me, but we were given orders to eliminate *all* the Naturals."

"And you're just going to take that order at face value?"

"*Da*, it's our duty."

"But why must we obey such a ridiculous order? Exterminate the Naturals? They haven't come after us! They're merely fighting in self-defense." A high pitched whistle was heard overhead, which triggered a reaction in Gulogulo. Pushing back Grigori, he quickly re-sheathed his swords and pulled out the black katana he had strapped to his back. Swinging it toward Benjamin, Gulogulo focused his energy into the blade and hoped for the best.

An arrow plunged into the ground just inches from Benjamin, the trajectory obviously altered by the swinging of the mysterious sword. Gulogulo breathed a sigh of relief as he addressed Benjamin, "Go to your friends and get out of here. I'll hold him off as long as I can."

"Very well, but how do I get away when I'm being held back like this?"

Slowly looking skyward, Gulogulo replied, "I don't think that's going to be a problem soon." Once again, a wave of ground and soldiers swept through the battlefield, knocking everyone to the ground. The soldiers who once held Benjamin lay in pieces on the ground, bits of armor strewn about.

It was now obviously clear that these soldiers were definitely hollow and, as they began to move again, something else entirely. One of the disembodied arms grabbed Benjamin's leg, which caused him to slash at it with his sword.

When the sword came in contact with the arm, sparks appeared, followed by a bright white flash and a small, smoldering fire on the ground. This phenomena caused the arm to let go of Benjamin's leg. Once again, Benjamin noticed a numbered disk on the soldier's armor. The number "12".

Now that Benjamin was finally released, he had no time to examine the empty, numbered soldiers. He quickly grabbed his weapon and flew into the air, watching as his savior confronted his mysterious, regenerating opponent. Quickly looking over the battlefield, he found Penny crouched down in a circle of downed soldiers.

Letting his wings disappear, he fell to the ground behind Penny, who was obviously running out of energy, her heavy breathing and sweat-soaked skin revealing how hard she had been fighting. Talking over her shoulder, she welcomed Benjamin, "So nice of you to drop by. Care to help me with these undead soldiers?"

"Undead? That's strange, I just ran into some soldiers who were completely hollow. How many weird soldiers does this army have?"

"Beats me. All I know is that my ground waves are becoming less effective."

"I thought that was you. Very impressive, Penny."

Penny smiled, but had no time to enjoy the compliment. The soldiers began their advance again and the two Naturals, back-to-back, readied their attacks.

"What's your problem, Gulogulo? I never saw you as the treasonous type."

"You know, Braun said the same thing."

"I'm assuming that's why you knew his shot was coming, right?"

"I've already seen it once before. I'm not letting it happen again."

"You do realize that I'm not nearly as lenient as Braun. In preventing me from completing my orders, I now need to see to it that you are killed along with the rest of the Naturals."

"So be it. At least I can die with a clean conscience. I doubt the rest of you will be so lucky."

"You're right on one point: I'm not going to die. Not now. Not ever."

"We'll just see about that." Both Generals prepared to fight each other by readying their weapons. Gulogulo knew that his fight would not only be futile, but could very well be fatal. Nevertheless, he held on to the six swords placed between his fingers, waiting for the first move. Grigori may have the experience, but Gulogulo knew that he certainly had the advantage in speed.

Grigori could see that his new opponent was biding his time, waiting for him to make the initial assault. Resting on his scythe's staff, he taunted, "You know, I've got all the time in the world. Take your time."

Somehow, Grigori's lax attitude made Gulogulo more nervous. Since it was apparent that he needed to start things off, he examined the situation.

Nervously flexing his fists caused the long blades in his hands to clink together rhythmically as he continued to think. Soon, he arrived at a decision. Taking a deep breath and letting it out slowly, Gulogulo crouched down and sprung forth toward Grigori's left side.

The wide, arching attack was easily blocked as Grigori sighed in frustration, "What is it with everyone attacking from the left side today? *Da*, I *know* I've got a blind spot, but you don't need to make it so obvious." Flipping his scythe around, he pushed off the three blades and swung wide with a counterattack. Gulogulo was quick enough to dodge it and took a few steps back to prepare his next attack.

For his second assault, Gulogulo repeated the swipe toward his opponent's left side, which Grigori took as a sign of unoriginality, "You know, if it didn't work the first time, I doubt it would work if you do it again." But what Grigori didn't realize was that the three swords which Gulogulo dragged along the ground were the second half of the attack. The added resistance of the ground increased the blades' speed once they got within range, landing a solid blow straight up Grigori's body.

Grigori merely laughed as the gaping wounds quickly disappeared, "You want to know the best part about this? It doesn't even hurt! With my body frozen in a single time state, I can be as reckless as I want." Deciding to turn the tide of the battle, Grigori began fervently attacking Gulogulo. The series of slashes and swipes were easily evaded by the quicker soldier, but he noticed that his hands were starting to bleed from the extended use of his swords.

From beyond the wall of soldiers, the battle of the Naturals could be heard. This momentary distraction helped Grigori disarm half of his opponent's swords, shattering them to pieces. Gulogulo knew his stamina couldn't hold out for much longer, so he decided to use his trump card. Re-sheathing the remaining three swords, he pulled the black katana from his back and took a two-hand stance with the weapon.

This change of swords intrigued Grigori, "So, you finally want to stoop to their level? I realize that your fluxion was a gift from Amedeo, as was mine, but it simply proves my point. The Naturals are stronger than we are. There's no doubt about that. We just evened the playing field. There's no way we could ever defeat them without using their own powers against them."

Gulogulo was tired of arguing with the people he had, up until recently, sided with. The real issue was that since he held no resentment towards the individuals, he didn't want to see them come to any real harm. Flipping the sword over to its blunt edge, Gulogulo readied the katana behind him and began to run toward Grigori, who once again chided, "I know that you've realized the sharp end of your swords won't work, but you're kind of going in the opposite direction."

Stopping a single step before his opponent, Gulogulo closed his eyes and focused all his energy into his sword, swinging it forward with unnatural speed and force. This caught Grigori off guard slightly, and he only had a moment to block with his staff. However, the energy of the blow was too great to block, and Gulogulo made contact with Grigori, sending the latter flying into the mass of soldiers behind him.

With a slow chuckle, Grigori got back on his feet, "That was a pretty good one, Gulogulo. What else you got?" From above, the high pitched whistle appeared again, but this time it sounded well rounded, different than the previous times. Looking to the smoke-filled sky, Gulogulo tried to see where it was coming from and where it was going. Two moments passed. In the first, he realized the attack was not meant for him. In the second, he realized the Naturals were being targeted again.

He tried to rush toward Benjamin and Penny, but the wall of soldiers prevented him from getting very far. Watching in horror, he saw the arrow multiply into a vast array of projectiles, all heading toward the two helpless fighters. A single breath escaped his lungs as he whispered in shock, "The Mount Charles method . . ."

From the edge of his peripheral vision, he saw something rise up to meet the flock of arrows. In a sudden burst of light, all that remained were splinters and shrapnel which rained down on the battlefield below. As he let out a sigh, Gulogulo noticed the next volley on its way and began to tense up again. But once more, the arrows were defeated, deflected by a deafening sound.

Knowing that Braun would not stop until his objective was completed, Gulogulo watched as the third volley of arrows rained down on the field. He waited for something spectacular to happen, but time kept passing by.

○

Benjamin found that fighting with an ally suddenly gave him more energy, and it seemed that the same was true of Penny as well. Fighting off the numerous hordes of minions actually became somewhat fun. At least it was more enjoyable than trying to fight someone who was actually skilled at battle. The two Naturals worked well as a team. Penny would take on the hollow shells of armor with her Resonance Crush and Benjamin would use his electric powers, combined with his recently made sword, to stop the reanimated corpses.

Together, they kept fighting the onslaught of soldiers until Benjamin noticed that, even though they had defeated many of the pawns, there weren't any less of them. "Where are they all coming from?" he shouted over the din of battle.

"Heck if I know!" Penny shouted back as she shattered another suit of armor, revealing the intertwining circuitry of snakes engraved on the inside. Suddenly, Benjamin heard a familiar sound from above. When he looked up, he couldn't see anything against the smoky backdrop, but soon a tiny speck began to spread, fanning out to an enormous swarm. Penny had noticed that Benjamin had stopped fighting, "What is it?!" she yelled.

"No time to explain. Just stay close." Grabbing his sword, Benjamin once again held the metal and let his electricity flow through the blade. With a swift motion, the metal spread across the entire handle that once held a hammer's head. His weapon had now evolved into a javelin. Focusing his lightning power into the weapon caused sparks to leap from the pointed tips.

Leaning backward, Benjamin threw the weapon high into the air. Sparks continued to fly as the lance sped upward toward the mass of black dots quickly growing bigger. Soon, a flash of bright light filled the sky as lightning erupted from the javelin, hitting every single arrow on its way to earth. The metal tips of the arrows attracted the electricity of the javelin and burst their wooden shafts into a cloud of splinters that rained down on the battlefield along with Benjamin's weapon, which stuck upright in the ground.

As some of the arrowheads landed on the ground and on the soldiers, still sparking from their recent electric encounter, something strange started to happen. The ones that fell on the soldiers made those particular soldiers bigger, turning them into giants. As for the arrowheads that fell on the ground, the earth seemed to sit up and take shape as fighters for the unending Army of Amedeo.

"What's going on?" Penny asked as the soil soldiers grabbed Benjamin, who found that his electricity could do nothing to help free him from their grasp.

"It's the arrowheads!" While Benjamin struggled, he tried to come up with an explanation, "They must have put some sort of human cores inside to make the ground take the form of soldiers." The whistling sound from above returned as both Benjamin and Penny looked up to see the same scene unfolding again. Shouting orders to his unrestrained partner, Benjamin kept trying to escape from the rocky grasp of the golems, "Penny! You're going to have to deal with this one. Just make sure the arrowheads don't land nearby!" Nodding in understanding, Penny stared upwards as she readied her stance, hands out at arm's length behind her.

As the arrows came closer, Benjamin became more nervous, "Any time now!"

"Just wait! They need to get in range!" A few moments passed and Benjamin closed his eyes in preparation for the worst. At once, a deafening boom was heard as Benjamin opened his eyes to see what caused the cacophonous sound. Penny had brought her hands together above her head; the resulting clap induced a sonic boom that shook the area. The shockwave ran through the air and diverted the arrows to a safe distance away. Still, as normal soldiers grew bigger and stone golems rose from the ground, they had only delayed the inevitable.

Since the stone soldiers nearby were unaffected by the sonic boom, they managed to grab Penny, thereby incapacitating the two Naturals. Penny gasped as they heard the sickening whistle above them a third time. She realized that if they could not get free, they were liable to be hit with the full force of the volley of arrows. Benjamin realized this as well and continued with increased vigor to escape from the grip of his captors.

Both Naturals struggled as the whistling grew louder. Penny helplessly looked at Benjamin and realized she didn't have much time left, "Benjamin!" she shouted. He looked up from examining the bodies of the stone soldiers, trying to find any weakness they had. Now that she had his attention, she swallowed back some tears, "I just want you to know that-" she lost her train of thought as the i-World symbol on Benjamin's forehead began to glow. Looking down, she noticed that her symbol was glowing as well. They both made eye contact and both had confused expressions on their faces.

A screech bellowed out over the whistle as a canopy of fire engulfed the entire area. Everyone crouched down, not only from the immense heat, but also due to the fact that a swarm of half a dozen dragons was swooping in from above. Through the dragons and snake-bat hybrids, Benjamin looked up to see a familiar face salute him as he flew away toward the source of the arrows. The glowing mark on his neck was partly obscured by his black cape, which fluttered behind him as he disappeared into the cloud of smoke.

Everyone stood still for a moment as the melted metal arrowheads sizzled on the ground, still glowing with latent heat. When the glowing Imaginary World marks began to fade, Benjamin noticed a familiar letter on the ground; he then noticed that the joints of the rock beast which was holding him were made of sand. At this point, he had run out of options. He knew that you could make glass out of sand with an application of fire, he just hoped that the Fire of Saint Erasmus would do the trick.

Focusing all the lightning energy he could into his hand, a bright blue orb appeared and seemed to flicker like fire in his palm. Benjamin thrust his palm to the golem's knee as he released the energy into the sand. Almost immediately, a shattering sound was heard from the knee as the leg broke at the joint, causing the stone soldier to fall away, releasing Benjamin in the process.

The remaining leg stood there, its shiny fragments revealing to Benjamin that he had indeed turned the sand into glass. Bending down to pick up the envelope, Benjamin was soon met by Penny, who now also knew the weakness of the soil soldiers. When Benjamin opened the letter, Penny noticed that it was the same exact note he sent out from Menlo Castle, "We got an answer?" she asked.

"It would appear so." Removing the note from the envelope, Benjamin saw the familiar design of a snake in an uroboros configuration, cut into pieces. The slogan "Join or Die" was emblazoned beneath the dissected serpent. Flipping the note over, he found that there was writing on the back. Just as he had suspected, it was from Bram:

To Lambda the Just:

It took me a while to realize that, in order to maintain peace for the whole, an occasional battle must be fought. I would look rather silly if peace were to be lost and I did nothing to prevent it. Consider the entire Order of the Dragon at your service.

Sincerely,
Umlaut the Dragon

With the addition of another fighter to their already miniscule resistance, Benjamin and Penny looked to the horizon to see the swarm of dragons engaging the swarm of arrows. When Penny glanced back to the battlefield, she noticed that one of the numbered soldiers had approached close enough to get his hand on Benjamin. She shouted, "Ben, look out!" but it was too late. The sweat on Benjamin's left arm reacted with the soldier, who wore an "11" Number Disk on his chest.

The reaction was quick and dramatic. In a small explosion, Benjamin was pushed to the ground. He grabbed at his sizzling arm in pain and was about to counterattack when Penny stepped in and blew the soldier into a multitude of pieces with a two-handed Resonance Crush. Helping Benjamin back to his feet, Penny was curious, "What was that?"

"I'm not too sure myself, but it seems like some of these armor soldiers have special powers connected to those numbered disks on their chests."

"What are we going to do about that?"

"Until we learn more, just stay alert."

The two Naturals prepared to fight again, but just before they were about to re-enter the fray, they heard a voice call out from the soldiers, "Wait just a minute!" The army men parted and out from the crowd appeared Nikola, slightly damaged, but victorious, "If you've got some time, Benjamin, I'd like my rematch now."

"Where's Thomas?"

"That old coot? He certainly put up a good fight, but it seems that youth and skill triumph over age and experience." Benjamin pulled his weapon from the ground and molded the metal back into that of a sword. A look of determination came across his face as he approached Nikola. This got Nikola rather excited, "I see you're finally serious, Ben," he then squinted in a bit of confusion, "so excited, in fact, that your forehead is glowing."

Benjamin's eyes widened as he looked back at Penny. Her mark was once again glowing as well. Looking to the sky, Benjamin couldn't see any hint of Bram nearby. When he looked back at Penny again, she began to think out loud, "You don't think Antonio actually came, do you?"

"Who else could there be? We don't even know who Breve the Lion *is*, and he's the only one left of the six who passed the trials in the Imaginary World."

Nikola was incredibly frustrated now. He was practically stomping toward Benjamin, yelling at the top of his lungs, "First you ran away from fighting me!

Now you're ignoring me! I will not suffer this indignation much longer! And furthermore-" a pillar of fire suddenly erupted from the ground, incinerating Nikola in an instant. The horde of soldiers cringed at this drastic turn of events. When the fire disappeared, all that was left was a hole in the ground, the rocks around the edge glowing from the latent heat.

But there was more to the hole; it appeared as though it was a set of stairs leading into the darkness of the earth. Penny and Benjamin heard footsteps climbing the red-hot, glowing steps as their symbols began to glow brighter and brighter.

○

Flying over the mountains on their approach to the valley of the Tower of Lebab, the Order of the Dragon kept their formation as they approached the towering pillar of black smoke that now stood in the spot of the razed structure. As they crested the final ridge and saw the battle below, one of the members to the right of Bram yelled over the howling wind, "Which side are we fighting for again? I hope it's that big one, because if so, this should be a very short battle."

"Sorry, we're the underdogs here. We can't always let those with more manpower dictate how the world will be run." Something in the sky caught Bram's attention, and he knew they had arrived just in the nick of time, "Looks like it's time to begin!" Leaning down to whisper to his dragon, Bram broke formation and dove toward the battlefield, the mark on his neck glowing ever brighter as he approached.

With a screech and a burst of fire, Bram's dragon incinerated the storm of arrows that were descending upon his fellow Imaginary World comrades. Flipping the note he received toward his allies, he caught Benjamin's attention and saluted as he pulled his dragon up and away from the battlefield. Rejoining the flying formation of the Order of the Dragon, he gave his commands, "We're here to keep the skies clear! Let's get to it!"

The group of dragons split up, but the snake-bat hybrids followed after Bram. There were many different types of snakes: cobras, rattlesnakes, and anacondas, just to name a few. Each species had a different style of flight, but they all remained with their lead. As they made their approach toward the point of the arrows' origin, the projectiles became less of a swarm, but were still many in number. The Dragonriders held tight to their mounts as they evaded the multitude of arrows. Occasionally, one of the riders would be able to get a shot off from one of their crossbows, but seconds later they would hear the high pitched "ping" of arrowhead colliding with arrowhead as they flew through a small cloud of splinters.

Bram was certainly impressed by this archer. Being able to shoot down an arrow from a crossbow, let alone in mid-flight, was something he had never seen before. Crouching down toward his dragon, he whispered another order and hung on. With a flap of its wings, the beast dove toward the archer, spinning its body to avoid the arrows flying toward it. As it got closer, the arrows became more difficult to dodge. With a deep breath, the dragon let out another burst of flame, burning the arrows and giving it an opportunity to land.

Opening its wings, the dragon slowed its descent just enough to smash into the ground with its hind legs, kicking up a cloud of dust in the process. Bram jumped off of the dragon's back and ran toward his enemy, who was covering his eyes to protect them from the dust and debris. This gave Bram just enough time to get to the archer and grab his bow. As the dust cleared, the swarm of snake-bat hybrids was seen circling above as the war in the valley raged on below.

Braun opened his eyes to see the only person who was ever able to get this close to him in battle. He smiled at Bram and said, "Well done. I must say that I've never faced a dragon before. I thought they were all dead."

"Not quite."

"So, let me ask you then: why are you fighting on behalf of the Naturals? Are you a Natural too?"

"*Nae*, I'm not a Natural, as you put it, but I do believe that there is more honor fighting against a bully than for one."

"Is that so? Well, that's a shame." Tapping on two notches in his bow, Braun looked Bram straight in the eyes, "I was hoping you were the last of Seasoned Compass. I'd already taken out two of them, and unfortunately one was killed before I had a chance to take a shot at them."

"Why would you even want to kill someone? Doesn't the guilt haunt you?"

"That's the great thing about being an archer, once the arrow leaves my bow; it's out of my hands. Where it comes down, and who it happens to hit is no longer my concern."

"Even if it happens to hit a comrade?"

"Like I said, it is no longer my concern." The rest of the Order of the Dragon landed in a circle surrounding Braun and aimed their crossbows at him. Looking down at the battlefield, he decided that his role in this war was complete, Braun let go of his longbow and put his hands in the air, "I might as well take a break now. I don't think this war will go on for much longer."

Bram turned around to see a spectacular fight occurring just above the heads of the vast myriads of soldiers. He became confused when it became obvious that two mythical beasts were battling against each other. He could only assume that it was the fight between two Naturals, as Braun had named them. But why was there infighting in their ranks? Didn't they know they had an enemy more numerous than any he had ever seen? At this point, there was little he could do but watch the incredible battle unfold.

Glowing ash from the incinerated remains of Nikola still slowly fell on the fighters as they watched a man, covered in flames, rise up out of the ground. The mark of Chi the Powerful was seen on the man's hand, glowing brighter than the flames which covered his body. A gust of wind snuffed out the fire to reveal a familiar face standing before them.

Penny shouted out in surprise, "Tecumseh! You're alive!"

"It's nice to see you again, Penny. I see you're still with Benjamin."

"But . . . how? We saw the entire tower collapse on top of you!"

"It's a little hard to explain without getting into the 'why'."

Benjamin noticed that Tecumseh now wore the uniform of the Army of Amedeo. He wondered how many other defectors he would see that day, "That brings up a good point, Tecumseh. Why *would* you fake your own death? And furthermore, why would you join the same army that is trying to kill off people just like you?"

Taking a few steps forward, Tecumseh chuckled, "I think the question you should be asking is why would I want to be the strongest Natural in the world? They may think that I'm fighting for them, but they're merely eliminating my competition. Naturally, I had to do my part as well, but I found that to be incredibly invigorating." Looking over at the still silent statue of Arma Ress, he smiled, "That piece of work over there definitely gave me a run for my money."

Penny made the connection and growled out through clenched teeth, "*You killed my brother?*"

"But of course! And your mother, and your father, and your other brothers," he paused as he let a smile creep across his lips, "and your younger sister. I *particularly* enjoyed killing that one."

This revelation made Penny snap. With a scream that rumbled the earth, she pushed off a wave of ground and launched herself toward Tecumseh, trident at the ready and poised to strike. Tecumseh lit his feet on fire and sunk through molten rock to dodge the attack. As Penny flew overhead, a stream of tears flowing from her angry eyes, Tecumseh thrust his pitchfork upward, catching Penny in her stomach, and flinging her into a wall of moving statues, the latter of which had just begun to appear from the hole that Tecumseh had made.

The statues each had a red disk set in their chest, an uroboros seal encircling the life-giving force. Penny collapsed on the ground and dropped her weapon as she clutched her side. A cough of blood followed as she glanced up at Tecumseh, who had pulled his legs out of the molten ground and shook off the remaining drops of magma as he approached the wounded woman. When he got close enough, Tecumseh knelt down to Penny's eye level and continued to explain, "You see, Penny. I knew that you would never be able to love me if you had others who loved you. Once you found that you had no one else to love, you would inevitably come back to me."

Penny spat in Tecumseh's face and growled, "Go to hell."

Wiping the bloody saliva from his cheek, Tecumseh sneered, "Where do you think I came from?" Standing up and turning around, he locked eyes with Benjamin, who had sprouted his wings and prepared his mind to fight a former ally. Tecumseh scowled and continued, "Of course, there was one person I knew you still loved, and I hoped that by this juncture in the war he would have been eliminated already. I suppose that in order to claim my prize, I must perform the finishing touches. I just need you to stay right there while I take care of this last detail. Then we can be together forever."

As Benjamin approached, he clenched his fist tighter, turning it into stone. When he got close enough, he wound up and struck Tecumseh squarely in the face. Staring at the ground, Tecumseh spat out some blood and one of his molars. He wiped the blood from his mouth with his sleeve as he began to chuckle, "I see you're as ready to fight as I am."

Benjamin opened up his fist and let the stones he had picked up drop back to the ground, returning his hand to its original state, "I can't figure you out, Tecumseh. You've got such great power. Power that could be used to help humanity. You could heat homes, or cook food, or provide an endless supply of light at night, but instead you squander your power for selfish gains."

"It's funny that I finally get to fight you, Benjamin. Since we first met, I knew this day would eventually come."

"I'm not going to fight you because you lied to us. I'm not going to fight you because you defected to our enemies. I'm not even going to fight you because of what you have done to Penny. I'm going to fight you to bring justice to this world."

Tecumseh leaned back and laughed heartily, "Justice! Justice means nothing. Power is the true equalizer. Of course, power is meaningless without money, without resources. When I saw the resources of the Army of Amedeo, I knew that my power could be so much greater than if I hung out with a few people who could wield power *almost* like I could."

"Is that why you faked your death? To get their attention?"

Touching his nose to indicate that Benjamin was right, Tecumseh focused on his Blood-fluxion as his legs began to turn into those of a bull, "Why don't we take this conversation up a little bit before we start fighting?" A blue fire burst forth from Tecumseh's hooves as he propelled himself into the sky.

While he still had a chance, Benjamin thrust his right arm upward toward the rising Tecumseh. A short burst of blue lightning erupted from his hand, but failed to gain momentum past his palm. This caused Tecumseh to quickly climb higher into the air. Mumbling something about his attack only being a "starter" and not a "jet", Benjamin flapped his wings a few times and rose into the air to meet his foe.

When both men had arrived at the same altitude, many yards above the heads of the soldiers below, Tecumseh spoke over the roar of his fire, "You know . . . our powers almost make us like brothers. Lightning can strike dry forests and start fires. The smoke of a fire can build up and eventually induce lightning. We are two halves of the same coin."

"I disagree, we are nothing alike. I strive to be honest and to live with honor. Trickery and treachery are the practices of fools who have not wits enough to be honest." With a flap of his wings, Benjamin made the first move, a thrust of his sword aimed right for Tecumseh's heart. Taking in a deep breath, Tecumseh blew out a fireball from his mouth, propelling him backwards and engulfing Benjamin in the process.

A bolt of lightning emerged from the fire and Benjamin appeared in a flash of light. Transforming his sword into a javelin once more, Benjamin charged the weapon and threw it into the smoky cloud above them. More of Tecumseh's body had become covered in flame, almost appearing like a brilliant blue armor of wavering fire. Now a set of horns emerged from his head to match his hooves, "Throwing away your weapon so soon?" he taunted. Flying higher into the sky, Benjamin hoped that Tecumseh would follow, "You're not getting away from me so easily!"

Benjamin knew he could not fly faster than Tecumseh, but he hoped that he could buy enough time to set his attack in motion. The javelin returned from the cloud and Benjamin caught it just as Tecumseh caught up to him. Rising above his opponent, Tecumseh wound up and delivered a fire-accelerated punch that knocked Benjamin toward the ground.

As he fell, Benjamin lifted up his javelin and began to charge it with energy. In response, the clouds began to spark, and soon multiple bolts of lightning found their way to Benjamin's weapon. Of course, since he was now directly below Tecumseh, the lightning had to travel through the fiery foe to get to its intended target. A direct hit!

Tecumseh momentarily lost his fire and began to fall, as the lightning had affected his nervous system, causing him to lose control. Just before he hit the ground, his fire returned, this time in a brilliant white, shining over the soldiers who gawked in awe of what they were witnessing. When he caught up to Benjamin again, Tecumseh chuckled, "That's an impressive trick you've got there."

"Well, while you were dead, I did a bit of training."

"Oh? So there's more?"

"Of course. In fact, here's something I learned from some research that one of your traitorous colleagues did before he left." Putting his weapon away to free up his hands, Benjamin clasped them together and focused on the Skybolt orb he wore around his neck. The light from the orb became brighter and began to pulse in sync with his heart. Soon, a similar light appeared between his hands. The resistance seemed to increase as his hands spread apart, revealing a swirling mass of electricity.

Tecumseh was still unimpressed, "What is *that?*"

"*This* is known as ball lightning." Holding the pulsing sphere of lightning in his right hand, Benjamin wound up and threw it at Tecumseh, who managed to just barely dodge. The ball lightning fell to the earth and quickly expanded outward, engulfing a few dozen legions with its destructive power.

Sweat soon started turning to steam from Tecumseh's forehead as it came in contact with his armor of flames. His eyes became wide as Benjamin began to prepare another round of ball lightning. Now that he knew what it could do, Tecumseh turned tail and ran, the panic causing his flames to briefly turn to blue then return to white. Benjamin flew after his opponent while still molding a bigger ball lightning than before. As was the case earlier, Benjamin was not as fast as Tecumseh in terms of flight, and he soon fell behind. To compensate for the lack of distance, Benjamin forced as much energy as he could into the ball lightning.

It happened in a single moment. The Skybolt orb, which up until now had behaved rather well, flickered. The massive amount of lightning that Benjamin had collected immediately tried to find the quickest way to dissipate itself. Travelling from his hands to his chest, the lightning hit something in his pocket, which began to glow.

With nothing restraining the ball lightning, it erupted in a huge explosion, one-hundred times more massive than the one that had come before it. The explosion created a shockwave which shook the area to its core. The black smoke stopped, the clouds cleared, and the entire battlefield immediately felt the effects of the eruption. Sparks ran across the ground and from soldier to soldier, spreading through the dense mass of fighters and destroying everything it could. Glass shattered, metal exploded, stone crumbled. The most destructive attack the world had ever seen did all this and more in a mere amount of seconds.

When the dust settled, the entire battlefield remained still. Not moving. Not fighting. The war to exterminate the Naturals had come to an end.

Epilogue

Millennial Erasure

From the nearby hill, Albert and company were amazed at the battle they had just witnessed. Now that the fight was over, they rushed down to see who had survived. Similarly, the Order of the Dragon took to the sky and descended upon the mass of downed soldiers. As everyone gathered, they realized that, despite the stupendous numbers involved, no one made it out alive.

The field was littered with soldiers. Many were men who fought for what they thought was right. Others were fluxion infused beasts, which were once again useless piles of armor or stone, as the glass vials holding their life-infusing Blood-fluxion cores were shattered from the explosion of the ball lightning.

As the survivors from the hills policed the area, they came upon Penny, who had died from the wound she had sustained from her scorned lover, moments before the explosion. The Seawave orb still churned away on the necklace she wore. Dr. Robert found the lone woman and took her fluxion core as he laid her flat on the ground and arranged her body in preparation for being buried. Nearby, Dmitri found the body of Mary, her fate was being crushed by a mound of her undead soldiers, now dead once again.

Bram found Chi's body, severely charred, not only from the lightning, but from his own fire. As was the case with Penny, the Hellfire orb which gave Chi his power still flickered with a sprightly energy that stood in stark contrast to the horrific scene around it. Noticing the others who were picking through the carnage, Bram approached Albert, hoping he was another ally.

Bram became defensive when he got close enough to realize that these men, while not wearing uniforms, bore the mark of the Army of Amedeo, "Are you all still willing to fight for this lost cause?"

Albert looked up, a distraught expression covering his face, "What? *Nein.*" He just shook his head, "We have done more damage here than I think should ever have happened. I have seen the results of our research, and I have come to the realization that humanity has not matured enough to handle such great power. I shudder to think what would have transpired had we perfected the Fluents."

Jules approached the two men, having overheard their conversation, "What do you suggest we do, Albert?"

"We need to hide this knowledge we have gained. Once we gather everything involved with these fluxions, we will split up the research and scatter it to the ends of the earth."

A pile of bodies moved behind them and immediately everyone became guarded. Pushing the bodies aside, General Gulogulo and General Grigori emerged from the pile. While they sported injuries from their own fight, they remained unscathed from the effects of the ball lightning. Gulogulo pulled Kuroni out of the ground and held it loosely, "We're done here, Grigori."

"I don't think so. While we still have two sides, we can still have a battle."

"I disagree. If I hadn't used Kuroni to draw in that lightning, it very well could have destroyed you. You may be immortal, but I doubt you wanted to test that theory in quite this way."

"Fine." Grigori turned to leave, "Just know that I will always be ready to fight. Wars will come and wars will go, but I will remain." Putting the blades back into the shaft of his scythe, Grigori left the battlefield. For a long time, Grigori wandered the earth, and his name became legend. Eventually, he was known as "The Grim Reaper", although that was merely an evolution from "Grigori the Reaper." Centuries later, he would be caught and imprisoned on charges of mass murder. He would sit in Pandora Prison for many more centuries, whittling away his immortal life.

Gulogulo turned around and noticed that Albert was on the battlefield, "I see you all have survived to tell the tale of this despicable place."

"We have. I for one am glad that I saw it, as it has humbled me and made me realize that, even though research can be used for good, it can just as easily be used to destroy."

Julius stood a small distance away and was overheard solemnly talking to himself, "Now we have become Death, the destroyer of worlds."

Mathison overheard Julius and responded, "It looks like Luvnac's wish has finally come true . . . but at what cost?"

Scanning across the masses of downed soldiers, Gulogulo asked, "Hey, where's Braun?"

Bram stepped forward and explained, "He's gone the way of your other General. Once he saw that there was no more fighting, he picked up his things and left."

Herbert was heard shouting a short distance away, "Hey, guys! Look who I found!"

As everyone gathered over the body, they realized that it was the mastermind and initiator of this entire conflict. General Amedeo lay beside a number of his precious soldiers, killed in the same way that they were. Herbert asked the question everyone was thinking, "Now that General Amedeo is dead, is the army dissolved?"

With a sigh, Albert responded, "I suppose so. All for the best, anyways. I do not know if anyone will really know what he was thinking, but he will certainly go down in history for it." Taking a moment of silence, Albert started giving orders, "All right, everyone. Let us search the battlefield for any more survivors, then let us return to the Library of Delaxanair to split up the fluxion research."

It took most of the day and night, but by the time the sun rose the next day, a large pile of soldiers was set where the Tower of Lebab once stood. Some individual graves were made for Penny, Chi, Arma Ress, Thomas, Mary, and General Amedeo, among others. Bram's dragon started the funeral pyre for the incredible amount of soldiers as Albert said a few words, "This place will no longer be known for the Tower of Lebab. From now on, it shall be known as the Trinity Site, as it is where The Triumvirate fought the Army of Amedeo, and each other." Turning from the fire, Albert led the way toward the open Q-Portal at the edge of the valley. As everyone gathered at the black opening, Albert turned to Bram and said, "Are you sure you are fine with us leaving you here?"

"*Aye* . . . I am. I think the rest of the Order of the Dragon and I need to consider what our role is in this new world after the war."

"*Wunderbar.* Just as long as you get that Hellfire orb back to where it belongs. If I remember from my research, it should have come from the Holy Cliffs of the 5th Kingdom. Hopefully it will return to obscurity. The obscurity it had been in until now."

Bram nodded as he mounted his dragon. Nudging the beast with his heels, it took off. Bram gave a salute as he joined his fellows from the Order in the sky. The group of researchers and General Gulogulo passed through the Q-Portal and arrived back at the Library of Delaxanair, where they began to collect everything that had led to the horrific war they had witnessed.

General Gulogulo was more than willing to help, and gathered many scrolls and items to take with him to a secret cave outside his hometown. While he kept Luvnac's last blade, Kuroni, he left the gravity fluxion core to be hidden far away from its seat in the black katana. Taking a few of the Q-Portal keys, he traveled back to his hometown to begin his retirement.

Just outside of New Town, Gulogulo opened a secret cave with a shout, "Where there's a Will, there's a way!" The stone rolled back, revealing an empty cave. When the stone closed behind him, Gulogulo lit a torch and continued into the cavern. He found a room further in, which had been originally used to store wine. Now its cubbies were empty and willing to accept the numerous scrolls which he carried in a pack slung over his shoulder. Along with the scrolls, he found a place for a glove with a Q-Portal key sewn into its fabric, the embroidery emulating that of an uroboros snake biting its tail, instead of eating the tail entirely. Holding the glove in his hand, Gulogulo wondered what such an item would have been used for, had it been involved with the war.

Finishing up the task at hand, Gulogulo made his way to the cave's entrance, where he purposely used one of the Q-Portal keys, instead of the normal key which was required to escape the cave. Creating a second keyhole with a black Q-Portal key, he pushed the door open and forced his way through the white hole. Once again, he found himself in the Library of Delaxanair.

Albert was a little surprised to see Gulogulo again, but the surprise turned into a smile as he greeted his friend. Gulogulo pointed to the open door behind him and offered, "You can use this cave to store as many things as you want."

"*Wunderbar*. We will just put a few things in it and you can go home to finally retire." Albert motioned for some of the researchers to take the first failed fluxion experiment and put the stone soldier in the cave, its horrified expression remained unchanged after the removal of its Soul-fusion fluxion.

Gulogulo finally made it home and, after a time, began to accept his nickname of "G. G.", even if it did sound very similar to a girl's name. Eventually, that nickname evolved into "G-squared". He built a family and eventually led New Town as the best leader the village had ever seen. When he died, a shrine was made in his honor; the only thing from his past that remained at the shrine was Kuroni, Luvnac's last blade.

Dmitri was distressed with the fact that he had to split up his massive Number Disk collection, but he eventually came to terms with it, having seen what they could potentially do. He split up the Number Disks into twenty groups and sent them to different parts of the world to be hidden. As for the noble Number Disks, he decided to return them to their respective Kingdoms. While the six Noble Swords were now destroyed, the least that could be done would be to return what was left: the Number Disks.

James and Garland, the discoverers of the knotted uroboros seal, took the 4th Kingdom's "36" Number Disk, the Seawave orb, and the 10 Caliber Sword of Selcomad and returned to their home on the Island Kingdom. During their journey to the 4th Kingdom, they decided it would be best if the Seawave orb were lost at the bottom of the ocean. Tossing the orb into the sea with an unimpressive "plop", the fluxion core vanished into the murky waters and from the memories of history.

Over time, James and Garland would be recognized for their efforts and a large statue of them was constructed near the stone structure that they used to test their sealing theories. The 10 Caliber Sword of Selcomad was eventually sealed in a stone and used to represent the arrival of a new King who would be able to remove the sword from the stone. Unfortunately, the sword and the stone disappeared and were not found for many centuries, evolving into legend.

Jules and Herbert were assigned a special task and were given the instructions to gather their families and meet back at the Library of Delaxanair.

Albert held up a short and thick black Q-Portal key and gave them an explanation, "This key is very special. It is the lowest frequency key that has ever been made. As such, there is a good chance that when it is used, it will transport you to an area that may not even be on this planet. This is why I have asked you to take the most powerful items of our research and to hide them away wherever this key will take you."

Both men were loaded down with numerous scrolls and fluxion cores. The all-important key to the Fluent of Light was one of the scrolls in their possession. As for fluxion cores, the gravity fluxion that was taken from Aki Nishi, the "–" fluxion core that Tecumseh stole, and the wind fluxion that was taken from Sunaru Suleac were some of the many cores that they now held. Albert opened the door with the key and gave them one last chance to back out, "Once you go through this door, there is no coming back. You will have no Q-Portal keys and there may be a good chance that you will never be seen from again."

Both men looked at their wives, who were in turn accepting of the circumstances. Herbert spoke for the group, "I think we've got all the people we need to see right here." All together, the group passed through the Q-Portal and were transported to an area which was incredibly bright and grey, even despite the black sky above them. Herbert and Jules looked at each other with surprise and immediate understanding. They had arrived on the moon. The moon they had both dreamed of being able to walk on.

Taking a few steps onto the virgin soil, the wives set down the cats they had been holding in their arms and took a look around while their husbands hugged each other and jumped up and down in excitement, each jump being higher than they had ever jumped while on earth. Herbert's wife, Amy, saw something in the distance and squinted her eyes, trying to recognize what it was, "Are those . . . cows?" Everyone stopped what they were doing and looked to where she was pointing. Indeed, those were cows.

While he no longer had something as miraculous and magnificent to study as the fluxions and Fluents, Albert was disturbed by one last question that was raised during the battle at the Trinity Site. While all the soldiers could be accounted for, due to their dog tags, not everyone from the opposing side was found. The one known as Benjamin, or Lambda the Just, had disappeared. Albert suspected that the energy of the ball lightning merely vaporized the man, but something about how the last explosion occurred gave him a slight doubt as to that hypothesis. It wasn't like how Nikola was killed, in an incinerating pillar of fire, it was more like he was pulled through the sky itself.

In his search for Benjamin, Albert came across a few Naturals who had escaped the wrath of Amedeo. One of the Naturals of note was Cremy Serehurm, the sole survivor of the family from Rancho de la Sol. Despite the threat of the Army of Amedeo being gone, Cremy Serehurm went into hiding for a while until he felt absolutely safe. Even then, he no longer used his powers as a Natural, as they would be too risky to expose. Returning to his love of speed, Cremy Serehurm started Transcontinental Express Airmail, or T.E.A. for short. This company still remains today and is the number one delivery service in the world.

Albert's obsession controlled him for the rest of his life, although no one is really sure when that was. Since he traveled so often, eventually people lost track of where he was. He just disappeared from the world's consciousness. Although, as he had hoped, the use of fluxions was erased from peoples' memories. The source of so much trouble, so much pain, so much suffering, finally ceased to exist. The world was a quiet place once again. People went about their daily lives, and nothing extraordinary really happened. And then, for a time, there was silence.

The Third Degree
A story about family, legacy, sacrifice, and most of all: science

Chapter 1

The Missing Key

The room was silent long past the point of being awkward. Irene and her father, Pierre, sat on the living room couch waiting for Isaac to continue. Irene was an ordinary girl with ordinary features and an ordinary life. Her straight, red hair was obviously inherited from her father, who still had some elements of color clinging to his scraggly beard. Of course, there was no remnant of this red hair on his head, as he was now completely bald.

Isaac, on the other hand, had shoulder-length white hair which matched the coat and headband draped over a chair in the corner. His features were rugged, worn from hardship. That's not to say he wasn't still young, as his true age was closer to a quarter century than his white hair would have one believe. Currently, he was sitting in an easy chair in Irene and Pierre's living room, staring at his broadsword, which he had placed on the coffee table.

While being somewhat longer than a normal broadsword, this weapon's unique feature was a triangular diamond core which was embedded in the tip of the blade, surrounded by a knotted snake in an uroboros configuration. The scabbard for this sword sat in the corner where his accoutrements lay, along with a katana held in a beautifully lacquered sheath with the boughs of an apple tree adorning its design. The broadsword had somehow entranced Isaac, causing him to stop the story he was recounting.

Irene and Pierre looked at each other with concerned expressions, then back at Isaac. Off in the distance, the sound of thunder could be heard, which motivated Pierre to clear his throat, snapping Isaac out of his daze, "You were saying, Isaac?"

"What's that?"

"You said that sometimes the truth is stranger than fiction, but then you just trailed off."

"Ah yes, that's right," picking up the cup and saucer he had placed on the coffee table, he lifted the tea cup and took a sip, the drink now considerably colder than when he had set it down, "The truth of the matter is that the Fluent which sits within this sword was developed around one thousand years ago. However, it hasn't been utilized until this era, when I found the scroll detailing its powers and put the research into practice." Glancing over to the corner, he continued, "In fact, that katana is likely to be one thousand years old as well."

Irene was becoming impatient, "That's great, but it's really not the story I've been expecting from you. I want to know about your adventures! Like, where did you find the scroll for the Fluent? I'm sure there's a great story behind that."

"Oh, that's easy. I found it on the moon."

"See? That wasn't so hard." Suddenly, the realization of what was said came to Irene and she did a double take, "Wait, did you say the *moon?*"

"Yes."

"You're pulling my chain."

"I can assure you that I'm not."

"Then spill the beans, Isaac! I'm getting restless here. If you don't let me know about your adventures, you've broken our promise."

Pierre looked at Irene, "What promise?"

As Irene turned to answer her father, a flash of light caused everyone to cover their eyes. At the same time, a cacophonous boom shook the house. Everyone tried to cover their ears, which was hard to do when there was barely enough time to react in order to cover their eyes as well. Pierre was the first to respond, "*Sacrebleu!* What was that?" he yelled, the ringing in his ears causing his boisterous response. Without waiting for an answer, the color dropped out of his face as he started running toward the front door, "Not the pier again! I swear, if it gets destroyed one more time, I'm done for!"

Irene had gotten up and quickly followed her father. Since her ears were also still ringing, she yelled behind her to Isaac as she grabbed him by the wrist and forced him outside, "If this is another one of your adventures, we might have to banish you from New Town altogether!"

Once outside, Irene saw her father standing on the end of his pier, slightly confused by the sudden event and the lack of damage to his property. Likewise, other dock owners were now making their way outside to assess the situation. They glanced at each other with quizzical looks as to the source of the unexpected explosion. Isaac was the first to notice, "There! The Square G shrine!" With an outstretched arm, he pointed to a lone tree on the top of a seaside cliff which was now ablaze, burning embers and tiny splinters falling from the sky above it.

Wrenching his arm free from Irene's grip, Isaac started running toward the site. Not wanting to be left out yet again, Irene ran after him, always a few lengths behind. When they arrived at the burning tree, the flames continued to crackle away at the aged bark. The apples from the tree had been thrown in every direction and some were hissing from being instantaneously baked by what could only be explained as a lightning strike. A dark gash down the trunk of the tree ran right through the middle of the carved plaque which sat above what used to be the resting place for Isaac's katana, Kuroni.

Isaac examined the sky, which gave no indication that the lightning could have come from its clear blue expanse. Looking toward the town, Isaac tried to see if there was some sort of cannon which would have shot the tree, but that still wouldn't have explained the flash of light. Irene tapped him on the shoulder to get his attention, "Look! Down there!"

Pointing toward the cliff, Irene ran right up to the edge so she could look over the precipice. When Isaac joined her, he didn't see anything out of the ordinary. Surf lazily crashed against the rocky wall as Isaac examined the water for something different. Looking up, he saw Pierre on his pier, pointing out further away from the cliff. For a brief moment, Isaac saw someone's head break the surface of the water, at which point he took a step forward and leapt off of the cliff and into the sea to rescue the individual.

Dragging the limp body to shore, Isaac met Irene, Pierre, and the rest of the dock owners who were still curious about what had happened. The body was that of a man in his early thirties, who wore outdated clothing and a pair of rectangular glasses. Isaac placed his ear to the man's chest and immediately pulled back in surprise. He had almost burnt his ear from something incredibly hot in the man's vest pocket.

Feeling for a pulse, Isaac scanned across the man's body and saw that he was still breathing. Looking up to those gathered around him, Isaac said, "He's breathing, but unconscious. And yet, his pace is a little fast for someone who was unconscious in the sea." Pointing to Pierre, he continued, "Let's get him indoors. Grab his legs!"

Once inside Pierre's dock house, the two men brought the stranger upstairs into the spare bedroom. As they lifted the body onto the bed, Isaac gave a short chuckle, "This seems like a little bit of déjà vu to me, but only because I was once in his position." Pierre took off the man's wet vest and shirt and laid them over the back of a solitary chair which sat in the corner of the room.

Irene entered the room with some towels and a water basin. She just rolled her eyes and smiled as she wrung out a moist towel and put it on the man's forehead. Pierre left the room and went back downstairs as Irene tended to the unconscious man. Isaac still stood there, but the grin of irony had left his face and was now replaced with a slight scowl of concern. Pulling the covers of the bed up over the half-naked body, Irene noticed Isaac's expression and asked, "What's wrong?"

"Either this is some sick joke, or it's an incredible coincidence."

"What do you mean?"

"This man looks exactly like the descriptions of Lambda the Just of The Triumvirate, but he died at the conclusion of Amedeo's War."

"What makes you think it's him?"

"Well, the glasses are a dead giveaway, but the scar on his right cheek is unmistakably that of Lambda the Just."

"That scar looks pretty real; do you think someone would go that far to look like Lambda?"

"I'm not really sure why anyone would." Something else caught Isaac's attention. A chain around the man's neck led to an object behind his back. As Isaac lifted the body up out of the bed, he pulled on the chain to dislodge the item pinned underneath the man.

Irene had her back to Isaac when she heard him fall to the wooden floor, "I hope you haven't fainted again, Isaac." When she turned around, she found him sitting on the floor, his arms propping him up from behind. A shocked expression of disbelief covered his face as he stared at the object which now lay on the man's chest. There, at the end of the chain, was an orb filled with electricity, its power seeming to grasp at the glass container holding it in. Irene was still confused, "Isaac? What is it?"

A barely audible whisper escaped his lips, "It *is* him."

"Huh?"

"Lambda the Just. He's lying right in front of me."

"How do you know? A moment ago you weren't so sure."

Arising from the floor, Isaac pointed to the glass orb on the man's chest, "*That* is how I know."

"And 'that' is?"

"*That* is the Skybolt orb, the source of Lambda's power, which was supposedly destroyed when he died. There's no mistaking it now. This is someone who lived over one thousand years ago. The legendary member of The Triumvirate. The man who single handedly ended Amedeo's War."

This news excited Irene, "Really?" Thinking to herself out loud, she mused, "I wonder what stories *he* could tell."

○

Outside the limits of New Town, an innocuous grove of aspen was rudely disrupted when the hillside behind the grove began to spark with lightning. The energy built, eventually revealing the outline of a door in the rock. At once, the electricity was released in a loud boom as the door swung open. From the darkness beyond, a man clad head-to-toe in a dark cloak emerged from the door, sparks still leaping from the opening and out onto the now blackened trees.

In his right, gloved hand, the man held a glowing key. The key sizzled in the man's grip as it began to lose its latent heat. Blowing over the item to cool it, the mysterious figure eventually put the key back into the recesses of his cloak as he gazed toward the town. Moments later, an electric orb appeared out of nowhere. It grew in size over a lone hill at the edge of the city, opposite from where the man stood.

With a release many times more powerful than the one the man just came from, the electric orb disappeared in a flash of light, transferring most of its energy to the nearest object: an apple tree which sat atop the coastal hill. Seconds later, the cloak of the man was blown backward as the acoustic shockwave of the ruptured electric bubble finally reached the outskirts of town. And yet, the only thing out of the ordinary shown underneath the cloak was a vest covered in hooks which held various keys of differing lengths, the most recent white key still dully glowing next to its brothers. As quickly as the keys were revealed, the cloak fell back in place, smothering the strange keys in darkness once again.

Although it was far away, the man saw someone fall from the recent explosion into the sea beyond. Partially obscured by the hood of his cloak, the man's face revealed a sly grin and nothing else, "*Wunderbar*. Right on time." Adjusting the large, cylindrical case he had strapped to his back, the man began walking toward New Town with a determined gait.

By the time the man had gotten well into the city, many of the townsfolk were talking about the loud explosion they had heard earlier that morning, speculating on the cause of such a sudden event. It was approaching noon, so the wares of many of the food stands were becoming increasingly appetizing. Being a coastal town, many of the vendors sold fish. One in particular skewered its catches on sharpened sticks, which were then barbecued. The man examined the options: halibut, salmon, trout, pike. While he was feeling a little hungry, he decided to move on toward his main objective.

Finally arriving at the opposite edge of town, the man focused on the smoldering remains of the apple tree which once proudly stood at the top of the nearby hill. Many of the townspeople were starting to gather on the cliff top, trying to figure out what had happened.

Turning his attention to the coastline, he stared out over the water to see if there was any sign of the person who fell in. Seeing that none of the townspeople were trying to rescue anybody, the man became concerned that his target may have drowned before anyone had gotten there. Turning toward the docks, which were in a flurry of business and confusion, he stopped one of the workers and asked, "What happened here? Was anyone hurt?"

A bit impatient, the worker replied, "I don't know and I don't care. I don't have time to figure it out either."

Before the worker could leave, the mysterious figure reached out and grabbed the man's shoulder with a thick glove, "I need to know if anyone was pulled from the sea."

The thick accent coming from the shadows of the hooded cloak made the worker answer purely on the impulse to escape from the awkward situation, "Yeah, they found some guy out in the water and pulled him ashore. He's at Pierre's place." With a jab of his thumb, the worker motioned toward the dock house which was clearly designated by the sign, "Pierre's Pier."

Patting the worker on the shoulder, the man replied, "*Wunderbar, dankeschön.*" Approaching the front door of the house, the cloaked man knocked twice and waited. His stomach growled again, but he ignored it as he pulled back the hood of his cloak to reveal a face that was kind, but had obviously been through a lot. The full head of white hair and thick moustache were absolutely uncontrollable and it appeared as though he didn't even try anymore. As he heard footsteps inside the house rushing to answer his knock, he smiled in preparation.

Pierre opened the door and was immediately greeted by the mysterious man, who shook Pierre's hand and made his way inside the house, "*Guten tag*, I believe that you have a friend of mine here, am I correct?" The man had already started to look through the various first-floor rooms as Pierre hurriedly tried to catch up.

"*Excusez-moi*, but are you a friend of Isaac's?" Pierre quickly asked while he tried to stop the intimidating intruder.

"*Nein*, I do not know who Isaac is. I am looking for the man you recently rescued from the sea." Noticing the staircase, the man deduced that the person he was looking for must be on the second floor, which is why he grabbed the banister and began to climb the stairs, two steps at a time.

At the bottom of the stairs, Pierre yelled past the intruder in a concerned voice, "Irene! You're about to have company!"

Isaac could hear the steps quickly approaching from downstairs, which made him realize both of his weapons were on the first floor. Nevertheless, he stepped out of the room and closed the door, putting himself between the unwanted guest and his new discovery. When the man arrived at the top of the stairs, he looked Isaac over, eventually settling on the dark disk embedded in his forehead, surrounded by a tattoo of two snake heads attempting to eat the disk, "I see fluxions have made a comeback. I suppose we did not hide things well enough."

This cryptic statement confused Isaac just long enough for the man to push him aside and get into the room beyond. Irene stood in front of the body, holding a knitting needle with both hands. She was confident, but was unsure if she would have the follow-through, should anything happen. The intruder saw past Irene to the man in the bed. Instantly, his face lit up as a smile came across his lips. Taking a step forward, the man stopped when Irene also stepped forward, "I don't know what you want, but I don't want to hurt you," her hands were trembling.

Letting out a hearty laugh, the mysterious man put up his right hand in a gesture of surrender, "There is no need to worry, *fräulein*. I am just glad to see Lambda the Just is doing well."

At the mention of Lambda the Just, Isaac re-entered the room, "I was right! But how do you know who this is? And furthermore, who are *you?*"

Setting down the cylindrical case from his back and pushing it into the corner of the room, the man sighed in relief, "Pardon my intrusion, but finding this man has been a goal of mine for a very long time," turning back to Isaac and Irene, he continued, "My name is Albert, and I know it may come as a shock to you, but I witnessed the disappearance of this man with my own eyes nearly one thousand years ago."

Isaac was dumbfounded, "Albert? As in *the* Albert who led the team of researchers who discovered fluxions? *That* Albert?"

"Ja."

For a moment, Isaac was speechless. Soon, he regained his senses and replied, "You know what? Since you've confirmed to me that this man is Lambda the Just, I really can't complain. And yet, if he's traveled here from the past, I don't see why you couldn't as well. Stranger stuff has happened."

Irene muttered to herself, "Not that I get to hear about any of it."

Glancing around the room, Albert was obviously searching for something as he spoke, "I see that you have a Soul-fusion fluxion, which tells me that fluxions are still in use today." A frown came over his face as he scrutinized Isaac, "From your knowledge of me, I would assume you have brought these powers back from the dead?"

"I have, but only to help mankind, not to harm it."

"There can be no good that can come from these things, which is why we must take their destruction one step further."

"What do you mean?"

"I cannot fully explain until our friend here wakes up, which brings me to my next question: when you brought him here, did he have a weapon with him?"

"A weapon? No. What kind of weapon?"

"It can take many forms, but I believe-" Albert closed his eyes to concentrate on a memory, "it is a javelin."

"I didn't see anything like that when I pulled him out of the water."

"Then it must still be in the sea." Albert walked over to the bed and gave Lambda the Just a few light slaps on the cheek with his right hand, "Wake up, sleepyhead!"

Isaac was hesitant, "I don't think that-" when Lambda groaned and began to stir, Isaac held his breath in anticipation.

Sitting up and rubbing his eyes, Lambda let his glasses fall back onto his nose as he surveyed his surroundings. When he saw a room filled with unfamiliar faces, he became startled and turned into lightning, which immediately discharged into the metal bedframe, leaving him back where he started. "Where am I?" he blurted out. Noticing that most of his clothes were gone, he pulled the sheets up to cover himself, "And what happened?"

Isaac and Irene stood with surprised expressions on their faces, but Albert seemed to expect this type of behavior, "Lambda the Just, my name is Albert. You have been transported to one thousand years in the future. I have come from that same timeframe to ask for your help."

"Wait! Hold on just one second!" Irene was shouting, "What just happened? Did he just turn into lightning?"

Lambda breathed a short laugh as he glanced at Albert, "They must not use powers like mine in the future," his expression became concerned, "But why do I feel like I'm not at my full potential?"

Albert's stomach grumbled once more, which caused him to clear his throat, "I can see there are going to be a lot of questions from all of you, so I suggest we move this conversation to another venue . . . like a restaurant." Almost as if in reply, Lambda's stomach growled as well.

Isaac chuckled as the atmosphere lightened, "I know just the place."

"*Wunderbar.* Lead the way."

Everyone collected their belongings as they prepared to head out. Lambda put on his shirt and vest, which were draped over a chair in the corner of the room. Albert picked up the cylindrical container he had set down earlier and strapped it onto his back. Isaac proceeded downstairs to fetch his jacket, headband, and swords. He waited at the front door for everyone to gather, at which point Irene shouted out to her father, "We're going to lunch! We'll be back later." The door slammed as Pierre emerged from his study and let out an exacerbated sigh. What had he done to deserve all this?

While more townspeople were arriving to gawk at the site of the explosion, many were satisfied with what they had seen and were starting to leave the area. The group from Pierre's Pier joined the throng of people who were leaving and could overhear much of the crowd's conversation. Most people couldn't explain what had happened, but since it really didn't affect their lives, they decided to leave the event in the realm of gossip as they returned to the activities they were performing before the explosion happened.

Isaac led the group through town to a tavern by the name of "Taurus", as evidenced by the sign hanging outside with the design of a menacing bull underneath the bold text of the tavern's name. Entering through the swinging doors beneath the sign, the group found that, since most people were working during this time of day and everyone else was most likely at the hill, the place was empty. Of course, it wasn't really the time to be drinking anyways.

Being of a circular construction, with the bar in the center of the room and booths on the outside, Isaac chose a booth near the door and set his weapons down, leaning them against the booth adjacent to theirs. Albert did the same with the container he carried on his back. Irene and Lambda slid into the booth as the others disarmed themselves.

The bartender had heard the group enter, so he made his way around to the front of the bar while wiping his hands with a rag. One look at Isaac and he pointed toward the door, "*You!* You're not here to cause any more trouble, are you?" Since the bartender was somewhat of a giant of a man, this question was very intimidating.

"No, I'm just here to talk with these people. Any trouble will come from someone else."

Putting his hand on his hip, the bartender relented, "OK, but I've got my eye on you." He squinted his eyes and used his other hand to point menacingly at Isaac.

"Very well. Can we have some food, please?"

"Four orders, coming right up," the bartender disappeared around to the other side of the bar, thereby revealing the stately grandfather clock which he was recently blocking.

Albert cleared his throat to gather everyone's attention, "I am certain you all have many questions, so I will do my best to explain before we get into any specifics." Turning to Lambda, he asked, "Do you have a key on you?"

"No, I don't know what-" suddenly, he remembered, "Actually, yes! I do have a key, but I'm not sure what this has to do with anything."

"You will know in time. May I please have this key?"

Lambda reached into the chest pocket of his vest and produced a white key but with a strange, bent tooth. He held it aloft and Albert's face lit up at the sight of it. When he reached out to grab the key, Lambda pulled it away, concerned by Albert's reaction, "Why do you want this key, again?"

Feeling a little hurt at Lambda's mistrust, Albert explained, "One of my titles is that of 'Keymaster'. I am in charge of a series of special keys and, as such, I need to account for every one of them. Before you disappeared, one of the keys went missing, and I just want to make sure the key you found is the same one I lost."

Holding the key in his fist, Lambda was still hesitant, "Once you figure out if this is the missing key, can I have it back?"

"But of course! I only need to know where all the keys are so, as long as we stick together, I am fine with you holding on to it for me." This answer seemed to satisfy Lambda, who reached out his hand and opened the fist above Albert's upturned palm. When the key was dropped into Albert's hand, he took it and struck it against the table, producing a pure tone. Listening to the key, he sighed, "A4 natural. This is it."

Isaac had been examining the key when it was revealed since it looked very similar, but not exactly the same as the ones he had used on his last adventure. Once he had determined that it was the same type of key, he asked, "That's a Q-Portal key, isn't it?"

Albert was surprised and skeptical, "*Ja*, it is! How do you know about them? With the exception of this one key, I hold every key that has ever been made. Now that the missing key is back in my collection, I can only wonder if your knowledge is purely academic. Unless . . ." Albert trailed off as he thought about one of the experiments conducted which would have multiplied the number of keys fivefold. But, even though he didn't have it on him, that key should be accounted for since it was sealed away in one of the research vaults. Did Isaac find this key? And if he did, what else from that vault was discovered?

"No, I found keys similar to that one in a cave that's just outside of town. That's how I traveled around in my quest to rid the abuse of fluxions from the world."

"Interesting," Albert was sure of it now: Isaac had found one of the research vaults. And yet, he was pleased that, at the very least, the keys were used to try and get rid of fluxions. Stroking his moustache thoughtfully, Albert said, "It seems your goals and mine intersect."

Observing that the two white-haired gentlemen were getting off topic, Lambda cleared his throat, "I'm not sure I see the correlation here. What's so important about my key?"

"Ah, let me explain," handing the key back to Lambda, who returned it to his vest pocket, Albert continued, "These keys are used to open Q-Portals, which exist to transport anyone instantaneously from one spot to another. However, these keys only work in specific, 'Q' shaped keyholes. And yet, what I have learned is that these keys do not merely control the transition between two spaces; they can be used to transit time itself."

"But if these keys need specific keyholes, how did *I* travel through time?" Lambda queried.

"Yours is a very special case, and it is what led me to eventually determine that the keys could be used to travel in time at all. You see, when you lost control of that large explosion of lightning during the battle against Chi the Powerful, it reacted with the key in your pocket, opening up a portal in mid-air that surrounded only yourself and some of your electric power. The fact that it did not need a keyhole was due to the sheer immensity of your power."

"That reminds me, why don't I feel as powerful here as I did back then?"

"This leads me to something already brought up by Isaac. I know we were not officially introduced, but I deduced that was your name when I invaded Pierre's house."

"That's right."

"Well, as Isaac already mentioned, he tried to rid the world of fluxion abuse. I tried to do the same after the end of Amedeo's War, but apparently my efforts were not enough. I assume that, despite Isaac's best efforts, we will eventually see the resurgence of bad people using fluxions." Albert stopped speaking when the bartender came over to the table and set down four plates of food in front of the customers.

Isaac reached into one of his pockets and produced a small brown bag, which he opened, looked inside, closed, and gave entirely to the bartender, merely stating, "Keep it. For your trouble before."

"Thanks," with that final word, the bartender returned to his post behind the bar.

Albert was hungry, but he also wanted to continue with his story. After gulping down a few bites of food, he returned to his point, "The real issue with fluxions is not stopping their use, but stopping their power source altogether."

"Power source?" Isaac seemed confused, "None of the documentation I saw ever said anything about a power source for the fluxions, other than the cores. But I assume you're not talking about them."

"That is correct, Isaac. I am the only one who knows about these power sources, and I have not allowed any of my notes to leave my sight."

Lambda interjected, "So, are you saying that the reason I don't feel as powerful in this time period is because some of these power sources have been destroyed in the last millennium?"

"That is correct, Lambda."

"Please, call me Benjamin."

"Very well," after a few more bites of food, Albert continued, "I am sure that Isaac is familiar with the snake seal on the fluxion core, as I have seen evidence that he is knowledgeable of these seals. These very snakes, in an uroboros configuration, are what power the fluxions throughout the earth. There are twelve such snakes which encircle the globe; each one has a statue at the interface between mouth and tail. These monuments are known as Caidoz statues. They are what give fluxions their power. They are what allow Naturals like Benjamin to control the fluxion cores without the uroboros seal. They are what we need to destroy in order for the fluxion threat to be eliminated."

Isaac was thoughtful, "Fascinating. I had always known about the effects of fluxions, but I never thought about where the source of their power came from. And if Benjamin says his powers aren't as effective as he remembers them being, then some statues must have been destroyed between the end of Amedeo's War and now."

"I know of four statues that have been destroyed, but this is only because I destroyed them myself. The real issue is that I am unsure where the other nine are located because the one hint of their existence is in a song. No one is sure where the song came from or why it mentions these statues, but it has been around for eons." Pulling a scroll from his cloak, Albert unrolled it on the table. Some of the stanzas were crossed out, "These are the lyrics of the song":

> Twelve statues: six above, six below
> Two Degrees from which power flow
> Four Elements and three Qualities
> Balanced in the sky above the trees

> The ram grazes in the valley's grass
> Avoiding the bite of the deadly asp
> The lion's red mouth opens and roars
> Protecting the island and its shores

> The water bearer holds the oceans
> Underneath the weight of many tons

~~The twins play in the mountain lakes~~
~~Which reflect their many mistakes~~

The centaur can see for miles and miles
Shooting an arrow to defeat its trials
The scales' balance must be intact
For unbiased justice it must enact

O those who come from nature's breast
Let your power flow from rest

That wars and fights cannot provide
But comes from harmony at your side

The maiden weeps her tears of joy
For being told she will bear a boy
The scorpion lies within the sand
Spreading poison throughout the land

The bull ran and jumped too soon
And got himself stuck on the moon
~~The fish both get caught together~~
~~A sailor's reward for enduring weather~~

~~The crab's pinch spreads its disease~~
~~Destroying the lives of all it sees~~

~~The sea goat frolics in the surf~~
~~Gnawing on the weeds of its turf~~

Beware the creator for he is jealous
These powers he created are not for us
But for himself to rule on high
To be the ruler of the sky

At the conclusion of the song, Benjamin and Isaac looked up and said in unison, "I know that song!" They both eyed each other and once again spoke at the same time, "But only part of it."

"Ah? Is that so?" Albert arched his eyebrow in curiosity.

Benjamin pointed to the middle stanza, "I heard Penny singing this verse when I met her, but I couldn't make out the rest of the lyrics she was singing."

Isaac pointed further down the sheet, "I can't read this, but if I'm right, this couplet is actually engraved on a plaque above that grandfather clock over there." He pointed to the clock behind the bar, at which point everyone got up and headed over to check it out. Sure enough, the words, "The bull ran and jumped too soon / and got himself stuck on the moon" were engraved above the clock. They also noticed that the part of the clock which showed the phase of the moon had a bull integrated into its design.

The bartender had overheard their conversation and came over to talk to the group, "Yeah, this clock was made with that couplet in mind. The founder of this tavern used it as the bar's centerpiece, which is why this tavern is called 'Taurus'." The clock also had other designs engraved on its sides, including mice running away from a cat playing a fiddle and various anthropomorphized kitchen utensils.

When the bartender had left, Isaac asked, "Even though we don't know where most of these statues are, how are we supposed to destroy them?"

"I can only think of three options, two of which are not available to us right now. This is why I asked if you knew where Benjamin's weapon was, because it is part of one of our choices. The third method is to use the Fluent of Light, but my research team was unsuccessful in getting it to work."

"It's funny you should mention that," Isaac grinned as he jogged over to where his swords were resting. Unsheathing the broadsword, he showed Albert the diamond tip with the uroboros seal. This was the Fluent of Light.

"*Wunderbar!*" Albert exclaimed, "A sword makes so much sense, now that I think about it. After all, what better way to split fluxions than through a sword that could cut light itself?"

"If you're sure that Benjamin traveled with his weapon to the future, we can go and look for it. That way we can have the three methods to destroy the statues and can split up to accomplish our goal faster."

Benjamin chimed in, "I was wondering where my weapon went, so I was going to eventually search for it. Shall we go look for it now?"

Albert nodded, "*Ja.*" The group gathered their belongings and headed back to the pier where they first met. Enough time had passed that the rest of the gawking townspeople had left the hill, content in not knowing what had happened.

Isaac took off his jacket and started to limber up, "I'm the one who pulled you from the sea, so what am I looking for, Benjamin?"

"If I remember correctly, it should be in the form of a metallic javelin." Albert nodded in agreement with Benjamin's statement.

"Got it." Isaac dove back into the water as the others watched.

Irene had been quiet for a long time, merely soaking in everything that had been discussed. She was having trouble wrapping her mind around everything, since it all sounded so extraordinary.

Off in the distance, Isaac's head came up from the waves of the sea. Taking two quick breaths, he descended to the rocky floor of the bay. This time he was underwater longer than before. Once again, Isaac's head burst forth from the sea, sputtering for air and coughing up water. Benjamin felt guilty for having Isaac retrieve his weapon, since it appeared he was having a difficult time doing so. Shouting out to him, Benjamin asked, "Is everything all right?"

Before Isaac could hear the question, he had taken a few more breaths and dove into the sea one more time. Time passed and the rest of the group waited on the shore impatiently. Isaac had been underwater far too long. Sensing that something was wrong, Benjamin started to head toward the pier so he could dive in to help Isaac. Irene was wringing her hands as Benjamin's pace grew faster. Just before he was about to dive in, Albert yelled out, "Benjamin, stop!"

From the sea, a hand broke the surface. A hand which held a long, metallic javelin. Moments later, Isaac breached the waves, gasping desperately for air, and began swimming to shore. Benjamin ran back down the pier and over to the shore where Isaac wearily crawled onto the dock, seawater dripping profusely from his clothes. Handing the javelin to Benjamin, he asked between coughs and sputters, "Is . . . this . . . it?"

Rolling the weapon in his hands, Benjamin gripped the shaft and made his electricity flow into the metal. While it took longer than he was used to, Benjamin eventually re-formed the javelin into a long-handled sledgehammer. The number "90" was engraved on the side of the head, "Yeah, this is it all right." Helping Isaac to his feet and handing him his white jacket, Benjamin meekly said, "If you needed help, you could have asked for it. I could have just as easily gotten my weapon."

Finally catching his breath, Isaac replied, "No, it was nothing. I knew where you had landed, so I had the best chance of finding your weapon," with a coughing laugh, he continued, "It's just a little harder to find when it's in that javelin form."

Albert approached Isaac and congratulated him, "*Wunderbar*, Isaac. We are now one step closer to destroying the statues. However, we still need the weapons from the other two members of The Triumvirate in order to complete the statue destroying device. Unfortunately, they have gone missing after we split them up in the wake of Amedeo's War."

"So, what you're saying is that, in order to finally get rid of fluxions, we need to find the rest of The Triumvirate weapons *and* we need to find the other eight Caidoz statues, right?"

"*Ja*. And I would like to get started as soon as possible."

Isaac looked over to Irene and asked, "Do you want to come with me this time?"

Staring at the soaking man who almost drowned in order to retrieve a magical javelin, Irene smiled and shook her head, "Nah, from what I've seen and overheard, I may be in way over my head." Squinting her eyes and pointing at Isaac, she continued, "But don't think you've gotten out of your promise yet, mister. I still want to hear about your adventures and you haven't told me squat yet."

Lifting up his right pinky finger and placing his left hand on his chest, Isaac replied, "The promise still stands." Irene mimicked the pose and went back inside, closing the door behind her.

Turning back to Albert, Isaac asked, "You said you now have the entire set of Q-Portal keys, right?"

"For the most part, *ja*. What do you have in mind?"

"I'd like to gather some friends of mine. They may be invaluable on this quest."

"Then, so be it. Where to first?"

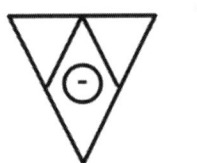 

Chapter 2

Collecting the Players

Armor Village exuded the same quaint charm that it did when Isaac first visited. Strolling through the small town in the light of the afternoon was nostalgic for him, especially when he saw the still broken chain that once connected the lakeshore to the floating island known as the Eagle's Nest. Eventually, Isaac led Albert and Benjamin to the biggest house in the village, where he was greeted by Milo, a woman with short, curly blonde hair and green armor covering her chest and arms.

When Milo opened the door, she was surprised at the sight of Isaac. She rushed out of the house and gave him a big hug, "Isaac! It's so good to see you! You should have told us you were coming."

"This was kind of a spur of the moment visit."

"Who are your friends?"

"This is Albert," Albert nodded in response, "and this is Benjamin," Benjamin did likewise.

Performing a slight curtsey, Milo introduced herself, "I'm Milo. Pleased to meet you."

Isaac got straight to the point, "Have you seen Artie around?"

"I think he's down at the Luvnac stable getting an armor upgrade."

"Thanks, Milo. I'm sorry we can't stay much longer, but it was nice to see you again."

"The feeling is mutual, Isaac," Milo waved as the three men headed back into the village.

Albert leaned over to Isaac and whispered, "I'm surprised Luvnac's legacy has lasted this long."

"What do you mean?"

"He was a legendary sword and armor blacksmith in our time, so it is interesting that his name is still associated with metalwork."

"That is impressive."

As the trio entered the stable, they saw the back of a man clad almost entirely in armor. The man made the armor covering complete when he put the right hand of his armor back on. However, this was somewhat out of the ordinary because there was no hand beyond the man's right wrist to protect with armor. What was more extraordinary was when the hand was re-attached to the armor, he flexed the newly attached fingers, nodding in approval. Speaking with a metallic voice he remarked, "Splendid. It still works."

"You're looking pretty upgraded, Artie."

Turning around, the man's glowing green eyes lit up even more at the sight of Isaac, "My friend! How are you? What has it been, six months?" Emblazoned on his breastplate was the serial number, R-3N3.

"I believe it has, Artie," Isaac extended his right hand to his comrade, who shook it in kind. However, Isaac pulled back almost immediately when he found that the armor was still hot.

Giving a slight chuckle, R-3N3 apologized, "I am sorry for that. It is still new to me."

"Very well, but I must say; your armor looks good. It has a lot more personality than your first set."

Albert approached the two men, fascinated by R-3N3. He muttered to himself, "I cannot believe these are still around." Scrutinizing R-3N3, he asked, "May I see the inside of your armor?"

"Certainly." Opening up the small door which bore his serial number, R-3N3 revealed the hollowed-out body of his armor. Albert thoughtfully stroked his moustache as he saw that the only thing keeping R-3N3 alive was a Blood-fluxion in a similar configuration to the one which Isaac wore beneath his headband.

Benjamin was defensive at this revelation, since he had to fight many hollow suits of armor in the final battle of Amedeo's War, "Is this *really* one of your friends, Isaac?"

"He is, and he's probably the most resilient of all of us."

Albert smiled solemnly as he finished inspecting R-3N3's seal work while the door in his chest was being closed, "I do not see why not. This type of fluxion application is meant for continuous battle."

"I know this query may be a bit late, but who are you?" R-3N3 inquired.

Having forgotten the introductions, Isaac apologized, "That's right, I forgot. R-3N3, this is Albert and Benjamin. Albert is the man partly responsible for the discovery of the Soul-fusion fluxion."

"Well, it was more of a team effort, but I am somewhat glad to see it is alive and well."

"As am I," R-3N3 chuckled. Benjamin was still slightly skeptical, but he was starting to lighten up as everyone laughed.

Isaac figured that now was as good a time as any to bring up why they were there, "This may come as a shock to you, Artie, but these men are from the past. One thousand years in the past, to be exact."

"That does not compute. How is that possible?"

"It's a little bit of a long story, but do you remember the small key I showed you after we defeated Testament?"

"Affirmative."

"Well, that key allows people to travel through space using specific keyholes. However, I'm still not clear on how they allow someone to travel through time. If I recall what Albert said, it has something to do with lightning-"

Albert interrupted to fill in some details, "Ah, I forgot to completely explain that point. It seems that an application of electricity, or in Benjamin's case, lightning, triggers an innate ability in the keys to also travel through time. The electric energy is used to break through the barrier which separates time from space. As such, while I have figured out how to accurately travel through space, I have not been able to fully control the time aspect yet. In fact, travelling forward in time seems to be much more difficult than travelling backwards, which is strange because we naturally travel forward in time, albeit at the same rate as everyone else."

"At any rate, Artie, it seems that defeating Testament was not enough to stop fluxion use and we need your help to destroy the Caidoz statues so that others won't abuse their power again."

"Seems logical to me. Count me in."

"*Wunderbar!* That makes one of your friends, so who do we need to get next, Isaac?"

"Sucari and Robin should be living near the Crystal Woods, if I'm not mistaken."

"Actually, Isaac," R-3N3 spoke up, "That would normally be true, but they just recently got married and traveled to Topal for their honeymoon."

Isaac raised his eyebrows, "Wow. That was pretty quick."

"Affirmative."

Albert had pulled out a map and was measuring the distance to Topal, "Benjamin, could you close that door please?" When Benjamin closed the door to the stable, Albert had finished with the calculation and was finding the key needed for the correct Q-Portal distance, "This may work to our advantage, as I need to check up on a few items we hid after Amedeo's War. Isaac, you and R-3N3 gather your friends while Benjamin and I take care of gathering these items."

"Very well, Albert." With a black key held in his right hand, Albert pushed the end into the door just above the existing, normal keyhole. The door swung open, revealing a white barrier directly beyond it. Albert immediately stepped through the door and disappeared. Benjamin and R-3N3 were amazed at the sight, having never seen a Q-Portal in action before. While Isaac had never seen a black-key Q-Portal in use before, he still goaded his partners on, "Don't worry. It doesn't hurt," he nervously chuckled as he added, "I think."

Everyone shielded their eyes from the soon-to-be setting desert sun when they emerged from the door on the other side. As the black opening closed with a blast of wind, the group turned around to see where they had arrived. Immediately, they had to crane their necks upward to see the top of a great sandstone wall. Isaac scanned the area and saw that they were close to the side gate of the walled city of Topal. He was impressed, "You weren't lying when you said you were accurate with your spatial travel."

Hooking the key back onto his vest, Albert chuckled, "They do not call me the Keymaster for nothing. Anyways, you and R-3N3 should go inside the city to find your friends. Benjamin and I need to head to the Holy Cliffs." Albert pointed to the bluish-white cliffs that stood in the distance to the east, their face covered with pockmarks and holes. "We will meet back here in a few hours."

"Very well. Let's go Artie." As Isaac and R-3N3 turned and walked toward the side gate, they heard a thunderous boom from behind, which caused them to turn around. Albert and Benjamin had vanished.

When they had roamed well into the city, Isaac could tell that things had changed. While the citizens were still afraid of outsiders, the atmosphere no longer felt like one of oppression. R-3N3 struck up a conversation as they walked, "I would deduce that you used this Q-Portal to get into Pandora Prison, since the door was still locked when we left."

"That's right. We were in a bit of a jam and the Q-Portal got us out of it."

"I am glad that it led you to me, as I would probably still be chained up in the Hope Wing to this day."

"I'm glad that you weren't as murderous as the legends painted you out to be."

"You were just fortunate that Erwin did not know about my past."

At the mention of their fallen comrade, both grew silent for a time. Since Isaac had been to the city before, he led them right to the palace, where he figured Sucari would go for his honeymoon. At the very least, he could ask King Niccolo if he knew where Sucari was. As Isaac and R-3N3 approached the front stairs of the palace, the guards saluted them and stood at attention. After Isaac had passed through, they crossed their weapons in front of R-3N3, blocking his path.

When Isaac heard the clash of metal, he turned around. Before the guards could respond, he simply said, "He's with me, guys." The guards were somewhat hesitant, but nonetheless uncrossed their weapons to let R-3N3 through. As they climbed the stairs together, Isaac mentioned, "Last time it wasn't so easy for me to get in, but after I helped save their King, I did receive some special treatment."

"Must be nice," R-3N3 replied in a tone that was flatly sardonic.

Entering into the castle, Isaac made his way to the throne room with R-3N3 in tow. Before he even entered the main chamber, King Niccolo saw Isaac down the hall and rose from the throne to greet his friend. Making a hand motion to one of his men, the guard nodded and left the room. With his arms wide open, Niccolo greeted Isaac with a big hug, "Isaac, my friend! Welcome back to the 5th Kingdom."

Finishing the hug, Niccolo was solemn for a moment when he said, "I heard what happened to Erwin, I'm so sorry that things turned out the way they did." Isaac nodded thoughtfully in remembrance of his fallen friend, which caused the King to change the subject, "I'm assuming you're here to see Sucari and his new bride. I must say that I was surprised when he came back to Topal with such a beautiful woman at his side."

"You are correct, we are here to see them," R-3N3 interjected.

"Who is this?" Niccolo asked, looking past Isaac to the intimidating suit of armor who stood behind him.

"This is R-3N3, or 'Artie' for short."

Niccolo was about to give R-3N3 a hug when he felt the latent heat from the metal of the armor and decided to merely bow instead, "I'm surprised you can stand the heat around here in that armor, Artie."

"It does not bother me."

"Well, make yourself at home, as any friend of Isaac's is a friend of mine."

From across the room, a familiar voice shouted out in excitement, "Isaac! Artie!" A woman with jet-black hair who used a pair of glasses for a headband and wore a flattering floral-patterned dress ran across the room to meet up with the group.

Behind her was a man with wild, blonde hair, tanned skin and dressed in some royal clothes, no doubt given to him by King Niccolo, "I've never seen you this excited before, Robin."

"Who wouldn't be excited to see these friends after our big day, Sucari?"

"Yes, I heard about that from Artie. Congratulations, you two," changing to a playful tone, he asked, "But why you didn't invite your uncle-in-law is beyond me."

Giving Isaac a hug, Robin replied, "Thank you, Isaac," and playing back, she replied, "And we would have sent you an invitation if you had actually told us where you were going."

"Very well, I guess I can forgive being left out," he said with a wink. Thinking back on the events of the last year, Isaac became more serious again, "Although, you only knew each other for a few months before you got married, right? Doesn't that seem kind of fast?"

Sucari laughed, "I suppose it does, but you can't argue with love at first sight."

"I suppose I can't," Isaac laughed back.

Looking over to R-3N3, Sucari smiled and said, "Thanks again for being my Best Man, Artie. I know it was kind of short notice."

"Please, the honor was mine."

"Your new armor looks awesome, by the way."

"Thank you, Sucari."

Robin spoke up, "So, what brings you two out here?"

Isaac's smile vanished, "Well, remember when we defeated Testament so that fluxions wouldn't be abused anymore?"

"Yeah, what about it?"

"Apparently that's not going to be enough."

Sucari interjected, "What do you mean?"

"It seems that we need to take care of the source of the fluxions' power. Stopping their proliferation won't completely stop their use. That's why I'm getting our team back together. Are you both with me?"

While Robin seemed excited, Sucari seemed hesitant, "I don't know Isaac. I think we might need to play it safe now that we're married."

Robin was disappointed, "Sucari, I was just talking about how we need to go on an adventure together. This is our chance!" She looked at him with her blue eyes and pouted just a little bit.

Sighing in futility, Sucari relented, "OK, let's do it."

Robin jumped with excitement and hugged Sucari, giving him a kiss on the lips, "You're the best, Sucari."

Blushing at the sudden display of affection, Sucari replied, "I suppose I am. Anyways, let's get our things and we can go." Robin ran off, dragging Sucari behind her as they prepared for a new adventure.

○

Removing the glove from his right hand with his mouth, Albert spoke to Benjamin through gritted teeth, "If you would not mind it, grab my hand and turn to lightning. We will both get to the cliffs faster that way." Benjamin nodded and complied, sending them both instantaneously to the base of the monolithic rocks.

When they arrived, Albert let out a gasp as he regained his breath. Putting his glove back on, he spoke through deep gulps of air, "I knew fluxion powers could be shared, but I never would have guessed that it would be so intense."

Benjamin was still trying to figure out Albert. While the researcher said that he wanted to destroy the fluxions' power source, Benjamin was struggling with the fact that Albert was partly responsible for the death of his friends and his sudden trip through time to a strange new land and era. Plus, he wasn't sure if he wanted to give up his lightning power, since he had just recently come to understand it better. At any rate, for the time being Benjamin would stay close to Albert to keep an eye on him, "Where to now?"

Scrutinizing the base of the cliffs, Albert squinted his eyes and eventually found a footprint of compacted sand a few hundred yards away. Pointing to the anomalous area in the sea of sand, he said, "Over there. That looks to be about the right spot for the Gates of Hell."

As they started hiking, Benjamin asked, "And why would we want to purposely go to something called the 'Gates of Hell'?"

"I need to check on the status of the Hellfire orb in order to make sure it is still protected and that it has not fallen into the wrong hands. I also think Chi's Pitchfork might have ended up here."

"Very well. Lead the way." When they arrived, they found two tall doors which had relief engravings on their surface depicting the terror Ruatonim dealt to many villages centuries ago. Benjamin let out a short laugh when he saw the scenes shown in the reliefs, "Tecumseh wasn't really that tall."

"I am sorry, who are you talking about?"

"Oh, I guess you probably knew him as Chi. Even though I never saw him actually terrorize villages like this, I had suspected it for a while." Looking behind him to the wasteland the area around Topal had become, Benjamin continued, "Although, I'd probably be filled with that much hate too if I had to run a farm in this desolate landscape." When he turned around, Albert had disappeared. However, the doors now stood open a crack. Rushing in after Albert, Benjamin yelled, "Hey! Wait up!"

The corridors of Ruatonim's Maze were dark and Benjamin had difficulty viewing the path past the small slit of light which was let in through the barely opened doors. Arcing some electricity across his fingers, he could see Albert well along the corridor in front of him. While he did his best to keep up with the researcher, Benjamin always seemed to be one turn behind Albert. Eventually, they both came to a stop outside a humble door. Taking a second to observe the area, Benjamin could see that the walls of the maze held unlit torches every so often, which led him to believe that at one time the labyrinth wasn't as pitch black as it was right now.

Softly knocking twice on the door, Albert opened it and let himself into the adjacent room. Holding the door open for Benjamin, the two Millennials soon stood in a humble bedroom. Examining the room's sparse decorations, Albert spotted a numbered disk framed on the wall of the room. He approached it and read the number: 61. Muttering to himself, Albert remarked, "We must be in the right place if this is here."

"What is that?" Benjamin asked.

"This Number-fluxion was given to the man who was supposed to guard the Hellfire orb from falling into the wrong hands. He would need to bestow it on someone from the next generation whom he felt was worthy enough of being able to protect such a terrible power. If this disk is here, it means that the Hellfire orb is still close by and protected." Finding another door, Albert once again led the way through it to the room beyond.

When Benjamin entered the room, his electricity still lighting the darkness, it was readily obvious that they were in a much larger chamber than anything they had been in up until now. A large statue of a half-man, half-bull was set in the middle of the room, its hands outstretched, cupping nothingness. Albert murmured with a concerned tone as he made his way to the front of the statue, "I could have sworn that the Hellfire orb would be here. I hope that the Order of the Dragon did not betray us and keep it for themselves."

"Albert! Look over here!" Benjamin yelled behind him as he crouched over a lifeless body.

As Albert rushed to Benjamin, he saw the charred remains of an old man, "Interesting." Reaching over to the walls of the chamber, he ran his finger across the stone and inspected the fresh soot that now stained his already black glove. "This body has died recently and, judging from the extensive burn coverage and the tremendous amount of soot on the walls, I would deduce that someone has come and stolen the Hellfire orb, killing its protector in the process. Probably within the last year or so."

Benjamin solemnly stood up as he wondered if the Hellfire orb would ever be used to help people, even centuries after it had caused so much harm to those he almost considered to be his family. Albert made his way back to the statue and began to examine it. Looking back over his shoulder, Benjamin asked, "Is this one of the Caidoz statues that we need to destroy? I remember something in the poem about a bull. Is this that bull?"

"*Nein*. This is not one of the statues, but we may still need to destroy it. First off, the stanza in the poem references the moon, which I have not found any evidence to link this statue to quite yet. However, the best evidence that this is not a Caidoz statue is that it is hollow." Striking the statue with his fist produced a rich tone, followed by a higher-pitched rattling sound, "And it seems that there may be more to this sculpture than first meets the eye." Stepping away from the memorial, Albert motioned to Benjamin, "Would you be so kind as to use that hammer of yours to help me see what is inside?"

"With pleasure." Even though the statue wasn't really Tecumseh, Benjamin couldn't help but enjoy destroying the image of his traitorous companion. Stepping forward, Benjamin sized up the memorial and pulled out the sledgehammer he received from passing through the Imaginary World. Crouching slightly, he held the hammer aloft with both hands as the Skybolt orb he wore on his chest began to spark with excitement. In a quick movement, enhanced by the electrical powers he could wield, Benjamin leapt upward, swinging the hammer in a complete circle, knocking the head of the statue cleanly away from its body.

The strike was such a powerful event that the entire room reverberated with the sound of the sculpture's natural frequency. With a gong, the head hit the ceiling then fell to the floor, repeating the sound. Using the hammer as a support, Benjamin proudly leaned against his weapon with his left hand as he used his right to once again light the room. The expected emptiness from the statue's shoulders instead revealed the four tines of Chi's Pitchfork, sticking out from the cavity where it calmly sat.

Albert climbed up onto the statue and managed to pull the pitchfork from its hiding place. Jumping back down and holding the weapon in a pose of triumph, he closely examined the silvery head of the pitchfork. First, he found the distinguishing mark of Chi the Powerful on the front of the item, the iconic χ symbol engraved in the metal. However, this wasn't enough for Albert as he turned the pitchfork over, obviously looking for something else. Since the sound had finally died down, Benjamin asked, "What are you looking for?"

"Both of your weapons have two marks on them. The first mark is that of your i-World symbol, which on your hammer just happens to be λ. The other mark is a number. Yours is just easier to see because the hammer has a larger surface area. Ah! Here it is." Flipping the pitchfork over to show Benjamin, Albert pointed to a small number engraved on the side opposite that which bore the χ symbol. Similar to Benjamin's hammer with its "90" engraving, Chi's Pitchfork sported the number "94". Holding the weapon as a walking staff, Albert joyfully announced, "With your hammer and this pitchfork, we are only missing one more weapon that will allow us to easily destroy Caidoz statues. And while it is disappointing that the Hellfire orb has gone missing, one can only assume that over a long period of time this sort of thing would eventually happen."

"Shall we go, then?"

"*Ja*, we shall." As the two Millennials left the large chamber, Albert spoke, "You seemed to derive great pleasure from destroying that statue, Benjamin."

With a short laugh, Benjamin replied, "Ha! I guess you're right. I think I just needed to get some frustration out, and what better way to do so than by destroying the likeness of someone who killed one of my best friends right in front of my eyes, betrayed me, and essentially sent me to the future with no closure to our battle."

"If you must know, he most certainly died in that final attack which sent you to this time, but I suppose that if you were not there to witness it, how would you ever know?"

"Yeah . . ." Benjamin's voice trailed off as he thought back over his fight with Tecumseh.

Before they knew it, both men were back at the entrance of the maze. Looking to the sky, aglow with the light of the recently set sun, Albert made a quick calculation and said, "We may be a little late, so let us hurry back to the others." Pulling off his glove, Albert handed the pitchfork to Benjamin, who put it away with his sledgehammer. Grabbing Albert's uncovered hand, Benjamin turned to lightning and quickly led them back to the side gate of the city of Topal where Isaac, R-3N3, and two more people now stood.

This sudden, booming appearance took Isaac's group by surprise, as they all jumped at Albert and Benjamin's electric arrival. The two newcomers to the group were now dressed differently than before, clad in clothes much more appropriate for travel and battle. While Robin wore her standard, knee-length pleated skirt with quivers strapped to her calves and a large crossbow attached to her back, Sucari was definitely the minimalist of the couple, wearing only a white vest and some short pants. The vest Sucari wore bore two fluxion cores. One was a Blood-fluxion on his back; but unfortunately, the other was an Elemental-fluxion with a fiery core right in the center of his chest. This core was the Hellfire orb.

When Benjamin saw the fiery orb being worn so brazenly, he couldn't help but threaten Sucari with the pitchfork that used to share the same master with the Hellfire orb. Locking his gaze with the young man, Benjamin spoke to Isaac, "I hope you have a good explanation for this, Isaac. We know the Hellfire orb was stolen recently, so there's a good chance that your friend here is a thief."

Isaac stepped in-between Benjamin and Sucari, pushing the pitchfork away in the process, "I'll have you know that Sucari's decision to bear the Hellfire orb came from my suggestion and that I was the one who had it stolen from Ruatonim's Maze."

"I don't think you're helping your case any, Isaac."

Sucari stepped forward, emboldened by his commitment to the orb's power, "I chose to wield this power for good, not for evil. I know it has had a sordid past, but I am trying to create a new future for it. A future of justice." Triggering something in Benjamin, the last word of Sucari's speech caused The Triumvirate member to lower his guard.

Bowing in apology, Benjamin softly spoke, "It seems that our ideals are in alignment. I am sorry if I doubted you or Isaac."

Pulling Sucari away, Robin tugged on his arm and spoke, "If we're done threatening each other, can we find out what the plan is?"

Isaac turned toward his comrades and asked, "Do any of you know where Vlad went?" When they all shook their heads, he sighed, "I'd like to have him along, but if we are uncertain of his location, we're liable to waste time trying to find him." Turning to Albert, who was already making preparations at the Q-Portal, Isaac transferred control, "Very well, Albert. Lead the way."

"*Wunderbar.*" Forcefully jamming a white key into the newly formed Q-hole, Albert opened up another Q-Portal and motioned for everyone to enter. Glancing behind him to check the surroundings, Albert passed through the door, which shut with a forceful gust of wind, briefly kicking up the dust and sand outside Topal's walls.

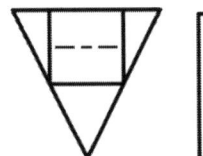 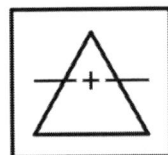

Chapter 3

The Fixed Oasis

Emerging from the Q-Portal, the group found themselves on the west coastline of the continent, the sun once again marching toward the horizon and its resting place for the day. The area was deserted with the exception of an ancient stone statue that looked like a vase, sitting on a circular stone plate. Directly to the left of the statue was another stone plate, but without the vase-like sculpture on top of it. Between the two stone plates was a staircase, also made of stone, which ran straight down into the ocean. A small rivulet stream ran beside the staircase and into the sea. The source of the stream was a small hole near the bottom of the stone vase.

Albert set down the cylindrical case that he carried and unlatched it in three places. Motioning for Benjamin to join him, Albert opened the case, which was now separated into two semi-circular sections. Whispering something to his Millennial partner caused Benjamin to hand the Imaginary World pitchfork to Albert, who stowed it away in the leftmost section of the container. In return, Albert gave Benjamin one of the keys he wore on his vest. Rummaging around in some of the shelves at the bottom of the case, Albert soon stood up and closed the container, allowing it to stand by itself as he and Benjamin joined the rest of the group.

Handing a white Q-Portal key and the scrolls he had pulled from the container to Isaac, Albert addressed the group, "Since most of you were brought here on Isaac's request, I shall let him lead you to destroy some of the Caidoz statues." Robin raised her hand, at which point Albert continued, "I will let *him* explain to the rest of the group why you will be destroying these statues." Robin put her hand down, at which point Sucari held it, intertwining his fingers with hers.

The couple smiled at each other, but Isaac still had a question, "Does that mean you're not coming with us?"

"That is correct, Isaac. Right now we have two of the three weapons that can destroy these statues, so I suggest we split up in order to accomplish our task in an expedient manner. To that end, I have given you a few scrolls which may help you. The most important of these is a scroll which can be used to translate the written language of my time into the written language of yours."

R-3N3 now had a question, pointing at the vase-like sculpture nearby, "Is this sculpture one of the Caidoz statues?"

"*Nein*, it is not. However, I have found that, in the lyrics of the song which I have given Isaac for reference, many of the couplets are alluded to in folklore. The statue before us has a story, much like many other locations, which leads me to believe that a Caidoz statue must be nearby."

Now it was Benjamin's turn, "When I destroyed the statue back at the Holy Cliffs, you said that it wasn't one of the Caidoz statues because it wasn't made of the right material."

"That is correct, Benjamin. Part of the reason the Caidoz statues can emit so much power into the world is that they are made of solid fluxionite. This metallic stone is more commonly known by the ore of the same name which was used to make the Q-Portal keys as well as the six Noble Swords and the pure fluxionite sword known as Kuroni."

Isaac coughed in surprise, which caused Albert to stop talking, wondering if the effects of almost drowning were starting to resurface. Standing to his feet and unsheathing his katana, Isaac spoke, "You mean *this* sword?"

Once again, Albert's jaw dropped as another legendary weapon made its appearance, "*Wunderbar!* I am impressed, Isaac. Not only did you figure out how to implement the Fluent of Light, but you found both Kuroni and its Gravity Core." For a moment, Albert was concerned because he knew where the Gravity Core ended up at the end of Amedeo's War. Isaac was certainly revealing a multitude of enigmas and Albert was having difficulty trying to figure out how they had been created.

When Isaac re-sheathed Kuroni, Albert continued, "Unfortunately, even though a sword made of pure fluxionite is itself indestructible, it cannot destroy other fluxionite objects. Furthermore, while Luvnac was the only person ever recorded to find fluxionite in nature and successfully infuse it into weapons; nevertheless, these nearly indestructible statues have existed for all of time, as far as I have been able to deduce."

Sucari, the last member of the group, finally spoke up with his own question, "So, if we're supposed to split up in order to cover more ground, how will our group do that if you have all the Q-Portal keys?"

"Good question! I have taken the liberty of calculating where another Caidoz statue may reside and I have given Isaac a Q-Portal key which he can use on the door from which we have just emerged. After you have destroyed the statue here, Benjamin and I will meet up with you at the next location. Hopefully, you will have destroyed that statue as well by the time we arrive."

Studying the group, Albert asked, "Are there any more questions?" When no one responded, he concluded, "*Wunderbar.* I believe that Isaac should have everything you will need. Now, if you will excuse us . . ." Albert trailed off as he stepped away and put a hand on Benjamin's shoulder to indicate that it was time to go.

Pulling out the black key Albert gave him earlier, Benjamin walked toward the Q-hole of the door the group just recently used. Strapping the cylindrical container onto his back yet again, Albert took off his glove and grabbed Benjamin's other hand. The electrical orb around Benjamin's neck became excited as the key began to glow. Turning around, Albert gave one last word, "Oh, and if you happen to find a trident down there, please bring it back with you." Benjamin thrust the key into the hole, at which point both Albert's and Benjamin's bodies emanated a bright light and disappeared with a loud boom.

○

A burst of sand blinded Benjamin and Albert as they both coughed and tried to cover their eyes, noses, and mouths. When the dust and grit had settled, both travelers coughed a few more times and opened their eyes to see where they ended up. Behind them was a large boulder, which now sported the distinctive Q-hole, glowing with an unnatural black light. Benjamin shouted out in pain and threw the Q-Portal key onto the sand where it sizzled. Albert put his glove back on and apologized, "I am sorry, but I suppose I should have given you my glove. The keys become incredibly hot when used for time travel."

"Time travel?" a voice shouted out behind them as the two Millennials turned around to see who had been eavesdropping. The shadow of a young man blocked out the sun, the silhouette preventing them from being able to see who it was. The figure turned and shouted behind him, "You didn't tell me anything about some random people showing up here due to *time travel!*"

In the distance, footsteps could be heard on the sand as a strong, yet old voice called out, "Arthur, these are the men we are here to meet."

Finally gaining an understanding of their surroundings, Albert saw that they were south of the Library of Delaxanair, which had almost been reduced completely to ruins from centuries of abandonment. The desert around them was vast and, with the exception of the boulder next to them and the Library many miles away, almost entirely empty. This was in comparison to the desert surrounding Topal, which obviously was not nearly as desolate.

When the old man caught up, he was partly out of breath, "You must forgive my young protégé, Mr. Keymaster. 'He is too satisfied with the present to dwell on the future'." Chuckling softly to himself as if he had just shared in an inside joke, the look of confusion on Albert's face soon spread to the man as he replied, "I can guess from your expression that we haven't met before . . . yet. My name is Reuel. Well . . . it is *now*, but I suppose that doesn't matter if we haven't met before." The old man had a kind and clean-shaven face, partially obscured by the shade produced from his pointy, yet floppy, hat. He held a walking staff which bore a small, white crystal embedded in its tip. On his right hand he wore a green ring. On his left was a yellow one.

The young man who was standing on top of the boulder jumped down and was introduced to the Millennials by Reuel, "Arthur, this is Lambda the Just and the Keymaster. They are here to help us on our quest." Benjamin was slightly confused, as was Albert, but Albert looked at Benjamin with a gaze that told him to use the names they were just given.

"I know you're some kind of wizard, Reuel, but I never knew that people could travel through time." While Reuel wore a simple, grey robe, Arthur wore some light armor emblazoned with the symbol of the 4th Kingdom: a scarlet lion. The symbol was repeated on a white headband which he wore diagonally across his face, covering his left eye and overlapping a golden crown with four points. Underneath the crown was a head of blonde hair and a face which sported a few freckles, some of which also seemed to form birthmarks on his neck and right hand. A scabbard held a broadsword on his left side, toward which his right hand was slowly reaching.

Benjamin spoke up, "Hey, I'm still new to this time travel thing myself."

Albert found it curious that this man knew not only his other moniker, but Benjamin's as well. Still, in time travel, anonymity helps to avoid any historical issues which may arise. Just to make sure, he pulled Reuel aside and whispered, "Did we perhaps meet at a different time before this?"

Observing from the corner of his eye that Arthur was reaching for his weapon, Reuel turned and loudly chastised the young man, "Arthur! These men are not our enemies, you can relax." Clearing his throat, he turned back toward Albert and lowered his voice, "I apologize for that. We did meet, long ago at the court of the 4th Kingdom. You told me that in four hundred years I should meet you in the desert to the south of the former Library of Delaxanair and to bring Arthur along with me. You mentioned something about a grail and a statue, but my memory of the finer details escapes me."

"Ah, I see. Very interesting. This must mean that after these events we will eventually go back further in time. I had never thought to use these connections to my advantage before, but now it seems almost obvious."

Meanwhile, now that he had let down his guard, Arthur and Benjamin were having their own conversation, "So, tell me Lambda, what do you know about the Holy Grail?"

"Honestly? Absolutely nothing."

"Hmmm. I guess the Keymaster knows what we're doing out here then. Reuel spoke of a legendary cup which could grant eternal life, so I gathered up some of the Knights of the Brotherhood to set out on a Crusade to find it. Unfortunately, Reuel and I are the only ones left on this quest."

"Wow. It sounds like you really demand some respect for someone so young."

"Why shouldn't I? I pulled the 10 Caliber Sword from the Ragna Rock and became King of the 4th Kingdom."

"I guessed as much by the crown," Benjamin remarked, offhandedly.

Arthur didn't notice and was on a roll, touting his accomplishments, "Of course, that was all *after* I had become the head of the Brotherhood of the Scarlet Lion." Pointing at the headband he wore diagonally across his face, Arthur explained, "That's what *this* is for."

"Arthur!" Reuel and Albert were done with their conversation, "If you wouldn't mind, please call Pen and let us depart."

"Sounds good to me." Placing two fingers in his mouth, Arthur breathed in deeply and whistled loudly. For a few moments, nothing happened, but soon the heavy sound of wings flapping through the air was heard in the distance. A loud roar which mimicked the tones of the whistle was heard just as a large shadow passed over the group and circled back to the solitary boulder in the field of sand.

While Albert and Benjamin had both seen dragons during the final battle of Amedeo's War, they were still stunned when the monstrous beast landed beside them and proceeded to lay its head down next to Arthur. Smiling and scratching beneath the beast's chin, Arthur said, "Our transportation has arrived. Say hello to Pen."

○

The remaining members of the group were dumbfounded, "Well . . . that was certainly something," Isaac remarked.

"What was that?" R-3N3 asked.

"I can only assume that is what traveling through time looks like."

Sucari spoke up, "OK, but what do we do now?"

Opening up one of the scrolls, Isaac said, "Let me do a bit of translation and we'll go off of what Albert gave us." Reading through the scroll that converted the old language to the new, Isaac nodded and muttered, "It's just a simple substitution cipher. That's convenient." Taking out a pencil, he quickly marked through the other scrolls he was given and now had an understanding of what needed to be done.

Motioning for the others to get closer, Isaac began with the scroll containing the lyrics to the Caidoz song, "There are twelve Caidoz statues which are the power sources to the fluxions. Unfortunately, when we defeated Testament, it didn't mean that the fluxions will never be used for evil again, so we need to cut their power off at the source. This song is the only clue we have as to where these statues are located. The one in particular that we seem to be near is described in the following couplet: 'The water bearer holds the oceans / Underneath the weight of many tons'."

"How do you know that?" Robin inquired.

"Well, this scroll here," Isaac held up the second of the three scrolls, "Goes into the details of the legend behind this vase statue behind us. It seems that it is known as the Aquarius Vase. The legend says that man was given fresh water from the bottom of the ocean. However, this fresh water needed to be brought by someone who lived on the ocean's floor, as no man could withstand the pressure of the water's weight at that depth. As a result, a goddess known as Aquarius climbed this staircase from the bottom of the ocean, carrying with her a vase full of fresh water. When she arrived at the top of the stairs, she would set down the vase and pick up the empty one which sat next to it, returning to the bottom of the ocean by the same staircase."

R-3N3 provided some insight, "I have come to the conclusion that the couplet's reference to being underneath the many tons of pressure which the water above induces is a direct tie to the legend of the Aquarius Vase, and that in order to find the Caidoz statue we must take this staircase to the bottom of the ocean."

"That's what I deduced as well, Artie."

"Aren't we forgetting something here?" Everyone looked at Robin, "How are we supposed to get to the bottom of the ocean? We can't just walk down this staircase with the water of an entire sea in the way."

Pulling out the last scroll, Isaac continued, "Fortunately, a lot of research was done on the Fluent of Light that resides in Hikari Shichidai. It seems that some researchers had already figured out ways to use the power before it technically even existed." Opening the scroll, he re-read some of the translated text as he started walking toward the stone staircase, "Apparently, one of the researchers thought that if the Fluent was placed in a club or staff, it could be used to part oceans for a long enough time that people could walk on the bed of the sea instead of having to swim across."

Isaac removed Hikari Shichidai from the scabbard on his back. The scabbard was an interesting, custom-built piece which was a brilliant white cover for the sword. However, the cover was only half of a normal sheath, due to the sword's unusual length. Seven colored straps held the sword in place and could be quickly broken through when the sword was drawn. The straps now loosely fell from the scabbard as he arrived at the edge of the water. Speaking toward the sea, he said, "Fortunately for us, I have it in a broadsword."

He pulled out Kuroni from its sheath and now held both swords together, "The name of this technique is the 'Sesom Strike', and it relies on the incredibly fast speed of the Fluent of Light. Unfortunately, it seems that part of the reason the technique was never successful was because, in order to get a great enough force to split the sea, the club or staff would be too heavy to wield," with a smile, he continued, "Fortunately, Kuroni should provide the weight we need." Lifting both swords above his head, Isaac took in a deep breath, "Let's hope this works."

Taking a single step forward, Isaac brought both swords down, making contact with the surface of the water. A breeze started to blow from behind them, growing in intensity until it was at gale force. Directly above them, and continuing on to the horizon, a small gap could be seen in the clouds which caused them to slowly spread apart. The gap was an impressive straight line. When the wind died down, R-3N3 remarked offhandedly, "I guess it did not work."

At that moment, the sound of rushing water was heard at the edge of the staircase as the sea began to separate. The roar of the event eventually became just as deafening as the wind which preceded it. Soon, the group was staring at an ocean, cleanly split in two. The staircase was still slightly wet, but could now be seen descending far into the depths of the sea. Isaac began running down the stairs, taking them two, sometimes three at a time, his voice quickly fading into the darkness, "We don't know how long this may last, so let's get going!"

With this urgency made clear, everyone was now running down the stairs toward the dark abyss below. Since the sun was just about to set, they lost light fairly quickly. Fortunately, the stairs were as straight as the strike that uncovered them. With the exception of occasionally running into the watery walls that surrounded them, which caused water to momentarily splash onto the steps, the group of adventurers were confidently descending into the dark of the ocean's bottom.

And yet, suddenly, something amazing happened. At a certain depth, there was light again. It started out in small amounts, but gradually grew as they continued to descend. Isaac slowed his pace momentarily to examine the phenomena. It seemed that certain sea creatures were born with luminescence in order to see and in order to lure prey to them. The physiology of these creatures was fascinating, as most looked like nothing anyone had ever seen before on the surface. The deeper they went, the larger the creatures became, and with the increase in size came an increase in light.

Unfortunately, the rushing sound of water could be heard behind the group. As they looked back to see the corridor between the walls of water quickly collapsing in a frothy torrent, everyone was suddenly motivated to move much faster toward the bottom of the ocean. Running at full tilt, everyone soon felt the splash of the water at their back, pushing them toward nothingness.

But, what luck! The end of the stairs came in sight, and just a moment before it was too late. When everyone had crossed the threshold, the last of the corridor the Sesom Strike had created came crashing down against the small temple. Fortunately, for an inexplicable reason, there was air inside the temple, a breathable oasis in the ocean's depths.

Most of the group lay on the stone floor of the temple, attempting to catch their breath. Yet, R-3N3 was already up and looking around. Examining the construction of the temple, R-3N3 was impressed with the architecture, but was more impressed that something like this could be built at the bottom of the ocean. Finally, he found what they were looking for, "I think I have found the statue we need to destroy."

Sitting up and glancing over to where R-3N3 stood, Isaac saw a smooth statue, carved out of a white rock which seemed to give off an unnatural amount of light. The statue was of a woman with the tail of a fish, holding a vase on her shoulder similar in style to the one which sat on the shoreline. Similar, except for the fact that it seemed to be made of a gem, a deep purple commonly associated with Amethyst. Isaac stood up and began to walk over to where R-3N3 was examining the sculpture.

Robin and Sucari still lay on their backs, catching their breath. Sucari put his hand out to Robin, who grabbed it and turned to look at her husband, speaking through deep breaths, "We haven't had an adventure like this in a long time."

"Agreed." The couple helped each other up and joined their two comrades at the statue. Casting their eyes upward at the large mermaid, Sucari asked, "So, how do we destroy this?"

"Not so fast, Sucari," Isaac warned, "I'd like to make sure we can get out of here first, should the destruction of the Caidoz statue also result in the destruction of this pocket of air." Walking over to the beginning of the stone staircase they just finished descending, Isaac once again took a stance and performed the Sesom Strike. No results. Humming in contemplation, Isaac noticed something that glinted against one of the pillars of the temple.

Bending down to pick up the item, Isaac stuck his hand past the watery barrier and grabbed the glass orb. Even though his interaction with the water was brief, Isaac could certainly tell that the line in the poem about the water pressure being many tons at the bottom of the ocean was certainly factual. The rest of the group joined Isaac as he rolled the glass orb around in his hand. The item seemed to contain some sort of fluid, but no matter how he held it, the fluid seemed to be producing waves inside the confines of its glass prison.

Everyone was mesmerized by the waves inside the glass. Robin monotonously asked, "What do you think it is?"

In the same monotonous tone, Isaac replied, "This may be one of the three Triumvirate powers," he paused, "I think this is the Seawave orb."

○

Over the howling wind high above the endless dunes of sand, Arthur shouted behind him to Albert, "What exactly are we looking for?"

Yelling back, Albert answered, "Anything out of the ordinary!" This answer was incredibly vague, but also incredibly apt as the landscape of the desert did not change for miles around.

"There!" Benjamin pushed between Arthur and Albert as he pointed toward a spot on the horizon. Everyone else couldn't quite make out what it was, but there was definitely something different about that part of the desert.

"Good eyes, Lambda," Albert replied. Benjamin merely smiled and adjusted his rectangular glasses, pushing them further up the arch of his nose. As they approached, it became definite: something was there. While most of the desert was a desolate, whitish tan, this part of the desert had a darker hue to it. It also sported some sickly looking trees. Not necessarily sickly from lack of water, but sickly in their eerie black color. The trees encircled a small oasis which consisted of a calm and clear pool of water, in the center of which was a solid rock hill. When Pen landed and everyone disembarked, it became obvious that they were in the literal middle of nowhere. In every direction was endless sand and desolation. No vegetation. No animals. Nothing.

Benjamin approached one of the palm trees and was about to touch the discolored bark when Albert nonchalantly shouted out, "I would not do that if I were you. The reason it is discolored is because it is poisoned." Pulling his hand back in disgust, Benjamin scrutinized the dark branches above him, then over to the other trees surrounding the oasis.

"By the way, what are we looking for here?" Benjamin asked.

"That's easy," Arthur replied confidently, "The Holy Grail."

"That's great, but I don't see any cups around here."

"Isn't the oasis an obvious clue? It holds water just like a grail would, keeping the liquid from spilling out over the entire desert."

"I still stand by my statement. Even if it is a clue, where do we go from here?"

Albert pointed to the rock mound which sat in the middle of the lake, "That is the only logical spot." Kicking over one of the trees into the lake, Albert continued, "Unfortunately, I see no way to cross this lake in order to get there. Obviously, the trees are not tall enough to make the transit safely."

"Why don't we swim?" Benjamin inquired.

Albert had to give him a look of doubt, "Because the reason why the trees are poisoned is due to the poisonous *water*."

"Sheesh. You don't need to get agitated over it."

Clearing his throat, Reuel interrupted as if they weren't arguing at all, "Now, I am sure some of you are not clear on the legend of the grail, so let me enlighten you. There are many things which led us to this particular oasis. Arthur is correct in deducing that the oasis is, in fact, a clue. This is the very desert in which Jesus was tempted by Satan for forty days and forty nights. After the ordeal, he found the spring of living water in the middle of this desert."

Arthur seemed a little put off, "Are you insinuating that this poison oasis is the spring of living water?"

"It used to be, yes. However, it seems that it has become tainted since that time," once more clearing his throat, Reuel continued, "I don't want to continue being sacrilegious, but many believe that this water is what gave Jesus his ability to heal people. Of course, there has been much debate as to whether or not God led him here to bestow upon him these powers, and I won't speculate further, lest I venture into a subject of which I am not the renowned expert."

Benjamin was still a bit impatient, "This still doesn't explain how we get to the rock. I know I can probably get over there with no problem, but I'll be at a loss for what to do next when I get there."

"In time, young man," was Reuel's reply. "Are you familiar with the concept of a 'Jesus Rock'?"

Shaking his head, Benjamin answered, "No. Is that a statue of Jesus somewhere?"

"No, quite the contrary," Reuel began walking along the edge of the water as he continued talking, "A Jesus Rock is in reference to a rock that goes unseen by sailors, which causes them to take Jesus' name in vain when they hit it with their ships. Of course, it has a double meaning as well," turning toward the shore and taking a step forward, Reuel smiled as everyone reacted with trepidation, "seeing as Jesus walked on the water." Continuing to walk forward, Reuel was unharmed, which allowed everyone the chance to breathe a collective sigh of relief.

Apparently, when flying overhead, Reuel had spied a small strip of rock which sat just below the water's surface. While it was difficult to distinguish in the air, it was nearly impossible to see while on the ground. Fortunately, even though Reuel's boots got wet, the poison did not affect him as its methods of transfer were through ingestion or contact with the skin. Everyone walked over to where Reuel's last step in the sand was and took a small leap of faith as they followed him out onto the water's surface.

When the group arrived at the rock, they waited as Reuel examined the monolithic barrier in front of them. Since they were in a single-file line, it was difficult for the others to see what was happening. "Is everything OK, Reuel?" Arthur asked.

"Indeed it is. I just need to find . . . ah! There it is," grabbing at a small hand-hold, Reuel pulled aside a stone barrier, revealing the entrance to a cave. Stepping inside, Reuel disappeared into the darkness beyond, followed by Arthur and Benjamin. Albert brought up the rear, but decided to leave the cave open in case they should need to escape quickly.

Benjamin noticed that, despite the enveloping darkness, he could still see around him. When they had walked about forty feet through the tight corridor, Benjamin could tell they were now in the large, hollow center of the rock. He could see the reflection of water just ahead of them, so he called out, "Stop!" Everyone turned to look at Benjamin, who knelt down to pick up a small pebble and throw it into the pool beyond, "If the water outside was poison, it's probably poison inside here as well."

Arthur seemed confused, "Lambda, since when has your forehead glowed like that?"

"What do you mean?" Placing his hand over his forehead, the light in the room became considerably dimmer. It was then that he noticed three glowing marks in front of him. The first was his own, shining in a golden reflection. However, of the remaining two, one mark was familiar and bright, whereas the other was less familiar and less luminous. Of course, both marks were considerably dimmer than the reflection of Benjamin's, which was the mark of Lambda the Just he received in the Imaginary World, "Oh, this? I got this mark from passing through the i-World. But what I can't figure out is who has those two marks there? I ask, since I knew the man who bore one of them."

"Now *I* must ask, what do you mean?" as Arthur spoke, the marks moved.

"Well, Arthur, the mark on your right hand is the mark of Breve the Lion, who I must admit I haven't met. Still, I would assume that you have a connection to him due to you telling us that you are the head of the Brotherhood of the Scarlet Lion. However-" Benjamin could hear someone rifling around in their pockets for a match, "that mark on your neck is that of Umlaut the Dragon, also known as Bram. He founded the Order of the Dragon, of which I can now assume you are also a part."

Albert struck the match and soon everyone could see each other once again. Arthur cringed in pain as he shut his eye tight. The headband of the Brotherhood which had once covered part of the left side of his face was now covering the right side. He had switched the sides of the headband when they entered the cave, since his left eye was more sensitive to light. Tattooed around the left eye was the symbol of the Order of the Dragon: a dragon eating its own tail in an uroboros configuration. Benjamin was right. Not only was Arthur the head of the Brotherhood of the Scarlet Lion, but he was part of the Order of the Dragon as well.

And yet, this revelation was just one of many interesting foibles about Arthur. When he eventually opened his left eye again, it was red. Benjamin could have sworn that Arthur's eyes were green, but a white, blotchy patch on Arthur's skin gave away some of his heredity. Somewhere along his family line, the recessive gene of an albino made its presence known on Arthur's face. This was part of the reason he wore the headband the way that he did: to cover up this shameful attribute.

"If you must know, Lambda: yeah, I am a member of the Order of the Dragon. I was given Pen by my mother, who was also a member of the Order. When I received my dragon, she told me that he was mightier than any sword, which is why dragons are so resilient and so desired by armor smiths. She also said our distant ancestor founded the Order, which must be this Bram character you knew."

"I soon became not only the youngest, but the best Dragonrider who ever existed, which gave me a chance to prove myself in the Brotherhood of the Scarlet Lion. This exclusive group which protects the 4th Kingdom is founded on riders, although most of them rode horses." Taking a breath and slowly letting it out, Arthur was slightly terse, "Now that we've delved into my history, can we please get on with what we're here for?"

Albert dropped the match as it reached his hand, bringing everyone back into darkness. Once again, the only light illuminating the cavern was that of the glowing marks from the Imaginary World. Soon, Albert lit another match and the group was able to survey their surroundings. Some of them soon wished that they hadn't.

Around the pool of water were a number of corpses, all in various states of decay. Many grasped cups and goblets in their hands, held over the years by the onset of rigor mortis after their deaths. And yet, despite the number of skeletons lining the water's edge, there were still more containers littering the ground. Arthur knelt down and started rummaging through the cups, tossing them behind him as he rejected them outright. He obviously knew what he was looking for. Suddenly, something caught his eye, as he pointed toward the depths of the pool, "There! That must be it." Down at the bottom of the liquid darkness, a cup reflected a small glint of gold.

Reuel came over to confirm, "By Jove, I think you're right. And yet–"

"It's at the bottom of a pool of poisonous water," Arthur finished the sentence, obviously dejected.

"I think we may have a solution, but it is incredibly dangerous." Albert was into his cylindrical case again and pulled out a fair-sized coil of wire. "Based off of a couplet from the song describing the Caidoz statues, which says, 'The scorpion lies within the sand / Spreading poison throughout the land', I can deduce that this oasis is the home of the scorpion Caidoz statue."

"What's that have to do with our solution?" Arthur asked.

"The *solution* is the solution," Albert answered. The second match went out, but Albert continued, "In my research of the statues, I found that the poisonous tip of the scorpion's tail is made up partially of Topaz. Now, any mineralogist could tell you that many gems consist of a few select elements, most of which can be found in a desert. Aluminum, Silicon, Oxygen: these elements are what make up the majority of sand. However, Topaz has an imperfection in its structure, and that imperfection is Fluorine. Also, if I were to guess, the Caidoz statue also lies at the bottom of this poisonous lake, since the scorpion's base Element is Water. Now stay with me, because this is where it gets tricky."

Lighting a third match, Albert handed the light to Benjamin as he began uncoiling the wire, sticking its split end into the poisonous lake. Albert began to walk backward out of the cave, causing the rest of the group to follow after him as he continued the explanation of his plan, "Fortunately for us, we have Benjamin here, and he can control lightning. My guess would be that the Fluorine from the Topaz tip of the scorpion has infiltrated into the water of this oasis, thereby adding the poisonous element to the formerly life-giving liquid. Where Benjamin's power comes in handy is that the electricity in lightning can be used to separate the individual elements of the water solution, thereby filling the cavern with Hydrogen, Oxygen, and Fluorine."

Now everyone was once again outside and following Albert along the Jesus Rock ridge back to the sandy shore. When Albert reached the end of the coil of wire, he stood up and held his lower back, "This is the reason we must perform this plan at a safe distance. Fluorine, let alone pure Hydrogen, is an incredibly volatile gas and any reactions that happen can be sudden and highly explosive."

Handing the end of the wire to Benjamin, Albert smiled and said, "If you would be so kind, Lambda. But please, do be careful. Not too much electricity now." Grabbing the wire, the Skybolt orb on Benjamin's chest began to glow. Soon afterward, the wire began to buzz with energy. Addressing Arthur and Reuel, Albert said, "This may take a while, so you might want to find some shade and get comfortable."

◯

No one knew how long they had been staring at the Seawave orb, but it must have felt like an eternity. Isaac remembered the task at hand and snapped out of his daze, pocketing the legendary fluxion core in his white coat. Gazing out into the dark depths of the ocean, he was racking his brain on how to safely get back to the surface. The multitude of glowing fish slowly floated by, giving Isaac an idea.

"Artie, I need you to go out and get something for me."

"I do not understand, Isaac."

"Well, we're all fairly organic beings, so we'll be crushed to death by the pressure of the water down here. However, you are made of metal, which means that, if we can use your powers correctly, you will be able to help us escape after we destroy the Caidoz statue."

"That makes sense. What do I need to do?"

"Go out and catch us one of those fish. It doesn't really matter which one, so long as you bring it back to me." R-3N3 nodded and began to head toward the wall of water. Before he went in, Isaac spoke one more warning, "Just make sure you fill yourself with water before you go out there so you can quickly equalize any pressure differentials. Otherwise, you might be crushed just like we would."

Removing the left hand of his armor, R-3N3 stuck the open wrist past the barrier of air and allowed water to quickly fill his body. When he was as full as he could get, the only air remaining in his helmet, he stepped out of the temple's barrier, reattaching his left hand. Some of the water spilled into the temple, but the bubble of air remained intact. The green glowing orbs of R-3N3's eyes allowed him to see in the darkness as he slowly made his way forward.

The water resistance was an incredible force. While R-3N3 wasn't crushed by the pressure, it did slow his movement. He then realized that, other than his bare hands, he had nothing to catch a fish with. As such, he decided he needed a weapon. Conveniently enough, in the distance directly in front of him was a long and straight piece of coral. It stuck up from the ground, begging to be used.

When he eventually arrived at the small reef, R-3N3 grabbed the end of the coral and broke it off, revealing the head of a gold-colored trident. While this discovery was certainly curious, a medium-sized fish was just passing by overhead, so R-3N3 knew he had his first chance to accomplish Isaac's task. Thrusting the trident upward, the tines of the weapon went through the fish and the barbs held it in place. While he could feel the fish struggle, R-3N3's strength was greater.

Turning toward the temple, R-3N3 began slowly making his way back to his friends, the dull light of the Caidoz statue lighting his path. As he proceeded, he noticed that his shadow was becoming more defined in front of him. This caused him to turn around and see what the greater source of light was. Unfortunately, he turned around just in time to see a gigantic fish start to swoop down and advance on him, its long and jagged teeth open and ready to devour everything in its path.

R-3N3 returned to his original course, now trying to run as fast as he could toward the Aquarius shrine. And yet, not being in his natural element, R-3N3 could soon feel the presence of the fish directly behind him. It was at that moment when he tripped over a rock and fell to the sandy ocean floor. The giant fish closed its mouth over the fish R-3N3 had caught earlier and started to drag him across the ground. As luck would have it, the trident worked its way loose and left R-3N3 lying face-down in a pile of sand, wanting nothing more than to get back into the safety of the shrine.

However, the large, lumbering fish, which was inadvertently fed by R-3N3, pulled up just a little too late, thereby nudging the shrine and causing some water to spill into the enclosure. R-3N3 watched in horror as this happened, but soon calmed down when it appeared that the shrine would remain intact.

Slowly rising to his feet, R-3N3 found another fish and pierced it with the trident, ready to rejoin his friends. When he re-entered the temple, spilling water on the floor again, the fish had stopped struggling. Robin and Sucari welcomed R-3N3 back and were almost in hysterics, not at the close call the shrine had encountered, but at having to watch their friend almost get eaten by a monster of a fish.

Isaac was on the floor, working on three strips of fabric he had torn from the edge of his white jacket, completely oblivious of what had just happened. R-3N3 dropped the fish on the floor, the trident still sticking out of its side. Isaac kept focused on his work and replied, "Yes, that will do quite nicely. Thank you, Artie."

"What do you plan to do with it?" R-3N3's voice was unusually deep, as the water inside the armor changed its tone.

Not noticing the change in his comrade's voice, Isaac kept working with the fabric, "I need its blood. We're going to make some rudimentary fluxions." On one end of each of the three strips, there was an uroboros seal drawn around a thick knot in the fabric. Since the fish was already bleeding from the trident wound, Isaac merely had to soak the fabric knots in the thick blood and set the strips aside. Wrapping one of the strips around his neck, Isaac briefly focused on the fluxion to test it out. Two sets of three slits appeared on the fabric around his neck, at which point Isaac stopped the experiment.

Taking a deep breath, Isaac said, "It looks like this will work." Finally looking up at R-3N3, whose front was scuffed from being dragged across the sandy ocean floor, Isaac asked, "What happened to you?"

"Didn't you see what happened out there?" Robin asked indignantly, "Artie almost got himself killed for that fish, and we almost didn't fare too well either."

Isaac was a bit surprised at this revelation, "Really? I guess I was too intently focused on creating the fluxion seals. If that's the case, we should probably continue with my plan pretty quickly."

Robin just had to laugh at the situation, because otherwise it would have been much too easy to cry, "So, what's the plan anyways, Isaac?"

Handing the two other strips of fabric to Sucari and Robin, Isaac explained, "After we destroy this statue, we will use these fluxions to grow gills, thereby allowing us to ascend to the surface safely. Plus, since the core we are using for these Blood-fluxions is that of a deep-sea fish, we should gain the pressure-resistant properties of our host. Similarly, as we ascend to the surface, I'm assuming some of the blood will probably wash out of the fabric, so the effect will be less as we progress."

"How did you ever think of something like this?"

"Actually, I modeled this after the scarf that Jacques wore when we were on Tanilats Dock."

Sucari smiled and nodded, "I remember that! Good work, Isaac."

"Thanks, but we're not done yet." Turning to study the daunting sculpture, Isaac frowned, "We still need to destroy this statue."

"You seem concerned."

"Well, based on what Albert said, this is made from the same material that Kuroni is, so I don't understand why it isn't black, but is instead pure white."

"I guess we'll just have to ask him when we see him again."

"I guess so. Besides, there were some symbols on the scroll which had the song lyrics on it, and this statue has a mark that matches one of them." Pulling out the lyric scroll, Isaac quickly found the symbol: a square with a triangle inscribed inside it. A line cut the square in half and intersected the triangle one third of the way from its tip. A plus sign was set within the triangle, aligned with the line. Pointing to the mermaid's crown, the symbol was evident.

Removing Hikari Shichidai from the scabbard on his back, Isaac gave everyone a warning, "I don't know what will happen, so be ready with the fluxions. With a diagonal slash, Isaac cut the statue. However, nothing happened. Isaac thrust the sword into the ground and was thoughtful with a murmur, "Hmmmm. That's curious. I knew Albert said the Fluent of Light should do the trick, so I don't know why it didn't work."

Pulling out the lyric scroll again, Isaac translated some of the notes on the back. "Very well, I see what we did wrong." Pointing to a diamond with four words written at its points, Isaac explained, "This must be what the song was referring to. Apparently, these statues exhibit different properties. Elements, if you will." Matching some of the symbols, Isaac continued, "This statue is of the Air Element," his voice changed when he read the sentence, expressing interest.

Looking up from the scroll, he smiled, "That would explain why there's this bubble of air down here. Although I'm certainly glad we have our escape route already figured out, because there's a good chance that this air will disappear when we destroy the statue." While Isaac was certainly glib about their possible demise, Sucari and Robin were worried and each took a step closer together. Glancing back down to the Element chart, Isaac came to a solution, "It seems that these Elements are weak against one of their brethren, so we need to use . . ." finding the weakness, Isaac was once again surprised at their luck, "Fire!"

Everyone stared at Sucari, who sighed as he smiled, "OK, I guess I'll help out this once." As Sucari approached the statue, Isaac readied Hikari Shichidai and Kuroni. They were going to do this in one shot. If it didn't work now, they might be out of options.

○

Arthur and Reuel had fallen asleep, leaning against Pen's side. The dragon was also asleep, his huge body rhythmically breathing, lulling the two men to sleep. Benjamin had become bored with the task given to him by Albert, who had taken to hiding behind his cylindrical container, which was now open. Every once in a while, Albert could be heard fiddling around with something inside, causing Benjamin to snap out of the daydream he was nodding off into.

Closing the case, Albert came over to where Benjamin was sitting cross-legged in the sand. His shadow gave Benjamin some relief from the sun, but the Natural was becoming impatient, "How much longer do I have to do this?"

"Electrolysis is a time-consuming procedure, especially if we are to remove all the water in that cavern pool." Peering toward the small entrance in the rock, Albert observed that there was some yellow gas now emanating from the hole, "It looks like we are about ready to begin, the Fluorine is starting to escape." Glancing over to the trio they met at the boulder, Albert chuckled, "What do you say to giving them a rude awakening?"

Benjamin lifted his eyebrows as if to question the juvenile act, especially from someone who was much older than him, but when he turned his head to look behind him, he saw that Albert had changed. He now wore his cloak as more of a cape, which revealed the vest he wore with Q-Portal keys hanging from hooks across its entire surface. White keys were exclusively on the right half of the vest, whereas black keys covered the left side.

But what was more surprising was that, strapped onto the left side of his body, he wore a large, metal arm which seemed to be encasing some sort of weapon. This revelation is what caused Benjamin to accidentally send more electricity down the wire, thereby igniting the volatile cave full of toxic and explosive gas.

In a deafening boom, the entire rock dome exploded, sending shrapnel everywhere. Pieces of stone were soon splashing into the poison lake as Albert was running along the Jesus Rock ridge, back to the ex-cavern's pool, Q-Portal keys jingling with each stride. Arthur and Reuel were shocked awake at the sound of the explosion, and were having trouble gaining their bearings. When they saw Benjamin running after Albert, they hurriedly grabbed their things and followed after them. Pen was also startled and took to the sky with a mighty beat of his wings and a roar, kicking up a small dust storm in the process.

Since most of the debris was small and inconsequential, the group ran unhindered toward the rock island, pelted by pebbles and sand. Still, larger pieces of rock rained down on the travelers, which meant that occasionally one of them would yell out, "Rock!" and point at the stony projectile, which usually landed in front of them. Occasionally, one of them had to run faster to avoid getting splashed by the poison water.

When Benjamin caught up with Albert, they were already well past where the stone door had once stood and blocked their path. The researcher had already jumped down into the empty pool and removed the metal covering from his left arm, revealing a most curious sight. Where his left arm should be, there was what appeared to be the pincer of a crab, but made entirely out of Ruby.

"What are you doing?" Benjamin shouted, the loud explosion long gone, but the ringing still persisting in his ears. He briefly wondered if he would develop permanent damage to his hearing if events like these were to be the norm around Albert.

"I will explain when I am done!" Albert lifted his left arm into the sky and let the sunlight charge the device, which began to whine at a higher and higher pitch. Arthur and Reuel arrived at the top of the hole which once held the cavern pool. They were as out of breath as they were dumbfounded by Albert's strange arm. As he listened to the increasing whine of the weapon, Albert stared down at his feet, where water was once again flowing. He muttered to himself, "Come on! Come on!"

In all the excitement, Arthur had forgotten why he was there, but when he saw water pouring back into the hole, he jumped down and grabbed the golden cup he had seen at the bottom of the pool earlier. Scrambling back to the edge of the hole, he lifted his hands, asking Reuel for help, "Could you get me out of here?"

Reuel reached down and pulled Arthur up out of the watery pit, never once breaking his gaze with the statue that now stood in plain sight at the bottom of the pool, water flowing from its claws. The statue was that of a scorpion, just as Albert had predicted. Also, as he had predicted, the poisonous tip of the scorpion's tail was made of a brilliant Topaz, its orange color almost overpowered by the deep black stone from which the sculpture was carved.

Benjamin could see the water rising as well and was slowly backing away, "Albert, whatever you're doing, you might want-"

"I am almost there!" he shouted. Suddenly, the Ruby pincer reached its peak and Albert yelled, "*Now!*" Leveling the pincer at the scorpion statue, a concentrated beam of red light penetrated the sculpture, causing small red cracks to permeate through its structure. "Keep going!" Albert shouted to himself and to the statue. With less fanfare than the explosion they had created to get in, the statue crumbled to the ground, its Topaz tail shattering when it landed.

The water stopped rising as Albert took a deep breath and let it out in a sigh of relief, "*Wunderbar*. It is finished."

"Very well, now that it is finished, do you mind explaining yourself?" Benjamin asked, clearly irritated, "First off, what is wrong with your left arm?"

"If you must know, I lost this arm when I defeated my first Caidoz statue," placing the metal cover back on the Ruby prosthetic, he continued, "And now we have destroyed another."

Benjamin pushed a spark between his fingers from the Skybolt orb on his chest. Albert was right, Benjamin felt slightly less powerful than he was just minutes ago. Calming down slightly, Benjamin inquired, "Losing your arm doesn't necessarily explain where you got that weapon, now does it?"

"In the defeat of my first Caidoz statue, the crab, I claimed this as my prize. I call it the C.L.A.W., or Cancer Light Amplification Weapon. The crab had a Ruby pincer which it used to destroy things. My hand got hit, and the destruction started creeping up my arm, which is why I had to cut it off. My only luck that day came from the fact that the crab statue was in a room full of treasure and I was able to find a reflective surface to bounce the amplified light back at it. In doing so, I destroyed the crab through its own power. After all, the couplet goes, 'The crab's pinch spreads its disease / Destroying the lives of all it sees'."

"Wait. Something about your story doesn't make sense. From the sounds of it, the statue was alive?" Jumping out of the hole with his electrically enhanced legs, Benjamin landed next to Arthur and Reuel, who were observing more amazing wonders by the second.

"Alive is a relative term, but it was indeed moving and attacking, probably as a protector to the treasure. We are merely lucky that *this* statue was immobile, considering its poisonous attributes." Reaching upward with his right hand, Albert accepted Benjamin's outstretched arm and was pulled out of the hole as he continued, "We are also fortunate that the weakness of the Water Element statues is Air, which is precisely why we needed to drain the pool." Now out of the drained pool, Albert breathed deeply in relief of having destroyed another Caidoz statue.

With the sun now streaming into the once dark cavern, something shiny glinted and caught Albert's attention. He saw that Arthur now held a golden goblet, which caused him to ask, "Is that what you were looking for?"

Arthur was lost in thought from the events that recently transpired before him and the fantastic tale which was given as a partial explanation. Realizing that he was asked a question, he finally examined the cup he had retrieved from the pool, hoping that it was the grail he had been searching for. The item was simple: made of gold, no jewel encrustments. Two words were engraved in a bold script on the edge of the cup, "Live" and "Crap". Arthur's face was excited, but at the same time concerned, "I think so, but I don't like the second word engraved on here."

Reuel was slightly assuring, "Let's just think about it for a moment, shall we? In the context of what we already know about this area, we must extend its connection with Jesus to the cup you now hold. Therefore, we must arrive at the conclusion that, while Jesus gave his life so that we could live, wasn't his life kind of crap? I mean, he was constantly persecuted by the religious establishment and he hung out with people who never quite understood him. Plus, the very people he was sent to save killed him in perhaps the most inhumane way possible. I think one word is a consequence of the other. The trick is to acknowledge that the responsibility of having the power to heal, like this Holy Grail touts, is to assume the role of a servant."

Arthur seemed a little dejected as he slowly made his way to the Jesus Rock ridge and back to the shore of the oasis. Everyone followed Arthur, as they had accomplished all they needed to in the former cavern. In an act of desperation, Arthur swung the cup down, filling it with some of the poison water in the lake and immediately taking a drink. Reuel was shocked, "What are you doing?" he shouted as he knocked the grail away.

As the cup landed in the sand, Arthur was laughing, "I sure got you, Reuel!" Everyone was confused until Reuel picked up the grail and examined it more closely. The stem of the goblet was hollow. In fact, there was a hole right through the bottom of the cup. Arthur hadn't drank any of the water, he had merely spilled some of it on his armor.

A resounding boom interrupted the two men as they immediately turned toward the destroyed rock dome. Nothing had changed. However, Benjamin and Albert had disappeared, much in the same way they appeared at the boulder just south of the Library of Delaxanair. Tousling Arthur's hair, Reuel chuckled, "You sure got me, Arthur." Putting the grail away in a bag, he patted the young man on his back, "Let's go home, shall we?"

"Sure thing, but who were those guys?"

"I don't think we'll ever fully know the answer to that, Arthur." With a whistle, Arthur once again called Pen, who circled the oasis a few times before landing and letting the two men mount its back. Their goal accomplished, the Wizard and the King rode the dragon into the sky, beginning their journey back to their home: the 4th Kingdom.

When Sucari caught fire, he immediately went to his white fire form, as he knew from past experience that it was hot enough to destroy stone. Isaac called out directions, "All right, everybody! Hold your breath, we might be getting soaked pretty soon." Sprouting his wings, which also caught fire, Sucari punched the Caidoz statue while flapping his wings, transferring all of the white fire to the already white statue. When it came in contact with the fluxionite, the fire suddenly got bigger, as if fueled by an unseen wind.

Isaac slashed again at the statue with Hikari Shichidai, followed by a blunt-force strike with Kuroni. The one-two punch did the trick, as the statue began to crumble, disintegrating with the fire. Isaac secured his swords as he watched the temple crumble around them, starting with the damage caused by the large fish that almost ate R-3N3. The wall of water that surrounded the temple began to leak in until it finally gave way, allowing the deep ocean to rush in and replace the oasis of air.

Everyone closed their eyes and immediately shivered when the cold water hit their bodies. The shock was so much that they almost let go of the breath in their lungs. Fortunately, they were prepared enough to activate the fluxion on their necks, and soon Isaac, Sucari, and Robin were swimming for the surface as fast as they could. As they ascended, they let the air out of their lungs slowly, but since the air was from the bottom of the ocean, it was expanding as they rose, so they didn't really need the gills to breathe, but rather they needed the bottom-dwelling fish's pressure resistance to prevent their bodies from being crushed.

However, just as Isaac had predicted, the Blood-fluxion was being washed away; and with it, the fish's powers. The three travelers could see the surface above them, but had run out of breath, both from their gills and their lungs. They frantically began to swim faster and harder, trying to do everything within their power to get to the air of the surface.

Their lungs were burning and the cold water was numbing their bodies as the Nitrogen was starting to invade their bloodstream. But, in one last push, they broke the surface of the ocean, gasping out for the fresh, salty air. Coughing and taking deep breaths, all three of them managed to work their way up to shore, laying down on the solid ground and staring up at the dark and starry sky.

Several minutes passed before any of them actually spoke. Sucari broke the silence, "That was intense. Can we not put ourselves at risk like that again?"

"Agreed," was Robin's answer.

"I've already almost drowned once today, so after this second time I'd rather not get in the water for quite a while," replied Isaac, who pulled the used fluxion from his neck and let its soggy fabric fall to the ground. Robin and Sucari merely glimpsed at each other, silently questioning what Isaac could have been doing to make this the second time in a day he had almost drowned.

Breathing deeply of the ocean air, the group lay on the ground, trying not to move. As they caught their breath, occasionally someone would adjust their aching body and would groan at the reminder of their recent physical exertion. The silence returned, but once again Sucari spoke, "Wait. Where's Artie?"

Isaac slowly sat up and stared out over the ocean, "That's right. He didn't need to get to the surface as quickly as we did . . . which means he's probably still making his way up here."

"OK, that's good. Since he's got that trident, and I know he's capable of using it, I think he can take care of himself, so we shouldn't worry."

Robin changed topics, "Where do we go next?"

Laying back down, Isaac answered, "I'm not sure. Albert gave me a Q-Portal key to use, but I don't know where it leads."

Yawning, not only due to a lack of Oxygen in his blood, but due to his fatigue as well, Sucari offered, "For the time being, let's get some sleep as we wait for Artie to catch up. We'll get going in the morning."

"Sounds like a plan," Robin remarked.

"I concur," said Isaac. With that last word, all three of them immediately fell asleep.

 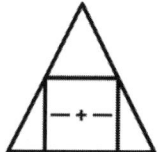

Chapter 4

Fight the Fire

Albert and Benjamin found themselves in a place very different from the desert they had left. While the desert had been bright and full of smooth, organic curves, they now stood in what appeared to be a dark quarry, its angular facets showing the influence of man. The light of the red moon above them took the color away from their surroundings, but they were pretty sure the stones, cut into cubes, were very white, regardless of the lighting. The Q-hole they had just created sizzled in the cool of the evening.

"Where do you think we are now?" Benjamin inquired.

"*Where* we are is most likely the Pablo Quarry on the edge of the 4th Kingdom. *When* we are is a completely different story," was Albert's reply.

As Benjamin started descending from a pile of white cubes, he asked, "Did we have to leave so suddenly? I think it was a bit rude. We should have at least thanked them for the ride, since it helped us find the statue much quicker than searching on our own."

"Perhaps, but we must not interfere with the past too much and we must keep our eyes on the mission at hand. Can you gauge how powerful you are? That should let us know how far back in time we have traveled."

Performing the same spark-gap test made Benjamin smile, "I'm more powerful now than I've ever been."

"Then that means we have traveled to a time before you received your powers. A time when all the Caidoz statues still existed." As they passed by some ships loaded down with white cubes of stone, they saw a message board which told where each of the vessels was heading. Both travelers picked up one of the documents and read the destinations in the hazy light of the moon, "A time before Pandora Prison was completely built, apparently."

The boats creaked silently in the night as Benjamin and Albert quietly made their way to the entrance of the quarry. Sure enough, a sign that read "Pablo Quarry at the White Cliffs" was emblazoned above the entrance. The lights of a city flickered in the distance to the west, which gave the two Millennials a destination to travel toward.

As they sauntered away from the cliff-side quarry, Benjamin determined that, since they were now alone, he could ask some questions, "So, Albert . . . why did you create the fluxions in the first place?"

"That is easy, I wanted respect."

"Respect?"

"Most scientific discoveries are never attributed to anyone, or if they are it is to the leader of a group. The group does the work, the leader gets the credit."

"I see."

"Of course, now that I have seen what a Natural can really do, when I saw you battling in Amedeo's War, I realized that while I said I wanted to help mankind with these powers, I really just wanted recognition for my genius."

"So the fluxion project was fueled by your pride?"

"You could say that, *ja*."

"But you obviously have discovered much more than the fluxions, so why did you even join the project in the first place?"

"Curiosity, mainly. I wanted to see the limits of what mankind could achieve. But now I have seen that evil can use these powers to carry out genocide, so I cannot idly stand by and let their existence continue. I am glad that you survived Amedeo's War and that I was able to find you, Benjamin. Perhaps someday you can find it in your heart to forgive us for what we did to you," Albert paused for a moment and softly continued, "For what I did to you."

Benjamin smiled at the heartfelt apology, "Luckily for you, I think I'm already there." Changing topics, Benjamin asked, "Am I the reason you were able to figure out the time traveling aspect of those keys?"

"*Ja*, if it was not for your massive electrical power and your mysterious disappearance, I would have never known that the Q-Portals could control travel through space *and* time."

"But I don't really get why we are using the black keys when I used a white one to go to the future."

"The reason for that is actually very simple: Degree."

"Degree?"

"Correct. The poem which describes the locations of the Caidoz statues talks about two Degrees. Black and White. Light and Dark. Forward and Backward. Half of the statues are white, and half are black. The white fluxionite is linked to the Degree known as 'Positive'. It is what can open white holes in space and it is what allows us to travel forward in time. Similarly, the black fluxionite Degree is 'Negative', and it opens black holes as well as the ability to travel backward in time."

"Interesting."

"It is, but what is more interesting is that you were able to travel one thousand years in the future somewhat effortlessly."

"Why is that?"

"When I had figured out where you had gone, I tried to travel forward in time, but I was only able to jump forward a few decades. A century if I was lucky. I needed to string together many time transitions to finally catch up to you. Now, on the flip side, I found that it was much easier to travel backward in time. I could go back a few centuries with ease. I think that since the Q-Portals rely on the use of fluxionite keys, the more Caidoz statues we destroy, the more difficult it will be to travel to the future. Inevitably, no matter how far forward we would try to travel, we would eventually come to the 'end of time', so to speak, when we finally achieve our goal and destroy the last statue."

"Incredible. I had no idea there was so much complexity to a simple set of keys."

Albert chuckled, "Well, they do not call me the 'Keymaster' for nothing."

A bell, tolling in the distance, reminded Benjamin of something else he had been meaning to ask Albert, "So, *Keymaster*, I would assume you traveled through time for quite a while before you eventually made it to me, right?"

"True, I did have to test out my ability before I made it to you. Why do you ask?"

"I noticed in the documentation that some of the boats back there were loaded with stones meant for the construction of the Tower of Lebab. Did you ever go back far enough to figure out why that tower was built in the first place?"

Albert awkwardly cleared his throat as he fumbled with some of his words, "Ah, well see, about that."

"Yes?"

"I think I may have had something to do with it."

"What did you do?"

"Remember the part of the song which talks about the bull on the moon? Well, at one point I was convinced that it was literal and so *I* convinced a very enthusiastic set of people known as the Lebabonians to build me a tower which could get me to the moon. They were an industrious people led by a fellow scientist named Archimedes."

"How did you get them to do that?"

"I worked a bit of my Q-Portal magic and made Archimedes think I was some sort of god. The rest of the convincing was easy, especially since *he* wanted to build some sort of elevator. However, by the time I realized the song may be speaking metaphorically, they had already started construction on it."

"Not that it mattered in the end, since Tecumseh destroyed the tower."

"True, but I thought that, maybe if I jumped forward in time from Archimedes' era to encourage the builders to continue on, I could change history and get the tower finished before it was destroyed," stroking his moustache thoughtfully, he said, "I never did succeed with that plan, though."

As the two Millennials approached the town, the continual tolling of a bell could still be heard. Upon closer inspection of the starless sky, the clouds seemed to be more of a hazy fog than actual clouds. The sky above the city glowed with an eerie orange color. These things were difficult to notice at the coast, but became clearer the closer they got to the city. Benjamin stopped walking for a moment and sniffed the air, "Do you smell . . . smoke?"

Albert stopped and took in a deep breath as well, "I do smell smoke." At once, the pieces all started to come together, "Which means we have arrived in the 4th Kingdom during the Great Fire of Old Non!"

"How far away do you think we are?"

"Well, the White Cliffs are about fifteen miles from the town and we've been walking for an hour, so I wouldn't put us any closer than twelve miles, considering our pace." Albert was now the curious one, "Why? What are you thinking?"

"We need to help them! Here, grab my hand." Benjamin extended his hand to Albert, who was already removing the glove from his right hand. In a flash, both travelers quickly made their way toward Old Non.

○

The soft light of morning began to light the sky above Isaac, Sucari, and Robin, all of whom had slept soundly due to the exhaustion they had endured in returning to the statue of the Aquarius Vase. Isaac awoke first and groaned at his soreness. When he stood up and started stretching, he noticed Robin and Sucari cuddling together and he let out a short laugh as he smiled. Newlyweds.

Glancing around their rudimentary campsite, Isaac grew concerned. Walking up a small hill to the east, Isaac once again examined their surroundings. From the hill, he shouted down to Sucari and Robin, "Hey! Have you two seen Artie yet?"

This inquiry woke the married couple and they both groaned at their own soreness as they began to get up. Still groggy with sleep, Sucari asked, "What was that, Isaac?"

Isaac had made his way back to the stone staircase which led to the ocean-bottom shrine and restated his question, "I'm just wondering if either of you noticed whether Artie came in during the night. I was sound asleep and didn't notice anything."

Both Sucari and Robin looked around the area and saw that Isaac was correct: R-3N3 was nowhere to be found. Sucari answered, "I slept just as well as you did. I didn't notice Artie come in either. How about you, honey?" Robin shook her head in concurrence.

"That's strange. I wonder if something happened to him when he was climbing back up."

"Do you think so?"

"I don't know, but I do know there were a lot of strange fish down there. Who knows if one of them swallowed him up?" Robin and Sucari looked at each other, not knowing if Isaac was being serious or not.

Almost as if on cue, R-3N3 slowly made his way out of the ocean, steadily climbing the stone steps that had led the group to the depths in the first place. Water drained from his armor as he apologized to everyone, his voice still much deeper than normal, "I apologize for taking so long. I hope you did not worry." Sitting down on the shore, R-3N3 removed his feet and let the water drain out of his body. Small fish flopped around on the shore as they were washed out to sea.

"To be honest, Artie, we were starting to wonder if something had happened to you."

R-3N3's voice was returning to its original pitch as the water drained from the armor, "I am not sure why, but after we destroyed the Caidoz statue, I suddenly felt weaker than I had before. As I saw all of you quickly rise to the surface, I tried to keep up, but just did not have the energy for it. When I lost sight of you, I decided to take it at my own pace, which was obviously considerably slower in the water, but it felt even slower than if I had been walking normally."

"Well, we're glad that you're back here with us, regardless." Isaac noticed a glint of something gold sitting next to R-3N3, "Hey Artie, what's that?"

R-3N3 held up the coral-encrusted trident he had found on the ocean's floor, "Oh, this? This is what I used to kill the fish, but I calculated that, since most of you have weapons, I would keep it as a weapon of my own."

"Do you mind if I take a look at it?"

"Not at all, go ahead." Handing the trident to Isaac, R-3N3 shook the last few drops of water from his armor and re-attached his feet.

Isaac examined the golden barbs which were no longer covered in coral. As he inspected them, his expression became more serious. Robin noticed and asked, "What is it, Isaac?"

"I don't think this is any ordinary trident." Grasping the long handle, Isaac wound up and struck the golden tips against the stone staircase. A pure tone, loud and clear, rang out from the trident. As he tried to hold on to the weapon, cracks started appearing on the coral and soon the entirety of the aquatic coverage had crumbled from the trident and lay in pieces on the ground. Isaac now held a beautifully crafted weapon, its blue-lacquered handle holding a silvery-golden head. Now that the coral was gone, the trident appeared to be almost brand new.

Examining the head one last time, Isaac nodded and gave the trident back to R-3N3, "Here you go Artie. Good as new."

"What did you do, Isaac?"

"As I had suspected, this is the trident of Psi the Sensitive. The small number opposite the side with the ψ mark on it confirms it. The number '93' is the distinguishing number of that member of The Triumvirate."

"Good work, Artie. I'm sure Albert will be glad to know we found what he was looking for." Sucari slapped R-3N3 on the back, which caused both the trident and R-3N3's armor to resonate.

"I am also sure this will come as great news, but I can't figure out why Psi's Trident was near the same location as the Seawave orb. This is almost too coincidental," Isaac mused.

Sucari was thoughtful for a moment, "But what about the pitchfork Benjamin held when we met up outside Topal? If this is Psi's Trident, wouldn't that have been Chi's Pitchfork? Remember that the Hellfire orb was located in the same area as well, right?"

Isaac nodded as he saw the logical connection, "The Imaginary World weapons must somehow be linked to their owners. Even when they're dead, the remaining vestiges of their power must have guided their weapons back to them, like a lost dog returning home."

R-3N3 was now a little concerned, "Does this mean I do not get to keep the trident?"

Isaac smiled, "You can keep it for the time being, but I wouldn't get too attached to it. I think Albert has bigger plans in store for that weapon."

"Understood. I guess I will keep it safe for now," R-3N3 relented in a bittersweet tone.

Robin spoke up, "Now that we're all here, should we get going?"

"Yes, we should," Isaac replied as he pulled the Q-Portal key from his pocket. Glimpsing at his comrades, he asked, "Do we have everything? I don't know if we'll be able to come back here any time soon." When everyone had looked around and made sure they were ready to go, Isaac inserted the white key into the keyhole which was created less than a day ago. When the door opened, its black mouth inviting them to enter, the team crossed the threshold and disappeared from the coastline.

The distance to Old Non was considerably further than Benjamin's lightning could travel in one leap. After a few attempts at extending the lightning's distance, he decided to take to the skies. Shooting upward into the smoky cloud, Benjamin took Albert and himself quickly over the city. When they reappeared, high above the burning capital of the 4th Kingdom, they could see the extent of the fire's coverage.

Much of the city was engulfed in flames, the glowing ash of people's homes floating into the sky. The few buildings made of non-flammable materials were illuminated from the inside, the fire burning their interiors like a twisted oven. Most of the townsfolk were out in the streets, trying in vain to put out the monstrous fire. A dedicated team was at the river which ran through the middle of the city, preventing the fire from advancing any farther south.

Now in the thick of the smoke, both Benjamin and Albert cupped their hands over their mouths and tried to not cough too hard. Unfortunately, as they began to fall, Albert reminded Benjamin that he was the only one who could successfully use the lightning power right now. Grabbing at Benjamin's hand with the only hand he had left, Albert yelled, "I hope you have a plan on getting us down from here, because I do not do so well with landings from this height!"

While Benjamin could control his lightning power in wide open spaces rather well, in the city he had trouble gauging where the closest metal that might conduct him would be. As such, when he turned into lightning, both Albert and Benjamin ended up standing at the top of a glass dome which sported a tall metal spire affixed to its peak. If the sudden release of electrical energy wasn't enough for the roof, the weight of two men certainly was. Spidery white lines spread across the dome as cracking sounds were heard underneath their feet.

When the dome broke way underneath them, they fell for a few feet before Benjamin sprouted his wings and grabbed onto Albert's hand, tighter than before, slowly allowing them both to land safely on the ornate marble floor now covered with shards of glass and metal. As Albert let out a sigh of relief, he soon found himself back-to-back with Benjamin due to the fact that a ring of twenty guards were now thrusting the pointed edges of their long-handled axes at two intruders to the throne room of the 4th Kingdom.

"What's going on here?" a commanding voice came from the front of the room as a man who appeared to be the King stood from his golden throne. The man had a full beard and wore a somewhat familiar crown on his head. However, aside from the four points on the crown which distinguished his position as the ruler of the 4th Kingdom, the headpiece was also a mask which covered his eyes and the top part of his nose. The uniform gold piece was as stately as it was mysterious.

"It's a little hard to explain, my brother, but it seems that a one-armed man and an angel have intruded upon our courtroom from the glass dome above us." Looking over to where the recognizable voice originated, Albert and Benjamin were slightly shocked to see a familiar face, albeit just a bit younger than they had remembered it. It was Reuel. He still wore rings on his fingers, but had three green ones on his right and three yellow ones on his left, as compared to one on each hand when they had first met him. And while his clothes were still somewhat loose, his hat was certainly stiffer and pointier than the one he wore in the desert.

"Well, we don't have time to deal with this right now, when we're presently facing the destruction of the entire city."

Albert smiled as he addressed Reuel, "He is too satisfied with the present to dwell on the future."

The King was furious now, "What's *that* supposed to mean?"

Reuel answered, "I am unsure, brother." Turning to Albert he asked, "Why do you taunt King Solepochs like that?"

"I must apologize, Reuel, but this whole situation reminded me of an inside joke I heard once upon a time."

Reuel was confused, but also concerned, "My name is not Reuel, it is Ronald, and now is not the time for jokes."

A loud roar from outside caused everyone to shudder in fear. Benjamin blurted out, "What was that?"

The back doors of the courtroom burst open and a young, handsome man ran into the room. He climbed to the stage where the four thrones were positioned and sat down on the silver chair which was set at the right side of the row, adjacent to the golden throne of the King. Finally catching his breath, the young man gave his report, "It has just taken the cathedral. I rode over here as fast as I could." With his report given, he at last had the chance to examine the scene in front of him. Observing two strange men standing on the shattered remains of the glass skylight, he asked, "Who are these people?"

"We were just about to find out, Prince Clive," Ronald responded.

Albert took the lead, pushing aside the guards' weapons as he approached the thrones, "You may call me the Keymaster, your majesties. As for my friend, he is known as Lambda the Just." When Albert turned to look back at Benjamin, he saw that the Imaginary World mark on his forehead was showing, which he communicated when they made eye contact.

Benjamin already knew that his mark was showing. Of the six people who had made it through the i-World, he had already met five of them. Having seen the images of his three predecessors memorialized in stained glass at the end of his journey through the strange dimension, when Prince Clive entered the room, he immediately recognized the visage of Breve the Lion. His round face and large eyes were a dead giveaway, but when Benjamin locked eyes with Prince Clive, he returned the gaze with a curious and knowing stare.

Continuing on, Albert elaborated, "It is our understanding that Old Non is burning to the ground as we speak."

On the opposite side of the podium, in a chair made of bronze, sat a young woman who wore a tiara and corrected Albert, "I don't know why you call it Old Non. This town is only known as Non."

Ronald was quick to chide her, "Please, don't interrupt, Princess Prohere."

Wanting to remain on the good side of the Princess, who was now pouting, Albert explained, "I must apologize, *fräulein*, but the time that I come from refers to this town as Old Non. I will try to remember that it has not gained that distinction yet." The Princess looked confused at this explanation, especially since the stranger referred to a different time, and not a different place.

King Solepochs was becoming more irate with each passing second, "Get to the point, Keymaster!"

"My point is that Lambda and I are here to help. In fact, if you would allow us to take charge, we can solve this problem in no time."

"So be it. What do you need? It has been three days and we cannot control this beast of a fire. At this juncture I am willing to try anything to save my Kingdom. Just keep in mind that if you fail us, your lives are forfeited."

"Understood, your highness. For right now all we need is the assistance of Ronald and Prince Clive."

Turning to his son, the King ordered, "Follow these men and do what they ask. They already sound pretty strange to me, so I have some hope that they've got some tricks up their sleeves."

Benjamin couldn't help but smirk as he glanced toward Albert and mouthed, ". . . or sleeve." Albert glared back at his Millennial partner, indicating that now was not the time or the place to be making jokes, since he had already been chastised for his humorous remarks in the courtroom moments before.

With a slight bow, Prince Clive answered, "I will do as you say, father." Heading back to the door he entered from, Prince Clive motioned for the two intruders and Ronald to join him, "Let's go guys."

As they were leaving, Benjamin pulled Albert aside, "Why are we using our other names, and furthermore, why is Reuel here?"

"As was the case in the desert, *Lambda*, history can sometimes be inadvertently changed by those who do not understand it. We must remain anonymous if we do not want to change the events of the past and become part of the history books ourselves. As for Reuel, I believe this is where he first met us, considering our last encounter with him was the first time *we* met him."

"So, what's our plan, if you don't mind me asking?"

"I suspect that the reason the town is on fire is because one of the Caidoz statues has come to life."

"Which one?"

"The lion. The 4th Kingdom is on an island, which matches with the couplet, 'The lion's red mouth opens and roars / Protecting the island and its shores.' Plus, have you ever given a thought as to where the Brotherhood of the Scarlet Lion came from?"

"Is this the event that founds it?"

"I believe so. Plus, I have a sneaking suspicion that Prince Clive may have gone through the Imaginary World, since your mark did not show itself until he arrived."

"I agree. I recognized him almost immediately from when I went through the i-World myself and the PHN-6 showed me those who passed through before me. Although, he was looking at me pretty intently in there. I think he knows I've been through it too, even though I accomplished it many years from now."

"Are you guys coming or not?" Prince Clive was heard beyond the open door, shouting to the two Millennials. When Albert and Benjamin left the courtroom, they could see Prince Clive had already mounted his horse, which was well behaved, under the circumstances.

Albert was giving orders now, relying on his limited memory of the event from what he had read in the history books, "Prince Clive, I need you to gather up as many riders as you can and meet us at the largest bridge in town. However, before you meet us, please tell all the citizens to make their way to the bank of the river." With a nod, Prince Clive was off and riding to accomplish his task.

Now that Prince Clive was gone, Ronald asked, "Why did you call me Reuel back there? You both seem to know me, but I haven't met you before in my life."

"We will explain when we are all done, but what we need from you is an explanation of the rings you wear."

"Ah, I see you noticed these. The people around here seem to think I can do magic with them, and they're only partially correct, I suppose. Are you interested in my magic?"

"Well, more accurately, we noticed that you have more of them. When we saw you last, you only had one on each finger. I would assume by the fact that you are not much younger than your future self, you use these rings to transport through time."

Ronald was a little hesitant, but eventually relented, "That's right. I have used these rings to transport myself to this time period. I used to be known as John, but that was one hundred years ago," Ronald was nostalgic for a moment, but quickly snapped out of it, "That's a story for another time, though."

Stroking his moustache thoughtfully, Albert wanted to be sure, "So they *do* transport you through time, correct?"

"I have only used these rings twice, and once was to travel through time. However, I was told they can transport through space as well."

Benjamin leaned over to Albert and whispered, "They seem to be like the Q-Portals you can control."

Albert whispered back, "Agreed, but without the need for a keyhole." Addressing Ronald, Albert asked, "Could you transport a large number of people?"

"I think so, but they could only go a short distance if it's a lot of them."

"That should be fine. I only have one more question: what is this country's largest boat?"

"That would be the *Twilight Runner*, although it's more of a barge, since it doesn't have any sails."

"*Wunderbar*. Where is that boat right now?"

"Actually, it's in port on the river."

"*Wunderbar*. Right now we just need you to go to where it is docked and bring it to the bridge."

"That might be a bit difficult, but I will do my best." Ronald hurried away, leaving Benjamin and Albert to themselves in the middle of the burning city, the cacophonous bell still continually sounding its alarm. Another roar rose above the sounds around them, somewhat confirming the existence of the Caidoz statue.

Albert now turned to Benjamin and said, "We need to lure the lion to the bridge and drop it in the river. If I remember my research correctly, this Caidoz statue's Element is Fire. But first, we must *find* the lion."

"Does that mean Water is the Fire Element's weakness?"

"Not quite, but you are catching on quickly. Now, take to the skies and see if you can spot the lion from up there."

Sprouting his eagle wings, Benjamin took to the sky and began flying in circles, taking advantage of the fire's updraft. As he surveyed the burning town, he saw what appeared to be a fire that slowly moved along the cobblestone streets. Diving down to get a closer look, he confirmed it was the lion. But what a sight it was. The statue was enormous and almost completely white. Its mane was made up of a deep red fire that billowed as it prowled down one of the main streets.

Landing back next to Albert, Benjamin saw the Keymaster had already attached the C.L.A.W. to his left side. With an apprehensive smile, Albert nervously spoke, "I have never operated this when the sun is not out, but I hope the light of these fires will be sufficient."

"I hope so too. Come on, I've found the lion." Grabbing Albert's right hand, Benjamin led the way through the streets and alleys. Finally, they both turned a corner, and there stood the lion. Its heat was almost as unbearable as the lime-green gaze of its Peridot eyes. Its Sardonyx claws clicked against the stone street as it slowly stalked toward the two men.

From behind them came a loud and commanding voice, "That's enough, Leo!" At the command, the lion stopped and laid down. Benjamin and Albert slowly turned around to see who could stop such a monstrous beast with only their voice.

○

When Isaac's group emerged from the Q-Portal, they found themselves in a very familiar valley. At least it was familiar to half of them. Sucari turned his face toward Isaac, eyes wide open in surprise, "This is just too weird."

"I remember part of the lyrics referring to an Asp, but I couldn't have ever thought it meant *that* Asp!" was Isaac's reply.

R-3N3 and Robin were confused. Speaking for those out of the loop, R-3N3 asked, "Am I to ascertain that you have both been here before?"

Sucari answered, "Yeah, this is the Pythagorean Triangle. This is where we met Vlad."

Glancing upward to the mountain in front of them, R-3N3 examined the snake-head-like peak and wavy ridge and came to his own conclusion, "I suppose it does look like an Asp."

Sucari asked Isaac, "Do you want to look for Vlad? I'm not sure, but I think he might have headed back here."

"He was a native of the area, so I'm sure he'd be of great help. At the very least, we can head into the village down the valley and ask around for information."

As Isaac guided the group down the valley toward the quaint mountain village, they passed by a familiar cottage with a stone wall around its inner yard. An old, somewhat disfigured man was just leaving his house when he happened to see the travelers passing by. He froze. The color drained from his face as he pointed at the group while they passed. Sucari saw the man and waved, "Hi, Posea! Nice to see you again!" As if he had seen a ghost, the man immediately fainted, passing out in his front yard.

Isaac chuckled, "Well, he's no fun . . . he fell right over!"

Robin held Sucari's hand as they strode side-by-side down the mountain path, "Who was that, Sucari?"

"That was Posea. He was the first person we met when we arrived in the valley."

"That's funny, I don't remember you ever mentioning that."

"I thought I did."

Playfully jabbing her husband in the ribs, Robin asked, "What else are you keeping from me, Sucari?"

With a quick peck on the cheek, Sucari answered, "If I knew the answer to that, I'd tell you."

R-3N3 had a similar question which he asked Isaac, "How did you know that man, Isaac?"

"Sucari, Erwin, and I met Posea when we took the Q-Portal from Sucari's home in the Holy Cliffs and ended up here. He's the one who got us oriented."

"Why do you think he fainted?"

"He probably thinks we're dead."

"Intriguing. Please explain."

"Well, when we used a Q-Portal to get to Pandora Prison, we just barely escaped an erupting volcano."

"I see. I doubt anyone could survive that, so I understand why he has gone into shock." The two travelers hiked on in silence for a bit longer, when Isaac let out a short laugh, "What is it, Isaac?"

"I can't believe I didn't realize this was the location of one of the Caidoz statues. It seems so obvious now. 'The ram grazes in the valley's grass / Avoiding the bite of the deadly asp.' I knew the legend of the Pythagorean Triangle, and I knew that these valleys were filled with sheep, so why I didn't make the connection until now is beyond me."

"Well, we have not found it yet," R-3N3 remarked.

Isaac laughed, "I suppose you're right. No sense in beating myself up for it just yet."

Sucari and Robin had been walking behind the other two when Robin noticed something different about Isaac. She ran forward and tapped him on the shoulder, "Is it me, or is your hair getting darker?"

Pulling a strand from his head, Isaac examined it. Indeed, his hair was starting to lose the white sheen that once reminded him of an experiment gone horribly wrong, "It certainly looks that way, Robin."

"I've heard of people's hair going white before, but never the opposite."

"I think this may have to do with a few factors, including the destruction of the Caidoz statues. It's also probably a side effect of my Soul-fusion fluxion being used up."

"Well, whatever it is, it looks good on you."

"Thanks, Robin."

By now, the group had reached the small mountain village at the bottom of the valley. The buildings were mostly made of stone, as was the street. What little wood that was available was used for doors and windows, but also for decoration on some of the fancier houses. The village bustled with activity as people went about their day. Occasionally, everyone had to move to the side of the road as a flock of sheep was herded through the streets.

Sucari asked Isaac, "You're the leader, so how do we find Vlad?"

"The same way I find information: a bar."

Robin stepped in, "Isn't it a little early to be drinking? I don't want a drunk uncle on my hands today."

"It is, but I don't go there for the alcohol. People have a poor understanding of what they divulge when they're drinking, and the one person who is *not* drinking at a bar is the bartender. If there's any information that will be useful to us, he would know." Quickly glancing around the village, he found the only bar in town, as indicated by the wooden sign depicting a full glass of beer hanging outside the door, "Excellent! There's a bar right here."

Leading the group inside the establishment, it seemed that Robin was right: the place was deserted. Chairs were upended on tables and no one was at the bar. However, upon hearing the entrance of the travelers, the bartender came out of the back, wiping his hands on his apron, "A little early to be drinking, don't you think?" he asked.

Robin gave Isaac a look as if to say "I told you so," at which Isaac just smiled and rolled his eyes. Approaching the bar, he began conversing with the bartender, "Agreed. We're just here to see if you have any information."

"I have lots of information, what do you want to know?"

"First of all, while some of us have been here before, we weren't here for long. You wouldn't happen to know anything about a large statue that looks like a ram, would you?"

"I haven't heard anything about a statue, but I have heard legends of a large ram roaming in the vicinity of Aries Pasture on the other side of Asp Peak."

"Were there any distinguishing features in the legend about the ram?"

"Not really, other than its size. It had white wool and black horns. Some renditions of the legend say its wool is either made with Diamonds or has Diamonds in it, because it seems to shimmer. No one's ever been able to confirm it, though, despite the best efforts of treasure hunters who occasionally come here looking for it."

"Very well, thanks." As Isaac turned to go, he remembered that he had another question, "Oh, one more thing."

"What?"

"Do you perchance know if a man by the name of Vlad lives in the area?"

The bartender's face scrunched up in a look of partial disgust, "I can't say I've seen him around here in a long time."

"Very well, thanks again." The bartender nodded and returned to the back room.

Isaac led the group from the bar and was about to make his way outside when he heard a voice, barely audible, from a booth near the door, "So you want to know where Vlad is, do you?"

This caused Isaac to stop in his tracks, half-way out the door, as he peered toward the darkened corner of the room. He squinted his eyes to try and see who was there, "Yes, he's a friend of ours. We want to find him so we can have him join us on a quest."

The voice was a bit louder now, and something about it seemed familiar, "The name of Vlad has not been heard in these parts in over six months." Finishing his drink with one final gulp and slamming the glass down onto the table, the man continued with a smile that showed his extended canine teeth, "But I haven't been one to draw attention to myself."

"Vlad? Is that you?" Isaac's voice was high with excitement.

"Around here, never. I'm merely a nameless man who stays up too late and drinks too early."

"So you're an alcoholic now?"

"By no means, but when my days are opposite everyone else's, it makes it seem that way. This is a nightcap for me, nothing more."

Everyone came over to the booth and sat down around it. They were smiling at the re-acquaintance of an old friend. "So, Mr. Nameless Man, are you up for an adventure?"

"I overheard your conversation earlier. Sounds alluring, especially the part about the Diamonds, but what's the catch?"

Isaac pulled out Albert's scroll and gave a brief explanation of the Caidoz statues, "We could really use as much help as we can get out there, since the song is somewhat cryptic. I figure that, if you're from this area, you'd be the best person to help us out."

"You know I'm always looking for a fight, and I haven't had a good adventure since I came back here a few months ago." Tossing a few coins on the table, Vlad pulled the hood of his cloak up over his head and slid out of the booth, "I guess this will just have to be a long night for me." With those words, Vlad exited the bar with the rest of the group in tow.

There, standing amidst the burning buildings of Non, was a man with grey complexion who stood about seven feet tall. His chiseled physique was somewhat intimidating, considering his above average size. His eyes seemed somewhat vacant, but were commanding. Albert was mainly impressed with the man's ability to control one of the Caidoz statues, "Who might you be?" he asked.

"Me? I am Ophiuchus."

"How on earth did you get the lion to stop?"

"That's easy. I set him loose."

Benjamin was immediately up in arms about this revelation, "What do you mean? Why would you do that?"

"I mean that I was getting bored and I wanted to spice things up a bit."

Albert was still concerned on the specifics, "But how? How can you command the statue like that?"

"Again, that's easy. I created them. Or, more accurately, had them created."

Albert's eyes grew wide as he recalled the last verse of the poem. This was bad. He hadn't calculated for the creator to be around, but having traveled back to a time before any of the statues were destroyed, he now realized this was indeed a possibility. "So, you can bring these statues to life?" Albert thought back to the crab statue which took his left arm and wondered how many other statues Ophiuchus had given life.

"I suppose that's the correct term for it, yes."

"But why would you have these statues created at all?"

"You know, I don't really have time for your questions right now. Just know that I created them so I could induce human suffering, and I'm actually a bit late to do just that."

As Ophiuchus turned to leave, Benjamin blocked his path in a flash of lightning, "Where do you think you're going?"

"If I know your plan correctly, you're about to get everyone in town onto a boat, and I mean to destroy that boat." Ophiuchus spoke with a calmness and monotony which came across as incredibly eerie. Albert was concerned. How did this man know of their plans, when they were just made mere minutes ago? Ophiuchus snapped his fingers and commanded, "Leo, you may play with these men. I've got a boat to catch." Pushing Benjamin down, Ophiuchus started running toward the river as the lion got up and roared.

Getting back on his feet, Benjamin watched Albert as the Keymaster started backing away from the giant, hunting feline, "What do we do? We need to stop him!"

"Then go after him! I am the only one with a weapon that even has a chance against this statue. I will lure the lion to the bridge, you take care of Ophiuchus!"

Glancing at Albert, then at the white lion covered in fire, Benjamin asked, "Are you sure you'll be fine?"

"*Just go!*" As Benjamin left, Albert knew why he was concerned. After all, scientists didn't necessarily do well in battle situations. But when it came to it, Benjamin was the only one who had a chance against someone like Ophiuchus. Albert knew that he just had to survive long enough to get the lion into the river. Listening to the humming C.L.A.W. on his left side, Albert was hoping that luck was also on his side.

Once Benjamin started running toward the bridge with his lightning powers enhancing his muscle movements, he realized that, in the maze-like city of Non, the time he spent talking to Albert was foolish. Ophiuchus could be anywhere by now, having turned off to a blind alley or ducked away down a side street. But catching him wasn't necessarily the solution, even if he did feel his powers were enhanced in this time period. No, the endgame was to prevent him from destroying the *Twilight Runner*. With that in mind, Benjamin continued to run toward the river.

When he got close, Benjamin saw someone on the corner of a street. They appeared to be looking for someone else. It was Ronald. Since Benjamin was running so quickly, Ronald just barely had enough time to notice him and shout after the Natural. Benjamin was moving so fast that the only way he could stop was to turn into lightning, suddenly appearing in front of Ronald with a loud boom.

This surprised Ronald, who fell down on the ground in shock. Benjamin helped him up, but was still in a great hurry, "What is it Ronald? I'm kind of busy at the moment."

"The *Twilight Runner* is at the bridge. Though, not everyone in town is at the river's edge yet."

"That doesn't matter right now! We've got more pressing things to worry about!" Benjamin was already running toward the bridge, hoping he could cut Ophiuchus off before the boat was damaged.

Ronald was still dumbfounded as he scrutinized the rings on his fingers, "And I thought *I* was a magician . . ."

Even though his muscles were enhanced by his electricity, Benjamin's lungs were not. They burned with a desperate need for Oxygen as he ran at full speed toward the river. When he turned a final corner, the bridge became visible, along with the river it crossed. There, almost touching the suspension bridge, was the *Twilight Runner*, although nothing on its simple wooden exterior would lead one to identify it as such.

The sight of the boat gave Benjamin a moment to pause as his mind began grinding away at what he saw. Breathing heavily, he stood near the entrance of the bridge and stared at the boat. Where had he seen it before? He knew it looked incredibly familiar, but from where? Was it just a similarly styled boat, or was he seeing things?

"So nice of you to join me, young sir!" A voice shouted out from the boat. It was Ophiuchus. He stood on the deck of the vessel, pacing back and forth. Benjamin's mind was really reeling now. Pushing his glasses back onto his face from the edge of his nose, Benjamin made sure he was actually seeing Ophiuchus on the boat.

After a second observation, he was sure of it. And yet, how could he have gotten here first? There was no way he could have moved that fast. Again, Ophiuchus shouted out to Benjamin, "I must apologize, but I don't know either of your names." Another roar from the lion echoed throughout the town, "But it sounds like I might just have to learn only *your* name, as Leo has probably taken care of your friend already."

Benjamin was goaded on by Ophiuchus' words, but more so by the chance to fight. His battle with Tecumseh at the end of Amedeo's War was tragically cut short, so he still wanted to try the few tricks up his sleeve he hadn't gotten a chance to exhibit earlier. Plus, with his powers at their ultimate peak, he was ready to see what he could do, "The name is Lambda. Lambda the Just."

"Well, Mr. Just . . . or is it Mr. Lambda? Whatever. I am assuming you are here to stop me from destroying this boat. And just how do you plan on stopping me?"

Clasping his hands together, Benjamin focused electrical energy into his palms. The Skybolt orb began to glow, its light illuminating Benjamin in the darkness of the night, tinged by the dull glow of the fire raging behind him. He closed his eyes as he tried to remember how to perform the attack he wanted. The energy between his hands began to crackle, waiting to be let out. Opening his hands a little to inspect the progress, he saw that the palms of both his hands were covered in what looked like blue fire.

In his training with Thomas at Menlo Castle, Benjamin knew that the Fire of Saint Erasmus was the base for one of his most powerful attacks. Of course, the Fire of Saint Erasmus wasn't fire, it was actually electricity. As he stared at his hands, he knew that the attack was finally ready, "How am I stopping you? I'll *show* you how I'm stopping you."

Ophiuchus knelt down and put his palm on the deck of the boat, positioning himself to dodge whatever Benjamin threw at him. With the townspeople starting to congregate around the bridge, Benjamin didn't have time to draw this battle out. He knew he needed to end this in one strike. Gritting his teeth and pouring all his power into his hands he yelled at the top of his lungs, "*Blue Jet!*" Pounding his wrists together and extending both palms out toward Ophiuchus, Benjamin let his attack fly. With all the speed of his other lightning attacks, a brilliant burst of what looked like blue fire erupted forth from Benjamin's palms.

That's when the strangest thing happened. Ophiuchus didn't dodge. He just knelt there and took the attack. Ophiuchus and the *Twilight Runner* emitted a blinding, white light for a brief moment and vanished. With the boat no longer displacing a large amount of water in the river, the remaining liquid poured into the empty space, causing the whole river to become agitated with waves.

"What the heck just happened?" It was Prince Clive. He had just arrived at the bridge with a posse of about twenty men on horseback. Benjamin still stood there, palms outward and sparking from his recent attack. He wasn't quite sure what he saw either. He had an inkling of what had happened, but absolutely no way of knowing how it could have occurred.

Ronald came running up and yelled, "I thought the boat was meant to save the people, so why did you make it disappear?"

"I didn't mean to do it; I was trying to defeat the man who was attempting to destroy it!"

"Well, a lot of good that did us. How are we going to save these people?" Ronald was soon joined by curious townsfolk who were also trying to contemplate what they just saw. A roar came from a block away, which caused most of the people to escape in panic.

Turning a corner and running toward the bridge, Albert saw that everyone was there as he shouted, "Where's the boat?"

"It's a long story!" Benjamin shouted back.

"Well, whatever, we do not have time to worry about that now. We need to work on defeating the lion." Almost as if on cue, the Caidoz statue pounced through a building, bursting it into shrapnel of stone, wood, and glowing ash. Once again, it roared and everyone knew they needed to act quickly.

○

If there was one thing Isaac did not like to do, it was backtracking. Unfortunately, the best way to get to Aries Pasture was to go back through Posea Pasture. Unfortunately, this meant that the group had to climb up to the ridge separating the two valleys. Unfortunately, even once they arrived at Aries Pasture, there was no guarantee that they'd know the location of the Caidoz statue.

Fortunately, Vlad took this time to get briefed on the Caidoz statues and why they had to be destroyed. As Vlad read through the scroll with the song lyrics describing the statues, he had a few questions for Isaac, "I would assume that, in order to destroy the statues, an opposing Element must first be applied, correct?"

"Correct."

"And right now the only weapon we have which can destroy these statues is your broadsword?"

"Correct."

Sighing through the metal visor which had fallen over his mouth, Vlad had to laugh just a little bit, "I know we've been in hopeless situations before, but this is ridiculous."

"What can I say? I like to be thorough."

Vlad laughed again, his metallic voice echoing off the mountains. Soon, he became serious again as he asked, "But the Elements are only part of the Caidoz statue's attributes, right? The poem clearly states that they have Qualities as well. Did Albert give any clues as to what these Qualities are? Is there any way we can use the Qualities to our advantage?"

"Those are some good questions, Vlad. I only picked up on the Elemental weakness from the chart he drew on the back. I don't know what the Qualities do exactly, just that there are three: Cardinal, Fixed, and Mutable. I've only seen one other statue, and that was the water bearer, which was Fixed. I'd assume from that statue that maybe the Quality has to do with a fixed sphere of influence since, when it was functioning, it held a bubble of air around itself. Either that, or they stay in one place, I'm not really sure."

"What is the Quality of the statue we're trying to find?"

Handing the scroll back to Isaac, Vlad waited for him to decipher its contents, "It seems that the ram is of the Cardinal Quality." Isaac kept reading, trying to find more information, but to no avail, "That's a bit vague, so I'll probably have to ask Albert when he gets back."

"When do you think he's coming back?"

"Beats me, but I hope it's soon, since he only gave us one Q-Portal key and not nearly enough information to find the rest of the statues." Pointing to the four crossed out couplets on the parchment, he continued, "It looks like four of these have been destroyed, we've destroyed one and we're on track to destroy another . . . but that still leaves six statues."

"Assuming that other statues aren't hidden in the rest of the lyrics, that is."

Isaac sighed, "Yes, that's a possibility too."

The group was nearing the ridge between the two valleys when R-3N3 picked up his pace so he could ask Vlad a question, "Vlad, what brought you back here? We lost contact with you pretty quickly. As a result, we could not bring you with us on our first statue destroying adventure."

"It's funny you should ask, because I came back to search for the very statue we're looking to destroy."

"That is incredible!"

"Well, first I wanted to come back to see the damage Sievuvus did inside the Pythagorean Triangle, and to visit home for a change. But when I remembered the legend of the Diamond ram, I figured I'd give it a shot. You know, try and restore some pride in the name of the Order of the Dragon."

"That is very noble of you."

"Well, I'm the last of the Order, so technically any riches I found would all go to me."

"Never mind."

"Hey, nice weapon by the way. Where'd you get that trident?"

"At the bottom of the ocean."

"Now that, my friend, is incredible. I guess I missed out by not staying in touch."

Robin overheard the conversation and chimed in, "You and Isaac, both." As everyone but Vlad laughed, he merely sighed and shook his head, unaware of the inside joke.

As the group crested the ridge, they could see the valley below, a very similar sight to the one they just came from, but with one big exception: burn marks. Sure, the grass was green and the pasture was littered with glacial erratics, but every so often one would come across a patch of burnt grass, almost like lightning had struck and a small fire was started and quickly went out.

Vlad spoke up, "Those burn marks in the valley are the trademark of the Diamond ram. Some say that its Diamond wool focuses the light of the sun to a point that starts the fires, but again, I have yet to see the ram to know if that's true or not."

Sucari seemed concerned, and he whispered to Isaac, "If that is or is not true, wouldn't that mean the ram can move around? I thought these statues stayed in little temples similar to the water bearer's."

"I'm starting to wonder that myself, but we've experienced random teleportation before with the Q-Portals, so it's not entirely out of the realm of possibilities."

"True, but this worries me."

"Don't worry, we'll figure it out. After all-"

"A new patch!" Vlad interrupted Sucari and Isaac's clandestine conversation when he pointed to a spot down the valley which sported one of the burned marks of the Diamond ram. Running down the valley, Vlad was overly excited at the new circle of burnt grass. Everyone tried to keep up with him, but it was difficult, since he was already acclimated to the altitude. When they arrived at the site, everyone stood in the grass at the edge of the burnt circle.

It was new all right. In fact, it was fresh. The ground was still smoldering as the patch gave off a terrible smell. Vlad had knelt down and examined the area. He muttered to himself, "It's got to be close. I've never been this close before." Standing up and gazing down the valley, he spotted something that caught his attention, "There!" he pointed.

Before anyone else could look, Vlad had gained a running start and leaped into the air, transforming his arms into bat wings and quickly flitting down the valley. Everyone else took their descent more casually as they tried to figure out what had gotten Vlad so excited. There, at the base of the valley, was the tail end of a flock of sheep, its last stragglers just visible as the rest of the flock had turned past the base of Boa Peak, the next mountain of the Pythagorean Triangle.

Soon, the travelers were letting gravity pull them down the valley as their pace increased. Vlad had just disappeared around the bend when everyone finally caught up to the flock of sheep, quietly grazing on the valley's grass. Robin knelt down and petted one of the lambs while Sucari watched. R-3N3 was still somewhat confused, "What does a flock of sheep have to do with Vlad getting so excited?"

Isaac answered with the best answer he had, "I'm not sure, but he's the native. Maybe he knows something we don't."

A moment later, they could hear Vlad shouting again, and soon he appeared, running toward them, up the valley. As he approached, Isaac yelled, "What's the matter?!"

"I've found it!" Vlad's voice was not excited, but instead very worried.

"That's great, but what's the matter?"

"Do we know what Element defeats it?"

"I'd have to check, but why?" Isaac got his answer as a ram, seven feet tall, turned the corner and began charging toward the group.

○

Albert saw Prince Clive had gathered some riders so, as he ran from the fiery lion, he started pulling keys off of his vest. Benjamin saw the lion was quickly catching up to Albert, so he decided to step in. Grabbing his weapon, already in its original sledgehammer form, he took a fighting stance a few steps from the group, waiting for the lion to pounce. The large cat stopped advancing and crouched down on its forepaws, its tail swishing, flinging glowing embers into the sky.

It was a sudden movement, but Benjamin was ready for it. The lion leapt forward, its Sardonyx claws ready to tear apart anyone who got in its way. Using his electrically enhanced response time, Benjamin ducked underneath the large cat and switched to attack mode. With his electrically enhanced muscle strength, Benjamin swung his sledgehammer upward, catching the lion by the jaw and sending it several blocks backward.

Prince Clive and the horsemen were astonished at the display Benjamin just put on, but when Albert whistled to get their attention, they looked down at a fist full of black keys. "All right, men! These keys are to be handled with extreme care. Please go along the river and find some walls which are facing the city. We are going to take this fire out in one shot."

As the men received the keys, each one creating high pitched clinks as they were handed out, Prince Clive asked, "What do you want them to do with these keys? What doors do they open?"

"There is no time to explain, but just find a blank wall, push the key in and turn. Simple as that. I have seen this done once before, so it is bound to work again." The lion roared once more, but this time a pillar of fire could be seen in the distance. "Now go! If we do not hurry, the town might be completely destroyed!" The horses whinnied as their riders headed out to execute Albert's plan.

With only Ronald left, Albert gave his last order, "Ronald! Where is the gunpowder kept for your armory?"

"Underneath us, at the base of the bridge."

Benjamin seemed shocked, "That doesn't seem like a smart place to put it."

"Ah, but it is. There are fail-safes which prevent fire from getting into the room and, as a final safeguard, the entire room can be flooded with water from the river."

Albert was smiling from ear-to-ear with a sinister grin, "Well, we are not going to have that water for much longer, and the gunpowder room's location is absolutely ideal."

"What do you mean, Keymaster?"

"Here is what I mean: blow up the bridge."

"What? That's insane! Do you know how much history that bridge has seen?"

"*Ja*, I do. I also know its future history and that is why we need to destroy it."

"You've gone mad. I refuse to do this."

Albert grabbed Ronald by the scruff of his shirt and was practically yelling in his face, "If you do *not* do this, the bridge will be destroyed anyway, along with the rest of the town! What will history say then, if not that we were unable to save Non from complete annihilation?"

This sudden outburst flustered Ronald, "But, but-"

"But nothing! The only way we can truly stop this fire is if we stop that lion!" As he spoke, the lion appeared again, clearly agitated, "And the only way we can do *that* is by blowing up the bridge!"

"Yes, sir!" Albert let go of Ronald as he ran to the gunpowder storage.

"I will give you the signal for when to blow the stash!" Albert yelled after him.

With no one else there but the two Millennials, Benjamin readied his weapon and stared straight at the angry lion as he spoke to Albert, "So, what's the plan on our end?"

"I need you to keep the lion busy on the bridge while Prince Clive's men drain the river."

"Drain the river? But I thought the Fire Element was weak against Water."

"I never said that, you came to that conclusion on your own. Furthermore, where is Ophiuchus? Did he get lost?"

"No, he beat me to the boat. I used one of my lightning attacks on him, but both he and the boat disappeared."

Albert faced Isaac with wide eyes, "What did you say?"

"They disappeared when I hit them with my most powerful lightning attack."

"Interesting. We will have to discuss this later." They were both slowly backing up as the lion approached, stalking its prey.

"So, I just need to be a decoy until we can blow the bridge, right?"

"Essentially, *ja*."

"All right, then. Let's go." Benjamin started running toward the middle of the bridge as Albert dove for cover near the entrance of the gunpowder store. The lion took the bait as it ran after Benjamin, clearly wanting revenge for the beating it took earlier. Fortunately, if there was one thing Benjamin was good at, it was dodging attacks.

Luring the beast further out onto the bridge, Benjamin waited for the lion to pounce again. When the Caidoz statue leapt at him, he turned to lightning and quickly made his way to a point behind the lion. He continued doing this for some time, and the lion kept turning around to find its agitator standing calmly behind it. With each leap, the heat of the lion's mane transferred into the thick metal cables holding the bridge aloft, causing them to glow red.

Benjamin almost got caught by the lion at one point when he heard a gurgling sound coming from the river beneath him. A hole had opened up and was draining the river. As he watched, more holes appeared, causing the waterline of the river to quickly drop. He also noticed a loud hissing sound was now heard across the town as a white wall of steam rose to the sky, mixing together with the smoke of the city which had succumbed to conflagration. Where *exactly* was Albert draining the river again?

Soon, the black holes that littered the riverbed had closed themselves, at which point Albert shouted down into the recesses beneath the bridge, "Ronald! Blow the bridge *now!*" A few moments later, Ronald came running up the stairs and Albert joined him in the escape from the doomed suspension structure.

With a deafening explosion, the towers holding up one side of the bridge were destroyed, causing the heated cables to stretch and eventually snap. As the bridge went down, the newly broken cables whipped through the air, hissing like snakes as they cooled, barely missing Benjamin on numerous occasions. Even though he knew it was coming, Benjamin was surprised by the collapse of the bridge as it threw him and the lion into the muddy riverbed below.

Albert ran up to the still burning edge of where the bridge once connected to the land and listened to the C.L.A.W. As the lion was rolling in the mud, trying to right itself, its fire was quickly going out. The pitch of the C.L.A.W. reached a crescendo, which caused Albert to slyly smile, "*Wunderbar*. Right on time." With a sudden release, Albert fired the concentrated beam of red light at the Caidoz statue, causing it to roar out in pain. The roar became softer as glowing red veins spread across its surface and the sculpture began to lose its sentient power.

Eventually, the lion's motion ceased altogether as it crumbled into the mud, sinking to the bottom of the murk and muck. Albert yelled down to Benjamin, "You may want to get back up here. The river is liable to return any minute now." Sure enough, with a wave of water from both ends, the river returned with a splash right at the site of the now downed bridge.

Ronald surveyed the city, now doused by the water of its own river, the fire completely out, "That is absolutely amazing. How did you do that, Keymaster?"

"Previous experience, my friend. Previous experience."

Prince Clive rode up on his horse, obviously soaked by the torrent of water that appeared when he opened one of the Q-Portals, "I'm not quite sure what just happened."

○

Immediately grabbing the scroll with the Elemental weaknesses detailed on it, Isaac found the answer, "It says that Fire's weakness is Earth!"

Vlad had almost reached the group when everyone started running away as well, "Earth? How in the world are we supposed to apply something like that? What does 'Earth' even mean?"

"I think it means dirt . . . or something similar," was Isaac's reply between breaths.

"Again, how are we supposed to apply something like that? We're in the mountains. Everything around us is rock!"

"Well, maybe we should stop the statue first, and figure out a solution later."

R-3N3 heard this and decided to take action. He stopped running and turned to face the charging beast. Vlad passed by R-3N3 and yelled behind him, "What are you doing?"

"I am going to try and stop it."

"Good luck!" was Vlad's reply as he continued running. After a day's worth of hiking through the mountains, everyone's exhaustion was really starting to set in. Even with the motivation of the ram charging behind them, some struggled to climb to the ridge between the Posea and Aries Pastures. Vlad was now out in front of the group and had arrived at the top of the ridge where he turned around and examined the scene below.

R-3N3 steadied himself, but the momentum of the ram was a bit too much for him to stop. With a clang, R-3N3's hands grabbed onto the black horns as he pushed back on the raging animal. Unfortunately, as the ram was much heavier, R-3N3 was slowly being pushed up the valley. The ram snorted in anger and short bursts of fire came from its nostrils. Leaning its head down, the ram lifted R-3N3 up off of the ground and continued charging headlong up the grassy valley.

As R-3N3 was dislodged from his position, Robin tripped and fell. In her distress, she called out, "Sucari!" Her husband was a few strides ahead of her, but when he heard her cry out, he turned around to see the ram bearing down on her, with R-3N3 barely holding on to its horns. Sucari knew he couldn't get there in time to stop Robin from being trampled if he didn't use his powers. In an instant, wings appeared on his back and his legs were engulfed in blue fire.

Unfortunately, Sucari wanted to call upon the highest level of power the fire would allow, so the decrease in output caused him to falter for a brief moment. Now it was going to be close. Pushing his limits, he thrust toward the soon-to-be accident, grabbing Robin just moments before the ram would have hit her. Flying a few yards above the ground, Sucari let out a deep breath as he sighed, "That was close."

Robin didn't respond, but instead buried her head in his chest as he watched the ram continue its upward climb, fiery hoofmarks burning the grass along the way, displaying its angry charge up the hillside. With a short buck, the ram threw R-3N3 to the side, where he tumbled down the hill for a short while before getting up and running after the fleeing statue.

Clouds were starting to quickly form above the group, as the weather often does in elevated areas. Vlad looked up and saw the conditions changing just as Isaac arrived at the ridge between the valleys, "I hope we get rain soon. It may not be Fire's weakness, but it might certainly help." Isaac was pulling out his swords and getting ready for battle. Vlad was surprised, "You're not thinking of fighting it, are you?"

"Do you have any better ideas?"

"Nope."

"Then shut up and let me think." Taking off the half-scabbard of Hikari Shichidai so that he could remove his jacket, Isaac gave Kuroni to Vlad, "Get this to Artie when he gets up here. He's the strongest among us."

"What are you going to do?"

"I'll distract it for a bit until Artie can make his way to the ridge. I'll use my coat to make myself look bigger."

"This is a ram we're talking about here, not a bull. And you aren't a matador."

"Don't you think I know that? Now get to Artie!"

Vlad took to the sky as the ram quickly approached Isaac, his jacket extended out as a makeshift cape. The entire group tensed up as the ram got within striking distance of Isaac. With a flourish, Isaac pulled the jacket back as the ram continued charging into the next valley. While everyone let out a sigh of relief, they couldn't see the statue quickly gaining its footing and turning around to charge at Isaac again.

Gliding along to R-3N3, who had almost made it to the top of the valley, Vlad gave him the black katana and explained, "Isaac wants you to use this when you get up there, so hurry!" R-3N3 nodded and quickened his pace toward the ridge. When he had almost reached the top, the ram had again charged right past Isaac and into the adjacent valley, almost hitting R-3N3 in the process.

When he arrived at the ridge next to Isaac, R-3N3 asked, "What do you want me to do?"

"I need you to try and stop the ram again, but this time use Kuroni and Psi's Trident to hold your ground. You'll only have a brief moment, but try to hook the weapons with the ram's horns. This will give me an opportunity to slash at the Caidoz statue with Hikari Shichidai."

"I hope you know what you are doing, Isaac."

"I hope so too, Artie."

Having been thwarted twice, the ram was beyond furious. It ran toward the top of the hill where R-3N3 was standing at the ready. Isaac descended a short distance into Posea Pasture with his sword prepared to strike. The air was starting to stir more rapidly and rumblings could be heard in the distance in anticipation of the event.

Once again, a clang was heard as the ram collided with R-3N3, but this time the momentum which pushed him down the valley was only from the gravity of travelling down from the ridge. Two large gashes appeared in the ground as the ram came to an eventual halt, just feet from where Isaac was standing, "Get out of the way, Artie!" As R-3N3 dove to the side, Isaac lifted Hikari Shichidai over his head and brought it down over the Caidoz statue. While the attack seemed to work, the ram continued to claw at the ground, eventually uprooting the two weapons holding it in place.

With a burst of fire, the ram collided with Isaac, causing him to lose hold of his broadsword, which clattered to the ground and slid down the grassy hill. As the ram continued forward, Isaac held onto the black horns for dear life. That's when the unexpected happened.

In an event that had been building for a few minutes, a sudden strike of lightning came from the sky. The bolt of electricity hit Isaac and the ram. For a brief moment, it seemed like there were three people holding onto the ram's horns before the entire lot disappeared into nothing. A few sparks of electricity jumped between the blades of grass, but this was all that remained of the sudden event.

Vlad, Sucari, and Robin had made it to the top of the ridge and saw that, on the other side, only R-3N3 remained. "What just happened?" was Sucari's question. "We saw lightning and heard the thunder, but where's the ram?" Noticing Hikari Shichidai on the ground, he continued, "And where's Isaac?"

R-3N3 just stood there, trying to process what he had seen, "I think that was Albert and Benjamin just now."

○

Morning had just broken on the recently extinguished city of Non. Of course, now that much rebuilding had to be done, the city had decided to rename itself to New Non, thereby classifying its burnt predecessor by the moniker, "Old Non". To this point, children were soon singing about the exciting conclusion to the catastrophic event, "Old Non town is burning down, burning down, burning down / Old Non bridge is falling down, my fair lady."

In the throne room of the 4th Kingdom, Albert and Benjamin were being recognized for their valiant efforts. As a result, they were given one request which would be granted by King Solepochs. They modestly requested to be kept out of the history books. When the ceremony was over, Albert leaned over to Ronald and whispered, "Why does the King wear a mask with his crown?"

"Well, you'd wear a mask too if you had torn your eyes out after you learned that you killed your father and married your mother."

"I suppose so."

Prince Clive strode over to Benjamin to congratulate him, "You did a bang-up job out there, Lambda the Just."

"You weren't too bad yourself, Prince Clive."

With a handful of keys he had retrieved from his men, the Prince gave them to Benjamin to return to Albert, "I just have one question, Lambda," he leaned in close and whispered, "You've been through the Imaginary World, haven't you?"

Surveying the courtroom to make sure that the coast was clear, Benjamin answered, "Yes, I have." Following with a question he already knew the answer to, he asked, "Have you?"

Showing Benjamin the back of his right fist, a mark, clear as his own, shone on the skin. The mark of ˘. "I didn't know anyone else had been through it. I thought I was the one and only."

"You may be the first, Breve the Lion, but you certainly weren't the last."

Prince Clive's eyes widened with the smile on his face, "So that *is* where you got your name."

"Yes, it is."

Albert and Ronald joined Benjamin and Prince Clive as Albert congratulated the Prince on his semi-promotion, "You did a fine job out there today, Prince Clive. I trust you will lead the newly founded Brotherhood of the Scarlet Lion with tenacity and bravery." Benjamin handed Albert the Q-Portal keys he had loaned out and Albert began placing them back in position on their hooks. As he worked, he offhandedly remarked, "I doubt this will be your last battle, Prince Clive."

"It surely isn't. We've already been tasked to advance on our northern borders, where an Ice Queen has been of particular trouble lately."

Benjamin shuddered briefly, which caused Albert to ask, "Are you all right?"

"Yes," rubbing his left shoulder, he muttered, "It's just that I haven't had much luck with ice in the past."

Interrupting the Natural, Prince Clive's horse whinnied, bringing Albert back to his previous conversation, "I'm sure your horse will enjoy the company on your journey up north."

"I don't see why not, I've had him since I was a boy. Heck, with my dad so focused on running the Kingdom, my horse practically raised me." Everyone laughed.

Turning to Ronald, Albert became more serious, "I still want to know your story, Ronald. What can those rings of yours actually do; and more importantly, where did you get them?"

"Yes, I suppose it's time I tell you about them. Prince Clive, you should probably hear about this too. You see, my story starts nearly one hundred years ago. Back then, I was a young man by the name of John, a bit younger than myself now. I fell in love with a woman. Her name was Gorgon."

Benjamin blurted out, "Wait! I know this story."

"Perhaps, but there is more to it than I think you realize. I loved Gorgon, as did most people. However, one day a man came to me with a box containing ten rings. Five green, five yellow. Each ring was designed as a snake in an uroboros configuration. He told me these rings granted wishes. This man never told me his name, but he asked that I refer to him as 'Serpent-bearer', which I suppose came from the fact that he had these snake rings in the first place, along with a single, golden ring which he wore on a chain that rested on his chest. The golden ring had strange writing on it, but was also of a snake in an uroboros configuration."

"He said the magic in these rings was from the ground-up remains of the serpent who deceived mankind around the beginning of time, and this was why they contained the power to grant wishes. Apparently, the trick to using the rings was that they were two halves which needed to be combined in order for the wish to work. This is why they were classified into two different colors and are required to be worn on separate hands. To show me that they really worked, the Serpent-bearer took two of them and asked me what the one thing in the world I desired was. When I told him that it was Gorgon, he touched the two rings together and they turned back to dust, carried off by the wind."

"Unfortunately, I learned a valuable lesson about magic that day: never let someone grant your wishes for you. When I found Gorgon again, her hair had turned to Pythons and she could turn things to stone with her eyes. I suppose the Serpent-bearer meant well, because no one would want to be with Gorgon, who now called herself Pythagoras, thereby making her mine for the taking. However, when she learned I had done this to her, she threw a fit and tried to kill me. From then on, I became known in legend as the wizard who created Pythagoras."

"I thought this story sounded familiar," Benjamin chimed in again, nudging his glasses up the arch of his nose.

"Yes, indeed it has become the stuff of legends, but it's all true."

Albert was stroking his moustache thoughtfully as he mused, "But that still does not explain why you are in *this* time."

"Well, as I said before, Pythagoras was hell bent on killing me, so my only recourse was to escape to the future. I figured the rings really did work, so I used them to transport myself to one hundred years in the future. In doing so, I could be sure the threat on my life would be gone by then. Of course, to be doubly sure, I changed my name to Ronald and befriended a man by the name of Solepochs. We became fast friends, especially since he was blind at the time, and I helped him to regain his humanity. Of course, I'm not actually his brother, but this bond might as well be tighter than a blood relation."

Albert had stopped stroking his moustache and was scribbling away on a piece of paper as he listened to the end of the story. When Ronald finished, Albert handed him the paper and explained, "I do not expect you to leave right away, but eventually I need you to travel another four hundred years in the future. I have detailed out a time and location on the outskirts of the Scorpio Desert where I need you to meet us. It will make more sense when you get to that time period, but make sure to bring Arthur with you, however you can get him out there."

"For all you've done for this town, I would be glad to help. I have heard rumors that the Serpent-bearer might still be alive, so I'm going to try and find him and destroy the ring he wore around his neck, since I think it's what gave him his power. After I'm done with that, I'll meet up with you both in the Scorpio Desert."

"*Wunderbar.* Well, we need to be going, but it was a pleasure working with you gentlemen." Everyone shook hands as the two Millennials left the court. Once outside, the sun was marching its way up into the mid-morning sky. Turning to Benjamin, Albert asked, "Do you think it is about time we headed back to see how Isaac is doing?"

"Sure thing."

From behind them came a slow, sarcastic clap, "Well done, gentlemen. Well done."

Turning around at the sound of a familiar voice, there stood Ophiuchus. And yet, something was different about him. While before his skin had been a pale grey, it was now a brilliant white, shining in the light of the rising sun. Benjamin reached for his weapon as he asked, "Where did the *Twilight Runner* go?"

"Oh, that old boat? I think you'll find it teetering on top of a volcano right about now. Albeit some time in the past."

Suddenly, the image of a large overturned boat next to a volcano spewing water entered into Benjamin's memory, "I knew that ship seemed familiar! How did you get it there?"

"Me? Why, you're the one who did all the work, Benjamin."

"That reminds me, how did you get to the boat so fast? Nobody could have outrun me." A shiver ran down his spine as Benjamin realized that he had only given his Imaginary World name to Ophiuchus. How much did this enemy know about him?

"Who said that was me?"

"What do you mean?"

"I mean, the me you first met might not have been the me on the boat. That's all."

Albert slipped Benjamin a white key with a nod to start charging it, "Are you insinuating that there were two of you here while this whole event took place?"

"Indeed . . . for a time. After all, if I traveled backward in time, there would, in theory, be two of me for the time which overlapped."

It was then that Albert noticed the ring which Ophiuchus wore on a chain around his neck, its gold color glinting in the sunlight of the dawn, "You are the Serpent-bearer, are you not?"

A sly grin crept across Ophiuchus' face, "It seems that I have found a fan of my work. I am indeed who you say I am."

"You might have someone gunning for you soon."

"Perhaps. Perhaps. But know that I have my sights set on you two," his tone became deadly serious, "You've destroyed one of my statues, and I'm not going to stand around and let you destroy more of them." With a sinister smile, he contemplated Albert's missing left arm as the scientist removed the glove on his right, "It looks to me like you had an unfortunate encounter with Cancer. I'll make a mental note to get the Ruby crab riled up before you stop by."

"It would be my pleasure. The outcome will still be the same," Albert replied in a monotonous tone with a smirk on his face, his eyes squinting in determination. Benjamin was behind Albert, back-to-back with the Keymaster. His hands were tight around the Q-Portal key as he charged it with a powerful attack of ball lightning. "Well, we hate to dash, but we have more Caidoz statues to destroy." With that final word, Albert reached his hand back and touched Benjamin's arm to signal that it was time to go. Releasing the energy, Albert and Benjamin disappeared with a boom which shattered all the remaining, unbroken windows in Old Non.

Traveling through a Q-Portal without using a Q-hole is an entirely different experience than travelling through a Q-Portal normally. Furthermore, travelling through time with a Q-Portal is normally much different than travelling through space with one. So, when Benjamin travelled through time without using a Q-hole, it was a new experience to him. Even though the first occurrence of him traveling through time without a Q-hole was when he escaped from Amedeo's War, he had gone unconscious by that point.

And yet, he finally experienced that sensation when he and Albert escaped from Ophiuchus. What an experience it was! The sensation was like being pulled through a tiny hole, your body tingling with electric shocks. When they came out on the other side of the time warp, they were above some clouds in a mountain range. Of course, the clouds obscured most of their view, so it was unclear what mountain range it was.

As is the case with non-Q-hole time travel, the electric orb containing Benjamin and Albert expanded until it reached capacity and discharged into the nearest object. Since Benjamin was conscious this time around, he was able to ride the lightning, bringing Albert along to their final destination. For a split moment after they descended below the clouds, Benjamin tried to stop their fall. Unfortunately, the electrical momentum carried them through to the point of contact: the ram's horns. It was then that the whole process started again. However, instead of a tingling sensation, it felt more like a friction burn.

When the group, now including Isaac and the Caidoz statue, emerged at the end of the time bridge, their new surroundings were dark, with the exception of a few candles lining a hallway of metal cages. While Albert, Benjamin, and Isaac were thrown off of the ram, the Caidoz statue continued charging forward, destroying the metal bars that got in its way.

"Curses! I overshot it," Benjamin swore as he dropped the Q-Portal key, which was even hotter than the first two times he had time traveled.

Albert comforted the Natural, "Do not be so hard on yourself. I think the reality is that we were spot on."

Isaac was absolutely dumbfounded, "I'm sorry, but what just happened? Where are we?" The animals which were once in cages were now creating quite the ruckus as the ram managed to turn around and start gaining momentum in order to charge the three time travelers.

Benjamin was equally confused. When he regarded his surroundings, the area seemed somehow nostalgic, but also somewhat inverted. Also, there was another member of their group who was now with them, "I agree, when did we pick up Isaac?"

Albert was shouting, trying to regain control of the situation, "We do not have time to be asking these meaningless questions! We are here now, and it seems we have an opportunity to destroy the statue of the ram." Surveying the darkness surrounding them, Albert knew that his C.L.A.W. wouldn't work here, "Isaac, do you have the Fluent of Light?"

Studying his empty hands, Isaac realized that it had been lost, "It must have been knocked away when the ram hit me."

"Did you happen to get a hit off?"

"I did, but where are we going to find any Earth Element in this wooden container?"

"We just need to send it to a volcano."

"That's easier said than done, Albert."

"*Nein!* Do you not see? We are in the hull of the *Twilight Runner!* Ophiuchus specifically told us it was sitting on top of a volcano." The ram was starting to get closer, its wool still sparking from the time travel.

The *Twilight Runner!* That was why it felt so familiar to Benjamin. Still, having been there before, he had a concern, "But there are no Q-Portals to that volcano! And besides, we need to cover the statue in Earth Element for Isaac's strike to have been effective. When I last saw this volcano, it had been sealed by Amedeo's Army and was full of water."

"But do you not see, Benjamin? The reason that the volcano needed to be sealed and the reason why it was full of water was because a Q-Portal had been created which was draining the Sea of Delaxanair. There *is* a Q-Portal here!"

Isaac's eyes became wide with a realization, "I've been through that Q-Portal! I was the one who unsealed it!"

As the pieces were falling into place, Benjamin pointed out one last gap in their reasoning, "But that still doesn't explain how we're going to cover the statue in Earth Element."

"When I went through the Q-Portal after I unsealed it, I know for a fact there was magma flowing. Unfortunately, it was because the volcano was erupting. It might be a bit of a long shot, but if we can use the Q-Portal right after I went through it, we might have a chance to cover the ram in molten Earth Element before the volcano explodes and destroys the Q-hole."

"*Wunderbar!* When did this happen?"

"It must have been exactly six and a half months ago." Having gained some momentum, the ram suddenly came to a stop as its black horn caught on one of the bars. A few moments later, some nearby cows disappeared into the floor, a white circle of light briefly appearing and disappearing. This jolt shook the entire boat and everyone took a step to steady themselves. Unfortunately, Isaac's step landed on the white Q-Portal key Benjamin had dropped on the floor, causing him to fall past the wooden planks and into a glowing black circle.

The circles disappeared. Albert and Benjamin looked at each other with surprise. Neither of them knew the keys could retain their energy and unexpectedly open Q-Portals. The ram finally became unhooked from the metal bar, revealing that part of its black horn had broken off, an obvious effect of Isaac's attack with Hikari Shichidai. As it continued its rampage forward, Albert quickly ran his fingers across the keys on his vest, trying to find the right one for the time and location they needed, "Benjamin! Start charging your energy, this will have to be quick!"

Finding the right key, Albert knelt down and, in one fluid motion, pulled the key Isaac had accidentally used out of the floor and shoved the new white key into the recently created Q-hole. Stepping back, Albert shouted, "Now!" at which point, Benjamin pointed his finger at the key and let a bolt of lightning transfer from his finger to the metal object.

The ram was almost upon them, but a black ring of light emerged around the key. When the Caidoz statue stepped into the ring of light, the door swung open, throwing the angry animal into a very different scene. Looking through the open door on the floor, Albert and Benjamin could see the blue sky above the volcano known as Sievuvus. The ram had completely destroyed a small hut that housed the Q-Portal and had landed on a large log cabin, ablaze and almost entirely covered in lava, a short distance away. Volcanic steam was shooting into the air and a hot, flowing stream of lava had almost made its way to the door from every direction.

Quickly sticking his head through the door to check on the destruction of the statue, Albert saw the ram, now covered in molten rock, slowly crumbling away. Benjamin already realized that, if they didn't act fast, the lava would be inside the boat, so he pulled Albert out of the hole and grabbed the door, slamming it shut, "Are you crazy? You could have gotten killed!"

"I had to be sure! I had to know the statue was destroyed."

Taking a moment to breathe and reassess the situation, Benjamin quietly asked, "So, what do we do now?"

"Now we head back to Isaac's group and continue to destroy the Caidoz statues. Isaac said the Fluent of Light must be back with his comrades."

"But what about Isaac? Aren't we going to find him?"

"I have no idea what happened to Isaac, and since I am unsure of the electrical power remaining in the key he used, there is no way of knowing either when or where he is."

"But we need to get him back, Albert! He's the leader of his team. I doubt they're going to let us take charge without him."

"*Nein*, the pressing need right now is to destroy the remaining statues."

"But a man has gone missing and-"

Albert pushed Benjamin up against the cages with his right arm. Talking through gritted teeth and trying to hold back a mixture of emotions, he growled, "Look! I know it is difficult for you to accept, but we cannot go after Isaac! Sacrifices would eventually be made!" Letting Benjamin down, Albert felt his left side where his arm used to be as he calmed down, "We cannot let a setback like this veer us off course."

Benjamin stared at the wooden floor, "What do we tell his friends?"

"The truth. He is alive somewhere and sometime, even if he is not here with us right now." Returning the most recently used Q-Portal key to its hook on his vest, he quietly said, "I hope they will understand." Finding the key they needed to return to Isaac's friends, Albert silently handed it to Benjamin, who charged it and pushed it into the floor. Once the black ring of light appeared again, the two Millennials burst out of the other side in the valley of Posea Pasture and lay on the grass, contemplating the difficult discussion they were about to have.

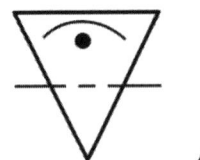 

Chapter 5

The Son's Birth

Isaac moaned as he lay on the ground. His head was throbbing. He rolled over onto his back, eyes still closed. He felt light-headed as he tried to determine if he was bleeding or not. No blood so far, but he did have a bit of a lump on the right side of his forehead. Taking in a deep breath of air, it felt strangely cool. Strangely crisp. Strangely fresh. Strangely thin. Strangely familiar.

He lay on the ground for another moment, soaking in the warmth of the sun. As he lay there, he replayed the events that just transpired. What happened? From the battle with the ram to the sudden transportation inside a ship to now, everything had happened so quickly. Isaac hardly knew what to think.

Finally opening his eyes, he stared out into the sky. Dark blackness. Looking around to make sure the sun was shining and not the moon; he saw the grey soil and realized what he suspected: he was back on the moon. "Not this again," he groaned. Sitting up, he examined his surroundings, trying to gain his bearings. Of course, given the current time, Isaac realized he wouldn't be able to figure out where he was on the moon because the last time he was there was during the dark month, and now it was obviously the light one.

Standing up, Isaac quickly came to the realization that he was almost completely unarmed. Both of his swords were back on Earth and, after rifling through his pockets, he found the only items to his name at the moment were a single throwing knife; a pad of paper and pencil; and the scroll containing the lyrics to the song describing the locations of the Caidoz statues. Besides being unarmed, he knew he possessed no Q-Portal keys to transport him back to Earth. Things were starting to look pretty bleak.

No food. No water. No money. No plan. Isaac had to sit back down and think. What he was going to do? The crater he found himself in was desolate and showed no signs of civilization. Lifting his gaze to the ridge of the crater, he decided that perhaps he needed a better perspective of the area.

As Isaac started walking toward the edge of the crater, he thought back to the last time he was on the moon. He had changed so much since then, and it was partly due to an energetic kid named Erwin. He was unsure if he would have ever been able to accomplish his objective of taking down Testament without Erwin's help. Even if the kid was naive at times, he balanced out Isaac's seriousness and eventually taught Isaac that he didn't have to tackle everything alone.

Of course, this led Isaac to think about Erwin's mother, Carroll. Now that he was back on the moon, he figured he should probably find her and give her the news that her son was dead. As he contemplated all possible simulations of this news, he soon came to the conclusion that it was better she not know this information, especially since Erwin's death was partly Isaac's fault.

This led Isaac to wonder if he had even arrived in the same timeframe as Carroll and Erwin. After all, Benjamin and Albert could freely travel through time, so did his accidental fall through space send him through time as well? Having traveled to the moon before, the Q-Portal sensation was much different this time around, which led him to believe that he had traveled through time as well. The question now was: how much time?

If he had gone backward in time to stop Erwin leaving with him in the first place, would he? After more thought, he realized this would be a bad idea. Much of what had brought him back to the moon hinged on Erwin following him to Earth. He then realized that, if he did travel to the same time period, he needed to protect his identity, in case he should inadvertently change history. He started running through names in his head, trying to pick one that was believable.

Letting his hair down over his eyes, he saw that it was almost completely brown now and the white had been banished from his head. Taking off the headband he wore to cover the Soul-fusion fluxion on his forehead, he flipped it inside-out to hide not only the fluxion, but the mark of the Brotherhood of the Scarlet Lion as well. He also turned his black shirt inside out to cover up the crossed bones of his coat of arms. These precautions were good steps, but if anyone confronted him about his true identity, he wasn't sure if he could maintain his cover.

While he was thinking, Isaac steadily trudged along the grey, gravelly dirt toward the ridge of the crater, slowly regaining his strength and his balance in the lighter gravity. Soon, he was jogging, then running with bounding leaps toward the edge of the crater. For the first time in a long time, he was having fun. The responsibility of destroying the statues seemed so far away up here, and he let out a long laugh as he ran.

Fate, however, can be a harsh mistress. Just as Isaac was starting to enjoy himself, he tripped on a small pile of rocks. Sliding to a stop several yards away, Isaac let out a sigh as he got up again and examined his arms and legs, now pretty torn up from the fall and starting to bleed. The stinging sensation on his extremities wasn't enough to stop him, though. Approaching the site of his fall, Isaac examined the pile of rocks and found it to be somewhat out of place.

Most of the rocks in the area were randomly scattered around and were a random assortment of sizes, but this pile was comprised of rocks which were all about the same size and all stacked together. This pile appeared to be man-made. Isaac never did get the complete history of why there were people on the moon, but he now knew he had arrived some time after the first ones had appeared.

Kicking the pile in playful anger, some of the stones fell away and revealed that there was something underneath the pile, covered by the collection of rocks. Removing the rest of the detritus, Isaac found a canvas bag, buried in the ground. Opening up the bag, his eyes widened at the treasure it held. Inside the innocuous sack was a plethora of fluxion cores and research scrolls. Of course, upon finding these items, he ravaged through the bag to see if luck was on his side. Could there be a Q-Portal key somewhere in the canvas duffel?

When the bag was empty, its contents scattered on the ground, Isaac let out a sigh when he realized there was no key. Quickly inspecting the various items, he wondered how they could help him get around, since the moon was a big place and he really didn't feel like walking across its entire surface. It was at this moment when a glass orb glinted the light of the sun into Isaac's eyes, grabbing his attention.

Leaning over and picking up the fluxion core, he examined it and found a familiar swirling inside. Not unlike the Seawave orb, which he now realized was still back on earth in the coat he had used as a matador's cape, this orb swirled with an intense gust of wind. Holding the orb in his palm and peering toward the black sky, Isaac was quickly narrowing down the timeframe he now lived in. It had to be before Erwin left.

Examining the other fluxion cores didn't give Isaac much more information, but one in particular did. Now that he knew he had arrived before Erwin left the moon, he also now knew he was at a time when Werner had not found one of the "lost" Number-fluxions. This was because Isaac now held the disk with the distinctive "–" mark in its center.

As he cradled the disk in his hand, his conscience was conflicted as he mulled over destroying the fluxion core, thereby eliminating a battle he would have to fight in the future. Still, how much of the future could he actually change, and how much *should* he change? It was then that, out of the corner of Isaac's eye, another familiar orb caught his attention.

As Robin and Sucari were picking up Isaac's belongings, R-3N3 was sitting on a rock, resting. As soon as the Caidoz statue had disappeared, R-3N3 felt dizzy and had almost passed out. He wasn't certain, but he suspected that he was slowly dying. The clouds above them were starting to clear as Vlad came up and put his hand on R-3N3's shoulder, "Are you doing any better, Artie?"

"Affirmative. I just needed to process what I observed."

"You're the only one of us who saw what happened, so we don't doubt what you say."

"Thank you, Vlad." Thinking for a moment, R-3N3 asked, "Say, Vlad, why do you think that statue was moving?"

"I was discussing the same thing with Isaac before we found the statue, and from what I remember, maybe it has to do with its Quality."

"Quality?"

"Indeed. It's kind of like the Element of a statue, but it's not as straightforward as Fire or Water."

"What was the ram's Quality?"

"Cardinal, if I remember correctly."

"You are correct, that is not straightforward."

"If I were to guess, maybe it didn't have to do with its Quality, but instead with the fact that it was a Fire Element. After all, the mountains tend to be cooler than other places, so maybe the sheep of the valley nuzzled next to it for warmth and brought it to life."

"At this point, I am unsure we will ever know what-" a loud boom interrupted R-3N3. Even though the echoes from the mountains made it difficult to determine the noise's origin, it seemed to come from the Q-Portal that the group had emerged from when they arrived in the area. As everyone focused their attention down the valley, they saw two men now lying on the grass outside of the Q-Portal, staring up at the sky. R-3N3 immediately recognized them, "It is Albert and Benjamin!" While this statement registered with the other members of the group, R-3N3 had already ran down the hill to where the Millennials were laying.

It became quickly apparent that someone was missing. When he got to Albert, he leaned down and picked up the man by his vest of keys. Shaking Albert, the keys jingled as R-3N3 yelled, "Where is Isaac?"

Averting his gaze from the red, glowing eyes before him, Albert mumbled, "He is gone."

"Gone? Gone where?"

Benjamin had gotten up and was trying to pull Albert away from R-3N3, "We don't know!" Everyone had caught up and could tell the situation was tense, "There was an accident. He slipped through a Q-Portal and was gone. We don't know to where or when he might have traveled."

At this solemn realization, R-3N3's eyes returned to their green state as he slowly put Albert down, "I am sorry I lashed out like that. But I must know: you were both in the lightning bolt that caused this whole mess, correct?"

"That's right. I thought we overshot our goal, but instead coincidence dealt us a bad hand."

Sucari spoke up, "So, what do we do now? Do we go after Isaac?"

Albert answered, "*Nein*. As Benjamin explained earlier, we do not know where or even when Isaac traveled to, so the chances of us finding him are beyond infinitesimally small."

Vlad now stepped in, "But there are six of us, surely if we split up we'd be able to-"

"Six times zero is still zero . . . I am sorry, but I do not believe that we have met."

R-3N3 gave the introduction, "Albert, this is Vlad, he is one of the people who helped us defeat Testament. Vlad, this is Albert, he is the reason we are finding these statues and destroying them." A somewhat terse handshake followed as the Keymaster and the Dragon finished their introduction.

"We still didn't get an answer to our question. What do we do now?" Robin inquired.

When Albert shifted his focus over to the woman who was holding the weapons used in the attempt to subdue the ram, he saw a familiar trident and became ecstatic, "You found it!"

"That's not an answer."

"I know it is not an answer, but you found Psi's Trident!"

"I didn't, Artie did." As Albert grabbed the trident out of her arms, Robin could only get out a single word in protest, "Hey!"

Examining the weapon, Albert found the ψ symbol and the number "93" on the head of the trident, "*Wunderbar! Wunderbar! Wunderbar!* Now that we have the weapons from the three members of The Triumvirate, we can create the final weapon able to destroy the Caidoz statues."

"Final weapon? What final weapon?" Benjamin asked, unaware of his sledgehammer's significance as part of a greater whole.

"Of the individuals who passed through the Imaginary World, only three were given weapons. I have done research which indicates that these three weapons were meant to be combined, as a symbol of the unity of the three who had the fortitude to do together what only three people before them had done individually. This weapon is known as 'The Spear of Trium'."

Robin still wasn't satisfied, "But we still don't have an answer to-" Sucari placed an understanding hand on his wife's shoulder which told her that to press now would be pointless. Albert was on a roll.

"Now that we have the three weapons, I think we might be ready to take Ophiuchus on."

Isaac's group was once again confused, "Ophiuchus?" R-3N3 asked, "Who is that?"

"I suppose I should explain." Taking out a blank scroll, Albert wrote down the lyrics to the song from memory and proceeded to cross out the seven couplets of the statues he knew were destroyed. Pointing to the last stanza of the poem, he continued, "The lyrics are a little ambiguous, but we came across the creator of the Caidoz statues when we were in the process of destroying the lion. Ophiuchus is the creator."

Vlad still wasn't quite up to speed, but broke in anyway, "But why do we need the three weapons which are supposed to be used to destroy the statues to defeat one man?"

Benjamin answered, "Well, since these statues are difficult to destroy with any conventional means, we're just making extra sure we can destroy him."

"I enjoy a good fight as much as the next man, but isn't that a bit overkill?"

"You haven't fought him. I have."

"All right, but if we aren't going to spend the time finding Isaac, why are we instead going to spend it trying to find Ophiuchus?"

Albert was solemn at this point, "We do not have to find Ophiuchus. He will find us."

"Why?"

"He knows we are out to destroy the statues he created, so chances are we will find him at these last five."

R-3N3 corrected Albert, "Four, actually. We destroyed the water bearer."

"That is right, I had forgotten. *Danke.*" Albert crossed off another two lines with a flourish.

Peeking over Albert's shoulder at the ancient script, Sucari asked, "So, what four do we have left?"

"The scales, the bull, the maiden, and the centaur."

Robin perked up at the mention of the last statue, "Did you say 'centaur'?"

"I did."

"What does the rest of the couplet say about it?"

"'The centaur can see for miles and miles / Shooting an arrow to defeat its trials'."

"I think I might know where that statue lies."

"What do you mean, Robin?" Sucari asked.

"Archery is my forte. In my training to become an archer, my mentor, Von, told me of an ancestor of his who found a legendary technique on the summit of Mount Charles. On top of that mountain lies a shrine called The Centaurcher shrine, and I believe *that* is where we will find our next Caidoz statue."

"*Wunderbar.*" Albert was rolling up the scroll with the poem written on it and replaced it with a map, which he unfurled, quickly measuring a distance and flicking a black key off of his vest and into the air where he caught it and said, "Now, let us depart!"

○

Staring at the solid black orb, Isaac wasn't quite sure what to make of the Gravity Core which sat on the ground, metaphorically staring back at him. He remembered the origin of the Gravity Core being the remains of a condensed comet which struck the moon, but now his faith in that statement was faltering. In fact, now he was starting to question whether or not he had arrived in an alternate dimension; something that ran parallel to the reality he had always known.

Isaac wasn't sure what to think anymore. The whole experience made his head spin. However, one thing was true: he now held a fluxion core which could get him quickly from one place to another. But now the question was not how he would get there, but where was he going? Should he search for Carroll and Erwin and give them the wind fluxion he would be using to get around? Should he search for the Caidoz statues? Were there even any Caidoz statues on the moon?

It was at that moment when Isaac remembered something he had read from the Caidoz statue location lyrics. Rifling through the scrolls he now had in his possession, he found the one given to him by Albert. Reading through the song, he came across the couplet, "The bull ran and jumped too soon / And got himself stuck on the moon." Was this metaphorical, or literal? The more Isaac thought about it, the more he was convinced there was a Caidoz statue on the moon. After all, if they were the source of power for fluxions, and he had used fluxions on the moon before, they must exist. But what if he managed to destroy the statues before the timeframe where he arrived on the moon in the first place? The time travelling paradox was becoming too much to think about, so Isaac just left it at that.

Of course, this meant he was now back to the situation of having to search the entire moon. And yet, performing this task haphazardly was unwise on many levels. First, Isaac needed to establish a base of operations, and the best place to set up camp would have to be in a town. After all, if he was going to spend all of his time searching for the Caidoz statues, he would not have time to worry about cooking food or setting up camp. In a town, he could pay people to do these things for him. Isaac frowned as he realized he didn't have any money, so the true first step he had to take was to get a job.

Still, the need for a job did not preclude him from travelling to a town. Grabbing the canvas duffel he had found, Isaac filled it back up with the scrolls and fluxion cores and did a glancing, once over of the area to make sure he didn't miss anything. Observing that the area was clear, he looked down at the wind fluxion he held in his hand. He was at a bit of a loss for how to apply an uroboros seal without any of the things he normally carried in his jacket, which was back on earth.

Pulling out what he had on him with his other hand, he saw the knife and contemplated using it to carve the uroboros symbol into his skin. Fortunately, he considered this only briefly. He then saw the pad of paper and pencil and wondered if it was enough to activate the core while keeping him safe from being controlled by the power. Drawing a quick, 7-1 knotted uroboros snake seal, Isaac held the paper in his hand, surrounding the windy orb. Closing his eyes, he hoped for the best.

While the sensation he felt was similar to the phenomenon when Erwin grabbed his hand and used the powers; when Isaac was in control, the feeling was much more intense but also felt much more stable. Turning into wind took the breath out of his lungs, but it gave him the experience of being able to transcend space. He felt like he was everywhere and nowhere, all at once. As this was the case, he could almost immediately tell which craters had people and which didn't. This was a tremendous accomplishment, considering the latter made up the majority of the craters on the moon's surface.

Choosing a town at random, he stopped travelling with a burst of air. Even though the whole process felt like it was endless, it only took a handful of seconds to accomplish. Still, Isaac was gasping for air and wondered how Erwin was able to do it so often. At any rate, Isaac put the fluxion away in his pocket, since he had now arrived outside a small village. All the houses were made of adobe, since it appeared that there were no trees anywhere on the moon's surface.

A man on the outskirts of the village was herding cattle. Isaac approached him and asked, "I'm new to this area, would you mind telling me what town this is?"

"This is Alden," the man replied.

Scrutinizing the area, Isaac was surprised this was the same town he ended up in before, mainly because there wasn't a large lake outside the village created from the collision of a comet with the moon. "Alden, huh? Really?"

"Yes, really. Don't you think I know my own town?"

"Sorry, but I remember it a little differently."

"I thought you said you were new to the area . . ."

Isaac faltered, "Well, I didn't immediately recognize the town, so I thought I was." Quickly changing topics, Isaac saw the man was rapidly losing control of his herd, "If you don't mind me asking, do you need any help?"

"Not today, but I have been looking to hire someone to watch the herd occasionally. Why? Are you looking for work?"

"Actually, yes I am." Isaac figured this would be a great way to earn some income while also perhaps gaining some insight as to the whereabouts of the bull statue.

"Come back here tomorrow and I'll be ready to put you to work." The man extended his hand as a form of understood agreement. Isaac grabbed the man's hand and they exchanged a hearty handshake.

As Isaac stood on the outskirts of Alden, the herd of cattle moved around the edge of town as the man led the cows back to their home. Just as the animals were leaving, Isaac overheard a ruckus coming from the town which grew louder as it approached the outskirts. From around a corner, Isaac could see what was happening. A few kids were chasing a middle-aged woman out of town, throwing rocks at her as she ran.

Her head was down and she cradled her midsection as she escaped her pursuers. Isaac watched as she ran by him, not even noticing he was there. Turning to face the persecuting children, Isaac caught two of the recently thrown rocks with his bare hands and knocked down a third with what he had caught. This stopped the kids in their tracks. Gripping the remaining of the two stones, Isaac broke it in his hand and let the dust and gravel fall to the ground. The children saw he meant business and started screaming for different reasons as they retreated back to their respective homes.

The woman didn't even notice the withdrawal of her aggressors as she continued running from town. Isaac saw that she had gained some distance, but still decided to let her know everything was now under control. Isaac grabbed the wind orb and uroboros seal paper from his pocket and blew past the woman. When he stopped in front of her, she almost knocked him over; but he had enough time to extend his arms and place his hands on her shoulders to stop her, "You can stop running. The kids are gone now."

Looking up at Isaac's face, the woman appeared distraught; rivulets of tears were streaming down her face as she asked, "Who are you? Why are you helping me?" Isaac was stunned. Even though she *looked* twenty, maybe even thirty years younger, despite actually being twelve years younger, there was no mistaking it. This was Carroll.

○

Emerging from a Q-Portal high in the Slap Mountain range, the combined group of warriors beheld the beauty of their surroundings, trying to gain their bearings. To the south, the sea could be seen, its waves calmly splashing the shores of an upscale coastal city. To the north, there sat the brunt of the Slap Mountains. The closest peak to their position was stately enough by itself, but the small temple, replete with columns and a domed roof, which sat upon the summit made the mountain appear much more esteemed. They had arrived on the approach to Mount Charles.

Off in the distance, a dozen miles away, another mountain could be seen to the northwest. Its summit was obscured by large clouds which towered above it in a menacing manner. This mountain was known as Meadow Peak. Albert considered the intimidating mountain in the distance and wondered how some of the researchers he had worked with while under the employ of General Amedeo ever managed to climb the monstrosity.

A cool, salty breeze blew across the top of the ridge on which they were standing, causing at least a few members of the group to shiver. Sucari took off Isaac's jacket, which he had decided to wear in his absence, and draped it over the shoulders of his wife. Unfortunately, since Robin wore a large crossbow on her back, the gesture didn't really work, but the thought was appreciated, "Thanks, Sucari, but I think I just need to get moving in order to warm up."

After the battle with the ram and Isaac's disappearance, his comrades had decided to hold on to his belongings until he returned. Most of them expected him to come back, as he had proven himself a very resourceful and intelligent man. And yet, for the time being, they had divided his possessions among themselves.

Vlad was somewhat fond of Kuroni, as it was through this sword that he first interacted with Isaac. He wore the katana at his side with pride. Sucari put on Isaac's white coat again, its bottom edge showing evidence of being singed. After Isaac tore the strips of fabric from the coat when they were on the bottom of the ocean, the coat was starting to unravel. Sucari had decided to fuse the frayed ends with his fire in order to keep its condition from deteriorating. He wore the jacket over his own white flight vest, but decided to hold Hikari Shichidai in its half-scabbard at his side instead of on his back, the way Isaac used to carry it.

As it was, Isaac's group wasn't quite sure who would assume command in his absence, but Sucari took it upon himself to step up and lead his friends to accomplish Isaac's goal of ridding the world of fluxions once and for all. While the group hiked along the ridge to the Centaurcher shrine, Sucari caught up to Albert and asked, "So, Albert . . . what does the Quality of a statue determine?"

"Ah, so you want to know about Quality, do you?"

"Yeah, we were kind of unclear about it when we were facing the ram, so I was wondering if you could explain it better."

"*Ja*, Quality is just one of three attributes held by each Caidoz statue."

"We know about the Element of the statues, obviously, and we know about the three types of Qualities, but we don't know what those three types really mean."

"I see. To start with, of the three Quality types, Cardinal is perhaps the most difficult to understand, which is probably why you are confused, since the ram exhibited this quality."

Benjamin was just ahead of Albert and Sucari and overheard the word "Cardinal", which caused him to ask, "Do the Cardinal statues have anything to do with Seasoned Compass?"

Albert was somewhat surprised, "Indeed they are! Why do you ask?"

Removing a ring from his pocket, Benjamin handed it to Albert as they continued hiking, "I met Tilde the Cardinal once. He was the leader of Seasoned Compass. He gave me this ring to help recruit former members to fight against Amedeo's Army, but to no avail. I just wondered if the Cardinal Quality had anything to do with him, or if it was merely coincidental."

"I see. Well, the four Cardinal statues were where the members of Seasoned Compass received the orbs that they drew their power from. Haru Higashi drew her regenerative power from the orb found with the ram. Natsu Minami gained his control over heat from the crab. While Aki Nishi's Gravity Core was created from the formation of Daniel Crater, it was not where he found it, as he would lead you to believe. *Nein*, his power was kept with the statue of the scales. Finally, Fuyu Kita's ice ability was originally stolen from the Ice Queen who terrorized the northern border of the 4th Kingdom, but she originally found it with the sea-goat statue."

Sucari shuddered briefly, which gave Benjamin and Albert a sense of déjà vu. As they both slowly turned to look at him with questioning glances, Sucari replied, "What?"

With a raised eyebrow, Benjamin asked, "Have you encountered this ice power before?"

"Yeah, I think so. The leader of Testament, Thomson, had the ability to make snowballs from the air itself. Artie and I defeated him when we stormed the Eagle's Nest about six months ago, although Artie already had a history with Thomson when we encountered him on that floating island." Sucari noticed Benjamin was smiling as he shook his head, "Why do you ask?"

Chuckling softly, Benjamin replied, "It seems that, while we lived a thousand years apart, we have many things in common, Sucari." Rubbing his left shoulder again, he continued, "I ran across that ability when I found Fuyu Kita, but he quite literally gave me the cold shoulder when I asked him to join my fight against Amedeo's Army."

"Even though I now realize that Amedeo's goals were not aligned with my own," Albert interjected, "I am still somewhat glad you were unable to get Fuyu Kita to join your cause, even if it would not have changed the outcome."

Benjamin mused, "Still, it's interesting that, even though Seasoned Compass might not have visited the shrines which held the statues with their powers, the powers were somehow inexplicably drawn to these people." This remark made Sucari recall something Isaac had said, which caused him to wonder if he was destined to bear the responsibility of the Hellfire orb.

"*Ja*, but there is one more attribute which ties the members of Seasoned Compass together."

"What would that be?"

"They were all Naturals, just like you, Benjamin."

"That is intriguing. I had suspected as much, considering their double names, but I only met half of them, so I wouldn't have been able to confirm it."

After a brief, awkward silence, Sucari sensed the thread of discussion was at its end, so he steered it back to the original topic, "So, now that we know about Seasoned Compass, what about the Cardinal Quality?"

"Ah, perhaps the best way to describe the statues with the Cardinal Quality is 'baseline'. Still a little vague, I know, but fortunately this means that they are the statues which are somewhat easier to destroy."

Thinking back on all the trouble they had with the ram statue, Sucari was worried, "If the Cardinal statues are the easiest, what makes the other two Qualities more difficult?"

"Well, the Fixed quality is really just stubborn, which means that it will not go down without a good fight. As for Mutable, that is the most difficult Quality due to its regenerative or multiplicative properties."

"Which one is the centaur?"

"Mutable."

"Great."

"Ah, but you see, Element and Quality are only two properties of these statues. The last property is known as Degree."

Benjamin chimed in, "I remember you telling me about this. There are two Degrees, right? Light and Dark?"

"Essentially, *ja*."

Sucari felt obliged to ask, "What do the Degrees actually do?"

"Degrees are usually only involved when using Q-Portals, either through space or time, so when we encounter them on the statues, it really just breaks down to what their color is: black or white."

"Is that why Isaac and you both traveled through time when you came back from the past?"

"I believe so, *ja*. I think Benjamin's electricity reacted with the Caidoz statue, sending us through time yet again," recalling the events in Old Non, Albert trailed off, "which would not be the first instance where something has been sent through time without a Q-Portal key." Albert began stroking his moustache as he considered the strange possibility that Ophiuchus was not actually human.

By this time, they had almost reached the Centaurcher shrine when Sucari noticed Robin was falling a bit behind. She had one hand on her stomach and another on her mouth. Allowing the rest of the group to continue on, Sucari jogged back to where his wife was slowly making progress up the ridge, "Are you OK, honey?"

"Yeah, I'm fine, but I have a bit of a headache and I'm a bit nauseous."

"Here, sit down for a minute and let's see if it passes."

As Sucari found a suitable rock for Robin to sit down, she proceeded to vomit off the side of the trail. After taking a few deep breaths, Robin regained her composure and sat down on the rock, "I think that made it better. I just needed to get it over with."

"What do you think it is? Food poisoning? Dehydration? Altitude Sickness?"

"I don't think it is any of those."

"What do you mean?"

"I felt this way the other day, when we came to Topal to visit Niccolo."

"So, it doesn't have to do with where we are right now?"

"Nah," Robin's mouth was slowly curling into a smile.

"Why are you smiling?"

"Sucari, you might want to be the one to sit down for this."

"Sit down? Sit down for what?"

"I think we may be pregnant." With those words, Sucari's eyes rolled back in his head and he fainted, landing flat on his back in the middle of the trail.

As Carroll stood up straight, Isaac soon realized why she was protecting her abdomen. A small bump protruded from her stomach, which caused Isaac to ask, "You're pregnant, aren't you?"

Tears began welling up in her eyes again as she bowed her head in shame, "Yes."

"Why are you ashamed? Is this why those kids were pestering you?"

"Yes. But there's more to it than that."

"Why would anyone want to harass a pregnant woman like that?"

The tears were steadily flowing again as Carroll's voice tightened at the emotions she was experiencing, "They think I'm a whore."

"Why would they think that?"

"I'm not married and everyone in town knows there are no men in my life, so when it came out that I was pregnant, I was treated like a pariah." She gazed up into Isaac's eyes, pleading for mercy, "But it's not like that, I swear! If I were to explain what really happened, no one would believe me."

"I've encountered some pretty strange stuff in my life," Isaac's eyes were twinkling, "Try me."

Carroll's face flushed, "You see, I'm not even sure why I'm pregnant either. The truth of the matter is," her voice dropped to a whisper, "I'm still a virgin."

Isaac's eyebrows were raised in surprise, "I have to admit, that's a new one for me."

"But I've wanted a child for so long that I feel this is more of a miracle than a curse. I've never had much luck with men, so the fact I could skip almost the entire process is definitely a blessing. I think my prayers to the maiden finally paid off."

"Maiden?" that word triggered some part of Isaac's memory, "What maiden?"

Looking around to make sure that no one else was present, she continued, "There's a shrine underground with the statue of a maiden, pregnant with child, just like I am now."

Reaching into his pocket and pulling out the Caidoz statue lyric scroll, Isaac glanced over the couplets until he found what he was looking for, "The maiden weeps her tears of joy / For being told she will bear a boy." While still reading the scroll, Isaac asked, "Can you show me where this shrine is?"

"Does that mean you believe me?" Carroll's voice was high with shock.

Rolling up the scroll and returning it to his pocket, Isaac replied, "I don't see why not. Like I said, I've seen some strange things in my life."

"You've been so kind to me, and I don't even know your name."

Isaac had to think quickly, since he hadn't settled on an alias yet, "Edmond," was the first thing which came to mind. In his head, he was now screaming at himself for being so stupid. He had heard that name before, and it was when he was on the moon. He believed he had just royally screwed up.

"Well, Edmond, my name is Carroll." She smiled as she wiped away the tears from her cheeks, "I'm so glad to meet you."

"Likewise, Carroll," this confirmed it: she was pregnant with Erwin, "Likewise."

"I stumbled across this shrine a while ago and I've secretly been visiting it for some time. No one else even knows it exists." Carroll started walking away from the town toward the large open space which had thrown Isaac for a loop earlier.

"When did you find out you were pregnant?" Isaac asked as he followed after her.

"Oh, I think probably four or five months ago. It was really quite a shock to me, but I was able to keep it a secret pretty well until a few weeks ago when it finally came out."

"Do you know what you want to name the child?"

"I do," she smiled as she looked toward the black, starry sky above, "Erwin."

"But what if it's a girl?" Isaac asked, only in order to not appear too suspicious. He knew the child would be a boy.

She just shook her head and cradled her torso with her hands, "No, it's clear to me that it will be a boy. I can just feel it."

"Your story reminds me of a couplet I read on that scroll I pulled out earlier, 'The maiden weeps her tears of joy / For being told she will bear a boy'."

"That's fascinating, since that very same couplet is inscribed on the walls of the shrine."

"Yes, that is fascinating." Isaac needed to make sure he didn't give away too much information on what he knew. He was doing a pretty good job of acting right now, but he wondered when or if he would ever slip up.

Carroll stopped suddenly and crouched down to the ground, dusting off something buried under the top layer of soil. It was a door. Inscribed on the stone façade was a symbol. An upside down triangle had a line intersecting it with a dash appearing inside the triangle. Above the dash was what looked like an eye inside the space of the triangle. The eye was represented by a single dot underneath a wide arc. Having already seen the symbol on the Caidoz scroll, Isaac knew this was the entrance to where the maiden statue was located.

Grabbing a small, grooved handle, Carroll tried to lift the door, but Isaac chivalrously put his hand on her shoulder and said, "I wouldn't be much of a gentleman if I were to allow a pregnant woman to do all the work, now would I?" Lifting the door revealed a long, dark tunnel which led down into the ground, the first few steps beckoning for them to enter, "After you, milady." Isaac held his hand out to allow Carroll into the corridor.

"Thank you, brave knight," Carroll smiled again, playing along with the show.

Closing the door behind them, the space suddenly became very dark as their eyes adjusted. Then, magic happened. The walls seemed to glow and sparkle with a spattered luminosity which reminded Isaac of a cathedral he had once visited. He still couldn't get used to the sight and let out a "Wow" in amazement.

"I know. Isn't it beautiful? But believe me; we haven't even gotten to the best part yet."

Carroll led Isaac down the dimly lit hall for some time. Isaac began to wonder how deep this shrine was, considering not only how far horizontally, but vertically, they had travelled. Suddenly, the corridor opened up into a chamber and Isaac had to step back for a moment, as the enclosed space had quickly become a precipice. Examining the enclosure, he observed that it seemed to resemble an upside down tetrahedron. Narrow bridges connected to the middle of the space, seeming to hold up a statue which stately sat in the center.

Thinking three dimensionally, Isaac realized this space mimicked the symbol used to designate the Caidoz statue of the maiden. It wasn't until he took a good look at the surroundings, and not the geometry, that he saw another familiar sight. Fireflies. Most were clinging to the walls, but a few flew through the air, giving a dizzying sensation of movement to the stationary cavern. As Isaac walked into the all-surrounding enclosure, it gave him the feeling of standing in the middle of outer space, all the stars of the universe twinkling in the distance in every direction.

When he had caught up with Carroll, Isaac beheld the jet-black statue above him and saw what the lyric was speaking of. While the figure was that of a beautiful woman, calm and composed, holding her torso, full with child, two streams of Sapphire tears poured from her Sapphire eyes. Pointing to a location behind the statue, Carroll said, "Look, there's the couplet you talked about earlier."

Sure enough, engraved in glowing letters, was the section of the poem described in the scroll. In fact, the words were inscribed on every face of the tetrahedron, all in the same dead language which Isaac was slowly becoming accustomed to. Standing behind Carroll, Isaac asked, "Before you realized you were pregnant, did you do anything differently than the times before when you came to pray to the maiden?"

"Let me think about that." Carroll was silent for a moment as she thought back, "If I remember correctly, I was becoming frustrated with myself and I cried out to the statue, grabbing its hand and pleading for it to let me become pregnant, even though I knew there was no possibility it would happen."

This intrigued Isaac, and he stored this information away in his mind to contemplate later. Placing a reassuring hand on her shoulder, Isaac said, "Thank you for showing me this. We can go back now." He turned around and began ascending the stairs to exit the underground shrine. While Isaac was excited to have found one of the Caidoz statues, he was incredibly concerned, because he now had nothing to destroy it with.

When the two of them emerged from the secret passage, Isaac kicked some dirt back onto the door to conceal it again. Carroll looked at Isaac and said,

"Thank you for believing my story, you don't know how much this means to me. I've held all these things inside my soul, and it feels good to know that someone else knows about them and doesn't doubt me. How can I ever repay you?"

Dredging the depths of his memory, Isaac had been thinking about how to correct his mistake in calling himself Edmond. He was also trying to figure out how to find a place to live, since he now had a job and needed to stick around long enough to figure out how to destroy the Caidoz statue he just found. Soon, a connection was made, and Isaac smiled at how simple the solution was, "Would you marry me?"

This came as a sudden shock to Carroll, who immediately blushed and stared down at the grey soil, "I just met you this morning. Don't you think we're going too fast?"

"I don't necessarily mean officially, but I don't want to see you harassed anymore. It might take some lying, but I think we can convince everyone that you had a secret husband who has just come back from a long journey."

Still staring at the ground, Carroll smiled as she brought her gaze up to Isaac's eyes, "I'd like that, Edmond," grabbing his hand and leading him back to town, she said, "Let's get married."

○

Vlad and R-3N3 ran back to Sucari and Robin when they saw Sucari fall to the ground. While Vlad knelt down and tried to get Sucari to wake up, R-3N3 asked, "What happened?"

Robin smiled and laughed as she replied, "I guess my husband doesn't do well with news like that."

With a solid slap to the face, Vlad got Sucari to wake up, his first words being a monotone, "I'm going to be a father."

Both Vlad and R-3N3 exclaimed, "What?"

Robin stood back up as she explained, "I think I'm pregnant."

Vlad helped Sucari up and gave him a pat on the back, "Way to go, old man!"

"Hey, I'm younger than you are, Vlad." Sucari laughed as everyone gave congratulations. Looking over to the Centaurcher shrine, Benjamin and Albert had already disappeared inside. Sucari brushed himself off as he said, "Anyway, shall we get back to the task at hand?" As Vlad and R-3N3 left to head to the shrine, Sucari came alongside Robin, holding her hand as the new family made their way to the top of Mount Charles.

Inside the domed temple, Sucari's group found Albert and Benjamin scrutinizing everything in the empty shrine, appearing to be confused and lost. There was no statue. Both of the Millennials were examining the walls, trying to find some clue as to where the statue might be. Turning to Robin, Albert asked, "Did your teacher tell you anything more about this shrine? Like if there was a secret chamber or anything hidden?"

"Nah, he had only said that it's where the legendary Mount Charles method came from. Obviously, with how close we are to civilization, I don't see why whatever was here before wouldn't have been stolen by now."

Benjamin asked, "What does the lyric say?"

Reciting from memory, Albert replied, "'The centaur can see for miles and miles / Shooting an arrow to defeat its trials.' Obviously up here you can see for quite a ways, but that couplet does not provide anything more in terms of useful information." Looking down at the floor in dejection, Albert noticed something familiar. Walking over to where R-3N3 was standing, he silently pushed the armored man to the side, still staring at the floor.

"A simple 'excuse me' would suffice," R-3N3 said in indignation. Albert stared at a mark engraved in the floor. The mark was of an "X" in the middle of a circle. Taking a few steps back and surveying the entire temple, Albert got a better look at the floor as a whole. The encircled X was underneath a long arc, making it look almost like an eyeball. This symbol was also inscribed inside an equilateral triangle, each of its three points touching the edges of the circular temple floor.

Noticing that his Millennial partner was on to something, Benjamin asked, "What do you see, Albert?"

"This is the symbol for the centaur, engraved on the floor, but it is not quite right."

"What do you mean?"

"This circle with an X in it should have a + instead. In fact-" bending down and putting his fingers in the groove of the X, Albert was able to turn the circular stone disk until it matched the centaur's symbol. With a heavy, grinding click, the temple began to rumble. Just outside the colonnade, a stone slab slid back and everyone gathered around to see what had happened. The stone slab was hiding a staircase which went down into the depths of the mountain.

Without asking any questions, Albert knew this new development was leading them in the right direction. Heading down the stairs, which curved slightly to match the outline of the temple, Albert soon stood in a chamber which sat underneath the Centaurcher shrine. Holes in the ceiling, that he hadn't noticed in the floor of the shrine, let the light of the afternoon stream into the darkness, piercing it with columns of luminescence.

Benjamin was right behind Albert and was amazed they had found the statue so easily, "Excellent! Good work, Albert."

Albert smiled and turned back to his Millennial partner to accept the compliment when he noticed that, once again, Benjamin's i-World symbol was glowing, albeit not as brightly as it had in the past, "Benjamin, I do not want to alarm you, but it seems that some of our group have once again inherited greatness."

Looking up toward his forehead, Benjamin asked, "You mean?"

"Ja. Your forehead is glowing, just like when we were with Arthur."

Benjamin decided to wait at the entrance to the cavern and examine everyone who came in, even though he had a hunch on who it might be. Sucari and Robin made it down first, but there was nothing glowing on their skin. R-3N3 obviously didn't have any skin to have the marks stick, so that only left the newest member of the group: Vlad. When the last representative of the Order of the Dragon entered, Benjamin noticed a very faint light on Vlad's neck which revealed the symbol of Umlaut the Dragon.

Pulling Vlad aside, Benjamin quietly asked, "Vlad, do you happen to know about your ancestry?"

"A little bit. My father told me we had descended from the original founder of the Order of the Dragon."

"That's right. There's a mark on your neck which confirms it, but do you know if you were also related to someone known as Breve the Lion?"

"I can't say I know anything that far back."

"How about Arthur?"

"You mean the legendary Dragonrider? Prodigy King of the 4th Kingdom?"

"That's the one."

"That would be amazing, but I don't think so."

"Do you mind if I take a look at your right hand?"

"Since we're inside now, not at all." Removing the black wrapping from his hand, Vlad soon noticed a mark on the back of his hand. It was lightly glowing, albeit dimmer than the mark on his neck, "What is that?"

"That is the mark of Breve the Lion, one of your ancient ancestors."

"I've never noticed that before. This is amazing."

"Arthur also had the same two marks on his body, so I want to say he's one of your distant ancestors."

"Wait, are you insinuating that you've actually *met* Arthur?"

"I did, when Albert and I visited the Scorpio Desert."

"Awesome! What was he like?"

"Certainly a confident man, that's for sure." Vlad reveled in this new knowledge as he re-wrapped his hand. Benjamin was still a little confused though, "There's one thing I don't quite understand about you, Vlad."

"What's that?"

"On Arthur, both of these marks react with one another to produce what look like birthmarks, but you said you have never noticed them before."

"It's probably because I'm an albino. We don't have any pigmentation, so things like birthmarks wouldn't show up on someone like me."

"Very interesting." Smiling and putting a reassuring hand on Vlad's back, Benjamin said, "You have some fine ancestors, Vlad. You should be proud to be a part of their ranks."

"Indeed, I am, Benjamin. Indeed, I am." Joining the rest of the group, Benjamin and Vlad looked up at the impressive statue before them. The statue was of a man with the lower body of a horse. This man was holding a bow, pulled back with an arrow ready to fly to its destination. With a short laugh, Vlad nudged R-3N3 with a clunk, "Kinda looks like Rigel, right Artie?"

"I suppose it does. Well, with a head, that is."

Robin was more interested in the bow the statue held. The arrow which was cocked on the bowstring was made of pure Turquoise. The arrowhead had a light, blue flame enveloping it, dimly lighting that area of the cavern. As she examined the stone weapon, she spoke to herself, "This is amazing, but it doesn't necessarily match with what I've heard about the Mount Charles method."

Albert overheard Robin and came over to ask, "What of the Mount Charles method do you know?" He had recalled that, since he was the archer of the Army, General Braun might have used the same attack during Amedeo's War. Albert was curious if this method was indeed the same.

"Well, it was my understanding that the method relied on a special type of projectile known as the Sagittarius Arrow. The material was never specified, but I know for certain that it wasn't Turquoise."

"What was so special about this projectile?"

"It was said that when one fired the Sagittarius Arrow, it would immediately multiply, taking every variable into consideration and propagating itself into a storm of arrows."

"Curious. That description matches what the Mutable Quality of the Caidoz statues can do." In contemplation, Albert was once again stroking his moustache. This description also matched what Albert had seen Braun use during the penultimate battle of the war.

"Really?"

"*Ja*, and this statue happens to be of the Mutable Quality." Taking a step to the side, Albert examined the statue again and remarked, "Why not take a look in the centaur's quiver?"

The quiver of the centaur was worn on its back and held a set of three arrows. Robin got Sucari to lift her up so she could reach the quiver and remove one of the arrows. Holding it in her hand, she saw the construction was similar to any other arrow, with feathered fletching and wooden shaft. However, the arrowhead was unique in that it exhibited the same smooth, white stone attributes which matched the rest of the statue.

Placing the arrow in one of the quivers she wore on her calves, Robin reached up to grab the rest of the arrows when she realized there were still three arrows in the centaur's quiver. Almost as if she had never taken it to begin with. This amazed her, "That is quite curious."

Albert noticed this as well and remarked, "That is the Mutable Quality for you."

Sucari grabbed the hilt of the broadsword he now wore on his hip and unsheathed the weapon, "Well, if we're done gawking, let's get to destroying."

"Hold on a moment, Sucari." Albert had his hand out in a gesture telling everyone to wait. "Let us not get too hasty here. I would like to put the Spear of Trium through a test drive so I can be sure it can destroy the statues like I think it can."

Re-sheathing Hikari Shichidai, Sucari relented, "OK, but how are three different weapons going to make a single weapon?"

Albert was already opening up the container he held on his back and pulling out two of the three Imaginary World weapons that were given to The Triumvirate. Setting Chi's Pitchfork and Psi's Trident on the stone floor, Albert motioned for Benjamin to lay down Lambda's Hammer next to its partner weapons. Examining the items as if they would magically come together to form the Spear of Trium, Benjamin asked, "Very well, now what?"

○

A few months had passed and Isaac was now fully integrated into the community of Alden. Carroll was overjoyed that she could have her child and no longer be persecuted for her unusual pregnancy. Even though some were still skeptical, most had accepted the false story about Isaac's involvement. After all, Carroll was the type of person who normally kept to herself and didn't let anyone know about her personal life.

As for Isaac, he was enjoying his life as Edmond. Herding cattle was an incredibly low-stress job which he found to be relaxing. While he did miss his friends back on earth, he had come to remember the simpler life of doing things by himself. In fact, as time went on, he had started to forget about the Caidoz statues. With each passing day, he spent less and less time looking for the statue of the bull. He had convinced himself that perhaps the maiden statue was the only statue on the moon. Even to that end, he had started to think of how to destroy it less and less.

With the pain of losing his first wife long behind him, Isaac was once again enjoying the married life, even if it was a sham. At the very least, he figured he could give Carroll some amount of happiness. For the time being, he felt it was his duty to do all that he could to help this single mother, since he knew his involvement in the future would eventually take her son away.

This nagging knowledge of the future was becoming less troubling as Carroll got closer to giving birth. One day, Isaac was out in the fields with the cows, watching them graze in a nearby crater when his boss ran up to him and asked, "What are you doing here, Edmond?"

"What do you mean? I've got this shift. It hasn't changed since I accepted the job."

"No, I mean what are you doing here, since Carroll is having her baby?"

"What?"

"Yeah, she just went into labor. The doctor is on his way." Isaac's boss covered his eyes when a burst of wind kicked up some dust. When the dust cleared, Isaac had vanished. His boss was dumbfounded, "I knew he needed to get back to Carroll, I just never figured he was that fast."

As was his method when he used the wind fluxion, Isaac appeared at the edge of town behind one of the buildings, so as to not draw attention to himself. As far as he knew, no one else on the moon was aware of the fluxions and he wanted it to stay that way. Running into town, Isaac arrived at his house and burst through the door. Some of Carroll's friends she had made since she "married" Isaac were there already.

"Wow, Edmond. That was fast. I just told your boss only about ten minutes ago that Carroll was going into labor, and you're here already."

"Thanks, Diana."

As Isaac reached for the door to the bedroom, another friend spoke up, "You can't go in there, Edmond. Doctor's orders."

"But she's my wife, Phoebe. I think I'm allowed the right." At that moment, Carroll screamed out in pain, at which point Isaac removed his hand from the doorknob and conceded, "Very well, maybe I'll just stay out here."

The last friend chimed in, "That's a wise choice."

"Thanks, Claire."

Another scream from behind the door, this time longer and more anguished than the last. Then, silence. The silence lasted longer than Isaac felt it should have. The silence was broken by the cry of a baby. Everyone in the room smiled as the tension immediately lifted. Strangely enough, the baby whistled at the end of each of his cries.

After a few moments, the doctor peeked his head out of the bedroom and said, "You can come in now, Edmond." When Isaac made his way into the room, the doctor pulled him to the side and whispered, "Did you know she was a virgin?"

"Yes, I knew."

"But how did she get pregnant in the first place? It doesn't make any sense."

"It's a long story, but we'd like it if you kept this to yourself." The doctor nodded with a blank stare on his face, not able to wrap his mind around the situation. He then opened the door and left the bedroom, leaving Isaac alone with Carroll and the newborn Erwin.

Erwin had stopped crying and was wrapped in some towels as he was cradled in his mother's arms. Carroll smiled as she gazed upon the face of the child she had wished for, "Welcome to the world, Erwin." When Isaac approached, she looked up and continued smiling, "Thank you so much, Edmond. You don't know how much your help has been appreciated since I met you," her cheeks flushed for a moment, "I wouldn't have had the hope to go on without you."

"Don't mention it, Carroll. After all, what are fake husbands for?"

This elicited a laugh from Carroll as she leaned over to give Isaac a kiss on the forehead. The door opened again and Carroll's three friends peeked their heads in, trying to get a look at the newest addition to the little family.

○

Albert was at a loss. He knew the weapons needed to come together, but he was still unsure on how. Looking to Benjamin, he asked, "You can change the shape of your weapon, right?"

"That's right."

"Well, perhaps your weapon would encompass the other two somehow."

"It's worth a shot, I suppose." Kneeling down and placing his hand on the hammer's head, Benjamin began to focus his electrical power into the metal. However, when the orb started to glow, it caused a reaction in the other two weapons. Chi's Pitchfork began to glow with heat and Psi's Trident vibrated, rattling on the stone floor. Benjamin stopped for a moment and the reactions with the other weapons stopped as well.

"That is most curious," Albert remarked, stroking his moustache. Perhaps the inherent properties of The Triumvirate's powers were linked to their weapons.

Sucari spoke up, "Wait a minute, Isaac said something similar when we found Psi's Trident."

"Then he must have deduced the same thing we are observing here." Motioning for Sucari to come closer, Albert asked, "You have the Hellfire orb, correct?"

"Yeah, that's right."

"Try putting that power into Chi's Pitchfork here." Sucari grabbed the handle of the weapon and focused on the orb embroidered into the chest of his vest. A faint flame erupted from the tines of the pitchfork and, as had happened before, the other two weapons reacted, except this time Lambda's Hammer started sparking. Albert was thoughtful, "It would appear we need the three Triumvirate powers in order to create this weapon." At this realization, he became downfallen, "Unfortunately, we have lost the Seawave orb, so this whole operation seems like it will be pointless."

"Wait! All is not lost yet." Placing Chi's Pitchfork back on the ground, Sucari reached into the pocket of Isaac's jacket and pulled out an orb on a chain, its contents vibrating and flowing in a very fluid manner, "We found this near Psi's Trident when we were on the bottom of the ocean."

At the sight of the Seawave orb, Albert was as ecstatic as he was when they first showed him Psi's Trident, "*Wunderbar! Wunderbar! Wunderbar!*" Grabbing the orb from Sucari, Albert said, "We do not have time to create a proper uroboros seal, so we will let Benjamin, who can use these powers naturally, control both the Skybolt orb and the Seawave orb. Are you fine with this, Benjamin?"

Nudging his glasses with his free hand, he replied, "Yes, I think I can handle it."

"*Wunderbar.* Now, let us get to work." Handing the Seawave orb to Benjamin, he put the chain around his neck and let the elemental core rest on his chest, next to his own. Each of the weapons were laid end-to-end on the floor. Benjamin knelt down and put one of each of his hands on his hammer and Psi's Trident. Benjamin motioned with his head for Sucari to do the same with Chi's Pitchfork.

When Sucari knelt down and placed his hands on the last weapon, he peered across at Benjamin, who nodded, indicating that they should start. At once, all three orbs began to glow and the respective weapons began to react to the influx of energy. The event happened quickly, but consisted of three subsequent events which all happened almost simultaneously. The metal of Chi's Pitchfork melted to the floor. The head of Lambda's Hammer began to flow and elongate. Psi's Trident vibrated at such a frequency that a pure tone rang out in the cavern.

In a flash, the event completed. On the floor now sat a long, metallic shaft with a pointed tip at one end. The silvery metal hissed as it cooled and a symbol appeared on the tip of the weapon. The symbol was of a large "9" with the numbers "0", "3", and "4" stacked on top of each other next to it. Everyone stared at the object in amazement. Vlad was the first to say something, "What just happened?"

Grabbing the elongated weapon with his gloved hand, Albert examined it, "It seems that all three shafts of the Imaginary Weapons were used as the structure of the spear and the heads of the weapons created an alloy which covered the shafts, much in the same way that Benjamin is able to transform his hammer into a javelin." Pointing at the symbol on the tip, he continued, "And since this item is a combination of the three Triumvirate weapons, the '9' is most apt, while also representing the individual units which constitute the spear's base elements."

The spear was almost seven feet long and as Benjamin examined the combined power, he had to ask, "So, Albert, how do we use this Spear of Trium?"

Determining it was now cool enough to touch with a bare hand, Albert handed the weapon to Benjamin as he returned to the cylindrical container which he normally held on his back. Opening the left side of the container, which used to house the individual weapons of the spear, Albert emerged with a rectangular ceramic box which was about six feet long. The box had a hole in one end and two handles, one metal at the end opposite the hole, and one ceramic in the middle of the box.

Setting the item on the ground with the hole end in the air, Albert motioned for Benjamin to place the spear in the mysterious box. Sliding the spear into the hole, it stuck out from the box a little bit. Albert handed the device to Benjamin, who examined it curiously and had to ask, "And what, may I ask, is this?"

"This, my electrical friend, is a rail gun. It works based off of your lightning powers. All you have to do is hold the two handles and let the entirety of your energy flow into the metal one. The coils inside will induce an accelerant force which will allow the Spear of Trium to reach destructive speeds in a minimal amount of space."

Grabbing the handles and leveling the weapon at the statue, Benjamin told everyone, "This might get dangerous. I'd suggest you get out of here while you can." As everyone else filed out of the chamber, the Skybolt orb on Benjamin's chest began to glow. He struggled to keep the energy in while building it to levels he had never handled before.

He worried that the flicker in the Skybolt orb, which occasionally occurred at the most inopportune times, would happen again. As a result, he tried to keep the charging at a controllable level. Soon, he couldn't hold it back anymore and let all the energy he had stored in his body transfer to the rail gun. In a flash, Benjamin was knocked to the back wall and the chamber resounded with an explosive sound.

As the room started to clear of dust and debris, Albert had rushed back down the stairs to examine the damage. The statue, which once stood in the middle of the room, was now no longer there and the Spear of Trium had embedded itself at least three feet into the solid rock wall on the opposite side of the chamber. Albert was overjoyed at the results of this experiment, "*Wunderbar!* Now we are ready to take on Ophiuchus."

Benjamin approached the other side of the room while rubbing his sore back. Examining the spear embedded in the wall, he tugged on it a few times to no avail. R-3N3 had come down to the room and was amazed at the destructive power of the device. He saw Benjamin struggling with removing the spear from the wall, so he went over to lend his assistance. Unfortunately, R-3N3's strength had decreased yet again. Vlad noticed this and came to assist them both. With all three of them working together, they managed to free the spear from the wall. Benjamin loaded it back into the rail gun and took the strap he was using to hold the hammer on his back and applied it to his new, enhanced weapon.

Everyone made their way outside and sighed in relief when they realized another statue had been destroyed. Both of the Millennials were relieved that they did not run into Ophiuchus, but they sensed that, with less statues to destroy, they would inevitably encounter him again. Albert pulled out the re-made sheet of Caidoz lyrics and crossed off another couplet. "*Wunderbar.* Only three statues remain."

"That's great, but where do we go next?" Sucari asked.

"Fortunately, I think I might know where one of them resides, and it is not too far away."

"OK, where?"

"Are you familiar with the Island of Stability?"

"Nah, not really."

"Well, it is a legendary island which rises above the clouds and I just happen to know a few researchers of mine who had actually visited it when we were studying the fluxions. In fact, you can see it from here." Albert pointed out across the mountains to the ominous peak which stood in the distance, clouds covering its top and a considerable amount of the airspace above it.

Robin pulled her glasses down from the top of her head and looked over to the mountain. Unfortunately, the glasses weren't working in the way she expected them to, so she put them back on top of her head as a headband to hold back her hair and merely asked, "So, do we have to walk over there, or will we use another Q-Portal?"

"Q-Portal, of course. But once we get there, we will need to discuss how to get to the top."

Vlad asked, "Why would we need to discuss it? Don't we just walk to the top?"

"This mountain is unlike anything you have ever experienced, Vlad. You will soon see what I mean." Albert headed back down the ridge of Mount Charles as he led the way to the Q-Portal they had used to arrive mere hours ago.

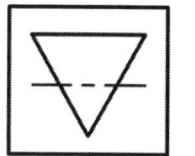 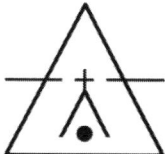

Chapter 6

Destroying the Statues

A few years had passed and Erwin was quickly growing to be a healthy and energetic young boy. Of course, he was a bit of a menace as he was learning to walk, which caused his mother to worry to no end. In fact, when he had just started learning to walk, he accidentally fell and knocked a tooth out, which also damaged his gums and the permanent tooth underneath, thereby leaving a set gap in his teeth. Now, whenever he spoke, he tended to whistle on the "s" of every word, which gained Carroll the moniker of "Whistler's Mother."

Now that Isaac was helping to raise Erwin, he had almost completely forgotten about the Caidoz statues and his goal to destroy them. His boss had eventually left the entire herd of cattle to Isaac and now was working in another pasture in another crater. Since the increased responsibility took most of Isaac's time, he didn't have much of it to search for methods to destroy the maiden statue. He had completely forgotten about even looking for the bull statue. Life moved on at a comfortable pace and nothing important really ever happened to Isaac, Carroll, or Erwin. That was, until a visitor came to Isaac's pasture one day.

It was a day like the others. Isaac sat on the ridge of the crater, watching his cows graze on the grey grass, occasionally stopping to moo. As he watched, he noticed something off in the distance. At first glance, it was a bull, completely black and charging the herd. However, Isaac kept examining the bull from afar, since something seemed off about it. The bull seemed like it was too big to be that far away, but he was also trying to figure out if it was from his herd or not. While there were a lot of cattle under his purview, this bull didn't seem familiar by any means.

Soon, the bull was closing the distance between itself and Isaac's herd, so he decided to step in. Now that Isaac had integrated the wind orb into his clothing, it allowed for use of both hands. In a burst of wind, he teleported to the top of the bull and grabbed onto its horns. Isaac was surprised to find the bull's skin to be cold and lifeless, despite the intense amount of its forward momentum. Since he was quickly approaching his herd, Isaac turned to wind, bringing the bull with him.

Appearing in a different crater, Isaac found himself and the bull in an area covered by the dark month, which meant that, when the bull bucked him off, he couldn't tell where the statue had gone. Since the blackness of the bull blended almost completely into the blackness of the surroundings, it was nearly impossible to see where it had ended up. The only parts of the bull which could even be seen were two Emerald eyes, glowing with anger. Isaac listened intently for the sounds of the bull's hooves on the ground, but realized that he still had a large herd of cattle to return to. As the sound of the bull got louder, Isaac transported back to his herd, out of breath and pumped with adrenaline.

Isaac's mind was reeling. What was that thing? It felt strangely familiar, but he was having trouble remembering from where. Deciding to forget about the incident for the time being, Isaac saw it was time to bring the cows back from grazing. Still, despite trying to put everything out of his mind, he couldn't stop thinking about the feel of the bull. It almost felt like rock, despite the fact that it acted like a real bull.

Arriving back home, Isaac was still obviously bothered by the event, since Carroll asked, "What's wrong, Edmond?"

"Nothing, just something at work today."

"Oh, what happened?"

"The herd was attacked by a strange bull, but the odd thing is that, when I tried to stop it, the interaction reminded me of something I experienced before, I'm just having trouble remembering what."

"Well, I'm sure you'll figure it out eventually."

"Yes, you're probably right." Changing topics, Isaac asked, "Say, do you want to go out and see the stars tonight?"

"Sure. I haven't gotten out of the house in a while, so it'll be nice to take some time to relax. Let me just check on Erwin and we can go."

"Very well." Isaac went to his room and was changing out of his work clothes when something in the closet caught his attention. It was the duffel bag which was filled with the items he had found when he first arrived on the moon two years ago. Opening it up, he saw the various orbs and scrolls which reminded him of a past which seemed like a distant memory. Pulling out the scroll which lay on the top of the pile, he read through it. It was the scroll which had the lyrics of a song on it; a few of its couplets had been crossed off.

Reading the poem, he got to the couplet, "The bull ran and jumped too soon / And got himself stuck on the moon", which triggered a connection in his mind. Was the bull that attacked his herd this same bull? Memories were starting to come back in pieces as he remembered that these statues were incredibly difficult to destroy and he had no weapons to destroy them. He then remembered where he had felt the same sensation he experienced while he rode the bull. Long ago, he had ridden a ram in a somewhat similar manner.

Had he finally found the bull? If he had, he still needed to figure out how to destroy it. He was pulled from his memories when he heard Carroll whispering behind him, "Edmond, are you in here?"

"Yes, I'm here."

"Erwin's asleep, we can go now." Returning the scroll and closing the bag, Isaac joined Carroll at the door as they made their way out of the house. Walking to the outskirts of town, Isaac and Carroll casually strolled through the open space outside the village, gazing upward at the vast expanse of stars above them. The dark month had just started in Alden and everyone had made the switch to extended darkness as easily as they had done for many dark months before.

As they strolled, Carroll reveled in the beauty of the sky above them, "There's really no comparison to this, even the inside of the Virgo shrine doesn't come close to this vast spectacle."

"To think that we're just one of those small dots floating out in space, really makes me contemplate the immensity of the universe."

"I'd rather focus on the beauty." Pointing up at the sky, Carroll exclaimed, "Look! There's something different from before." Sure enough, out among the throng of stars was a bright object, its blue, luminescent tail trailing behind it as it slowly travelled through space.

"You're right! It looks like a comet has appeared since our last dark month." Another memory came floating to Isaac's mind, which changed his mood to one of solemnity once again.

Carroll noticed the change and asked, "Are you OK?"

"Yes, just a memory of something from my past."

"You know, I haven't really gotten a chance to ask about your past."

"I'd rather not talk about it."

"Is it painful?"

"Sort of, but I think it's best if I keep you in the dark about a lot of it. For your own safety. After all, I wouldn't want you getting harassed again on my account."

Nuzzling up against Isaac's arm, Carroll cooed, "Thanks for looking out for me, Edmond."

"Hey, what are fake husbands for?"

Arriving at the base of the clouds, just short of the summit of Meadow Peak, the group of Caidoz statue destroyers transitioned to the misty reaches of the top of the mountain. Climbing the straight ridge, they eventually arrived at a peculiar sight. On the top of the mountain was a pillar which seemed to be holding up a large mass above it. Albert stopped at the column and explained, "This is where we need to figure out how to get to the top."

"Is this not the top?" R-3N3 asked.

"*Nein*. In fact, it is more like the middle." Motioning with his hand, Albert tried to give an idea of the mountain's shape, "Think of this mountain as an hourglass. We are at the midpoint of the hourglass, which means that Meadow Peak is the bottom half. The top half is known as the Island of Stability."

Vlad spoke up, "Well, if that's the case, then how on earth are we going to get to the Island of Stability? We can't very well climb up an inverted slope like this."

"I must ask you all, because I do not know your powers yet, how many of you can fly?" Vlad and Sucari rose their hands, along with Benjamin. "*Wunderbar*. It seems like we have enough people to make this work. My only question now is how long do you think you can carry someone while still maintaining flight?" Everyone gave their own answers, but it seemed like the lowest value was about ten minutes. This concerned Albert, "This task might take all of your fortitude, but if you would rather not carry one of our team members, we would need to figure out who will stay behind right now."

Everyone glanced at everyone else and, from the looks in their eyes, it didn't seem like anyone wanted to give up the chance to participate. Sucari gave their answer, "I think we just need to make it work . . . somehow."

"Very well. Here is the plan. Sucari, I am assuming that you can use the Hellfire orb for thrust, so you will be carrying R-3N3. Benjamin, you will carry me, and Vlad will carry Robin. Is everyone fine with these arrangements?" Everyone nodded in agreement, "*Wunderbar*. Now, when we get to the top, we need everyone to land in a circle around the center of the island. If we cannot do this correctly, the entire island is liable to fall over. Is everybody ready to go?" With nods from all parties, everyone paired up with their respective partner.

In one organized movement, everyone jumped off of the mountain and began to climb into the sky. Albert was giving out orders as they flew, "Stay close to the island, otherwise you might get lost as you ascend! Just be careful, as you cannot merely fly straight up." Sure enough, the cloud was very disorienting, so as the group flew into the sky, the people who couldn't fly were charged with letting the fliers know how close they were getting to the inverted slope of the island.

Vlad was the first to start struggling, as Robin was hanging on around his waist, he began having to flap more often to gain altitude. Next, Benjamin started to show fatigue. Since Sucari was using his fire to do most of the heavy lifting, he was still fine, but he could tell it would only be a matter of time before even his fire gave out.

The clouds were starting to become brighter and brighter as they climbed higher and higher. In a blinding flash, they broke the surface of the clouds and rose above a wide expanse, littered with concentric circles of pillars topped with fire. This was the Island of Stability. Now that they didn't have to fly upward, the three fliers slowly made their way to the middle of the island, gliding as much as possible. When they arrived at the temple in the center of the island, they flew inside and landed as close to the exact center as they possibly could.

When they landed, the fliers collapsed on the ground, breathing heavily as they tried to regain their strength. Since the group wasn't entirely balanced around the center of the island, the ground began to tilt and groan in protest. Instinctively, the members of the group who were still standing took a few steps away from their initial positions and the island soon settled back into its balanced state.

With the excitement of the shifting island now over, Albert stood still as he examined the temple, which seemed similar to the one they had just visited on top of Mount Charles, "Good work, men. We would not have been able to get here this quickly without your assistance." Glancing at the surroundings, Albert saw some random rocks sitting on the ground, but he also saw an engraved mantra encircling the floor of the temple. It said, "Silence induces Neutrality. Neutrality induces Equilibrium. Equilibrium induces Balance. Balance induces Stability. Stability induces Peace. Peace induces Silence." With the last statement, the mantra was back at its beginning, continuing its saying in an infinite loop.

Examining the temple, R-3N3 and Robin were standing still, trying to find some indication of where the statue would lie. Robin asked, "Do you see anything, Artie?"

"Negative. But I also am not sure what I am looking for."

"Well, since the statue isn't here, like it was in the Aquarius shrine, I would assume that the Centaurcher shrine is our precedent and the statue would be underneath us." A low rumble was heard below, causing the non-fliers to look beneath them, "I think I may be right, but how do we get down there?" A loud crack was heard as a fissure appeared around the edge of the engraved mantra, "Actually, I don't think I want to know how we'll get down there."

Another loud crack finished connecting the fissure, which made the entire circle drop deep into the Island of Stability. The group was caught off guard and didn't even have enough time to scream by the time they realized what was happening. From the bright ambiance of the top of the Island of Stability, they were quickly plunged into a darkness that was not only disorienting in terms of direction, but in the speed at which they fell.

As suddenly as the event had begun, it stopped, knocking everyone to the stone slab, or at least everyone who wasn't already lying on it. The first person to regain his verbal faculties was Sucari, "What just happened?"

Albert was slowly getting up and scrutinizing their new location. He looked up to the pinpoint of light which shone above them, showing him how far they had really fallen. Surveying the edge of the stone slab they were resting on, he noticed that the separation was clean, and not jagged, "I think we may have put too much weight on this slab."

R-3N3 was using his green, lighted eyes to illuminate the area, "But where do we go from here?" Just as he asked the question, he found a dark gap in the wall and said, "Never mind, I think I found a staircase to the area below us."

When R-3N3 took a step toward the opening, Albert shouted, "Wait! You will offset the balance of the whole island!" This caused R-3N3 to falter, taking a few more steps than he intended toward the opening. Everyone tensed up as they waited for the island to shift again. And yet, nothing happened. When a few moments passed, Albert relaxed, but was still confused, "How can this be?" Pulling out the lyric scroll, Albert read the couplet about the scales, "'The scales' balance must be intact / For unbiased justice it must enact.' Obviously this island is based off of the concept of balance, but why are we not affected by it here?"

Noticing the symbol used to designate this particular Caidoz statue, it suddenly came to Albert what was going on, "Ah! We must be at the centroid of the island."

R-3N3 had to ask, "Centroid, what is that?"

"The centroid is the complete center of a body of mass. If the centroid of any object can be found, it can be balanced. This is why the island does not shift when we move around down here." This revelation allowed everyone to relax as they stood up and followed R-3N3 to the opening in the wall. Down the dark, spiral staircase, the group descended, the only indication of their progress being how close they were to the inexplicable light at the end of the corridor.

When the group emerged at the other side, they stood before a large statue, carved of a brilliant white fluxionite which seemed to emit its own light, much like the water bearer's statue had on the bottom of the ocean. This statue was the scales.

The next day, Isaac was once again watching over his herd of cattle as he thought about what he had seen last night. He was trying to remember the timeframe in which everything occurred when he came to the moon the first time. He knew that Erwin was about twelve when he first met him and that Edmond's comet collided with the moon ten years prior to that, but why was the comet named after his assumed identity?

Isaac knew he wasn't supposed to affect history negatively, but what if he was supposed to enact history? What if he was supposed to cause the comet to crash into the back of the moon? He knew the effects of that singular event were great enough to block out the sun on the earth for an entire year, so he was hesitant to carry through with any plan which would put that into action. Still, he didn't want to change what had already happened, as the paradox he had created would cease to exist if he didn't somehow get the comet to collide with the moon.

Suddenly, pieces started to fall into place. He needed to destroy two Caidoz statues. Pulling out the scroll he had taken from the bag in his closet, he found both the bull and the maiden were of the Earth Element, which was weak against the Water Element. He knew comets were made mostly of ice, so this destructive event would work completely to his advantage. Now he had a way to destroy the statues, but not a means to enact that plan.

Another piece fell into place. He remembered seeing the Gravity Core in the duffel bag which he had found, and he found it odd that the core was already there, when he had thought the comet bearing his alter ego's moniker had brought the core to the moon. If he could somehow activate the Gravity Core and draw it to the maiden statue, he would destroy the statues and create the lake he had distinctly remembered seeing outside of Alden.

Now he just had to lure the bull statue to the Virgo shrine and he could kill two birds with one stone, literally. But first, he needed to figure out how to activate the Gravity Core so as to draw the comet down to the moon. He needed to act quickly on this aspect of the plan, as the comet wasn't going to be around forever. And yet, he was concerned with the realization that, when he had gotten to the moon in the future, Edmond was no longer around. In fact, he remembered that Edmond had died tragically in the comet catastrophe. Still, Isaac tried to be optimistic about it. Did he really die, or was he able to escape in time and use the event to disappear from Erwin and Carroll's lives?

Deciding to take an early day, Isaac started leading the cattle back home as he continued thinking about how to implement his plan to crash the comet into the moon. When he arrived back at his house, he snuck inside and found Carroll was out with Erwin. This was good, as it gave him time to gather some important things and steal away to the Virgo shrine. Using his wind power to quickly teleport to the door of the hidden cavern, Isaac lifted the stone slab and carefully closed it behind him.

At the chamber housing the maiden statue, Isaac felt the walls to see what kind of material he would be working with. While they were sturdy, they did allow him to quickly carve out some simple designs with his throwing knife. Opening up the duffel bag, he rifled through the scrolls until he found one which described a long-distance sealing technique which would allow the capture of more intangible items. A note scrawled on the bottom of the scroll detailed the successful capture of sunlight as an example of its use. The uroboros design and note brought back nostalgic memories from his former life, when he had just started his research on fluxions.

Unrolling the scroll and pinning it underneath the duffel bag to keep it open, Isaac started carving the uroboros snake design into the walls of the chamber. The work was simple enough, but tedious and time consuming. After a few hours, he had managed to carve across one third of the chamber, at which point he packed everything up and hid it behind the maiden statue. Leaving the shrine, Isaac appeared back at his home and entered, pretending as if he had just come home from work, "I'm home!" he announced.

"Hi, Edmond. How was work?"

"Pretty good, how was your day?"

"It went well. Erwin and I had a play date at Eugene's house."

"That's nice. Erwin should make a lot of friends."

"I agree, but friends aren't the end all be all. After all, I only gained my three friends after you had 'married' me."

"True. Very true."

"You seem distant again, Edmond. Is something wrong?"

"No, I'm just thinking about something."

Carroll was a little excited about this. Since Isaac's encounter with the bull a few weeks ago, he had been acting strangely, but Carroll thought it might be because he was going to ask her to actually marry him. No sham, no fake. Really get married. "OK. If you ever want to talk, let me know."

With a smile, Isaac replied, "OK."

The next day, Isaac repeated the engraving process and managed to get another third of the uroboros seal completed in the Virgo shrine. The day after, he completed the seal and put the Gravity Core in the link between the snake's tail and mouth. Placing his hands on the mouth and tail interface, Isaac took a deep breath and proceeded to focus his energy into the fluxion he had created in the underground cavern. The uroboros seal began to glow with a white light as Isaac took the first step toward sealing his fate.

When he emerged from the shrine that night, he looked up at the sky and saw the comet far off in the distance. And yet, something about it had changed. It appeared as though the tail was shorter than it used to be, and the head of the comet was now considerably bigger. This was evidence that the plan would work. Now the next step was to find the bull statue again and lure it to the Virgo shrine. He wasn't quite sure how he was going to continue using the fluxion with the huge black beast also inside the cramped quarters, but maybe the bull didn't have to be *inside* the shrine at all, but merely on top of it.

At the door to the underground shrine, Isaac started pacing until he had arrived at a location that he believed was directly above the Virgo shrine which sat unnoticed deep below. Kneeling down, he marked the spot with an "X" using his knife and proceeded to make his way back home. In order for everything to go smoothly, there were a few things he needed to get ready.

The scales were certainly a sight. Not only were they a glowing, white stone, but each plate was a different, brilliant gem. The left plate was a stunning Opal while the right plate was a fantastic Tourmaline. When everyone filed into the chamber, Albert removed the metal protector from the C.L.A.W. he wore on his left side and said, "Let me use the light to charge this weapon and we will be done with this statue and can move on to the last two."

A voice, coming seemingly from nowhere, spoke to the group, "Oh, but how little you know." Everyone jumped at the sound, and looked around to see where it was coming from. The voice had changed location and continued, "This is actually the last surviving member of the Caidoz statues that you have so brutally destroyed."

Benjamin's and Albert's veins went cold. They recognized the voice. Albert called out, "Ophiuchus? Is that you?"

"It is."

"Where are you?"

"Can't you see? I'm right here in the room with you." Albert was struck from behind and fell to the ground. Everyone turned toward Albert to see if the assailant was there, but the most they could see was a black silhouette, quickly moving into the darkness beyond the reach of the scales' light.

Benjamin grabbed the rail gun and shouted orders to the others, "We need to destroy the statue quickly! He's here to prevent us from accomplishing our goal!"

Moaning on the ground, Albert tugged on Isaac's coat which Sucari was wearing, attempting to get himself upright, "Sucari, the scales are of the Air Element, which means Fire is its weakness. If Benjamin cannot get the rail gun charged in time, you will be our only hope."

Vlad and R-3N3 were frantically trying to find where Ophiuchus was in the dimly lit room. Standing back-to-back, Vlad asked, "This takes me back. Do you see anything, Artie?"

R-3N3's eyes glowed green as he scanned the room, "Negative, he is moving too quickly for me to get a lock on his position."

"Yeah, I'm having the same problem. Even though I can see well in the dark, if he keeps moving around like this, we're liable to-" another strike from the shadows and Vlad went silent and fell to the floor.

"Vlad?" R-3N3 turned around and found his comrade on the floor, "Vlad! Are you all right?"

The Skybolt orb was glowing brighter and brighter as Benjamin charged the energy inside his body. He was muttering to himself, "Come on. Hurry! Hurry!"

Adrenaline was pumping through Robin's veins as more members of the team started going down. Her breathing was rapid as she backed up toward the glowing statue in the middle of the room, hoping the light would give her enough time to react, should the shadowy figure go after her next. In a bright flash, Sucari caught fire, his body covered in red flames. When Robin regained her sight, she saw a pitch black figure directly in front of her, his arm poised for attack.

Another flash and Sucari was now covered in blue flames, immediately forcing himself between Robin and Ophiuchus. Hikari Shichidai was drawn and used to block the attack meant for his wife. Even though the blade was meant to be so sharp as to be able to cut light itself, Ophiuchus had taken the hit from the sword and seemed unfazed. With Sucari lighting the room with his fire, it was shown that Ophiuchus was indeed a black and featureless figure, instead of just someone who stayed in the shadows to hide his movements. And yet, parts of his body appeared damaged, despite being of a black color which seemed to absorb what little light there was in the room.

Ophiuchus chuckled softly as Sucari struggled to hold him back, "I am assuming this woman means something to you, otherwise you wouldn't have put yourself in such a defenseless position."

Through gritted teeth, Sucari growled, "That's none of your business."

"Oh, but it's simple deduction, young man. I've already incapacitated two within your group without so much as a reaction from anyone, so when I attacked her, I was surprised to find someone who could stand up to me. After all, if your relationship is much more than one of a battle companion, then the others would have been saved as well."

Still struggling, Sucari turned his head slightly and spoke to his wife, "Robin, I need you to move out of the way soon."

"Oh? What do you plan on doing?" Ophiuchus taunted.

"This!" In a moment, Sucari's wings appeared, covered in blue fire, and Robin dove out of the way. With more energy being required to turn his blue fire white, Sucari was pushed back by Ophiuchus, Hikari Shichidai inching closer and closer to his face. The fire was flickering between the point of blue and white, not quite making it to the next level.

With the edge of his sword uncomfortably close, Sucari's adrenaline was pumping in overdrive and he yelled to give himself enough motivation to make the switch from blue fire to white. Suddenly, the fire became white and stayed white, at which point Sucari stepped to the side, letting Hikari Shichidai fall to where he was standing. Quickly using the force Ophiuchus had been applying to his advantage, Sucari thrust the sword and struck the statue of the scales which stood behind him.

Flapping his wings in tandem with his attack, the white fire flew from Sucari's body and onto the Caidoz statue, immediately engulfing it with a heat which caused almost everybody to take a step backwards. As the statue burned, Ophiuchus laughed, "Ha ha ha! Do you really think that is enough to destroy a statue? Fluxions defeating the very thing that gives them power? If this worked before, it certainly won't work now."

From across the room, Benjamin yelled, "You're right! *This* will be enough." Everyone looked over to where the Natural was standing against the back wall, bracing himself for the eventual recoil of his weapon. Electricity was sparking all across his body, little blue arcs jumping from point to point. The air in the room was buzzing with the energy he had charged into his body. Those who had seen the destructive power of the Spear of Trium fell to the ground and covered their bodies in defensive positions. In a quick release, he poured all the electricity he had into the rail gun. A bright flash followed immediately afterward, resulting in flaming pieces of crumbling rubble raining over everyone as the scales disintegrated. Finally, the last statue had been destroyed.

For the good part of a week, Isaac had been visiting the Virgo shrine whenever he had a spare moment in order to activate the Gravity Core and pull the comet toward the moon. Each time he used the fluxion, the comet would become larger in the sky. He knew comets traveled at high speeds, but he needed to make absolutely sure his plan would work. The faster the better. Often, he would pour so much energy into the fluxion that he would pass out, only to awaken half an hour later, physically exhausted.

Carroll was increasingly worried about Isaac. He was becoming more and more distant from her and Erwin and she wasn't sure why. She had observed the comet they had noticed a few weeks ago growing bigger and brighter in the sky and she wondered if that was why she was losing him. One day, she breached the subject that had been on her mind for some time, "Edmond?"

"Yes, Carroll?"

"Do you want to get married?"

"What do you mean? Aren't we already married?"

"Unofficially, yes. But I mean, do you want to get married for real?"

Isaac was obviously distracted, thinking of something else, "What purpose would it serve?"

"Well, we've been living in this sham marriage for two years now, and I just would feel better if we made it official."

"So, what? Like have a ceremony in front of a priest?"

Carroll was starting to lose her confidence, "Not necessarily, maybe just fill out some paperwork." Isaac was silent, his mind elsewhere, "Are you thinking about the comet we saw?"

This comment snapped Isaac out of his daze, "What? What do you mean?"

"That comet we saw at the beginning of the dark month. It's obviously getting bigger."

Isaac sighed, "Yes, I am thinking about it. I'm worried what will happen to the town if it gets too close."

"Too close? What do you mean?"

"I mean, what if it were to collide with our town?"

"That's terrible! Why would you even think that?"

"I'm just considering the worst case scenario here."

"Is that why you don't want to get married?"

"I hardly think these two things are related."

Tears welled up in Carroll's eyes as she got up and started to leave the room, "OK, I get it. It must be me then." Her voice cracked as she quickly left the house.

Isaac had to admit it: he had been a real jerk. Now that he was focused on his original goal of eliminating the Caidoz statues, he had forgotten how much time had passed since he came to the moon. While it was his best intention to help Carroll raise Erwin, as he felt guilty for his fate, now the situation had enough time to develop into something he had not initially intended.

And yet, time was quickly running out. He didn't know how much longer it would take to get the comet to the moon, but from what he observed, it couldn't be but another week until the impact happened. With Carroll gone for the moment, Isaac went and retrieved the duffel bag with the fluxion scrolls and cores which he had placed back in his closet. He opened it and found a few familiar items from his first time on the moon. Right now, he was focused on setting the stage for his eventual arrival.

Grabbing the bag, he turned to wind and rushed off to another part of the moon. Arriving at the Peak of Eternal Light, he rummaged around in the duffel bag and found the scroll he was looking for: the seal for the Fluent of Light. Building a small pedestal out of the rocks on the summit, Isaac placed the scroll down and stepped back, surveying the sky where he first saw the earth silently hovering in the inky blackness. His home looked so foreign now. Strange how a few years on the moon can change one's perspective.

Now a piece of the stage was set. The next part of the setup was more difficult, because he knew that he had to supply a past enemy from the future with the supplies he needed to manipulate many people into following him. He had heard rumors of a failing church in a different town a few craters away from Herbert crater, where Alden quietly sat. Turning to wind, he left the Peak of Eternal Light to go and pay a visit to the Church of Werner.

The building was dilapidated and obviously in need of repair, but when Isaac made his way inside, he saw a priest in simple robes walking the aisles of the deserted sanctuary. Standing in the shadows of the narthex, Isaac called out, trying to mask his voice, "Priest Werner!"

The man stopped and asked, "Who's there?" He started to walk towards the call of the shadowy figure.

"Stop right there!"

With his hands in the air, Werner pleaded, "I swear, we don't have any money."

Isaac sighed as he continued, "I'm not here to rob you. I'm here to help you."

"Help me? How so?" Isaac threw the duffel bag on the ground. It slid toward Priest Werner, who scrutinized it questioningly, "What's this?"

"In a week, a terrible tragedy is about to befall the town of Alden, two craters over."

"What do you want me to do about it?"

"Take the tragedy and turn it to your advantage. That bag contains scrolls and items which will help you rise to power, quickly gaining a following that will do whatever you say." Isaac wasn't about to mention the lost Number-fluxion specifically, since he didn't want to give Werner an advantage in the future. He figured that the Priest would need to work out how to use the fluxion on his own. After all, the documentation he needed to create it was in the bag which now sat at his feet.

"That's great, but what's in it for you?"

"You may only accept that bag on a few conditions."

"All right, what are they?"

"First, the people of Alden will refer to the comet as 'Edmond's comet'. As such, you should build a shrine on the site of the disaster and name it after Edmond."

"That's easy enough, what else?"

"I need you to give me a blank, signed marriage certificate."

"Why would I want to do that?"

"Do you want to continue failing here?"

Relenting to the fraud he was about to commit, Werner sighed, "All right. Do you want anything else?"

"No, that will be all."

Picking up the bag, Werner made his way past Isaac, still obscured by shadows, as he sighed, "Let me get the certificate from my office." A few moments later, he reappeared with a form, completely blank except for his signature at the bottom of the page, "Here you go." Isaac grabbed the paper, quickly examined it and turned to wind to escape. Werner stood there in stunned silence. What had just happened?

Back in his office, Werner was rummaging through the canvass duffel. He chose one of the scrolls at random and opened it. Inside the scroll was a map to the Peak of Eternal Light. He read some of the notes on the map, but was still confused about what it was trying to tell him. He had no idea what a Fluent of Light was or why a scroll detailing its seal creation was placed on the top of the famous peak. Placing the scroll back in the bag, he decided that he had experienced enough strange things for one day and headed home.

Back at Alden, Isaac used his power to quickly knock on everyone's door. Soon, an irate mob was gathering in the middle of town, demanding answers. A burly gentleman shouted out, "What's the big deal, Edmond?"

"I'm glad you've all come here. I have to tell you all something."

Another rowdy crowd member shouted, "What is it?"

Pointing to the sky, everyone followed Isaac's finger, "Do you all see that? That is a comet which will strike the moon not far from this town."

The mumbling and jeering continued, "Yeah, right. How do you know?"

"I've been tracking this comet for a few weeks now, and it's definitely on a collision course with this town."

"Oh? And what do you expect us to do about it?"

"It's inevitable at this point, so I only ask that you leave town for a week, just to be safe."

"Leave town? Why? So you can loot us?"

"No! It's for your safety!"

The crowd started to disperse, "Yeah, right. Whatever, Edmond."

Obviously not being able to reason with the townspeople, Isaac headed to the Virgo shrine and spent the rest of the day putting all of his energy into the Gravity Core fluxion. As a result, the next day the comet was significantly closer. So much so that it almost seemed to take up a fifth of the sky. People were in a panic and they finally heeded his warning and left town. Just to make sure, Isaac used his wind power to check every house. Everyone had gone. Well, everyone but two people.

Carroll held Erwin in her arms as she asked, "Why won't you evacuate with us?"

"I still have some work to do, then I'll be right there with you."

"OK, I trust you, but if you don't show up, I'll never forgive you."

Giving her a peck on the cheek, Isaac said, "I know, dear." When he was sure Carroll and Erwin were safely away, he performed the last of his preparations. Transforming to wind, he traveled to a nearby abandoned crater where he had brought the bull statue. It was calmly grazing on the short grey grass and was no longer as angered as when he had first encountered it. Isaac gently touched its back as the bull continued to graze. Turning to wind, he transported both of them to the "X" he had marked above the Virgo shrine.

With no more grass to chew, the bull was slightly surprised, but merely lay down on the ground, too bored to do anything else. Isaac took a few steps away from the bull and transported himself back to his house. He got a few things together and put them in a box which he set on the kitchen table. First, he took the wind fluxion and put it in a different shirt that he had prepared. The shirt was long-sleeved, grey, and much smaller than the one he wore. It had the uroboros seal around the newly emplaced wind core.

Placing the shirt back in the box, Isaac fished an envelope out of his back pocket and also put it in the box. The envelope had Carroll's name on it, but he still pulled out another sheet of paper and sat down to write. Closing the box, he prepared himself to write one of the most difficult things he had ever come to terms with. This is what he wrote:

My dearest Carroll,

You must forgive me, but I am not coming back.

Don't get me wrong, this has nothing to do with you or Erwin and everything to do with my fate and my destiny. It's a little hard to explain, but the disaster which has just befallen you had to happen. Don't question it, but rather embrace it as the significant event that it is.

In the two years I have known you, you've helped me to forget a lot of the pain I've experienced in my past. I know I jokingly made light of our sham marriage, but I really do want to do right by you. In the envelope inside this box, you will find a marriage certificate, filled out, signed, and dated for our supposed marriage date more than two years ago. Even though I will no longer be around, you only need sign it and our sham marriage will become official. I know that in hindsight I should have done this a long time ago, but I've been looking to the future for far too long.

Please keep Erwin safe as I am certain he will be a handful in the years to come. Also in this box is a gift that I want you to give him when he turns ten years old. For the sake of restraint, tell him not to use the power which is embroidered on the chest, but just know that, as kids are prone to do, he will ignore you. Do not be angry with him, but just know he is a free spirit and he will always consider you his mother. As such, please do not tell him of me, as odds are he will not understand why I left, and will most likely blame himself.

In closing, just know that what I did, I did for the greater benefit of mankind. I love you and I love Erwin and I always will.

With all my heart,
Edmond

Placing the letter on the table, he stood up and began to walk to the Virgo shrine. When he arrived at the door, he looked towards the plain and saw the bull still sitting on the ground, unaware of what was about to happen. Gently pulling on a chain he placed around the beast's neck, Isaac guided the black statue to the entrance of the Virgo shrine.

Surveying the sky, Isaac saw the blue mass of the comet looming above them. He hoped he had given it enough of a pull to get down to the shrine, but to make absolutely sure, he was going to see this to the bitter end. He had thought about escaping and trying to start another new life somewhere else on the moon, but he knew that eventually the paradox would catch up to him. This was the only solution.

Lifting up the door to the shrine, Isaac took the end of the chain from the bull and attached it to the door handle to make sure the Caidoz statue would stay in place while the comet collided with the moon. With a deep, apprehensive sigh, Isaac closed the door behind him and shut himself off from the rest of the world for the last time. Slowly descending the dark corridor, Isaac contemplated his life up to this point. Was he merely a cog in the machine of the universe? At the very least, he now knew his actions would have lasting repercussions, since he already knew how this event would end.

Descending into the underground cavity, Isaac ran his hand along the walls of the tunnel, enjoying the small glowing specks embedded in the rock one last time. He felt like a dead man walking to his execution, his legs numb from the anticipation. Finally arriving at the shrine, Isaac knelt down and started to focus his energy into the Gravity Core fluxion. Tears started flowing from his eyes as the uroboros seal began to glow. The tears fell from his face and landed on the back of his hands, shaking from the inevitability of his death.

Then, out of the periphery of his vision, Isaac noticed some of the phosphorescent glass was being blocked by something. Not only that, but the blockage seemed to move, a dark black silhouette which suddenly grew bigger. In a moment, Isaac's vision went white as the dark figure kicked Isaac in the chin, flinging him away from the fluxion, which immediately lost its light. A deep voice came from the shadowy figure, "So someone found the statues I had hidden up here after all. I must say I'm impressed."

The voice came as a bit of a shock to Isaac, who was still trying to regain his senses, "What do you mean? Who are you?" He closed his eyes briefly, trying to concentrate enough to be able to see clearly in the darkness.

"I am Ophiuchus, but I must admit that I didn't expect anyone to be able to capture the bull after I set it loose."

"Wait, *you* made that bull into an animate object?"

"Indeed I did. Nothing like a little bit of chaos to really get things more interesting up here."

"Did you also do the same thing to the ram?"

Ophiuchus' tone changed, "Oh, so you know about the ram as well? I can't say I've given it life yet, but that's a good idea."

Isaac was trying to crawl back to the fluxion seal to continue his work. He mumbled, "Great. Next time I'll remember to keep my big mouth shut."

Another kick from Ophiuchus knocked the wind out of Isaac's lungs, "Your determination to kill yourself is impressive, but if you want me to speed it along, I'm more than willing."

After a few coughs and deep breaths, Isaac replied, "No thanks, but if I can take you with me, all the better."

"I think you'll find I'm not so easy to defeat as these statues."

"We'll see about that. I have yet to meet someone who can survive a direct impact with a comet." When Ophiuchus kicked him again, he was ready for it. Grabbing the leg of his assailant, Isaac used his other hand to stab at the leg with his throwing knife. With a loud clink, the knife shattered into pieces.

"What did I tell you?" Ophiuchus punched Isaac off his leg and continued to taunt him, "But since you went to the trouble of attempting to destroy two of my statues, why don't you tell me your name? Maybe I can let your next of kin know of your fate."

Isaac was still trying to figure out why Ophiuchus was completely black, let alone hard as stone. He had fought a few people who exhibited similar qualities before, but not nearly to this magnitude or duration. Spitting up blood on the ground, Isaac noticed that some of it touched the uroboros seal and it gained a dim glow because of it, "You can tell those who would ask that Isaac of the Brotherhood of the Scarlet Lion was the one who defeated you."

Going down on all fours once again, Isaac now knew that Ophiuchus' solitary goal was to keep Isaac from his. He prepared himself for the inevitable blows as he remained steadfast, both hands on the fluxion seal, its light filling the small room. Despite Ophiuchus' best efforts, Isaac remained on the seal.

The event happened quickly. An initial jolt told Isaac that the comet had made contact with the surface of the moon. Now he hoped he had given it enough acceleration. The jolt was followed by a dull rumbling which increased exponentially toward a violent crescendo in the next few moments. As the room shook, the noise became deafening until that brief moment of release when the comet broke through to the chamber of the Virgo shrine. All at once, a fury of dust, ice, and fire consumed the tiny room and all who resided therein.

Chapter 7

The Third Degree

As the dust settled, everyone found themselves in utter darkness. The only way they could actually tell the dust had settled was after they had finished coughing. With no way to know which way to exit, most of them lay on the ground, waiting for their strength to return. With a deep sigh, a familiar voice spoke into the void, "Well, now you've done it. You must feel proud of yourselves. At least that's the feeling I got from Isaac when he destroyed two statues simultaneously on the moon."

Sucari shouted into the darkness, "What? What did you say about Isaac?"

Albert similarly shouted a question, "What did you say about two statues on the moon?"

Ophiuchus let out a short laugh as he said, "I see you all have many questions, so I think it's only fair, since you've destroyed all twelve Caidoz statues, I give you a full explanation of their origins." Clearing his throat, he began, "You see, long ago, before any of the six Kingdoms were founded, there was a sculptor by the name of Auguste who came across the most magnificent material ever. This rock had the ability to adapt to its surroundings. As sculptors do, Auguste carved out the statue of a man with this stone. When he was done, he accidentally touched it in admiration, giving it life."

"In fact, the rock had absorbed a portion of his life force, which meant the statue was, in essence, another version of Auguste. Observing the great power this sculpture held, Auguste was convinced by this statue to make twelve more sculptures so that this power could be used all over the world. When the sculptures were completed, the first statue killed Auguste so the secret of their existence would disappear."

"Since the first statue fully understood the properties of what you know as 'fluxionite', he was able to transport the twelve statues to various locations through the use of what you call 'Q-Portals' so his power wouldn't be limited by any locational constraints. However, over time, word got out about these statues, which is where that cursed song came from which gave clues as to their whereabouts."

"Unfortunately, a limitation arose with the fluxionite. There were two Degrees which needed to be kept in balance in order for the universe to not collapse in on itself. The two Degrees were Positive and Negative. However, something interesting happened when the first Caidoz statue was destroyed: the very first statue took on the Degree of the destroyed one."

"In this way, the 13th Caidoz statue exhibited what is known as the Third Degree. The Third Degree maintained balance in the world. In its neutrality, it could become either black or white, depending on the Degrees of the statues that still existed. Because of this duality, the 13th statue not only had more control over the fluxionite power, but is much more difficult to destroy."

"In case you haven't figured it out by now-" Ophiuchus clapped his hands, activating everyone's fluxions at once, "I am Ophiuchus the Serpent-bearer. I am the 13th Caidoz statue. I am the Third Degree." With Sucari's fire and Benjamin's lightning once again illuminating the small room, everyone could see Ophiuchus standing on the pile of rubble which was once the scales statue, his grey skin frighteningly eerie in the limited lighting. Half of his body seemed to be scarred from a traumatic event that happened long ago.

Albert was surprised at the state of Ophiuchus' body, "What happened to you?"

"That's right; I haven't seen you since you destroyed the first statue." Sweeping a hand across his body, he continued, "This is the result of Isaac's feeble attempt to defeat me. Your friend, at least I would assume so based on your reaction, decided to crash a comet into the back of the moon and this was the only scratch I received from it. Needless to say, you'll have to do much better than that if you want to beat me."

Sucari leaned over to Robin and whispered, "That happened ten years ago, I didn't think Isaac had anything to do with it. I thought it was an act of God."

Robin whispered back, "Maybe that's where he ended up when he disappeared?"

"It must be."

Vlad was tiring of the endless talking. Standing up, he pulled out his retractable spear and flicked it to its full length, "Well, I'm ready to try and defeat you, if none of my comrades are." As he charged Ophiuchus, the statue of a man just rolled his eyes. With a snap of his fingers, the fluxions turned off, plunging the room back into darkness. A loud clang was heard and tiny pings on the floor heralded the destruction of Vlad's weapon.

In the darkness, Ophiuchus spoke, "Silly mortals, no mere weapons can harm me." Almost as if in response to the taunt, the room started to groan. Loud cracks were soon heard as the chamber began to lean to the side. Ophiuchus laughed maniacally, "Ha ha ha! Now that you've destroyed the one thing that was keeping the balance of the island, it's ready to fall!"

The noise was disorienting, but it didn't prevent Robin from shouting out over the uproar, "What do we do?"

Sucari grunted as he managed to produce a faint, red flame around his fists, dimly lighting the room, "We get out of here, that's what we do."

"But how?"

The room was starting to accelerate in its rotation as the island continued to fall. Ophiuchus crouched down and jumped into the air. With a kick, he shattered the circular slab the team had used to descend to the chamber in the first place. Now the shaft was quickly becoming a tunnel, the light at the end a faint dot in the distance. Pointing toward the exit, Sucari responded, "We follow the light!"

Benjamin hurried to the other side of the chamber and pulled out the Spear of Trium from the wall. It wasn't nearly as imbedded in the stone as it had been previously, an obvious sign that the power had decreased with the destruction of the centaur statue. Everyone else was scrambling up to the opening which was once the ceiling of the small room, following after Ophiuchus while escaping from the doomed island at the same time.

Chunks of rock were starting to fall as the cracking and grinding of stone continued, foretelling the limited time the Island would continue to be somewhat stable. As everyone was running, some of the rocks came loose and started to fall toward them. Benjamin saw this first and knew he had to act quickly. His mind raced as he tried to think of a solution. He determined that his lightning wouldn't do anything, but it was then that he felt the other Triumvirate orb hanging from his neck. As he ran, he forced some energy into the eagle Blood-fluxion he carried on him, causing his back to sprout wings, which he used to fly to a point past where the rocks were falling. Now he had to remember how Penny used the Seawave orb. Benjamin struggled as he focused into his former teammate's power source and clapped his hands together, creating a sonic boom which sent the falling rocks back behind where his team was running.

Of course, as these rocks began to crumble, Benjamin found that the recoil of the sonic boom had sent him flying toward Ophiuchus at an incredible speed. Ophiuchus realized something was approaching quickly from behind, so in response he disappeared, allowing Benjamin to pass right through where he was once standing. When the Caidoz statue destroyers caught up, they were confused, due to the fact that their foe had entirely vanished.

Suddenly, Ophiuchus reappeared out of the air, in the same spot he was standing before he disappeared. Unfortunately, he was poised to attack the person closest to him at that time: Robin. Since everyone was still running, trying to escape the crumbling mountain, it was difficult to adjust course to protect their comrade. Sucari struggled to get his fire to a higher energy level in order to save his wife and unborn child.

Fortunately, Robin handled the situation expertly. In one fluid movement, she pulled the large crossbow she wore from her back with her left hand while her right hand reached down to the quiver on her right calf. Gracefully, she loaded the only arrow in the quiver into the bow and leveled it at Ophiuchus. As the arrow was quickly released from the bow, it immediately began to multiply, creating a small bunch of arrows which headed toward their target. This was the power of the Mount Charles method.

When the arrows hit Ophiuchus, they burst into an array of splinters and arrowheads, doing no discernible damage to the statue's skin. Fortunately, this attack provided an adequate amount of force to push him back enough to give Robin time to dodge his punch, already in mid-execution. At this same moment, Sucari gained the necessary power to assist, his body now covered in a brighter, orange flame. He had also managed to sprout his wings and, as he leapt into the air, Ophiuchus had finished his punch, completely missing the intended target.

With an accelerating burst of flame, Sucari kicked Ophiuchus in the head with both feet, sending him further down the crumbling tunnel. The exit was becoming much clearer now, but the slope was also becoming much more drastic. Ophiuchus took advantage of the increased momentum Sucari had given him, and used it to slide out the end of the collapsing tunnel. Everyone else was having trouble keeping their footing, and soon they had to resort to sliding on the smooth rock surface much like Ophiuchus had.

Then came the impact. Everyone was thrown into the air momentarily and hung in free fall as the Island of Stability came in contact with the ground. The jolt created more cracks and now the complete destruction of the tunnel was imminent. Benjamin yelled to everyone as he managed to turn around, "Grab on to me! I'll get us out of here." Since they were all relatively close together, they grabbed onto Benjamin and held tight. Rocks were falling with them and ahead of them, rapidly closing them into a rocky tomb. Once more, Benjamin focused some of his energy into the Seawave orb and created a sonic boom, propelling the freefalling team down the collapsing tunnel and out the exit.

The roof of the shrine had been torn off in the crash so, when everyone fell out of the Island of Stability, they flew through the air for a while before hitting the ground, tumbling to a stop on the mountainous tundra nearby. As they began to pick themselves up, they saw the once mighty balancing mountain finish its death throes, rumbling to its final end of ruins and rubble. The veil that once surrounded the island had been torn asunder by its fall, leaving a huge gap in the towering pillar of clouds.

The landing wasn't smooth for most of the team, and as they got up, they noticed Ophiuchus standing in the distance, sarcastically clapping as he slowly sauntered toward them on the wide expanse of tundra on which they had landed, "I am impressed. Most mortals wouldn't be able to escape something like that. Unfortunately, you'll-" before he could even finish, Sucari was upon him, fighting with a rage that continued from Ophiuchus' attempt to injure his wife a second time. Body covered in orange flames and Hikari Shichidai drawn, Sucari began battling the last Caidoz statue.

Albert was trying to assess the situation. He quickly counted and found out someone was missing, "Where is R-3N3?" Everyone else glanced around and found that R-3N3 was nowhere to be seen.

Vlad spoke up when he came to the same realization, "Do you think he even made it out of the Island?" Everyone focused on the pile of rubble, rocks still clattering as it settled. Even though R-3N3 was different from the rest of the group, most of them doubted he could survive something like that. The sun appeared from behind the clouds, causing Vlad to catch sight of something shiny caught in the rubble, "There he is!"

Albert looked up at the shining sun and gave the orders, "You all go and help him. I need to charge my weapon." As he lifted the C.L.A.W. to the sky, everyone else ran back to the site of the now razed Island of Stability.

Vlad arrived first and he found the armor-man trapped under a few large boulders. When he saw that R-3N3's eyes were black, he yelled at his friend, "Artie! Are you all right?"

A dim green light began to fill R-3N3's eyes again as he regained consciousness, "How am I still alive?"

This lightened the mood a little as Vlad replied, "Heck if I know, you magnificent marvel. I know I wouldn't be so hot after being crushed by boulders."

"Negative, I mean, did we not destroy the last statue?"

"We did, but it turns out this Ophiuchus guy is actually the last one. What does that have to do with anything?"

"Never mind." R-3N3 slowly began to move, which caused everyone to help remove the boulders that were pinning him down. When he got out of the pile of rocks, he brushed his metal exterior with his hands, removing the last pieces of dust and debris. While he had survived, his armor was pretty beaten up, scuffed and dented from the adventure he had endured up until this point. Now that R-3N3 was saved, everyone turned back to the battle scene unfolding before them.

Ophiuchus was half-heartedly blocking attacks as Sucari furiously fought against the last obstacle between him and accomplishing the goal Isaac had gathered them to complete. At Sucari's attempts to injure him, Ophiuchus merely laughed, "If you're trying to kill me, you're going to have to do better than that, although I do admit the slices from your sword itch a little bit."

Sucari didn't know how much longer his anger could fuel his fight. He was certainly fortunate that his attacks were at a frequency which prevented Ophiuchus from countering with attacks of his own. Behind him, Sucari heard Albert yell, "Sucari! Get out of the way!" When he turned around, he saw Albert leveling a strange, Ruby weapon that was attached to his left side.

With a burst of fire, Sucari flew into the air as Albert's glowing weapon released its energy, sending a concentrated beam of light toward Ophiuchus. The beam hit Ophiuchus square in the chest and spread a circuitry of red light across his torso. When the attack finished, the circuitry of red light began to spread, but Ophiuchus let out a short laugh as he brushed the attack off of his skin, revealing that it had little to no effect.

Landing back with his teammates, Sucari could tell Albert was crushed by the failure of his attack, "I could have sworn this would work. I even overcharged it a bit just to be sure. At this point, I do not-" Albert gripped his left side as he groaned in pain and fell to his knees.

Benjamin shouted out in surprise, "Albert! What's wrong?"

"It is nothing."

"It is not nothing! You're in pain." Grabbing Albert's shirt, Benjamin ripped part of it away to reveal the C.L.A.W., which Albert wore in place of his left arm, had begun to take over his body. The crystalline structure was invading into Albert's chest and was visibly spreading. Benjamin stood back in shock, "What's happening, Albert?"

Mustering the strength to return to his feet, Albert replied, "I knew this would eventually happen."

"What's happening, Albert?" Benjamin asked again, his voice clearly showing concern.

"The fluxionite is starting to fuse with my body. At this point, I cannot stop it. This is why I made it a rule to rarely wear this weapon."

"But why would you do this to yourself?"

Through struggled breathing, Albert replied, "I had no other choice! If I did not take the initiative to destroy these statues, then the tyranny of fluxions could remain on this earth indefinitely! Besides-" Albert coughed up some blood as he lifted the weapon toward the sky again, charging it for another attack, "We are not done yet. Ophiuchus still stands."

Observing that Ophiuchus was once again advancing toward their position, Robin took the lead and began firing arrows from her crossbow. Each time she used the Mount Charles method, the arrow regenerated in her quiver, so she had no worries about running out of ammunition. The spread of arrows continued to hit Ophiuchus, but didn't do any damage. However, they still pushed him back enough so that his forward progress was essentially halted.

Sucari asked Albert, "But why are you throwing your life away, if you already know your attack isn't going to work?"

"I just need to try again."

"No, we need a plan!" Turning to Benjamin, Sucari took control, "Benjamin, you need to start charging the Spear of Trium. If Albert's weapon doesn't work again, we'll have to use yours. I already know mine is pretty much useless."

A realization came to Albert, "Wait! I have a better idea." Motioning with his head to Benjamin, he spoke, "Come next to me, Benjamin. We will use our weapons together for a combined attack. However-"

As Benjamin pulled out the rail gun and arrived at Albert's left side, he asked, "However, what?"

"However, we need Ophiuchus to stand completely still if this is to work. We only have one shot at this."

R-3N3 spoke up, "Vlad, can you still turn to mist?"

"I think so."

"Splendid. Please do so. Provide me some cover."

"What are you planning on doing?"

"I am going to give us the best chance at that one shot."

Vlad resigned himself to trusting R-3N3 knew what he was doing and focused his energy into the fluxion he wore on his chest. As mist started to gather at his feet, Benjamin interrupted him, "Wait! Before you go, I want you to do something for me."

"What now?"

"I need to use your sword to help absorb the recoil in my weapon."

"All right." Unsheathing Kuroni, Vlad focused some of his energy into the katana as he thrust it into the ground behind Benjamin, who used the hilt to brace himself.

"Thank you, Vlad."

"Don't mention it." The last member of the Order of the Dragon was now disappearing, his mist beginning to rise up and surround the group. Soon, it moved and enveloped Ophiuchus. R-3N3 ran into the mist and disappeared into its milky depths.

Robin, no longer able to see her target, had overheard the plan and came over to help, "You both tell me when you're ready to attack, I'll help by aiming you." As she said this, she pulled her glasses down from the top of her head and placed them on her face.

Both Albert and Benjamin replied, "Understood." As Albert's weapon was charging, Benjamin could see the Ruby-red crystal was spreading quickly over his comrade's body. With his friend's life on the line, Benjamin put all of his might into charging the rail gun. Sparks soon began to appear on Benjamin's skin, jumping off into the dry mountain air.

A deep rumble was heard behind them. Sucari glanced backward to see if the destroyed Island of Stability was still in the process of dying. What he saw was the tower of clouds which once hid the Island were now churning, brief flashes of lightning jumping through its misty mass in response to Benjamin's charging.

Suddenly, there were some indistinguishable shouts coming from Vlad's mist as it slowly dissipated in front of the group. Vlad slowly re-appeared next to the team, clearly shook up. Sucari noticed this and asked, "What's wrong?" Vlad could do nothing more than point ahead of him. There, in a spot which was once in the middle of his field of mist, stood Ophiuchus. Except, now R-3N3 had grabbed on to the last Caidoz statue and was holding him still, despite Ophiuchus' struggles to escape R-3N3's grasp.

Vlad softly spoke, "He wants us to fire through both of them."

Sucari was shocked, "What?"

"He said fluxions are the only reason he's alive to begin with. If we destroy Ophiuchus, he will die because the fluxions won't work anymore." Vlad choked up for a moment, "Either way, Artie is going to die."

From the distance, R-3N3 could be heard shouting, "What are you waiting for? Shoot already!"

Everyone now understood the inevitability of R-3N3's fate, but couldn't cope with his sacrifice. Sucari yelled back, "Are you sure you're OK with this?"

"There is no other outcome! Shoot!"

Robin had to wipe the tears from her eyes in order to aim the weapons at her friend. Readjusting her glasses, she gave orders, "Benjamin, aim a little to the right. OK, that's good. Albert, a little to your left. Right there." Looking to her husband, she spoke through a tight throat, "We're ready."

Benjamin was focused on gathering energy, and replied, "Not yet! I don't have the power yet!" Turning his gaze toward Albert, Benjamin saw most of his friend's body was now comprised of Ruby. They were running out of time. As if in response, the clouds above them rumbled once more and a single bolt of lightning came down and struck Benjamin, completing the charging of the Spear of Trium. As everyone recoiled from the sudden event, Benjamin shouted, "Now!"

In a sudden release, the rail gun quickly accelerated the Spear of Trium toward Ophiuchus and R-3N3. A moment later, Albert fired the C.L.A.W., allowing the red light to fuse with the spear, combining their power and rushing headlong toward their target. The whole event took a fraction of a second, which was more than enough to finish the battle. A moment later, a loud boom knocked most everyone to the ground, the sound waves finally catching up to the blinding speed of the combined attack.

Ophiuchus still stood there, a look of shock on his once haughty face. A large hole now stood in his chest, showing daylight beyond. At the edges of the hole, a red light slowly crumbled away at Ophiuchus' body. R-3N3 fell away from Ophiuchus' back, his armor sporting the same hole as his foe. With wide eyes, Ophiuchus clawed at his chest, trying to stop the decay that was introduced to his body. Looking toward the team that had been able to damage him so severely, he shouted in panic, "What did you do? How could you even do something like this? Don't you know who I am? I created these powers, so how could you use them to defeat me? Who are you?"

In a flash of blue flame, Sucari appeared in front of Ophiuchus, Hikari Shichidai at the ready to attack, "Who are we? We are the finishers. Others may have started our journey, but we are here to finish it." With that last word, Sucari thrust the broadsword into the hole created by the Spear of Trium. Turning around, he pulled the sword upward, slicing Ophiuchus cleanly in two. The shocked look on Ophiuchus remained as the red light from the C.L.A.W. quickly spread over his body, disintegrating him into a small pile of useless fluxionite on the ground.

Sucari was joined by Robin and Vlad, both of whom had rushed over to check on R-3N3. While the gaping hole in his chest revealed that the Soulfusion fluxion which had powered him for many years was barely missed by the attack, it was clearly obvious: the power of fluxions was no more. Upon the sight of their fallen friend, Robin burst into tears, burying her head in Sucari's shoulder. Tears were flowing freely from Sucari's eyes as well while he stood there, contemplating R-3N3's sacrifice.

Vlad was very stoically gathering nearby rocks and placing them around R-3N3's body. He worked alone and soon had created a grave for his friend. As he stood over the pile of rocks which covered R-3N3, he spoke softly, "He may have been a hollow shell of a man, but he was more of a man than anyone I have ever known."

As Benjamin watched Ophiuchus crumble to the ground, he let out a sigh of relief, "It's over. We won, Albert!" Looking over to his Millennial partner, he saw that, while the growth of the Ruby had stopped, it was far too late to save Albert.

The only part of Albert's body which remained unaffected was the right side of his face. He managed to smile as he croaked out one final word, "*Wun . . . der . . . bar.*" With that last statement, his smile vanished and his eye closed. Albert had died standing in victory over the power that not only had become his obsession, but also the cause of his death. He stood as a statue made completely of Ruby, his body still covered with fluxionite keys and a dark cloak, gently fluttering in the mountain wind.

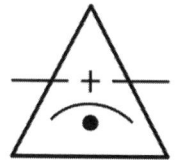

Epilogue

Ending the Story

"Come on, Isaac! It's time to go!" Sucari called into his house as a boy, about the age of three, came rushing out of the open door.

"I'm coming, daddy," said the boy, the spitting image of his father. Tousled blonde hair gently bounced on his head as his green eyes gazed up at his father. A small hand reached up to grab a hold of Sucari's as they walked down the street.

Sucari's other hand was occupied as well. While he held the hand of his wife, her other hand was used to cradle her torso, once again pregnant with child. The small family sauntered down the main street of New Town, their new home quickly growing smaller behind them. It was a busy day in the city and the streets were bustling with activity.

Seagulls squawked overhead as Sucari, Robin, and their son, whom they had named Isaac, strolled toward the shore of the town. The gentle sound of waves became louder as they approached a hill with a scraggly, dead tree on its peak. As they climbed, Isaac asked, "Where are we going, daddy?"

"Well son, we're going to see some friends of ours we met before you were born."

"Oh, OK."

Cresting the hill, they found they were the first ones to arrive. The gnarly tree had something carved in its trunk, but the damage sustained from a lightning strike, which occurred long ago, made it unreadable. Next to the tree, a sword was stuck in the ground, a white jacket loosely hanging on its hilt and calmly fluttering in the sea breeze.

Isaac pointed to the sword and asked, "What's that, daddy?"

Kneeling down to his son's level, Isaac explained, "That's a memorial, Isaac. In fact, it's a memorial to the man you were named after."

From behind them, a feminine voice was heard, "That's right, and he never did keep his promise." Sucari turned around and stood up at the sight of Irene, who herself had a young girl in tow. The girl was about two years old and had the same red hair as her mother.

Isaac was afraid of these unfamiliar people, so he hid behind Sucari's leg. Robin saw this and gently spoke to her son, "Isaac, there's no need to be scared. These are friends of ours."

Another voice came up the hill and spoke to Irene's daughter, "Penny! You forgot your glasses." It was Benjamin. While he appeared a little older, as evidenced by some grey starting to infiltrate his hair, he still sported the scar on his face from his younger days. He handed a pair of glasses, which were similar in style to his own, to the little girl, who unfolded them and put them on. Looking up at Sucari and Robin, Benjamin couldn't help but laugh, "She may look like her mother, but she's got my eyesight."

Sucari returned the laugh as he approached Benjamin for a hug, "Good to see you, Ben."

"And it's good to see you too, Sucari. I see you guys are pregnant again."

Robin smiled as Benjamin came over to hug her as well, "Indeed we are."

"What are you going to name it?"

Looking over to Sucari, who nodded in response, she replied, "We were thinking of Erwin."

Irene chimed in, "That's wonderful! And how fitting. Benjamin has been reading to me what you've sent about your adventures," she laughed for a moment, "It's about time I've heard what Isaac was really up to."

"Mommy, what does she mean by that?"

Picking up her son, Robin laughed, "Not you, Isaac. The Isaac you're named after."

Sucari tousled his boy's hair as he said, "I've filled in what I can, but I still can't believe Erwin was from the moon, or that Isaac even traveled there to begin with. A lot of what I gave you was definitely hearsay, but I trust it is true, considering its sources. I'm just glad he kept a journal in that white coat of his."

Benjamin spoke, "I can't thank you enough for your help on this. I've wanted to document the history of the fluxions for some time now, and I want to get the inside story on everything, considering most people nowadays don't even know what really happened."

Irene came up behind Benjamin and put her arm around his, "When he came back to tell me Isaac wasn't going to return, I couldn't have imagined that Ben's adventures were as equally impressive as Isaac's, if not more so."

Changing topics, Benjamin asked, "By the way, Sucari, have you heard from Vlad lately?"

"Not really. The last I had heard, he was now the ruler of the 3rd Kingdom, since they had recently changed the way they elect their leaders."

"So he's probably not coming today, then. Is he?"

From behind the twisted tree came another voice, "I wouldn't be so sure about that. After all, if one doesn't remember his roots, there's no chance to advance." Appearing from the shadow of the dead tree was Vlad, still covered from head to toe, but now with royal robes of a deep green color. He wore a three-pointed crown over the hood of his cloak.

Sucari shouted out, "Vlad! You came!"

Accepting the sudden hug, Vlad said, "Are you kidding? Even though I'm some big shot politician, I wouldn't miss this for the world." After greeting everyone else, he sighed and said solemnly, "Has it really been four years since we met?"

Sucari replied, "I know. How time has flown."

"It feels kind of weird that fluxions don't even exist anymore, but at least we can be confident in the fact we won't have to worry about them destroying the world anymore."

"True. We may have peace now, and we can be sure it won't be disturbed by the use of fluxions."

"Indeed, peace is merely a temporary state, but at least we can somewhat control how long it will last."

Remembering one of the reasons for coming to this particular spot, Sucari asked, "So, Vlad. Did you remember to bring it?"

"I did." From the folds of his cloak, Vlad brought out Kuroni, the jet black katana, briefly glinting in the sunlight. Gingerly holding the blade in his hands, he said nostalgically, "It seems only fitting that this blade return to the spot where it was meant to rest. Grabbing the hilt, Vlad knelt down at the tree and found the notch where the sword used to rest. Sliding the katana into the tree trunk, he stood up and took a few steps back to survey the hill.

The hill now stood as a shrine for many people who had done the right thing, even though it went against easy and simple paths. It represented the battles fought for freedom from fluxion tyranny. Everyone stood silently for a moment, contemplating everything they had done to make freedom possible.

Penny tugged on her mother's dress, "Mommy, I'm hungry." This broke the silence and everyone couldn't help but laugh.

Picking up her daughter, Irene said, "Well, let's go back to the house and have some lunch then, shall we?"

Everyone left the hill and made their way to the dock house that had started the adventure so many years ago. In solitude and peace, the white coat of Isaac, member of the Brotherhood of the Scarlet Lion, fluttered contentedly in the salty breeze of the sea. Overhead, the sky was an unusual shade of deep blue, a serene expanse above the memorial hill.

Appendix
WARNING: SPOILERS!

Section 1

Introduction

Greetings, and welcome to the Appendix for *The Fluxion Trilogy!* You may be asking yourself why there is such a section tacked on to these three novels. If you haven't already noticed, I have placed many hidden references throughout my books. Some are obvious, while others are not. In an attempt to make what appears to be a standard adventure story much deeper, I have developed many characters, settings, and items that are linked to real world counterparts. It is my hope that you will use this Appendix to deepen your understanding of what I have hidden in the text, and therefore gain a deeper appreciation for the references and their connections.

It all started about three years ago with the planning for the first novel in this trilogy: *First Name Basis*. I wasn't quite sure what to title my book initially, but when I made the realization that many famous people in literature, art, history, psychology, and (most of all) science were known by their last names, I thought to myself, "Why don't I exclusively use their first names?" In this way, many of the idols of their respective fields have made their marks in this trilogy.

The next year, I continued with the prequel: *Second to None*. When I was editing *First Name Basis*, I found there was a lot of material that I did not use, as well as many references to events in the past that I could draw on to develop the history of the world I had created. While the title is a play on words that highlights the fact that this was my second novel, it also is enhanced by the story. Not only can it be seen as Amedeo's drive to be the most powerful army in the world, but the "to none" part hints at the eventual demise of said army.

Finally, after writing two novels and naming them in such a way, this naturally led to book three: *The Third Degree*. Surprisingly enough, I still had quite a few leftover ideas that I wanted to cover, and this last novel in the trilogy helped to explore them as well as wrap up any loose ends and questions

I may have created in books one and two. The title for this novel took a while to congeal, but needless to say, it had to have "third" in it.

Now, remember that these novels are works of fiction, and I, as the author, have put my own spin and characterizations on these references. Not everything I have written is truth, but much of it is based on real people and real phenomena. It is my hope that people would find a few of the easier references, then start examining other aspects of the books for other ones. This Appendix is to be used to clarify what references I've made through the trilogy so that those who are unfamiliar with some of the concepts I've presented might learn about them and realize how incredible they are in the world we live in right now.

If you are skipping to this section while reading through the trilogy for the first time, I hope that you would reconsider. Aside from the plethora of spoilers in this section, I ask that you please read through the novels without referring to the Appendix so that you can figure out as much as you can by yourself. Then, once you're done, use these following pages to enhance your understanding and to uncover the "Easter eggs" hidden in the text.

So, without further ado, I present you with the Appendix to *The Fluxion Trilogy*. Enjoy!

- Benjamin M. Weilert

Section 2

Characters

In this section of the Appendix, I would like to give some insight into the characters who appear in these novels. While there may be some settings and items based off of real people, this section will focus solely on those referenced people who are manifested in human forms. This section will go through each book and highlight the main characters, followed by the minor characters, explaining each person and who they link to in our world. The name in bold is the name used in the trilogy, which is followed by the name of the reference made.

FIRST NAME BASIS

Isaac: Isaac Newton

This historical figure is someone I've been writing about since Elementary school. As such, it is no wonder that he was the main character of my very first novel. In fact, the two chapters bounding *First Name Basis* are written with capital letters because they are supposed to be his initials. Chapter 1 is "IN" which stands for "Isaac Newton", whereas Chapter 8 is "SIN", which adds on hit title to create "Sir Isaac Newton". Although the choice to name Chapter 8 "SIN" was mostly due to the climactic battle of Isaac and the growth of the character culminating in that eighth chapter. That being said, he was knighted in real life as well, and this is further explained under the organization of The Brotherhood of the Scarlet Lion in Section 5.

The first descriptions of Isaac in *First Name Basis* are based off of a few things. First, the white hair, which in the novel was attributed to the interaction with Radium, was a characteristic of Isaac Newton in real life due to his work with telescopes. In creating the precise mirrors needed to make the new type of telescope he invented, Newton dealt with a lot of Mercury, which was also a

Figure 2.1: Coat of Arms

key component in his love of alchemy (*see also: Section 4 – "Fluxions"*). Therefore, the early onset of white hair was thought to have been due to Mercury, and Mercury poisoning was thought to be a contributor to his death. Secondly, the white jacket he wears through *The Fluxion Trilogy* is meant to convey his life as a scientist. However, the black shirt underneath with the crossed bones is not the designation of a pirate, but is in fact Isaac Newton's personal coat of arms (see Figure 2.1). Therefore, there were definitely a few moments of confusion inserted into the novel for humorous effect.

One of the most common associations people make with Isaac Newton is that of his discovery of gravity by an apple falling on his head. As such, the apple motif makes many appearances in the trilogy. However, since the gravity theme is closely tied to the katana Kuroni, I will leave further explanation to under that item in Section 4.

Similarly, Newton was well known for his work in optics. The aforementioned telescope was the first instance of a reflecting telescope (which used mirrors to focus light) instead of a refracting telescope (which uses glass lenses to focus light). And yet, the decomposition of white light into its spectral colors is definitely his defining work in this realm. I started off this paragraph with "similarly" because this discovery is also closely tied to one of Isaac's swords: the broadsword Hikari Shichidai. More details on this topic can be found under this item in Section 4.

These two swords represent the third of Newton's laws of motion. The first law states that an object in action (or inaction) tends to stay in action/inaction unless acted upon by an outside force, whereas the second law states that the aforementioned force is equal to the mass of an object multiplied by its acceleration. However, this third law is what brought about the quote on the back of *First Name Basis*, "For every action, there is a consequence." This same law is why the character of Isaac does not believe in random chance or fate: everything must have a cause, and every action must cause something else to happen. Furthermore, the idea of "equal and opposite forces" is a great way to drive plot, since one of the most common conflicts is that of good and evil, light and dark, justice and injustice. And yet, the more interesting conflict in this story has to do with what is known as "The Calculus Wars".

The Calculus Wars hearken back to a time where thoughts weren't immediately available through the internet. When somebody discovers something, usually the first to do so is given the credit. But what if two people independently arrive at the same discovery? This was just such the case with the mathematics behind calculus. Gottfried Leibniz discovered calculus at almost the exact same time that Newton did, but when it came down to who was to receive the credit, the fighting began. Many centuries later, most students are taught some form of both of these, but the Leibniz method is usually more useful and used more often in higher level mathematics, even to the point that we call it by the name Leibniz used: calculus.

So, what did Newton call it? His version of calculus was known as Fluxions and Fluents. Sound familiar? It was from this naming convention that I pulled the superpowers that we see in this trilogy: Fluxions and Fluents. These powers are also linked to the ideas of alchemy, which has been mentioned as one of Newton's many intellectual pursuits. In fact, if you look closely at the powers and functions of the fluxions in this trilogy, you might find some similarities to the Japanese manga and anime *Fullmetal Alchemist*. For more information on the fluxions and Fluents, please refer to their respective sections later in this Appendix.

Overall, Newton has been an inspiration to me over the years, and it was quite fun writing an "action hero" version of him in this trilogy. That being said, there are still many more references to Newton throughout the novels, including the dried figs the group eats on their way to the top of Asp Peak (Fig Newtons, anyone?), as well as the name of the town that starts and ends the trilogy: New Town.

Erwin: Erwin Schrödinger

Mostly known for his Schrödinger's Cat thought experiment, this scientist helped found what we know today as Quantum Physics. Because Quantum Physics deals with particles which are very small, observations of these particles can be very difficult. One of these particles is light, which can be observed as a particle (a photon), or as a wave. The trick with observing light is that you aren't quite sure if it will behave as a particle or a wave until you actually observe it. In fact, light is both a particle and a wave, which is called a superposition of states. However, if we measure light as a particle or a wave, we "collapse the wave function" and arrive at a single state.

What does this have to do with cats, you ask? Well, the Schrödinger's Cat thought experiment has to do with a cat in a sealed box with a device which will release poison whenever a radioactive substance decays. Since there is no known time in which the radioactive substance will decay, there is no known time in which the cat will die. Therefore, since the cat cannot be observed, it is both alive and dead: a superposition of states. This thought experiment was extended by Eugene Wigner, where the results of the experiment are observed by someone, but then passed on to the scientist, thus earning the title of "Wigner's friend". In the novel, Eugene is mentioned briefly as Erwin's friend, and this is the reference being made.

I took the cat association and played it through a few different relations. First is the moon. Not only is there a crater on the moon named after Schrödinger (as is the case for many scientists), but when it is nearing the new moon phase, the sliver of light seen from earth is often referred to as the smile of the Cheshire cat (which is explained more under the character of Carroll).

Secondly, the idiom of curiosity killing the cat was one of the main reasons Erwin was killed off near the end of *First Name Basis*. Children are naturally curious, so that is why I made the character of Erwin a bit younger than the others.

However, back on the subject of Quantum Physics, Schrödinger worked with atomic electron transition, which is also known as "Quantum jumping". This Quantum jumping is represented in the novel by the wind Elemental-fluxion he wears. Not only can wind not be observed, thus needing to be observed by its interaction with other objects (a very Quantum physics phenomenon), but it has the ability to be everywhere and nowhere at once (a similarity to the superposition of states). Wind is very unpredictable as well, and (like most weather) is merely understood based on probabilities, since it is difficult to tie down exactly where and when something will happen when dealing with particles which are so small.

The two other characters who bore the wind fluxion were Sunaru Suleac and Isaac. While Sunaru Suleac was the original owner of the wind fluxion core, Isaac was the one who gave it to Erwin in *The Third Degree*. In fact, the reason why Isaac's experience with this fluxion core is much more intense than when he experienced it with Erwin is due to the fact that the fluxions were more powerful on the moon when he arrived in *The Third Degree*, since by *First Name Basis* two Caidoz statues were destroyed (by Isaac, through Edmond's comet), thus reducing the power of the fluxions.

Sucari: Icarus

One of many mythological characters who made an appearance in the trilogy, Icarus did not have a last name, so I decided that the characters who were known by their first (and only) name would have their name made into an anagram in order to hide their true identity. The legend of Icarus was about a boy who was escaping a prison with his father, Daedalus. Daedalus was an inventor (*see also: Section 3 – "Ruatonim's Maze"*) who made wings of feathers and wax for them to escape prison. Unfortunately, Icarus flew too high and the heat from the sun melted the wax on his wings and he fell down and drowned in the sea.

I took this legend and flipped it around a little. While Sucari's father still gifted him with flight (through the eagle wing vest), instead of this character being a cautionary tale, I infused the fire of the sun into his ability to fly, as if he had succeeded in his ambitions and actually reached the sun. The different colors of the fire he is able to call forth are extracted from the colors of the stars based on their temperatures. Cooler stars are red, followed by orange, yellow, blue, and white, increasing in temperature with each color designation.

Vlad: Vlad III, the Impaler (aka *Dracula*)

Some of the characters I used were based on famous literary figures. Vampires have been the rage in literature recently, but I didn't really want to jump on that bandwagon. Instead, I went back and examined the character's origins and pulled from them to develop this character. Plus, within the constraints of the world I had created, I wanted a logical explanation for "vampires". In my world, vampires are created by a Blood-fluxion of a bat and snake. The bat provides the light sensitivity, good hearing, wings, and bloodlust that are often associated with vampires, whereas the snake provides the fangs most often associated with the bite of the vampire. In order to make his skin sensitive to light (instead of just his eyes), I went with the albino tactic, which is a skin disorder that results from having no pigmentation. This disorder is evident in white skin, white hair, and red irises in the eyes. In this way, I could capture most of the mythos associated with vampires while still holding to some reality of our world. Still, there were certain powers of Dracula that I had to work in somehow (like turning into mist) that couldn't have much more of an explanation than "the fluxion did it".

Of course, I went a bit further and researched the background of the most famous vampire: Dracula. This fictional character created by Bram Stoker was based on Vlad III, the Impaler. As such, his weapon is a retractable spear, which can be used for impaling. What's more interesting is that Vlad III was called Dracula because his father was a part of the Order of the Dragon (as was he). This is a real organization and more can be learned about it in Section 5. And yet, the character of Count Dracula was why I made Vlad an accountant: since they count money and money is horded by the novel's Order of the Dragon.

Two other references made in relation to Vlad are those of Abraham and George. Abraham would be Abraham Van Helsing, the vampire hunter whose expertise is called upon to get rid of the titular *Dracula*. The main way to kill a vampire is to drive a wooden stake through its heart, so I made a play on words between stake and steak in making Abraham a butcher. Secondly, George would be a reference to St. George and the Dragon. Seeing as Vlad is the last member of the Order of the Dragon, it would stand to reason that he would be the last dragon, and therefore persecuted by George the vicar.

R-3N3 (aka Artie, aka The Crimson Front): René Descartes

Even though this character was based off of the most well-known of Descartes' philosophy, "I think, therefore I am", the real depth of this character comes from Isaac Asimov's three rules of robotics, as well as the Turing test. In fact, the "Isaac" referenced upon the R-3N3's introduction is that of Asimov, whose first name just so happens to happily coincide with the first name of the main character. These three rules were essentially the same rules set forth in the novel, merely rewritten to be less about robots and more about a moral code. R-3N3's nickname of "Artie" is partly inspired from the *Star Wars* character, R2-D2, and its nickname of "Artoo", further expounding on the robot theme

R-3N3 was Dr. Paul's greatest creation and was one of the simultaneous rediscoveries of the fluxion age: the discovery of the Soul-fusion fluxion. Isaac's discovery of this fluxion happened a little later, but since this fluxion is taboo, due to it involving the use of human souls, anyone who re-discovered it kept it quiet for that very reason. At any rate, since R-3N3 was Dr. Paul's greatest creation, he gave the sentient suit of armor the highest numerical designation of his experiments: #1. Unfortunately, R-3N3 escaped the island of Sievuvus and made his way to the town of Mathiston, where he met Isaac (Asimov) and was rehabilitated, having since lost his memory of his time on the island. Mathiston is the town named after Mathison, one of the researchers in Amedeo's Army. More information on this character (and the relation to R-3N3) is explained later.

The discovery of R-3N3 in Pandora Prison was very much an homage to *The Phantom of the Opera*, in that organ music was being played in an area not normally meant for people to inhabit. The reason for his imprisonment was the same reason he had the nickname of Crimson Front: he killed enough people to cover his front with blood, all to obey the first law of robotics (preventing more death). Furthermore, as some might have guessed by now, R-3N3 is also a reference to the character Alphonse from *Fullmetal Alchemist*. When I was writing *The Third Degree*, I knew R-3N3's predicament would allow for a sacrificial moment, which I modeled after Goku's sacrifice in the early part of *Dragon Ball Z*.

Robin (aka Hellen): Hermann Snellen / Robin Hood

While some characters are left pretty intact, this one was a conglomeration of a few different ideas. The first idea was the creator of the eye chart, Hermann Snellen (ergo, the "Snellen chart"). This eye chart reference is retained in her fluxion glasses, as the number 20/1, which appears engraved on them, is the absolute best eyesight anybody could have. This ratio means that someone with this eyesight could read something at 20 feet that a person with normal eyesight would need to be 1 foot away in order to read. These glasses were passed on to her by her father, Hermann, who died in an unspecified altercation with Testament. Her name is the closest I could get to her father's, but still remaining feminine. Hellen is a brief reference to Helen of Troy, a woman so beautiful that she single-handedly started the Trojan War. As such, she became the romantic interest of Sucari. However, since a name like "Hellen Snellen" would probably be hated by most girls, I chose to give her the nickname referencing the famed English archer, Robin Hood. As such, since the character of Robin is also an archer, her glasses make her quite the sniper.

Marie / Maria: Marie Curie

If someone were to ask you who the most famous woman scientist was, you would almost always say Marie Curie. In researching the effects of radiation with her husband, they discovered Radium, atomic element #88.

Marie's death in the novel is the same thing that happens to Radium when it is exposed to air. The atomic element #96 is named Curium in memoriam of this couple's valiant research.

Even though Marie died before the events of the first novel, I still wanted some connection to her to eventually come into play, so I gave her a sister named Maria, who was wife to Hermann and mother of Robin. I realize the confusion that a household would have with two daughters named almost the same thing, but I really needed something to drive home the connection.

Pierre: Pierre Curie

A few characters had names that I couldn't resist using some clever wordplay with. As such, even though Pierre is not connected to Marie or their combined radioactivity research in the novels, he is the owner of a Pier in New Town. Still, Pierre's daughter in real life was Irene Curie, which leads me to . . .

Irene: Irene Curie

While it would be easy to imply the infidelity of Marie to Isaac, based on the real-life child of Marie and Pierre Curie being Irene, this is a work of fiction. I did, however, maintain the relationship of Irene to her father, Pierre. However, since Irene, Marie, and Isaac are somewhat similar in age in *First Name Basis*, the first sentence of this paragraph would never make sense.

At any rate, there are a few things about Irene which should be mentioned. First is her red hair. In *First Name Basis*, she makes a pinky swear with Isaac that they will meet again. This is a reference to the "red string of fate", which (while implying a more romantic destiny) states that two people are connected by their pinkies with an invisible red string. This string cannot be broken and is seen as the reason how two soul mates can find each other even despite tremendous odds against them. Original drafts of *First Name Basis* had Irene tie the red string from a strip of fabric she tore from her dress. This then progressed to her tying a strand of her red hair around their pinkies, finally arriving at not tying anything around the fingers at all. As such, this reference is a bit more of an ambiguous stretch as to the importance of her red hair.

Secondly, is Irene's name. Irene is based in Greek and stands for "Peace". There is a depth to the story between Isaac and Irene in that Isaac has not found peace when he arrives in New Town. As such, he does not want to bring Irene along because then he would have found peace. It's not until the end of the novel, when he has obtained closure from his relationship with Marie, that can finally go back and find peace. Also of note is her connection to the sea, since Eirene (a different spelling of Irene) is a daughter of Poseidon. As such, her role as the daughter of a dock owner is most apt. If Penny had lived past *Second to None*, I would have found a way to make her Irene's mother.

Robert: Robert Hooke

While there is another Robert referenced in *Second to None* (which happens in the past, in relation to *First Name Basis*), this is not the same Robert referenced when the "Reign of Robert" is brought up. Robert Hooke was a scientist who lived around the exact same time that Isaac Newton did. In fact, while Newton went to Cambridge, Hooke studied at Oxford, showing interest in many of the same subjects which made Newton famous (such as optics and gravitation), but also making his mark on science in his own way as well. This was mainly with Hooke's Law, a description of spring elasticity.

Furthermore, Hooke tended to criticize many of Newton's ideas, which led to both men essentially becoming enemies. This was on top of allegations that Hooke stole other peoples' work. Therefore, the novel version of Robert had a hook for a hand (a play on his last name), which was gained after his hand was cut off as punishment for theft (not to mention that, with a left hand removed, he would always be "right"). While it was never mentioned outright, part of the downfall of the Reign of Robert was due to the fluxions that Isaac discovered, thus tying this real-life conflict into a brief, occasional mention of the past which transpired before the rise of the New Testament.

Felix: Felix Klein

First Name Basis holds a lot of references to interesting geometries, and the Klein bottle (see Figure 2.2) is the first one. In simple terms, a Klein bottle is a two-dimensional area with only one side (*see also: Section 3 – "Ferdinand Freeway"*). As such, the space contained by a Klein bottle has no "inside" or "outside". Nevertheless, the bottle's descriptor, Felix Klein, was placed in the novel as a reference to the bottle.

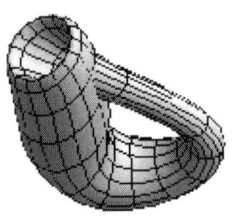

Figure 2.2: Klein bottle

When one thinks of a bottle, there are usually two connotations: babies and drunks. I decided to go with the latter, which led to the connection of a Chinese concept known as Zui Quan, but most often referred to as "drunken boxing". The fact that Felix uses a fluxion which turns his fists into flint is merely linking up the delicious alliteration that results in "Flint fist Felix". But even deeper than that is the fact that flint and steel are often used as a fire-starter when matches are unavailable. With the flint of Felix's fists combined with the steel of Isaac's knives, I got the imagery of sparks that I wanted to convey.

Jason: Jason of the Argo

Back when I wasn't sure if I was going to use last names in these novels, this character was originally designated as Jason Stalfos, the last name being a reference to the skeleton warriors in the *Legend of Zelda* video game series. Still, while the last name did not survive, the idea of skeleton keys did. Each of the fingers used to activate Q-Portals had a significance to the next part of the story (*see also: Section 4 – "Q-Portals"*). Even if Stalfos did not survive, the name of Jason did, and the explanation of his connection to the 3rd Kingdom is better explained in the section which discusses the 6 Kingdoms. Needless to say, the third noble gas is known as Argon, which is a short jump from Argo: the ship Jason captained in ancient Greek legend.

Carroll / Lewis: Lewis Carroll

One of the few split characters, both Carroll and the much more minor character of Lewis are based off of the literary works of Lewis Carroll. Mainly: *Alice in Wonderland*. We'll start with the more brief character of Lewis. This character is based off of the Mad Hatter, as evidenced by his top hat and the fact that he works for Transcontinental Express Airmail (or T.E.A. for short), since the character of Mad Hatter is always in a perpetual tea party. Furthermore, the fact that Lewis is a messenger and has winged sandals is in reference to the element which gave many haberdashers the mad hatter's disease: Mercury. More explanation on the Mercury connection can be found in the section about Cremy Serehurm.

Now, Carroll is a reference only due to her association with her cat (which is a Cheshire cat, by the way). The Cheshire cat is the smiling feline from Lewis Carroll's stories and has already been explained as a linked reference to the moon. However, Carroll's description is that of the painting *Arrangement in Grey and Black No. 1* by James McNeill Whistler. This piece is known more often as "Whistler's Mother". So, why did I describe Erwin's mother like this? Well, if there's one thing that wind can do well, it's whistle. Since Erwin's tooth gap created a whistle when he talked, and his wind powers can whistle through the town of Alden, it would come to reason that she would earn the moniker of "Whistler's Mother".

In *The Third Degree*, Carroll took on another reference: Mary, mother of Jesus. Even though the Caidoz statue of the Maiden was the actual, direct reference here, Carroll's circumstances were somewhat similar, especially when you consider Erwin's demise, both in its brutality and in the prime of his youth. Now, I'm not saying that Erwin is a reference to Jesus, but merely that some of their circumstances ended up being very similar.

Phoebe / Diana / Claire: N/A

While many names are shrouded in mystery, these three are just obscure enough that I can use them as they are. While two of them are of similar origin, all three have to do with the moon, which is why they all live there. Phoebe and Diana were straight pulls from Greek and Roman mythology, respectively. They are both lunar deities. Claire is a reference to the term "Clair de Lune", which is French for "moonlight" and is most often associated with the song of the same name by Claude Debussy.

Priest Werner: Werner Heisenberg

If Erwin Schrödinger was one of the fathers of Quantum Physics, Werner Heisenberg is the other one. The formulation of Quantum Physics that Heisenberg created is known as "Matrix mechanics". This matrix is referenced in the chess set that Priest Werner is first seen using in *First Name Basis*, mainly because this 8 by 8 grid can be seen as a matrix.

Most people know Heisenberg by his uncertainty principle: you can know how fast something is moving, but not where it is, or you can know where something is, but not how fast it's moving. This uncertainty is best shown in the behavior of electrons, which is why the character of Priest Werner uses the "–" lost Number-fluxion, which references the electron.

Operation Alsos was a mission meant to determine whether or not the Germans had an atomic bomb program. As a result, Werner Heisenberg was a part of this Operation because he was put in prison by the allies due to his work on the nuclear energy project in Germany. I had originally wanted to anagram the name to Operation Lasso, but figured the original reference was obscure enough not to be noticed.

Prince Niccolo: Niccolo Machiavelli

This character was an interesting one to write, mainly because Prince Niccolo wasn't very Machiavellian himself. Niccolo Machiavelli is best known for his political writing, and especially his book "The Prince", from which we get Machiavellianism. Ergo, since his most famous work was titled as such, I gave this character the distinction of himself being a prince. However, even though Prince Niccolo was a bit naïve and young, this meant that his royal advisor, Allan, needed to exhibit a more Machiavellian attitude in order to get the reference across. This attitude employs a lot of cunning and a lot of duplicity, much like the other political figures I emplaced in *First Name Basis* (who are, of course, "Flint Fist" Felix and Harry).

Edgar (aka Allan): Edgar Allan Poe

People with two names were very helpful in character development, especially when I can't use the last name. Not only could I split the person I'm referencing into two different characters (like I did for Carl Friedrich Gauss), but I could also give split personalities, or an identity change. The last option is what I went with for this gothic American poet. Even though his regicide was closer to that of William Shakespeare's *Hamlet*, a few of his stories were infused in this character. Of note is that since the plot to kill the King was a creation of a William, Edgar held the position of Number 7 in Testament, a fact that never made it into *First Name Basis* outright. At any rate, stories like *The Tell-Tale Heart* and poems like *The Raven* were at the forefront of this character.

King Sadim: King Midas

The first of the characters with an inverted name (read: spelled backwards), the King who held the legendary "golden touch" was represented in a similar way here. Instead of being a magical power, the power to turn things Gold (and the consequences of it) are represented through a Number-fluxion. The number "79" is that of the atomic number of Gold. More explanation of Number-fluxions is in Section 4 of this Appendix.

Pruthesemo: Prometheus

While Prometheus, the Greek Titan, is known for a few things, the main theme with this character is the theft of fire from the gods. It is no coincidence that the fluxion glove he wears allows him to "hold fire". The glove is based off of the Sulfur (chemical element #16) heads that are found on "strike anywhere" matches, which is why he was able to set his hand ablaze by dragging it across the stone wall of the chamber. I intended the position of Pruthesemo to be handed down from one guardian to another. As such, the "61" Number Disk held by the guardian of the Hellfire orb is passed on to the next guardian when one gets too old. 61 is the atomic number of Promethium.

As punishment for giving man the fire of the gods, Zeus had Prometheus chained to a rock and his liver pecked out by an eagle every day (the liver regenerated daily). This connection to an eagle is most appropriate for the eventual linking of the Hellfire orb and Sucari, since Sucari's flight vest uses an eagle Blood-fluxion. Some versions of the myth have Hercules rescuing Prometheus, which is what was referenced with the connection between Pruthesemo and Fred. The reference to Cinderella, Pruthesemo's incinerated wife, is a play on the word "cinder", which is the remnant of a fire.

Even though the figure of Prometheus is a symbol of progress and civilization, I decided to take an opposite approach, much like how Icarus was handled in the novels. The story I tried to convey was one of hesitation to accept all progress as good for humanity. We may develop technologies that can solve many world problems, but if these technologies can be used to destroy, we must be cautious with their use. This theme comes into play more in *Second to None* (see also: Section 4 – *"Fluxions"*).

Posea: Aesop

Another in the "spelled backwards" set of characters, Aesop was most well-known for his fables. One such fable is "The Boy Who Cried Wolf". While many people think that "Wolf in Sheep's Clothing" is one of his fables, this term is actually one of Biblical origin. Either way, the fact that some of the sheep in the area turn into wolves on the full moon references both of these idioms because it would only happen at night and only in specific conditions.

Dr. Paul (aka Number 5): Dr. Paul Moreau / Paul Lévy

Have I mentioned how I love "twofer" characters? Dr. Paul was originally a reference to Dr. Paul Moreau of the H.G. Wells story *The Island of Dr. Moreau*, but when I started doing some research into different fractals, I came across Paul Lévy. Dr. Moreau is the titular character from the Wells' story, whose goal in life was to remove the line between humanity and animals. On the other hand, Paul Lévy was a French mathematician who first described the Lévy C curve. This curve is also known as a C Dragon. Is it no wonder that in the lake of the Pythagorean Triangle there just happens to be a *Sea* Dragon?

Now, you may be asking yourself what the numbers mean? Why does the Sea Dragon have a "5" on it? Why did the sheep have "359" on it? Why did the two-headed dragon have a "2" on it? Let's go down the line, shall we?:

- *#1*: This number was R-3N3, but he escaped.
- *#2*: This number was for the twindragon, Horace and Donald. This dragon used to be the dragon of Harter under the name of Heigway. This is a reference to the Harter-Heigway dragon, which is a fractal curve. William Harter and John Heigway are the mathematicians who share the name of this dragon fractal. The twindragon's heads are the names of the mathematicians Horace Chandler Davis and Donald Ervin Knuth. They are the ones responsible for discovering it.
- *#3*: Not explicitly stated, but the dog with three heads had this number and is a reference to the beast which guards the gates of hell: Cerberus.
- *#5*: This is the number for the Sea Dragon, as mentioned earlier. I chose "5" based on the homestarrunner.com creation, "Trogdor the Burninator". The instructions on how to draw this dragon is to start by drawing an "S", for "dragon". The number which most closely represents an "S" is a "5".
- *#359*: The sheep that had this number branded into it was one of the sheep which turned into wolves during the full moon. Therefore, this is a reference to the 6th closest star to earth: Wolf 359. Interesting fact: this star is in the constellation Leo, which we eventually encounter in *The Third Degree*.

Because Dr. Moreau specialized in animal hybrids, some of the animals referenced on the island were fictional, but others are real. I didn't number these creatures, since I just wanted to reference as many as I could in a short amount of space. A moose with the face of a piranha is a reference to the webcomic *Wondermark* by David Malki. The creature known as Pirhanhamoose is the reference here. A horse with the horn of a narwhal is a reference to a unicorn. A beaver with the bill of a duck is a reference to a platypus. Finally, the fact that Dr. Paul's beast transformation had his right arm turn into that of a bear is a play on words and a reference to the 2nd Amendment to the Constitution: the right to bear arms.

Jacques: Jacques Cousteau

While some will accuse me of the wordplay I purposely put toward "Pierre's Pier", the fact that Jacques lives on a dock was merely a subconscious coincidence. However, this "Old Man and the Sea" (which references Ernest Hemmingway, as does the character's connection to writing about bull fights) is best known for the development of the **S**elf **C**ontained **U**nderwater **B**reathing **A**pparatus (aka SCUBA). This device's appearance in the fantasy world of *The Fluxion Trilogy* was made through the application of a Blood-fluxion, infused with the blood of a fish, to a person's neck, thereby giving them gills and the ability to breathe underwater.

Ivan: Ivan Pavlov

Are you familiar with the experiment where a dog starts salivating when it hears a bell? This is an example of what is known as classical conditioning. A more common name for this is a Pavlovian response. Who discovered this response? Why Ivan Pavlov, of course. This psychological trigger is based on repeated negative or positive consequences to a somewhat arbitrary action. This response is seen in the character of Ivan every time he uses Dr. Paul's name instead of calling him "Number 5". This is due to Dr. Paul beating Ivan every time he used the wrong name. As a result, every time he accidentally uses the wrong name, he cowers in pain, even if the punishment didn't come with it.

Michael: Michael Faraday

Chapter 6 in *First Name Basis* was heavily influenced by electromagnetism. One of the most influential scientists to do work in electromagnetism was Michael Faraday. Not only did he establish the concept of the electromagnetic field, he discovered electromagnetic induction, which states that a magnetic field can be created by coiling electrified wire. This is also known as an electromagnet. While Faraday was one of the most influential scientists in history, many are unfamiliar with his work, which also included the Faraday cage (which I was unfortunately unable to work into *First Name Basis*).

In the novel, much of Faraday's involvement comes in the Dendritic Forest. This forest is electrically charged due to the idea of induction heating, which is caused by the resistance of certain metals when charged with an electric current. The molten metal pool underneath the forest causes the trees above to be electrically charged, creating an electromagnetic field. Michael's weapon, the long copper whip, is used to wrap around the metal trees and absorb the electric current used to induce a magnetic field when the other end of the whip is coiled around a metal weapon (i.e. a sword). Since the trees are magnetized, this created magnetic field incapacitates any metal weapons, which now stick to the trees.

Rigel: Rigel Kentaurus

Not an actual person, per sé, but rather a reference to one of the stars closest to earth, which also goes by the name of Alpha Centauri. However, the reference can be taken one step further to that of *The Legend of Sleepy Hollow* by Washington Irving. Since a centaur is a creature which is half horse and half man, it would lead to Rigel being called a horse-man. Add to this the fact that the inhabitants of Armor Village have birth defects which cause them to not grow body parts, to which Rigel did not grow a head. You now have a headless horse-man. It's no wonder that the armor Rigel wears to cover his deformity is a helmet in the shape of a pumpkin.

Milo: Venus de Milo

When one thinks of famous works of art which are missing extremities, the first one that comes to mind is that of Venus de Milo (with the Sphinx being a close second). Therefore, in a village filled with characters who are missing limbs, I would be amiss not to include Venus de Milo. The insect used in the Blood-fluxion, which is harnessed to give her working arms, is that of the praying mantis, chosen only because of the very distinct arms which are present on this insect.

A brief, but omitted idea was for her arms to have short swords integrated into their design in much the same fashion as a butterfly knife. This would be easy to implement, since the interior of the armored arms would be hollow. This also would link again to the praying mantis motif. However, since this character did not have an opportunity to fight, it was left out.

Carl / Fred: Carl Friedrich Gauss

If Faraday was one of the fathers of electromagnetism, Gauss was the other one. While Faraday was more involved with the electric side of electromagnetism, Gauss was responsible for the magnetic side. As such, these characters were given the power of magnetism. As you may know, all magnets are polarized, with a north and south pole. As such, the two characters of Carl and Fred were born as Siamese twins, and both have very opposite personalities.

- *Carl*: Atlas
    - The "blue" side of the magnet pair, Carl is modeled after the Greek Titan known as "Atlas". Not only was this seen in the feeling that his brother (a reference to Hercules) tricked him into "carrying the world on his back", but that he was interested in cartography (map making). A collection of maps is known as an Atlas. Furthermore, one of the rhinoceros beetles is known as Atlas, which is why his armor was designed with this insect in mind.

Appendix   Section 2: Characters

- *Fred*: Hercules
  - The "red" side of the magnet pair (easily connected to the name "F<u>red</u>"), this character is modeled after the divine hero of Hercules. Since Hercules shared some mythology with Prometheus (saving him from the liver-eating eagles), the connection between the two characters was definitely one I made sure to include. Hercules was also a bit of a momma's boy, which is why Fred was manipulated by Valerie so easily, since she impersonated his dead mother. His armor also references a rhinoceros beetle known as Hercules. As the evil twin, he was born on the left side, therefore he had his "right" removed when Carl and Fred were separated. His Li-berator attack uses a "3" Number Disk, which is a reference to the chemical element of Lithium, also known as "Li", which reacts violently when it comes in contact with water.

John: John William Strutt (aka 3rd Baron Rayleigh)

Have you ever wondered, "Why is the sky blue?" Well, the answer to that is Rayleigh scattering, which is named after John William Strutt, also known as Lord Rayleigh. This phenomenon occurs because light will scatter at different wavelengths depending on how much atmosphere it has to travel through. The different wavelengths of light represent different colors, which is why the sky is blue during the day, since the wavelength for blue light is scattered the most based on the amount of atmosphere the sunlight travels through. Similarly, this is why sunsets and sunrises are red: there is more atmosphere for the light to travel through, so the longer wavelength of red light is the color that makes it through.

Due to Rayleigh scattering being a large contributor to the color of the sky, the "Chapelle Wing" in Maurits Manor is a reference to the Parisian chapel, Sainte-Chapelle (literally "The Holy Chapel"), which is best known for its stunning and extensive stained glass windows. Similarly, John is the heir to the throne of the 2nd Kingdom, which is referencing Neon, a chemical element which can produce many different colored lights.

Governor Harry: Harry Houdini (aka Erik Weisz)

The world's most famous illusionist, Harry Houdini suffered a tragic death, having simply been punched in the stomach, which ruptured his appendix. Most of Houdini's illusions had to do with escapes, but most "magic" has been described as "smoke and mirrors", which is why Harry is a cigar smoking politician (Governor of the Timberland region) who works in a mirrored office. Often, playing cards are used in illusions, so his use of cards as weapons (and the verbal linkages to the cards he throws) would be within the character's theme. The playing card theme is also continued with David and Rachel.

Snellius: Willebrord Snellius

As will be explained in Section 5 about Testament, Snellius is another one of the villains who just happens to have "Will" in his name. Even though Snellius didn't officially make it into Testament, he was certainly a contender, considering his "invisibility" power. In reality, this power was just refracting light around his body so that it would appear as though he was not there. In order to do this, the density of the air around him needs to be increased so that light is bent around him. This concept is described in the Snell-Descartes law, also known as the law of refraction.

In simple terms, it says that the path of light changes at the interface of two mediums of differing densities. This is why Snellius' power is not invisibility, but instead is the power of density. Of the two names referenced in the law's name, Snellius (a Dutch astronomer) is usually the one credited with describing the law, even if it had been observed long before him. Of course, the second name is that of our friend: René Descartes. So, who should be the one to defeat Snellius but R-3N3 himself?

David / Rachel: N/A

Once more, the real names of these characters were used unchanged, not only because they don't have last names, but because the references are a little more hidden due to the commonness of the names. These characters are based off of the Biblical characters of the same names; however, this is only because of their representative playing cards. Each of the "royal" cards in a deck are references to historical figures. David, the King of Israel, is represented by the King of Spades, while Rachel, wife to Isaac (the Biblical one, not Newton or Asimov), is represented by the Queen of Diamonds. Diamonds are made from Carbon, usually through a process that requires a lot of heat and pressure. This element just so happens to be #6 on the periodic table and is also the Number Disk Rachel uses.

Valerie / the Kyries: Valkyries

While there was only one moment where Valerie (or Val, for short) and her Kyrie soldiers are mentioned together in *First Name Basis*, the reference here was of the Norse figures known as Valkyries. The Ride of the Valkyries is referenced in many pieces of art and music, the most common of which is the title of the song composed by Richard Wagner (think of the quintessential opera singer with armor and a winged helmet, and you've got it).

Even though the leader of the Kyries, Valerie, possessed a dove Blood-fluxion core, the rest of the Kyries were outfitted with raven Blood-fluxions because Valkyries were often seen together and associated with these black birds. It's no wonder that the raven makes another appearance as a villain, considering Edgar's use of it earlier in the novel.

Alfred (aka The Peacemaker): Alfred Nobel

Those who have heard of the Nobel Prize know that this annual award is given for many different categories, ranging from Physics to Literature to Economics. Of course, the most referenced of these prizes is awarded for outstanding contributions to the world in the realm of Peace. Ergo, the character of Alfred, which references the Prize's namesake: Alfred Nobel, is known as "The Peacemaker". The idea of "peace" was perpetuated in the character of Alfred, who was designed to be similar to a Buddhist monk, an individual who spends his life searching for peace. Nobel decided to start the Nobel Prizes after he felt guilty that his invention, dynamite, could be used for a lot of destruction and a lot of actions which were not very peaceful. The staff weapon he uses has a dynamite fluxion on the tips, and is colored bright red to take the connection to dynamite even further.

Along with Grigori "The Reaper", Alfred wore a mask and had a staff weapon. The staff was meant to signify that they were part of Testament's "staff", but the masks they wore were a reference to the two masks associated with the theatre. Alfred's was a smiling face, which referenced Thalia, the mask of Comedy.

Thomson (aka Number 1): William Thomson (aka 1st Baron Kelvin)

The power held by Thomson was not necessarily that of ice, but rather of cold. This fluxion core was passed down or stolen from the Ice Queen on Ice Island, to William of Seasoned Compass, and finally to Thomson of Testament. Kelvin is the temperature scale which is set so that there can be no negative temperatures. Zero Kelvin is when all molecular movement stops, and has yet to be attained by scientists (even outer space is at a constant 5 Kelvin). When temperatures get this cold, elements which are usually in a gaseous state start to become liquid, and eventually start to freeze. The attack "Zero Hour" is a reference to this lower limit of the Kelvin temperature scale, but the "snowballs" Thomson throws are of solid Oxygen and solid Nitrogen. Because air is mostly made of Nitrogen (about 70% of all air), the Nitrogen ball is much bigger than the Oxygen ball (which is the remaining 30%). His power allows him to compress the air into its solid form because of the properties of these gasses in extremely cold temperatures.

Gottfried (aka Number 4): Gottfried Wilhelm Leibniz

In the Calculus Wars, the side opposite Isaac Newton was Gottfried Leibniz. While his notation and name for this area of mathematics are still used today, and in greater frequency than Newton's, most people tend to attribute Newton to the discovery, mainly because he discovered so many other things as well. Gottfried's version of calculus was the summation of small rectangles to determine the area underneath a curve. As such, Gottfried's version of fluxions used multiple snakes instead of a long, knotted one.

Leibniz also had some principles of logic that broke down to two rules: 1. There are a small number of simple ideas and 2. Complex ideas are merely combinations of these simple ideas. Therefore, Gottfried was very adept at combining fluxions to create more complex ones. This is also why he possessed, and was able to use, The Omnipotence. One of these "combination attacks" was that of methane (CH_4), an odorless, highly explosive gas which is a combination of four Hydrogen atoms (atomic number 1) and one Carbon atom (atomic number 6). Of course, with a "final boss" like Gottfried, I had to cover the powers previously seen in the enemies earlier in the novel.

Similarly, we have the "Gottfried Gun", which is formed by wearing a glove with four different fluxions on it: flint on the middle finger, steel on the thumb, gunpowder on the base of the index finger and any type of metal or heavy element on the tip of the index finger. The gun is shot by snapping the fingers together, creating a spark and igniting the gunpowder, which thrusts the metal fingertip toward the target. Even though I attributed it to Gottfried, this gun is actually a reference to the "Gosper Gun", which is a version of cellular automation first discovered by William Gosper (*see also: Section 3 – "The Eagle's Nest"*).

SECOND TO NONE

Benjamin: Benjamin Franklin

Many people have pointed out that my name is identical to the main character of *Second to None*. And while I do infuse parts of my personality into the main characters of my novels, this character is mainly based on the American revolutionary philosopher, Benjamin Franklin. In fact, the slogan "Join, or Die", which depicted a snake cut into eight sections, was a political cartoon drawn by Franklin leading up to the American Revolution, which fit nicely into the fluxion motif since the Naturals did not need the uroboros seal in order to use the fluxion cores.

Much like the character of Benjamin was once employed as a librarian, Franklin was responsible for creating a group of individuals who eventually started the first library in America. Similarly, Franklin's relationship with his wife was similar to that of the character of Benjamin, since she did not join him on his travels or adventures. Of the few times a newspaper is used in the Trilogy, Benjamin is the one reading it, a reference to his success as a newspaper editor. Aside from his inventions, like the Franklin Stove and Bifocals (those square glasses the character wears as well), Franklin was most known for his exploration of lightning and electricity. The zigzag scar on his cheek was meant to show this connection, and not as a reference to Harry Potter. His Imaginary World name of Lambda the Just was a similar reference to lightning, as the symbol "λ" looks like forked lightning. Furthermore,

Lambda in Greek numerals stands for the number "30", which is why Benjamin was 30 years old in the novels.

Back when *First Name Basis* was written, I had decided that The Triumvirate of Power would consist of references to three Greek gods: Zeus, Poseidon, and Hades. Since Franklin's kite experiment (which was why his possession of a Q-Portal key was so fundamental to the climax of *Second to None*) was foundational in understanding the nature of lightning, he was a prime candidate to take the role of "Zeus". Because of his research on lightning (even before the kite experiment), Franklin also invented the lightning rod which, ironically enough, attracted more lightning than it prevented. Still, the pointed rods translated well into Zeus' lightning bolt, which I represented as the javelin form of Benjamin's weapon.

Some of the key attacks Benjamin performs with the Skybolt orb are tied to mysterious lightning effects. I'll leave the explanation of ball lightning to Nikola Tesla's section, but attacks like the Blue Jet are examples of lightning not usually seen while on the ground. A Blue Jet is lightning that shoots upward into the ionosphere and looks exactly the way you'd think it would. Blue Starters are merely Blue Jets that are shorter and brighter. Finally, the Fire of Saint Erasmus goes by a different name in real life: St. Elmo's Fire. This phenomenon was first observed by sailors who encountered charged electrical fields with their ships. The points of these ships would show a light blue flame which was the manifestation of the electricity in the field and was caused much in the same way that Franklin's lightning rod worked. The Fire of Saint Erasmus is used in the novel to create fulgurite (glass created by the interaction of lightning and sand) in the knees of the stone soldiers.

Furthermore, when I used Benjamin in *The Third Degree*, I used his lightning as a method to power some scientific experiments. The first experiment was that of electrolysis, which uses direct current (like lightning) to separate elements. Usually this is performed to transform water into Oxygen and Hydrogen; but in 1886, Fluorine was discovered by French chemist, Henri Moissan. Of note here is that Fluorine is actually toxic, and is the one element in Topaz ($Al_2SiO_4(F,OH)_2$) that is not commonly found in sand, both facts that are brought forth in *The Third Degree*. The second experiment was that of a railgun. This is explained in more detail in the section about the "Spear of Trium".

And yet, the theme of lightning is so deep that I couldn't resist making quite a few more references. As was already mentioned, Benjamin's character has some attributes pulled from Zeus, whose Roman counterpart was Jupiter (thus his "Natural" name of Reptiju Suez). However, the weapon Benjamin received after his Imaginary World adventure was not a javelin, but rather a hammer. This hammer, along with the number "90" engraved on its side is meant to reference the Norse lightning deity: Thor (the chemical element #90 being Thorium). Part of why Benjamin's weapon could change shape is due to the fact that metal is often conductive of electricity, but not without some resistance. The electrical resistance heats the metal and allows it to be more malleable. Therefore, the head of a hammer could be spread across its handle to create a javelin or sword.

I wanted all three of the members of The Triumvirate to be human-animal hybrids, which is why I gave Benjamin the power of flight: to make him an angel. This can be read into further, considering many circumstances surrounding the character of Benjamin and his mysterious disappearance. Of course, a flying lightning man could also be construed as a "thunderbird", which is yet another lightning deity, this time from the Native Americans. This attribute meant that his Elemental affinity was really one of "Air" (thus: Skybolt orb). When Benjamin was given a Blood-fluxion from Noah, the reason he chose a turkey before finally settling on a bald eagle has to do with Franklin's desire to have the wild turkey be the national bird of the United States instead of what eventually was agreed upon: the bald eagle.

Finally, one of the more obscure references involving Benjamin came with his arrival in the future. The apple tree, which was also the Square G shrine, was struck by lightning when he re-appeared, thus instantaneously baking all the apples which were hanging from its branches. One of Benjamin Franklin's favorite foods was Baked Apples, thereby easily linking him to the lore I had already incorporated into *The Fluxion Trilogy*.

Tecumseh: William Tecumseh Sherman

This Civil War General from the Union was well known for his march to the Atlantic, incinerating everything in his path. This "scorched earth" policy was used to lower the morale of the opposing side. Also, as the trend was throughout *First Name Basis*, I couldn't resist a villain with the name of "William". Of course, the villain who easily comes to mind throughout history would be that of Satan.

Satan, Lucifer, and the Devil are all names for the force of evil in the world, but the mythological gods associated with this power of the underworld were Hades (Greek) and Pluto (Roman), which created the "Natural" name of Lotup Sedah. Hell has often been linked to fire, which is why this character's Fire affinity was easily linked to the Civil War General who was responsible for burning down Atlanta, Georgia. Thus, the Hellfire orb completely matches the Element of "Fire" for this character.

Even though the Devil is often shown as a half-man, half-goat, I decided to model this character closer to that of the Minotaur, which (if spelled backwards) is Ruatonim. Even though the reason Tecumseh burned down the villages was due to the connection between his Roman god reference, and the political ruling state known as a Plutocracy: rule by the rich, the images of villagers on fire and thatched roof cottages aflame comes from the homestarrunner.com creation of Trogdor the Burninator (also referenced in *Dr. Paul's Sea Dragon*).

The traditional weapon of Satan has been that of the pitchfork, which is why Tecumseh's weapon of choice was modeled similarly, explained by his farming background. When he emerged victorious over the Imaginary World, Tecumseh's weapon now sported a number, "94", which is the atomic number of Plutonium, yet a final reference to the Roman god of Pluto.

Penny (aka Penneut Psinodeo): Neptune / Poseidon

Another semi-original character who was birthed out of the fact that I have very few strong female characters in my novels. Plus, I wanted the "three gods of Olympus" to have more of a love triangle. It was a little difficult to come up with a name which was common, but also managed to capture the references to Poseidon and Neptune. Therefore, the nickname "Penny" from "Penneut Psinodeo" was a good compromise. In fact, since the "Natural" names are somewhat tied to the Imaginary World names, I was glad I could fit "Psi" in the anagram to complete the connection.

Traditionally, these mythological gods have been in charge of the sea and the waves (ergo: Seawave orb). The weapon associated with these gods has been the trident, but when this weapon is "evolved" in the Imaginary World, it picks up the number "93", the atomic number of Neptunium. Furthermore, the symbol for Psi, "ψ", looks very much like a trident, thus adding even more referential depth to the character.

Being associated with the sea meant that Penny's animal-hybrid was that of a mermaid and also explains why both her weapon and fluxion core were attracted to the Aquarius shrine in *The Third Degree*. In fact, both of these cores were given to her as birthday presents. The Seawave orb was a gift on her 6th birthday (which was the age of "it" in the Imaginary World), whereas the trout Blood-fluxion was a gift on her 12th birthday. Each of the children from Rancho de la Sol received their fluxion cores on these two birthdays.

Much like Benjamin's attacks were based on more scientific concepts surrounding lightning, Penny's attacks were similarly associated to waves. This is partly because The Triumvirate name of "Psi" is a reference to Quantum Physics. Psi is the most common symbol for the wave function, which is the description of how a particle behaves in quantum space. This symbol is further used in the Schrödinger equation, which describes the evolution of the wave function over time. At any rate, the form of "wave" that I chose to manipulate was closer to that of physical waves instead of quantum ones.

The three attacks which Penny uses are all some variation of what can happen with waves. Once more, I'll leave the Resonance Crush to be described with Nikola Tesla, but the attack which requires two subsequent Wave Punches works off of the idea of positive interference. This concept states that when two waves come in contact with each other, their amplitudes (how tall they are) are either added or subtracted from each other, depending on where the wave is in relation to the origin line. If two waves are added, they become taller. However, if they are subtracted, the two waves can cancel each other out! This wave matching is how noise-cancelling headphones work: creating a sound wave that is the inverse of the ambient noise.

Just like there can be waves through solids and liquids, the waves we hear through the air is called sound. This is why Penny was a great singer and could mimic any sound she heard. This is also why her third, and final attack was the Sonic Boom. When an object travels faster than the speed of sound, the sound barrier is broken and a sonic boom is heard. And yet, before the sound barrier is broken, much of the sound is compressed in front of the object, waiting to be released. When the waves are finally released, by breaking the sound barrier, they are released all at once. This very loud sound wave actually compresses the air to a point where it can provide a concussive force: being pushed over by sound!

In reading through *The Fluxion Trilogy*, one might notice that the characters of Erwin (from *First Name Basis*) and Penny (from *Second to None*) are very similar. Both are very gifted at using fluxions at a young age (Erwin at ten, Penny at six), but are forbidden from using these fluxions by their parents. Both characters left home to join the main characters of their respective novels, but were eventually killed tragically. These similarities are due to what I like to call "sidekick syndrome", which usually goes hand-in-hand with having a knowledgeable main character.

Amedeo: Amedeo Avagadro

If you're wondering why General Amedeo wanted an army 1 septillion soldiers strong, it would be because he is referencing a common unit in chemistry: Avagadro's number (also designated as N_A). This constant is 6.02×10^{23}, and it represents the number of atoms in a mol of a substance. Mol is also referenced by the caves which were dug out underneath the Tower of Lebab, since the mammal known as a mole is well known for digging tunnels.

For reference, a septillion of something would be 1.0×10^{24}. This is why, when the final numbers for the army's total personnel came in at 60% of a septillion, it was meant to represent the 6.02×10^{23} of Avagadro's number. Since it is such a large number, Avagadro's constant is a little difficult to visualize, especially when associated with people. Since there are only a few billion people on earth, to reach a septillion people would be a million billion billion (or one million billions of a billion). That's a lot of people!

Grigori (aka The Reaper): Grigori Rasputin

Grigori Rasputin, also known as the "Mad Monk" (despite not actually being a monk), was a Russian mystic who was killed multiple times, but miraculously survived most of them. The Grigori in *First Name Basis* and *Second to None* is the only character to be physically present in both stories due to the Time Thread stasis experiment performed on him near the end of *Second to None*. This experiment gave Grigori immortality, which is a reference to the myth that he could not be killed. Due to his weapon being a switchblade scythe, the nickname of "the Grim Reaper" was an easy derivation from his name and an apt description based on his immortality and clothing. In *First Name Basis*, he wore a skull mask which mirrored the mask Alfred wore in that it was a theatre mask which represented Melpomene, the mask of Tragedy. Grigori was finally killed in the novel due to the idea that gravity can affect both space and time, as referenced when the Time Thread was tied to Kuroni (the gravity sword).

Bram: Bram Stoker

The author who wrote *Dracula* was modeled more after the titular character he wrote than the real life Bram. In *First Name Basis* I was trying to mimic the powers of Dracula, but in *Second to None*, I tried to get the feel of the character of Dracula. How he holds himself. How he looks. How he reacts. Granted, I did make him a protagonist, instead of the standard antagonist that vampires generally fall in to. But that just makes it more exciting! While never mentioned in the novel, the town where Bram lives goes by the name of Styla Nirvana, which is an anagram of Transylvania. The fact that he had a butler named Alfred is a reference to Bruce Wayne (a similar, rich individual) and his alter ego of Batman (bats of course being a reference to vampires).

Thomas: Thomas Edison

After writing *First Name Basis*, I felt that *Second to None* would need another good rivalry similar to the Calculus Wars referenced earlier. This is where Thomas Edison came in. Lining up well with the Benjamin Franklin lightning reference, Thomas and Nikola both worked to control electricity. Edison's version was known as DC power, which stands for Direct Current. This is the type of power you'd receive from a battery or (as luck would have it), a bolt of lightning. The character of Alessandro is a reference to Alessandro Volta, who first described the electrochemical battery (and where we get the unit of "Volts"). In the novel, Alessandro was able to capture the power of lightning in the Skybolt orb for Thomas to use in his electrical, direct current experiments.

In real life, Edison had the nickname of "The Wizard of Menlo Park", which fit in nicely with the fantasy theme I had begun back in book one. As such, Menlo Castle is a reference to this moniker. It was at Menlo Park where Edison invented the first light bulb which would last longer than a few moments. In fact, Alessandro Volta was one of the earlier inventors of the light bulb, but Edison made it more practical to be used commercially. The first filaments used in these light bulbs were made of Tungsten, which is chemical element #74. These filaments produced light when an electrical current passed through them.

Nikola: Nikola Tesla

As was mentioned in Thomas' section, the other side of the electrical rivalry was Nikola Tesla. One of the aspects of the differences between these two men that I kept in their characters was their age difference, with Nikola being about 10 years younger than Thomas. And while I made Nikola a character who wanted to be a magician with electricity (a reference to his appearance in the 2006 Christopher Nolan film, *The Prestige*) as compared to Thomas' "wizard" moniker, another aspect of their differences was definitely their different beliefs on electricity.

While Edison was adamant that DC power was the way to go, Tesla was a firm believer in his solution: AC power. This power relies on Alternating Currents, which is part of the reason I made him switch sides to that of Amedeo's Army (alternating allegiances). This is also aside from the fact that he did actually work for Thomas Edison for a time before heading out on his own. And yet, his work with electricity did not stop at AC power.

Tesla's lightning rod was an improvement on Franklin's design and actually provided protection from lightning instead of attracting it. Even though the novel version attracted lightning, this lightning rod was referenced when the "Frankenstein" experiment was performed in the mountain chapel. Furthermore, Tesla was able to create lightning with a device which we now know as a "Tesla Coil". He is also the only person to have been able to create ball lightning in a laboratory. Ball lightning is exactly what it sounds like: a sphere of electricity which lasts a bit longer than a bolt of lightning. Finally, Tesla worked on wireless electricity, which was referenced in the revival of the corpses in the mountainous graveyard.

Even though Tesla worked on a lot of electrical projects, he also had other discoveries. Even though Wilhelm Conrad is usually given the credit for discovering X-Rays (*see also: Section 5 – "Testament"*), Nikola Tesla was actually the one who first discovered and used them. Furthermore, he performed many experiments involving the idea of resonance, which is when a wave is produced that builds upon itself with constructive interference until the material cannot hold the energy of the wave anymore and breaks apart (thus: Penny's Resonance Crush attack). All in all, Tesla was truly an amazing scientist and I wish I could have included more of this character in my novels.

Braun: Werner von Braun

Of all the characters based on real people, this one was a little tricky because I had already used Werner in *First Name Basis* for Werner Heisenberg. In the end, I had to go with Braun, even though it wasn't his first name. This was in part due to the brief reference in *First Name Basis* (and again in *The Third Degree*) of a character by the name of Von, thereby leaving only one name left to use. In fact, in the timeline of the story, Von is a distant grandchild to Braun, which is why he could teach Robin her archery skills.

The trick of having an archaic fantasy world infused with modern science is the transfer between old and new. Werner von Braun is mostly known for his work as a German scientist in the realm of rockets. It has been jokingly said that he didn't care about the targets of his missiles, merely saying (according to comedian Tom Lehrer), "Once the rockets are up, who cares where they come down? That's not my department." Missiles are technologically advanced from arrows, so the reference still makes sense in a fantasy setting when I made him an archer.

And yet, a lot of variables go into hitting a target. Minute variations in velocity, wind speed, and angle can make the difference between a bull's-eye and a miss. This is why simulations are often run using the Monte Carlo method. Named after the famous gambling town, this simulation method changes a lot of variables, one at a time, and plots the result. By using a normal distribution of what these variables could be, a set of possible outcomes is produced. If you haven't guessed by now, the Mount Charles method is in reference to Monte Carlo simulations. When Braun would launch one of these arrows (also known as the Sagittarius Arrow), it would multiply to all its different variables, raining down a storm of arrows that followed all the different paths they could take. We learn in *The Third Degree* that the Mount Charles method is a direct attribute of the Sagittarius Arrow's Mutable Quality.

Gulogulo: Galileo Galilei

OK, I'll be the first to admit that this is a little bit of a stretch. However, I didn't want to use either Galileo's first or last name, since both are easily recognized. While "G-squared" worked for the Square G shrine in *First Name Basis*, I needed a name that I could use, but would still be able to induce the necessary shortening to G². This G² needed to represent Galileo's initials (G.G., much like Isaac Newton was I.N.), but was also representative of the universal gravitational constant: G (also known as Newton's constant). Even though these references were great, I still didn't have a name to use.

This was when I arrived at the binomial nomenclature for "wolverine": *Gulo gulo*. If these two names were smashed together and said with a slur, you could almost arrive at "Galileo". For those familiar with Marvel superheroes, they would recognize that the six swords held in Gulogulo's two hands mimic the adamantium claws of the X-Men character of Wolverine. However, the length of the swords being longer than Wolverine's trademark claws is attributed to a reference to the villain known as Captain Kuro from the Japanese manga and anime, *One Piece*.

And yet, even though I referenced some non-scientific works with his name, Galileo's influence on science was very distinct. In terms of gravity, a precursor to Isaac Newton's discovery (and perhaps a direct inspiration too), was a thought experiment involving Galileo standing atop the Tower of Pisa and dropping two balls of differing masses. These two balls would hit the ground at the same time, which proves that objects fall at the same rate, regardless of their mass. This rate is gravity. Even though this thought experiment did not come out in the novels, his connection to the gravity sword, Kuroni, is a direct reference to this scientific principle.

Galileo stood in direct opposition to the thought that the earth was the center of the universe. Much like Gulogulo opposed the genocide of the Naturals, Galileo stood up for the idea that the sun was the center of the solar system, based on observations he made through his telescope. While such ideas like the earth revolving around the sun seem so simple now, back in Galileo's time it was a very serious claim to make and was not agreed upon by most people.

Mary: Mary Shelly

Much in the same way that Bram Stoker was the writer of *Dracula*, Mary Shelly was the writer of *Frankenstein*. In fact, *Second to None* seemed to have quite a few references to authors when compared to *First Name Basis*. And yet, I treated Mary the same way I treated Bram: as the creator of her famous work. Her story deals with bringing life to the dead, so I had her character do just that. Considering the lack of strong female characters in the first part of this trilogy, Mary was a welcome addition to the ranks, even if she was quite aloof.

Victor: Victor Frankenstein

People often mislabel the monster created in Mary Shelly's *Frankenstein*, but in *Second to None*, the name of the monster created when bringing a corpse back to life is that of the original scientist: Victor Frankenstein. Aside from the obvious wordplay about being a victor over death, in a sense Victor was Mary Shelly's creation, even if he then created the monster we commonly recognize as "Frankenstein". The key to the creation of Victor is that much of the body is controlled by our nervous system, which is itself a series of electrical impulses. This is why a heart can be restarted (or stopped) with electricity. Likewise, muscles can be triggered with electricity, which is why Benjamin was able to enhance his movements and strength by using the power of the Skybolt orb. Finally, the character of Victor was similar to Frankenstein's monster due to their aversion to fire.

Mathison: Alan Mathison Turing

Mathison is a character that I pulled from my work on *First Name Basis*. I figured that the named towns a millennium later must have been named after certain people, so I decided to give a bit of back story to these characters. Even though the town in *First Name Basis* was Mathiston, not Mathison, that was merely because many towns have the "-ton" suffix, and it was a matter of "close enough". Of course, the character of Mathison was based off of the character of Igor in Mary Shelly's *Frankenstein*, but only because the Turing test accomplishes a very similar concept: convincing us that the dead are alive.

Alan Turing is credited with giving us the Turing test, which is a test run in computer science to examine the proficiency of an artificial intelligence. The idea behind the Turing test is to have a computer respond to a question in much the same way that a human would. In this way, if the person asking the question cannot see who is answering, the answer should make them question whether or not there is a computer or a human on the other end. Therefore, this idea fits nicely in the realm of creating life from death, since it is interpreting a human signal from something that is not human. This is why R-3N3 and Isaac (Asimov) were in Mathiston before Testament's raid on Pandora Prison: to link them to this concept of artificial intelligence.

Herbert: Herbert George Wells (aka H.G. Wells)
One of the great founders of science fiction, H.G. Wells wrote many stories which are easily recognized today. Stories like:
- *The Time Machine*
- *The Island of Dr. Moreau*
- *The War of the Worlds*
- *The Invisible Man*
- *The First Men in the Moon*

The character of Herbert was based off of this author, not only from his appearance, but his wife as well (Amy Catherine Robbins). Wells was one of the main inspirational authors who got me into writing my own stories. Needless to say, much like Mathison, I gave some background to this character so that we would know why a crater on the moon would come to be called Herbert Crater.

Jules: Jules Verne
If H.G. Wells was one of the great founders of science fiction, Jules Verne was right up there with him. As was the case between Thomas and Nikola, I tried to put the two characters of Herbert and Jules at ages that reflected their real-life age difference (with Jules being older than Herbert). The other similarities linking Jules to Herbert were their wives (Jules' being Honorine de Viane Morel), and the fact that they have craters on the moon named after them (Jules Crater being the reference in *The Fluxion Trilogy*). Of course, once again we have an author with many recognizable titles, including:
- *20,000 Leagues Under the Sea*
- *Journey to the Center of the Earth*
- *From the Earth to the Moon*
- *Around the World in 80 Days*
- *Michael Strogoff: The Courier of the Czar*

While Wells was good at the personal aspects of science fiction, Verne absolutely nailed a lot of the science. For instance, in his story *From the Earth to the Moon*, he predicted we would be able to go to the moon if we put a launching station in Florida. This was in 1865! The chemistry used in that story (as well as in *20,000 Leagues Under the Sea*) is what inspired my take on how people would be able to live and breathe on the moon. Air is created by the extended light of the sun during the day (which lasts almost an entire month) reacting with potassium chlorate. The CO_2 produced by the people breathing the air is absorbed by caustic potash.

And yet, I didn't want the entire surface of the moon to have an atmosphere, because then it would look different from earth. By mixing in silicon with the potassium chlorate and caustic potash, I created a system that would develop glass bubbles of air each time a meteor would strike the surface of the moon. The heat generated with the crater creation would fuse the silicon into a glass bubble covering for the crater, which would then trap the reactions of the other two chemicals, both of which were uncovered by the violence of the meteor strike.

Another Verne reference was the dead volcano, Sievuvus. Not only did the crew of the Nautilus in *20,000 Leagues Under the Sea* find themselves inside a dead volcano, but the method in which they arrived there was very similar to the underwater tunnel that I used in my novel.

Noah: Noah Webster

Some of the names referenced in this trilogy are combinations of a few different ideas, but this one is a beautiful "twofer". The obvious reference, considering his location, is that of the Noah from the Bible. This Noah was a collector of animals. Noah Webster, on the other hand, was a collector of words, compiling them into what we now know today as the dictionary.

The Biblical Noah built an ark and collected two of every animal, which is why the character in the novel has two sets of Blood-fluxion cores of every animal. Furthermore, the novel character also lived in a giant boat balancing on a volcano, since the Biblical ark rested on top of Mount Ararat when the flood was over (instead of being knocked off the volcano by a flood, like what happened in *Second to None*).

When Noah offers Benjamin a Blood-fluxion, he suggests both a raven and a dove, which were the two birds sent out after the flood. The fact that one of these Blood-fluxion collections is called "The Spectrum" is a reference to the rainbow which appeared after the flood as God's promise to never flood the earth again (much like the Pythagorean Triangle uroboros seal stopped the Sievuvus flood). This collection is held in a box which matches the description of the Ark of the Covenant, yet one more link to the "Noah's ark" reference. This boat is supposed to look like an arc of a circle, yet another play on words.

Joan: Joan of Arc

This one might come as a bit of a groaner to people, but Joan living in Noah's Ark would make her Joan of Ark. Luckily, since the ark in the novel is shaped more like an arc, she can still be referred to as Joan of Arc. Unfortunately, her real-life death of being burned alive for heresy, even though she led the French to a military victory over the English, is just marginally less painful than her character's death in the novel: death by volcano.

This character was covered in armor, much like the character of Milo was in *First Name Basis*. Of course, both of these women in armor is a reference to the character of Erza Scarlet from *Fairy Tail*. Of note here is that the event which caused Joan to fall into the volcano is the exact same event in *The Third Degree* that sent Isaac to the moon, thereby linking the two novels together.

Camille: Camille Saint-Saëns

This French composer is known for many pieces of music, but is best known for his *Carnival of the Animals* suite. I liked how well this fit in with the characters of Noah and Joan. His mother is French. His father collects animals. This character almost wrote itself.

Dmitri: Dmitri Mendeleev

Mendeleev is credited with creating the periodic table of the elements that we use today. This table (which was a literal table in the novel) is based on the atomic number of each of the elements, which is determined by how many protons are in the atom's nucleus. As such, Dmitri holds the "+" lost Number Disk because of its reference to protons. The "101" Number Disk represents Mendelevium, an element named for this very scientist. The character of Dmitri is obsessed with finding these Number Disks (all of which represent the chemical elements), as well as using the Philosopher's Stone and the "lost" Number Disks to create more Number Disks. He is a collector by nature and as such gets a little obsessive when searching for these Number Disks.

Dr. Robert / Mr. Louis: Robert Louis Stevenson

Robert Louis Stevenson was a writer whose works include *Treasure Island* and *Dr. Jekyll and Mr. Hyde*. As such, the Treasure Island referenced in *Second to None* is none other than the Island of Stability. The character of Dr. Robert is not only a reference to the Beatles' song "Doctor Robert", but his wooden leg is a reference to Long John Silver, the pirate from *Treasure Island*. However, since Dr. Robert turns into Mr. Louis through the Soul-fusion fluxion (which we see similarly with Isaac in *First Name Basis*), it can be obviously inferred which literary reference is made here. Briefly after Mr. Louis' introduction, there is a short mention of "Dante", who would be a reference to Dante Alighieri and his *Inferno*, and the seven deadly sins referenced therein.

Johann: Johann David Wyss

The stone house outside of Meadow Peak is one filled with references. First is the reference to *The Swiss Family Robinson*, written by Johann David Wyss. This reference is made when Johann offers his guests cheese (Swiss cheese) and hot chocolate (Swiss Miss hot chocolate). This was as far as that reference

went, but the rest of the Johann references are all linked to composers and are as follows:
- ➤ *Johann:* Johann Strauss, who popularized the waltz and was the father of Johann Strauss II.
- ➤ *Junior:* Johann Strauss II, known as "The Waltz King" and for works including *The Blue Danube* and *Die Fledermaus*.
- ➤ *Pachelbel:* Johann Pachelbel, known for the piece *Canon and Gigue in D*.
- ➤ *Sebastian:* Johann Sebastian Bach, known for many pieces of baroque music including *The Brandenburg Concertos*.

Antonio: Antonio Vivaldi

Anyone who is familiar with Antonio Vivaldi will know that he was the composer of *The Four Seasons*, a series of four violin concertos. These concertos were then referenced by the organization Antonio created: Seasoned Compass. This reference breaks into two parts. First, is the aforementioned musical piece, whereas the second has to do with Vivaldi's nickname of "The Red Priest". Not only was he actually a Catholic priest, but his hair was quite red. And thus, the character's nickname of "Tilde the Cardinal" was born. Of course, wanting to join together the four cardinal seasons with the four cardinal directions was made that much easier by this nickname. To even further the reference, the character of Antonio was a Cardinal priest, hence the red outfit and the bird in the tree. Once more, the monastery where Benjamin and Penny found Antonio was never mentioned, but it was Alive Ild Abbey, which is an anagram of Vivaldi. Furthermore, the monk who meets them at the door of the Abbey was named Thelonious, a reference to the jazz musician, Thelonious Monk.

Luvnac (aka Natsu Minami): Vulcan

Referenced originally in *First Name Basis*, Luvnac was a member of Seasoned Compass. His power of heat is a reference to the Roman god of Vulcan, who is often associated with not only fire, but volcanoes (hence his forge being in Daniel Volcano). Vulcan is usually seen as a blacksmith, which is a direct carry over into the character of Luvnac and his creation of the six Noble Swords and Kuroni. However, the ideology that fire can be useful, as well as harmful, was a good link in the chain to the Manhattan Project (*see also: Section 4 – "Fluxions"*) and the mixed usage for nuclear energy. This idea was seen in Luvnac's refusal to make any more weapons (nuclear bombs) with his powers, but instead form metal into armor (nuclear energy) in order to protect people from the weapons.

Trea Raiga (aka Haru Higashi): Mother Earth

Also a member of Seasoned Compass, who better to be more in tune with the "Natural world" than that of the reference to "Mother Earth"? Her ability to be able to learn the "Natural" name of someone was something I used to my advantage when dispensing the few "double names" in *Second to None*.

Because of the system I set up in *First Name Basis*, with people only having one name, adding a second name to a character was definitely something different. I did this mainly because I had too many references to fit into certain characters, so I had to double up. The "double names" Trea Raiga (which is an anagram of "Terra" and "Gaia") produced were only for those who were denoted as "Naturals", so as to give an easy way to know when a character was a Natural or not.

Of course, if I'm giving a character the attributes of the earth, there were a few references I needed to make. First, was the fact that her inherent ability was one of "life", since earth is the only planet we know of that can sustain life (at least in this solar system). Secondly, was the reference to the Kármán Line, which is essentially the "boundary" of the earth's atmosphere: around 100 km above sea level. I used this Line as a sort of "barrier" to keep people from discovering Rancho de la Sol, just like the earth's atmosphere is a "barrier" to incoming particulate, like meteors. The only way to get through the Line is to either be really big, or to know how to enter it, much like space shuttles do when they re-enter the earth's atmosphere.

Gustav: Gustav Holst

Second to None may have had fewer references to scientists, but one thing it was not lacking in was references to composers. Gustav Holst is another one of these references. The work he is best known for is "The Planets", and it covers the mythological gods instead of the actual planets themselves. It was the titles for these planets (like "Mercury, the Winged Messenger") which led to many of the attributes of the "Naturals family" that the character of Gustav fathered with Trea Raiga (*see also: Section 5 – "Rancho de la Sol"*).

Salvador: Salvador Dali

If there's one person who we think of when we think of surrealist art, it's Salvador Dali. This Spanish artist is best known for his work *The Persistence of Memory*, which is usually known as the "melted clock" painting. As such, when dealing with pocket watches and certain Time Thread stasis experiments, who better to provide the timepiece than the character of Salvador?

PHN-6: Sphinx

An anagram of "sphinx", PHN-6 (or the **P**sychological **H**eightened e**N**igma) is the final challenge for those passing through the Imaginary World. The sphinx is known for its riddle (the question about man), which was asked of Tecumseh when The Triumvirate passed through the i-World. Since the sphinx is known for these riddles, I included two more "unsolvable questions" to be asked of the other two members of The Triumvirate when they passed through the i-World. Normally, only one person passes through the Imaginary World at a time, so the sphinx's riddle would be the only question asked.

The symbols given to those who pass the test of PHN were grouped into two sets: diacritics and Greek letters (*see also: Section 5 – "The Triumvirate of Power"*). These symbols, much like the Naturals' ability to use fluxions, are passed down to the children of those who pass PHN's quiz, although the luminosity of these symbols decreases with each generation. As such, if there is enough i-World ancestry in an individual, these symbols will look like birthmarks and will react in much the same way that they would when the i-World victors would gather. In order to hide the accomplishment of finding and successfully passing through the Imaginary World, these symbols would only reveal themselves to others who had passed through the i-World:

➢ Where two are gathered, the symbols appear like tattoos on the skin.
➢ When three are together, the symbols glow.
➢ If four meet, the symbols emit a sound much like the blip on a radar screen.
➢ In the unlikely event that five are near each other, they all are given the ability to see through solid matter, with the exception of their Imaginary World comrades.
➢ Finally, if all six symbol bearers come together, PHN can be summoned and used to do the bidding of these individuals.

While the Greek letter symbols need very little explanation, diacritics are the little marks added to letters to change the way a letter sounds. I originally wanted the diacritic set of characters to be a "First Triumvirate", but this didn't work out with the way the timeline was constructed. The three diacritic characters were as follows:

➢ *Breve the Lion* [Prince Clive]
   o Shaped like the bottom half of a circle, this symbol was used mainly because "Breve" sounds a lot like "Brave", which is usually associated with lions. The symbol also looks a little bit like the nose of a lion.
➢ *Umlaut the Dragon* [Bram]
   o Often seen gracing the titles of heavy metal albums, these two dots were a great way to make a reference to vampires, since the bite of a vampire often looks like an umlaut on the neck.
➢ *Tilde the Cardinal* [Priest Antonio]
   o A Tilde is the wavy accent mark usually seen in Spanish words (especially above the "n"). As was the case with Breve, Tilde was used because it's close to "Tide", as in "the changing tide of the seasons". Also, the symbol looks like air/wind, which a cardinal would use to fly.

Julius: J. (aka Julius) Robert Oppenheimer
One of the men in charge of the Manhattan Project, Oppenheimer was horrified at the destructive power they had created. As a result, I made a minor

part for Julius in the fluxion research department, mainly so that he could comment on the destruction brought about at the end of Amedeo's War.

James & Garland: James Wadell Alexander II & Garland Baird Briggs

Figure 2.3: 6-2 Knot

These two gentlemen are best known for their work on knotting theory. This geometric pursuit is just what it sounds like: exploring knots. However, these knots are created with a single loop of rope so as to be continuous. There are different notations for knots, but I decided to go with the Alexander-Briggs notation, which starts with how many intersections there are, followed by the "order" that the knot would be in for similar intersections. For instance, the knot 6_2 (also notated as 6-2) would be the knot seen in Figure 2.3. Notice how there are six intersections?

In the novels, I used this notation to designate the strength of the seal, followed by how many fluxion cores were incorporated into it. Figure 2.3 shows Sucari's seal after Isaac had completed working on it. Notice how the top looks like wings? That's partly why I chose to have that knot be the one for Sucari. Anyways, since Sucari had the Blood-fluxion and Elemental-fluxion as part of his flight vest, he needed the order of the knot on his seal to be "2", even though the 6_1 knot (see Figure 2.4) would have worked better visually, with both fluxion cores being held in the two loops along the centerline. However, as Isaac explained in *First Name Basis*, if the first number is too large, the power cannot be accessed; but if the number is too low, the user would be taken over by the power of the fluxion (*see also: Section 4 – "Fluxions"*).

Figure 2.4: 6-1 Knot

THE THIRD DEGREE

Albert: Albert Einstein

I am aware that the real Albert Einstein perhaps did not say *"Wunderbar"* nearly as much as my character did, but when you have someone so excited about science, what better way to express it? Much like many of the other scientists referenced throughout the trilogy, Einstein is considered to be one of the most influential of the modern era. Much of his work was in theoretical physics, which has many fantastical ideas that were easy to pull into a fantasy world. Along with the chemical element #99, Einsteinium, bearing his name, one of his ideas was the Einstein-Rosen Bridge, which is more commonly known as a wormhole. This connection and reference were why Albert was so adept at using the Q-Portal keys.

Of course, at the root of these wormholes is Einstein's contribution to the knowledge of Space-time. Knowing that space and time are connected is a key point to *The Third Degree*, which uses the Q-Portals not only as transitions through space (which is what they had been used for in the previous two novels), but also though time. The "Time Thread" referenced in the novels, and used to make Grigori immortal, is linked to Einstein's Theory of Relativity and the idea that, as one moves faster toward the speed of light, the individual remains younger.

Einstein was one of the scientists who helped start the Manhattan Project, which is why I made him the lead researcher of the fluxions in *Second to None*. As was the case with most involved with the Manhattan Project, they eventually felt guilty for what they had created, much like Albert felt guilty for his work on the fluxions, since it essentially eradicated all Naturals from the planet. This guilt is what drove him to eventually discover the Caidoz statues. One statue in particular, the crab, was used to create the laser known as "C.L.A.W." This reference, and the fact that Albert uses it as a weapon, is due to Einstein's theoretical foundations for the device (*see also: Section 4 – "C.L.A.W."*).

Arthur: Arthur Pendragon

While King Arthur is mainly known through his legends, he did lead the British in the early 6th century. The legends he is mostly known for involve the search for the Holy Grail and the more modern legend of the Sword in the Stone, both of which are represented in the novel. Arthur is also linked to the wizard Merlin, who was represented by the character of Ronald. Furthermore, Arthur's dragon (named "Pen") is a reference to Arthur's last name of Pendragon, a fact which I used to incorporate him into the Order of the Dragon. Of course, with a dragon named Pen, I couldn't resist making it mightier than any sword. His inclusion in the Brotherhood of the Scarlet Lion was due to his heritage as an English King.

Prince Clive: Clive Staples Lewis (aka C.S. Lewis)

Some of the books from my earliest childhood that I remember were written by C.S. Lewis. I refer, of course, to the *Chronicles of Narnia*. While he wrote many other books on or about Christianity, including *The Screwtape Letters*, I made it a point to reference all seven of the *Chronicles of Narnia* in the character of Prince Clive:

- ➢ *The Lion, the Witch, and the Wardrobe*: Aside from founding the Brotherhood of the Scarlet Lion, I hinted at his next quest: defeating an Ice Queen to the north.
- ➢ *Prince Caspian*: This one's easy. He's a Prince.
- ➢ *Voyage of the Dawn Treader*: While Clive didn't have much direct contact with the *Twilight Runner*, the reference was still there.

- *The Silver Chair*: The four thrones for each royal member not only mimic the four thrones meant for the "sons of Adam" and "daughters of Eve", but also reference this fourth book in the series.
- *A Horse and His Boy*: Members of the Brotherhood of the Scarlet Lion were initially meant to have some sort of riding experience, regardless of the animal. As such, Prince Clive was almost raised by his horse.
- *The Magician's Nephew*: Ronald, the magician, was King Solepoch's brother, which would make Clive the Magician's Nephew. Also, the rings which give Ronald his power are the same color and on the same hands as the rings presented in the C.S. Lewis tale.
- *The Last Battle*: Briefly mentioned, but the Great Fire of Old Non was not Clive's Last Battle.

John / Ronald / Reuel: John Ronald Reuel Tolkein (aka J.R.R. Tolkien)

I couldn't well include a reference to C.S. Lewis without including a reference to J.R.R. Tolkien. This author of *The Hobbit* and *The Lord of the Rings* was great to use, especially in the part of the trilogy that covered time travel. I had three names to work with here! At any rate, the gold uroboros ring that Ophiuchus wears is a reference to the "one ring" from the *Lord of the Rings* trilogy, but in a sense Tolkien's character in my novel was the "Lord of the Rings", since he had the green and yellow rings given to him by Ophiuchus, thereby making him the eponymous Lord of them, even if the reference there is to the Magician's Nephew of the *Chronicles of Narnia* series.

While I first modeled Reuel after Gandalf the Grey (Reuel in the Scorpio Desert), the time traveling aspect also made it useful to include a reference to Merlin, King Arthur's trusted wizard (the model for Ronald). While the overall characterization was closer to Gandalf than Merlin, I believe the reference I tried to infuse made its point.

King Solepochs / Princess Prohere: Sophocles / Antigone

One of the dramatic authors of Ancient Greece, Sophocles is best known for his trilogy based around the character of Oedipus the King. For those unfamiliar with the story, Oedipus essentially killed his father and married his mother. After the latter action, and once he realized what he had done, he ripped his eyes out, which is why King Solepochs wears a masked crown.

The daughter of Oedipus was Antigone, and she helped him survive after he maimed himself. Her story is the conclusion of the Oedipus trilogy. All three stories are Greek tragedies, which means that the heroes never live. Antigone is represented in *The Third Degree* by Princess Prohere, with "pro" being the opposite of "anti" and "here" being the antithesis of "gone".

Ophiuchus (aka Serpent-bearer): N/A

Originally, I wanted Ophiuchus to have an anagrammed name, but once I started writing, I decided it would be easier to leave it as it is. After all, the other Zodiac signs weren't anagrammed, so why should he be? This constellation is considered to be the 13th Zodiac sign, only because it exists in the same plane that the other 12 signs inhabit. This made for a great plot twist at the end of *The Third Degree* when the twelve Caidoz statues were finally destroyed. He is *in* the Zodiac, but not *of* the Zodiac. This also comes into play in my next trilogy: *The Constellation Tournament*.

As was explained in the novel, Ophiuchus was the Third Degree. This meant that he would become the Degree that would balance out the rest of the statues so that the fluxions would still work. As such, when Benjamin and Albert first met Ophiuchus, before any statues were destroyed, he was grey. However, when the lion statue was destroyed, he became white fluxionite (the Positive Degree) because it was now the Degree that was missing. And yet, since the next three statues destroyed were of the Negative Degree, Ophiuchus was forced deeper and deeper into the Negative Degree just to balance everything out. By the time the last statue was destroyed, he returned to the neutral grey of the Third Degree.

Of course, with a character made out of fluxionite, one of the aspects of this trait was not only that he could control everything (much like Gottfried tried to do in *First Name Basis* with The Omnipotence), but that he could freely travel through space and time. The Q-Portals were based in the fluxionite keys of the two different Degrees, so Ophiuchus only had to stick his finger into a wall to open up a Q-Portal anywhere. Similarly, if he was struck by lightning, he could travel through time (as shown when he disappeared with the *Twilight Runner*). This system was never explained in the novels, but is the reason why he showed up on the moon when Isaac was destroying the statues. It also links back to the finger keys obtained from Jason's skeleton in *First Name Basis*. Finally, the sculptor by the name of Auguste who created Ophiuchus and the rest of the Caidoz statues is a reference to Auguste Rodin, the artist responsible for the sculpture known as *The Thinker*.

Section 3

Settings

Not all of the people who I reference in *The Fluxion Trilogy* are in the form of characters. Sometimes the ideas conveyed by these individuals are best captured by a location. However, this doesn't mean that every setting is based on a person. Many of the locations are also based on real world areas and features. This section follows a similar format to the previous one in that the name used in the novels is in bold, followed by the real-world reference.

FIRST NAME BASIS

New Town: Isaac Newton

What better way to start a trilogy than in a place called New Town? While the name is a direct pull from Isaac Newton's name, the feel of this port city is extracted from "Rulers of the Waves Chronicles", the forum role playing story which was the spark that ignited this whole endeavor in the first place. Of course, in that story, the city was an island called Trade Town, but the functions it served were the same. The pier functioned as a good starting place, and the bar was a good place to meet characters. Furthermore, considering the returns to New Town at the end of all three parts of *The Fluxion Trilogy*, there is an implication that new adventures will start out from this port after the last words are read on the page.

Taurus Tavern: Toroid / Constellation

If you haven't been able to figure it out yet, I tend to enjoy a good amount of wordplay, and the Taurus Tavern is no exception. The shape of the Tavern described in the books is that of a torus (see Figure 3.1), which is pronounced in the same fashion of the constellation of the bull: Taurus. Of course, this

Figure 3.1: Toroid/Torus

worked out to my advantage when I pulled in the Zodiac signs into the plot of *The Third Degree*.

The grandfather clock, which is set as the centerpiece of the Tavern, is decorated with the designs of some of the lines from the children's nursery rhyme "Hey Diddle Diddle", in which a cow jumps over the moon (*see also: Section 4 – "Caidoz statues"*). Furthermore, the cows on the moon did jump there, but it was a "Quantum jump" from the incident in the *Twilight Runner* which caused Isaac to travel to the future and Joan to fall into the volcano. With cows now on the moon, dairies could be used to make cheese, which was part of Priest Werner's Operation Alsos. This also helped link to the reference of the erroneous statement that the moon is made of cheese, further perpetuated by the "Wallace & Gromit" short *A Grand Day Out*. At any rate, I mainly needed the clock for Isaac's directed eavesdropping, but when the rhyme fit with the theme so well (especially considering the cows on the moon), I couldn't resist. Nevertheless, this homophonic link between what I had written in *First Name Basis* to the ideas presented in *The Third Degree* was a great way to tie things together through the trilogy.

Peak of Eternal Light: N/A

The beauty of some of the references in these novels is that sometimes I don't even have to make up the names. The name that already exists is too awesome to change. This is just such a location. There is a spot on the moon that, due to its rotation and tilt, is always bathed in sunlight. This area, located near the north pole of the moon, is known as the Peak of Eternal Light, for obvious reasons. And yet, even though this point is always in sunlight, it is important to understand how the light of the sun hits the moon. Because the moon always shows the earth the same face, the back side of the moon is called the "Dark Side". It is not dark because there is no light, but rather that we cannot see it. For instance, when the moon is in its "new" phase, the entire dark side of the moon is covered in light! A lunar day lasts as long as a lunar cycle, about 28 days. This means a day (or night) on the moon is almost an entire month! What's also nice is that, since the moon is less massive than the earth, it has less gravity, which means that everything on the moon feels "light".

Alden: Neil Alden Armstrong

Even though there is a crater on the moon named after Neil Armstrong, I decided that I would name the town of the first people we meet on the moon after him. Also fitting is that the town of Alden sits within Herbert crater, a reference to the actual crater "H.G. Wells" on the dark side of the moon. I say that it is fitting because H.G. Wells wrote a story entitled *The First Men in the Moon*. At any rate, Neil Armstrong was the mission commander on Apollo 11, a spaceflight which culminated in the first human lunar landing in July 1969. He is credited for christening this momentous occasion with the words, "One small step for man, one giant leap for mankind."

Edmond shrine: Edmond Halley

Even though it was eventually revealed that Isaac was in fact Edmond, this was something I did not necessarily plan on from the beginning. Still, the Edmond in reference here is Edmond Halley, for whom Halley's Comet is named. This shrine was built on the spot where Edmond's comet collided with the back of the moon. When the comet created a new crater in Herbert Crater, it also melted in the process. This is why Edmond shrine is surrounded by a lake: comets are made out of dust and ice. Furthermore, as is also the case with Daniel Volcano, this crater is a complex crater due to the fact that it has a hill in the middle of the impact zone.

Of course, back on earth, the incident of Edmond's comet crashing into the back of the moon created enough debris that the light of the sun was blocked out for an entire year. This was known as "The Dark Year", which is a reference to the Great Plague of London, which was a lesser outbreak of the massive Black Death that occurred in the mid-14th century. During the two-year London outbreak of Bubonic Plague, Isaac Newton was not able to go to school, but instead stayed home and made many breakthroughs in his research of calculus and optics. As such, the rediscovery of fluxions happened during the Dark Year in the novels.

Topal: Plato

This capitol of the 5th Kingdom is loosely based on the best known work of the Greek philosopher, Plato. In *The Republic,* Plato details out how his idea of a perfect political state would work. Essentially, everyone who lives in the Republic has a role which fits their skills and requires a specific set of skills. As such, everyone works in the Republic and there is no need for outsiders or those who do no work. I took this concept to mean that once all the roles were filled, they would shut the doors and not let anyone else in, ergo: xenophobic. What does this fear of outsiders sound like? That's right: Xenon, the 5th noble gas. While *The Republic* is very deep and complex, I only took a few light concepts from it when developing the city of Topal.

Ruatonim's Maze: Daedalus' Labyrinth

Daedalus, the father of Icarus, was quite the inventor. Not only did he invent some wings to help him and Icarus escape prison, but he also designed the Labyrinth of Crete, which housed the Minotaur, of which "Ruatonim" is merely "Minotaur" spelled backwards. A labyrinth can also be seen as a maze, which is why this location is known as Ruatonim's Maze. Fortunately, Ruatonim only existed for a short amount of time before being killed. A memorial statue was set up in the Maze to protect the Hellfire orb.

Pythagorean Triangle: Bermuda Triangle

One of the less hidden references in the trilogy, the Pythagorean Triangle is first a reference to the geometric figure, but secondly a reference to the Bermuda Triangle. The latter triangle is well known for many mysterious events and disappearances, based on numerous theories. However, the mathematical reference for this location goes a little deeper than just the title. A Pythagorean triangle is a right triangle with three sides labeled a, b, and c (*see also: Section 6 – "The Pythagorean Triangle"*). The right angle is opposite the longest side ("c"), which is also known as the hypotenuse. A right angle can be represented by a square, which is exactly what Tanilats Dock does in the novel. If you could not tell by now, the three letters which denote the sides of the Pythagorean triangle are represented by the three snakes: Asp, Boa, and Cobra. Furthermore, the Guardian of the Fangs whose remains were found in the cave on Cobra Peak further exemplified the unique characteristics of the Cobra, not only with the hooded cloak, but the "V" shaped fluxion on the back of the hood.

The character of Pythagoras herself, while never seen, but often mentioned, is a reference to the mythological monster known as Medusa. This snake-haired woman, also known as a Gorgon, usually had venomous snakes for hair, of which pythons do not qualify. However, the combination of Python and Gorgon was simple enough to continue onward to Pythagoras. It has been said that the gaze of Medusa would turn someone into stone, which is why this part of the legend behind the Pythagorean Triangle and Pythagoras tree are included as such. The Pythagoras tree is a fractal that is made by squares which have the same sides as a Pythagorean triangle (see Figure 3.2). However, the citrus fruit which hung from this tree was meant as a deterrent for scurvy, which often plagued sailors who were on the sea for so long without vitamin C.

Figure 3.2: Pythagoras tree

Tanilats Dock: Atlantis

Yet another reference to the works of Plato, Atlantis was briefly mentioned in some writings by this philosopher, but is better known for its mysterious disappearance. Even though it would be more likely that Atlantis resides in the Mediterranean, some have placed it in the Bermuda Triangle, which is essentially what I have done by putting it inside the Pythagorean Triangle. And even though Tanilats Dock is not underwater, the fact that it is almost completely vacant is a reference to this missing city.

Sievuvus: Mount Vesuvius / Mount Ararat / The Island of Dr. Moreau

The volcano of Mount Vesuvius was the cause of the great tragedy of Italian city of Pompeii. This eruption happened in 79 AD and resulted in the destruction and burial of the entire city of Pompeii. The energy of this eruption was almost 100,000 times more powerful than the nuclear bombings in World War II. While I modeled this volcano after the one visited in *20,000 Leagues Under the Sea*, it also holds the reference of Mount Ararat, the mountain where Noah's Ark eventually settled after the flood. Finally, due to Dr. Paul's animal research taking place on this island volcano in *First Name Basis*, Sievuvus also references *The Island of Dr. Moreau*.

Pandora Prison (aka "The Box"): Pandora's Box

The story of Pandora Prison is much the same as that of Pandora's Box, the Grecian artifact that held all of the world's evils. Much like a prison must contain the evils of the world, separating them from decent society, Pandora Prison held all the worst criminals in the world. However, in the myth of Pandora's Box, Pandora's curiosity got the better of her after she was told not to open the Box under any circumstance. In the same way, Erwin's curiosity caused him to venture into the depths of this prison. And yet, the emptying of Pandora Prison of all its evils was performed by Testament five years before the start of *First Name Basis* (see also: Section 7 – *"Year 1274"*).

Yet, with all this evil now in the world, the one thing that remained in Pandora's Box was "hope". This take on hope was adapted to Pandora Prison by being the "Hope Wing", the area which held the absolute worst criminals in the world in the hope that they would never escape. However, the inscription above the door of the Hope Wing is a loose usage of the last line of the inscription above the gate of Hell from Dante's *Inferno*.

The Molten Forests: Petrified Forests

Petrified Forests are generally formed due to underground fossilization, when minerals replace the cellular structure of buried trees. However, the idea of plants pulling up liquids from their roots, regardless of the liquid content, is something that anyone with a white rose and some food coloring would know. The idea for these forests initially came from the process that metal goes through when it cools. In metallurgy, as molten metal cools (or freezes, even though it's at room temperature), the structures produced by the metal are called "dendrites", which look just like trees. It's no wonder that the Greek word "dendrite" is translated literally to "tree". In fact, dendrites can be seen when water freezes as well (see Figure 3.3).

With the idea of dendrites in hand, I started with the Dendritic Forest, which is a forest filled with metal trees. In order to explain this metal forest, I made the trees heartier than normal, hence their presence in the "Timberland" region of the 3rd Kingdom. With hearty trees, they were able to pull up any liquid beneath them, even if it was molten metal. When the metal was integrated with the trees' structure, the tree died, but

Figure 3.3: Ice Dendrite

the metal cooled and remained. A similar process occurred in the Granite Grove to the northwest with molten rock, and the Crystal Woods to the northeast with molten sand. This type of forest was seen again in *The Third Degree* around the Scorpio Oasis, the trees having absorbed the poison of the scorpion Caidoz statue.

The Eagle's Nest (aka Ralph Island): Germany / Ralph Gosper
As was mentioned earlier in the section about Gottfried, the Eagle's Nest is a reference to Germany's coat of arms, which depicts a black eagle. Not only is the 3rd Kingdom where the Eagle's Nest resides a reference to Germany, but the forested region, Timberland, where it is located is a reference to the Black Forest of Germany. Furthermore, when the Eagle's Nest rose from the lake, and Testament Tower was built, the entire island was set ablaze, resulting in yet another reference to the color black.

The original name of the island, before it was lifted into the sky by four large chains, was Ralph Island, which is a reference to Ralph William Gosper. Gosper is a mathematician whose name is lent to the fractal known as the Gosper Curve, and subsequently the Gosper Island. The four chains holding up the Eagle's Nest work off of the induced magnetism from the volcanic pools of metal under the surface of the Molten Forests, much like the fluctuating magnetic forces do in an induction furnace.

Ferdinand Freeway: August Ferdinand Möbius
Much like the Klein bottle is a two-dimensional manifold with the inside being the same surface as the outside, the Möbius strip is a surface with only one side. As such, if someone were to travel along the Möbius strip (or in the case of the novel, the Ferdinand Freeway), they would eventually arrive back where they started. Even though it happens a little later, this is a hint at Isaac eventually returning to New Town in the Epilogue.

Maurits Manor: Maurits Cornelis Escher (aka M.C. Escher)
The butler of Maurits Manor, Cornelis (also named after Escher) was added because Escher had two names and I could use both. This artist was best known for his optical illusions and repeated tiling (tessellation) artwork. As such, the Manor is filled with many fractals and optical illusion references:
- ➢ *Wactaw Carpet*: Wactaw Franciszek Sierpinski, creator of the Sierpinski triangle and Sierpinski carpet.
- ➢ *Karl Sponge*: Karl Menger, creator of the Menger sponge.
- ➢ *Gaston Tea Set*: Gaston Julia and Pierre Fatou, creators of the Julia Set, which is related to . . .
- ➢ *Benoit Chess Set*: Benoit Mandlebrot, creator of the Mandelbrot Set.
- ➢ *Adrien Rabbit*: Adrien Douady, creator of the Douady Rabbit.

> *Helge*: Helge von Koch, creator of the Koch snowflake. This brief mention of a weatherman named Helge always predicting snow is the reference here.
> *Roger Staircase*: Roger Penrose, creator of the Penrose Triangle and Penrose Stairs. While not actually a fractal, this optical illusion fits right in with the works of M.C. Escher.

Morgana: Fata Morgana

If you haven't figured it out yet, most of Chapter 7 ("Light") has references to optical illusions and fractals. Fata Morgana is just such a reference. Even though we see the character of Morgana in *Second to None* (as Tranus Sunroc's wife and Luvnac's apprentice), Fata Morgana is in fact a term for a very complex mirage that is often seen at sea. Caused by refraction of light in the atmosphere beyond the curvature of the earth, images often seen in a Fata Morgana are those of floating objects in the sky near the horizon. As such, the legend of the "Flying Dutchman" might have been perpetuated by images of distant ships appearing in the sky due to this mirage.

Thurston Ring: William Thurston/Stonehenge

One of the beautiful little coincidences in these novels came when I was ready to make the cover for *First Name Basis*. In the stock imagery on the online cover creator I was using was this picture of Stonehenge in silhouette, the moon hovering above it and light emanating from the confines of the stone circle. Considering the plot of *First Name Basis*, I had no other choice: I had to use this image for the cover of my book. As such, the covers for the following novels in the trilogy were actually created before they were even written, so that I could incorporate the cover images into the plots.

At any rate, the Thurston Ring not only references Stonehenge, but also William Thurston, a modern mathematician who won the Fields Medal for his study of 3-manifolds. In simple terms, this means that he was involved with knotting theory, and is the reason why the Thurston Ring had a knotted uroboros seal underneath its stone structures. Furthermore, the way the uroboros seal was activated by James and Garland is a reference to *Fullmetal Alchemist*.

SECOND TO NONE

Library of Delaxanair: Library of Alexandria

Considered to be one of the 7 Wonders of the Ancient World, this Egyptian Library was one of the largest and most extensive libraries. Unfortunately, it was eventually destroyed and lost to the ages. In the novel, the Library of Delaxanair was used as the main hub of fluxion research, but once Amedeo's War was concluded, much of the contents of the library were split up and distributed to the four corners of the world. By the time Arthur and Reuel arrived in the Scorpio Desert to the south of the Library, the building had been in a state of disrepair for a few centuries, having been essentially abandoned for 277 years at that point (*see also: Section 7 – "Year 545"*).

Imaginary World (aka i-World): Sigmund Freud

A slight nod to Apple's naming convention (with everything they make starting with " i "), the i-World is actually a reference to the mathematical notation of imaginary numbers. The guardian to the Imaginary World was none other than Sigmund, a reference to Sigmund Freud, the German psychologist. Regardless of your opinions on his theories involving dreams (or your mother), one accepted piece of his work is that of the three parts of the psyche. The journey of The Triumvirate through the Imaginary World was a confrontation of each character by the three parts of their psyche: the id, the ego, and the super ego. Of course, for hiding the references, I chose to go with the literal, German translations of "das Es", "das Ich", and "das Über-Ich", which stand for "the it", "the I", and the "Super-I":

- *it*: Usually associated with children and their many, and sometimes contrary, impulses (especially pleasure). This part of the i-World asks everyone about their relationships. The significance of it being a 6 year old is partly to link to PHN-6, as well as being a naturally inquisitive age for children.
- *I*: More cautious than the it, I is concerned with reducing risk, which is why The Triumvirate is asked about their decisions to set out on their quests by this part of the i-World.
- *Super-I*: Seen as an idealized version of ourselves, the Super-I is used in the novel as a test of fighting skill and fluxion control (ergo: Super) as well as the final test of The Triumvirate before moving on to the PHN.

One might also wonder why the text in the i-World is sideways. Not only did I want to convey that all three journeys were happening at the same time, with the same responses from the Imaginary World, but there's a mathematical reason as well. In order to enter into the Imaginary World, The Triumvirate traveled underneath the Angular Mangroves to reach an arch with a negative sign (the "lost" Number Disk of "–" (pull)). This represented a negative number underneath a square root, since most of the roots of the Angular Mangroves were at 90 degrees, the angle most commonly associated with squares. In mathematics, you cannot take a square root of a negative number. Or rather, you can, but the result will be "imaginary". Numbers can fall into two categories: Real and Imaginary. In order to plot numbers that have both real and imaginary parts to them, a grid must be formed. The x-axis is the real-axis, whereas the y-axis is the imaginary-axis. Therefore, in order to get to the Imaginary World, one must be orthogonal (or perpendicular to) the Real World. All orthogonal orientations are at 90 degrees, which is why the book needed to be flipped 90 degrees in order to read the Imaginary World sections.

Appendix — Section 3: Settings

Meadow Peak: The Matterhorn

Translating to English can hide a few references, and Meadow Peak is one of them. In its native language, Meadow Peak is known as The Matterhorn. This famous mountain in the Alps (on the border of Switzerland and Italy) is not nearly as easy to climb as I have depicted in my novel, but it is in a pyramid formation, which led to its establishment as a "four corners" of sorts between four different Kingdoms. Of course, wanting to hide the reference to the well-known Alps, I anagrammed the name so that Meadow Peak was in the Slap Mountains. Another location included in the Alps is that of Monte Carlo, of which Mount Charles is the equivalent reference in the novels.

Island of Stability: Copernicium

When I was researching the different elements on the periodic table, I naturally gravitated toward the end of the list. As of the writing of *Second to None*, the highest named element was that of 112: Copernicium (It's now 114 with Flerovium). Named after Niccolaus Copernicus (the monk in the center of the island is named Niccolaus for this very reason), this element lies in a very interesting "island of stability". This "island" in nuclear physics deals with very heavy elements. As is the case with many laboratory made elements, the heavier the atom, the quicker it decomposes into more stable elements through radioactive decay. The time that it takes to decompose is called the half-life and is usually very short. However, for elements like Copernicium, the half-life is much longer (almost 9 minutes), partly because the electrons line up in "shells" needed for stabilitiy. In fact, Copernicium almost acts like a noble gas!

As for Copernicus himself, he was the first scientist to postulate that the Sun is the center of our solar system, and not the earth. In honor of this, the "orbits" of the electrons (the pillars of fire leading to the temple in the middle of the island) represent this idea, even if it is done so very loosely. Not only does the temple in the middle of the island represent the nucleus of Copernicium, but it also represents the sun.

Of course, when I started introducing the Zodiac signs into the story, I had to put the Libra shrine (for the scales) inside the Island of Stability. Everything there focused on balance, just like the 10 Caliber Sword of Selcomad, and the "lost" Number Disk of "0" (representing neutrons). Of course, Albert's explanation of the centroid is the key concept on which all balance hinges. The Matterhorn (or Meadow Peak) is in the Swiss Alps, and we all know that Switzerland is very neutral. One piece of information that didn't make it into the novels was that the "War of Swords" between the four kingdoms which share the Island of Stability was the reason why the Sword of Selcomad was put there in the first place.

Tower of Lebab / Trinity Site: Tower of Babel / Leaning Tower of Pisa

While the Tower of Lebab is a direct reference to the Tower of Babel, the design description is somewhat closer to that of the Leaning Tower of Pisa, replete with bell at the top. The multitude of stone soldiers inside the Tower is a reference to the Terracotta Army of Qin Shi Huang, the first Emperor of China.

This Tower was built, not to reach heaven to talk to God, as the original Babel tower was, but rather to reach the moon so that one of the Caidoz statues could be destroyed. Unfortunately, the Tower of Lebab ceased construction for mysterious reasons, but not until some Archimedes Elevators (based off of the Archimedes' screw) were installed to aid in upward construction. Its destruction came before the great battle of Amedeo's War, and is now considered "The Trinity Site".

The Trinity Site is a direct reference to the location of the first atomic bomb test in New Mexico. This test was the culmination of the work done by the Manhattan Project. The similar amount of destruction caused by Benjamin's ball lightning attack is supposed to evoke the same emotion from the researchers who watched the battle from afar as the scientists who witnessed the detonation of the world's first nuclear device..

Daniel Volcano: Daniel Barringer

Even though the moon is covered with craters, occasionally earth's atmosphere doesn't destroy incoming projectiles, and a meteor eventually makes its way through and impacts the earth's surface. One of the largest and best examples of this is Barringer Crater, located in Arizona. This crater is named after the first person to suggest that the crater was a product of a meteor: Daniel Barringer.

Now, the crater I envisioned is much larger than Barringer Crater. I see it as a more complex crater, similar to that of the crater created with Edmond's comet, one which creates a hill in the middle. I also envisioned this crater being formed in an area that is closer to geothermal heat (like Yellowstone), so that, when the meteor hit, it essentially "popped the zit" on the earth's surface, creating the volcano. This meteor was then condensed inside the volcano and was eventually spat out as the Gravity Core, which Ophiuchus put in the Island of Stability.

THE THIRD DEGREE

Pablo Quarry: Pablo Picasso

Picasso is best known for his use of the cubist style in his art. As such, a quarry that produces cubes of stone for use on building projects would be a great connection to this artist. This quarry is also a reference to the White Cliffs of Dover, which are located about 70 miles southeast of London (and not fifteen miles, like it is in the novel).

Old Non: London

An anagram of London, this city is the capitol of the 4th Kingdom, much like London is the capitol of England. There are a few similarities between the two capitols, including a bridge over a river in the middle of town (which would be London Bridge and the River Thames, respectively), as well as a Great Fire which destroyed most of the city. The Great Fire of London took place in 1666 and consumed most of the city near the River Thames and London Bridge.

The rhyme after the Great Fire of Old Non is meant to reference "London Bridge is Falling Down", which has been considered as a lyric referencing the state of London Bridge after the Great Fire of 1666, although not due to a battle with a large lion statue which led to its destruction by a gunpowder explosion.

The *Twilight Runner*: The *Dawn Treader*

Another reference to one of the *Chronicles of Narnia* written by C.S. Lewis, the *Twilight Runner* is also a reference to Noah's Ark, but only after it is transported to Sievuvus Volcano. The ship is large and is shaped much like the arc of a circle would be. As such, in the novels it is referred to as Noah's Arc.

Section 4

Items

In creating a fantasy world, filled with real science, one of the best ways to convey some of the more difficult ideas is through items. These items can be weapons (like swords) or they can be an orb or disk which can grant superpowers to normal humans.

FIRST NAME BASIS

Fluxions: Calculus

When I was in the initial planning stages for *First Name Basis*, I was having trouble coming up with a name for the "superpowers" that would be utilized by the characters. I wanted something similar to the Devil Fruit powers from *One Piece*, but with their own weaknesses and implementation. As I drew closer to realizing the main conflict between Isaac Newton and Gottfried Leibniz was at the core of my story, I finally arrived at the name: fluxions. This is a fitting name, considering what these powers do. A fluxion changes the physical properties of whatever object it comes in contact with, thereby making it a changed object: an object in flux.

Because the fluxions in *First Name Basis* represented the simultaneous discovery of calculus by both Newton and Leibniz, I needed two different ways to use them. As was explained in the novels, fluxions are made with three principles:

> *Willpower:* A certain amount of strength is needed to use a fluxion. A weak person cannot use a fluxion because the core would likely take them over. On the other extreme, someone who wants the fluxion to work and has too much willpower will short circuit the seal and it won't work. This is why people could get worn out from using their fluxion

too much, or would be in danger of being taken over by a fluxion if they combine too many of them together.

➤ *Core*: This is the energy source of the fluxion. If the core is too powerful, it will take over someone with not enough willpower. However, if the seal is too tight, the power of the core cannot be accessed. Fluxion cores fall into three further categories:
  o *Blood*: By using the blood of an animal, a fluxion user can obtain the special skills or features of the animal. Most of the time, the Blood-fluxion will change a person's body, but if the "blood" used is that of an insect, the exoskeleton attribute is acquired, but only through a piece of armor and extensive seal-work. A special type of Blood-fluxion uses human blood cores and a special seal and is known as a Soul-fusion fluxion. This fluxion is taboo.
  o *Elemental*: These cores generally contain some sort of element (e.g. fire, lightning, sand, wind, etc.) which can be used and controlled by the fluxion user. The three most coveted Elemental-fluxions are those held by The Triumvirate.
  o *Number*: A Number Disk is needed to use one of these specialized fluxions. The numbers on the discs are directly related to the atomic number of the periodic element being referenced. There are three "lost" Number Disks which correlate to the particles which make up atoms (*see also: Section 4 – "Philosopher's Stone"*).

➤ *Seal*: At the base of the fluxion seal is an uroboros snake (see Figure 4.1), which is a snake eating its own tail. This symbol is common in alchemy (especially in *Fullmetal Alchemist*), and is one of the reasons I chose it as part of the fluxion, due to Isaac Newton's interest in alchemy. The idea behind using the uroboros snake is that, as the core is used through the seal, the seal gets tighter (the snake eats more of its tail), thus eventually restricting the fluxion's use based on how powerful the core is. If the seal is not powerful enough, the user will be taken over by the core. Seals can be engraved in metal, sewn in fabric, tattooed on skin, or branded on flesh, as well as many other methods. As long as the seal surrounds the core, the fluxion will work. However, if the seal is too powerful, the user won't have enough willpower to access the effects of the core. There are two sealing methods:

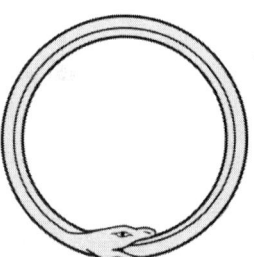

Figure 4.1: Uroboros

  o *Newton*: Isaac's method uses a single snake with a single outlet for the core's power. In order to adequately seal the core, a very long snake is used, but in a knotted formation to decrease

its area. This method isn't directly related to Newton's form of calculus, but is merely a different way to seal the fluxions when compared to the alternative.
- *Leibniz*: Gottfried's method uses multiple snakes linked together to form a seal around the core. The more snakes used means the power of the core can be accessed in more points. This sealing method references Leibniz' version of calculus, which uses the area of a multitude of small rectangles to estimate the area underneath a curve.

Q-Portals: Quantum jumping

As mentioned in the section about Jason Stalfos, the Q-Portal keys were literal skeleton keys which could transport people to many different areas. The "Q" in "Q-Portals" stands for "Quantum", which is why Priest Werner knew about them. Q-Portals work on the idea that an electron cannot be pinned to an exact location, but is instead in a "ring of probability" (further explained later). Even though Q-Portals are explained in more detail in *Second to None*, by using a Q-Portal in *First Name Basis*, the user will not know where they will end up, but is relying mainly on luck to get to where they need to go. That being said, each of the fingers used to activate Q-Portals in *First Name Basis* has a significance and a reference to the next part of the story. Here's what they meant:

➢ Thumb
  - *Destination*: Jules Crater [Moon]
  - *Reference*: The Hitchhiker's Guide to the Galaxy
  - *Used*: First
➢ Index finger
  - *Destination*: Pandora Prison
  - *Reference*: Creation of Adam (giving life to lifeless objects)
  - *Used*: Fourth
➢ Middle finger
  - *Destination*: Posea Pasture
  - *Reference*: Dr. Moreau playing God (giving Him the finger)
  - *Used*: Third
➢ Ring finger
  - *Destination*: Holy Cliffs of Topal
  - *Reference*: a ringed wall around the city
  - *Used*: Second
➢ Pinky
  - *Destination*: New Town
  - *Reference*: the pinky swear made in the first chapter
  - *Used*: Fifth

Kuroni: Gravity

One of the many Japanese names in the trilogy, Kuroni is actually a portmanteau of two words: Kuro and Oni. In Japanese, "Kuro" is "black" and "Oni" means "demon". Therefore, "Kuro Oni" would translate as "Black Demon", which is an apt description of the power of gravity, especially when considering black holes. The portmanteau merely fused the two "o"s together to create "Kuroni". Furthermore, the kanji for these two words (see Figure 4.2) have the same window-like box on the top of the symbols, so the combination of the two, made by flipping over the "Oni" kanji, would look like Figure 4.3.

As was mentioned before, Kuroni is the embodiment of the idea of gravity. While this is achieved with the addition of the Gravity Core and swirling vortex of snakes that makes up the uroboros seal on the sword (much like a black hole), there are other attributes which hint at the power of gravity. First is the fact that Kuroni is a katana, which is generally a curved sword. Since gravity is a pulling force on everything in the universe, if an item has a certain amount of inertia already, its path will be curved. In fact, gravity is so powerful it can curve light, space, and even time (theoretically). Secondly, since gravity gives objects their weight, Kuroni is a heavy sword at times, dealing more force than a normal sword would. Third, is an examination of Newton's second law: Force equals mass times acceleration ($F=ma$, which also, conveniently enough, is the initials commonly associated with **Fu**llmetal **A**lchemist (*FMA*)). Gravity is an acceleration, so even though Kuroni is a heavy sword, it is a fast sword. This acceleration is also seen as a "pull" (the same pull that creates the aforementioned curves), so Kuroni has the ability to pull foes toward it.

Figure 4.2: Kuro Oni

The Gravity Core is another aspect of this sword, and is what gives it the power over gravity. This core was not forged by the crashing of Edmond's comet into the back of the moon, but instead from a similar collision on earth which created Daniel Volcano. This core is the condensed remains of the large meteor. Something so small and so dense acts in much the same way that a black hole would. After forming the volcano and crater, Ophiuchus saw how much power this core had, so he took the Gravity Core and hid it away in the Island of Stability. It was there, with the Cardinal Caidoz statue of the scales, that Aki Nishi found the Gravity Core and brought it back to his home in the Granite Grove, just outside Daniel Volcano. This is where Gulogulo found the Gravity Core and fused it with Kuroni.

Even though Kuroni is made of pure negative (or black) Fluxionite, it did not obtain its association with apples until after Amedeo's War. Gulogulo, who we have discussed before, was definitely a prime candidate to wield Kuroni but, after the war, he saw that it was a power too great to let

Figure 4.3: Kuroni

anyone handle and he decided to let it lie on a quiet hill outside a fishing village. A millennium later, an apple tree had grown up and around the sword so that, when Isaac finally came along and pulled the katana from the trunk of the tree, its scabbard had been fully ingrained as part of the Square G shrine. Isaac then took one of the tree's branches and had a scabbard made which bore the scene of an apple falling from its branches, thus linking to the legend that Isaac Newton discovered gravity from a falling apple.

Hikari Shichidai: Prism

There's just something about objects with Japanese names which I really enjoy. This sword is no exception. Meant as the counterpart to Kuroni (in the "equal and opposite" sense), Hikari Shichidai does loosely translate to "The Seventh Light" (with "Hikari" being "Light" and "Shichidai" meaning "The Seventh"), which is a reference not only to the seven sword pieces which were brought together to create the sword, but also that light is seen as having seven different colors in its spectrum (*see also: Section 4 – "Six Noble Swords"*)

This sword takes advantage of one of the two Fluents: the Fluent of Light. This is a power that was meant to counteract the Fluent of Darkness, otherwise known as "The Omnipotence". Since the Fluent of Darkness was all powers combined, the Fluent of Light is meant to separate powers. As such, it has the ability to separate anything, even light itself. This is a reference to the optical experiments of Isaac Newton involving prisms separating white light into its discrete spectrum of colors.

This is why the core and seal for this Fluent are in the shape of a prism. The core is that of diamond, which often is cut so that it acts somewhat like a prism. However, the seal scroll for the Fluent of Light is yet another reference. The scroll is held on the dark side of the moon. Those who are familiar with the cover of the Pink Floyd album of the name *Dark Side of the Moon* know that the art on this album is that of a prism taking white light and separating it out into a spectrum of color.

Even though this broadsword is very large, as it is a combination of seven different swords, its weight is very low, because it is "light". Partly because of its light weight, it is a very fast sword. This is also referencing the speed of light, which is the fastest speed in the universe at nearly 300 million meters per second.

Finally, the Sesom Strike works on the concept that the sword which is so sharp "it can cut light itself" could cut an entire ocean in two. Of course, those who know that I like to spell things backwards would notice that "Sesom" is the inverse of the name of "Moses". Those who also know the Biblical story of the exodus of the Israelites from Egypt would know that God, through Moses, split the Red Sea so that the Israelites could flee Egyptian slavery. As such, in the novel, the Sesom Strike splits the ocean along the staircase down to the Aquarius shrine.

Six Noble Swords: Noble gasses

Much like there are 6 Kingdoms, each of these Kingdoms has a noble Number Disk, which references the noble gas that each Kingdom represents (*see also: Section 5 – "6 Kingdoms"*). These swords are made with white fluxionite and pull their power from the noble Number Disks. Luvnac forged these blades, but regretted the decision when he saw what they were being used for. Over time, these six swords were eventually used to seal a Q-Portal that had opened in the Pythagorean Triangle and would not close.

The names of the six Noble Swords all have colors associated with them. These six colors are the most common colors associated with the rainbow: red, orange, yellow, green, blue, and violet (or purple). These colors were paired up in each of the three caves to be complimentary pairs so that Asp Peak had red/green, Boa Peak had orange/blue, and Cobra Peak had yellow/violet. The colored names of the swords were mostly linked to their respective Kingdoms based on the colors that the noble gasses emit when electrified. The fragments of these swords, along with the hilt of the 10 Caliber Sword, were then used to forge Hikari Shichidai, the sword so sharp it can cut light itself.

The 10 Caliber Sword of Selcomad: Excalibur / Damocles

Here we have two different references, each one added at a different point in the trilogy. The first reference is that of Excalibur, the legendary sword of Arthurian legend. Caliber is used as a unit of size for diameters, which would then translate to the diameter of the hilt (think: larger hilt = larger sword). If you were to write the name as X-Calibur, the "X" could be translated as a roman numeral "10", and thus we arrive at "10 Caliber".

The "of Selcomad" bit was added when it was put in the shrine atop the Island of Stability. "Selcomad" is merely "Damocles" spelled backwards. The dangling sword of Damocles is a story about a sword which is held aloft by a very small string, keeping the blade in a state of pensive doom. The moral is essentially that life cannot be enjoyed if there is a constant state of fear involved. Finally, since the Excalibur legend involved pulling a sword from a stone, I chose to name the stone "Ragna Rock" after the Norse Ragnarök, an event which essentially equates to the end of the world.

This sword was placed on the Island of Stability after the "War of the Swords" between the 3rd, 4th, 5th, and 6th Kingdoms. After Amedeo's War, the sword was placed in the Ragna Rock until Arthur came along and removed it, becoming the rightful King of the 4th Kingdom. When he died, the sword was returned to the Ragna Rock. Decades later, the 5th Kingdom found the original treaty from the War of the Swords and determined that, since the 4th Kingdom had the sword, this broke the centuries old armistice agreement between the four Kingdoms. As such, a special team from the 5th Kingdom infiltrated Old Non and stole the sword and the stone and brought them back to Topal, where they resided in secret. None of the other three Kingdoms knew what happened to the sword, until Isaac came across it underneath Topal's palace, centuries later.

Supages: Pegasus

A straight pull from the mythological creature, I decided that the best way to make a flying horse would be the same way that I would make a flying man. This is why Sucari was the original owner of Supages: due to the similar nature of their powers.

SECOND TO NONE

Fluxions: The Manhattan Project

While fluxions may have represented the Calculus Wars in *First Name Basis*, in *Second to None* they had a different reference. I hinted at the supreme power of fluxions in the first novel, but I also hinted at the research which initially brought them into the world. Fluxions carry a lot of power, but they can also be very useful. Much like nuclear energy can be used to destroy entire cities, or power said cities for decades. Furthermore, much like the fluxion research in *Second to None*, the Manhattan Project looked to weaponize nuclear energy.

Part of the fluxion research was also linked to the Naturals, who could use fluxions without the need for the seals. The reason they did not need the uroboros seals was that their DNA looped back on itself, essentially becoming the knotted uroboros seal that the fluxion users would need in order to access the power of the core. The "Friedrich" who was interested in studying the blood of the Naturals is a reference to Friedrich Miescher, a Swiss biologist who was the first person to isolate and identify nucleic acid.

Because the Naturals can use fluxions without the seal, and because their DNA has this attribute, if two Naturals were to have a child, the effectiveness and power of the fluxion would not diminish. However, in the case where a non-Natural has a child with a Natural, the power of the fluxion is split in half. Therefore, since the majority of Naturals were killed during Amedeo's War, by the time the events of *First Name Basis* took place, very few individuals would have the pure Natural power, but many would have a small amount of this ability. This is partly why the fluxions made a resurgence: the seals didn't need to be quite as strong anymore because everyone would have a little bit of Natural power in their blood.

Fluents: N/A

I put the section on Fluents in *Second to None* because it was in this book that they were researched and created. Originally, I wanted Isaac to have both Fluents by the time he arrived to fight Gottfried, but then I reconsidered and thought, "What if the Fluents fought each other?" As mentioned earlier, the name for Isaac Newton's calculus was "Fluxions and Fluents", so I merely applied the second word to the most powerful fluxions. If fluxions are changing some part of a person's genetic code, Fluents were meant to make this change more permanent. And yet, as I got writing, I decided that the two Fluents would be the Fluent of Light and the Fluent of Darkness.

The Fluent of Light has the power to split any combined fluxions into their separate parts. The Fluent of Darkness, also known as "The Omnipotence", which stands for "all powers", is just that: a combination of all fluxions. One separating, one combining. The Omnipotence was meant to be used as a "super soldier" Fluent, and the Fluent of Light was only supposed to be used as a means to keep the Fluent of Darkness in check. However, due to the incredibly complicated sealing needed to keep all the powers in The Omnipotence in check, it was never completed. Similarly, the Fluent of Light's seal was completed, but it was never implemented.

Q-Portals: Electron rings

While Q-Portals were essentially tied to Quantum jumping in *First Name Basis*, it wasn't until *Second to None* that I really explored how they worked. With the addition of Albert Einstein to the novels, I had a lot of material I could pull from. The idea of an Einstein-Rosen Bridge was a natural fit to the idea of Q-Portals. Albert Einstein and Nathan Rosen's concept of portals between two locations in space goes by a much simpler moniker: wormholes.

In the world of *Second to None*, the Q-Portals consist of two parts: a key and a bridge. This is why Albert is the Keymaster and Nathan is the Bridgekeeper. The bridge is established when a key is used, but the key is truly the lynchpin of the operation. There are two key colors: black and white. And yes, I do realize the hokey wordplay with having Q-Portal keys linked to piano keys. Anyways, since the keys used in *First Name Basis* were all created from a skeleton's hand, these keys were all white and acted in the same manner. When a white key is used in a Q-hole, a black hole opens up from the key. Somewhere else, a white hole is also created and links to the black hole by the bridge. This bridge is essentially the two event horizons of the black and white holes.

The black key works in a similar way, except that it can be used without a Q-hole. In fact, the black keys create Q-holes. When a black key is used, a white hole opens from the key and a black hole is created somewhere else. Because black holes suck in material and white holes emit material, Q-Portals can only be used in one direction. It is nearly impossible to go through a Q-Portal opened with a black key. White keys transport to somewhere, whereas black keys transport something to you.

The other concept presented with Q-Portals in this novel is that the distance can be controlled. Each key is made of metal and exhibits a certain natural frequency, much like a tuning fork. This frequency has a wavelength, and that wavelength determines how far away the black and white holes are from each other. The deeper tones have longer wavelengths, which puts the two ends of the portal further away than the higher tones. In this way, a thick key (like that of a thumb, for instance) could get you to the moon.

However, knowing the distance is only part of the problem. Much like the Quantum jumping problem presented in *First Name Basis*, there's still an unknown to where you'll end up. By knowing the wavelength, you will have a radius that will provide you with an idea of how far away you'll be from your starting location. However, you'll never quite know in which direction that might be. It's all based off of probability.

Number Disks: Periodic Table of the Elements

Since *Second to None* had a lot of Number Disks in it, I decided I would explain it a little more here. Each Number Disk directly correlates to an atomic number of an element on the periodic table of the elements. Many of these disks have very specific powers based on what element is being referenced. Many elements are volatile when they come in contact with water, or even air! Others provide weight to be used as a force assist on an attack. However, there are three "lost" Number Disks, which leads me to . . .

Philosopher's Stone: Subatomic particles

Each element is made with only three subatomic particles: electrons, neutrons, and protons. These three particles are the "lost" Number Disks:

> "–": Known as "pull", this power is used by Priest Werner as an "uncertainty power", since it is extremely difficult to know where an electron actually is at any point in time. Electrons can also be used to create electricity and magnetism, so this "lost" Number Disk is probably the most complex and most powerful of the three.

> "0": Known as "neutrality", this "lost" disk has the power to nullify any fluxion power used, be it through a traditional seal or used by a Natural. This power can even be used to nullify the other two "lost" disks. It is unfortunate that I did not get to explore using this power more in the novels, as it could have provided for some interesting plot twists.

> "+": Known as "push", this power could be used to enact a barrier of sorts. It can also be used to nullify "pull", but it cannot nullify any other fluxions. Since I only ever focused on "pull", I never fleshed out this power much past its name.

These Number Disks weren't "lost" in the sense that nobody knew where they were, even if they were difficult to find. They were "lost" in the sense that they did not fit into the 1-112 number scheme for the periodic table. However, when they are used together with the Philosopher's Stone, they can be used to make any of the 112 Number Disks. Furthermore, while never explicitly stated, the Philosopher's Stone could be used to fuse two Number Disks into a new Number Disk, much in the same way that nuclear fusion combines lighter elements (like Hydrogen) and fuses them together to create larger ones (like Helium).

This idea of creating elements out of nothing, or at least mutating an element into different one is a base concept in alchemy. Most people were interested in turning Lead into Gold, but in order to do so, one would have to add neutrons, protons, and electrons to the Lead atoms. In order to get to Gold (#79) from Lead (#82) would require a lot of work, and would probably be impossible. It would almost be easier to change Gold (#79) into Mercury (#80). The Philosopher's Stone was thought to be able to perform this feat, along with many other impossible things. This was just a fantasy in the end.

The Spectrum: Rainbow

When God flooded the earth in the Bible, He made a promise to never to it again. This promise is the rainbow we now see in the sky after/during a rainstorm. As such, this spectrum of colors is associated with Noah and his Ark. I took this idea and applied it to the large variety of animals that had to weather the storm on Noah's Ark. They exhibited the wide spectrum of animal life on earth.

THE THIRD DEGREE

Fluxions: Nuclear energy

The final piece of the fluxion puzzle comes in the last part of *The Fluxion Trilogy*: *The Third Degree*. Not only do we learn that there is a material known as fluxionite, but that the Caidoz statues are the power source to all the fluxions on earth (and the moon). Each statue stands at the intersection of an uroboros seal, and thus powers the uroboros seals used in all fluxions (or the blood of Naturals). With the statues destroyed, fluxions would lose all their power and be completely useless.

Q-Portals: Time travel

Expounding upon the idea of wormholes presented in *Second to None*, I added in a hint at the end of that novel as to another ability of Q-Portals. While they had originally been relegated to being only able to travel in space, with the addition of electricity they could now be used to travel through time as well. The wavelength of the keys still determine the distance in space traveled, but the amount of electrical charge applied to the keys will determine how far in time someone will travel. More electricity, like with Benjamin's ball lightning, means a further jump in time.

The fluxionite keys made from both the "positive" (white) and "negative" (black) fluxionite not only have different effects when used to travel through space, but they allow for two-directional time travel as well. The white keys, when charged with electricity, can break through the space barrier and send a user forward in time. Similarly, the black keys will transport someone backward in time.

Because the Q-Portal keys rely on the power of fluxions, once the Caidoz statues are destroyed, they cannot be used to travel through either space or time. This is why it is easier to travel backward in time in large chunks and more difficult to travel forward in time: as the Caidoz statues were destroyed, the effectiveness of the Q-Portals decreases. All strange and supernatural powers can be explained in this world by the presence of the Caidoz statues.

Caidoz statues: Zodiac signs

Those following along up to this point will readily realize that the twelve Caidoz statues are directly linked to the twelve Zodiac signs. But, how much do you know about these signs? Did you know each has an Element, Quality, and Polarity? Much like a large game of "Rock, Paper, Scissors", I went ahead and applied a few weaknesses and strengths to these attributes in order to make things more interesting. I also managed to organize things so that the Caidoz statues fall into a grid (which actually ends up forming a sphere). Let's get things started with:

> *Element*: Consider this to be your standard "elements of the universe", which are often invoked in many fantasy stories. Anyways, think of the Element of the statue as the "y-axis" of a graph.
> - *Air*: The top of the Elements. Associated with Autumn. Hot, wet, light. All Air Elements are of the Positive polarity. This Element defeats Water Element because water evaporates in air. However, Air is defeated by Fire Element, because wind makes fire stronger. Gemini, Libra, and Aquarius are all Air signs. The symbol for Air is an upward pointing triangle with a line through it. Lambda the Just is an Air Element.
> - *Water*: Heading down the y-axis, we arrive at Water. Associated with Winter. Cold, wet, soft. All Water Elements are of the Negative polarity. Shares the aforementioned weakness to Air Element. Powerful against Earth Element because water erodes earth. Cancer, Scorpio, and Pisces are all Water signs. The symbol for Water is a downward pointing triangle. Psi the Sensitive is a Water Element.
> - *Earth*: While Water is on top of the "x-axis", Earth is directly below it. Associated with Spring. Cold, dry, heavy. All Earth Elements are of the Negative polarity. Shares the aforementioned weakness to Water Element. Powerful against Fire Element because earth smothers a fire. Taurus, Virgo, and Capricorn are all Earth signs. The symbol for Earth is a downward pointing triangle with a line through it.

- *Fire*: The bottom of the y-axis, Fire is the last Element. However, consider the y-axis looping back on itself and connecting back into Air at the top. Associated with Summer. Hot, dry, ardent. All Fire Elements are of the Positive polarity. Shares the aforementioned weakness to Water Element and strength to Air Element. Aries, Leo, and Sagittarius are all Fire signs. The symbol for Fire is an upward pointing triangle. Chi the Powerful is a Fire Element.

➢ *Quality*: If Element is the "y-axis", Quality is the "x-axis".
- *Mutable*: This Quality has the ability to be adjustable and adaptable. Statues with this Quality can regenerate or have the ability to multiply. This is the left-most Quality on the graph and loops back and connects to Cardinal. Gemini, Virgo, Sagittarius, and Pisces are all Mutable signs. The symbol for Mutable Quality is a curve with a dot underneath it.
- *Fixed*: The Fixed statues are resistant to change, and are therefore very stubborn and difficult to destroy. They need multiple hits or strong attacks in order to finally fail. This is the central Quality on the graph and intersects the y-axis. Taurus, Leo, Scorpio, and Aquarius are all Fixed signs. The symbol for Fixed Quality is a square with a line through it.
- *Cardinal*: The Zodiac signs which exhibit the Cardinal Quality are all signs associated with the change in seasons. As such, the fluxion cores held by the members of Seasoned Compass were found at these four shrines. This is the right-most Quality on the graph. Aries, Cancer, Libra, and Capricorn are all Cardinal signs. The symbol for Cardinal Quality is an upward "V" with a dot in it.

➢ *Polarity*: Also known as "Degree" in the novel, the polarity is exactly what it sounds like. There are two polarities, Positive and Negative. Each is represented by a plus or minus sign, respectively. Originally, I wanted the Positive statues to be above ground, and the Negative ones to be underground, but that didn't end up working out in the end. However, the first couplet of the Caidoz song does detail out this key plot point: "Twelve statues: six above, six below / Two Degrees from which power flow."

As you can see, each sign has a specific symbol associated to its Element, Quality, and Polarity. I was able to combine each of these symbols for each Caidoz statue in order to create unique symbols for each of the twelve signs, many of which I tried to do so in a way that ties to what the statue is. Now that we have an idea where everything lies on the x-y graph, let's look at it:

	Mutable	_Fixed_	_Cardinal_
Air	Gemini	Aquarius	Libra
Water	Pisces	Scorpio	Cancer
Earth	Virgo	Taurus	Capricorn
Fire	Sagittarius	Leo	Aries

On top of the normal associations with the Zodiac signs, as mentioned above, each of the twelve Caidoz statues has a birthstone association tied to it. Since the Zodiac signs are not completely aligned with each month, I chose the birthstone for each statue that fit with the month that overlapped the most with its correlated Zodiac sign. Because there are a lot of references made with each Caidoz statue, please see Section 5 for details about all twelve.

C.L.A.W.: Laser

The **C**ancer **L**ight **A**mplification **W**eapon, or C.L.A.W. for short, is a direct reference to the Laser, which stands for **L**ight **A**mplification by **S**timulated **E**mission of **R**adiation. Einstein was the first person to discover the theoretical concept of the laser, so this is why Albert was the one to wield the weapon. The earliest lasers were made with synthetic rubies, so the fact that the sign of Cancer lined up with the birthstone for July just drove home a few more connections. A red laser is usually what most people would think of when they think of this device, and the fact that I could create an acronym for something that represented an acronym itself was pretty nice. Even though the red color associated with crabs is due to the crabs being cooked, the destructive red light that was emitted from the C.L.A.W. is actually more a reference to the disease of cancer than it is to the constellation of the same name.

The Holy Grail: Percival

This Arthurian legend fit well with introducing and using the character of Arthur. I modified the legend slightly by linking the "water of life" that Jesus describes in the gospels of the Bible to the Holy Grail: a cup which can provide eternal life. Those unfamiliar with the legend of the grail would not know that one of the Knights of the Round Table, Percival, was the one to initially find the Holy Grail. Therefore, the words "Crap / Live" engraved on the chalice are merely words pulled from an anagram of Percival's name. Of course, as I had done in *First Name Basis* (and the Holy Cliffs), I also transposed the meaning of "holey" on the word "holy", as evidenced by the hole in the bottom of the grail.

And yet, this oasis was more than just a reference to Jesus' "water of life". Anyone who has gone canoeing will know that the concept of a "Jesus Rock" matches the description given in the novel: a shallow stone that goes unseen by boaters, but can also give the illusion that someone can walk on water. Furthermore, having to roll away a stone in order to get into the cave of the scorpion statue is a reference to the stone which blocked Jesus' tomb after his crucifixion, while the large dome-shaped rock which contains the statue is a reference to the Dome of the Rock, considered by many to be the site of the Temple that Jesus frequented while he was alive.

Spear of Trium: Spear of Triam

While not official Greek mythology (it's part of the plot of the 2012 movie, *Wrath of the Titans*), the Spear of Trium is a weapon created by combining Zeus' thunderbolt, Hades' pitchfork, and Poseidon's trident. As we'll learn in Section 5 about The Triumvirate, these three gods are represented in the characters of Lambda the Just, Chi the Powerful, and Psi the Sensitive, with each having a hammer/javelin, pitchfork, and trident, respectively. These weapons were earned from their journey through the Imaginary World, where they also earned the name of "The Triumvirate". Therefore, it's not much of a stretch to make the weapon the Spear of Trium, which is short for Triumvirate.

Furthermore, the three weapons used to create the Spear of Trium are made out of the three atomic elements that would reference the Greek gods who held these weapons. Thorium (#90), Plutonium (#94), and Neptunium (#93) refer to gods of similar elements, even if they are not the Greek versions of the gods who held the weapons in *Wrath of the Titans*. As such, since they all share the tens digit, "9", and since this number is the square of three, we see the numerical code on the Spear of Trium represent all three as individuals (with the numbers 0, 3, and 4 stacked next to the 9), but also as a larger whole.

And yet, the device which is used to propel the Spear of Trium, the "rail gun" is exactly that. Railguns use massive amounts of direct current electricity to launch projectiles at incredible speeds in short distances by using the force caused by electrical conductivity induced in two, parallel metal rails. Of course, the best source for direct current electricity is that of lightning. Fortunately enough, I just happened to have a character who could control lightning so that the weapon could be used.

Section 5

Organizations

If there's one thing I love, it's connections. These threads tie together random characters and give them a common purpose and theme. In fact, if you look closely at the titles of the chapters of each of the novels, you can see these connections. For *First Name Basis*, each chapter title is a single word. For *Second to None*, the connections get a little more complex. The two words for each chapter represent what happens with each storyline, which is why the chapter where the plots intersect is represented by only one word: War. Finally, *The Third Degree* not only has chapters which are three words long, but one of those words in each title is "the", alternating from the first and second positions of the titles, since the title of the novel had that article as well.

So, if you couldn't tell already, I really like grouping things together. In this section, we'll cover the groups and organizations that appear in *The Fluxion Trilogy*. Some of the connections are fictional and came from my imagination, but others are a little deeper than you might think at first glance. If there's one thing about these novels, it's that they work on many layers that sometimes go very deep into multiple references.

FIRST NAME BASIS

Testament

As was the case with some of the other names in this Trilogy, Testament started out as something closer to "League of Barons". When I was researching possible characters, I noticed that two of them were Barons (Kelvin and Rayleigh). Since they had different numbers associated with their Baron title, I wanted to create an organization that had a ranking system involving numbers. It was at this point where I realized another thing they had in common: "William" was in their name. From here, things started falling into place rather quickly, especially when I realized that my main antagonist (Gottfried) had a version of "Will" in his name as well. From this realization, I linked "Will" to "Will and Testament" and thus, Testament was born. Now, most people are familiar with the Biblical Testament (both Old and New), so once I came upon the name, I decided to have two iterations of the group just so there could be an Old Testament and a New Testament.

This link between "Will" and "Testament" is what led to the secret password to the cave outside of New Town: "Where there's a Will there's a way". This cave is not necessarily a *Lord of the Rings* reference, but actually a reference to a cautionary tale that my paternal grandfather used to tell his grandchildren. The conditions changed, based on what the lesson to be learned was, but the one unifying aspect of the story was a cave that needed two keys: one to get in and one to get out. The key to get in was usually some sort of password, which was overheard by the treasure hunter, not knowing that, in order to get out, a different key was needed. This cave was meant to be a storehouse of Testament equipment, discovered by the Old Testament (after it was filled following Amedeo's War) and used by the New Testament to quietly equip individuals with political power and overthrow the landscape of the 6 Kingdoms. When the cave was discovered, the password was reset to indicate the "Will" association to Testament.

The idea for the numbering system of Testament was to have ten numbered positions (similar to the Arrancar in the Japanese manga and anime, *Bleach*). These positions were meant to be filled by the most powerful members of the organization. By the time Isaac arrived at Testament Tower, most of the members had died, quit, or left the Old Testament because their goal of defeating Robert was accomplished. Because so many members were gone, some of the numbered positions were not as much fighters as they were support members. Of course, the two fugitives that New Testament broke out of Pandora Prison weren't in the organization long enough to be ranked, but they were merely the start of a plan to rebuild Testament to a world domination power. Grigori and Alfred would likely sit at Numbers 2 and 3, respectively, to replace old members who had retired.

Some of the members of Testament were never explicitly stated, and a few don't have "Will" in their name, but many of them have numbered designations, regardless. This was due to Old Testament wanting to maintain the "Will" designator for numbered positions, but the New Testament had no need for an arbitrary system and decided to fill numbers by physical strength. Below are the members of New Testament and their ranks:

➢ *Number 1*: Thomson [William Thomson, 1st Baron Kelvin]
➢ *Number 2*: Thurston [William Thurston] {DEAD – FORMER #1}
➢ *Number 3*: John [John William Strutt, 3rd Baron Rayleigh] {RETIRED}
➢ *Number 4*: Gottfried [Gottfried Wilhelm Leibniz]
➢ *Number 5*: Harter [William Harter] to Dr. Paul [Paul Lévy/Dr. Moreau]
➢ *Number 6*: Val [Valkyries]

- *Number 7*: Edgar / Allan [Edgar Allan Poe]
- *Number 8*: Ralph [Ralph William "Bill" Gosper] {RETIRED}
- *Number 9*: Felix [Felix Klein]
- *Number 10*: Conrad [Wilhelm Conrad Röntgen] {DEAD}
- Alfred the Peacemaker [Alfred Nobel]
- Grigori the Reaper [Grigori Rasputin]

6 Kingdoms

When you hear the word "Noble" what do you think of? Kingdoms, right? I thought so. This is why I chose to create six Kingdoms to rule over the world. These six Kingdoms are directly related to the six noble gasses from the periodic table of the elements. As such, each Kingdom has a Number Disk and a sword which can wield the power of the Number-fluxion.

- *1st Kingdom*: Helium (chemical element #2) [Orange Crush]
    - Never mentioned in the trilogy, but many of the residents would have high-pitched voices, much like your voice would be if you breathed Helium. The 1st Kingdom occupies the northern realm of the world.
- *2nd Kingdom*: Neon (chemical element #10) [Red Flood]
    - *Capital*: The Meadows [Las Vegas]
    - Ruled by King Edward and Queen Lalande, who await the return of their prodigal son: John. The King and Queen are references to Edward Barnard (Barnard's star is named after him) and Lalande 21185, respectively. These are the 5th and 7th nearest stars to us. Barnard's star is in the constellation Ophiuchus so, even though it was never mentioned, King Edward is a descendant of Ophiuchus. Lalande 21185 is in Ursa Major. Because these two rulers are named after stars, it's only fitting that they live in a capital which references Las Vegas ("The Meadows" is the English translation of this), since this Nevada city is well known for its neon lights. As such, the 2nd Kingdom occupies much of the desert area of the world, as well as what is known as the "southern continent", a vastly unexplored and undeveloped area. This southern continent is where the Serpentes Tribe resides.
- *3rd Kingdom*: Argon (chemical element #18) [Violet Violence]
    - *Capital*: Morgana [Fata Morgana]
    - Very briefly mentioned, but home to Jason and his grandson, Michael, who lived on the west coast of the Kingdom. The 3rd Kingdom is mostly filled with the region known as Timberland, and is a reference to the Black Forest of Germany.
- *4th Kingdom*: Krypton (chemical element #36) [Blue Division]
    - *Capital*: Old Non [London]

- At one time ruled by King Solepochs, then by his son, Prince Clive, this area, also known as the Island Kingdom, is home to Isaac (among many other characters), and was the origin of the Reign of Robert. Krypton was the fictional planet of Superman (also known as the "Man of Steel", hence Luvnac's armor connection), a character created by Jerry Siegel and Joe Shuster. The Sechilla Ceremony is a reference to Superman, but also to Achilles (of which "Sechilla" is an anagram) because Superman's one weakness is Kryptonite, just like Achilles' one weakness was his heel. Krypton is used in high powered lasers, but is narcotic if inhaled. Of course, one of the most powerful kingdoms in the real world was that of the British empire. The 4th Kingdom spans the islands and oceans to the west, including Ice Island to the north (a direct reference to Iceland).
- *5th Kingdom*: Xenon (chemical element #54) [Yellow Flash]
  - *Capital*: Topal [Plato's Republic]
  - Ruled by King Sadim and followed by his son, Prince Niccolo, and homeland to Tecumseh. The residents of the 5th Kingdom do not like outsiders, due to their phobia. This fear is known as xenophobia, which shares its word root with the 5th noble gas. Furthermore, solid Xenon has a sky blue color, which is why the Holy Cliffs to the east of Topal have this distinctive hue as well. Of course, solid Xenon doesn't have holes in it, like the cliffs do. This characteristic is merely a play on the words "holy" and "holey". The cliffs are also a reference to the White Cliffs of Dover, although not nearly as direct as Pablo Quarry.
- *6th Kingdom*: Radon (chemical element #86) [Green Legion]
  - Also never explicitly mentioned in the novels, but the residents here would probably be radioactive. The 6th Kingdom covers the wasteland realm to the west and south.

SECOND TO NONE

Army of Amedeo

One thing I wanted to convey with Amedeo's Army was the ranking system of the Generals. It's too simple to merely say "one star General", so I used some constellations and stars with very specific numbers to convey the ranks I wanted. It's no wonder that I ended up using more constellations in *The Third Degree*, eventually writing a whole trilogy about them, starting with *The Constellation Tournament*.

- *Polaris-Class*: Equivalent to a Brigadier (or one-star) General, this rank is referencing the North Star.

- *Gemini-Class*: Equivalent to a Major (or two-star) General, this rank references the Zodiac constellation of the twins.
- *Orion-Class*: Equivalent to a Lieutenant (or three-star) General, this rank references Orion's belt, which is comprised of a line of three stars.
- *Cross-Class*: Equivalent to a Full (or four-star) General, this rank references the four stars that make up the constellation of Crux, also known as the Southern Cross.
- *Aquila-Class*: Equivalent to the highest ranking (or five-star) General, this rank references the constellation of Aquila, the eagle.

The Triumvirate of Power

Ever since High School, I have been somewhat obsessed with the word "Triumvirate". It's no wonder that it would pop up in my first novel and perpetuate into a novel of their own. These three characters were meant to represent the three Greek gods of Zeus, Poseidon, and Hades. When I wrote *Second to None*, the three members of The Triumvirate also took on the reference to the three bearers of the triforce from *The Legend of Zelda*.

However, I found that groups of three were really easy to make, so I made sure to fit in as many triads as I could into this group. A short list of these triads would be mythical human hybrids, colors, and moral systems. I wanted the three previous Imaginary World members to be a different Triumvirate, but that didn't work out, and was probably for the best.

- *Lambda the Just*: Benjamin [Reptiju Suez]
    - *Symbol*: λ [meant to symbolize forked lightning]
    - *Power*: Lightning
    - *Greek god*: Zeus
    - *Hybrid*: Angel
    - *Affinity*: Good
    - *Weapon*: Hammer / Javelin
    - *Core*: Skybolt orb
    - *Roman god*: Jupiter
    - *Element*: Air
    - *Color*: Yellow
- *Psi the Sensitive*: Penny [Penneut Psinodeo]
    - *Symbol*: ψ [meant to symbolize her trident]
    - *Power*: Waves
    - *Greek god*: Poseidon
    - *Hybrid*: Mermaid
    - *Affinity*: Neutral
    - *Weapon*: Trident
    - *Core*: Seawave orb
    - *Roman god*: Neptune
    - *Element*: Water
    - *Color*: Blue
- *Chi the Powerful*: Tecumseh [Lotup Sedah]
    - *Symbol*: χ [meant to symbolize banishment]
    - *Power*: Fire
    - *Greek god*: Hades
    - *Hybrid*: Minotaur
    - *Affinity*: Evil
    - *Weapon*: Pitchfork
    - *Core*: Hellfire orb
    - *Roman god*: Pluto
    - *Element*: Fire
    - *Color*: Red

Seasoned Compass

At a time before the events of *Second to None*, there was a group of Naturals brought together by Tilde the Cardinal. These four Naturals were the most powerful beings in the world, especially after they all obtained their unique (and Elementally aligned) fluxion core abilities. During the events of Amedeo's War, which focused on the eradication of the Naturals, the fates of the members of this organization were questionable, at best. It is thought that perhaps one of the Naturals survived, but nobody was ever quite sure. The name of each of the four members is a combination of a direction and season in Japanese. The members of Seasoned Compass were:

- *Tilde the Cardinal*: Antonio
  - After earning his Imaginary World title, Antonio was given a vision of four Naturals who he was meant to bring together. These four people (with Antonio's guidance) set out to find their individual powers (located with Cardinal Caidoz statues).
- *Haru Higashi*: Trea Raiga [Spring / East]
  - *Power*: Regeneration [found in Aries Pasture]
  - A fitting power for "Mother Earth", considering it is the only planet with self-sustaining life on it. Also fitting for the connection to the season of Spring: a time of regeneration and rebirth.
- *Natsu Minami*: Luvnac [Summer / South]
  - *Power*: Heat [found in the Hoard of the Order of the Dragon]
  - Luvnac's power was actually given to him by the Order as payment for some dragon armor. He had heard they might have something that would allow him to work metal with his bare hands, but since their hoard is so secretive, he never actually got inside to see where this fluxion core was located.
- *Aki Nishi*: Abraham [Fall / West]
  - *Power*: Gravity [found in the Island of Stability]
  - Not the same Abraham referenced in *First Name Basis*, but rather the Biblical Abraham, father of Isaac. Since this is a prequel, I had to give the gravity power to whoever was before Isaac, even if his real name was never mentioned.
- *Fuyu Kita*: William [Winter / North]
  - *Power*: Cold [found in the Capricorn Glacier]
  - The cold power never saw an owner who wasn't evil. From the Ice Queen (a *Chronicles of Narnia* reference), to William, to Thomson, it always brought pain. Considering the "William" connection to Testament, it's only fitting that William Rankine (of the Rankine Temperature scale, which also goes to Absolute Zero) held this power at one time. His residence in "Mount Jack" is a reference to Jack Frost.

Rancho de la Sol

Literally translated as "Ranch of the Sun", this farm was meant to hold many of the characters which are references to the planets of our solar system. It almost seems fitting that Lotup Sedah (Pluto) wasn't included and was the one who killed off everyone at the Ranch, considering that it is no longer officially considered a planet.

And yet, I took the "planet" theme a bit further. Rancho de la Sol sat close to the Olympus River, which is a reference to Mount Olympus, the place where the gods congregated, and each planet being named after a god. English composer Gustav Holst's orchestral suite, *The Planets*, was the inspiration for many of the characterizations, based merely on the few words that accompanied each planet's name for each of the seven movements:

- *Gustav*: Gustav Holst
    - *Family position*: Father
    - *Age*: 60
- *Trea Raiga*: Terra / Gaia [N/A]
    - *Family position*: Mother
    - *Age*: 61
    - Reference to Mother Earth. Gave each of the "double names".
- *Cremy Serehurm*: Mercury / Hermes [The Winged Messenger]
    - *Family position*: Youngest son (5th child)
    - *Age*: 20
    - References the chemical element, as well as being the founder of Transcontinental Express Airmail: a messaging service. He flips sides from Amedeo's Army to the Naturals' cause because to be mercurial is to be changeable, flighty, and fickle.
- *Suev Tideorphan*: Venus / Aphrodite [The Bringer of Peace]
    - *Family position*: Youngest daughter (6th child)
    - *Age*: 18
    - The nickname of "Sue" is similar to her sister's "Penny".
- *Arma Ress*: Mars / Ares [The Bringer of War]
    - *Family position*: 2nd Eldest son (2nd child)
    - *Age*: 32
    - Member of Amedeo's Army. Elemental affinity to iron, a reference to the planet Mars' red color, due to rust.
- *Reptiju Suez*: Jupiter / Zeus [The Bringer of Jollity]
    - *Family position*: N/A
    - *Age*: 30
    - One of the two non-family members.
- *Tranus Sunroc*: Saturn / Cronos [The Bringer of Old Age]
    - *Family position*: Eldest son (1st child)
    - *Age*: 40
    - Center-pivot irrigation produces circular crops so, not only is it a reference to Saturn's rings, but the god's association with

agriculture. The fact that Tranus Sunroc is married (to the character of Morgana), with a wedding ring obvious on his finger, is another reference to the planet's rings.
- ➢ *Sunaru Suleac*: Uranus / Caelus [The Magician]
  - ○ *Family position*: 2nd Youngest son (3rd child)
  - ○ *Age*: 28
  - ○ Original owner of the wind Elemental-fluxion core, which is used for his "magic".
- ➢ *Penneut Psinodeo*: Neptune / Poseidon [The Mystic]
  - ○ *Family position*: Eldest daughter (4th child)
  - ○ *Age*: 25
  - ○ The "Mountain Mystic" is the reference to the Holst designation.
- ➢ *Lotup Sedah*: Pluto / Hades [N/A]
  - ○ *Family position*: N/A
  - ○ *Age*: 26
  - ○ Not only was Lotup Sedah not one of the family members, he's not even included in Holst's suite. Probably just as well, considering that it is no longer considered a planet.

Order of the Dragon

If there was one incredible coincidence that I just had to use, it would have to be the Order of the Dragon. Once I had decided on the uroboros snake seal as one of the main parts of the fluxions, I delved into some research on Vlad the Impaler. When I learned that he (and his father) were part of an organization called the "Order of the Dragon", I knew I had to use it. When I learned that the symbol of the Order is a dragon in an uroboros configuration, I about passed out. Now I absolutely had to use this organization in my novels! Of course, one can't have an organization of Dragons without a few Dragonriders, a bit of a reference to *How to Train Your Dragon*. Here are the three members (in chronological order) of the Order of the Dragon in *The Fluxion Trilogy*:
- ➢ *Bram*: Much like Mary was the "mother" of *Frankenstein*, Bram was the "father" of *Dracula*. As such, he ended up being the "father" of the Order of the Dragon in the novels. He founded the Order after earning the title of "Umlaut the Dragon" in the Imaginary World, partly due to his expert Dragonriding ability.
- ➢ *Arthur*: The only character to be a member of both the Order of the Dragon and the Brotherhood of the Scarlet Lion, Arthur earned this distinction because his real-life reference, Arthur Pendragon had "dragon" in his name, while also being a mythical King of England. Considered to be one of the last Dragonriders.
- ➢ *Harter / Vlad*: Because I wanted to keep the "father/son" dynamic that existed with the real-life Vlad, I made Harter a member of the Order of

the Dragon along with his son, Vlad. Harter was the true last Dragonrider, but after he was killed by Dr. Paul, Vlad became the last of the Order completely. Of all the members over all time, Vlad was the only one to truly become a dragon.

THE THIRD DEGREE

Brotherhood of the Scarlet Lion

In finding a suitable animal to face off against Germany's "Onyx Eagle", I eventually settled on the lion, mainly due to its prominent display on England's coat of arms. This was decided in *First Name Basis* to represent the knighthood, but once *The Third Degree* came around, and I realized that Leo (the lion) was a Fire sign, the fact that I had already set up the Brotherhood of the Scarlet Lion was almost too good to be coincidence.

As the name indicates, the majority of the members of this organization are men, which is in reference to the title bestowed upon those who enter the knighthood: Sir. In the novels, the Brotherhood originally began as a society for riders, specifically horses. As time went on, they had to include other animal riders as well, the most famous being Arthur, the Dragonrider. Of the characters who were part of the Brotherhood of the Scarlet Lion, these three (in chronological order) are:

- ➤ *Clive*: The founder of the Brotherhood, mainly due to the first book in the *Chronicles of Narnia: The Lion, the Witch, and the Wardrobe*.
- ➤ *Arthur*: Many Kings started off as members of the Brotherhood, in order to show their leadership potential. Arthur gained his membership as the Brotherhood's only Dragonrider. Much like Isaac would eventually do, Arthur used his Brotherhood headband to cover up something he was ashamed of: his albino heritage.
- ➤ *Isaac*: Of the three members of the Brotherhood mentioned here, Isaac was the only one to be knighted and obtain the title of "Sir Isaac Newton". By this point in the timeline, the Brotherhood accepted people into its ranks also on their contribution to the betterment of the 4th Kingdom. He used his headband to cover the taboo Soul-fusion fluxion he implanted on his forehead.

Caidoz statues

Since there are twelve different Caidoz statues, each with their own location and attributes, I would do a disservice if I put the list of them under Section 4, which already explained the Element, Quality, and Polarity of these fluxionite carvings. Therefore, here is the complete list with all the information you'd ever need to know about them, in the order in which they were destroyed (chronologically):

- Leo (the lion)
  - Symbol:
  - Location: Old Non
  - Lyric: The lion's red mouth opens and roars
             Protecting the island and its shores
  - Destroyed: Year 144
  - Attributes: Fire / Fixed / Positive
  - Birthstone: Peridot / Sardonyx [August]
- Capricorn (the sea-goat)
  - Symbol:
  - Location: Capricorn Glacier on Ice Island (north of Old Non)
  - Lyric: The sea-goat frolics in the surf
             Gnawing on the weeds of its turf
  - Destroyed: Year 271
  - Attributes: Earth / Cardinal / Negative
  - Birthstone: Garnet [January]
- Cancer (the crab)
  - Symbol:
  - Location: Hoard of the Order of the Dragon
  - Lyric: The crab's pinch spreads its disease
             Destroying the lives of all it sees
  - Destroyed: Year 274
  - Attributes: Water / Cardinal / Negative
  - Birthstone: Ruby [July]
- Pisces (the fish)
  - Symbol:
  - Location: Pisces Islands (border between 5th & 6th Kingdoms)
  - Lyric: The fish both get caught together
             A sailor's reward for enduring weather
  - Destroyed: Year 277
  - Attributes: Water / Mutable / Negative
  - Birthstone: Aquamarine [March]
- Scorpio (the scorpion)
  - Symbol:
  - Location: Scorpio Desert (southwest of Library of Delaxanair)
  - Lyric: The scorpion lies within the sand
             Spreading poison throughout the land
  - Destroyed: Year 545
  - Attributes: Water / Fixed / Negative
  - Birthstone: Topaz [November]
- Gemini (the twins)
  - Symbol:
  - Location: Mirror Lakes (near Rancho de la Sol)
  - Lyric: The twins play in the mountain lakes
             Which reflect their many mistakes
  - Destroyed: Year 548
  - Attributes: Air / Mutable / Positive
  - Birthstone: Pearl / Moonstone [June]

➢ *Taurus (the bull)*
  - Symbol:
  - Destroyed: Year 1269
  - Attributes: Earth / Fixed / Negative
  - Birthstone: Emerald [May]
  - Location: Taurus Field (near Jules Crater)
  - Lyric: The bull ran and jumped too soon
            And got himself stuck on the moon

➢ *Virgo (the maiden)*
  - Symbol:
  - Destroyed: Year 1269
  - Attributes: Earth / Mutable / Negative
  - Birthstone: Sapphire [September]
  - Location: Virgo shrine (near Alden)
  - Lyric: The maiden weeps her tears of joy
            For being told she will bear a boy

➢ *Aquarius (the water bearer)*
  - Symbol:
  - Destroyed: Year 1280
  - Attributes: Air / Fixed / Positive
  - Birthstone: Amethyst [February]
  - Location: Aquarius shrine (southwest of New Town)
  - Lyric: The water bearer holds the oceans
            Underneath the weight of many tons

➢ *Aries (the ram)*
  - Symbol:
  - Destroyed: Year 1280
  - Attributes: Fire / Cardinal / Positive
  - Birthstone: Diamond [April]
  - Location: Aries Pasture (next to Posea Pasture and Asp Peak)
  - Lyric: The ram grazes in the valley's grass
            Avoiding the bite of the deadly asp

➢ *Sagittarius (the archer)*
  - Symbol:
  - Destroyed: Year 1280
  - Attributes: Fire / Mutable / Positive
  - Birthstone: Turquoise [December]
  - Location: Centaurcher shrine on Mount Charles
  - Lyric: The centaur can see for miles and miles
            Shooting an arrow to defeat its trails

➢ *Libra (the scales)*
  - Symbol:
  - Destroyed: Year 1280
  - Attributes: Air / Cardinal / Positive
  - Birthstone: Opal / Tourmaline [October]
  - Location: Island of Stability
  - Lyric: The scales' balance must be intact
            For unbiased justice it must enact

Section 6

Maps

What fantasy realm wouldn't be complete without a couple of maps? Since the locations in *The Fluxion Trilogy* are somewhat based on real places, this section would give you a good idea of where things are in relation to each other. Many of these maps were useful to me in determining where the sun would lie when a Q-Portal is used and the characters are suddenly in a new location.

Map #1: The Moon

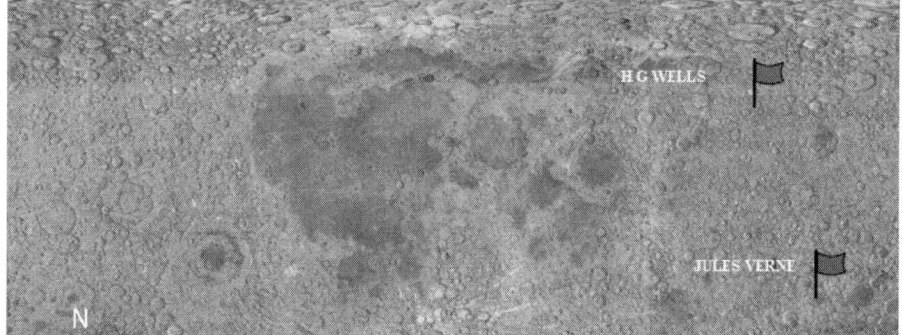

These two locations are the real locations of the craters H.G. Wells and Jules Verne. As such, the craters in the novels are Herbert Crater and Jules Crater, respectively. Both craters are on the dark side of the moon, which is why Isaac couldn't see the earth until he was at the Peak of Eternal Light. Since the Peak of Eternal Light is at the north pole, it can't be displayed on this map, but just know that it is the very top part of the image.

Herbert Crater is home to the town of Alden, Edmond shrine, and the former site of the Virgo shrine, which was underground. This was also the same site where Edmond's comet crashed into the back of the moon, which created the debris field that caused the Dark Year back on earth.

Because the moon is a vast area, many of the other areas were not named. The Taurus Field, where the bull was sent to roam, is just one of these places. Similarly, the crater where Priest Werner originally had his church is unnamed. Needless to say, most of the areas and craters are adjacent to either Jules Crater or Herbert Crater.

Map #2: World Map

As you can obviously see, this is a map of Europe. However, the scale is a bit different, mainly because I wanted places to be within a walking distance for my characters. There's nothing more boring than long journeys without getting anywhere, am I right? This map was most useful for determining where the sun would be when the characters instantaneously transported to somewhere new using the Q-Portals. There are about four time zones, so the people at the Library of Delaxanair (#12) are roughly an hour ahead of Topal (#2), two hours ahead of Mathiston (#4), and three hours ahead of Old Non (#22).

This map also shows the distribution of the 6 Kingdoms, even down to their water boundaries. As you can see, most of the action in *The Fluxion Trilogy* takes place in the 3rd, 4th, and 5th Kingdoms. These Kingdoms exist simultaneously, and are always vying for more land.

Because it would be too cluttered to write all the locations on this map, here is the legend for the numbered locations, in roughly chronological order where they appear in the Trilogy:

1. New Town / Taurus Tavern / Pierre's Pier / Square G shrine
2. Topal / Holy Cliffs / Ruatonim's Maze
3. Pythagorean Triangle (Asp Ridge & Peak, Boa Ridge & Peak, Cobra Ridge & Peak) / Posea Pasture / Aries Pasture / Tanilats / Sievuvus
4. Pandora Prison / Mathiston
5. Dendritic Forest / Armor Village
6. Granite Grove
7. Maurits Manor / Morgana
8. Crystal Woods
9. Thurston Ring / James Garland Arch
10. Eagle's Nest / Testament Tower / Ralph Island
11. Menlo Castle
12. Library of Delaxanair / Scorpio Desert
13. Mirror Lakes / Rancho de la Sol
14. Angular Mangroves / Olympus River Delta
15. Meadow Peak / Island of Stability / Libra shrine
16. Tower of Lebab / Trinity Site
17. Styla Nirvana / Hoard of the Order of the Dragon
18. Alive Ild Abbey / Mount Jack
19. Daniel Volcano
20. Salvador's Clock Tower
21. Aquarius shrine
22. Old Non / Pablo Quarry
23. Centaurcher shrine / Mount Charles
24. Capricorn Glacier / Ice Island
25. Pisces Islands

Map #3: The Pythagorean Triangle

This diagram was definitely helpful when writing about the mysterious Pythagorean Triangle. In order to know where everything stood in relation to everything else, I had to have this diagram to make sure I wasn't inadvertently putting something in the wrong place in relation to something else.

As you can see, the Pythagorean Triangle is the same configuration as the real-world mathematical concept. This concept says that for a right triangle, the length of the square of the hypotenuse (the side opposite the 90° angle) is equal to the sum of the squares of the other sides. In other words, $a^2 + b^2 = c^2$. As such, the three ridges follow this same naming convention, with the hypotenuse starting with "c" (Cobra Ridge) and the two other sides starting with "a" and "b" (Asp Ridge and Boa Ridge, respectively). Similarly, Tanilats dock is square and at the base of Boa Peak to represent the right angle of the triangle. A common Pythagorean triangle has sides of lengths 3, 4, and 5 (or multiples thereof), which means that this triangle has distances of 3 miles for Asp Ridge, 4 miles for Boa Ridge, and 5 miles for Cobra Ridge.

Sievuvus Volcano is as close to the centroid of the Pythagorean Triangle as possible and is just a bit shorter than the heights of the three peaks, which are all the same elevation. The prominence of these peaks is about 3,000 feet. Even though there are two Q-Portals shown on the map, the one in Posea Pasture was the one most commonly used. The Q-Portal to the north of Boa Peak was used by Gulogulo and his company of soldiers when they came to seal the Triangle.

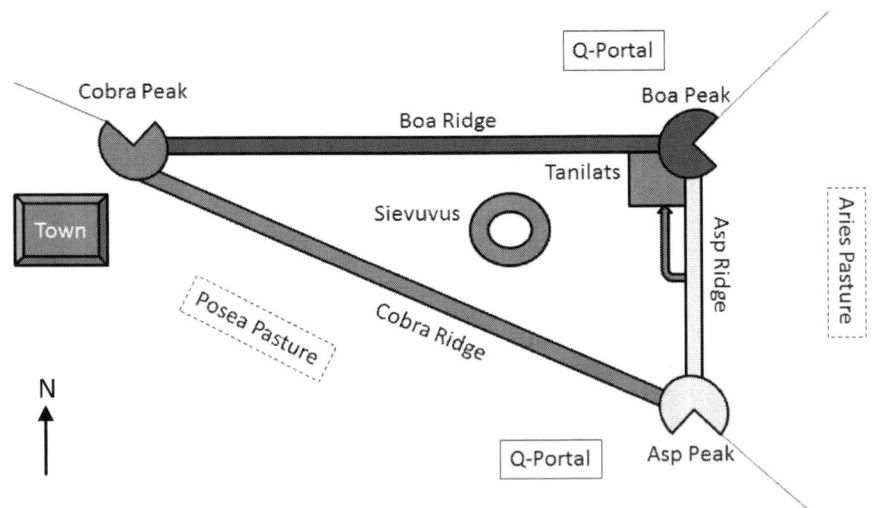

Section 7

Timeline

Knowing when things happen is important. When there's a gap of 1,000 years separating stories, it is *very* important. It's even more important for stories that deal with time travel. This section gives a timeline of the events in, and referenced by, *The Fluxion Trilogy*.

Year 0: The Fall of Man.
Year 1: Pythagoras is born.
Year 2: Lost Number Disks created.
Year 3: Lost Number Disks & Philosopher's Stone create 112 Number Disks.
Year 4: Hellfire orb is created.
Year 5: Ruatonim's Maze created in the Holy Cliffs.
Year 6:
Year 7: Ruatonim is killed and the Hellfire orb is stolen for the first time.
Year 8:
Year 9: Jesus' trials in the Scorpio Desert.
Year 10: Forging of the 10 Caliber Sword of Selcomad.
Year 11: Creation of Ophiuchus.
Year 12:
Year 13: Creation of the Caidoz statues.
Year 14: Imaginary World is discovered by Sigmund.
Year 15: 1st World Council and the Foundation of the 6 Kingdoms.
Year 16: The *Twilight Runner* arrives on top of Sievuvus Volcano.
Year 17: Noble Number Disks given to the rulers of the 6 Kingdoms.
Year 18: Island of Stability discovered. Map created.
Year 19: Caidoz statue poem written.
Year 20: War of the Swords between the 3rd, 4th, 5th, and 6th Kingdoms.
Year 21:
Year 22: 10 Caliber Sword of Selcomad sealed away in Island of Stability.

Year 23: Cows arrive on the moon.
Year 24:
Year 25: John (aka Ronald, aka Reuel) turns Pythagoras into stone.

[*100 Years*]

Year 125: John arrives in the future, changes name to Ronald.
Year 126: Archimedes Elevators created.
Year 127: King Solepochs established as King of the 4th Kingdom.
Year 128: Princess Prohere born.
Year 129:
Year 130: Prince Clive born.
Year 131: Albert travels the farthest back in time, meets Lebabonians.
Year 132: Construction begins on the Tower of Lebab.
Year 133:
Year 134: Seawave orb is created.
Year 135: Construction begins on the *Twilight Runner*.
Year 136:
Year 137: Daniel Volcano created when a meteor struck the earth.
Year 138: Ophiuchus seals the Gravity Core away in the Libra shrine.
Year 139:
Year 140: Hellfire orb returned to Ruatonim's Maze.
Year 141: Construction begins on Pandora Prison.
Year 142:
Year 143: Prince Clive earns the title of "Breve the Lion".
Year 144: The Great Fire of Old Non. 1st Caidoz statue [the lion] destroyed.
Year 145: Brotherhood of the Scarlet Lion officially founded.
Year 146: Pandora Prison completed.
Year 147:
Year 148: Prince Clive defeats the Ice Queen of the northern Ice Island.
Year 149: Albert tries to revive construction on Tower of Lebab.
Year 150: Ronald seals the Ice Core away in the Capricorn Glacier.

[*100 Years*]

Year 250: Library of Delaxanair completed.
Year 251: Bram earns the title of "Umlaut the Dragon".
Year 252: Amedeo rises to power over the 5th Kingdom's military.
Year 253: Albert and Nathan discover Q-Portals.
Year 254: Antonio earns the title of "Tilde the Cardinal".
Year 255: Amedeo defeats and acquires the 3rd Kingdom's military.
Year 256: Seasoned Compass is founded.
Year 257: Members of Seasoned Compass find their power cores.
Year 258: Noah moves his family into the *Twilight Runner*.

Year 259: Amedeo defeats and acquires the 4th Kingdom's military.
Year 260: Thomas and Alessandro create the Skybolt orb.
Year 261: Seasoned Compass disbanded.
Year 262: Luvnac creates the six Noble Swords.
Year 263: Trea Raiga and Gustav move their family to Rancho de la Sol.
Year 264: Luvnac creates his final sword: Kuroni.
Year 265: Amedeo defeats and acquires the 2nd Kingdom's military.
Year 266: James and Garland's expedition to the Serpentes tribe.
Year 267: Benjamin first discovers his powers.
Year 268: EVENTS OF *SECOND TO NONE*.
Year 269:
Year 270: Albert's first journey backwards in time.
Year 271: 2nd Caidoz statue [the sea-goat] destroyed.
Year 272:
Year 273: Albert discovers existence of Caidoz statues.
Year 274: 3rd Caidoz statue [the crab] destroyed.
Year 275:
Year 276:
Year 277: 4th Caidoz statue [the fish] destroyed.
Year 278: Albert discovers Q-Portal time travel, goes back to Year 270.
Year 279:
Year 280: Albert travels forward in time.

[*260 Years*]

Year 540: Ronald arrives in the future, changes name to Reuel.
Year 541: Arthur pulls the 10 Caliber Sword from the Ragna Rock.
Year 542: Arthur's coronation as King of the 4th Kingdom.
Year 543: Quest for the Holy Grail begins.
Year 544:
Year 545: 5th Caidoz statue [the scorpion] destroyed.
Year 546: Albert's first arrival forward in time.
Year 547:
Year 548: 6th Caidoz statue [the twins] destroyed.

[*690 Years*]

Year 1238: Robert conquers 4th Kingdom.
Year 1239: Harry born.
Year 1240: Robert conquers 6th Kingdom.
Year 1241: Maria born.
Year 1242: Hermann born.
Year 1243: Felix born.
Year 1244: Robert conquers 2nd Kingdom.

Year 1245: Thomson born.
Year 1246: Alfred born.
Year 1247: Werner born.
Year 1248: Edgar born.
Year 1249: Robert conquers 1st Kingdom.
Year 1250: Gottfried born.
Year 1251: Marie born.
Year 1252: Isaac born.
Year 1253: Robert conquers 3rd Kingdom.
Year 1254: David born.
Year 1255: Vlad born.
Year 1256: Rachel born.
Year 1257: Robert conquers 5th Kingdom, completes conquest of continent.
Year 1258: Reign of Robert begins.
Year 1259: Thurston Ring discovered.
Year 1260: Robin born.
Year 1261: Prince Niccolo born.
Year 1262: Sucari born.
Year 1263: Priest Werner starts a church.
Year 1264: Testament founded by Thurston.
Year 1265: Pruthesemo's wife (Cinderella) dies.
Year 1266: Isaac arrives on moon, changes name to Edmond.
Year 1267: Erwin born.
Year 1268: Millennial Erasure ends, fluxions rediscovered.
Year 1269: 7th/8th Caidoz statues [bull/maiden] destroyed. Dark Year begins.
Year 1270: Marie dies. Edgar becomes Isaac's assistant. Dark Year ends.
Year 1271: Isaac rediscovers the uroboros knotting seal.
Year 1272: Edgar banished from 4th Kingdom.
Year 1273: Reign of Robert ends. Old Testament disbanded.
Year 1274: New Testament founded. Raid on Pandora Prison.
Year 1275: Dr. Paul becomes Number 5 of New Testament.
Year 1276: Vlad sets out to avenge his father, Harter.
Year 1277: Eagle's Nest created.
Year 1278: King Sadim dies.
Year 1279: EVENTS OF *FIRST NAME BASIS*.
Year 1280: EVENTS OF *THE THIRD DEGREE*.
Year 1281: Benjamin and Irene get married.
Year 1282: Benjamin and Irene have their first child (Penny).
Year 1283: Epilogue of *The Fluxion Trilogy*.

ABOUT THE AUTHOR

Benjamin M. Weilert was born in Colorado in 1985. As a hobby, he has won National Novel Writing Month four years in a row, the most recent win (writing 50,000 words of a novel) completed in a mere 10 days! The first three years of NaNoWriMo completed *The Fluxion Trilogy* with *First Name Basis*, *Second to None*, and *The Third Degree*. He has already begun work on his next trilogy: *The Constellation Tournament*, and has plans for one more trilogy and a memoir centered around hiking Colorado's 14,000 ft. peaks with his father.

His advice to aspiring novelists is threefold:
1. Write what you know – It's easier to make it sound plausible if you're already an expert on it. If you love the subject, you'll love writing about it.
2. Preparation, preparation, preparation – Don't just jump in to writing a novel once you get a good idea. Flesh it out, let it grow and develop before finally putting it to paper.
3. Get outside opinions – You may think your work is perfect, but maybe there's something you missed or that doesn't make sense to someone else. With another perspective, it helps make the work solid. Just don't take the criticism personally; they're only trying to help.